TALES OF
O. Henry

TALES OF
O. Henry

SIXTY-TWO
STORIES

BARNES
&NOBLE
BOOKS
NEW YORK

This edition published by Barnes & Noble, Inc.

1993 Barnes & Noble Books

ISBN 0-8802-9942-8 *casebound*
ISBN 0-7607-1575-0 *paperback*
ISBN 0-7607-0342-6 *leatherbound*

Printed and bound in the United States of America

02 03 MC 9 8
02 03 MP 9 8 7 6 5
00 01 02 03 ML 9 8 7 6 5 4 3 2

QF

CONTENTS

Contents   vii

TALES OF
O. Henry

The Gift of the Magi

ONE DOLLAR and eighty-seven cents. That was all. And sixty cents of it was in pennies. Pennies saved one and two at a time by bulldozing the grocer and the vegetable man and the butcher until one's cheeks burned with the silent imputation of parsimony that such close dealing implied. Three times Della counted it. One dollar and eighty-seven cents. And the next day would be Christmas.

There was clearly nothing to do but flop down on the shabby little couch and howl. So Della did it. Which instigates the moral reflection that life is made up of sobs, sniffles, and smiles, with sniffles predominating.

While the mistress of the home is gradually subsiding from the first stage to the second, take a look at the home. A furnished flat at $8 per week. It did not exactly beggar description, but it certainly had that word on the lookout for the mendicancy squad.

In the vestibule below was a letter-box into which no letter would go, and an electric button from which no mortal finger could coax a ring. Also appertaining thereunto was a card bearing the name "Mr. James Dillingham Young."

The "Dillingham" had been flung to the breeze during a former period of prosperity when its possessor was being paid $30 per week. Now, when the income was shrunk to $20, the letters of "Dillingham" looked blurred, as though they were thinking seriously of contracting to a modest and unassuming D. But whenever Mr. James Dillingham Young came home and reached his flat above he was called "Jim" and greatly hugged by Mrs. James Dillingham Young, already introduced to you as Della. Which is all very good.

Della finished her cry and attended to her cheeks with the powder rag. She stood by the window and looked out dully at a gray cat walking a gray fence in a gray backyard. Tomorrow would be Christmas Day, and she had only $1.87 with which to buy Jim a present. She had been saving every penny she could for months, with this result. Twenty dollars a week doesn't go far. Expenses had been greater than she had calculated. They always are. Only $1.87 to buy a present for Jim. Her Jim. Many a happy hour she had spent planning for something nice for him. Something fine and rare and sterling—something just a little bit near to being worthy of the honor of being owned by Jim.

There was a pier-glass between the windows of the room. Perhaps you have seen a pier-glass in an $8 flat. A very thin and very agile person may, by observing his reflection in a rapid sequence of longitudinal strips, obtain a fairly accurate conception of his looks. Della, being slender, had mastered the art.

Suddenly she whirled from the window and stood before the glass. Her eyes were shining brilliantly, but her face had lost its color within twenty seconds. Rapidly she pulled down her hair and let it fall to its full length.

Now, there were two possessions of the James Dillingham Youngs in which they both took a mighty pride. One was Jim's gold watch that had been his father's and his grandfather's. The other was Della's hair. Had the Queen of Sheba lived in the flat across the airshaft, Della would have let her hair hang out the window some day to dry just to depreciate Her Majesty's jewels and gifts. Had King Solomon been the janitor, with all his treasures piled up in the basement, Jim would have pulled out his watch every time he passed, just to see him pluck at his beard from envy.

So now Della's beautiful hair fell about her rippling and shining like a cascade of brown waters. It reached below her knee and made itself almost a garment for her. And then she did it up again nervously and quickly. Once she faltered for a minute and stood still while a tear or two splashed on the worn red carpet.

On went her old brown jacket; on went her old brown hat. With a whirl of skirts and with the brilliant sparkle still in her eyes, she fluttered out the door and down the stairs to the street.

Where she stopped the sign read: "Mme. Sofronie. Hair Goods of All Kinds." One flight up Della ran, and collected herself, panting. Madame, large, too white, chilly, hardly looked the "Sofronie."

"Will you buy my hair?" asked Della.

"I buy hair," said Madame. "Take yer hat off and let's have a sight at the looks of it."

Down rippled the brown cascade.

"Twenty dollars," said Madame, lifting the mass with a practised hand.

"Give it to me quick," said Della.

Oh, and the next two hours tripped by on rosy wings. Forget the hashed metaphor. She was ransacking the stores for Jim's present.

She found it at last. It surely had been made for Jim and no one else. There was no other like it in any of the stores, and she had turned all of them inside out. It was a platinum fob chain simple and chaste in design, properly proclaiming its value by substance alone and not by meretricious ornamentation—as all good things should do. It was even worthy of The Watch. As soon as she saw it she knew that it must be Jim's. It was like him. Quietness and value—the description applied to both. Twenty-one dollars they took from her for it, and she hurried home with the 87 cents. With that chain on his watch Jim might be properly anxious about the time in any company. Grand as the watch was, he sometimes looked at it on the sly on account of the old leather strap that he used in place of a chain.

When Della reached home her intoxication gave way a little to prudence and reason. She got out her curling irons and lighted the gas and went to work repairing the ravages made by generosity added to love. Which is always a tremendous task, dear friends—a mammoth task.

Within forty minutes her head was covered with tiny, close-lying curls that made her look wonderfully like a truant school-boy. She looked at her reflection in the mirror long, carefully, and critically.

"If Jim doesn't kill me," she said to herself, "before he takes a second look at me, he'll say I look like a Coney Island chorus girl. But what could I do—oh! what could I do with a dollar and eighty-seven cents?"

At 7 o'clock the coffee was made and the frying-pan was on the back of the stove hot and ready to cook the chops.

Jim was never late. Della doubled the fob chain in her hand and sat on the corner of the table near the door that he always entered. Then she heard his step on the stair away down on the first flight, and she turned white for just a moment. She had a habit of saying little silent prayers about the simple everyday things, and now she whispered: "Please God, make him think I am still pretty."

The door opened and Jim stepped in and closed it. He looked thin and very serious. Poor fellow, he was only twenty-two—and to be burdened with a family! He needed a new overcoat and he was without gloves.

Jim stopped inside the door, as immovable as a setter at the scent of quail. His eyes were fixed upon Della, and there was an expression in them that she could not read, and it terrified her. It was not anger, nor surprise, nor disapproval, nor horror, nor any of the sentiments that she had been prepared for. He simply stared at her fixedly with that peculiar expression on his face.

Della wriggled off the table and went for him.

"Jim, darling," she cried, "don't look at me that way. I had my hair cut off and sold it because I couldn't have lived through Christmas without giving you a present. It'll grow out again—you won't mind, will you? I just had to do it. My hair grows awfully fast. Say 'Merry Christmas!' Jim, and let's be happy. You don't know what a nice—what a beautiful, nice gift I've got for you."

"You've cut off your hair?" asked Jim, laboriously, as if he had not arrived at that patent fact yet even after the hardest mental labor.

"Cut it off and sold it," said Della. "Don't you like me just as well, anyhow? I'm me without my hair, ain't I?"

Jim looked about the room curiously.

"You say your hair is gone?" he said, with an air almost of idiocy.

"You needn't look for it," said Della. "It's sold, I tell you—sold and gone, too. It's Christmas Eve, boy. Be good to me, for it went for you. Maybe the hairs of my head were numbered," she went on with a sudden serious sweetness, "but nobody could ever count my love for you. Shall I put the chops on, Jim?"

Out of his trance Jim seemed quickly to wake. He enfolded his Della. For ten seconds let us regard with discreet scrutiny some inconsequential object in the other direction. Eight dollars a week or a million a year—what is the difference? A mathematician or a wit would give you the wrong answer. The magi brought valuable gifts, but that was not among them. This dark assertion will be illuminated later on.

Jim drew a package from his overcoat pocket and threw it upon the table.

"Don't make any mistake, Dell," he said, "about me. I don't think there's anything in the way of a haircut or a shave or a shampoo that could make me like my girl any less. But if you'll unwrap that package you may see why you had me going a while at first."

White fingers and nimble tore at the string and paper. And then an ecstatic scream of joy; and then, alas! a quick feminine change to hysterical tears and wails, necessitating the immediate employment of all the comforting powers of the lord of the flat.

For there lay The Combs—the set of combs, side and back, that Della had worshipped for long in a Broadway window. Beautiful combs, pure tortoise shell, with jewelled rims—just the shade to wear in the beautiful vanished hair. They were expensive combs, she knew, and her heart had simply craved and yearned over them without the least hope of possession. And now, they were hers, but the tresses that should have adorned the coveted adornments were gone.

But she hugged them to her bosom, and at length she was able to look up with dim eyes and a smile and say: "My hair grows so fast, Jim!"

And then Della leaped up like a little singed cat and cried, "Oh, oh!"

Jim had not yet seen his beautiful present. She held it out to him eagerly upon her open palm. The dull precious metal seemed to flash with a reflection of her bright and ardent spirit.

"Isn't it a dandy, Jim? I hunted all over town to find it. You'll have to look at the time a hundred times a day now. Give me your watch. I want to see how it looks on it."

Instead of obeying, Jim tumbled down on the couch and put his hands under the back of his head and smiled.

"Dell," said he, "let's put our Christmas presents away and keep 'em a while. They're too nice to use just at present. I sold the watch to get the money to buy your combs. And now suppose you put the chops on."

The magi, as you know, were wise men—wonderfully wise men —who brought gifts to the Babe in the manger. They invented the art of giving Christmas presents. Being wise, their gifts were no doubt wise ones, possibly bearing the privilege of exchange in case of duplication. And here I have lamely related to you the uneventful chronicle of two foolish children in a flat who most unwisely sacrificed for each other the greatest treasures of their house. But in a last word to the wise of these days let it be said that of all who give gifts these two were the wisest. Of all who give and receive gifts, such as they are wisest. Everywhere they are wisest. They are the magi.

A Cosmopolite in a Café

AT MIDNIGHT the café was crowded. By some chance the little table at which I sat had escaped the eye of incomers, and two vacant chairs at it extended their arms with venal hospitality to the influx of patrons.

And then a cosmopolite sat in one of them, and I was glad, for I held a theory that since Adam no true citizen of the world has existed. We hear of them, and we see foreign labels on much luggage but we find travellers instead of cosmopolites.

I invoke your consideration of the scene—the marble-topped tables, the range of leather-upholstered wall seats, the gay company, the ladies dressed in demi-state toilets, speaking in an exquisite visible chorus of taste, economy, opulence or art; the sedulous and largess-loving garçons, the music wisely catering to all with its raids upon the composers; the mélange of talk and laughter—and, if you will, the Würzburger in the tall glass cones that bend to your lips as a ripe cherry sways on its branch to the beak of a robber jay. I was told by a sculptor from Mauch Chunk that the scene was truly Parisian.

My cosmopolite was named E. Rushmore Coglan, and he will be heard from next summer at Coney Island. He is to establish a new "attraction" there, he informed me, offering kingly diversion. And then his conversation rang along parallels of latitude and longitude. He took the great, round world in his hand, so to speak, familiarly, contemptuously, and it seemed no larger than the seed of a Maraschino cherry in a table d'hôte grape fruit. He spoke disrespectfully of the equator, he skipped from continent to continent, he derided the zones, he mopped up the high seas with his napkin. With a wave of his hand he would speak of a certain bazaar in Hyderabad. Whiff! He would have you on skis in Lapland. Zip! Now you rode the breakers with the Kanakas at Kealaikahiki. Presto! He dragged you through an Arkansas post-oak swamp, let you dry for a moment on the alkali plains of his Idaho ranch, then whirled you into the society of Viennese archdukes. Anon he would be telling you of a cold he acquired in a Chicago lake breeze and how old Escamila cured it in Buenos Ayres with a hot infusion of the *chuchula* weed. You would have addressed a letter to "E. Rushmore Coglan, Esq., the Earth, Solar System, the Universe," and mailed it, feeling confident that it would be delivered to him.

I was sure that I had found at last the one true cosmopolite since Adam, and I listened to his world-wide discourse fearful lest I should discover in it the local note of the mere globe-trotter. But his opinions never fluttered or drooped; he was as impartial to cities, countries, and continents as the winds or gravitation.

And as E. Rushmore Coglan prattled of this little planet I thought with glee of a great almost-cosmopolite who wrote for the whole world and dedicated himself to Bombay. In a poem he has to say that there is pride and rivalry between the cities of the earth, and that "the men that breed from them, they traffic up and down, but cling to their cities' hem as a child to the mother's gown." And whenever they walk "by roaring streets unknown" they remember their native city "most faithful, foolish, fond: making her mere-breathed name their bond upon their bond." And my glee was roused because I had caught Mr. Kipling napping. Here I had found a man not made from dust; one who had no narrow boasts of birthplace or country, one who, if he bragged at all, would brag of his whole round globe against the Martians and the inhabitants of the Moon.

Expression on these subjects was precipitated from E. Rushmore Coglan by the third corner to our table. While Coglan was describing to me the topography along the Siberian Railway the orchestra glided into a medley. The concluding air was "Dixie," and as the exhilarating notes tumbled forth they were almost overpowered by a great clapping of hands from almost every table.

It is worth a paragraph to say that this remarkable scene can be witnessed every evening in numerous cafés in the City of New York. Tons of brew have been consumed over theories to account for it. Some have conjectured hastily that all Southerners in town hie themselves to cafés at nightfall. This applause of the "rebel" air in a Northern city does puzzle a little; but it is not insolvable. The war with Spain, many years' generous mint and watermelon crops, a few long-shot winners at the New Orleans race track, and the brilliant banquets given by the Indiana and Kansas citizens who compose the North Carolina Society have made the South rather a "fad" in Manhattan. Your manicure will lisp softly that your left forefinger reminds her so much of a gentleman's in Richmond, Va. Oh, certainly; but many a lady has to work now—the war, you know.

When "Dixie" was being played a dark-haired young man sprang up from somewhere with a Mosby guerrilla yell and waved frantically his soft-brimmed hat. Then he strayed through the smoke, dropped into the vacant chair at our table and pulled out cigarettes.

The evening was at the period when reserve is thawed. One of us mentioned three Würzburgers to the waiter; the dark-haired young man acknowledged his inclusion in the order by a smile and a nod. I hastened to ask him a question because I wanted to try out a theory I had.

"Would you mind telling me," I began, "whether you are from——"

The fist of E. Rushmore Coglan banged the table and I was jarred into silence.

"Excuse me," said he, "but that's a question I never like to hear asked. What does it matter where a man is from? Is it fair to judge a man by his post-office address? Why, I've seen Kentuckians who hated whiskey, Virginians who weren't descended from Pocohontas, Indianians who hadn't written a novel, Mexicans who didn't wear velvet trousers with silver dollars sewed along the seams, funny Englishmen, spendthrift Yankees, cold-blooded Southerners, narrow-minded Westerners, and New Yorkers who were too busy to stop for an hour on the street to watch a one-armed grocer's clerk do up cranberries in paper bags. Let a man be a man and don't handicap him with the label of any section."

"Pardon me," I said, "but my curiosity was not altogether an idle one. I know the South, and when the band plays 'Dixie' I like to observe. I have formed the belief that the man who applauds that air with special violence and ostensible sectional loyalty is invariably a native of either Secaucus, N. J., or the district between Murray Hill Lyceum and the Harlem River, this city. I was about to put my opinion to the test by inquiring of this gentleman when you interrupted with your own—larger theory, I must confess."

And now the dark-haired young man spoke to me, and it became evident that his mind also moved along its own set of grooves.

"I should like to be a periwinkle," said he, mysteriously, "on the top of a valley, and sing too-ralloo-ralloo."

This was clearly too obscure, so I turned again to Coglan.

"I've been around the world twelve times," said he. "I know an Esquimau in Upernavik who sends to Cincinnati for his neckties, and I saw a goat-herder in Uruguay who won a prize in a Battle Creek breakfast food puzzle competition. I pay rent on a room in Cairo, Egypt, and another in Yokahama all the year around. I've got slippers waiting for me in a tea-house in Shanghai, and I don't have to tell 'em how to cook my eggs in Rio Janeiro or Seattle. It's a mighty little old world. What's the use of bragging about being from the North, or the South, or the old manor house in the dale, or Euclid Avenue, Cleveland, or Pike's Peak, or Fairfax County, Va., or Hooligan's Flats or any place? It'll be a better world when we quit being fools about some mildewed town or ten acres of swampland just because we happened to be born there."

"You seem to be a genuine cosmopolite," I said, admiringly. "But it also seems that you would decry patriotism."

"A relic of the stone age," declared Coglan, warmly. "We are all brothers—Chinamen, Englishmen, Zulus, Patagonians and the people in the bend of the Kaw River. Some day all this petty pride in one's city or state or section or country will be wiped out, and we'll all be citizens of the world, as we ought to be."

"But while you are wandering in foreign lands," I persisted, "do not your thoughts revert to some spot—some dear and——"

"Nary a spot," interrupted E. R. Coglan, flippantly. "The terrestrial, globular, planetary hunk of matter, slightly flattened at the poles, and known as the Earth, is my abode. I've met a good many object-bound citizens of this country abroad. I've seen men from Chicago sit in a gondola in Venice on a moonlight night and brag about their drainage canal. I've seen a Southerner on being introduced to the King of England hand that monarch, without batting his eyes, the information that his grand-aunt on his mother's side was related by marriage to the Perkinses, of Charleston. I knew a New Yorker who was kidnapped for ransom by some Afghanistan bandits. His people sent over the money and he came back to Kabul with the agent. 'Afghanistan?' the natives said to him through an interpreter. 'Well, not so slow, do you think?' 'Oh, I don't know,' says he, and he begins to tell them about a cab driver at Sixth Avenue and Broadway. Those ideas don't suit me. I'm not tied down to anything that isn't 8,000 miles in diameter. Just put me down as E. Rushmore Coglan, citizen of the terrestrial sphere."

My cosmopolite made a large adieu and left me, for he thought he saw some one through the chatter and smoke whom he knew. So I was left with the would-be periwinkle, who was reduced to Würzburger without further ability to voice his aspirations to perch, melodious, upon the summit of a valley.

I sat reflecting upon my evident cosmopolite and wondering

how the poet had managed to miss him. He was my discovery and I believed in him. How was it? "The men that breed from them they traffic up and down, but cling to their cities' hem as a child to the mother's gown."

Not so E. Rushmore Coglan. With the whole world for his——

My meditations were interrupted by a tremendous noise and conflict in another part of the café. I saw above the heads of the seated patrons E. Rushmore Coglan and a stranger to me engaged in terrific battle. They fought between the tables like Titans, and glasses crashed, and men caught their hats up and were knocked down, and a brunette screamed, and a blonde began to sing "Teasing."

My cosmopolite was sustaining the pride and reputation of the Earth when the waiters closed in on both combatants with their famous flying wedge formation and bore them outside, still resisting.

I called McCarthy, one of the French *garçons*, and asked him the cause of the conflict.

"The man with the red tie" (that was my cosmopolite), said he, "got hot on account of things said about the bum sidewalks and water supply of the place he come from by the other guy."

"Why," said I, bewildered, "that man is a citizen of the world—a cosmopolite. He——"

"Originally from Mattawamkeag, Maine, he said," continued McCarthy, "and he wouldn't stand for no knockin' the place."

The Skylight Room

FIRST Mrs. Parker would show you the double parlors. You would not dare to interrupt her description of their advantages and of the merits of the gentleman who had occupied them for eight years. Then you would manage to stammer forth the confession that you were neither a doctor nor a dentist. Mrs. Parker's manner of receiving the admission was such that you could never afterward entertain the same feeling toward your parents, who had neglected to train you up in one of the professions that fitted Mrs. Parker's parlors.

Next you ascended one flight of stairs and looked at the second-floor-back at $8. Convinced by her second-floor manner that it was worth the $12 that Mr. Toosenberry always paid for it until he left to take charge of his brother's orange plantation in Florida near Palm Beach, where Mrs. McIntyre always spent the winters that had the double front room with private bath, you managed to babble that you wanted something still cheaper.

If you survived Mrs. Parker's scorn, you were taken to look at Mr. Skidder's large hall room on the third floor. Mr. Skidder's room was not vacant. He wrote plays and smoked cigarettes in it all day long. But every room-hunter was made to visit his room to admire the lambrequins. After each visit, Mr. Skidder, from the fright caused by possible eviction, would pay something on his rent.

Then—oh, then—if you still stood on one foot, with your hot

hand clutching the three moist dollars in your pocket, and hoarsely proclaimed your hideous and culpable poverty, nevermore would Mrs. Parker be cicerone of yours. She would honk loudly the word "Clara," she would show you her back, and march downstairs. Then Clara, the colored maid, would escort you up the carpeted ladder that served for the fourth flight, and show you the Skylight Room. It occupied 7 x 8 feet of floor space in the middle of the hall. On each side of it was a dark lumber closet or storeroom.

In it was an iron cot, a washstand and a chair. A shelf was the dresser. Its four bare walls seemed to close in upon you like the sides of a coffin. Your hand crept to your throat, you gasped, you looked up as from a well—and breathed once more. Through the glass of the little skylight you saw a square of blue infinity.

"Two dollars, suh," Clara would say in her half-contemptuous, half-Tuskegeenial tones.

One day Miss Leeson came hunting for a room. She carried a typewriter made to be lugged around by a much larger lady. She was a very little girl, with eyes and hair that had kept on growing after she had stopped and that always looked as if they were saying: "Goodness me! Why didn't you keep up with us?"

Mrs. Parker showed her the double parlors. "In this closet," she said, "one could keep a skeleton or anæsthetic or coal——"

"But I am neither a doctor nor a dentist," said Miss Leeson, with a shiver.

Mrs. Parker gave her the incredulous, pitying, sneering, icy stare that she kept for those who failed to qualify as doctors or dentists, and led the way to the second-floor-back.

"Eight dollars?" said Miss Leeson. "Dear me! I'm not Hetty if I do look green. I'm just a poor little working girl. Show me something higher and lower."

Mr. Skidder jumped and strewed the floor with cigarette stubs at the rap on his door.

"Excuse me, Mr. Skidder," said Mrs. Parker, with her demon's smile at his pale looks. "I didn't know you were in. I asked the lady to have a look at your lambrequins."

"They're too lovely for anything," said Miss Leeson, smiling in exactly the way the angels do.

After they had gone Mr. Skidder got very busy erasing the tall, black-haired heroine from his latest (unproduced) play and inserted a small, roguish one with heavy, bright hair and vivacious features.

"Anna Held'll jump at it," said Mr. Skidder to himself, putting his feet up against the lambrequins and disappearing in a cloud of smoke like an aërial cuttlefish.

Presently the tocsin call of "Clara!" sounded to the world the state of Miss Leeson's purse. A dark goblin seized her, mounted a Stygian stairway, thrust her into a vault with a glimmer of light in its top and muttered the menacing and cabalistic words "Two dollars!"

"I'll take it!" sighed Miss Leeson, sinking down upon the squeaky iron bed.

Every day Miss Leeson went out to work. At night she brought home papers with handwriting on them and made copies with her typewriter. Sometimes she had no work at night, and then she would sit on the steps of the high stoop with the other roomers. Miss Leeson was not intended for a skylight room when the plans were drawn for her creation. She was gay-hearted and full of tender, whimsical fancies. Once she let Mr. Skidder read to her three acts of his great (unpublished) comedy, "It's No Kid; or, The Heir of the Subway."

There was rejoicing among the gentlemen roomers whenever Miss Leeson had time to sit on the steps for an hour or two. But Miss Longnecker, the tall blonde who taught in a public school and said, "Well, really!" to everything you said, sat on the top step and sniffed. And Miss Dorn, who shot at the moving ducks at Coney every Sunday and worked in a department store, sat on the bottom step and sniffed. Miss Leeson sat on the middle step and the men would quickly group around her.

Especially Mr. Skidder, who had cast her in his mind for the star part in a private, romantic (unspoken) drama in real life. And especially Mr. Hoover, who was forty-five, fat, flush and foolish. And especially very young Mr. Evans, who set up a hollow cough to induce her to ask him to leave off cigarettes. The men voted her "the funniest and jolliest ever," but the sniffs on the top step and the lower step were implacable.

I pray you to let the drama halt while Chorus stalks to the footlights and drops an epicedian tear upon the fatness of Mr. Hoover. Tune the pipes to the tragedy of tallow, the bane of bulk, the calamity of corpulence. Tried out, Falstaff might have rendered more romance to the ton than would have Romeo's rickety ribs to the ounce. A lover may sigh, but he must not puff. To the train of Momus are the fat men remanded. In vain beats the faithfullest heart above a 52-inch belt. Avaunt, Hoover! Hoover, forty-five, flush and foolish, might carry off Helen herself; Hoover, forty-five, flush, foolish and fat is meat for perdition. There was never a chance for you, Hoover.

As Mrs. Parker's roomers sat thus one summer's evening, Miss Leeson looked up into the firmament and cried with her little gay laugh:

"Why, there's Billy Jackson! I can see him from down here, too."

All looked up—some at the windows of skyscrapers, some casting about for an airship, Jackson-guided.

"It's that star," explained Miss Leeson, pointing with a tiny finger. "Not the big one that twinkles—the steady blue one near it. I can see it every night through my skylight. I named it Billy Jackson."

"Well, really!" said Miss Longnecker. "I didn't know you were an astronomer, Miss Leeson."

"Oh, yes," said the small star gazer, "I know as much as any of them about the style of sleeves they're going to wear next fall in Mars."

"Well, really!" said Miss Longnecker. "The star you refer to is

Gamma, of the constellation Cassiopeia. It is nearly of the second magnitude, and its meridian passage is——"

"Oh," said the very young Mr. Evans, "I think Billy Jackson is a much better name for it."

"Same here," said Mr. Hoover, loudly breathing defiance to Miss Longnecker. "I think Miss Leeson has just as much right to name stars as any of those old astrologers had."

"Well, really!" said Miss Longnecker.

"I wonder whether it's a shooting star," remarked Miss Dorn. "I hit nine ducks and a rabbit out of ten in the gallery at Coney Sunday."

"He doesn't show up very well from down here," said Miss Leeson. "You ought to see him from my room. You know you can see stars even in the daytime from the bottom of a well. At night my room is like the shaft of a coal mine, and it makes Billy Jackson look like the big diamond pin that Night fastens her kimono with."

There came a time after that when Miss Leeson brought no formidable papers home to copy. And when she went out in the morning, instead of working, she went from office to office and let her heart melt away in the drip of cold refusals transmitted through insolent office boys. This went on.

There came an evening when she wearily climbed Mrs. Parker's stoop at the hour when she always returned from her dinner at the restaurant. But she had had no dinner.

As she stepped into the hall Mr. Hoover met her and seized his chance. He asked her to marry him, and his fatness hovered above her like an avalanche. She dodged, and caught the balustrade. He tried for her hand, and she raised it and smote him weakly in the face. Step by step she went up, dragging herself by the railing. She passed Mr. Skidder's door as he was red-inking a stage direction for Myrtle Delorme (Miss Leeson) in his (unaccepted) comedy, to "pirouette across stage from L to the side of the Count." Up the carpeted ladder she crawled at last and opened the door of the skylight room.

She was too weak to light the lamp or to undress. She fell upon the iron cot, her fragile body scarcely hollowing the worn springs. And in that Erebus of a room she slowly raised her heavy eyelids, and smiled.

For Billy Jackson was shining down on her, calm and bright and constant through the skylight. There was no world about her. She was sunk in a pit of blackness, with but that small square of pallid light framing the star that she had so whimsically and oh, so ineffectually, named. Miss Longnecker must be right: it was Gamma, of the constellation Cassiopeia, and not Billy Jackson. And yet she could not let it be Gamma.

As she lay on her back, she tried twice to raise her arm. The third time she got two thin fingers to her lips and blew a kiss out of the black pit to Billy Jackson. Her arm fell back limply.

"Good-bye, Billy," she murmured, faintly. "You're millions of miles away and you won't even twinkle once. But you kept where I could see you most of the time up there when there wasn't anything else but darkness to look at, didn't you? . . . Millions of miles. . . . Good-bye, Billy Jackson."

Clara, the coloured maid, found the door locked at 10 the next day, and they forced it open. Vinegar, and the slapping of wrists and burnt feathers proving of no avail, some one ran to 'phone for an ambulance.

In due time it backed up to the door with much gong-clanging, and the capable young medico, in his white linen coat, ready, active, confident, with his smooth face half debonair, half grim, danced up the steps.

"Ambulance call to 49," he said, briefly. "What's the trouble?"

"Oh, yes, doctor," sniffed Mrs. Parker, as though her trouble that there should be trouble in the house was the greater. "I can't think what can be the matter with her. Nothing we could do would bring her to. It's a young woman, a Miss Elsie—yes, a Miss Elsie Leeson. Never before in my house——"

"What room?" cried the doctor in a terrible voice, to which Mrs. Parker was a stranger.

"The skylight room. It——"

Evidently the ambulance doctor was familiar with the location of skylight rooms. He was gone up the stairs, four at a time. Mrs. Parker followed slowly, as her dignity demanded.

On the first landing she met him coming back bearing the astronomer in his arms. He stopped and let loose the practised scalpel of his tongue, not loudly. Gradually Mrs. Parker crumpled as a stiff garment that slips down from a nail. Ever afterwards there remained crumples in her mind and body. Sometimes her curious roomers would ask her what the doctor said to her.

"Let that be," she would answer. "If I can get forgiveness for having heard it I will be satisfied."

The ambulance physician strode with his burden through the pack of hounds that follow the curiosity chase, and even they fell back along the sidewalk abashed, for his face was that of one who bears his own dead.

They noticed that he did not lay down upon the bed prepared for it in the ambulance the form that he carried, and all that he said was: "Drive like h—l, Wilson," to the driver.

That is all. Is it a story? In the next morning's paper I saw a little news item, and the last sentence of it may help you (as it helped me) to weld the incidents together.

It recounted the reception into Bellevue Hospital of a young woman who had been removed from No. 49 East —— Street, suffering from debility induced by starvation. It concluded with these words:

"Dr. William Jackson, the ambulance physician who attended the case, says the patient will recover."

Man About Town

THERE WERE two or three things that I wanted to know. I do not care about a mystery. So I began to inquire.

It took me two weeks to find out what women carry in dress suit cases. And then I began to ask why a mattress is made in two pieces. This serious query was at first received with suspicion because it sounded like a conundrum. I was at last assured that its double form of construction was designed to make lighter the burden of woman, who makes up beds. I was so foolish as to persist, begging to know why, then, they were not made in two equal pieces; whereupon I was shunned.

The third draught that I craved from the fount of knowledge was enlightenment concerning the character known as A Man About Town. He was more vague in my mind than a type should be. We must have a concrete idea of anything, even if it be an imaginary idea, before we can comprehend it. Now, I have a mental picture of John Doe that is as clear as a steel engraving. His eyes are weak blue; he wears a brown vest and a shiny black serge coat. He stands always in the sunshine chewing something; and he keeps half-shutting his pocket knife and opening it again with his thumb. And, if the Man Higher Up is ever found, take my assurance for it, he will be a large, pale man with blue wristlets showing under his cuffs, and he will be sitting to have his shoes polished within sound of a bowling alley, and there will be somewhere about him turquoises.

But the canvas of my imagination, when it came to limning the Man About Town, was blank. I fancied that he had a detachable sneer (like the smile of the Cheshire cat) and attached cuffs; and that was all. Whereupon I asked a newspaper reporter about him.

"Why," said he, "a 'Man About Town' is something between a 'rounder' and a 'clubman.' He isn't exactly—well, he fits in between Mrs. Fish's receptions and private boxing bouts. He doesn't —well, he doesn't belong either to the Lotos Club or to the Jerry McGeogheghan Galvanized Iron Workers' Apprentices' Left Hook Chowder Association. I don't exactly know how to describe him to you. You'll see him everywhere there's anything doing. Yes, I suppose he's a type. Dress clothes every evening; knows the ropes; calls every policeman and waiter in town by their first names. No; he never travels with the hydrogen derivatives. You generally see him alone or with another man."

My friend the reporter left me, and I wandered further afield. By this time the 3126 electric lights on the Rialto were alight. People passed, but they held me not. Paphian eyes rayed upon me, and left me unscathed. Diners, heimgangers, shop-girls, confidence men, panhandlers, actors, highwaymen, millionaires, and outlanders hurried, skipped, strolled, sneaked, swaggered, and scurried by me; but I took no note of them. I knew them all; I had read their hearts; they had served. I wanted my Man About Town. He was a type, and to drop him would be an error— a typograph—but no! let us continue.

Let us continue with a moral digression. To see a family reading the Sunday paper gratifies. The sections have been separated. Papa is earnestly scanning the page that pictures the young lady exercising before an open window, and bending—but there, there! Mamma is interested in trying to guess the missing letters in the word N—w Yo—k. The oldest girls are eagerly perusing the financial reports, for a certain young man remarked last Sunday night that he had taken a flyer in Q., X. & Z. Willie, the eighteen-year-old son, who attends the New York public school, is absorbed in the weekly article describing how to make over an old shirt, for he hopes to take a prize in sewing on graduation day.

Grandma is holding to the comic supplement with a two-hours' grip; and little Tottie, the baby, is rocking along the best she can with the real estate transfers. This view is intended to be reassuring, for it is desirable that a few lines of this story be skipped. For it introduces strong drink.

I went into a café to—and while it was being mixed I asked the man who grabs up your hot Scotch spoon as soon as you lay it down what he understood by the term, epithet, description, designation, characterization or appellation, viz.: a "Man About Town."

"Why," said he, carefully, "it means a fly guy that's wise to the all-night push—see? It's a hot sport that you can't bump to the rail anywhere between the Flatirons—see? I guess that's about what it means."

I thanked him and departed.

On the sidewalk a Salvation lassie shook her contribution receptacle gently against my waistcoat pocket.

"Would you mind telling me," I asked her, "if you ever meet with the character commonly denominated as 'A Man About Town' during your daily wanderings?"

"I think I know whom you mean," she answered, with a gentle smile. "We see them in the same places night after night. They are the devil's body guard, and if the soldiers of any army are as faithful as they are, their commanders are well served. We go among then, diverting a few pennies from their wickedness to the Lord's service."

She shook the box again and I dropped a dime into it.

In front of a glittering hotel a friend of mine, a critic, was climbing from a cab. He seemed at leisure; and I put my question to him. He answered me conscientiously, as I was sure he would.

"There is a type of 'Man About Town' in New York," he answered. "The term is quite familiar to me, but I don't think I was ever called upon to define the character before. It would be difficult to point you out an exact specimen. I would say, offhand, that it is a man who had a hopeless case of the peculiar New York disease of wanting to see and know. At 6 o'clock each day life begins with him. He follows rigidly the conventions of dress and manners; but in the business of poking his nose into places where he does not belong he could give pointers to a civet cat or a jackdaw. He is the man who has chased Bohemia about the town from rathskeller to roof garden and from Hester Street to Harlem until you can't find a place in the city where they don't cut their spaghetti with a knife. Your 'Man About Town' has done that. He is always on the scent of something new. He is curiosity, impudence, and omnipresence. Hansoms were made for him, and gold-banded cigars; and the curse of music at dinner. There are not so many of him; but his minority report is adopted everywhere.

"I'm glad you brought up the subject; I've felt the influence of this nocturnal blight upon our city, but I never thought to analyze it before. I can see now that your 'Man About Town' should have been classified long ago. In his wake spring up wine agents and cloak models; and the orchestra plays 'Let's All Go Up to Maud's' for him, by request, instead of Händel. He makes his rounds every evening; while you and I see the elephant once a week. When the cigar store is raided, he winks at the officer, familiar with his ground, and walks away immune, while you and I search among the Presidents for names, and among the stars for addresses to give the desk sergeant."

My friend, the critic, paused to acquire breath for fresh eloquence. I seized my advantage.

"You have classified him," I cried with joy. "You have painted his portrait in the gallery of city types. But I must meet one face to face. I must study the Man About Town at first hand. Where shall I find him? How shall I know him?"

Without seeming to hear me, the critic went on. And his cab-driver was waiting for his fare, too.

"He is the sublimated essence of Butt-in; the refined, intrinsic extract of Rubber; the concentrated, purified, irrefutable, unavoidable spirit of Curiosity and Inquisitiveness. A new sensation is the breath in his nostrils; when his experience is exhausted he explores new fields with the indefatigability of a——"

"Excuse me," I interrupted, "but can you produce one of this type? It is a new thing to me. I must study it. I will search the town over until I find one. Its habitat must be here on Broadway."

"I am about to dine here," said my friend. "Come inside, and if there is a Man About Town present I will point him out to you. I know most of the regular patrons here."

"I am not dining yet," I said to him. "You will excuse me. I am going to find my Man About Town this night if I have to rake New York from the Battery to Little Coney Island."

I left the hotel and walked down Broadway. The pursuit of my type gave a pleasant savor of life and interest to the air I breathed. I was glad to be in a city so great, so complex and diversified. Leisurely and with something of an air I strolled along with my heart expanding at the thought that I was a citizen of great Gotham, a sharer in its magnificence and pleasures, a partaker in its glory and prestige.

I turned to cross the street. I heard something buzz like a bee, and then I took a long, pleasant ride with Santos-Dumont.

When I opened my eyes I remembered a smell of gasoline, and I said aloud: "Hasn't it passed yet?"

A hospital nurse laid a hand that was not particularly soft upon my brow that was not at all fevered. A young doctor came along, grinned, and handed me a morning newspaper.

"Want to see how it happened?" he asked, cheerily. I read the article. Its headlines began where I heard the buzzing leave off the night before. It closed with these lines:

"——Bellevue Hospital, where it was said that his injuries were not serious. He appeared to be a typical Man About Town."

The Cop and the Anthem

ON HIS BENCH in Madison Square Soapy moved uneasily. When wild geese honk high of nights, and when women without sealskin coats grow kind to their husbands, and when Soapy moves uneasily on his bench in the park, you may know that winter is near at hand.

A dead leaf fell in Soapy's lap. That was Jack Frost's card. Jack is kind to the regular denizens of Madison Square, and gives fair warning of his annual call. At the corners of four streets he hands his pasteboard to the North Wind, footman of the mansion of All Outdoors, so that the inhabitants thereof may make ready.

Soapy's mind became cognizant of the fact that the time had come for him to resolve himself into a singular Committee of Ways and Means to provide against the coming rigor. And therefore he moved uneasily on his bench.

The hibernatorial ambitions of Soapy were not of the highest. In them were no considerations of Mediterranean cruises, of soporific Southern skies or drifting in the Vesuvian Bay. Three months on the Island was what his soul craved. Three months of assured board and bed and congenial company, safe from Boreas and bluecoats, seemed to Soapy the essence of things desirable.

For years the hospitable Blackwell's had been his winter quarters. Just as his more fortunate fellow New Yorkers had bought their tickets to Palm Beach and the Riviera each winter, so Soapy had made his humble arrangements for his annual hegira to the

Island. And now the time was come. On the previous night three Sabbath newspapers, distributed beneath his coat, about his ankles and over his lap, had failed to repulse the cold as he slept on his bench near the spurting fountain in the ancient square. So the Island loomed big and timely in Soapy's mind. He scorned the provisions made in the name of charity for the city's dependents. In Soapy's opinion the Law was more benign than Philanthropy. There was an endless round of institutions, municipal and eleemosynary, on which he might set out and receive lodging and food accordant with the simple life. But to one of Soapy's proud spirit the gifts of charity are encumbered. If not in coin you must pay in humiliation of spirit for every benefit received at the hands of philanthropy. As Cæsar had his Brutus, every bed of charity must have its toll of a bath, every loaf of bread its compensation of a private and personal inquisition. Wherefore it is better to be a guest of the law, which, though conducted by rules, does not meddle unduly with a gentleman's private affairs.

Soapy, having decided to go to the Island, at once set about accomplishing his desire. There were many easy ways of doing this. The pleasantest was to dine luxuriously at some expensive restaurant; and then, after declaring insolvency, be handed over quietly and without uproar to a policeman. An accommodating magistrate would do the rest.

Soapy left his bench and strolled out of the square and across the level sea of asphalt, where Broadway and Fifth Avenue flow together. Up Broadway he turned, and halted at a glittering café, where are gathered together nightly the choicest products of the grape, the silkworm, and the protoplasm.

Soapy had confidence in himself from the lowest button of his vest upward. He was shaven, and his coat was decent and his neat black, ready-tied four-in-hand had been presented to him by a lady missionary on Thanksgiving Day. If he could reach a table in the restaurant unsuspected success would be his. The portion of him that would show above the table would raise no doubt in the waiter's mind. A roasted mallard duck, thought Soapy, would be about the thing—with a bottle of Chablis, and then Camembert, a demi-tasse and a cigar. One dollar for the cigar would be enough. The total would not be so high as to call forth any supreme manifestation of revenge from the café management; and yet the meat would leave him filled and happy for the journey to his winter refuge.

But as Soapy set foot inside the restaurant door the head waiter's eye fell upon his frayed trousers and decadent shoes. Strong and ready hands turned him about and conveyed him in silence and haste to the sidewalk and averted the ignoble fate of the menaced mallard.

Soapy turned off Broadway. It seemed that his route to the coveted Island was not to be an epicurean one. Some other way of entering limbo must be thought of.

At a corner of Sixth Avenue electric lights and cunningly displayed wares behind plate-glass made a shop window conspicuous. Soapy took a cobblestone and dashed it through the glass. People came running around the corner, a policeman in the lead. Soapy stood still, with his hands in his pockets, and smiled at the sight of brass buttons.

"Where's the man that done that?" inquired the officer, excitedly.

"Don't you figure out that I might have had something to do with it?" said Soapy, not without sarcasm, but friendly, as one greets good fortune.

The policeman's mind refused to accept Soapy even as a clue. Men who smash windows do not remain to parley with the law's minions. They take to their heels. The policeman saw a man halfway down the block running to catch a car. With drawn club he joined in the pursuit. Soapy, with disgust in his heart, loafed along, twice unsuccessful.

On the opposite side of the street was a restaurant of no great pretensions. It catered to large appetites and modest purses. Its crockery and atmosphere were thick; its soup and napery thin. Into this place Soapy took his accusive shoes and telltale trousers without challenge. At a table he sat and consumed beefsteak, flapjacks, doughnuts and pie. And then to the waiter he betrayed the fact that the minutest coin and himself were strangers.

"Now, get busy and call a cop," said Soapy. "And don't keep a gentleman waiting."

"No cop for youse," said the waiter, with a voice like butter cakes and an eye like the cherry in a Manhattan cocktail. "Hey, Con!"

Neatly upon his left ear on the callous pavement two waiters pitched Soapy. He arose joint by joint, as a carpenter's rule opens, and beat the dust from his clothes. Arrest seemed but a rosy dream. The Island seemed very far away. A policeman who stood before a drug store two doors away laughed and walked down the street.

Five blocks Soapy travelled before his courage permitted him to woo capture again. This time the opportunity presented what he fatuously termed to himself a "cinch." A young woman of a modest and pleasing guise was standing before a show window gazing with sprightly interest at its display of shaving mugs and inkstands, and two yards from the window a large policeman of severe demeanor leaned against a water plug.

It was Soapy's design to assume the rôle of the despicable and execrated "masher." The refined and elegant appearance of his victim and the contiguity of the conscientious cop encouraged him to believe that he would soon feel the pleasant official clutch upon his arm that would insure his winter quarters on the right little, tight little isle.

Soapy straightened the lady missionary's ready-made tie, dragged his shrinking cuffs into the open, set his hat at a killing cant and sidled toward the young woman. He made eyes at her, was taken with sudden coughs and "hems," smiled, smirked and went brazenly through the impudent and contemptible litany of the "masher." With half an eye Soapy saw that the policeman was watching him fixedly. The young woman moved away a few steps, and again bestowed her absorbed attention upon the shaving mugs. Soapy followed, boldly stepping to her side, raised his hat and said:

"Ah there, Bedelia! Don't you want to come and play in my yard?"

The policeman was still looking. The persecuted young woman had but to beckon a finger and Soapy would be practically en route for his insular haven. Already he imagined he could feel the cozy warmth of the station-house. The young woman faced him and, stretching out a hand, caught Soapy's coat sleeve.

"Sure, Mike," she said, joyfully, "if you'll blow me to a pail of suds. I'd have spoke to you sooner, but the cop was watching."

With the young woman playing the clinging ivy to his oak Soapy walked past the policeman overcome with gloom. He seemed doomed to liberty.

At the next corner he shook off his companion and ran. He halted in the district where by night are found the lightest streets, hearts, vows and librettos. Women in furs and men in greatcoats moved gaily in the wintry air. A sudden fear seized Soapy that some dreadful enchantment had rendered him immune to arrest. The thought brought a little of panic upon it, and when he came upon another policeman lounging grandly in front of a transplendent theatre he caught at the immediate straw of "disorderly conduct."

On the sidewalk Soapy began to yell drunken gibberish at the top of his harsh voice. He danced, howled, raved, and otherwise disturbed the welkin.

The policeman twirled his club, turned his back to Soapy and remarked to a citizen.

"'Tis one of them Yale lads celebratin' the goose egg they give to the Hartford College. Noisy; but no harm. We've instructions to lave them be."

Disconsolate, Soapy ceased his unavailing racket. Would never a policeman lay hands on him? In his fancy the Island seemed an unattainable Arcadia. He buttoned his thin coat against the chilling wind.

In a cigar store he saw a well-dressed man lighting a cigar at a swinging light. His silk umbrella he had set by the door on entering. Soapy stepped inside, secured the umbrella and sauntered off with it slowly. The man at the cigar light followed hastily.

"My umbrella," he said, sternly.

"Oh, is it?" sneered Soapy, adding insult to petit larceny. "Well, why don't you call a policeman? I took it. Your umbrella! Why don't you call a cop? There stands one on the corner."

The umbrella owner slowed his steps. Soapy did likewise, with a presentiment that luck would again run against him. The policeman looked at the two curiously.

"Of course," said the umbrella man—"that is—well, you know how these mistakes occur—I—if it's your umbrella I hope you'll excuse me—I picked it up this morning in a restaurant——If you recognize it as yours, why—I hope you'll——"

"Of course it's mine," said Soapy, viciously.

The ex-umbrella man retreated. The policeman hurried to assist a tall blonde in an opera cloak across the street in front of a street car that was approaching two blocks away.

Soapy walked eastward through a street damaged by improvements. He hurled the umbrella wrathfully into an excavation. He muttered against the men who wear helmets and carry clubs. Because he wanted to fall into their clutches, they seemed to regard him as a king who could do no wrong.

At length Soapy reached one of the avenues to the east where the glitter and turmoil was but faint. He set his face down this toward Madison Square, for the homing instinct survives even when the home is a park bench.

But on an unusually quiet corner Soapy came to a standstill. Here was an old church, quaint and rambling and gabled. Through one violet-stained window a soft light glowed, where, no doubt, the organist loitered over the keys, making sure of his mastery of the coming Sabbath anthem. For there drifted out to Soapy's ears sweet music that caught and held him transfixed against the convolutions of the iron fence.

The moon was above, lustrous and serene; vehicles and pedestrians were few; sparrows twittered sleepily in the eaves—for a little while the scene might have been a country churchyard. And the anthem that the organist played cemented Soapy to the iron fence, for he had known it well in the days when his life contained such things as mothers and roses and ambitions and friends and immaculate thoughts and collars.

The conjunction of Soapy's receptive state of mind and the influences about the old church wrought a sudden and wonderful change in his soul. He viewed with swift horror the pit into which he had tumbled, the degraded days, unworthy desires, dead hopes, wrecked faculties and base motives that made up his existence.

And also in a moment his heart responded thrillingly to this novel mood. An instantaneous and strong impulse moved him to battle with his desperate fate. He would pull himself out of the mire; he would make a man of himself again; he would conquer the evil that had taken possession of him. There was time; he was comparatively young yet: he would resurrect his old eager ambitions and pursue them without faltering. Those solemn but sweet organ notes had set up a revolution in him. To-morrow he would go into the roaring downtown district and find work. A fur importer had once offered him a place as driver. He would find him to-morrow and ask for the position. He would be somebody in the world. He would——

Soapy felt a hand laid on his arm. He looked quickly around into the broad face of a policeman.

"What are you doin' here?" asked the officer.

"Nothin'," said Soapy.

"Then come along," said the policeman.

"Three months on the Island," said the Magistrate in the Police Court the next morning.

The Love-Philtre of Ikey Schoenstein

THE Blue Light Drug Store is downtown, between the Bowery and First Avenue, where the distance between the two streets is the shortest. The Blue Light does not consider that pharmacy is a thing of bric-à-brac, scent and ice-cream soda. If you ask it for pain-killer it will not give you a bonbon. The Blue Light scorns the labor-saving arts of modern pharmacy. It macerates its opium and percolates its own laudanum and paregoric. To this day pills are made behind its tall prescription desk—pills rolled out on its own pill-tile, divided with a spatula, rolled with the finger and thumb, dusted with calcined magnesia and delivered in little round paste-board pill-boxes. The store is on a corner about which coveys of ragged-plumed, hilarious children play and become candidates for the cough drops and soothing syrups that wait for them inside.

Ikey Schoenstein was the night clerk of the Blue Light and the friend of his customers. Thus it is on the East Side, where the heart of pharmacy is not glacé. There, as it should be, the druggist is a counsellor, a confessor, an adviser, an able and willing missionary and mentor whose learning is respected, whose occult wisdom is venerated and whose medicine is often poured, untasted, into the gutter. Therefore Ikey's corniform, bespectacled nose and narrow, knowledge-bowed figure was well known in the vicinity of the Blue Light, and his advice and notice were much desired.

Ikey roomed and breakfasted at Mrs. Riddle's two squares away. Mrs. Riddle had a daughter named Rosy. The circumlocution has been in vain—you must have guessed it—Ikey adored Rosy. She tinctured all his thoughts; she was the compound extract of all that was chemically pure and officinal—the dispensatory contained nothing equal to her. But Ikey was timid, and his hopes remained insoluble in the menstruum of his backwardness and fears. Behind his counter he was a superior being, calmly conscious of special knowledge and worth; outside he was a weak-kneed, purblind, motorman-cursed rambler, with ill-fitting clothes stained with chemicals and smelling of socotrine aloes and valerianate of ammonia.

The fly in Ikey's ointment (thrice welcome, pat trope!) was Chunk McGowan.

Mr. McGowan was also striving to catch the bright smiles tossed about by Rosy. But he was no out-fielder as Ikey was; he picked them off the bat. At the same time he was Ikey's friend and customer, and often dropped in at the Blue Light Drug Store to have a bruise painted with iodine or get a cut rubber-plastered after a pleasant evening spent along the Bowery.

One afternoon McGowan drifted in in his silent, easy way, and sat, comely, smooth-faced, hard, indomitable, good-natured, upon a stool.

"Ikey," said he, when his friend had fetched his mortar and sat opposite, grinding gum benzoin to a powder, "get busy with your ear. It's drugs for me if you've got the line I need."

Ikey scanned the countenance of Mr. McGowan for the usual evidence of conflict, but found none.

"Take your coat off," he ordered. "I guess already that you have been stuck in the ribs with a knife. I have many times told you those Dagoes would do you up."

Mr. McGowan smiled. "Not them," he said. "Not any Dagoes. But you've located the diagnosis all right enough—it's under my coat, near the ribs. Say! Ikey—Rosy and me are goin' to run away and get married to-night."

Ikey's left forefinger was doubled over the edge of the mortar, holding it steady. He gave it a wild rap with the pestle, but felt it not. Meanwhile Mr. McGowan's smile faded to a look of perplexed gloom.

"That is," he continued, "if she keeps in the notion until the time comes. We've been layin' pipes for the getaway for two weeks. One day she says she will; the same evenin' she says nixy. We've agreed on to-night, and Rosy's stuck to the affirmative this time for two whole days. But it's five hours yet till the time, and I'm afraid she'll stand me up when it comes to the scratch."

"You said you wanted drugs," remarked Ikey.

Mr. McGowan looked ill at ease and harassed—a condition opposed to his usual line of demeanor. He made a patent-medicine almanac into a roll and fitted it with unprofitable carefulness about his finger.

"I wouldn't have this double handicap make a false start to-night for a million," he said. "I've got a little flat up in Harlem all ready, with chrysanthemums on the table and a kettle ready to boil. And I've engaged a pulpit pounder to be ready at his house for us at 9.30. It's got to come off. And if Rosy don't change her mind again!"—Mr. McGowan ceased, a prey to his doubts.

"I don't see then yet," said Ikey, shortly, "what makes it that you talk of drugs, or what I can be doing about it."

"Old man Riddle don't like me a little bit," went on the uneasy suitor, bent upon marshalling his arguments. "For a week he hasn't let Rosy step outside the door with me. If it wasn't for losin' a boarder they'd have bounced me long ago. I'm makin' $20 a week and she'll never regret flyin' the coop with Chunk McGowan."

"You will excuse me, Chunk," said Ikey. "I must make a prescription that is to be called for soon."

"Say," said McGowan, looking up suddenly, "say, Ikey, ain't there a drug of some kind—some kind of powders that'll make a girl like you better if you give 'em to her?"

Ikey's lip beneath his nose curled with the scorn of superior enlightenment; but before he could answer, McGowan continued:

"Tim Lacy told me he got some once from a croaker uptown and fed 'em to his girl in soda water. From the very first dose he was ace-high and everybody else looked like thirty cents to her. They was married in less than two weeks."

Strong and simple was Chunk McGowan. A better reader of men than Ikey was could have seen that his tough frame was strung upon fine wires. Like a good general who was about to invade the enemy's territory he was seeking to guard every point against possible failure.

"I thought," went on Chunk, hopefully, "that if I had one of them powders to give Rosy when I see her at supper to-night it might brace her up and keep her from reneging on the proposition to skip. I guess she don't need a mule team to drag her away, but women are better at coaching than they are at running bases. If the stuff'll work just for a couple of hours it'll do the trick."

"When is this foolishness of running away to be happening?" asked Ikey.

"Nine o'clock," said Mr. McGowan. "Supper's at seven. At eight Rosy goes to bed with a headache, at nine old Parvenzano lets me through to his backyard, where there's a board off Riddle's fence, next door. I go under her window and help her down the fire-escape. We've got to make it early on the preacher's account. It's all dead easy if Rosy don't balk when the flag drops. Can you fix me one of them powders, Ikey?"

Ikey Schoenstein rubbed his nose slowly.

"Chunk," said he, "it is of drugs of that nature that pharmaceutists must have much carefulness. To you alone of my acquaintance would I intrust a powder like that. But for you I shall make it, and you shall see how it makes Rosy to think of you."

Ikey went behind the prescription desk. There he crushed to a powder two soluble tablets, each containing a quarter of a grain of morphia. To them he added a little sugar of milk to increase the bulk, and folded the mixture neatly in a white paper. Taken by an adult this powder would insure several hours of heavy slumber without danger to the sleeper. This he handed to Chunk McGowan, telling him to administer it in a liquid if possible, and received the hearty thanks of the backyard Lochinvar.

The subtlety of Ikey's action becomes apparent upon recital of his subsequent move. He sent a messenger for Mr. Riddle and disclosed the plans of Mr. McGowan for eloping with Rosy. Mr. Riddle was a stout man, brick-dusty of complexion and sudden in action.

"Much obliged," he said, briefly, to Ikey. "The lazy Irish loafer! My own room's just above Rosy's. I'll just go up there myself after supper and load the shot-gun and wait. If he comes in my backyard he'll go away in a ambulance instead of a bridal chaise."

With Rosy held in the clutches of Morpheus for a many-hours deep slumber, and the blood-thirsty parent waiting, armed and forewarned, Ikey felt that his rival was close, indeed, upon discomfiture.

All night in the Blue Light Drug Store he waited at his duties for chance news of the tragedy, but none came.

At eight o'clock in the morning the day clerk arrived and Ikey started hurriedly for Mrs. Riddle's to learn the outcome. And, lo! as he stepped out of the store who but Chunk McGowan sprang from a passing street car and grasped his hand—Chunk McGowan with a victor's smile and flushed with joy.

"Pulled it off," said Chunk with Elysium in his grin. "Rosy hit the fire-escape on time to a second, and we was under the wire at the Reverend's at 9.30¼. She's up at the flat—she cooked eggs this mornin' in a blue kimono—Lord! how lucky I am! You must pace up some day, Ikey, and feed with us. I've got a job down near the bridge, and that's where I'm heading for now."

"The—the—powder?" stammered Ikey.

"Oh, that stuff you gave me!" said Chunk, broadening his grin; "well, it was this way. I sat down at the supper table last night at Riddle's, and I looked at Rosy, and I says to myself, 'Chunk, if you get the girl get her on the square—don't try any hocus-pocus with a thoroughbred like her.' And I keeps the paper you give me in my pocket. And then my lamps fall on another party present, who, I says to myself, is failin' in a proper affection toward his comin' son-in-law, so I watches my chance and dumps that powder in old man Riddle's coffee—see?"

Mammon and the Archer

OLD Anthony Rockwall, retired manufacturer and proprietor of Rockwall's Eureka Soap, looked out the library window of his Fifth Avenue mansion and grinned. His neighbour to the right—the aristocratic clubman, G. Van Schuylight Suffolk-Jones—came out to his waiting motor-car, wrinkling a contumelious nostril, as usual, at the Italian renaissance sculpture of the soap palace's front elevation.

"Stuck-up old statuette of nothing doing!" commented the ex-Soap King. "The Eden Musée'll get that old frozen Nesselrode yet if he don't watch out. I'll have this house painted red, white, and blue next summer and see if that'll make his Dutch nose turn up any higher."

And then Anthony Rockwall, who never cared for bells, went to the door of his library and shouted "Mike!" in the same voice that had once chipped off pieces of the welkin on the Kansas prairies.

"Tell my son," said Anthony to the answering menial, "to come in here before he leaves the house."

When young Rockwall entered the library the old man laid aside his newspaper, looked at him with a kindly grimness on his big, smooth, ruddy countenance, rumpled his mop of white hair with one hand and rattled the keys in his pocket with the other.

"Richard," said Anthony Rockwall, "what do you pay for the soap that you use?"

Richard, only six months home from college, was startled a little. He had not yet taken the measure of this sire of his, who was as full of unexpectedness as a girl at her first party.

"Six dollars a dozen, I think, dad."

"And your clothes?"

"I suppose about sixty dollars, as a rule."

"You're a gentleman," said Anthony, decidedly. "I've heard of these young bloods spending $24 a dozen for soap, and going over the hundred mark for clothes. You've got as much money to waste as any of 'em, and yet you stick to what's decent and moderate. Now I use the old Eureka—not only for sentiment, but it's the purest soap made. Whenever you pay more than 10 cents a cake for soap you buy bad perfumes and labels. But 50 cents is doing very well for a young man in your generation, position and condition. As I said, you're a gentleman. They say it takes three generations to make one. They're off. Money'll do it as slick as soap grease. It's made you one. By hokey! it's almost made one of me. I'm nearly as impolite and disagreeable and ill-mannered as these two old knickerbocker gents on each side of me that can't sleep of nights because I bought in between 'em."

"There are some things that money can't accomplish," remarked young Rockwall, rather gloomily.

"Now, don't say that," said old Anthony, shocked. "I bet my money on money every time. I've been through the encyclopædia down to Y looking for something you can't buy with it; and I expect to have to take up the appendix next week. I'm for money against the field. Tell me something money won't buy."

"For one thing," answered Richard, rankling a little, "it won't buy one into the exclusive circles of society."

"Oho! won't it?" thundered the champion of the root of evil. "You tell me where your exclusive circles would be if the first Astor hadn't had the money to pay for his steerage passage over?"

Richard sighed.

"And that's what I was coming to," said the old man, less boisterously. "That's why I asked you to come in. There's something going wrong with you, boy. I've been noticing it for two weeks.

Out with it. I guess I could lay my hands on eleven millions within twenty-four hours, besides the real estate. If it's your liver, there's the *Rambler* down in the bay, coaled, and ready to steam down to the Bahamas in two days."

"Not a bad guess, dad; you haven't missed it far."

"Ah," said Anthony, keenly; "what's her name?"

Richard began to walk up and down the library floor. There was enough comradeship and sympathy in this crude old father of his to draw his confidence.

"Why don't you ask her?" demanded old Anthony. "She'll jump at you. You've got the money and the looks, and you're a decent boy. Your hands are clean. You've got no Eureka soap on 'em. You've been to college, but she'll overlook that."

"I haven't had a chance," said Richard.

"Make one," said Anthony. "Take her for a walk in the park, or a straw ride, or walk home with her from church. Chance! Pshaw!"

"You don't know the social mill, dad. She's part of the stream that turns it. Every hour and minute of her time is arranged for days in advance. I must have that girl, dad, or this town is a blackjack swamp forevermore. And I can't write it—I can't do that."

"Tut!" said the old man. "Do you mean to tell me that with all the money I've got you can't get an hour or two of a girl's time for yourself?"

"I've put it off too late. She's going to sail for Europe at noon day after to-morrow for a two years' stay. I'm to see her alone to-morrow evening for a few minutes. She's at Larchmont now at her aunt's. I can't go there. But I'm allowed to meet her with a cab at the Grand Central Station to-morrow evening at the 8.30 train. We drive down Broadway to Wallack's at a gallop, where her mother and a box party will be waiting for us in the lobby. Do you think she would listen to a declaration from me during that six or eight minutes under those circumstances? No. And what chance would I have in the theatre or afterward? None. No, dad, this is one tangle that your money can't unravel. We can't buy one minute of time with cash; if we could, rich people would live longer. There's no hope of getting a talk with Miss Lantry before she sails."

"All right, Richard, my boy," said old Anthony, cheerfully. "You may run along down to your club now. I'm glad it ain't your liver. But don't forget to burn a few punk sticks in the joss house to the great god Mazuma from time to time. You say money won't buy time? Well, of course, you can't order eternity wrapped up and delivered at your residence for a price, but I've seen Father Time get pretty bad stone bruises on his heels when he walked through the gold diggings."

That night came Aunt Ellen, gentle, sentimental, wrinkled, sighing, oppressed by wealth, in to Brother Anthony at his evening paper, and began discourse on the subject of lovers' woes.

"He told me all about it," said Brother Anthony, yawning. "I told him my bank account was at his service. And then he began to knock money. Said money couldn't help. Said the rules of society couldn't be bucked for a yard by a team of ten-millionaires."

"Oh, Anthony," sighed Aunt Ellen, "I wish you would not think so much of money. Wealth is nothing where a true affection is concerned. Love is all-powerful. If he only had spoken earlier! She could not have refused our Richard. But now I fear it is too late. He will have no opportunity to address her. All your gold cannot bring happiness to your son."

At eight o'clock the next evening Aunt Ellen took a quaint old gold ring from a moth-eaten case and gave it to Richard.

"Wear it to-night, nephew," she begged. "Your mother gave it to me. Good luck in love she said it brought. She asked me to give it to you when you had found the one you loved."

Young Rockwall took the ring reverently and tried it on his smallest finger. It slipped as far as the second joint and stopped. He took it off and stuffed it into his vest pocket, after the manner of man. And then he 'phoned for his cab.

At the station he captured Miss Lantry out of the gabbing mob at eight thirty-two.

"We mustn't keep mamma and the others waiting," said she.

"To Wallack's Theatre as fast as you can drive!" said Richard, loyally.

They whirled up Forty-second to Broadway, and then down the white-starred lane that leads from the soft meadows of sunset to the rocky hills of morning.

At Thirty-fourth Street young Richard quickly thrust up the trap and ordered the cabman to stop.

"I've dropped a ring," he apologized, as he climbed out. "It was my mother's, and I'd hate to lose it. I won't detain you a minute—I saw where it fell."

In less than a minute he was back in the cab with the ring.

But within that minute a crosstown car had stopped directly in front of the cab. The cab-man tried to pass to the left, but a heavy express wagon cut him off. He tried the right and had to back away from a furniture van that had no business to be there. He tried to back out, but dropped his reins and swore dutifully. He was blockaded in a tangled mess of vehicles and horses.

One of those street blockades had occurred that sometimes tie up commerce and movement quite suddenly in the big city.

"Why don't you drive on?" said Miss Lantry impatiently. "We'll be late."

Richard stood up in the cab and looked around. He saw a congested flood of wagons, trucks, cabs, vans and street cars filling the vast space where Broadway, Sixth Avenue, and Thirty-fourth Street cross one another as a twenty-six inch maiden fills her twenty-two inch girdle. And still from all the cross streets they were hurrying and rattling toward the converging point at full speed, and hurling themselves into the straggling mass, locking wheels and adding their drivers' imprecations to the clamor. The entire traffic of Manhattan seemed to have jammed itself around them. The oldest New Yorker among the thousands of spectators that lined the sidewalks had not witnessed a street blockade of the proportions of this one.

"I'm very sorry," said Richard, as he resumed his seat, "but it looks as if we are stuck. They won't get this jumble loosened up in an hour. It was my fault. If I hadn't dropped the ring we—"

"Let me see the ring," said Miss Lantry. "Now that it can't be helped, I don't care. I think theatres are stupid, anyway."

At 11 o'clock that night somebody tapped lightly on Anthony Rockwall's door.

"Come in," shouted Anthony, who was in a red dressing-gown, reading a book of piratical adventures.

Somebody was Aunt Ellen, looking like a gray-haired angel that had been left on earth by mistake.

"They're engaged, Anthony," she said, softly. "She has promised to marry our Richard. On their way to the theatre there was a street blockade, and it was two hours before their cab could get out of it.

"And oh, Brother Anthony, don't ever boast of the power of money again. A little emblem of true love—a little ring that symbolized unending and unmercenary affection—was the cause of our Richard finding his happiness. He dropped it in the street, and got out to recover it. And before they could continue the blockade occurred. He spoke to his love and won her there while the cab was hemmed in. Money is dross compared with true love, Anthony."

"All right," said old Anthony. "I'm glad the boy has got what he wanted. I told him I wouldn't spare any expense in the matter if—"

"But, Brother Anthony, what good could your money have done?"

"Sister," said Anthony Rockwall. "I've got my pirate in a devil of a scrape. His ship has just been scuttled, and he's too good a judge of the value of money to let drown. I wish you would let me go on with this chapter."

The story should end here. I wish it would as heartily as you who read it wish it did. But we must go to the bottom of the well for truth.

The next day a person with red hands and a blue polka-dot necktie, who called himself Kelly, called at Anthony Rockwall's house, and was at once received in the library.

"Well," said Anthony, reaching for his check-book, "it was a good bilin' of soap. Let's see—you had $5,000 in cash."

"I paid out $300 more of my own," said Kelly. "I had to go a little above the estimate. I got the express wagons and cabs mostly for $5; but the trucks and two-horse teams mostly raised me to $10. The motormen wanted $10, and some of the loaded teams $20. The cops struck me hardest—$50 I paid two, and the rest $20 and $25. But didn't it work beautiful. Mr. Rockwall? I'm glad William A. Brady wasn't onto that little outdoor vehicle mob scene. I wouldn't want William to break his heart with jealousy. And never a rehearsal, either! The boys was on time to the fraction of a second. It was two hours before a snake could get below Greeley's statue."

"Thirteen hundred—there you are, Kelly," said Anthony, tearing off a check. "Your thousand, and the $300 you were out. You don't despise money, do you, Kelly?"

"Me?" said Kelly. "I can lick the man that invented poverty."

Anthony called Kelly when he was at the door.

"You didn't notice," said he, "anywhere in the tie-up, a kind of a fat boy without any clothes on shooting arrows around with a bow, did you?"

"Why, no," said Kelly, mystified. "I didn't. If he was like you say, maybe the cops pinched him before I got there."

"I thought the little rascal wouldn't be on hand," chuckled Anthony. "Good-by, Kelly."

Springtime à la Carte

It was a day in March.

Never, never begin a story this way when you write one. No opening could possibly be worse. It is unimaginative, flat dry, and likely to consist of mere wind. But in this instance it is allowable. For the following paragraph, which should have inaugurated the narrative, is too wildly extravagant and preposterous to be flaunted in the face of the reader without preparation.

Sarah was crying over her bill of fare.

Think of a New York girl shedding tears on the menu card!

To account for this you will be allowed to guess that the lobsters were all out, or that she had sworn ice-cream off during Lent, or that she had ordered onions, or that she had just come from a Hackett matinée. And then, all these theories being wrong, you will please let the story proceed.

The gentleman who announced that the world was an oyster which he with his sword would open made a larger hit than he deserved. It is not difficult to open an oyster with a sword. But did you ever notice any one try to open the terrestrial bivalve with a typewriter? Like to wait for a dozen raw opened that way?

Sarah had managed to pry apart the shells with her unhandy weapon far enough to nibble a wee bit at the cold and clammy world within. She knew no more shorthand than if she had been a graduate in stenography just let slip upon the world by a business college. So, not being able to stenog, she could not enter that bright galaxy of office talent. She was a free-lance typewriter and canvassed for odd jobs of copying.

The most brilliant and crowning feat of Sarah's battle with the world was the deal she made with Schulenberg's Home Restaurant. The restaurant was next door to the old red brick in which she hall-roomed. One evening after dining at Schulenberg's 40-cent, five-course *table d'hôte* (served as fast as you throw the five base-balls at the colored gentleman's head) Sarah took away with her the bill of fare. It was written in an almost unreadable script neither English nor German, and so arranged that if you were not careful you began with a toothpick and rice pudding and ended with soup and the day of the week.

The next day Sarah showed Schulenberg a neat card on which the menu was beautifully typewritten with the viands temptingly marshalled under their right and proper heads from "hor d'œuvre" to "not responsible for over-coats and umbrellas."

Schulenberg became a naturalized citizen on the spot. Before Sarah left him she had him willingly committed to an agreement. She was to furnish typewritten bills of fare for the twenty-one tables in the restaurant—a new bill for each day's dinner, and new ones for breakfast and lunch as often as changes occurred in the food or as neatness required.

In return for this Schulenberg was to send three meals per diem to Sarah's hall room by a waiter—an obsequious one if possible—and furnish her each afternoon with a pencil draft of what Fate had in store for Schulenberg's customers on the morrow.

Mutual satisfaction resulted from the agreement. Schulenberg's patrons now knew what the food they ate was called even if its nature sometimes puzzled them. And Sarah had food during a cold, dull winter, which was the main thing with her.

And then the almanac lied, and said that spring had come. Spring comes when it comes. The frozen snows of January still lay like adamant in the cross-town streets. The hand-organs still played "In the Good Old Summertime," with their December vivacity and expression. Men began to make thirty-day notes to

buy Easter dresses. Janitors shut off steam. And when these things
happen one may know that the city is still in the clutches of
winter.

One afternoon Sarah shivered in her elegant hall bedroom;
"house heated; scrupulously clean; conveniences; seen to be ap-
preciated." She had no work to do except Schulenberg's menu
cards. Sarah sat in her squeaky willow rocker, and looked out the
window. The calendar on the wall kept crying to her: "Springtime
is here, Sarah—springtime is here, I tell you. Look at me, Sarah,
my figures show it. You've got a neat figure yourself, Sarah—a—
nice springtime figure—why do you look out the window so sadly?"

Sarah's room was at the back of the house. Looking out the
window she could see the windowless rear brick wall of the box
factory on the next street. But the wall was clearest crystal; and
Sarah was looking down a grassy lane shaded with cherry trees
and elms and bordered with raspberry bushes and Cherokee roses.

Spring's real harbingers are too subtle for the eye and ear. Some
must have the flowering crocus, the wood-starring dogwood, the
voice of bluebird—even so gross a reminder as the farewell handshake of the retiring buckwheat and oyster before they can welcome the Lady in Green to their dull bosoms. But to old earth's
choicest kind there come straight, sweet messages from his newest
bride, telling them they shall be no stepchildren unless they
choose to be.

On the previous summer Sarah had gone into the country and
loved a farmer.

(In writing your story never hark back thus. It is bad art, and
cripples interest. Let it march, march.)

Sarah stayed two weeks at Sunnybrook Farm. There she learned
to love old Farmer Franklin's son Walter. Farmers have been
loved and wedded and turned out to grass in less time. But young
Walter Franklin was a modern agriculturist. He had a telephone in
his cow house, and he could figure up exactly what effect next
year's Canada wheat crop would have on potatoes planted in
the dark of the moon.

It was in this shaded and raspberried lane that Walter had wooed and won her. And together they had sat and woven a crown of dandelions for her hair. He had immoderately praised the effect of the yellow blossoms against her brown tresses; and she had left the chaplet there, and walked back to the house swinging her straw sailor in her hands.

They were to marry in the spring—at the very first signs of spring, Walter said. And Sarah came back to the city to pound her typewriter.

A knock at the door dispelled Sarah's visions of that happy day. A waiter had brought the rough pencil draft of the Home Restaurant's next day fare in old Schulenberg's angular hand.

Sarah sat down to her typewriter and slipped a card between the rollers. She was a nimble worker. Generally in an hour and a half the twenty-one menu cards were written and ready.

To-day there were more changes on the bill of fare than usual. The soups were lighter; pork was eliminated from the entrées, figuring only with Russian turnips among the roasts. The gracious spirit of spring pervaded the entire menu. Lamb, that lately capered on the greening hillsides, was becoming exploited with the sauce that commemorated its gambols. The song of the oyster, though not silenced, was *dimuendo con amore*. The frying-pan seemed to be held, inactive, behind the beneficent bars of the broiler. The pie list swelled; the richer puddings had vanished; the sausage, with his drapery wrapped about him, barely lingered in a pleasant thanatopsis with the buckwheats and the sweet but doomed maple.

Sarah's fingers danced like midgets above a summer stream. Down through the courses she worked, giving each item its position according to its length with an accurate eye.

Just above the desserts came the list of vegetables. Carrots and peas, asparagus on toast, the perennial tomatoes and corn and succotash, lima beans, cabbage—and then——

Sarah was crying over her bill of fare. Tears from the depths of some divine despair rose in her heart and gathered to her eyes.

Down went her head on the little typewriter stand; and the keyboard rattled a dry accompaniment to her moist sobs.

For she had received no letter from Walter in two weeks, and the next item on the bill of fare was dandelions—dandelions with some kind of egg—but bother the egg!—dandelions, with whose golden blooms Walter had crowned her his queen of love and future bride—dandelions, the harbingers of spring, her sorrow's crown of sorrow—reminder of her happiest days.

Madam, I dare you to smile until you suffer this test: Let the Marechal Niel roses that Percy brought you on the night you gave him your heart be served as a salad with French dressing before your eyes at a Schulenberg *table d'hôte*. Had Juliet so seen her love tokens dishonored the sooner would she have sought the lethean herbs of the good apothecary.

But what witch is Spring! Into the great cold city of stone and iron a message had to be sent. There was none to convey it but the little hardy courier of the fields with his rough green coat and modest air. He is a true soldier of fortune, this *dent-de-lion*—this lion's tooth, as the French chefs call him. Flowered, he will assist at love-making, wreathed in my lady's nut-brown hair; young and callow and unblossomed, he goes into the boiling pot and delivers the word of his sovereign mistress.

By and by Sarah forced back her tears. The cards must be written. But, still in a faint, golden glow from her dandelion dream, she fingered the typewriter keys absently for a little while, with her mind and heart in the meadow lane with her young farmer. But soon she came swiftly back to the rock-bound lanes of Manhattan, and the typewriter began to rattle and jump like a strike-breaker's motor car.

At 6 o'clock the waiter brought her dinner and carried away the typewritten bill of fare. When Sarah ate she set aside, with a sigh, the dish of dandelions with its crowning ovarious accompaniment. As this dark mass had been transformed from a bright and love-indorsed flower to be an ignominious vegetable, so had her summer hopes wilted and perished. Love may, as Shakespeare said, feed on itself: but Sarah could not bring herself to eat the dandelions that had graced, as ornaments, the first spiritual banquet of her heart's true affection.

At 7.30 the couple in the next room began to quarrel: the man in the room above sought for A on his flute; the gas went a little lower; three coal wagons started to unload—the only sound of which the phonograph is jealous; cats on the back fences slowly retreated toward Mukden. By these signs Sarah knew that it was time for her to read. She got out "The Cloister and the Hearth," the best non-selling book of the month, settled her feet on her trunk, and began to wander with Gerard.

The front door bell rang. The landlady answered it. Sarah left Gerard and Denys treed by a bear and listened. Oh, yes; you would, just as she did!

And then a strong voice was heard in the hall below, and Sarah jumped for her door, leaving the book on the floor and the first round easily the bear's.

You have guessed it. She reached the top of the stairs just as her farmer came up, three at a jump, and reaped and garnered her, with nothing left for the gleaners.

"Why haven't you written—oh, why?" cried Sarah.

"New York is a pretty large town," said Walter Franklin. "I came in a week ago to your old address. I found that you went away on a Thursday. That consoled some; it eliminated the possible Friday bad luck. But it didn't prevent my hunting for you with police and otherwise ever since!"

"I wrote!" said Sarah, vehemently.

"Never got it!"

"Then how did you find me?"

The young farmer smiled a springtime smile.

"I dropped into that Home Restaurant next door this evening," said he. "I don't care who knows it; I like a dish of some kind of greens at this time of the year. I ran my eye down that nice typewritten bill of fare looking for something in that line. When I got below cabbage I turned my chair over and hollered for the proprietor. He told me where you lived."

"I remember," sighed Sarah, happily. "That was dandelions below cabbage."

"I'd know that cranky capital W 'way above the line that your typewriter makes anywhere in the world," said Franklin.

"Why, there's no W in dandelions," said Sarah in surprise.

The young man drew the bill of fare from his pocket and pointed to a line.

Sarah recognised the first card she had typewritten that afternoon. There was still the rayed splotch in the upper right-hand corner where a tear had fallen. But over the spot where one should have read the name of the meadow plant, the clinging memory of their golden blossoms had allowed her fingers to strike strange keys.

Between the red cabbage and the stuffed green peppers was the item:

"DEAREST WALTER, WITH HARD-BOILED EGG."

From the Cabby's Seat

THE CABBY has his point of view. It is more single-minded, perhaps, than that of a follower of any other calling. From the high, swaying seat of his hansom he looks upon his fellow-men as nomadic particles, of no account except when possessed of migratory desires. He is Jehu, and you are goods in transit. Be you President or vagabond, to cabby you are only a Fare. He takes you up, cracks his whip, joggles your vertebræ and sets you down.

When time for payment arrives, if you exhibit a familiarity with legal rates you come to know what contempt is; if you find that you have left your pocketbook behind you are made to realize the mildness of Dante's imagination.

It is not an extravagant theory that the cabby's singleness of purpose and concentrated view of life are the results of the hansom's peculiar construction. The cock-of-the-roost sits aloft like Jupiter on an unsharable seat, holding your fate between two thongs of inconstant leather. Helpless, ridiculous, confined, bobbing like a toy mandarin, you sit like a rat in a trap—you, before whom butlers cringe on solid land—and must squeak upward through a slit in your peripatetic sarcophagus to make your feeble wishes known.

Then, in a cab, you are not even an occupant; you are contents. You are a cargo at sea, and the "cherub that sits up aloft" has Davy Jones's street and number by heart.

One night there were sounds of revelry in the big brick tene-

ment house next door but one to McGary's Family Café. The
sounds seemed to emanate from the apartments of the Walsh
family. The sidewalk was obstructed by an assortment of interested neighbors, who opened a lane from time to time for a hurrying messenger bearing from McGary's goods pertinent to festivity
and diversion. The sidewalk contingent was engaged in comment
and discussion from which it made no effort to eliminate the news
that Norah Walsh was being married.

In the fulness of time there was an eruption of the merry-makers
to the sidewalk. The uninvited guests enveloped and permeated
them, and upon the night air rose joyous cries, congratulations,
laughter, and unclassified noises born of McGary's oblations to the
hymeneal scene.

Close to the curb stood Jerry O'Donovan's cab. Night-hawk was
Jerry called; but no more lustrous or cleaner hansom than his ever
closed its doors upon point lace and November violets. And Jerry's
horse! I am within bounds when I tell you that he was stuffed with
oats until one of those old ladies who leave their dishes unwashed
at home and go about having expressmen arrested, would have
smiled—yes, smiled—to have seen him.

Among the shifting, sonorous, pulsing crowd glimpses could
be had of Jerry's high hat, battered by the winds and rains of
many years; of his nose like a carrot, battered by the frolicsome,
athletic progeny of millionaires and by contumacious fares; of his
brass-buttoned greencoat, admired in the vicinity of McGary's.
It was plain that Jerry had usurped the functions of his cab, and
was carrying a "load." Indeed, the figure may be extended and
he be likened to a bread-wagon if we admit the testimony of a
youthful spectator, who was heard to remark "Jerry has got a bun."

From somewhere among the throng in the street or else out of
the thin stream of pedestrians a young woman tripped and stood
by the cab. The professional hawk's eye of Jerry caught the movement. He made a lurch for the cab, overturning three or four on-
lookers and himself—no! he caught the cap of a water-plug and
kept his feet. Like a sailor shining up the ratlins during a squall

Jerry mounted to his professional seat. Once he was there McGary's liquids were baffled. He seesawed on the mizzenmast of his craft as safe as a Steeple Jack rigged to the flagpole of a skyscraper.

"Step in, lady," said Jerry, gathering his lines.

The young woman stepped into the cab; the doors shut with a bang; Jerry's whip cracked in the air; the crowd in the gutter scattered, and the fine hansom dashed away 'crosstown.

When the oat-spry horse had hedged a little his first spurt of speed Jerry broke the lid of his cab and called down through the aperture in the voice of a cracked megaphone, trying to please:

"Where, now, will ye be drivin' to?"

"Anywhere you please," came up the answer, musical and contented.

"'Tis drivin' for pleasure she is," thought Jerry. And then he suggested as a matter of course:

"Take a thrip around in the park, lady. 'Twill be ilegant cool and fine."

"Just as you like," answered the fare, pleasantly.

The cab headed for Fifth Avenue and sped up that perfect street. Jerry bounced and swayed in his seat. The potent fluids of McGary were disquieted and they sent new fumes to his head. He sang an ancient song of Killisnook and brandished his whip like a baton.

Inside the cab the fare sat up straight on the cushions, looking to right and left at the lights and houses. Even in the shadowed hansom her eyes shone like stars at twilight.

When they reached Fifty-ninth Street Jerry's head was bobbing and his reins were slack. But his horse turned in through the park gate and began the old familiar nocturnal round. And then the fare leaned back, entranced, and breathed deep the clean, wholesome odors of grass and leaf and bloom. And the wise beast in the shafts, knowing his ground, struck into his by-the-hour gait and kept to the right of the road.

Habit also struggled successfully against Jerry's increasing torpor.

He raised the hatch of his storm-tossed vessel and made the inquiry that cabbies do make in the park.

"Like shtop at the Cas-sino, lady? Gezzer r'freshm's, 'n lish'n the music. Ev'body shtops."

"I think that would be nice," said the fare.

They reined up with a plunge at the Casino entrance. The cab doors flew open. The fare stepped directly upon the floor. At once she was caught in a web of ravishing music and dazzled by a panorama of lights and colors. Some one slipped a little square card into her hand on which was printed a number—34. She looked around and saw her cab twenty yards away already lining up in its place among the waiting mass of carriages, cabs, and motor cars. And then a man who seemed to be all shirt-front danced backward before her; and next she was seated at a little table by a railing over which climbed a jessamine vine.

There seemed to be a wordless invitation to purchase; she consulted a collection of small coins in a thin purse, and received from them license to order a glass of beer. There she sat, inhaling and absorbing it all—the new-colored, new-shaped life in a fairy palace in an enchanted wood.

At fifty tables sat princes and queens clad in all the silks and gems of the world. And now and then one of them would look curiously at Jerry's fare. They saw a plain figure dressed in a pink silk of the kind that is tempered by the word "foulard," and a plain face that wore a look of love of life that the queens envied.

Twice the long hands of the clocks went round. Royalties thinned from their *al fresco* thrones, and buzzed or clattered away in their vehicles of state. The music retired into cases of wood and bags of leather and baize. Waiters removed cloths pointedly near the plain figure sitting almost alone.

Jerry's fare rose, and held out her numbered card simply:

"Is there anything coming on the ticket?" she asked.

A waiter told her it was her cab check, and that she should give it to the man at the entrance. This man took it, and called the number. Only three hansoms stood in line. The driver of one

of them went and routed out Jerry asleep in his cab. He swore
deeply, climbed to the captain's bridge and steered his craft to
the pier. His fare entered, and the cab whirled into the cool
fastnesses of the park along the shortest homeward cuts.

At the gate a glimmer of reason in the form of sudden suspicion seized upon Jerry's beclouded mind. One or two things
occurred to him. He stopped his horse, raised the trap and
dropped his phonographic voice, like a lead plummet, through the
aperture:

"I want to see four dollars before goin' any further on th' thrip.
Have ye got th' dough?"

"Four dollars!" laughed the fare, softly, "dear me, no. I've only
got a few pennies and a dime or two."

Jerry shut down the trap and slashed his oat-fed horse. The
clatter of hoofs strangled but could not drown the sound of his
profanity. He shouted choking and gurgling curses at the starry
heavens; he cut viciously with his whip at passing vehicles; he
scattered fierce and everchanging oaths and imprecations along
the streets, so that a late truck driver, crawling homeward, heard
and was abashed. But he knew his recourse, and made for it at
a gallop.

At the house with the green lights beside the steps he pulled
up. He flung wide the cab doors and tumbled heavily to the
ground.

"Come on, you," he said, roughly.

His fare came forth with the Casino dreamy smile still on her
plain face. Jerry took her by the arm and led her into the police
station. A gray-moustached sergeant looked keenly across the desk.
He and the cabby were no strangers.

"Sargeant," began Jerry in his old raucous, martyred, thunderous
tones of complaint. "I've got a fare here that——"

Jerry paused. He drew a knotted, red hand across his brow. The
fog set up by McGary was beginning to clear away.

"A fare, sargeant," he continued, with a grin, "that I want to introduce to ye. It's me wife that I married at ould man Walsh's this evening. And a divil of a time we had, 'tis thrue. Shake hands wit th' sargeant, Norah, and we'll be off to home."

Before stepping into the cab Norah sighed profoundly.

"I've had such a nice time, Jerry," said she.

An Unfinished Story

WE NO LONGER groan and heap ashes upon our heads when the flames of Tophet are mentioned. For, even the preachers have begun to tell us that God is radium, or ether or some scientific compound, and that the worst we wicked ones may expect is a chemical reaction. This is a pleasing hypothesis; but there lingers yet some of the old, goodly terror of orthodoxy.

There are but two subjects upon which one may discourse with a free imagination, and without the possibility of being controverted. You may talk of your dreams; and you may tell what you heard a parrot say. Both Morpheus and the bird are incompetent witnesses; and your listener dare not attack your recital. The baseless fabric of a vision, then, shall furnish my theme—chosen with apologies and regrets instead of the more limited field of pretty Polly's small talk.

I had a dream that was so far removed from the higher criticism that it had to do with the ancient, respectable, and lamented bar-of-judgment theory.

Gabriel had played his trump; and those of us who could not follow suit were arraigned for examination. I noticed at one side a gathering of professional bondsmen in solemn black and collars that buttoned behind; but it seemed there was some trouble about their real estate titles; and they did not appear to be getting any of us out.

A fly cop—an angel policeman—flew over to me and took me

by the left wing. Near at hand was a group of very prosperous-looking spirits arraigned for judgment.

"Do you belong with that bunch?" the policeman asked.

"Who are they?" was my answer.

"Why," said he, "they are——"

But this irrelevant stuff is taking up space that the story should occupy.

Dulcie worked in a department store. She sold Hamburg edging, or stuffed peppers, or automobiles, or other little trinkets such as they keep in department stores. Of what she earned, Dulcie received six dollars per week. The remainder was credited to her and debited to somebody else's account in the ledger kept by G—— Oh, primal energy, you say, Reverend Doctor—— Well, then, in the Ledger of Primal Energy.

During her first year in the store, Dulcie was paid five dollars per week. It would be instructive to know how she lived on that amount. Don't care? Very well; probably you are interested in larger amounts. Six dollars is a larger amount. I will tell you how she lived on six dollars per week.

One afternoon at six, when Dulcie was sticking her hat pin within an eighth of an inch of her *medulla oblongata*, she said to her chum, Sadie—the girl that waits on you with her left side:

"Say, Sade, I made a date for dinner this evening with Piggy."

"You never did!" exclaimed Sadie, admiringly. "Well, ain't you the lucky one? Piggy's an awful swell; and he always takes a girl to swell places. He took Blanche up to the Hoffman House one evening, where they have swell music, and you see a lot of swells. You'll have a swell time, Dulce."

Dulcie hurried homeward. Her eyes were shining, and her cheeks showed the delicate pink of life's—real life's—approaching dawn. It was Friday; and she had fifty cents left of her last week's wages.

The streets were filled with the rush-hour floods of people. The electric lights of Broadway were glowing—calling moths from miles, from leagues, from hundreds of leagues out of darkness around to come in and attend the singeing school. Men in accurate clothes, with faces like those carved on cherry stones by the old salts in sailors' homes, turned and stared at Dulcie as she sped, unheeding, past them. Manhattan, the night-blooming cereus, was beginning to unfold its dead-white, heavy-odored petals.

Dulcie stopped in a store where goods were cheap and bought an imitation lace collar with her fifty cents. That money was to have been spent otherwise—fifteen cents for supper, ten cents for breakfast, ten cents for lunch. Another dime was to be added to her small store of savings; and five cents was to be squandered for licorice drops—the kind that made your cheek look like the toothache, and last as long. The licorice was an extravagance—almost a carouse—but what is life without pleasures?

Dulcie lived in a furnished room. There is this difference between a furnished room and a boarding-house. In a furnished room, other people do not know it when you go hungry.

Dulcie went up to her room—the third-floor-back in a West Side brownstone-front. She lit the gas. Scientists tell us that the diamond is the hardest substance known. Their mistake. Landladies know of a compound beside which the diamond is as putty. They pack it in the tips of gas-burners; and one may stand on a chair and dig at it in vain until one's fingers are pink and bruised. A hairpin will not remove it; therefore let us call it immovable.

So Dulcie lit the gas. In its one-fourth-candle-power glow we will observe the room.

Couch-bed, dresser, table, washstand, chair—of this much the landlady was guilty. The rest was Dulcie's. On the dresser were her treasures—a gilt china vase presented to her by Sadie, a calendar issued by a pickle works, a book on the divination of dreams, some rice powder in a glass dish, and a cluster of artificial cherries tied with a pink ribbon.

Against the wrinkly mirror stood pictures of General Kitchener, William Muldoon, the Duchess of Marlborough, and Benvenuto Cellini. Against one wall was a plaster of Paris plaque of an

O'Callahan in a Roman helmet. Near it was a violent oleograph of lemon-colored child assaulting an inflammatory butterfly. This was Dulcie's final judgment in art; but it had never been upset. Her rest had never been disturbed by whispers of stolen copes; no critic had elevated his eyebrows at her infantile entomologist.

Piggy was to call for her at seven. While she swiftly makes ready, let us discreetly face the other way and gossip.

For the room, Dulcie paid two dollars per week. On week-days her breakfast cost ten cents; she made coffee and cooked an egg over the gaslight while she was dressing. On Sunday mornings she feasted royally on veal chops and pineapple fritters at "Billy's" restaurant, at a cost of twenty-five cents—and tipped the waitress ten cents. New York presents so many temptations for one to run into extravagance. She had her lunches in the department-store restaurant at a cost of sixty cents for the week; dinners were $1.05. The evening papers—show me a New Yorker going without his daily paper!—came to six cents; and two Sunday papers—one for the personal column and the other to read—were ten cents. The total amounts to $4.76. Now, one has to buy clothes, and——

I give it up. I hear of wonderful bargains in fabrics, and of miracles performed with needle and thread; but I am in doubt. I hold my pen poised in vain when I would add to Dulcie's life some of those joys that belong to woman by virtue of all the unwritten, sacred, natural, inactive ordinances of the equity of heaven. Twice she had been to Coney Island and had ridden the hobby-horses. 'Tis a weary thing to count your pleasures by summers instead of by hours.

Piggy needs but a word. When the girls named him, an undeserving stigma was cast upon the noble family of swine. The words-of-three-letters lesson in the old blue spelling book begins with Piggy's biography. He was fat; he had the soul of a rat, the habits of a bat, and the magnanimity of a cat. . . . He wore expensive clothes; and was a connoisseur in starvation. He could look at a shop-girl and tell you to an hour how long it had been since she had eaten anything more nourishing than marshmallows and tea. He hung about the shopping districts, and prowled around in department stores with his invitations to dinner. Men who escort dogs upon the streets at the end of a string look down upon him. He is a type; I can dwell upon him no longer; my pen is not the kind intended for him; I am no carpenter.

At ten minutes to seven Dulcie was ready. She looked at herself in the wrinkly mirror. The reflection was satisfactory. The dark blue dress, fitting without a wrinkle, the hat with its jaunty black feather, the but-slightly-soiled gloves—all representing self-denial, even of food itself—were vastly becoming.

Dulcie forgot everything else for a moment except that she was beautiful, and that life was about to lift a corner of its mysterious veil for her to observe its wonders. No gentleman had ever asked her out before. Now she was going for a brief moment into the glitter and exalted show.

The girls said that Piggy was a "spender." There would be a grand dinner, and music, and splendidly dressed ladies to look at and things to eat that strangely twisted the girls' jaws when they tried to tell about them. No doubt she would be asked out again.

There was a blue pongee suit in a window that she knew—by saving twenty cents a week instead of ten in—let's see—— Oh, it would run into years! But there was a second-hand store in Seventh Avenue where——

Somebody knocked at the door. Dulcie opened it. The landlady stood there with a spurious smile, sniffing for cooking by stolen gas.

"A gentleman's downstairs to see you," she said. "Name is Mr. Wiggins."

By such epithet was Piggy known to unfortunate ones who had to take him seriously.

Dulcie turned to the dresser to get her handkerchief; and then she stopped still, and bit her underlip hard. While looking in her mirror she had seen fairyland and herself, a princess, just awakening from a long slumber. She had forgotten one that was watching her with sad, beautiful, stern eyes—the only one there was to approve or condemn what she did. Straight and slender and tall, with a look of sorrowful reproach on his handsome, melancholy face, General Kitchener fixed his wonderful eyes on her out of his gilt photograph frame on the dresser.

Dulcie turned like an automatic doll to the landlady.

"Tell him I can't go," she said, dully. "Tell him I'm sick, or something. Tell him I'm not going out."

After the door was closed and locked, Dulcie fell upon her bed, crushing her black tip, and cried for ten minutes. General Kitchener was her only friend. He was Dulcie's ideal of a gallant knight. He looked as if he might have a secret sorrow, and his wonderful moustache was a dream, and she was a little afraid of that stern yet tender look in his eyes. She used to have little fancies that he would call at the house sometime, and ask for her, with his sword clanking against his high boots. Once, when a boy was rattling a piece of chain against a lamp post she had opened the window and looked out. But there was no use. She knew that General Kitchener was away over in Japan, leading his army against the savage Turks; and he would never step out of his gilt frame for her. Yet one look from him had vanquished Piggy that night. Yes, for that night.

When her cry was over Dulcie got up and took off her best dress, and put on her old blue kimono. She wanted no dinner. She sang two verses of "Sammy." Then she became intensely interested in a little red speck on the side of her nose. And after that was attended to, she drew up a chair to the rickety table, and told her fortune with an old deck of cards.

"The horrid, impudent thing!" she said aloud. "And I never gave him a word or a look to make him think it!"

At nine o'clock Dulcie took a tin box of crackers and a little pot of raspberry jam out of her trunk and had a feast. She offered General Kitchener some jam on a cracker; but he only looked at her as the sphinx would have looked at a butterfly—if there are butterflies in the desert.

"Don't eat if you don't want to," said Dulcie. "And don't put on so many airs and scold so with your eyes. I wonder if you'd be so superior and snippy if you had to live on six dollars a week."

It was not a good sign for Dulcie to be rude to General Kitchener. And then she turned Benvenuto Cellini face downward with a severe gesture. But that was not inexcusable; for she had always thought he was Henry VIII, and she did not approve of him.

At half-past nine Dulcie took a last look at the pictures on the dresser, turned out the light and skipped into bed. It's an awful thing to go to bed with a good-night look at General Kitchener, William Muldoon, the Duchess of Marlborough, and Benvenuto Cellini.

This story doesn't really get anywhere at all. The rest of it comes later—sometime when Piggy asks Dulcie again to dine with him, and she is feeling lonelier than usual, and General Kitchener happens to be looking the other way; and then——

As I said before, I dreamed that I was standing near a crowd of prosperous-looking angels, and a policeman took me by the wing and asked if I belonged with them.

"Who are they?" I asked.

"Why," said he, "they are the men who hired working-girls, and paid 'em five or six dollars a week to live on. Are you one of the bunch?"

"Not on your immortality," said I. "I'm only a fellow that set fire to an orphan asylum, and murdered a blind man for his pennies."

The Romance of a Busy Broker

PITCHER, confidential clerk in the office of Harvey Maxwell, broker, allowed a look of mild interest and surprise to visit his usually expressionless countenance when his employer briskly entered at half-past nine in company with his young lady stenographer. With a snappy "Good-morning, Pitcher," Maxwell dashed at his desk as though he were intending to leap over it, and then plunged into the great heap of letters and telegrams waiting there for him.

The young lady had been Maxwell's stenographer for a year. She was beautiful in a way that was decidedly unstenographic. She forewent the pomp of the alluring pompadour. She wore no chains, bracelets, or lockets. She had not the air of being about to accept an invitation to luncheon. Her dress was gray and plain, but it fitted her figure with fidelity and discretion. In her neat black turban hat was the gold-green wing of a macaw. On this morning she was softly and shyly radiant. Her eyes were dreamily bright, her cheeks genuine peach-blow, her expression a happy one, tinged with reminiscence.

Pitcher, still mildly curious, noticed a difference in her ways this morning. Instead of going straight into the adjoining room, where her desk was, she lingered, slightly irresolute, in the outer office. Once she moved over by Maxwell's desk, near enough for him to be aware of her presence.

The machine sitting at that desk was no longer a man; it was a busy New York broker, moved by buzzing wheels and uncoiling springs.

"Well—what is it? Anything?" asked Maxwell, sharply. His opened mail lay like a bank of stage snow on his crowded desk. His keen gray eye, impersonal and brusque, flashed upon her half impatiently.

"Nothing," answered the stenographer, moving away with a little smile.

"Mr. Pitcher," she said to the confidential clerk, "did Mr. Maxwell say anything yesterday about engaging another stenographer?"

"He did," answered Pitcher. "He told me to get another one. I notified the agency yesterday afternoon to send over a few samples this morning. It's 9.45 o'clock, and not a single picture hat or piece of pineapple chewing gum has showed up yet."

"I will do the work as usual, then," said the young lady, "until some one comes to fill the place." And she went to her desk at once and hung the black turban hat with the gold-green macaw wing in its accustomed place.

He who has been denied the spectacle of a busy Manhattan broker during a rush of business is handicapped for the profession of anthropology. The poet sings of the "crowded hour of glorious life." The broker's hour is not only crowded, but minutes and seconds are hanging to all the straps and packing both front and rear platforms.

And this day was Harvey Maxwell's busy day. The ticker began to reel out jerkily its fitful coils of tape, the desk telephone had a chronic attack of buzzing. Men began to throng into the office and call at him over the railing, jovially, sharply, viciously, excitedly. Messenger boys ran in and out with messages and telegrams. The clerks in the office jumped about like sailors during a storm. Even Pitcher's face relaxed into something resembling animation.

On the Exchange there were hurricanes and landslides and snowstorms and glaciers and volcanoes, and those elemental disturbances were reproduced in miniature in the broker's offices.

Maxwell shoved his chair against the wall and transacted business after the manner of a toe dancer. He jumped from ticker to 'phone, from desk to door with the trained agility of a harlequin.

In the midst of this growing and important stress the broker became suddenly aware of a high-rolled fringe of golden hair under a nodding canopy of velvet and ostrich tips, and imitation sealskin sacque and a string of beads as large as hickory nuts, ending near the floor with a silver heart. There was a self-possessed young lady connected with these accessories; and Pitcher was there to construe her.

"Lady from the Stenographer's Agency to see about the position," said Pitcher.

Maxwell turned half around, with his hands full of papers and ticker tape.

"What position?" he asked, with a frown.

"Position of stenographer," said Pitcher. "You told me yesterday to call them up and have one sent over this morning."

"You are losing your mind, Pitcher," said Maxwell. "Why should I have given you any such instructions? Miss Leslie has given perfect satisfaction during the year she has been here. The place is hers as long as she chooses to retain it. There's no place open here, madam. Countermand that order with the agency, Pitcher, and don't bring any more of 'em here."

The silver heart left the office, swinging and banging itself independently against the office furniture as it indignantly departed. Pitcher seized a moment to remark to the bookkeeper that the "old man" seemed to get more absentminded and forgetful every day of the world.

The rush and pace of business grew fiercer and faster. On the floor they were pounding half a dozen stocks in which Maxwell's customers were heavy investors. Orders to buy and sell were coming and going as swift as the flight of swallows. Some of his own holdings were imperilled, and the man was working like some high-geared, delicate, strong machine—strung to full tension, going at full speed, accurate, never hesitating, with the proper word and decision and act ready and prompt as clockwork. Stocks and bonds, loans and mortgages, margins and securities—here was a world of finance, and there was no room in it for the human world or the world of nature.

When the luncheon hour drew near there came a slight lull in the uproar.

Maxwell stood by his desk with his hands full of telegrams and memoranda, with a fountain pen over his right ear and his hair hanging in disorderly strings over his forehead. His window was open, for the beloved janitress, Spring had turned on a little warmth through the waking registers of the earth.

And through the window came a wandering—perhaps a lost—odor—a delicate, sweet odor of lilac that fixed the broker for a moment immovable. For this odor belonged to Miss Leslie; it was her own, and hers only.

The odor brought her vividly, almost tangibly before him. The world of finance dwindled suddenly to a speck. And she was in the next room—twenty steps away.

"By George, I'll do it now," said Maxwell, half aloud. "I'll ask her now. I wonder I didn't do it long ago."

He dashed into the inner office with the haste of a short trying to cover. He charged upon the desk of the stenographer.

She looked up at him with a smile. A soft pink crept over her cheek, and her eyes were kind and frank. Maxwell leaned one elbow on her desk. He still clutched fluttering papers with both hands and the pen was above his ear.

"Miss Leslie," he began, hurriedly, "I have but a moment to spare. I want to say something in that moment. Will you be my wife? I haven't had time to make love to you in the ordinary way, but I really do love you. Talk quick, please—those fellows are clubbing the stuffing out of Union Pacific."

"Oh, what are you talking about?" exclaimed the young lady. She rose to her feet and gazed upon him, round-eyed.

"Don't you understand?" said Maxwell, restively. "I want you to marry me. I love you, Miss Leslie. I wanted to tell you, and I snatched a minute when things had slackened up a bit. They're calling me for the 'phone now. Tell 'em to wait a minute, Pitcher. Won't you, Miss Leslie?"

The stenographer acted very queerly. At first she seemed overcome with amazement; then tears flowed from her wondering eyes; and then she smiled sunnily through them, and one of her arms slid tenderly about the broker's neck.

"I know now," she said, softly. "It's this old business that has driven everything else out of your head for the time. I was frightened at first. Don't you remember, Harvey? We were married last evening at 8 o'clock in the Little Church around the Corner."

After Twenty Years

THE POLICEMAN on the beat moved up the avenue impressively. The impressiveness was habitual and not for show, for spectators were few. The time was barely 10 o'clock at night, but chilly gusts of wind with a taste of rain in them had well nigh depeopled the streets.

Trying doors as he went, twirling his club with many intricate and artful movements, turning now and then to cast his watchful eye adown the pacific thoroughfare, the officer, with his stalwart form and slight swagger, made a fine picture of a guardian of the peace. The vicinity was one that kept early hours. Now and then you might see the lights of a cigar store or of an all-night lunch counter; but the majority of the doors belonged to business places that had long since been closed.

When about midway of a certain block the policeman suddenly slowed his walk. In the doorway of a darkened hardware store a man leaned, with an unlighted cigar in his mouth. As the policeman walked up to him the man spoke up quickly.

"It's all right, officer," he said, reassuringly. "I'm just waiting for a friend. It's an appointment made twenty years ago. Sounds a little funny to you, doesn't it? Well, I'll explain if you'd like to make certain it's all straight. About that long ago there used to be a restaurant where this store stands—'Big Joe' Brady's restaurant."

"Until five years ago," said the policeman. "It was torn down then."

The man in the doorway struck a match and lit his cigar. The light showed a pale, square-jawed face with keen eyes, and a little white scar near his right eyebrow. His scarfpin was a large diamond, oddly set.

"Twenty years ago to-night," said the man, "I dined here at 'Big Joe' Brady's with Jimmy Wells, my best chum, and the finest chap in the world. He and I were raised here in New York, just like two brothers, together. I was eighteen and Jimmy was twenty. The next morning I was to start for the West to make my fortune. You couldn't have dragged Jimmy out of New York; he thought it was the only place on earth. Well, we agreed that night that we would meet here again exactly twenty years from that date and time, no matter what our conditions might be or from what distance we might have to come. We figured that in twenty years each of us ought to have our destiny worked out and our fortunes made, whatever they were going to be."

"It sounds pretty interesting," said the policeman. "Rather a long time between meets, though, it seems to me. Haven't you heard from your friend since you left?"

"Well, yes, for a time we corresponded," said the other. "But after a year or two we lost track of each other. You see, the West is a pretty big proposition, and I kept hustling around over it pretty lively. But I know Jimmy will meet me here if he's alive, for he always was the truest, stanchest old chap in the world. He'll never forget. I came a thousand miles to stand in this door to-night, and it's worth it if my old partner turns up."

The waiting man pulled out a handsome watch, the lids of it set with small diamonds.

"Three minutes to ten," he announced. "It was exactly ten o'clock when we parted here at the restaurant door."

"Did pretty well out West, didn't you?" asked the policeman.

"You bet! I hope Jimmy has done half as well. He was a kind of plodder, though, good fellow as he was. I've had to compete with some of the sharpest wits going to get my pile. A man gets in a groove in New York. It takes the West to put a razor-edge on him."

The policeman twirled his club and took a step or two.

"I'll be on my way. Hope your friend comes around all right. Going to call time on him sharp?"

"I should say not!" said the other. "I'll give him half an hour at least. If Jimmy is alive on earth he'll be here by that time. So long, officer."

"Good-night, sir," said the policeman, passing on along his beat, trying doors as he went.

There was now a fine, cold drizzle falling, and the wind had risen from its uncertain puffs into a steady blow. The few foot passengers astir in that quarter hurried dismally and silently along with coat collars turned high and pocketed hands. And in the door of the hardware store the man who had come a thousand miles to fill an appointment, uncertain almost to absurdity, with the friend of his youth, smoked his cigar and waited.

About twenty minutes he waited, and then a tall man in a long overcoat, with collar turned up to his ears, hurried across from the opposite side of the street. He went directly to the waiting man.

"Is that you, Bob?" he asked, doubtfully.

"Is that you, Jimmy Wells?" cried the man in the door.

"Bless my heart!" exclaimed the new arrival, grasping both the other's hands with his own. "It's Bob, sure as fate. I was certain I'd find you here if you were still in existence. Well, well, well!—twenty years is a long time. The old restaurant's gone, Bob; I wish it had lasted, so we could have had another dinner there. How has the West treated you, old man?"

"Bully; it has given me everything I asked it for. You've changed lots, Jimmy. I never thought you were so tall by two or three inches."

"Oh, I grew a bit after I was twenty."

"Doing well in New York, Jimmy?"

"Moderately. I have a position in one of the city departments.

Come on, Bob; we'll go around to a place I know of, and have a good long talk about old times."

The two men started up the street, arm in arm. The man from the West, his egotism enlarged by success, was beginning to outline the history of his career. The other, submerged in his overcoat, listened with interest.

At the corner stood a drug store, brilliant with electric lights. When they came into this glare each of them turned simultaneously to gaze upon the other's face.

The man from the West stopped suddenly and released his arm.

"You're not Jimmy Wells," he snapped. "Twenty years is a long time, but not long enough to change a man's nose from a Roman to a pug."

"It sometimes changes a good man into a bad one," said the tall man. "You've been under arrest for ten minutes, 'Silky' Bob. Chicago thinks you may have dropped over our way and wires us she wants to have a chat with you. Going quietly, are you? That's sensible. Now, before we go to the station here's a note I was asked to hand to you. You may read it here at the window. It's from Patrolman Wells."

The man from the West unfolded the little piece of paper handed him. His hand was steady when he began to read, but it trembled a little by the time he had finished. The note was rather short.

Bob: I was at the appointed place on time. When you struck the match to light your cigar I saw it was the face of the man wanted in Chicago. Somehow I couldn't do it myself, so I went around and got a plain clothes man to do the job.

                                                    Jimmy

The Furnished Room

RESTLESS, shifting, fugacious as time itself is a certain vast bulk of the population of the red brick district of the lower West Side. Homeless, they have a hundred homes. They flit from furnished room to furnished room, transients forever—transients in abode, transients in heart and mind. They sing "Home, Sweet Home" in ragtime; they carry their *lares et penates* in a bandbox; their vine is entwined about a picture hat; a rubber plant is their fig tree.

Hence the houses of this district, having had a thousand dwellers, should have a thousand tales to tell, mostly dull ones, no doubt; but it would be strange if there could not be found a ghost or two in the wake of all these vagrant guests.

One evening after dark a young man prowled among these crumbling red mansions, ringing their bells. At the twelfth he rested his lean hand-baggage upon the step and wiped the dust from his hatband and forehead. The bell sounded faint and far away in some remote, hollow depths.

To the door of this, the twelfth house whose bell he had rung, came a housekeeper who made him think of an unwholesome, surfeited worm that had eaten its nut to a hollow shell and now sought to fill the vacancy with edible lodgers.

He asked if there was a room to let.

"Come in," said the housekeeper. Her voice came from her throat; her throat seemed lined with fur. "I have the third-floor back, vacant since a week back. Should you wish to look at it?"

The young man followed her up the stairs. A faint light from no particular source mitigated the shadows of the halls. They trod noiselessly upon a stair carpet that its own loom would have forsworn. It seemed to have become vegetable; to have degenerated in that rank, sunless air to lush lichen or spreading moss that grew in patches to the stair-case and was viscid under the foot like organic matter. At each turn of the stairs were vacant niches in the wall. Perhaps plants had once been set within them. If so they had died in that foul and tainted air. It may be that statues of the saints had stood there, but it was not difficult to conceive that imps and devils had dragged them forth in the darkness and down to the unholy depths of some furnished pit below.

"This is the room," said the housekeeper, from her furry throat. "It's a nice room. It ain't often vacant. I had some most elegant people in it last summer—no trouble at all, and paid in advance to the minute. The water's at the end of the hall. Sprowls and Mooney kept it three months. They done a vaudeville sketch. Miss B'retta Sprowls—you may have heard of her—Oh, that was just the stage names—right there over the dresser is where the marriage certificate hung, framed. The gas is here, and you see there is plenty of closet room. It's a room everybody likes. It never stays idle long."

"Do you have many theatrical people rooming here?" asked the young man.

"They comes and goes. A good proportion of my lodgers is connected with the theatres. Yes, sir, this is the theatrical district. Actor people never stays long anywhere. I get my share. Yes, they comes and they goes."

He engaged the room, paying for a week in advance. He was tired, he said, and would take possession at once. He counted out the money. The room had been made ready, she said, even to towels and water. As the housekeeper moved away he put, for the thousandth time, the question that he carried at the end of his tongue.

"A young girl—Miss Vashner—Miss Eloise Vashner—do you remember such a one among your lodgers? She would be singing on the stage, most likely. A fair girl, of medium height and slender, with reddish, gold hair and dark mole near her left eyebrow."

"No, I don't remember the name. Them stage people has names they change as often as their rooms. They comes and they goes. No, I don't call that one to mind."

No. Always no. Five months of ceaseless interrogation and the inevitable negative. So much time spent by day in questioning managers, agents, schools and choruses; by night among the audiences of theatres from all-star casts down to music halls so low that he dreaded to find what he most hoped for. He who had loved her best had tried to find her. He was sure that since her disappearance from home this great, water-girt city held her somewhere, but it was like a monstrous quicksand, shifting its particles constantly, with no foundation, its upper granules of to-day buried to-morrow in ooze and slime.

The furnished room received its latest guest with a first glow of pseudo-hospitality, a hectic, haggard, perfunctory welcome like the specious smile of a demirep. The sophistical comfort came in reflected gleams from the decayed furniture, the ragged brocade upholstery of a couch and two chairs, a foot-wide cheap pier glass between the two windows, from one or two gilt picture frames and a brass bedstead in a corner.

The guest reclined, inert, upon a chair, while the room, confused in speech as though it were an apartment in Babel, tried to discourse to him of its divers tenantry.

A polychromatic rug like some brilliant-flowered, rectangular, tropical islet lay surrounded by a billowy sea of soiled matting. Upon the gay-papered wall were those pictures that pursue the homeless one from house to house—The Huguenot Lovers, The First Quarrel, The Wedding Breakfast, Psyche at the Fountain. The mantel's chastely severe outline was ingloriously veiled behind some pert drapery drawn rakishly askew like the sashes of the Amazonian ballet. Upon it was some desolate flotsam cast aside by the room's marooned when a lucky sail had borne them to a fresh port—a trifling vase or two, pictures of actresses, a medicine bottle, some stray cards out of a deck.

One by one, as the characters of a cryptograph became explicit, the little signs left by the furnished rooms' procession of guests developed a significance. The threadbare space in the rug in front of the dresser told that lovely woman had marched in the throng. The tiny fingerprints on the wall spoke of little prisoners trying to feel their way to sun and air. A splattered stain, raying like the shadow of a bursting bomb, witnessed where a hurled glass or bottle had splintered with its contents against the wall. Across the pier glass had been scrawled with a diamond in staggering letters the name "Marie." It seemed that the succession of dwellers in the furnished room had turned in fury—perhaps tempted beyond forbearance by its garish coldness—and wreaked upon it their passions. The furniture was chipped and bruised; the couch, distorted by bursting springs, seemed a horrible monster that had been slain during the stress of some grotesque convulsion. Some more potent upheaval had cloven a great slice from the marble mantel. Each plank in the floor owned its particular cant and shriek as from a separate and individual agony. It seemed incredible that all this malice and injury had been wrought upon the room by those who had called it for a time their home; and yet it may have been the cheated home instinct surviving blindly, the resentful rage at false household gods that had kindled their wrath. A hut that is our own we can sweep and adorn and cherish.

The young tenant in the chair allowed these thoughts to file, soft-shod, through his mind, while there drifted into the room furnished sounds and furnished scents. He heard in one room a tittering and incontinent, slack laughter; in others the monologue of a scold, the rattling of dice, a lullaby, and one crying dully; above him a banjo tinkled with spirit. Doors banged somewhere; the elevated trains roared intermittently; a cat yowled miserably upon a back fence. And he breathed the breath of the house—a dank savor rather than a smell—a cold, musty effluvium as from underground vaults mingled with the reeking exhalations of linoleum and mildewed and rotten woodwork.

Then suddenly, as he rested there, the room was filled with the strong, sweet odor of mignonette. It came as upon a single buffet of wind with such sureness and fragrance and emphasis that it almost seemed a living visitant. And the man cried aloud: "What, dear?" as if he had been called, and sprang up and faced about. The rich odor clung to him and wrapped him around. He reached out his arms for it, all his senses for the time confused and commingled. How could one be peremptorily called by an odor? Surely it must have been a sound. But, was it not the sound that had touched, that had caressed him?

"She has been in this room," he cried, and he sprang to wrest from it a token, for he knew he would recognize the smallest thing that had belonged to her or that she had touched. This enveloping scent of mignonette, the odor that she had loved and made her own—whence came it?

The room had been but carelessly set in order. Scattered upon the flimsy dresser scarf were half a dozen hairpins—those discreet, indistinguishable friends of womankind, feminine of gender, infinite mood and uncommunicative of tense. These he ignored, conscious of their triumphant lack of identity. Ransacking the drawers of the dresser he came upon a discarded, tiny, ragged handkerchief. He pressed it to his face. It was racy and insolent with heliotrope; he hurled it to the floor. In another drawer he found odd buttons, a theatre programme, a pawnbroker's card, two lost marshmallows, a book on the divination of dreams. In the last was a woman's black satin hair bow, which halted him, poised between ice and fire. But the black satin bow also is femininity's demure, impersonal common ornament and tells no tales.

And then he traversed the room like a hound on the scent, skimming the walls, considering the corners of the bulging matting on his hands and knees, rummaging mantel and tables, the curtains and hangings, the drunken cabinet in the corner, for a visible sign, unable to perceive that she was there beside, around, against, within, above him, clinging to him, wooing him, calling him so poignantly through the finer senses that even his grosser ones became cognizant of the call. Once again he answered loudly: "Yes, dear!" and turned, wild-eyed, to gaze on vacancy, for he could not yet discern form and color and love and outstretched arms in the odor of mignonette. Oh, God! whence that odor, and since when have odors had a voice to call? Thus he groped.

He burrowed in crevices and corners, and found corks and cigarettes. These he passed in passive contempt. But once he found in a fold of the matting a half-smoked cigar, and this he ground beneath his heel with a green and trenchant oath. He sifted the room from end to end. He found dreary and ignoble small records of many a peripatetic tenant; but of her whom he sought, and who may have lodged there, and whose spirit seemed to hover there, he found no trace.

And then he thought of the housekeeper.

He ran from the haunted room downstairs and to a door that showed a crack of light. She came out to his knock. He smothered his excitement as best he could.

"Will you tell me, madam," he besought her, "who occupied the room I have before I came?"

"Yes, sir. I can tell you again. 'Twas Sprowls and Mooney, as I said. Miss B'retta Sprowls it was in the theatres, but Missis Mooney she was. My house is well known for respectability. The marriage certificate hung, framed, on a nail over——"

"What kind of a lady was Miss Sprowls—in looks, I mean?"

"Why, black-haired, sir, short, and stout, with a comical face. They left a week ago Tuesday."

"And before they occupied it?"

"Why, there was a single gentleman connected with the draying business. He left owing me a week. Before him was Missis Crowder and her two children, that stayed four months; and back of them was old Mr. Doyle, whose sons paid for him. He kept the room six months. That goes back a year, sir, and further I do not remember."

He thanked her and crept back to his room. The room was dead. The essence that had vivified it was gone. The perfume of mignonette had departed. In its place was the old, stale odor of mouldy house furniture, of atmosphere in storage.

The ebbing of his hope drained his faith. He sat staring at the yellow, singing gaslight. Soon he walked to the bed and began to tear the sheets into strips. With the blade of his knife he drove them tightly into every crevice around windows and door. When all was snug and taut he turned out the light, turned the gas full on again and laid himself gratefully upon the bed.

It was Mrs. McCool's night to go with the can for beer. So she fetched it and sat with Mrs. Purdy in one of those subterranean retreats where housekeepers foregather and the worm dieth seldom.

"I rented out my third-floor-back this evening," said Mrs. Purdy, across a fine circle of foam. "A young man took it. He went up to bed two hours ago."

"Now, did ye, Mrs. Purdy, ma'am?" said Mrs. McCool, with intense admiration. "You do be a wonder for rentin' rooms of that kind. And did ye tell him, then?" she concluded in a husky whisper laden with mystery.

"Rooms," said Mrs. Purdy, in her furriest tones, "are furnished for to rent. I did not tell him, Mrs. McCool."

" 'Tis right ye are, ma'am; 'tis by renting rooms we kape alive. Ye have the rale sense for business, ma'am. There be many people will rayjict the rentin' of a room if they be tould a suicide has been after dyin' in the bed of it."

"As you say, we has our living to be making," remarked Mrs. Purdy.

"Yis, ma'am; 'tis true. 'Tis just one wake ago this day I helped ye lay out the third-floor-back. A pretty slip of a colleen she was to be killin' herself wid the gas—a swate little face she had, Mrs. Purdy, ma'am."

"She'd a-been called handsome, as you say," said Mrs. Purdy, assenting but critical, "but for that mole she had a-growin' by her left eyebrow. Do fill up your glass again, Mrs. McCool."

From
HEART OF THE WEST

✤

Hearts and Crosses

BALDY WOODS reached for the bottle, and got it. Whenever Baldy went for anything he usually—but this is not Baldy's story. He poured out a third drink that was larger by a finger than the first and second. Baldy was in consultation; and the consultee is worthy of his hire.

"I'd be king if I was you," said Baldy, so positively that his holster creaked and his spurs rattled.

Webb Yeager pushed back his flat-brimmed Stetson, and made further disorder in his straw-colored hair. The tonsorial recourse being without avail, he followed the liquid example of the more resourceful Baldy.

"If a man marries a queen, it oughtn't to make him a two-spot," declared Webb, epitomizing his grievances.

"Sure not," said Baldy, sympathetic, still thirsty, and genuinely solicitous concerning the relative value of the cards. "By rights you're a king. If I was you, I'd call for a new deal. The cards have been stacked on you—I'll tell you what you are, Webb Yeager."

"What?" asked Webb, with a hopeful look in his pale-blue eyes.

"You're a prince-consort."

"Go easy," said Webb. "I never black-guarded you none."

"It's a title," explained Baldy, "up among the picture-cards; but it don't take no tricks. I'll tell you, Webb. It's a brand they've got for certain animals in Europe. Say that you or me or one of them Dutch dukes marries in a royal family. Well, by and by our wife gets to be queen. Are we king? Not in a million years. At the coronation ceremonies we march between little casino and the Ninth Grand Custodian of the Royal Hall Bedchamber. The only use we are is to appear in photographs, and accept the responsibility for the heir-apparent. That ain't any square deal. Yes, sir, Webb, you're a prince-consort; and if I was you, I'd start a interregnum or a habeas corpus or somethin'; and I'd be king if I had to turn from the bottom of the deck."

Baldy emptied his glass to the ratification of his Warwick pose.

"Baldy," said Webb, solemnly, "me and you punched cows in the same outfit for years. We been runnin' on the same range, and ridin' the same trails since we was boys. I wouldn't talk about my family affairs to nobody but you. You was line-rider on the Nopalito Ranch when I married Santa McAllister. I was foreman then; but what am I now? I don't amount to a knot in a stake rope."

"When old McAllister was the cattle king of West Texas," continued Baldy with Satanic sweetness, "you was some tallow. You had as much to say on the ranch as he did."

"I did," admitted Webb, "up to the time he found out I was tryin' to get my rope over Santa's head. Then he kept me out on the range as far from the ranch-house as he could. When the old man died they commenced to call Santa the 'cattle queen.' I'm boss of the cattle—that's all. She 'tends to all the business; she handles all the money; I can't sell even a beef-steer to a party of campers, myself. Santa's the 'queen'; and I'm Mr. Nobody."

"I'd be a king if I was you," repeated Baldy Woods, the royalist. "When a man marries a queen he ought to grade up with her— on the hoof—dressed—dried—corned—any old way from the chaparral to the packing-house. Lots of folks thinks it's funny, Webb, that you don't have the say-so on the Nopalito. I ain't reflectin' none on Miz Yeager—she's the finest little lady between the Rio Grande and next Christmas—but a man ought to be boss of his own camp."

The smooth, brown face of Yeager lengthened to a mask of wounded melancholy. With that expression, and his rumpled yellow hair and guileless blue eyes, he might have been likened to a schoolboy whose leadership had been usurped by a youngster of superior strength. But his active and sinewy seventy-two inches and his girded revolvers forbade the comparison.

"What was that you called me, Baldy?" he asked. "What kind of a concert was it?"

"A 'consort,'" corrected Baldy—"'a prince-consort.' It's a kind of short-card pseudonym. You come in sort of between Jack-high and a four-card flush."

Webb Yeager sighed, and gathered the strap of his Winchester scabbard from the floor.

"I'm ridin' back to the ranch to-day," he said, half-heartedly. "I've got to start a bunch of beeves for San Antone in the morning."

"I'm your company as far as Dry Lake," announced Baldy. "I've got a round-up camp on the San Marcos cuttin' out two-year-olds."

The two *compañeros* mounted their ponies and trotted away from the little railroad settlement, where they had foregathered in the thirsty morning.

At Dry Lake, where their routes diverged, they reined up for a party cigarette. For miles they had ridden in silence save for the soft drum of the ponies' hoofs on the matted mesquite grass, and the rattle of the chaparral against their wooden stirrups. But in Texas discourse is seldom continuous. You may fill in a mile, a meal, and a murder between your paragraphs without detriment to your thesis. So, without apology, Webb offered an addendum to the conversation that had begun ten miles away.

"You remember, yourself, Baldy, that there was a time when Santa wasn't quite so independent. You remember the days when old McAllister was keepin' us apart, and how she used to send

me the sign that she wanted to see me? Old man Mac promised to
make me look like a colander if I ever come in gun-shot of the
ranch. You remember the sign she used to send, Baldy—the heart
with a cross inside of it?"

"Me?" cried Baldy, with intoxicated archness.

"You old sugar-stealing coyote! Don't I remember! Why, you
dad-blamed old long-horned turtle-dove, the boys in camp was
all cognoscious about them hieroglyphs. The 'gizzard-and-crossbones' we used to call it. We used to see 'em on truck that was
sent out from the ranch. They was marked in charcoal on the sacks
of flour and in lead-pencil on the newspapers. I see one of 'em once
chalked on the back of a new cook that old man McAllister sent
out from the ranch—danged if I didn't."

"Santa's father," exclaimed Webb gently, "got her to promise
that she wouldn't write to me or send me any word. That heart-
and-cross sign was her scheme. Whenever she wanted to see me
in particular she managed to put that mark on somethin' at the
ranch that she knew I'd see. And I never laid eyes on it but what
I burnt the wind for the ranch the same night. I used to see her in
that coma mott back of the little horse-corral."

"We knowed it," chanted Baldy; "but we never let on. We was
all for you. We knowed why you always kept that fast paint in
camp. And when we see that gizzard-and-crossbones figured out
on the truck from the ranch we knowed old Pinto was goin' to eat
up miles that night instead of grass. You remember Scurry—that
educated horse-wrangler we had—the college fellow that tangle-
foot drove to the range? Whenever Scurry saw that come-meet-
your-honey brand on anything from the ranch, he'd wave his hand
like that, and say, 'Our friend Lee Andrews will again swim the
Hell's point to-night.'"

"The last time Santa sent me the sign," said Webb, "was once
when she was sick. I noticed it as soon as I hit camp, and I
galloped Pinto forty mile that night. She wasn't at the coma
mott. I went to the house; and old McAllister met me at the
door. 'Did you come here to get killed?' says he; 'I'll disoblige you
for once. I just started a Mexican to bring you. Santa wants you.

Go in that room and see her. And then come out here and see me.'

"Santa was lyin' in bed pretty sick. But she gives out a kind of a smile, and her hand and mine lock horns, and I sets down by the bed—mud and spurs and chaps and all. 'I've heard you ridin' across the grass for hours, Webb,' she says. 'I was sure you'd come. You saw the sign?' she whispers. 'The minute I hit camp,' says I. ' 'Twas marked on the bag of potatoes and onions.' 'They're always together.' says she, soft like—'always together in life.' 'They go well together,' I says, 'in a stew.' 'I mean hearts and crosses,' says Santa. 'Our sign—to love and to suffer—that's what they mean.'

"And there was old Doc Musgrove amusin' himself with whisky and a palm-leaf fan. And by and by Santa goes to sleep; and Doc feels her forehead; and he says to me: 'You're not such a bad febrifuge. But you'd better slide out now, for the diagnosis don't call for you in regular doses. The little lady'll be all right when she wakes up.'

"I seen old McAllister outside. 'She's asleep,' says I. 'And now you can start in with your colander-work. Take your time; for I left my gun on my saddle-horn.'

"Old Mac laughs, and he says to me: 'Pumpin' lead into the best ranch-boss in West Texas don't seem to me good business policy. I don't know where I could get as good a one. It's the son-in-law idea, Webb, that makes me admire for to use you as a target. You ain't my idea for a member of the family. But I can use you on the Nopalito if you'll keep outside of a radius with the ranch-house in the middle of it. You go upstairs and lay down on a cot, and when you get some sleep we'll talk it over.' "

Baldy Woods pulled down his hat, and uncurled his leg from his saddle-horn. Webb shortened his rein, and his pony danced, anxious to be off. The two men shook hands with Western ceremony.

"*Adios*, Baldy," said Webb. "I'm glad I seen you and had this talk."

With a pounding rush that sounded like the rise of a covey of quail, the riders sped away toward different points of the compass. A hundred yards on his route Baldy reined in on the top of a bare knoll and emitted a yell. He swayed on his horse; had he been on foot, the earth would have risen and conquered him; but in the saddle he was a master of equilibrium, and laughed at whisky, and despised the centre of gravity.

Webb turned in his saddle at the signal.

"If I was you," came Baldy's strident and perverting tones, "I'd be king!"

At eight o'clock on the following morning Bud Turner rolled from his saddle in front of the Nopalito ranch-house, and stumbled with whizzing rowels toward the gallery. Bud was in charge of the bunch of beef-cattle that was to strike the trail that morning for San Antonio. Mrs. Yeager was on the gallery watering a cluster of hyacinths growing in a red earthenware jar.

"King" McAllister had bequeathed to his daughter many of his strong characteristics—his resolution, his gay courage, his contumacious self-reliance, his pride as a reigning monarch of hoofs and horns. *Allegro* and *fortissimo* had been McAllister's tempo and tone. In Santa they survived, transposed to the feminine key. Substantially, she preserved the image of the mother who had been summoned to wander in other and less finite green pastures long before the waxing herds of kine had conferred royalty upon the house. She had her mother's slim, strong figure and grave, soft prettiness that relieved in her the severity of the imperious McAllister eye and the McAllister air or royal independence.

Webb stood on one end of the gallery giving orders to two or three sub-bosses of various camps and outfits who had ridden in for instructions.

" 'Morning," said Bud, briefly. "Where do you want them beeves to go in town—to Barber's, as usual?"

Now, to answer that had been the prerogative of the queen. All the reins of business—buying, selling, and banking—had been held by her capable fingers. The handling of the cattle had been entrusted fully to her husband. In the days of "King" McAllister,

Santa had been his secretary and helper; and she had continued her work with wisdom and profit. But before she could reply, the prince-consort spake up with calm decision:

"You drive thàt bunch to Zimmerman and Nesbit's pens. I spoke to Zimmerman about it some time ago."

Bud turned on his high boot-heels.

"Wait!" called Santa quickly. She looked at her husband with surprise in her steady gray eyes.

"Why, what do you mean, Webb?" she asked, with a small wrinkle gathering between her brows. "I never deal with Zimmerman and Nesbit. Barber has handled every head of stock from this ranch in that market for five years. I'm not going to take the business out of his hands." She faced Bud Turner. "Deliver those cattle to Barber," she concluded positively.

Bud gazed impartially at the water-jar hanging on the gallery, stood on his other leg, and chewed a mesquite-leaf.

"I want this bunch of beeves to go to Zimmerman and Nesbit," said Webb, with a frosty light in his blue eyes.

"Nonsense," said Santa impatiently. "You'd better start on, Bud, so as to noon at the Little Elm waterhole. Tell Barber we'll have another lot of culls ready in about a month."

Bud allowed a hesitating eye to steal upward and meet Webb's. Webb saw apology in his look, and fancied he saw commiseration.

"You deliver them cattle," he said grimly, "to——"

"Barber," finished Santa sharply. "Let that settle it. Is there anything else you are waiting for, Bud?"

"No, m'm," said Bud. But before going he lingered while a cow's tail could have switched thrice; for a man is man's ally; and even the Philistines must have blushed when they took Samson in the way they did.

"You hear your boss!" cried Webb, sardonically. He took off his hat, and bowed until it touched the floor before his wife.

"Webb," said Santa rebukingly, "you're acting mighty foolish to-day."

"Court fool, your Majesty," said Webb, in his slow tones, which had changed their quality. "What else can you expect? Let me tell you. I was a man before I married a cattle-queen. What am I now? The laughing-stock of the camps. I'll be a man again."

Santa looked at him closely.

"Don't be unreasonable, Webb," she said calmly. "You haven't been slighted in any way. Do I ever interfere in your management of the cattle? I know the business side of the ranch much better that you do. I learned it from Dad. Be sensible."

"Kingdoms and queendoms," said Webb, "don't suit me unless I am in the pictures, too. I punch the cattle and you wear the crown. All right. I'd rather be High Lord Chancellor of a cow-camp than the eight-spot in a queen-high flush. It's your ranch; and Barber gets the beeves."

Webb's horse was tied to the rack. He walked into the house and brought out his roll of blankets that he never took with him except on long rides, and his "slicker," and his longest stake-rope of plaited rawhide. These he began to tie deliberately upon his saddle. Santa, a little pale, followed him.

Webb swung up into the saddle. His serious, smooth face was without expression except for a stubborn light that smouldered in his eyes.

"There's a herd of cows and calves," said he, "near the Hondo Waterhole on the Frio that ought to be moved away from timber. Lobos have killed three of the calves. I forgot to leave orders. You'd better tell Simms to attend to it."

Santa laid a hand on the horse's bridle, and looked her husband in the eye.

"Are you going to leave me, Webb?" she asked quietly.

"I am going to be a man again," he answered.

"I wish you success in a praiseworthy attempt," she said, with a sudden coldness. She turned and walked directly into the house.

Webb Yeager rode to the southeast as straight as the topography of West Texas permitted. And when he reached the horizon he might have ridden on into blue space as far as knowledge of him on the Nopalito went. And the days, with Sundays at their head, formed into hebdomadal squads; and the weeks, captained by the full moon, closed ranks into menstrual companies carrying "Tempus fugit" on their banners; and the months marched on toward the vast camp-ground of the years; but Webb Yeager came no more to the dominions of his queen.

One day a being named Bartholomew, a sheep-man—and therefore of little account—from the lower Rio Grande country, rode in sight of the Nopalito ranch-house, and felt hunger assail him. *Ex consuetudine* he was soon seated at the mid-day dining-table of that hospitable kingdom. Talk like water gushed from him: he might have been smitten with Aaron's rod—that is your gentle shepherd when an audience is vouchsafed him whose ears are not overgrown with wool.

"Missis Yeager," he babbled, "I see a man the other day on the Rancho Seco down in Hidalgo County by your name—Webb Yeager was his. He'd just been engaged as manager. He was a tall, light-haired man, not saying much. Maybe he was some kin of yours, do you think?"

"A husband," said Santa cordially. "The Seco has done well. Mr. Yeager is one of the best stockmen in the West."

The dropping out of a prince-consort rarely disorganizes a monarchy. Queen Santa had appointed as *mayordomo* of the ranch, a trusty subject, named Ramsay, who had been one of her father's faithful vassals. And there was scarcely a ripple on the Nopalito ranch save when the gulf-breeze created undulations in the grass of its wide acres.

For several years the Nopalito had been making experiments with an English breed of cattle that looked down with aristocratic contempt upon the Texas long-horns. The experiments were found satisfactory; and a pasture had been set apart for the blue-bloods. The fame of them had gone forth into the chaparral and pear as far as men ride in saddles. Other ranches woke up, rubbed their eyes, and looked with new dissatisfaction upon the long-horns.

As a consequence, one day a sunburned, capable, silk-kerchiefed nonchalant youth, garnished with revolvers, and attended by three Mexican *vaqueros*, alighted at the Nopalito ranch and presented the following business-like epistle to the queen thereof.

Mrs. Yeager—The Nopalito Ranch:

Dear Madam:
I am instructed by the owners of the Rancho Seco to purchase 100 head of two and three-year-old cows of the Sussex breed owned by you. If you can fill the order please deliver the cattle to the bearer; and a check will be forwarded to you at once.

Respectfully,
Webster Yeager,
Manager of the Rancho Seco.

Business is business, even—very scantily did it escape being written "especially"—in a kingdom.

That night the 100 head of cattle were driven up from the pasture and penned in a corral near the ranch-house for delivery in the morning.

When night closed down and the house was still, did Santa Yeager throw herself down, clasping that formal note to her bosom, weeping, and calling out a name that pride (either in one or the other) had kept from her lips many a day? Or did she file the letter, in her business way, retaining her royal balance and strength?

Wonder, if you will; but royalty is sacred; and there is a veil. But this much you shall learn.

At midnight Santa slipped softly out of the ranch-house, clothed in something dark and plain. She paused for a moment under the live-oak trees. The prairies were somewhat dim, and the moonlight was pale orange, diluted with particles of an impalpable, flying mist. But the mock-bird whistled on every bough of vantage; leagues of flowers scented the air; and a kindergarten of little shadowy rabbits leaped and played in an open space near by. Santa turned her face to the southeast and threw kisses thitherward; for there was none to see.

Then she sped silently to the blacksmith-shop, fifty yards away; and what she did there can only be surmised. But the forge glowed red; and there was a faint hammering such as Cupid might make when he sharpens his arrow-points.

Later she came forth with a queer-shaped, handled thing in one hand, and a portable furnace, such as are seen in branding-camps, in the other. To the corral where the Sussex cattle were penned she sped with these things swiftly in the moonlight.

She opened the gate and slipped inside the corral. The Sussex cattle were mostly a dark red. But among this bunch was one that was milky white—notable among the others.

And now Santa shook from her shoulder something that we had not seen before—a rope lasso. She freed the loop of it, coiling the length in her left hand, and plunged into the thick of the cattle.

The white cow was her object. She swung the lasso, which caught one horn and slipped off. The next throw encircled the forefeet and the animal fell heavily. Santa made for it like a panther; but it scrambled up and dashed against her, knocking her over like a blade of grass.

Again she made the cast, while the aroused cattle milled round the four sides of the corral in a plunging mass. This throw was fair; the white cow came to earth again; and before it could rise Santa had made the lasso fast around a post of the corral with a swift and simple knot, and had leaped upon the cow again with the rawhide hobbles.

In one minute the feet of the animal were tied (no record-breaking deed) and Santa leaned against the corral for the same space of time, panting and lax.

And then she ran swiftly to her furnace at the gate and brought the branding-iron, queerly shaped and white-hot.

The bellow of the outraged white cow, as the iron was applied, should have stirred the slumbering auricular nerves and consciences of the near-by subjects of the Nopalito, but it did not. And it was amid the deepest nocturnal silence that Santa ran like a lapwing back to the ranch-house and there fell upon a cot and sobbed—sobbed as though queens had hearts as simple ranchmen's wives have, and as though she would gladly make kings of prince-consorts, should they ride back again from over the hills and far away.

In the morning the capable, revolvered youth and his *vaqueros* set forth, driving the bunch of Sussex cattle across the prairies to the Rancho Seco. Ninety miles it was; a six days' journey, grazing and watering the animals on the way.

The beasts arrived at Rancho Seco one evening at dusk; and were received and counted by the foreman of the ranch.

The next morning at eight o'clock a horseman loped out of the brush to the Nopalito ranch-house. He dismounted stiffly, and strode, with whizzing spurs, to the house. His horse gave a great sigh and swayed foam-streaked, with down-drooping head and closed eyes.

But waste not your pity upon Belshazzar, the flea-bitten sorrel. Today, in Nopalito horse-pasture he survives, pampered, beloved, unridden, cherished record-holder of long-distance rides.

The horseman stumbled into the house. Two arms fell around his neck and someone cried out in the voice of woman and queen alike: "Webb—oh, Webb!"

"I was a skunk," said Webb Yeager.

"Hush," said Santa, "did you see it?"

"I saw it," said Webb.

What they meant God knows; and you shall know, if you rightly read the primer of events.

"Be the cattle-queen," said Webb; "and overlook it if you can. I was a mangy, sheep-stealing coyote."

"Hush!" said Santa again, laying her fingers upon his mouth. "There's no queen here. Do you know who I am? I am Santa Yeager, First Lady of the Bedchamber. Come here."

She dragged him from the gallery into the room to the right.

There stood a cradle with an infant in it—a red, ribald, unintelligible, babbling, beautiful infant, sputtering at life in an unseemly manner.

"There's no queen on this ranch," said Santa again. "Look at the king. He's got your eyes, Webb. Down on your knees and look at his Highness."

But jingling rowels sounded on the gallery, and Bud Turner stumbled there again with the same query that he had brought, lacking a few days, a year ago.

"'Morning. Them beeves is just turned out on the trail. Shall I drive 'em to Barber's, or——"

He saw Webb and stopped, open-mouthed.

"Ba-ba-ba-ba-ba-ba!" shrieked the king in his cradle, beating the air with his fists.

"You hear your boss, Bud," said Webb Yeager, with a broad grin—just as he had said a year ago.

And that is all, except that when old man Quinn, owner of the Rancho Seco, went out to look over the herd of Sussex cattle that he had bought from the Nopalito ranch, he asked his new manager:

"What's the Nopalito ranch brand, Wilson?"

"X Bar Y," said Wilson.

"I thought so," said Quinn. "But look at that white heifer there; she's got another brand—a heart with a cross inside of it. What brand is that?"

The Ransom of Mack

ME and old Mack Lonsbury, we got out of that Little Hide-and-Seek gold mine affair with about $40,000 apiece. I say "old" Mack; but he wasn't old. Forty-one, I should say; but he always seemed old.

"Andy," he says to me, "I'm tired of hustling. You and me have been working hard together for three years. Say we knock off for a while, and spend some of this idle money we've coaxed our way."

"The proposition hits me just right," says I. "Let's be nabobs a while and see how it feels. What'll we do—take in the Niagara Falls, or buck at faro?"

"For a good many years," says Mack, "I've thought that if I ever had extravagant money I'd rent a two-room cabin somewhere, hire a Chinaman to cook, and sit in my stocking feet and read Buckle's History of Civilization."

"That sounds self-indulgent and gratifying without vulgar ostentation," says I; "and I don't see how money could be better invested. Give me a cuckoo clock and a Sep Winner's Self-Instructor for the Banjo, and I'll join you."

A week afterward me and Mack hits this small town of Piña, about thirty miles out from Denver, and finds an elegant two-room house that just suits us. We deposited half-a-peck of money in the Piña bank and shook hands with every one of the 340 citizens in the town. We brought along the Chinaman and the cuckoo clock and Buckle and the Instructor with us from Denver; and they made the cabin seem like home at once.

Never believe it when they tell you riches don't bring happiness. If you could have seen old Mack sitting in his rocking-chair with his blue-yarn sock feet up in the window and absorbing in that Buckle stuff through his specs you'd have seen a picture of content that would have made Rockefeller jealous. And I was learning to pick out "Old Zip Coon" on the banjo, and the cuckoo was on time with his remarks, and Ah Sing was messing up the atmosphere with the handsomest smell of ham and eggs that ever laid the honeysuckle in the shade. When it got too dark to make out Buckle's nonsense and the notes in the Instructor, me and Mack would light our pipes and talk about science and pearl diving and sciatica and Egypt and spelling and fish and tradewinds and leather and gratitude and eagles, and a lot of subjects that we'd never had time to explain our sentiments about before.

One evening Mack spoke up and asked me if I was much apprised in the habits and policies of women folks.

"Why, yes," says I, in a tone of voice; "I know 'em from Alfred to Omaha. The feminine nature and similitude," says I, "is as plain to my sight as the Rocky Mountains is to a blue-eyed burro. I'm onto all their little sidesteps and punctual discrepancies."

"I tell you, Andy," says Mack, with a kind of sigh. "I never had the least amount of intersection with their predispositions. Maybe I might have had a proneness in respect to their vicinity, but I never took the time. I made my own living since I was fourteen; and I never seemed to get my ratiocinations equipped with the sentiments usually depicted toward the sect. I sometimes wish I had," says old Mack.

"They're an adverse study," says I, "and adapted to points of view. Although they vary in rationale, I have found 'em quite often obviously differing from each other in divergences of contrast."

"It seems to me," goes on Mack, "that a man had better take 'em in and secure his inspirations of the sect when he's young and so preordained. I let my chance go by; and I guess I'm too old now to go hopping into the curriculum."

"Oh, I don't know," I tells him. "Maybe you better credit yourself with a barrel of money and a lot of emancipation from a quantity of uncontent. Still, I don't regret my knowledge of 'em," I says. "It takes a man who understands the symptoms and by-plays of women-folks to take care of himself in this world."

We stayed on in Piña because we liked the place. Some folks might enjoy their money with noise and rapture and locomotion; but me and Mack we had had plenty of turmoils and hotel towels. The people were friendly; Ah Sing got the swing of the grub we liked; Mack and Buckle were as thick as two body-snatchers, and I was hitting out a cordial resemblance to "Buffalo Gals, Can't You Come Out To-night," on the banjo.

One day I got a telegram from Speight, the man that was working a mine I had an interest in out in New Mexico. I had to go out there; and I was gone two months. I was anxious to get back to Piña and enjoy life once more.

When I struck the cabin I nearly fainted. Mack was standing in the door; and if angels ever wept, I saw no reason why they should be smiling then.

That man was a spectacle. Yes; he was worse; he was a spy-glass; he was the great telescope in the Lick Observatory. He had on a coat and shiny shoes and a white vest and a high silk hat; and a geranium as big as an order of spinach was spiked onto his front. And he was smirking and warping his face like an infernal storekeeper or a kid with colic.

"Hello, Andy," says Mack, out of his face. "Glad to see you back. Things have happened since you went away."

"I know it," says I, "and a sacrilegious sight it is. God never made you that way, Mack Lonsbury. Why do you scarify His works with this presumptious kind of ribaldry?"

"Why, Andy," said he, "they've elected me justice of the peace since you left."

I looked at Mack close. He was restless and inspired. A justice of the peace ought to be disconsolate and assuaged.

Just then a young woman passed on the sidewalk; and I saw Mack kind of half snicker and blush, and then he raised up his hat and smiled and bowed, and she smiled and bowed, and went on by.

"No hope for you," says I, "if you've got the Mary-Jane infirmity at your age. I thought it wasn't going to take on you. And patent leather shoes! All this in two little short months!"

"I'm going to marry the young lady who just passed to-night," says Mack, in a kind of a flutter.

"I forgot something at the post-office," says I, and walked away quick.

I overtook that young woman a hundred yards away. I raised my hat and told her my name. She was about nineteen; and young for her age. She blushed, and then looked at me cool, like I was the snow scene from the "Two Orphans."

"I understand you are to be married to-night," I said.

"Correct," says she. "You got any objections?"

"Listen, sissy," I begins.

"My name is Miss Rebosa Reed," says she in a pained way.

"I know it," says I. "Now, Rebosa, I'm old enough to have owed money to your father. And that old, specious, dressed-up, garbled, sea-sick ptomaine prancing around avidiously like an irremediable turkey gobbler with patent leather shoes on is my best friend. Why did you go and get him invested in this marriage business?"

"Why, he was the only chance there was," answered Miss Rebosa.

"Nay," says I giving a sickening look of admiration at her complexion and style of features; "with your beauty you might pick any kind of a man. Listen, Rebosa. Old Mack ain't the man you want. He was twenty-two when you was *née* Reed, as the papers say. This bursting into bloom won't last with him. He's all ventilated with oldness and rectitude and decay. Old Mack's down with a case of Indian summer. He overlooked his bet when he was young; and now he's suing Nature for the interest on the promissory note he took from Cupid instead of the cash. Rebosa, are you bent on having this marriage occur?"

"Why, sure I am," says she, oscillating the pansies on her hat, "and so is somebody else, I reckon."

"What time is it to take place?" I asks.

"At six o'clock," says she.

I made up my mind right away what to do. I'd save old Mack if I could. To have a good, seasoned, ineligible man like that turn chicken for a girl that hadn't quit eating slate pencils and buttoning in the back was more than I could look on with easiness.

"Rebosa," says I, earnest, drawing upon my display of knowledge concerning the feminine intuitions of reason—"ain't there a young man in Piña—a nice young man that you think a heap of?"

"Yep," says Rebosa, nodding her pansies—"Sure there is! What do you think! Gracious!"

"Does he like you?" I asks. "How does he stand in the matter?"

"Crazy," says Rebosa. "Ma has to wet down the front steps to keep him from sitting there all the time. But I guess that'll be all over after to-night," she winds up with a sigh.

"Rebosa," says I, "you don't really experience any of this adoration called love for old Mack, do you?"

"Lord! no," says the girl, shaking her head. "I think he's as dry as a lava bed. The idea!"

"Who is this young man that you like, Rebosa?" I inquires.

"It's Eddie Bayles," says she. "He clerks in Crosby's grocery. But he don't make but thirty-five a month. Ella Noakes was wild about him once."

"Old Mack tells me," I says, "that he's going to marry you at six o'clock this evening."

"That's the time," says she. "It's to be at our house."

"Rebosa," says I, "listen to me. If Eddie Bayles had a thousand dollars cash—a thousand dollars, mind you, would buy him a store of his own—if you and Eddie had that much to excuse matrimony on, would you consent to marry him this evening at five o'clock?"

The girl looks at me a minute; and I can see these inaudible cogitations going on inside of her, as women will.

"A thousand dollars?" says she. "Of course I would."

"Come on," says I. "We'll go and see Eddie."

We went up to Crosby's store and called Eddie outside. He looked to be estimable and freckled; and he had chills and fever when I made my proposition.

"At five o'clock?" says he, "for a thousand dollars? Please don't wake me up! Well, you *are* the rich uncle retired from the spice business in India. I'll buy out old Crosby and run the store myself."

We went inside and got old man Crosby apart and explained it. I wrote my check for a thousand dollars and handed it to him. If Eddie and Rebosa married each other at five he was to turn the money over to them.

And then I gave 'em my blessing, and went to wander in the wild-wood for a season. I sat on a log and made cogitations on life and old age and the zodiac and the ways of women and all the disorder that goes with a lifetime. I passed myself congratulations that I had probably saved my old friend Mack from his attack of Indian summer. I knew when he got well of it and shed his infatuation and his patent leather shoes, he would feel grateful. "To keep old Mack disinvolved," thinks I, "from relapses like this, is worth more than a thousand dollars." And most of all I was glad that I'd made a study of women, and wasn't to be deceived any by their means of conceit and evolution.

It must have been half-past five when I got back home. I stepped in; and there sat old Mack on the back of his neck in his old clothes with his blue socks on the window and the History of Civilization propped up on his knees.

"This don't look like getting ready for a wedding at six," I says, to seem innocent.

"Oh," says Mack, reaching for his tobacco, "that was postponed back to five o'clock. They sent me a note saying the hour had been changed. It's all over now. What made you stay away so long, Andy?"

"You heard about the wedding?" I asks.

"I operated it," says he. "I told you I was justice of the peace. The preacher is off East to visit his folks, and I'm the only one in town that can perform the dispensations of marriage. I promised Eddie and Rebosa a month ago I'd marry 'em. He's a busy lad; and he'll have a grocery of his own some day."

"He will," says I.

"There was lots of women at the wedding," says Mack, smoking up. "But I didn't seem to get any ideas from 'em. I wish I was informed in the structure of their attainments like you said you was."

"That was two months ago," says I, reaching up for the banjo.

Telemachus, Friend

RETURNING FROM a hunting trip, I waited at the little town of Los Piños, in New Mexico, for the south-bound train, which was one hour late. I sat on the porch of the Summit House and discussed the functions of life with Telemachus Hicks, the hotel proprietor.

Perceiving that personalities were not out of order, I asked him what species of beast had long ago twisted and mutilated his left ear. Being a hunter, I was concerned in the evils that may befall one in the pursuit of game.

"That ear," says Hicks, "is the relic of true friendship."

"An accident?" I persisted.

"No friendship is an accident," said Telemachus; and I was silent.

"The only perfect case of true friendship I ever knew," went on my host, "was a cordial intent between a Connecticut man and a monkey. The monkey climbed palms in Barranquilla and threw down cocoanuts to the man. The man sawed them in two and made dippers, which he sold for two *reales* each and bought rum. The monkey drank the milk of the nuts. Through each being satisfied with his own share of the graft, they lived like brothers.

"But in the case of human beings, friendship is a transitory act, subject to discontinuance without further notice.

"I had a friend once, of the entitlement of Paisley Fish, that I imagined was sealed to me for an endless space of time. Side by side for seven years we had mined, ranched, sold patent churns, herded sheep, took photographs and other things, built wire fences, and picked prunes. Thinks I, neither homicide nor flattery nor riches nor sophistry nor drink can make trouble between me and Paisley Fish. We was friends an amount you could hardly guess at. We was friends in business, and we let our amicable qualities lap over and season our hours of recreation and folly. We certainly had days of Damon and nights of Pythias.

"One summer me and Paisley gallops down into these San Andrés mountains for the purpose of a month's surcease and levity, dressed in the natural store habiliments of man. We hit this town of Los Piños, which certainly was a roof-garden spot of the world, and flowing with condensed milk and honey. It had a street or two, and air, and hens, and a eating-house; and that was enough for us.

"We strikes the town after supper-time, and we concludes to sample whatever efficacy there is in this eating-house down by the railroad tracks. By the time we had set down and pried up our plates with a knife from the red oil-cloth, along intrudes Widow Jessup with the hot biscuit and fried liver.

"Now, there was a woman that would have tempted an anchovy to forget his vows. She was not so small as she was large; and a kind of welcome air seemed to mitigate her vicinity. The pink of her face was the *in hoc signo* of a culinary temper and a warm disposition, and her smile would have brought out the dogwood blossoms in December.

"Widow Jessup talks to us a lot of garrulousness about the climate and history and Tennyson and prunes and the scarcity of mutton, and finally wants to know where we came from.

" 'Spring Valley,' says I.

" 'Big Spring Valley,' chips in Paisley, out of a lot of potatoes and knuckle-bone of ham in his mouth.

"That was the first sign I noticed that the old *fidus Diogenes* business between me and Paisley Fish was ended forever. He knew how I hated a talkative person, and yet he stampedes into the conversation with his amendments and addendums of syntax. On the map it was Big Spring Valley; but I had heard Paisley himself call it Spring Valley a thousand times.

"Without saying any more, we went out after supper and set on the railroad track. We had been pardners too long not to know what was going on in each other's mind.

"'I reckon you understand,' says Paisley, 'that I've made up my mind to accrue that widow woman as part and parcel in and to my hereditaments forever, both domestic, sociable, legal, and otherwise, until death us do part.'

"'Why, yes,' says I, 'I read it between the lines, though you only spoke one. And I suppose you are aware,' says I, 'that I have a movement on foot that leads up to the widow's changing her name to Hicks, and leaves you writing to the society column to inquire whether the best man wears a japonica or seamless socks at the wedding!'

"'There'll be some hiatuses in your program,' says Paisley, chewing up a piece of a railroad tie. 'I'd give in to you,' says he, 'in 'most any respect if it was secular affairs, but this is not so. The smiles of woman,' goes on Paisley, 'is the whirlpool of Squills and Chalybeates, into which vortex the good ship Friendship is often drawn and dismembered. I'd assault a bear that was annoying you,' says Paisley, 'or I'd indorse your note, or rub the place between your shoulder-blades with opodeldoc the same as ever; but there my sense of etiquette ceases. In this fracas with Mrs. Jessup we play it alone. I've notified you fair.'

"And then I collaborates with myself, and offers the following resolutions and by-laws:

"'Friendship between man and man,' says I, 'is an ancient historical virtue enacted in the days when men had to protect each other against lizards with eighty-foot tails and flying turtles. And they've kept up the habit to this day, and stand by each other till the bellboy comes up and tells them the animals are not really there. I've often heard,' I says, 'about ladies stepping in and breaking up a friendship between men. Why should that be?

I'll tell you, Paisley, the first sight and hot biscuit of Mrs. Jessup appears to have inserted a oscillation into each of our bosoms. Let the best man of us have her. I'll play you a square game, and won't do any underhanded work. I'll do all my courting of her in your presence, so you will have an equal opportunity. With that arrangement I don't see why our steamboat of friendship should fall overboard in the medicinal whirlpools you speak of, whichever of us wins out.'

" 'Good old hoss!' says Paisley, shaking my hand. 'And I'll do the same,' says he. 'We'll court the lady synonymously, and without any of the prudery and bloodshed usual to such occasions. And we'll be friends still, win or lose.'

"At one side of Mrs. Jessup's eating-house was a bench under some trees where she used to sit in the breeze after the south-bound had been fed and gone. And there me and Paisley used to congregate after supper and make partial payments on our respects to the lady of our choice. And we was so honorable and circuitous in our calls that if one of us got there first we waited for the other before beginning any gallivantery.

"The first evening that Mrs. Jessup knew about our arrangement I got to the bench before Paisley did. Supper was just over, and Mrs. Jessup was out there with a fresh pink dress on, and almost cool enough to handle.

"I sat down by her and made a few specifications about the moral surface of nature as set forth by the landscape and the contiguous perspective. That evening was surely a case in point. The moon was attending to business in the section of sky where it belonged, and the trees was making shadows on the ground according to science and nature, and there was a kind of conspicuous hullabaloo going on in the bushes between the bull-bats and the orioles and the jack-rabbits and other feathered insects of the forest. And the wind out of the mountains was singing like a jew's-harp in the pile of old tomato-cans by the railroad track.

"I felt a kind of sensation in my left side—something like dough rising in a crock by the fire. Mrs. Jessup had moved up closer.

" 'Oh, Mr. Hicks,' says she, 'when one is alone in the world, don't they feel it more aggravated on a beautiful night like this?'

"I rose up off the bench at once.

"'Excuse me, ma'am,' says I, 'but I'll have to wait till Paisley comes before I can give a audible hearing to leading questions like that.'

"And then I explained to her how we was friends cinctured by years of embarrassment and travel and complicity, and how we had agreed to take no advantage of each other in any of the more mushy walks of life, such as might be fomented by sentiment and proximity. Mrs. Jessup appears to think serious about the matter for a minute, and then she breaks into a species of laughter that makes the wildwood resound.

"In a few minutes Paisley drops around, with oil of bergamot on his hair, and sits on the other side of Mrs. Jessup, and inaugurates a sad tale of adventure in which him and Pieface Lumley has a skinning-match of dead cows in '95 for a silver-mounted saddle in the Santa Rita valley during the nine months' drought.

"Now, from the start of that courtship I had Paisley Fish hobbled and tied to a post. Each one of us had a different system of reaching out for the easy places in the female heart. Paisley's scheme was to petrify 'em with wonderful relations of events that he had either come across personally or in large print. I think he must have got his idea of subjugation from one of Shakespeare's shows I see once called 'Othello.' There is a colored man in it who acquires a duke's daughter by disbursing to her a mixture of the talk turned out by Rider Haggard, Lew Dockstader, and Dr. Parkhurst. But that style of courting don't work well off the stage.

"Now, I give you my own recipe for inveigling a woman into that state of affairs when she can be referred to as *'née* Jones.' Learn how to pick up her hand and hold it, and she's yours. It ain't so easy. Some men grab at it so much like they was going to set a dislocation of the shoulder that you can smell the arnica and hear 'em tearing off bandages. Some take it up like a hot horseshoe, and hold it off at arm's length like a druggist pouring tincture of asafœtida in a bottle. And most of 'em catch hold of it and drag it right out before the lady's eyes like a boy finding a baseball in the grass, without giving her a chance to forget that the hand is growing on the end of her arm. Them ways are all wrong.

"I'll tell you the right way. Did you ever see a man sneak out in the backyard and pick up a rock to throw at a tomcat that was sitting on a fence looking at him? He pretends he hasn't got a thing in his hand, and that the cat don't see him, and he don't see the cat. That's the idea. Never drag her hand out where she'll have to take notice of it. Don't let her know that you think she knows you have the least idea she is aware you are holding her hand. That was my rule of tactics; and as far as Paisley's serenade about hostilities and misadventure went, he might as well have been reading to her a time-table of the Sunday trains that stop at Ocean Grove, New Jersey.

"One night when I beat Paisley to the bench by one pipeful, my friendship gets subsidized for a minute, and I asks Mrs. Jessup if she didn't think a 'H' was easier to write than a 'J'. In a second her head was mashing the oleander flower in my button-hole, and I leaned over and—but I didn't.

" 'If you don't mind,' says I, standing up, 'we'll wait for Paisley to come before finishing this. I've never done anything dishonorable yet to our friendship, and this won't be quite fair.'

" 'Mr. Hicks,' says Mrs. Jessup, looking at me peculiar in the dark, 'if it wasn't for but one thing, I'd ask you to hike yourself down the gulch and never disresume your visits to my house.'

" 'And what is that, ma'am?' I asks.

" 'You are too good a friend not to make a good husband,' says she.

"In five minutes Paisley was on his side of Mrs. Jessup.

" 'In Silver City, in the summer of '98,' he begins, 'I see Jim Bartholomew chew off a Chinaman's ear in the Blue Light Saloon on account of a crossbarred muslin shirt that—what was that noise?'

"I had resumed matters again with Mrs. Jessup right where we had left off.

" 'Mrs. Jessup,' says I, 'has promised to make it Hicks. And this is another of the same sort.'

"Paisley winds his feet around a leg of the bench and kind of groans.

" 'Lem,' says he, 'we been friends for seven years. Would you mind not kissing Mrs. Jessup quite so loud? I'd do the same for you.'

" 'All right,' says I. 'The other kind will do as well.'

" 'This Chinaman,' goes on Paisley, 'was the one that shot a man named Mullins in the spring of '97, and that was——'

"Paisley interrupted himself again.

" 'Lem,' says he, 'if you was a true friend you wouldn't hug Mrs. Jessup quite so hard. I felt the bench shake all over just then. You know you told me you would give me an even chance as long as there was any.'

" 'Mr. Man,' says Mrs. Jessup, turning around to Paisley, 'if you was to drop in to the celebration of mine and Mr. Hicks's silver wedding, twenty-five years from now, do you think you could get it into that Hubbard squash you call your head that you are *nix cum rous* in this business? I've put up with you a long time because you was Mr. Hicks's friend; but it seems to me it's time for you to wear the willow and trot off down the hill.'

" 'Mrs. Jessup,' says I, without losing my grasp on the situation as fiancé, 'Mr. Paisley is my friend, and I offered him a square deal and a equal opportunity as long as there was a chance.'

" 'A chance!' says she. 'Well, he may think he has a chance; but I hope he won't think he's got a cinch, after what he's been next to all the evening.'

"Well, a month afterwards me and Mrs. Jessup was married in the Los Piños Methodist Church; and the whole town closed up to see the performance.

"When we lined up in front and the preacher was beginning to sing out his rituals and observances, I looks around and misses Paisley. I calls time on the preacher. 'Paisley ain't here,' says I. 'We've got to wait for Paisley. A friend once, a friend always—

that's Telemachus Hicks,' says I. Mrs. Jessup's eyes snapped some; but the preacher holds up the incantations according to instructions.

"In a few minutes Paisley gallops up the aisle, putting on a cuff as he comes. He explains that the only dry-goods store in town was closed for the wedding, and he couldn't get the kind of a boiled shirt that his taste called for until he had broke open the back window of the store and helped himself. Then he ranges up on the other side of the bride, and the wedding goes on. I always imagined that Paisley calculated as a last chance that the preacher might marry him to the widow by mistake.

"After the proceedings was over we had tea and jerked antelope and canned apricots, and then the populace hiked itself away. Last of all Paisley shook me by the hand and told me I'd acted square and on the level with him and he was proud to call me a friend.

"The preacher had a small house on the side of the street that he'd fixed up to rent; and he allowed me and Mrs. Hicks to occupy it till the ten-forty train the next morning, when we was going on a bridal tour to El Paso. His wife had decorated it all up with hollyhocks and poison ivy, and it looked real festal and bowery.

"About ten o'clock that night I sets down in the front door and pulls off my boots a while in the cool breeze, while Mrs. Hicks was fixing around in the room. Right soon the light went out inside; and I sat there a while, reverberating over old times and scenes. And then I heard Mrs. Hicks call out, 'Ain't you coming in soon, Lem?'

" 'Well, well!' says I, kind of rousing up. 'Durn me if I wasn't waiting for old Paisley to——'

"But when I got that far," concluded Telemachus Hicks, "I thought somebody had shot this left ear of mine off with a forty-five. But it turned out to be only a lick from a broomhandle in the hands of Mrs. Hicks."

The Handbook of Hymen

'TIS THE OPINION of myself, Sanderson Pratt, who sets this down, that the educational system of the United States should be in the hands of the weather bureau. I can give you good reasons for it; and you can't tell me why our college professors shouldn't be transferred to the meteorological department. They have been learned to read; and they could very easily glance at the morning papers and then wire in to the main office what kind of weather to expect. But there's the other side of the proposition. I am going on to tell you how the weather furnished me and Idaho Green with an elegant education.

We was up in the Bitter Root Mountains over the Montana line prospecting for gold. A chin-whiskered man in Walla-Walla, carrying a line of hope as excess baggage, had grubstaked us; and there we was in the foothills pecking away, with enough grub on hand to last an army through a peace conference.

Along one day comes a mail-rider over the mountains from Carlos, and stops to eat three cans of green-gages, and leave us a newspaper of modern date. This paper prints a system of premonitions of the weather, and the card it dealt Bitter Root Mountains from the bottom of the deck was "warmer and fair, with light westerly breezes."

That evening it began to snow, with the wind strong in the east. Me and Idaho moved camp into an old empty cabin higher up the mountain, thinking it was only a November flurry. But after falling three foot on a level it went to work in earnest; and we knew we was snowed in. We got in plenty of firewood before it got deep, and we had grub enough for two months, so we let the elements rage and cut up all they thought proper.

If you want to instigate the art of manslaughter just shut two men up in a eighteen-by-twenty-foot cabin for a month. Human nature won't stand it.

When the first snowflakes fell me and Idaho Green laughed at each other's jokes and praised the stuff we turned out of a skillet and called bread. At the end of three weeks Idaho makes this kind of a edict to me. Says he:

"I never exactly heard sour milk dropping out of a balloon on the bottom of a tin pan, but I have an idea it would be music of the spears compared to this attenuated stream of asphyxiated thought that emanates out of your organs of conversation. The kind of half-masticated noises that you emit every day puts me in mind of a cow's cud, only she's lady enough to keep hers to herself, and you ain't."

"Mr. Green," says I, "you having been a friend of mine once, I have some hesitations in confessing to you that if I had my choice for society between you and a common yellow three-legged cur pup, one of the inmates of this here cabin would be wagging a tail just at present."

This way we goes on for two or three days, and then we quits speaking to one another. We divides up the cooking implements, and Idaho cooks his grub on one side of the fireplace, and me on the other. The snow is up to the windows, and we have to keep a fire all day.

You see me and Idaho never had any education beyond reading and doing "if John had three apples and James five" on a slate. We never felt any special need for a university degree, though we had acquired a species of intrinsic intelligence in knocking around the world that we could use in emergencies. But snow-bound in that cabin in the Bitter Roots, we felt for the first time that if we had studied Homer or Greek and fractions and the

higher branches of information, we'd have had some resources in
the line of meditation and private thought. I've seen them
Eastern college fellows working in camps all through the West,
and I never noticed but what education was less of a drawback
to 'em than you would think. Why, once over on Snake River,
when Andrew McWilliams' saddle horse got the botts, he sent a
buckboard ten miles for one of these strangers that claimed to be
a botanist. But that horse died.

One morning Idaho was poking around with a stick on top of a
little shelf that was too high to reach. Two books fell down to the
floor. I started toward 'em but caught Idaho's eye. He speaks for
the first time in a week.

"Don't burn your fingers," says he. "In spite of the fact that
you're only fit to be the companion of a sleeping mud-turtle, I'll
give you a square deal. And that's more than your parents did
when they turned you loose in the world with the sociability of a
rattlesnake and the bedside manner of a frozen turnip. I'll play
you a game of seven-up, the winner to pick up his choice of the
book, the loser to take the other."

We played; and Idaho won. He picked up his book; and I took
mine. Then each of us got on his side of the house and went to
reading.

I never was as glad to see a ten-ounce nugget as I was that
book. And Idaho looked at his like a kid looks at a stick of candy.

Mine was a little book about five by six inches called "Herkimer's Handbook of Indispensable Information." I may be wrong,
but I think that was the greatest book that ever was written.
I've got it to-day; and I can stump you or any man fifty times in
five minutes with the information in it. Talk about Solomon or
the New York *Tribune!* Herkimer had cases on both of 'em. That
man must have put in fifty years and travelled a million miles to
find out all that stuff. There was the population of all cities in it,
and the way to tell a girl's age, and the number of teeth a camel
has. It told you the longest tunnel in the world, the number of the
stars, how long it takes for chicken pox to break out, what a lady's

neck ought to measure, the veto powers of Governors, the dates of the Roman aqueducts, how many pounds of rice going without three beers a day would buy, the average annual temperature of Augusta, Maine, the quantity of seed required to plant an acre of carrots in drills, antidotes for poisons, the number of hairs on a blond lady's head, how to preserve eggs, the height of all the mountains in the world, and the dates of all wars and battles, and how to restore drowned persons, and sunstroke, and the number of tacks in a pound, and how to make dynamite and flowers and beds, and what to do before the doctor comes—and a hundred times as many things besides. If there was anything Herkimer didn't know I didn't miss it out of the book.

I sat and read that book for four hours. All the wonders of education was compressed in it. I forgot the snow, and I forgot that me and old Idaho was on the outs. He was sitting still on a stool reading away with a kind of partly soft and partly mysterious look shining through his tanbark whiskers.

"Idaho," says I, "what kind of a book is yours?"

Idaho must have forgot, too, for he answered moderate, without any slander or malignity.

"Why," says he, "this here seems to be a volume by Homer K. M."

"Homer K. M. what?" I asked.

"Why, just Homer K. M.," says he.

"You're a liar," says I, a little riled that Idaho should try to put me up a tree. "No man is going 'round signing books with his initials. If it's Homer K. M. Spoopendyke, or Homer K. M. McSweeney, or Homer K. M. Jones, why don't you say so like a man instead of biting off the end of it like a calf chewing off the tail of a shirt on a clothesline?"

"I put it to you straight, Sandy," says Idaho, quiet. "It's a poem book," says he, "by Homer K. M. I couldn't get colour out of it at first, but there's a vein if you follow it up. I wouldn't have missed this book for a pair of red blankets."

"You're welcome to it," says I. "What I want is a disinterested statement of facts for the mind to work on, and that's what I seem to find in the book I've drawn."

"What you've got," says Idaho, "is statistics, the lowest grade of information that exists. They'll poison your mind. Give me old K. M.'s system of surmises. He seems to be a kind of a wine agent. His regular toast is 'nothing doing,' and he seems to have a grouch, but he keeps it so well lubricated with booze that his worst kicks sound like an invitation to split a quart. But it's poetry," says Idaho, "and I have sensations of scorn for that truck of yours that tries to convey sense in feet and inches. When it comes to explaining the instinct of philosophy through the art of nature, old K. M. has got your man beat by drills, rows, paragraphs, chest measurement, and average annual rainfall."

So that's the way me and Idaho had it. Day and night all the excitement we got was studying our books. That snowstorm sure fixed us with a fine lot of attainments apiece. By the time the snow melted, if you had stepped up to me suddenly and said: "Sanderson Pratt, what would it cost per square foot to lay a roof with twenty by twenty-eight tin at nine dollars and fifty cents per box?" I'd have told you as quick as light could travel the length of a spade handle at the rate of one hundred and ninety-two thousand miles per second. How many can do it? You wake up 'most any man you know in the middle of the night, and ask him quick to tell you the number of bones in the human skeleton exclusive of the teeth, or what percentage of the vote of the Nebraska Legislature overrules a veto. Will he tell you? Try him and see.

About what benefit Idaho got out of his poetry book I didn't exactly know. Idaho boosted the wine-agent every time he opened his mouth; but I wasn't so sure.

This Homer K. M., from what leaked out of his libretto through Idaho, seemed to me to be a kind of a dog who looked at life like it was a tin can tied to his tail. After running himself half to death, he sits down, hangs his tongue out, and looks at the can and says:

"Oh, well, since we can't shake the growler, let's get it filled at the corner, and all have a drink on me."

Besides that, it seems he was a Persian; and I never hear of Persia producing anything worth mentioning unless it was Turkish rugs and Maltese cats.

That spring me and Idaho struck pay ore. It was a habit of ours to sell out quick and keep moving. We unloaded on our grub-staker for eight thousand dollars apiece; and then we drifted down to this little town of Rosa, on the Salmon River, to rest up, and get some human grub, and have our whiskers harvested.

Rosa was no mining-camp. It laid in the valley, and was as free of uproar and pestilence as one of them rural towns in the country. There was a three-mile trolley line champing its bit in the environs; and me and Idaho spent a week riding on one of the cars, dropping off of nights at the Sunset View Hotel. Being now well read as well as travelled, we was soon *pro re nata* with the best society in Rosa, and was invited out to the most dressed-up and high-toned entertainments. It was at a piano recital and quail-eating contest in the city hall, for the benefit of the fire company, that me and Idaho first met Mrs. D. Ormond Sampson, the queen of Rosa society.

Mrs. Sampson was a widow, and owned the only two-story house in town. It was painted yellow, and whichever way you looked from you could see it as plain as egg on the chin of an O'Grady on a Friday. Twenty-two men in Rosa besides me and Idaho was trying to stake a claim on that yellow house.

There was a dance after the song books and quail bones had been raked out of the Hall. Twenty-three of the bunch galloped over to Mrs. Sampson and asked for a dance. I side-stepped the two-step, and asked permission to escort her home. That's where I made a hit.

On the way home says she:

"Ain't the stars lovely and bright to-night, Mr. Pratt?"

"For the chance they've got," says I, "they're humping themselves in a mighty creditable way. That big one you see is sixty-six billions of miles distant. It took thirty-six years for light to reach us. With an eighteen-foot telescope you can see forty-three millions of 'em, including them of the thirteenth magnitude, which, if one was to go out now, you would keep on seeing it for twenty-seven hundred years."

"My!" says Mrs. Sampson. "I never knew that before. How warm it is! I'm as damp as I can be from dancing so much."

"That's easy to account for," says I, "when you happen to know that you've got two million sweat-glands working all at once. If every one of your perspiratory ducts, which are a quarter of an inch long, was placed end to end, they would reach a distance of seven miles."

"Lawsy!" says Mrs. Sampson. "It sounds like an irrigation ditch you was describing, Mr. Pratt. How do you get all this knowledge of information?"

"From observation, Mrs. Sampson," I tells her. "I keep my eyes open when I go about the world."

"Mr. Pratt," says she, "I always did admire a man of education. There are so few scholars among the sap-headed plug-uglies of this town that it is a real pleasure to converse with a gentleman of culture. I'd be gratified to have you call at my house whenever you feel so inclined."

And that was the way I got the goodwill of the lady in the yellow house. Every Tuesday and Friday evenings I used to go there and tell her about the wonders of the universe as discovered, tabulated, and compiled from nature by Herkimer. Idaho and the other gay Lutherans of the town got every minute of the rest of the week that they could.

I never imagined that Idaho was trying to work on Mrs. Sampson with old K. M.'s rules of courtship till one afternoon when I was on my way over to take her a basket of wild hog-plums. I met the lady coming down the lane that led to her house. Her eyes were snapping, and her hat made a dangerous dip over one eye.

"Mr. Pratt," she opens up, "this Mr. Green is a friend of yours, I believe."

"For nine years," says I.

"Cut him out," says she. "He's no gentleman!"

"Why, ma'am," says I, "he's a plain incumbent of the mountain, with asperities and the usual failings of a spendthrift and a liar, but I never on the most momentous occasion had the heart to deny that he was a gentleman. It may be that in haberdashery and the sense of arrogance and display Idaho offends the eye, but inside, ma'am, I've found him impervious to the lower grades of crime and obesity. After nine years of Idaho's society, Mrs. Sampson," I winds up, "I should hate to impute him, and I should hate to see him imputed."

"It's right plausible of you, Mr. Pratt," says Mrs. Sampson, "to take up the curmudgeons in your friend's behalf; but it don't alter the fact that he has made proposals to me sufficiently obnoxious to ruffle the the ignominy of any lady."

"Why, now, now, now!" says I. "Old Idaho do that! I could believe it of myself sooner. I never knew but one thing to deride in him; and a blizzard was responsible for that. Once while we was snowbound in the mountains he became a prey to a kind of spurious and uneven poetry, which may have corrupted his demeanor."

"It has," says Mrs. Sampson. "Ever since I knew him he has been reciting to me a lot of irreligious rhymes by some person he calls Ruby Ott, and who is no better than she should be, if you judge by her poetry."

"Then Idaho has struck a new book," says I, "for one he had was by a man who writes under the *nom de plume* of K. M."

"He'd better have stuck to it," says Mrs. Sampson, "whatever it was. And to-day he caps the vortex. I get a bunch of flowers from him, and on 'em is pinned a note. Now, Mr. Pratt, you know a lady when you see her; and you know how I stand in Rosa society. Do you think for a moment that I'd skip out to the woods with a man along with a jug of wine and a loaf of bread, and go singing and cavorting up and down under the trees with him? I take a little claret with my meals, but I'm not in the habit of packing a jug of it into the brush and raising Cain in any such style as that. And of course he'd bring his book of verses along, too. He said so. Let him go on his scandalous picnics alone! Or let him take his Ruby Ott with him. I reckon she wouldn't kick unless it was on account of there being too much bread along. And what do you think of your gentleman friend now, Mr. Pratt?"

"Well, 'm," says I, "it may be that Idaho's invitation was a kind of poetry, and meant no harm. Maybe it belonged to the class of rhymes they call figurative. They offend law and order, but they get sent through the mails on the grounds that they mean something that they don't say. I'd be glad on Idaho's account if you'd overlook it," says I, "and let us extricate our minds from the low regions of poetry to the higher planes of fact and fancy. On a beautiful afternoon like this, Mrs. Sampson," I goes on, "we should let our thoughts dwell accordingly. Though it is warm here, we should remember that at the equator the line of perpetual frost is at an altitude of fifteen thousand feet. Between the latitudes of forty degrees and forty-nine degrees it is from four thousand to nine thousand feet."

"Oh, Mr. Pratt," says Mrs. Sampson, "it's such a comfort to hear you say them beautiful facts after getting such a jar from that minx of a Ruby's poetry!"

"Let us sit on this log at the roadside," says I, "and forget the inhumanity and ribaldry of the poets. It is in the glorious columns of ascertained facts and legalized measures that beauty is to be found. In this very log we sit upon, Mrs. Sampson," says I, "is statistics more wonderful than any poem. The rings show it was sixty years old. At the depth of two thousand feet it would become coal in three thousand years. The deepest coal mine in the world is at Killingworth, near Newcastle. A box four feet long, three feet wide, and two feet eight inches deep will hold one ton of coal. If an artery is cut, compress it above the wound. A man's leg contains thirty bones. The Tower of London was burned in 1841."

"Go on, Mr. Pratt," says Mrs. Sampson. "Them ideas is so

original and soothing. I think statistics are just as lovely as they can be."

But it wasn't till two weeks later that I got all that was coming to me out of Herkimer.

One night I was waked up by folks hollering "Fire!" all around. I jumped up and dressed and went out of the hotel to enjoy the scene. When I seen it was Mrs. Sampson's house, I gave forth a kind of yell, and I was there in two minutes.

The whole lower story of the yellow house was in flames, and every masculine, feminine, and canine in Rosa was there, screeching and barking and getting in the way of the firemen. I saw Idaho trying to get away from six firemen who were holding him. They was telling him the whole place was on fire downstairs, and no man could go in it and come out alive.

"Where's Mrs. Sampson?" I asks.

"She hasn't been seen," says one of the firemen. "She sleeps upstairs. We've tried to get in, but we can't, and our company hasn't got any ladders yet."

I runs around to the light of the big blaze, and pulls the Handbook out of my inside pocket. I kind of laughed when I felt it in my hands—I reckon I was some daffy with the sensation of excitement.

"Herky, old boy," I says to it, as I flipped over the pages, "you ain't ever lied to me yet, and you ain't ever throwed me down at a scratch yet. Tell me what, old boy, tell me what!" says I.

I turned to "What to do in Case of Accidents," on page 17. I run my finger down the page, and struck it. Good old Herkimer, he never overlooked anything! It said:

SUFFOCATION FROM INHALING SMOKE OR GAS. —There is nothing better than flaxseed. Place a few seed in the corner of the eye.

I shoved the Handbook back in my pocket, and grabbed a boy that was running by.

"Here," says I, giving him some money, "run to the drug store and bring a dollar's worth of flaxseed. Hurry, and you'll get another one for yourself. Now," I sings out to the crowd, "we'll have Mrs. Sampson!" And I throws away my coat and hat.

Four of the firemen and citizens grabs hold of me. It's sure death, they say, to go in the house, for the floors was beginning to fall through.

"How in blazes," I sings out, kind of laughing yet, but not feeling like it, "do you expect me to put flaxseed in a eye without the eye?"

I jabbed each elbow in a fireman's face, kicked the bark off of one citizen's shin, and tripped the other one with a side hold. And then I busted into the house. If I die first I'll write you a letter and tell you if it's any worse down there than the inside of that yellow house was; but don't believe it yet. I was a heap more cooked than the hurry-up orders of broiled chicken that you get in restaurants. The fire and smoke had me down on the floor twice, and was about to shame Herkimer, but the firemen helped me with their little stream of water, and I got to Mrs. Sampson's room. She'd lost conscientiousness from the smoke, so I wrapped her in the bed clothes and got her on my shoulder. Well, the floors wasn't as bad as they said, or I never could have done it— not by no means.

I carried her out fifty yards from the house and laid her on the grass. Then, of course, every one of them other twenty-two plaintiffs to the lady's hand crowded around with tin dippers of water ready to save her. And up runs the boy with the flaxseed.

I unwrapped the covers from Mrs. Sampson's head. She opened her eyes and says:

"Is that you, Mr. Pratt?"

"S-s-sh," says I. "Don't talk till you've had the remedy."

I runs my arm around her neck and raises her head, gentle, and breaks the bag of flaxseed with the other hand; and as easy as I could I bends over and slips three or four of the seeds in the outer corner of her eye.

Up gallops the village doc by this time, and snorts around, and grabs at Mrs. Sampson's pulse, and wants to know what I mean by any such sandblasted nonsense.

"Well, old Jalap and Jerusalem oak seed," says I, "I'm no regular practitioner, but I'll show you my authority, anyway."

They fetched my coat, and I gets out the Handbook.

"Look on page 117," says I, "at the remedy for suffocation by smoke or gas. Flaxseed in the outer corner of the eye, it says. I don't know whether it works as a smoke consumer or whether it hikes the compound gastro-hippopotamus nerve into action, but Herkimer says it, and he was called to the case first. If you want to make it a consultation, there's no objection."

Old doc takes the book and looks at it by means of his specs and a fireman's lantern.

"Well, Mr. Pratt," says he, "you evidently got on the wrong line in reading your diagnosis. The recipe for suffocation says: 'Get the patient into fresh air as quickly as possible, and place in a re-clining position.' The flaxseed remedy is for 'Dust and Cinders in the Eye,' on the line above. But, after all——"

"See here," interrupts Mrs. Sampson, "I reckon I've got some-thing to say in this consultation. That flaxseed done me more good than anything I ever tried." And then she raises up her head and lays it back on my arm again, and says: "Put some in the other eye, Sandy dear."

And so if you was to stop off at Rosa to-morrow, or any other day, you'd see a fine new yellow house with Mrs. Pratt, that was Mrs. Sampson, embellishing and adorning it. And if you was to step inside you'd see on the marble-top centre table in the parlor, "Herkimer's Handbook of Indispensable Information," all re-bound in red morocco, and ready to be consulted on any subject pertaining to human happiness and wisdom.

Hygeia at the Solito

IF YOU ARE knowing in the chronicles of the ring you will recall to mind an event in the early 'nineties when, for a minute and sundry odd seconds, a champion and a "would-be" faced each other on the alien side of an international river. So brief a conflict had rarely imposed upon the fair promise of true sport. The reporters made what they could of it, but, divested of padding, the action was sadly fugacious. The champion merely smote his victim, turned his back upon him, remarking, "I know what I done to dat stiff," and extended an arm like a ship's mast for his glove to be removed.

Which accounts for a trainload of extremely disgusted gentlemen in uproar of fancy vests and neckwear being spilled from their Pullman in San Antonio in the early morning following the fight. Which also partly accounts for the unhappy predicament in which "Cricket" McGuire found himself as he tumbled from his car and sat upon the depot platform, torn by a spasm of that hollow, racking cough so familiar to San Antonian ears. At that time, in the uncertain light of dawn, that way passed Curtis Raidler, the Nueces County cattleman—may his shadow never measure under six feet two.

The cattleman, out this early to catch the south-bound for his ranch station, stopped at the side of the distressed patron of sport and spoke in the kindly drawl of his ilk and region, "Got it pretty bad, bud?"

"Cricket" McGuire, exfeather-weight prize-fighter, tout, jockey, follower of the "ponies," all-around sport, and manipulator of the gum balls and walnut shells, looked up pugnaciously at the imputation cast by "bud."

"G'wan," he rasped, "telegraph pole. I didn't ring for yer."

Another paroxysm wrung him, and he leaned limply against a convenient baggage truck. Raidler waited patiently, glancing around at the white hats, short overcoats, and big cigars thronging the platform. "You're from the No'th, ain't you, bud?" he asked when the other was partially recovered. "Come down to see the fight?"

"Fight!" snapped McGuire. "Puss-in-the-corner! 'Twas a hypodermic injection. Handed him just one like a squirt of dope, and he's asleep, and no tanbark needed in front of his residence. Fight!" He rattled a bit, coughed, and went on, hardly addressing the cattleman, but rather for the relief of voicing his troubles. "No more dead sure t'ings for me. But Rus Sage himself would have snatched at it. Five to one dat de boy from Cork wouldn't stay t'ree rounds is what I invested in. Put my last cent on, and could already smell the sawdust in dat all-night joint of Jimmy Delaney's on T'irty-seventh Street I was goin' to buy. And den —say, telegraph pole, what a gazaboo a guy is to put his whole roll on one turn of the gaboozlum!"

"You're plenty right," said the big cattleman; "more 'specially when you lose. Son, you get up and light out for a hotel. You got a mighty bad cough. Had it long?"

"Lungs," said McGuire comprehensively. "I got it. The croaker says I'll come to time for six months longer—maybe a year if I hold my gait. I wanted to settle down and take care of myself. Dat's why I speculated on dat five to one perhaps. I had a t'ousand iron dollars saved up. If I winned I was goin' to buy Delaney's café. Who'd a t'ought dat stiff would take a nap in de foist round —say?"

"It's a hard deal," commented Raidler, looking down at the diminutive form of McGuire crumpled against the truck. "But you go to a hotel and rest. There's the Menger and the Maverick, and—"

"And the Fi'th Av'noo, and the Waldorf-Astoria," mimicked McGuire. "Told you I went broke. I'm on de bum proper. I've got one dime left. Maybe a trip to Europe or a sail in me private yacht would fix me up—pa'per!"

He flung his dime at a newsboy, got his *Express*, propped his back against the truck, and was at once rapt in the account of his Waterloo, as expanded by the ingenious press.

Curtis Raidler interrogated an enormous gold watch, and laid his hand on McGuire's shoulder.

"Come on, bud," he said. "We got three minutes to catch the train."

Sarcasm seemed to be McGuire's vein.

"You ain't seen me cash in any chips or call a turn since I told you I was broke, a minute ago, have you? Friend, chase yourself away."

"You're going down to my ranch," said the cattleman, "and stay till you get well. Six months'll fix you good as new." He lifted McGuire with one hand, and half-dragged him in the direction of the train.

"What about the money?" said McGuire, struggling weakly to escape.

"Money for what?" asked Raidler, puzzled. They eyed each other, not understanding, for they touched only as at the gear of bevelled cog-wheels—at right angles, and moving upon different axes.

Passengers on the south-bound saw them seated together, and wondered at the conflux of two such antipodes. McGuire was five feet one, with a countenance belonging to either Yokohama or Dublin. Bright-beady of eye, bony of cheek and jaw, scarred, toughened, broken and reknit, indestructible, grisly, gladiatorial as a hornet, he was a type neither new nor unfamiliar. Raidler was the product of a different soil. Six feet two in height, miles broad, and no deeper than a crystal brook, he represented the

union of the West and South. Few accurate pictures of his kind
have been made, for art galleries are so small and the mutoscope
is as yet unknown in Texas. After all, the only possible medium
of portrayal of Raidler's kind would be the fresco—something
high and simple and cool and unframed.

They were rolling southward on the International. The timber
was huddling into little, dense green motts at rare distances before
the inundation of the downright, vert prairies. This was the land
of the ranches; the domain of the kings of the kine.

McGuire sat, collapsed into his corner of the seat, receiving
with acid suspicion the conversation of the cattleman. What was
the "game" of this big "geezer" who was carrying him off? Altruism
would have been McGuire's last guess. "He ain't no farmer,"
thought the captive, "and he ain't no con man, for sure. W'at's his
lay? You trail in, Cricket, and see how many cards he draws.
You're up against it, anyhow. You get a nickel and gallopin' consumption, and you better lay low. Lay low and see w'at's his
game."

At Rincon, a hundred miles from San Antonio, they left the
train for a buckboard which was waiting there for Raidler. In
this they travelled the thirty miles between the station and their
destination. If anything could, this drive should have stirred the
acrimonious McGuire to a sense of his ransom. They sped upon
velvet wheels across an exhilarant savanna. The pair of Spanish
ponies struck a nimble, tireless trot, which gait they occasionally
relieved by a wild, untrammelled gallop. The air was wine and
seltzer, perfumed, as they absorbed it, with the delicate redolence
of prairie flowers. The road perished, and the buckboard swam
the uncharted billows of the grass itself, steered by the practised
hand of Raidler, to whom each tiny distant mott of trees was a
signboard, each convolution of the low hills a voucher of course
and distance. But McGuire reclined upon his spine, seeing nothing but a desert, and receiving the cattleman's advances with sullen distrust. "W'at's he up to?" was the burden of his thoughts;
"w'at kind of a gold brick has the big guy got to sell?" McGuire

was only applying the measure of the streets he had walked to a range bounded by the horizon and the fourth dimension.

A week before, while riding the prairies, Raidler had come upon a sick and weakling calf deserted and bawling. Without dismounting he had reached and slung the distressed bossy across his saddle, and dropped it at the ranch for the boys to attend to. It was impossible for McGuire to know or comprehend that, in the eyes of the cattleman, his case and that of the calf were identical in interest and demand upon his assistance. A creature was ill and helpless; he had the power to render aid—these were the only postulates required for the cattleman to act. They formed his system of logic and the most of his creed. McGuire was the seventh invalid whom Raidler had picked up thus casually in San Antonio, where so many thousand go for the ozone that is said to linger about its contracted streets. Five of them had been guests of Solito Ranch until they had been able to leave, cured or better, and exhausting the vocabulary of tearful gratitude. One came too late, but rested very comfortably, at last, under a ratama tree in the garden.

So, then, it was no surprise to the ranchhold when the buckboard spun to the door, and Raidler took up his debile *protégé* like a handful of rags and set him down upon the gallery.

McGuire looked upon things strange to him. The ranch-house was the best in the country. It was built of brick hauled one hundred miles by wagon, but it was of but one story, and its four rooms were completely encircled by a mud floor "gallery." The miscellaneous setting of horses, dogs, saddles, wagons, guns, and cow-punchers' paraphernalia oppressed the metropolitan eye of the wrecked sportsman.

"Well, here we are at home," said Raidler, cheeringly.

"It's a h—l of a looking place," said McGuire promptly, as he rolled upon the gallery floor, in a fit of coughing.

"We'll try to make it comfortable for you, buddy," said the cattleman, gently. "It ain't fine inside; but it's the outdoors, anyway, that'll do you the most good. This'll be your room, in here. Anything we got, you ask for it."

He led McGuire into the east room. The floor was bare and clean. White curtains waved in the gulf breeze through the open windows. A big willow rocker, two straight chairs, a long table covered with newspapers, pipes, tobacco, spurs, and cartridges stood in the centre. Some well-mounted heads of deer and one of an enormous black javeli projected from the walls. A wide, cool cot-bed stood in a corner. Nueces County people regarded this guest chamber as fit for a prince. McGuire showed his eye teeth at it. He took out his nickel and spun it up to the ceiling.

"T'ought I was lyin' about the money, did ye? Well, you can frisk me if you wanter. Dat's the last simoleon in the treasury. Who's goin' to pay?"

The cattleman's clear gray eyes looked steadily from under his grizzly brows into the huckleberry optics of his guest. After a little he said simply, and not ungraciously, "I'll be much obliged to you, son, if you won't mention money any more. Once was quite a plenty. Folks I ask to my ranch don't have to pay anything, and they very scarcely ever offers it. Supper'll be ready in half an hour. There's water in the pitcher, and some, cooler, to drink in that red jar hanging on the gallery."

"Where's the bell?" asked McGuire, looking about.

"Bell for what?"

"Bell to ring for things. I can't—see here," he exploded in a sudden weak fury, "I never asked you to bring me here. I never held you up for a cent. I never gave you a hard-luck story till you asked me. Here I am fifty mile from a bellboy or a cocktail. I'm sick. I can't hustle. Gee! but I'm up against it!" McGuire fell upon the cot and sobbed shiveringly.

Raidler went to the door and called. A slender, bright-complexioned Mexican youth about twenty came quickly. Raidler spoke to him in Spanish.

"Ylario, it is in my mind that I promised you the position of *vaquero* on the San Carlos range at the fall *rodeo*."

"*Sí señor*, such was your goodness."

"Listen. This *señorito* is my friend. He is very sick. Place your-self at his side. Attend to his wants at all times. Have much pa-tience and care with him. And when he is well, or—and when he is well, instead of *vaquero* I will make you *mayordomo* of the Rancho de las Piedras. *Está bueno?*"

"*Sí, sí—mil gracias, señor*." Ylario tried to kneel upon the floor in his gratitude, but the cattleman kicked at him benevolently, growling, "None of your opery-house antics, now."

Ten minutes later Ylario came from McGuire's room and stood before Raidler.

"The little *señor*," he announced, "presents his compliments" (Raidler credited Ylario with the preliminary) "and desires some pounded ice, one hot bath, one gin feez-z, that the windows be all closed, toast, one shave, one Newyorkheral', cigarettes, and to send one telegram."

Raidler took a quart bottle of whisky from his medicine cabinet. "Here, take him this," he said.

Thus was instituted the reign of terror at the Solito Ranch. For a few weeks McGuire blustered and boasted and swaggered before the cow-punchers who rode in for miles around to see this latest importation of Raidler's. He was an absolutely new experi-ence to them. He explained to them all the intricate points of sparring and the tricks of training and defence. He opened to their minds' view all the indecorous life of a tagger after profes-sional sports. His jargon of slang was a continuous joy and sur-prise to them. His gestures, his strange poses, his frank ribaldry of tongue and principle fascinated them. He was like a being from a new world.

Strange to say, this new world he had entered did not exist to him. He was an utter egoist of bricks and mortar. He had dropped out, he felt, into open space for a time, and all it contained was an audience for his reminiscences. Neither the limitless freedom of the prairie days nor the grand hush of the close-drawn, spangled nights touched him. All the hues of Aurora could not win him from the pink pages of a sporting journal. "Get something for nothing," was his mission in life; "T'irty-seventh" Street was his goal.

Nearly two months after his arrival he began to complain that he felt worse. It was then that he became the ranch's incubus, its harpy, its Old Man of the Sea. He shut himself in his room like some venomous kobold or flibbertigibbet, whining, complaining, cursing, accusing. The keynote of his plaint was that he had been inveigled into a gehenna against his will; that he was dying of neglect and lack of comforts. With all his dire protestations of increasing illness, to the eye of others he remained unchanged. His currant-like eyes were as bright and diabolic as ever; his voice was as rasping; his callous face, with the skin drawn tense as a drum-head, had no flesh to lose. A flush on his prominent cheek bones each afternoon hinted that a clinical thermometer might have revealed a symptom, and percussion might have established the fact that McGuire was breathing with only one lung, but his appearance remained the same.

In constant attendance upon him was Ylario, whom the coming reward of the *mayordomoship* must have greatly stimulated, for McGuire chained him to a bitter existence. The air—the man's only chance for life—he commanded to be kept out by closed windows and drawn curtains. The room was always blue and foul with cigarette smoke; whosoever entered it must sit, suffocating, and listen to the imp's interminable gasconade concerning his scandalous career.

The oddest thing of all was the relation existing between McGuire and his benefactor. The attitude of the invalid toward the cattleman was something like that of a peevish, perverse child toward an indulgent parent. When Raidler would leave the ranch McGuire would fall into a fit of malevolent, silent sullenness. When he returned, he would be met by a string of violent and stinging reproaches. Raidler's attitude toward his charge was quite inexplicable in its way. The cattleman seemed actually to assume and feel the character assigned him by McGuire's intemperate accusations—the character of tyrant and guilty oppressor. He seemed to have adopted the responsibility of the fellow's condition, and he always met his tirades with a pacific, patient, and even remorseful kindness that never altered.

One day Raidler said to him, "Try more air, son. You can have the buckboard and a driver every day if you'll go. Try a week or two in one of the cow camps. I'll fix you up plum comfortable. The ground, and the air next to it—them's the things to cure you. I knowed a man from Philadelphy, sicker than you are, got lost on the Guadalupe, and slept on the bare grass in sheep camps for two weeks. Well, sir, it started him getting well, which he done. Close to the ground—that's where the medicine in the air stays. Try a little hossback riding now. There's a gentle pony——"

"What've I done to yer?" screamed McGuire. "Did I ever double-cross yer? Did I ask you to bring me here? Drive me out to your camps if you wanter; or stick a knife in me and save trouble. Ride! I can't lift my feet. I couldn't sidestep a jar from a five-year-old kid. That's what you d--d ranch has done for me. There's nothing to eat, nothing to see, and nobody to talk to but a lot of Reubens who don't know a punching bag from a lobster salad."

"It's a lonesome place, for certain," apologized Raidler abashedly. "We got plenty, but it's rough enough. Anything you think of you want, the boys'll ride up and fetch it down for you."

It was Chad Murchison, a cow-puncher from the Circle Bar outfit, who first suggested that McGuire's illness was fraudulent. Chad had brought a basket of grapes for him thirty miles, and four out of his way, tied to his saddle-horn. After remaining in the smoke-tainted room for a while, he emerged and bluntly confided his suspicions to Raidler.

"His arm," said Chad, "is harder'n a diamond. He interduced me to what he called a shore-perplexus punch, and 'twas like being kicked twice by a mustang. He's playin' it low down on you, Curt. He ain't no sicker'n I am. I hate to say it, but the runt's workin' you for range and shelter."

The cattleman's ingenuous mind refused to entertain Chad's

view of the case, and when, later, he came to apply the test, doubt entered not into his motives.

One day, about noon, two men drove up to the ranch, alighted, hitched, and came in to dinner; standing and general invitations being the custom of the country. One of them was a great San Antonio doctor, whose costly services had been engaged by a wealthy cowman who had been laid low by an accidental bullet. He was now being driven to the station to take the train back to town. After dinner Raidler took him aside, pushed a twenty-dollar bill against his hand, and said:

"Doc, there's a young chap in that room I guess has got a bad case of consumption. I'd like for you to look him over and see just how bad he is, and if we can do anything for him."

"How much was that dinner I just ate, Mr. Raidler?" said the doctor bluffly, looking over his spectacles. Raidler returned the money to his pocket. The doctor immediately entered McGuire's room, and the cattleman seated himself upon a heap of saddles on the gallery, ready to reproach himself in the event the verdict should be unfavorable.

In ten minutes the doctor came briskly out. "Your man," he said promptly, "is as sound as a new dollar. His lungs are better than mine. Respiration, temperature, and pulse normal. Chest expansion four inches. Not a sign of weakness anywhere. Of course I didn't examine for the bacillus, but it isn't there. You can put my name to the diagnosis. Even cigarettes and a vilely close room haven't hurt him. Coughs, does he? Well, you tell him it isn't necessary. You asked if there is anything we could do for him. Well, I advise you to set him digging post-holes or breaking mustangs. There's our team ready. Good-day, sir." And like a puff of wholesome, blustery wind the doctor was off.

Raidler reached out and plucked a leaf from a mesquite bush by the railing, and began chewing it thoughtfully.

The branding season was at hand, and the next morning Ross Hargis, foreman of the outfit, was mustering his force of some twenty-five men at the ranch, ready to start for the San Carlos range, where the work was to begin. By six o'clock the horses were all saddled, the grub wagon ready, and the cow-punchers were swinging themselves upon their mounts, when Raidler bade them wait. A boy was bringing up an extra pony, bridled and saddled, to the gate. Raidler walked to McGuire's room and threw open the door. McGuire was lying on his cot, not yet dressed, smoking.

"Get up," said the cattleman, and his voice was clear and brassy, like a bugle.

"How's that?" asked McGuire, a little startled.

"Get up and dress. I can stand a rattlesnake, but I hate a liar. Do I have to tell you again?" He caught McGuire by the neck and stood him on the floor.

"Say, friend," cried McGuire wildly, "are you bug-house? I'm sick—see? I'll croak if I got to hustle. What've I done to yer?" —he began his chronic whine—"I never asked yer to——"

"Put on your clothes," called Raidler, in a rising tone.

Swearing, stumbling, shivering, keeping his amazed, shiny eyes upon the now menacing form of the aroused cattleman, McGuire managed to tumble into his clothes. Then Raidler took him by the collar and shoved him out and across the yard to the extra pony hitched at the gate. The cow-punchers lolled in their saddles, open-mouthed.

"Take this man," said Raidler to Ross Hargis, "and put him to work. Make him work hard, sleep hard, and eat hard. You boys know I done what I could for him, and he was welcome. Yesterday the best doctor in San Antone examined him, and says he's got the lungs of a burro and the constitution of a steer. You know what to do with him, Ross."

Ross Hargis only smiled grimly.

"Aw," said McGuire, looking intently at Raidler, with a peculiar expression upon his face, "the croaker said I was all right, did he? Said I was fakin', did he? You put him onto me. You t'ought I wasn't sick. You said I was a liar. Say, friend, I talked rough, I know, but I didn't mean most of it. If you felt like I did—aw! I forgot—I ain't sick, the croaker says. Well, friend, now I'll go work for yer. Here's where you play even."

He sprang into the saddle easily as a bird, got the quirt from the horn, and gave his pony a slash with it. "Cricket," who once brought in Good Boy by a neck at Hawthorne—and a 10 to 1 shot—had his foot in the stirrups again.

McGuire led the cavalcade as they dashed away from San Carlos, and the cow-punchers gave a yell of applause as they closed in behind his dust.

But in less than a mile he had lagged to the rear, and was last man when they struck the patch of high chaparral below the horse pens. Behind a clump of this he drew rein, and held a handkerchief to his mouth. He took it away drenched with bright, arterial blood, and threw it carefully into a clump of prickly pear. Then he slashed with his quirt again, gasped "G'wan" to his astonished pony, and galloped after the gang.

That night Raidler received a message from his old home in Alabama. There had been a death in the family; an estate was to divide, and they called for him to come. Daylight found him in the buckboard, skimming the prairies for the station. It was two months before he returned. When he arrived at the ranchhouse he found it well-nigh deserted save for Ylario, who acted as a kind of steward during his absence. Little by little the youth made him acquainted with the work done while he was away. The branding camp, he was informed, was still doing business. On account of many severe storms the cattle had been badly scattered, and the branding had been accomplished but slowly. The camp was now in the valley of the Guadalupe, twenty miles away.

"By the way," said Raidler, suddenly remembering, "that fellow I sent along with them—McGuire—is he working yet?"

"I do not know," said Ylario. "Man's from the camp come verree few times to the ranch. So plentee work with the leetle calves. They no say. Oh, I think that fellow McGuire he dead much time ago."

"Dead!" said Raidler. "What you talking about?"

"Verree sick fellow, McGuire," replied Ylario, with a shrug of his shoulder. "I theenk he no live on, two month when he go away."

"Shucks!" said Raidler. "He humbugged you, too, did he? The doctor examined him and said he was sound as a mesquite knot."

"That doctor," said Ylario, smiling, "he tell you so? That doctor no see McGuire."

"Talk up," ordered Raidler. "What the devil do you mean?"

"McGuire," continued the boy tranquilly, "he getting drink water outside when that doctor come in room. That doctor take me and pound me all over here with his fingers"—putting his hand to his chest—"I not know for what. He put his ear here and here and here, and listen—I not know for what. He put his little glass stick in my mouth. He feel my arm here. He make me count like whisper—so—twenty, *treinta, cuarenta*. Who knows," concluded Ylario, with a deprecating spread of his hands, "for what that doctor do those verree droll and such-like things?"

"What horses are up?" asked Raidler, shortly.

"Paisano is grazing out behind the little corral, *señor*."

"Saddle him for me at once."

Within a very few minutes the cattleman was mounted and away. Paisano, well named after that ungainly but swift-running bird, struck into his long lope that ate up the road like a strip of macaroni. In two hours and a quarter Raidler, from a gentle swell, saw the branding camp by a water hole in the Guadalupe. Sick with expectancy of the news he feared, he rode up, dismounted, and dropped Paisano's reins. So gentle was his heart that at that moment he would have pleaded guilty to the murder of McGuire.

The only being in the camp was the cook, who was just arranging the hunks of barbecued beef, and distributing the tin coffee cups for supper. Raidler evaded a direct questioning concerning the one subject in his mind.

"Everything all right in camp, Pete?" he managed to inquire.

"So, so," said Pete, conservatively. "Grub give out twice.

Wind scattered the cattle, and we've had to rake the brush for forty mile. I need a new coffee-pot. And the mosquitoes is some more hellish than common."

"The boys—all well?"

Pete was no optimist. Besides, inquiries concerning the health of cow-punchers were not only superfluous, but bordered on flaccidity. It was not like the boss to make them.

"What's left of 'em don't miss no calls to grub," the cook conceded.

"What's left of 'em?" repeated Raidler in a husky voice. Mechanically he began to look around for McGuire's grave. He had in his mind a white slab such as he had seen in the Alabama church-yard. But immediately he knew that was foolish.

"Sure," said Pete; "what's left. Cow camps change in two months. Some's gone."

Raidler nerved himself.

"That—chap—I sent along—McGuire—did—he——"

"Say," interrupted Pete, rising with a chunk of corn bread in each hand, "that was a dirty shame, sending that poor, sick kid to a cow camp. A doctor that couldn't tell he was graveyard meat ought to be skinned with a cinch buckle. Game as he was, too— it's a scandal among snakes—lemme tell you what he done. First night in camp the boys started to initiate him in the leather breeches degree. Ross Hargis busted him one swipe with his chaparreras, and what do you reckon the poor child did? Got up, the little skeeter, and licked Ross. Licked Ross Hargis. Licked him good. Hit him plenty and everywhere and hard. Ross'd just get up and pick out a fresh place to lay down on agin.

"Then that McGuire goes off there and lays down with his head in the grass and bleeds. A hem'ridge they calls it. He lays there eighteen hours by the watch, and they can't budge him. Then Ross Hargis, who loves any man who can lick him, goes to work and damns the doctors from Greenland to Poland Chiny; and him and Green Branch Johnson they gets McGuire in a tent, and spells each other feedin' him chopped raw meat and whisky.

"But it looks like the kid ain't got no appetite to git well, for they misses him from the tent in the night and finds him rootin' in the grass, and likewise a drizzle fallin'. 'Gwan,' he says, 'lemme go and die like I wanter. He said I was a liar and a fake and I was playin' sick. Lemme alone.'

"Two weeks," went on the cook, "he laid around, not noticin' nobody, and then——"

A sudden thunder filled the air, and a score of galloping centaurs crashed through the brush into camp.

"Illustrious rattlesnakes!" exclaimed Pete, springing all ways at once: "here's the boys come, and I'm an assassinated man if supper ain't ready in three minutes."

But Raidler saw only one thing. A little brown-faced, grinning chap, springing from his saddle in the full light of the fire. McGuire was not like that, and yet——

In another instant the cattleman was holding him by the hand and shoulder.

"Son, son, how goes it?" was all he found to say.

"Close to the ground, says you," shouted McGuire, crunching Raidler's fingers in a grip of steel; "and dat's where I found it—healt' and strengt', and tumbled to what a cheap skate I been actin'. T'anks fer kickin' me out, old man. And—say! de joke's on dat croaker, ain't it? I looked t'rough the window and see him playin' tag on dat Dago kid's solar plexus."

"You son of a tinker," growled the cattleman, "whyn't you talk up and say the doctor never examined you?"

"Aw—g'wan!" said McGuire, with a flash of his old asperity, "nobody can't bluff me. You never ast me. You made your spiel, and you t'rowed me out, and I let it go at dat. And, say, friend, dis chasin' cows is outer sight. Dis is de whitest bunch of sports I ever travelled with. You'll let me stay, won't yer, old man?"

Raidler looked wonderingly toward Ross Hargis.

"That cussed little runt," remarked Ross tenderly, "is the Jo-dartin'est hustler—and the hardest hitter in anybody's cow camp."

The Hand that Riles the World

"MANY of our great men," said I (apropos of many things), "have declared that they owe their success to the aid and encouragement of some brilliant woman."

"I know," said Jeff Peters. "I've read in history and mythology about Joan of Arc and Mme. Yale and Mrs. Caudle and Eve and other noted females of the past. But, in my opinion, the woman of to-day is of little use in politics or business. What's she best in, anyway?—men make the best cooks, milliners, nurses, housekeepers, stenographers, clerks, hairdressers and launderers. About the only job left that a woman can beat a man in is female impersonator in vaudeville."

"I would have thought," said I, "that occasionally, anyhow, you would have found the wit and intuition of woman valuable to you in your lines of-er-business."

"Now, wouldn't you," said Jeff, with an emphatic nod— "wouldn't you have imagined that? But a woman is an absolutely unreliable partner in any straight swindle. She's liable to turn honest on you when you are depending upon her most. I tried 'em once."

"Bill Humble, an old friend of mine in the Territories, conceived the illusion that he wanted to be appointed United States Marshal. At that time me and Andy was doing a square, legitimate business of selling walking canes. If you unscrewed the head of one and turned it up to your mouth a half pint of good rye whiskey would go trickling down your throat to reward you for your act of intelligence. The deputies was annoying me and Andy some, and when Bill spoke to me about his officious aspirations, I saw how the appointment as Marshal might help along the firm of Peters & Tucker.

" 'Jeff,' says Bill to me, 'you are a man of learning and education, besides having knowledge and information concerning not only rudiments but facts and attainments.'

" 'I do,' says I, 'and I have never regretted it. I am not one,' says I, 'who would cheapen education by making it free. Tell me,' says I, 'which is of the most value to mankind, literature or horse racing?'

" 'Why—er—, playing the po—I mean, of course, the poets and the great writers have got the call, of course,' says Bill.

" 'Exactly,' says I. 'Then why do the master minds of finance philanthropy,' says I, 'charge us $2 to get into a race-track and let us into a library free? Is that distilling into the masses,' says I, 'a correct estimate of the relative value of the two means of self-culture and disorder?'

" 'You are arguing outside of my faculties of sense and rhetoric,' says Bill. 'What I wanted you to do is to go to Washington and dig out this appointment for me. I haven't no ideas of cultivation and intrigue. I'm a plain citizen and I need the job. I've killed seven men,' says Bill; 'I've got nine children; I've been a good Republican ever since the first of May; I can't read nor write, and I see no reason why I ain't illegible for the office. And I think your partner, Mr. Tucker,' goes on Bill, 'is also a man of sufficient ingratiation and connected system of mental delinquency to assist you in securing the appointment. I will give you preliminary,' says Bill, '$1,000 for drinks, bribes and carfare in Washington. If you land the job I will pay you $1,000 more, cash down, and guarantee you impunity in boot-legging whiskey for twelve months. Are you patriotic to the West enough to help me put this thing through the White-washed Wigwam of the Great Father of the most eastern flag station of the Pennsylvania Railroad?' says Bill.

"Well, I talked to Andy about it, and he liked the idea immense. Andy was a man of an involved nature. He was never content to plod along, as I was, selling to the peasantry some little tool like a combination steak beater, shoe horn, marcel waver, monkey wrench, nail file, potato masher and Multum in Parvo tuning fork. Andy had the artistic temper, which is not to be judged as a preacher's or a moral man's is by purely commercial deflections. So we accepted Bill's offer, and strikes out for Washington.

"Says I to Andy, when we get located at a hotel on South Dakota Avenue, G. S. S. W. 'Now Andy, for the first time in our lives we've got to do a real dishonest act. Lobbying is something we've never been used to; but we've got to scandalize ourselves for Bill Humble's sake. In a straight and legitimate business,' says I, 'we could afford to introduce a little foul play and chicanery, but in a disorderly and heinous piece of malpractice like this it seems to me that the straightforward and aboveboard way is the best. I propose,' says I, 'that we hand over $500 of this money to the chairman of the national campaign committee, get a receipt, lay the receipt on the President's desk and tell him about Bill. The President is a man who would appreciate a candidate who went about getting office that way instead of pulling wires.

"Andy agreed with me, but after we talked the scheme over with the hotel clerk we give that plan up. He told us that there was only one way to get an appointment in Washington, and that was through a lady lobbyist. He gave us the address of one he recommended, a Mrs. Avery, who he said was high up in sociable and diplomatic rings and circles.

"The next morning at 10 o'clock me and Andy called at her hotel, and was shown up to her reception room.

"This Mrs. Avery was a solace and a balm to the eyesight. She had hair the color of the back of a twenty-dollar gold certificate, blue eyes and a system of beauty that would make the girl on the cover of a July magazine look like a cook on a Monongahela coal barge.

"She had on a low necked dress covered with silver spangles, and diamond rings and ear bobs. Her arms was bare; and she was using a desk telephone with one hand, and drinking tea with the other.

"'Well, boys,' says she after a bit, 'what is it?'

"I told her in as few words as possible what we wanted for Bill, and the price we could pay.

"'Those western appointments,' says she, 'are easy. Le'me see, now,' says she, 'who could put that through for us. No use fooling with Territorial delegates. I guess,' says she, 'that Senator Sniper would be about the man. He's from somewheres in the West. Let's see how he stands on my private menu card.' She takes some papers out of a pigeonhole with the letter 'S' over it.

"'Yes,' says she, 'he's marked with a star; that means "ready to serve." Now, let's see. "Age 55; married twice; Presbyterian, likes blondes, Tolstoi, poker and stewed terrapin; sentimental at third bottle of wine." Yes,' she goes on, 'I am sure I can have your friend, Mr. Bummer, appointed Minister to Brazil.'

"'Humble,' says I: 'And United States Marshal was the berth.'

"'Oh, yes,' says Mrs. Avery. 'I have so many deals of this sort I sometimes get them confused. Give me all the memoranda you have of the case, Mr. Peters, and come back in four days. I think it can be arranged by then.'

"So me and Andy goes back to our hotel and waits. Andy walks up and down and chews the left end of his mustache.

"'A woman of high intellect and perfect beauty is the rare thing, Jeff,' says he.

"'As rare,' says I, 'as an omelet made from the eggs of the fabulous bird known as the epidermis,' says I.

"'A woman like that,' says Andy, 'ought to lead a man to the highest positions of opulence and fame.'

"'I misdoubt,' says I, 'if any woman ever helped a man to secure a job any more than to have his meals ready promptly and spread a report that the other candidate's wife had once been a shoplifter. They are no more adapted for business and politics,' says I, 'than Algernon Charles Swinburne is to be floor manager at one of Chuck Connor's annual balls. I know,' says I to Andy, 'that sometimes a woman seems to step out into the kalsomine light as the charge d'affaires of her man's political job. But how does it come out? Say, they have a neat little berth somewhere as foreign consul of record to Afghanistan or lockkeeper on the Delaware and Raritan Canal. One day this man finds his wife putting on her overshoes and three months' supply of bird seed into the canary's cage. "Sioux Falls?" he asks with a kind of hopeful look in his eye. "No, Arthur," says she, "Washington. We're wasted here," says she. "You ought to be Toady Extraordinary to the Court of St. Bridget or Head Porter of the Island of Porto Rico. I'm going to see about it."

" 'Then this lady,' I says to Andy, 'moves against the authorities at Washington with her baggage and munitions, consisting of five dozen indiscriminating letters written to her by a member of the Cabinet when she was 15; a letter of introduction from King Leopold to the Smithsonian Institution, and a pink silk costume with canary colored spats.

" 'Well, and then what?' I goes. 'She has the letters printed in the evening papers that match her costume, she lectures at an informal tea given in the palm room of the B. & O. Depot and then calls on the President. The ninth Assistant Secretary of Commerce and Labor, the first aide-de-camp of the Blue Room and an unidentified colored man are waiting there to grasp her by the hands—and feet. They carry her out to S. W. B. street and leave her on a cellar door. That ends it. The next time we hear of her she is writing postal cards to the Chinese Minister asking him to get Arthur a job in a tea store.'

" 'Then,' says Andy, 'you don't think Mrs. Avery will land the Marshalship for Bill?'

"'I do not,' says I. 'I do not wish to be a septic, but I doubt if she can do as well as you and me could have done.'

"'I don't agree with you,' says Andy. 'I'll bet you she does. I'm proud of having a higher opinion of the talent and the powers of negotiation of ladies.'

"We was back at Mrs. Avery's hotel at the time she appointed. She was looking pretty and fine enough, as far as that went, to make any man let her name every officer in the country. But I hadn't much faith in looks, so I was certainly surprised when she pulls out a document with the great seal of the United States on it, and 'William Henry Humble' in a fine, big hand on the back.

"'You might have had it the next day, boys,' says Mrs. Avery, smiling. 'I hadn't the slightest trouble in getting it,' says she. 'I just asked for it, that's all. Now, I'd like to talk to you a while,' she goes on, 'but I'm awfully busy, and I know you'll excuse me. I've got an Ambassadorship, two Consulates and a dozen other minor applications to look after. I can hardly find time to sleep at all. You'll give my compliments to Mr. Humble when you get home, of course.'

"Well, I handed her the $500, which she pitched into her desk drawer without counting. I put Bill's appointment in my pocket and me and Andy made our adieus.

"We started back for the Territory the same day. We wired Bill: 'Job landed; get the tall glasses ready,' and we felt pretty good.

"Andy joshed me all the way about how little I knew about women.

"'All right,' says I. 'I'll admit that she surprised me. But it's the first time I ever knew one of 'em to manipulate a piece of business on time without getting it bungled up in some way,' says I.

"Down about the edge of Arkansas I got out Bill's appointment and looked it over, and then I handed it to Andy to read. Andy read it, but didn't add any remarks to my silence.

"The paper was for Bill, all right, and a genuine document, but it appointed him post-master of Dade City, Fla.

"Me and Andy got off the train at Little Rock and sent Bill's appointment to him by mail. Then we struck northeast toward Lake Superior.

"I never saw Bill Humble after that."

The Exact Science of Matrimony

"As I have told you before," said Jeff Peters, "I never had much confidence in the perfidiousness of woman. As partners or coeducators in the most innocent line of graft they are not trustworthy."

"They deserve the compliment," said I. "I think they are entitled to be called the honest sex."

"Why shouldn't they be?" said Jeff. "They've got the other sex either grafting or working overtime for 'em. They're all right in business until they get their emotions or their hair touched up too much. Then you want to have a flat-footed, heavy-breathing man with sandy whiskers, five kids and a building and loan mortgage ready as an understudy to take her desk. Now there was that widow lady that me and Andy Tucker engaged to help us in that little matrimonial agency scheme we floated out in Cairo.

"When you've got enough advertising capital—say a roll as big as the little end of a wagon tongue—there's money in matrimonial agencies. We had about $6,000 and we expected to double it in two months, which is about as long as a scheme like ours can be carried on without taking out a New Jersey charter.

"We fixed up an advertisement that read about like this:

"Charming widow, beautiful, home loving, 32 years, possessing $3,000 cash and owning valuable country property, would remarry. Would prefer a poor man with affectionate disposition to one with means, as she realizes that the solid virtues are oftenest to be found in the humble walks of life. No objection to elderly man or one of homely appearance if faithful and true and competent to manage property and invest money with judgment. Address, with particulars.

Lonely,

Care of Peters & Tucker, agents, Cairo, Ill.

" 'So far, so pernicious,' says I, when we had finished the literary concoction. 'And now,' says I, 'where is the lady?'

"Andy gives me one of his looks of calm irritation.

" 'Jeff,' says he, 'I thought you had lost them ideas of realism in your art. Why should there be a lady? When they sell a lot of watered stock on Wall Street would you expect to find a mermaid in it? What has a matrimonial ad got to do with a lady?'

" 'Now listen,' says I. 'You know my rule, Andy, that in all my illegitimate inroads against the legal letter of the law the article sold must be existent, visible, producible. In that way and by a careful study of city ordinances and train schedules I have kept out of all trouble with the police that a five-dollar bill and a cigar could not square. Now, to work this scheme we've got to be able to produce bodily a charming widow or its equivalent with or without the beauty, hereditaments and appurtenances set forth in the catalogue and writ of errors, or hereafter be held by a justice of the peace.'

" 'Well,' says Andy, reconstructing his mind, 'maybe it would be safer in case the post office or the peace commission should try to investigate our agency. But where,' he says, 'could you hope to find a widow who would waste time on a matrimonial scheme that had no matrimony in it?'

"I told Andy that I thought I knew of the exact party. An old friend of mine, Zeke Trotter, who used to draw soda water and teeth in a tent show, had made his wife a widow a year before by drinking some dyspepsia cure of the old doctor's instead of the liniment that he always got boozed up on. I used to stop at their house often, and I thought we could get her to work with us.

"'Twas only sixty miles to the little town where she lived, so I jumped out on the I. C. and finds her in the same cottage with the same sunflowers and roosters standing on the washtub. Mrs. Trotter fitted our ad first rate except, maybe, for beauty and age and property valuation. But she looked feasible and praiseworthy to the eye, and it was a kindness to Zeke's memory to give her the job.

"'Is this an honest deal you are putting on, Mr. Peters?' she asks me when I tell her what we want.

"'Mrs. Trotter?' says I, 'Andy Tucker and me have computed the calculation that 3,000 men in this broad and fair country will endeavor to secure your fair hand and ostensible money and property through our advertisement. Out of that number something like thirty hundred will expect to give you in exchange, if they win you, the carcass of a lazy and mercenary loafer, a failure in life, a swindler and contemptible fortune seeker.

"'Me and Andy,' says I, 'propose to teach these preyers upon society a lesson. It was with difficulty,' says I, 'that me and Andy could refrain from forming a corporation under the title of the Great Moral and Millennial Malevolent Matrimonial Agency. Does that satisfy you?'

"'It does, Mr. Peters,' says she. 'I might have known you wouldn't have gone into anything that wasn't opprobrious. But what will my duties be? Do I have to reject personally these 3,000 ramscallions you speak of, or can I throw them out in bunches?'

"'Your job, Mrs. Trotter,' says I, 'will be practically a cynosure. You will live at a quiet hotel and will have no work to do. Andy and I will attend to all the correspondence and business end of it.

"'Of course,' says I, 'some of the more ardent and impetuous suitors who can raise the railroad fare may come to Cairo to personally press their suit or whatever fraction of a suit they may be wearing. In that case you will be probably put to the inconvenience of kicking them out face to face. We will pay you $25 per week and hotel expenses.'

"'Give me five minutes,' says Mrs. Trotter, 'to get my powder rag and leave the front door key with a neighbor and you can let my salary begin.'

"So I conveys Mrs. Trotter to Cairo and establishes her in a family hotel far enough away from mine and Andy's quarters to be unsuspicious and available, and I tell Andy.

" 'Great,' says Andy. 'And now that your conscience is appeased as to the tangibility and proximity of the bait, and leaving mutton aside, suppose we revenoo a noo fish.'

"So, we began to insert our advertisement in newspapers covering the country far and wide. One ad was all we used. We couldn't have used more without hiring so many clerks and marcelled paraphernalia that the sound of the gum chewing would have disturbed the Postmaster-General.

"We placed $2,000 in a bank to Mrs. Trotter's credit and gave her the book to show in case anybody might question the honesty and good faith of the agency. I knew Mrs. Trotter was square and reliable and it was safe to leave it in her name.

"With that one ad Andy and me put in twelve hours a day answering letters.

"About one hundred a day was what came in. I never knew there was so many large hearted but indigent men in the country who were willing to acquire a charming widow and assume the burden of investing her money.

"Most of them admitted that they ran principally to whiskers and lost jobs and were misunderstood by the world, but all of 'em were sure that they were so chock full of affection and manly qualities that the widow would be making the bargain of her life to get 'em.

"Every applicant got a reply from Peters & Tucker informing him that the widow had been deeply impressed by his straightforward and interesting letter and requesting them to write again stating more particulars; and enclosing photograph if convenient. Peters & Tucker also informed the applicant that their fee for handing over the second letter to their fair client would be $2, enclosed therewith.

"There you see the simple beauty of the scheme. About 90 per cent. of them domestic foreign noblemen raised the price somehow and sent it in. That was all there was to it. Except that me and Andy complained an amount about being put to the trouble of slicing open them envelopes, and taking the money out.

"Some few clients called in person. We sent 'em to Mrs. Trotter and she did the rest; except for three or four who came back to strike us for carfare. After the letters began to get in from the r. f. d. districts Andy and me were taking in about $200 a day.

"One afternoon when we were busiest and I was stuffing the two and ones into cigar boxes and Andy was whistling 'No Wedding Bells for Her' a small, slick man drops in and runs his eye over the walls like he was on the trail of a lost Gainsborough painting or two. As soon as I saw him I felt a glow of pride, because we were running our business on the level.

" 'I see you have quite a large mail to-day,' says the man.

"I reached and got my hat.

" 'Come on,' says I. 'We've been expecting you. I'll show you the goods. How was Teddy when you left Washington?'

"I took him down to the Riverview Hotel and had him shake hands with Mrs. Trotter. Then I showed him her bank book with the $2,000 to her credit.

" 'It seems to be all right,' says the Secret Service.

" 'It is,' says I. 'And if you're not a married man I'll leave you to talk a while with the lady. We won't mention the two dollars.'

" 'Thanks,' says he. 'If I wasn't, I might. Good day, Mr. Peters.'

"Toward the end of three months we had taken in something over $5,000, and we saw it was time to quit. We had a good many complaints made to us; and Mrs. Trotter seemed to be tired of the job. A good many suitors had been calling to see her, and she didn't seem to like that.

"So we decides to pull out, and I goes down to Mrs. Trotter's hotel to pay her last week's salary and say farewell and get her check for $2,000.

"When I get there I found her crying like a kid that don't want to go to school.

" 'Now, now,' says I, 'what's it all about? Somebody sassed you or you getting homesick?' "

" 'No, Mr. Peters,' says she. 'I'll tell you. You was always a friend of Zeke's, and I don't mind. Mr. Peters, I'm in love. I just love a man so hard I can't bear not to get him. He's just the ideal I've always had in mind.'

" 'Then take him,' says I. 'That is, if it's a mutual case. Does he return the sentiment according to the specifications and painfulness you have described?'

" 'He does,' says she. 'But he's one of the gentlemen that's been coming to see me about the advertisement and he won't marry me unless I give him the $2,000. His name is William Wilkinson.' And then she goes off again in the agitations and hysterics of romance.

" 'Mrs. Trotter,' says I, 'there's no man more sympathizing with a woman's affections than I am. Besides, you was once a life partner of one of my best friends. If it was left to me I'd say take this $2,000 and the man of your choice and be happy.

" 'We could afford to do that, because we have cleaned up over $5,000 from these suckers that wanted to marry you. But,' says I, 'Andy Tucker is to be consulted.

'He is a good man, but keen in business. He is my equal partner financially. I will talk to Andy,' says I, 'and see what can be done.'

"I goes back to our hotel and lays the case before Andy.

" 'I was expecting something like this all the time,' says Andy. 'You can't trust a woman to stick by you in any scheme that involves her emotions and preferences.'

" 'It's a sad thing, Andy,' says I, 'to think that we've been the cause of the breaking of a woman's heart.'

" 'It is,' says Andy, 'and I tell you what I'm willing to do, Jeff. You've always been a man of a soft and generous disposition. Perhaps I've been too hard and worldly and suspicious. For once

I'll meet you half way. Go to Mrs. Trotter and tell her to draw the $2,000 from the bank and give it to this man she's infatuated with and be happy.'

"I jumps and shakes Andy's hand for five minutes, and then I goes back to Mrs. Trotter and tells her, and she cries as hard for joy as she did for sorrow.

"Two days afterward me and Andy packed to go.

"'Wouldn't you like to go down and meet Mrs. Trotter once before we leave?' I asks him. 'She'd like mightily to know you and express her encomiums and gratitude.'

"'Why, I guess not,' says Andy. 'I guess we'd better hurry and catch that train.'

"I was strapping our capital around me in a memory belt like we always carried it, when Andy pulls a roll of large bills out of his pocket and asks me to put 'em with the rest.

"'What's this?' says I.

"'It's Mrs. Trotter's two thousand,' says Andy.

"'How do you come to have it?' I asks.

"'She gave it to me,' says Andy. 'I've been calling on her three evenings a week for more than a month.'

"'Then you are William Wilkinson?' says I.

"'I was,' says Andy."

Conscience in Art

"I NEVER could hold my partner, Andy Tucker, down to legitimate ethics of pure swindling," said Jeff Peters to me one day.

"Andy had too much imagination to be honest. He used to devise schemes of money-getting so fraudulent and high-financial that they wouldn't have been allowed in the bylaws of a railroad rebate system.

"Myself, I never believed in taking any man's dollars unless I gave him something for it—something in the way of rolled gold jewelry, garden seeds, lumbago lotion, stock certificates, stove polish or a crack on the head to show for his money. I guess I must have had New England ancestors away back and inherited some of their stanch and rugged fear of the police.

"But Andy's family tree was in different kind. I don't think he could have traced his descent any further back than a corporation.

"One summer while we was in the middle West, working down the Ohio valley with a line of family albums, headache powders and roach destroyer, Andy takes one of his notions of high and actionable financiering.

"'Jeff,' says he, 'I've been thinking that we ought to drop these rutabaga fanciers and give our attention to something more nourishing and prolific. If we keep on snapshooting these hinds for their egg money we'll be classed as nature fakers. How about plunging into the fastnesses of the skyscraper country and biting some big bull caribous in the chest?'

" 'Well,' says I, 'you know my idiosyncrasies. I prefer a square, non-illegal style of business such as we are carrying on now. When I take money I want to leave some tangible object in the other fellow's hands for him to gaze at and to distract his attention from my spoor, even if it's only a Komical Kuss Trick Finger Ring for Squirting Perfume in a Friend's Eye. But if you've got a fresh idea, Andy,' says I, 'let's have a look at it. I'm not so wedded to petty graft that I would refuse something better in the way of a subsidy.'

" 'I was thinking,' says Andy, 'of a little hunt without horn, hound or camera among the great herd of the Midas Americanus, commonly known as the Pittsburg millionaires.'

" 'In New York?' I asks.

" 'No, sir,' says Andy, 'in Pittsburg. That's their habitat. They don't like New York. They go there now and then just because it's expected of 'em.'

" 'A Pittsburg Millionaire in New York is like a fly in a cup of hot coffee—he attracts attention and comment, but he don't enjoy it. New York ridicules him for "blowing" so much money in that town of sneaks and snobs, and sneers. The truth is, he don't spend anything while he is there. I saw a memorandum of expenses for a ten days' trip to Bunkum Town made by a Pittsburg man worth $15,000,000 once. Here's the way he set it down:

R. R. fare to and from	$ 21 00
Cab fare to and from hotel	2 00
Hotel bill @ $5 per day	50 00
Tips	5,750 00
TOTAL	$5,823 00

" 'That's the voice of New York,' goes on Andy. 'The town's nothing but a head waiter. If you tip it too much it'll go and stand by the door and make fun of you to the hat check boy.

When a Pittsburger wants to spend money and have a good time he stays at home. That's where we'll go to catch him.'

"Well, to make a dense story more condensed, me and Andy cached our paris green and antipyrine powders and albums in a friend's cellar, and took the trail to Pittsburg. Andy didn't have any especial prospectus of chicanery and violence drawn up, but he always had plenty of confidence that his immoral nature would rise to any occasion that presented itself.

"As a concession to my ideas of self-preservation and rectitude he promised that if I should take an active and incriminating part in any little business venture that we might work up, there should be something actual and cognizant to the senses of touch, sight, taste or smell to transfer to the victim for the money so my conscience might rest easy. After that I felt better and entered more cheerfully into the foul play.

" 'Andy,' says I, as we strayed through the smoke along the cinderpath they call Smithfield Street, 'had you figured out how we are going to get acquainted with these coke kings and pig iron squeezers? Not that I would decry my own worth or system of drawing-room deportment, and work with the olive fork and pie knife,' says I, 'but isn't the entree nous into the salons of the stogie smokers going to be harder than you imagined?'

" 'If there's any handicap at all,' says Andy, 'it's our own refinement and inherent culture. Pittsburg millionaires are a fine body of plain, wholehearted, unassuming, democratic men.

" 'They are rough but uncivil in their manners, and though their ways are boisterous and unpolished, under it all they have a great deal of impoliteness and discourtesy. Nearly every one of 'em rose from obscurity,' says Andy, 'and they'll live in it till the town gets to using smoke consumers. If we act simple and unaffected and don't go too far from the saloons and keep making a noise like an import duty on steel rails we won't have any trouble in meeting some of 'em socially.'

"Well, Andy and me drifted about town three or four days getting our bearings. We got to know several millionaires by sight.

"One used to stop his automobile in front of our hotel and have a quart of champagne brought out to him. When the waiter opened it he'd turn it up to his mouth and drink it out of the bottle. That showed he used to be a glass-blower before he made his money.

"One evening Andy failed to come to the hotel for dinner. About 11 o'clock he came into my room.

" 'Landed one, Jeff,' says he. 'Twelve millions. Oil, rolling mills, real estate and natural gas. He's a fine man; no airs about him. Made all his money in the last five years. He's got professors posting him up now on education—art and literature and haberdashery and such things.

" 'When I saw him he'd just won a bet of $10,000 with a Steel Corporation man that there'd be four suicides in the Allegeheny rolling mills to-day. So everybody in sight had to walk up and have drinks on him. He took a fancy to me and asked me to dinner with him. We went to a restaurant in Diamond Alley and sat on stools and had sparkling Moselle and clam chowder and apple fritters.

" 'Then he wanted to show me his bachelor apartment on Liberty Street. He's got ten rooms over a fish market with privilege of the bath on the next floor above. He told me it cost him $18,-000 to furnish his apartment, and I believe it.

" 'He's got $40,000 worth of pictures in one room, and $20,-000 worth of curios and antiques in another. His name's Scudder, and he's 45, and taking lessons on the piano and 15,000 barrels of oil a day out of his wells.'

" 'All right,' says I. 'Preliminary canter satisfactory. But, kay vooly, voo? What good is the art junk to us? And the oil?'

" 'Now, that man,' says Andy, sitting thoughtfully on the bed, 'ain't what you would call an ordinary scutt. When he was showing me his cabinet of art curios his face lighted up like the door of a coke oven. He says that if some of his big deals go through he'll make J. P. Morgan's collection of sweatshop tapestry and Augusta, Me., beadwork look like the contents of an ostrich's craw thrown on a screen by a magic lantern.

" 'And then he showed me a little carving,' went on Andy, 'that anybody could see was a wonderful thing. It was something like 2,000 years old, he said. It was a lotus flower with a woman's face in it carved out of a solid piece of ivory.

" 'Scudder looks it up in a catalogue and describes it. An Egyptian carver named Khafra made two of 'em for King Rameses II about the year B.C. The other one can't be found. The junk shops and antique bugs have rubbered all Europe for it, but it seems to be out of stock. Scudder paid $2,000 for the one he has.'

" 'Oh, well,' says I, 'this sounds like the purling of a rill to me. I thought we came here to teach the millionaires business, instead of learning art from 'em?'

" 'Be patient,' says Andy, kindly. 'Maybe we will see a rift in the smoke ere long.'

"All the next morning Andy was out. I didn't see him until about noon. He came to the hotel and called me into his room across the hall. He pulled a roundish bundle about as big as a goose egg out of his pocket and unwrapped it. It was an ivory carving just as he had described the millionaire's to me.

" 'I went in an old second-hand store and pawnshop a while ago,' says Andy, 'and I see this half hidden under a lot of old daggers and truck. The pawnbroker said he'd had it several years and thinks it was soaked by some Arabs or Turks or some foreign dubs that used to live down by the river.

" 'I offered him $2 for it, and I must have looked like I wanted it, for he said it would be taking the pumpernickel out of his children's mouths to hold any conversation that did not lead up to a price of $335. I finally got it for $25.

" 'Jeff,' goes on Andy, 'this is the exact counterpart of Scudder's carving. It's absolutely a dead ringer for it. He'll pay $2,000 for it as quick as he'd tuck a napkin under his chin. And why shouldn't it be the genuine other one, anyhow, that the old gypsy whittled out?'

"'Why not, indeed?' says I. 'And how shall we go about compelling him to make a voluntary purchase of it?'

"Andy had his plan all ready, and I'll tell you how we carried it out.

"I got a pair of blue spectacles, put on my black frock coat, rumpled my hair up and became Prof. Pickleman. I went to another hotel, registered, and sent a telegram to Scudder to come to see me at once on important art business. The elevator dumped him on me in less than an hour. He was a foggy man with a clarion voice, smelling of Connecticut wrappers and naphtha.

"'Hello, Profess!' he shouts. 'How's your conduct?'

"I rumpled my hair some more and gave him a blue glass stare.

"'Sir,' says I. 'Are you Cornelius T. Scudder? Of Pittsburg, Pennsylvania?'

"'I am,' says he. 'Come out and have a drink.'

"'I have neither the time nor the desire,' says I, 'for such harmful and deleterious amusements. I have come from New York,' says I, 'on a matter of busi—on a matter of art.

"'I learned there that you are the owner of an Egyptian ivory carving of the time of Rameses II., representing the head of Queen Isis in a lotus flower. There were only two of such carvings made. One has been lost for many years. I recently discovered and purchased the other in a pawn—in an obscure museum in Vienna. I wish to purchase yours. Name your price.'

"'Well, the great ice jams, Profess!' says Scudder. 'Have you found the other one? Me sell? No. I don't guess Cornelius Scudder needs to sell anything that he wants to keep. Have you got the carving with you, Profess?'

"I shows it to Scudder. He examines it careful all over.

"'It's the article,' says he. 'It's a duplicate of mine, every line and curve of it. Tell you what I'll do,' he says. 'I won't sell, but I'll buy. Give you $2,500 for yours.'

"'Since you won't sell, I will,' says I. 'Large bills please. I'm a man of few words. I must return to New York to-night. I lecture to-morrow at the aquarium.'

"Scudder sends a check down and the hotel cashes it. He goes off with the piece of antiquity and I hurry back to Andy's hotel, according to arrangement.

"Andy is walking up and down the room looking at his watch.

" 'Well?' he says.

" 'Twenty-five hundred,' says I. 'Cash.'

" 'We've got just eleven minutes,' says Andy, 'to catch the B. & O. westbound. Grab your baggage.'

" 'What's the hurry?' says I. 'It was a square deal. And even if it was only an imitation of the original carving it'll take him some time to find it out. He seemed to be sure it was the genuine article.'

" 'It was,' says Andy. 'It was his own. When I was looking at his curios yesterday he stepped out of the room for a moment and I pocketed it. Now, will you pick up your suitcase and hurry?'

" 'Then,' says I, 'why was that story about finding another one in the pawn——'

" 'Oh,' says Andy, 'out of respect for that conscience of yours. Come on.' "

ROADS OF DESTINY

✿

Roads of Destiny

> I go to seek on many roads
>   What is to be.
> True heart and strong, with love to light—
> Will they not bear me in the fight
> To order, shun or wield or mould
>   My Destiny?

UNPUBLISHED POEMS.OF DAVID MIGNOT

THE SONG was over. The words were David's; the air, one of the countryside. The company about the inn table applauded heartily, for the young poet paid for the wine. Only the notary, M. Papineau, shook his head a little at the lines, for he was a man of books, and he had not drunk with the rest.

David went out into the village street, where the night air drove the wine vapor from his head. And then he remembered that he and Yvonne had quarrelled that day, and that he had resolved to leave his home that night to seek fame and honor in the great world outside.

"When my poems are on every man's tongue," he told himself, in a fine exhilaration, "she will, perhaps, think of the hard words she spoke this day."

Except the roysterers in the tavern, the village folk were abed. David crept softly into his room in the shed of his father's cottage and made a bundle of his small store of clothing. With this upon a staff, he set his face outward upon the road that ran from Vernoy.

He passed his father's herd of sheep huddled in their nightly pen—the sheep he herded daily, leaving them to scatter while he wrote verses on scraps of paper. He saw a light yet shining in Yvonne's window, and a weakness shook his purpose of a sudden. Perhaps that light meant that she rued, sleepless, her anger, and that morning might—— But, no! His decision was made. Vernoy was no place for him. Not one soul there could share his thoughts. Out along that road lay his fate and his future.

Three leagues across the dim, moonlit champaign ran the road, straight as a plowman's furrow. It was believed in the village that the road ran to Paris, at least; and this name the poet whispered often to himself as he walked. Never so far from Vernoy had David travelled before.

THE LEFT BRANCH *Three leagues, then, the road ran, and turned into a puzzle. It joined with another and a larger road at right angles. David stood, uncertain, for a while, and then took the road to the left.*

Upon this more important highway were, imprinted in the dust, wheel tracks left by the recent passage of some vehicle. Some half an hour later these traces were verified by the sight of a ponderous carriage mired in a little brook at the bottom of a steep hill. The driver and postilions were shouting and tugging at the horses' bridles. On the road at one side stood a huge, black-clothed man and a slender lady wrapped in a long, light cloak.

David saw the lack of skill in the efforts of the servants. He quietly assumed control of the work. He directed the outriders to cease their clamor at the horses and to exercise their strength upon the wheels. The driver alone urged the animals with his familiar voice; David himself heaved a powerful shoulder at the rear of the carriage, and with one harmonious tug the great vehicle rolled up on solid ground. The outriders climbed to their places.

David stood for a moment upon one foot. The huge gentleman waved a hand. "You will enter the carriage," he said, in a voice large, like himself, but smoothed by art and habit. Obedience belonged in the path of such a voice. Brief as was the young poet's hesitation, it was cut shorter still by a renewal of the command. David's foot went to the step. In the darkness he perceived dimly the form of the lady upon the rear seat. He was about to seat himself opposite, when the voice again swayed him to its will. "You will sit at the lady's side."

The gentleman swung his great weight to the forward seat. The carriage proceeded up the hill. The lady was shrunk, silent, into her corner. David could not estimate whether she was old or young, but a delicate, mild perfume from her clothes stirred his poet's fancy to the belief that there was loveliness beneath the mystery. Here was an adventure such as he had often imagined. But as yet he held no key to it, for no word was spoken while he sat with his impenetrable companions.

In an hour's time David perceived through the window that the vehicle traversed the street of some town. Then it stopped in front of a closed and darkened house, and a postilion alighted to hammer impatiently upon the door. A latticed window above flew wide and a night-capped head popped out.

"Who are ye that disturb honest folk at this time of night? My house is closed. 'Tis too late for profitable travellers to be abroad. Cease knocking at my door, and be off."

"Open!" spluttered the postilion, loudly; "open for Monseigneur the Marquis de Beaupertuys."

"Ah!" cried the voice above. "Ten thousand pardons, my lord. I did not know—the hour is so late—at once shall the door be opened, and the house placed at my lord's disposal."

Inside was heard the clink of chair and bar, and the door was flung open. Shivering with chill and apprehension, the landlord of the Silver Flagon stood, half clad, candle in hand, upon the threshold.

David followed the marquis out of the carriage. "Assist the lady," he was ordered. The poet obeyed. He felt her small hand tremble as he guided her descent. "Into the house," the next command.

The room was the long dining-hall of the tavern. A great oak table ran down its length. The huge gentleman seated himself in a chair at the nearer end. The lady sank into another against the wall, with an air of great weariness. David stood, considering how best he might now take his leave and continue upon his way.

"My lord," said the landlord, bowing to the floor, "h-had I ex-expected this honor, entertainment would have been ready. T-t-there is wine and cold fowl and m-m-maybe——"

"Candles," said the marquis, spreading the fingers of one plump white hand in a gesture he had.

"Y-yes, my lord." He fetched half a dozen candles, lighted them, and set them upon the table.

"If monsieur would, perhaps, deign to taste a certain Burgundy —there is a cask——"

"Candles," said monsieur, spreading his fingers.

"Assuredly—quickly—I fly, my lord."

A dozen more lighted candles shone in the hall. The great bulk of the marquis overflowed his chair. He was dressed in fine black from head to foot save for the snowy ruffles at his wrist and throat. Even the hilt and scabbard of his sword were black. His expression was one of sneering pride. The ends of an upturned moustache reached nearly to his mocking eyes.

The lady sat motionless, and now David perceived that she was young, and possessed a pathetic and appealing beauty. He was startled from the contemplation of her forlorn loveliness by the booming voice of the marquis.

"What is your name and pursuit?"

"David Mignot. I am a poet."

The moustache of the marquis curled nearer to his eyes.

"How do you live?"

"I am also a shepherd; I guarded my father's flock," David answered, with his head high, but a flush upon his cheek.

"Then listen, master shepherd and poet, to the fortune you have blundered upon to-night. This lady is my niece, Mademoiselle Lucie de Varennes. She is of noble descent and is possessed of ten thousand francs a year in her own right. As to her charms, you have but to observe for yourself. If the inventory pleases your shepherd's heart, she becomes your wife at a word. Do not interrupt me. To-night I conveyed her to the château of the Comte de Villemaur, to whom her hand had been promised. Guests were present; the priest was waiting; her marriage to one eligible in rank and fortune was ready to be accomplished. At the altar this demoiselle, so meek and dutiful, turned upon me like a leopardess, charged me with cruelty and crimes, and broke, before the gaping priest, the troth I had plighted for her. I swore there and then, by ten thousand devils, that she should marry the first man we met after leaving the château, be he prince, charcoal-burner, or thief. You, Shepherd, are the first. Mademoiselle must be wed this night. If not you, then another. You have ten minutes in which to make your decision. Do not vex me with words or questions. Ten minutes, shepherd; and they are speeding."

The marquis drummed loudly with his white fingers upon the table. He sank into a veiled attitude of waiting. It was as if some great house had shut its doors and windows against approach. David would have spoken, but the huge man's bearing stopped his tongue. Instead, he stood by the lady's chair and bowed.

"Mademoiselle," he said, and he marvelled to find his words flowing easily before so much elegance and beauty. "You have heard me say I was a shepherd. I have also had the fancy, at times, that I am a poet. If it be the test of a poet to adore and cherish the beautiful, that fancy is now strengthened. Can I serve you in any way, mademoiselle?"

The young woman looked up at him with eyes dry and mournful.

His frank, glowing face made serious by the gravity of the adventure, his strong, straight figure and the liquid sympathy in his blue eyes, perhaps, also, her imminent need of long-denied help and kindness, thawed her to sudden tears.

"Monsieur," she said, in low tones, "you look to be true and kind. He is my uncle, the brother of my father, and my only relative. He loved my mother, and he hates me because I am like her. He has made my life one long terror. I am afraid of his very looks, and never before dared to disobey him. But to-night he would have married me to a man three times my age. You will forgive me for bringing this vexation upon you, monsieur. You will, of course, decline this mad act he tries to force upon you. But let me thank you for your generous words, at least. I have had none spoken to me in so long."

There was now something more than generosity in the poet's eyes. Poet he must have been, for Yvonne was forgotten; this fine, new loveliness held him with its freshness and grace. The subtle perfume from her filled him with strange emotions. His tender look fell warmly upon her. She leaned to it, thirstily.

"Ten minutes," said David, "is given me in which to do what I would devote years to achieve. I will not say I pity you, mademoiselle; it would not be true—I love you. I cannot ask love from you yet, but let me rescue you from this cruel man, and, in time, love may come. I think I have a future, I will not always be a shepherd. For the present I will cherish you with all my heart and make your life less sad. Will you trust your fate to me, mademoiselle?"

"Ah, you would sacrifice yourself from pity!"

"From love. The time is almost up, mademoiselle."

"You will regret it, and despise me."

"I will live only to make you happy, and myself worthy of you."

Her fine small hand crept into his from beneath her cloak.

"I will trust you," she breathed, "with my life. And—and love—may not be so far off as you think. Tell him. Once away from the power of his eyes I may forget."

David went and stood before the marquis. The black figure stirred, and the mocking eyes glanced at the great hall clock.

"Two minutes to spare. A shepherd requires eight minutes to decide whether he will accept a bride of beauty and income! Speak up, shepherd, do you consent to become mademoiselle's husband?"

"Mademoiselle," said David, standing proudly, "has done me the honor to yield to my request that she become my wife."

"Well said!" said the marquis. "You have yet the making of a courtier in you, master shepherd. Mademoiselle could have drawn a worse prize, after all. And now to be done with the affair as quick as the Church and the devil will allow!"

He struck the table soundly with his sword hilt. The landlord came, knee-shaking, bringing more candles in the hope of anticipating the great lord's whims. "Fetch a priest," said the marquis, "a priest; do you understand? In ten minutes have a priest here, or——"

The landlord dropped his candles and flew.

The priest came heavy-eyed and ruffled. He made David Mignot and Lucie de Varennes man and wife, pocketed a gold piece that the marquis tossed him, and shuffled out again into the night.

"Wine," ordered the marquis, spreading his ominous fingers at the host.

"Fill glasses," he said, when it was brought. He stood up at the head of the table in the candlelight, a black mountain of venom and conceit, with something like the memory of an old love turned to poison in his eye, as it fell upon his niece.

"Monsieur Mignot," he said, raising his wine-glass, "drink after I say this to you: You have taken to be your wife one who will make your life a foul and wretched thing. The blood in her is an inheritance running black lies and red ruin. She will bring you shame and anxiety. The devil that descended to her is there in her eyes and skin and mouth that stoop even to beguile a peasant. There is your promise, monsieur poet, for a happy life. Drink your wine. At last, mademoiselle, I am rid of you."

The marquis drank. A little grievous cry, as if from a sudden wound, came from the girl's lips. David, with his glass in his hand, stepped forward three paces and faced the marquis. There was little of a shepherd in his bearing.

"Just now," he said calmly, "you did me the honor to call me 'monsieur.' May I hope, therefore, that my marriage to mademoiselle has placed me somewhat nearer to you in—let us say, reflected rank—has given me the right to stand more as an equal to monseigneur in a certain little piece of business I have in my mind?"

"You may hope, shepherd," sneered the marquis.

"Then," said David, dashing his glass of wine into the contemptuous eyes that mocked him, "perhaps you will condescend to fight me."

The fury of the great lord outbroke in one sudden curse like a blast from a horn. He tore his sword from its black sheath; he called to the hovering landlord: "A sword there, for this lout!" He turned to the lady, with a laugh that chilled her heart, and said: "You put much labor upon me, madame. It seems I must find you a husband and make you a widow in the same night."

"I know not sword-play," said David. He flushed to make the confession before his lady.

"'I know not sword-play,'" mimicked the marquis. "Shall we fight like peasants with oaken cudgels? *Hola!* François, my pistols!"

A postilion brought two shining great pistols ornamented with carven silver from the carriage holsters. The marquis tossed one upon the table near David's hand. "To the other end of the table," he cried; "even a shepherd may pull a trigger. Few of them attain the honor to die by the weapon of a De Beaupertuys."

The shepherd and the marquis faced each other from the ends of the long table. The landlord, in an ague of terror, clutched the air and stammered: "M-M-Monseigneur, for the love of Christ! not in my house!—do not spill blood—it will ruin my custom——" The look of the marquis, threatening him, paralyzed his tongue.

"Coward," cried the lord of Beaupertuys, "cease chattering your teeth long enough to give the word for us, if you can."

Mine host's knees smote the floor. He was without a vocabulary. Even sounds were beyond him. Still, by gestures he seemed to beseech peace in the name of his house and custom.

"I will give the word," said the lady, in a clear voice. She went up to David and kissed him sweetly. Her eyes were sparkling bright, and color had come to her cheek. She stood against the wall, and the two men levelled their pistols for her count.

"*Un—deux—trois!*"

The two reports came so nearly together that the candles flickered but once. The marquis stood, smiling, the fingers of his left hand resting, outspread, upon the end of the table. David remained erect, and turned his head very slowly, searching for his wife with his eyes. Then, as a garment falls from where it is hung, he sank, crumpled, upon the floor.

With a little cry of terror and despair, the widowed maid ran and stooped above him. She found his wound, and then looked up with her old look of pale melancholy. "Through his heart," she whispered. "Oh, his heart!"

"Come," boomed the great voice of the marquis, "out with you to the carriage! Daybreak shall not find you on my hands. Wed you shall be again, and to a living husband, this night. The next we come upon, my lady, highwayman or peasant. If the road yields no other, then the churl that opens my gates. Out with you to the carriage!"

The marquis, implacable and huge, the lady wrapped again in the mystery of her cloak, the postilion bearing the weapons—all moved out to the waiting carriage. The sound of its ponderous wheels rolling away echoed through the slumbering village. In the hall of the Silver Flagon the distracted landlord wrung his hands above the slain poet's body, while the flames of the four and twenty candles danced and flickered on the table.

THE RIGHT BRANCH *Three leagues, then, the road ran, and turned into a puzzle. It joined with another and a larger road at right angles. David stood, uncertain, for a while, and then took the road to the right.*

Whither it led he knew not, but he was resolved to leave Vernoy far behind that night. He travelled a league and then passed a large château which showed testimony of recent entertainment. Lights shone from every window; from the great stone gateway ran a tracery of wheel tracks drawn in the dust by the vehicles of the guests.

Three leagues farther and David was weary. He rested and slept for a while on a bed of pine boughs at the roadside. Then up and on again along the unknown way.

Thus for five days he travelled the great road, sleeping upon Nature's balsamic beds or in peasants' ricks, eating of their black, hospitable bread, drinking from streams or the willing cup of the goat-herd.

At length he crossed a great bridge and set his foot within the smiling city that has crushed or crowned more poets than all the rest of the world. His breath came quickly as Paris sang to him in a little undertone her vital chant of greeting—the hum of voice and foot and wheel.

High up under the eaves of an old house in the Rue Conti, David paid for lodging, and set himself, in a wooden chair, to his poems. The street, once sheltering citizens of import and consequence, was now given over to those who ever follow in the wake of decline.

The houses were tall and still possessed of a ruined dignity, but many of them were empty save for dust and the spider. By night there was the clash of steel and the cries of brawlers straying restlessly from inn to inn. Where once gentility abode was now but a rancid and rude incontinence. But here David found housing commensurate to his scant purse. Daylight and candlelight found him at pen and paper.

One afternoon he was returning from a foraging trip to the lower world, with bread and curds and a bottle of thin wine. Halfway up his dark stairway he met—or rather came upon, for she she rested on the stair—a young woman of a beauty that should balk even the justice of a poet's imagination. A loose, dark cloak, flung open, showed a rich gown beneath. Her eyes changed swiftly with every little shade of thought. Within one moment they would be round and artless like a child's, and long and cozening like a gypsy's. One hand raised her gown, undraping a little shoe, high-heeled, with its ribbons dangling, untied. So heavenly she was, so unfitted to stoop, so qualified to charm and command! Perhaps she had seen David coming, and had waited for his help there.

Ah, would monsieur pardon that she occupied the stairway, but the shoe!—the naughty shoe! Alas! it would not remain tied. Ah! if monsieur *would* be so gracious!

The poet's fingers trembled as he tied the contrary ribbons. Then he would have fled from the danger of her presence, but the eyes grew long and cozening, like a gypsy's, and held him. He leaned against the balustrade, clutching his bottle of sour wine.

"You have been so good," she said, smiling. "Does monsieur, perhaps, live in the house?"

"Yes, madame. I—I think so, madame."

"Perhaps in the third story, then?"

"No, madame; higher up."

The lady fluttered her fingers with the least possible gesture of impatience.

"Pardon. Certainly I am not discreet in asking. Monsieur will forgive me? It is surely not becoming that I should inquire where he lodges."

"Madame, do not say so. I live in the——"

"No, no, no; do not tell me. Now I see that I erred. But I cannot lose the interest I feel in this house and all that is in it. Once it was my home. Often I come here but to dream of those happy days again. Will you let that be my excuse?"

"Let me tell you, then, for you need no excuse," stammered the poet. "I live in the top floor—the small room where the stairs turn."

"In the front room?" asked the lady, turning her head sidewise.

"The rear, madame."

The lady sighed, as if with relief.

"I will detain you no longer, then, monsieur," she said, employing the round and artless eye. "Take good care of my house. Alas! only the memories of it are mine now. Adieu, and accept my thanks for your courtesy."

She was gone, leaving but a smile and a trace of sweet perfume. David climbed the stairs as one in slumber. But he awoke from it, and the smile and the perfume lingered with him and never afterward did either seem quite to leave him. This lady of whom he knew nothing drove him to lyrics of eyes, chansons of swiftly conceived love, odes to curling hair, and sonnets to slippers on slender feet.

Poet he must have been, for Yvonne was forgotten; this fine, new loveliness held him with its freshness and grace. The subtle perfume about her filled him with strange emotions.

On a certain night three persons were gathered about a table in a room on the third floor of the same house. Three chairs and the table and a lighted candle upon it was all the furniture. One of the persons was a huge man, dressed in black. His expression was one of sneering pride. The ends of his upturned moustache reached nearly to his mocking eyes. Another was a lady, young and beautiful, with eyes that could be round and artless, like a child's, or long and cozening, like a gypsy's, but were now keen and ambitious, like any other conspirator's. The third was a man of action, a combatant, a bold and impatient executive, breathing fire and steel. He was addressed by the others as Captain Desrolles.

This man struck the table with his fist, and said, with controlled violence:

"To-night. To-night as he goes to midnight mass. I am tired of the plotting that gets nowhere. I am sick of signals and ciphers and secret meetings and such *baragouin*. Let us be honest traitors. If France is to be rid of him, let us kill in the open, and not hunt with snares and traps. To-night, I say. I back my words. My hand will do the deed. To-night, as he goes to mass."

The lady turned upon him a cordial look. Woman, however wedded to plots, must ever thus bow to rash courage. The big man stroked his upturned moustache.

"Dear captain," he said, in a great voice, softened by habit, "this time I agree with you. Nothing is to be gained by waiting. Enough of the palace guards belong to us to make the endeavor a safe one."

"To-night," repeated Captain Desrolles, again striking the table. "You have heard me, marquis; my hand will do the deed."

"But now," said the huge man, softly, "comes a question. Word must be sent to our partisans in the palace, and a signal agreed upon. Our stanchest men must accompany the royal carriage. At this hour what messenger can penetrate so far as the south doorway? Ribout is stationed there; once a message is placed in his hands, all will go well."

"I will send the message," said the lady.

"You, countess?" said the marquis, raising his eyebrows. "Your devotion is great, we know, but——"

"Listen!" exclaimed the lady, rising and resting her hands upon the table; "in a garret of this house lives a youth from the provinces as guileless and tender as the lambs he tended there. I have met him twice or thrice upon the stairs. I questioned him, fearing that he might dwell too near the room in which we are accustomed to meet. He is mine, if I will. He writes poems in his garret, and I think he dreams of me. He will do what I say. He shall take the message to the palace."

The marquis rose from his chair and bowed. "You did not permit me to finish my sentence, countess," he said. "I would have said: 'Your devotion is great, but your wit and charm are infinitely greater.'"

While the conspirators were thus engaged, David was polishing some lines addressed to his *amorette d'escalier*. He heard a timorous knock at his door, and opened it, with a great throb, to behold her there, panting as one in straits, with eyes wide open and artless, like a child's.

"Monsieur," she breathed, "I come to you in distress. I believe you to be good and true, and I know of no other help. How I flew through the streets among the swaggering men! Monsieur, my mother is dying. My uncle is a captain of guards in the palace of the king. Some one must fly to bring him. May I hope——"

"Mademoiselle," interrupted David, his eyes shining with the desire to do her service, "your hopes shall be my wings. Tell me how I may reach him."

The lady thrust a sealed paper into his hand.

"Go to the south gate—the south gate, mind—and say to the guards there, 'The falcon has left his nest.' They will pass you, and you will go to the south entrance to the palace. Repeat the words, and give this letter to the man who will reply 'Let him strike when he will.' This is the password, monsieur, entrusted to me by my uncle, for now when the country is disturbed and men plot against the king's life, no one without it can gain entrance to the palace grounds after nightfall. If you will, monsieur, take him this letter so that my mother may see him before she closes her eyes."

"Give it me," said David, eagerly. "But shall I let you return home through the streets alone so late? I——"

"No, no—fly. Each moment is like a precious jewel. Some time," said the lady, with eyes long and cozening, like a gypsy's, "I will try to thank you for your goodness."

The poet thrust the letter into his breast, and bounded down the stairway. The lady, when he was gone, returned to the room below.

The eloquent eyebrows of the marquis interrogated her.

"He is gone," she said, "as fleet and stupid as one of his own sheep, to deliver it."

The table shook again from the batter of Captain Desrolles' fist.

"Sacred name!" he cried; "I have left my pistols behind! I can trust no others."

"Take this," said the marquis, drawing from beneath his cloak a shining, great weapon, ornamented with carven silver. "There are none truer. But guard it closely, for it bears my arms and crest, and already I am suspected. Me, I must put many leagues between myself and Paris this night. To-morrow must find me in my château. After you, dear countess."

The marquis puffed out the candle. The lady, well cloaked, and the two gentlemen softly descended the stairway and flowed into the crowd that roamed along the narrow pavements of the Rue Conti.

David sped. At the south gate of the king's residence a halberd was laid to his breast, but he turned its point with the words: "The falcon has left his nest."

"Pass, brother," said the guard, "and go quickly."

On the south steps of the palace they moved to seize him, but again the *mot de passe* charmed the watchers. One among them stepped forward and began: "Let him strike——" But a flurry among the guards told of a surprise. A man of keen look and soldierly stride suddenly pressed through them and seized the letter which David held in his hand. "Come with me," he said, and led him inside the great hall. Then he tore open the letter and read it. He beckoned to a man uniformed as an officer of musketeers, who was passing. "Captain Tetreau, you will have the guards at the south entrance and the south gate arrested and confined. Place men known to be loyal in their places." To David he said: "Come with me."

He conducted him through a corridor and an anteroom into a spacious chamber, where a melancholy man, sombrely dressed, sat brooding in a great leather-covered chair. To that man he said:

"Sire, I have told you that the palace is as full of traitors and spies as a sewer is of rats. You have thought, sire, that it was my fancy. This man penetrated to your very door by their connivance. He bore a letter which I have intercepted. I have brought him here that your majesty may no longer think my zeal excessive."

"I will question him," said the king, stirring in his chair. He looked at David with heavy eyes dulled by an opaque film. The poet bent his knee.

"From where do you come?" asked the king.

"From the village of Vernoy, in the province of Eure-et-Loir, sire."

"What do you follow in Paris?"

"I—I would be a poet, sire."

"What did you in Vernoy?"

"I minded my father's flock of sheep."

The king stirred again, and the film lifted from his eyes.

"Ah! in the fields?"

"Yes, sire."

"You lived in the fields; you went out in the cool of the morning and lay among the hedges in the grass. The flock distributed itself upon the hillside; you drank of the living stream; you ate your sweet brown bread in the shade; and you listened, doubtless, to blackbirds piping in the grove. Is not that so, shepherd?"

"It is, sire," answered David, with a sigh; "and to the bees at the flowers, and, maybe, to the grape gatherers singing on the hill."

"Yes, yes," said the king, impatiently; "maybe to them; but surely to the blackbirds. They whistled often, in the grove, did they not?"

"Nowhere, sire, so sweetly as in Eure-et-Loir. I have endeavored to express their song in some verses that I have written."

"Can you repeat those verses?" asked the king, eagerly. "A long time ago I listened to the blackbirds. It would be something better than a kingdom if one could rightly construe their song. And at night you drove the sheep to the fold and then sat, in peace and tranquillity, to your pleasant bread. Can you repeat those verses, shepherd?"

"They run this way, sire," said David, with respectful ardor:

"Lazy shepherd, see your lambkins
        Skip, ecstatic, on the mead;
See the firs dance in the breezes,
        Hear Pan blowing at his reed.

"Hear us calling from the tree-tops,
    See us swoop upon your flock;
    Yield us wool to make our nests warm
    In the branches of the——"

"If it please your majesty," interrupted a harsh voice, "I will ask a question or two of this rhymester. There is little time to spare. I crave pardon, sire, if my anxiety for your safety offends."

"The loyalty," said the king, "of the Duke d'Aumale is too well proven to give offence." He sank into his chair, and the film came again over his eyes.

"First," said the duke, "I will read you the letter he brought:

"To-night is the anniversary of the dauphin's death. If he goes, as is his custom, to midnight mass to pray for the soul of his son, the falcon will strike, at the corner of the Rue Esplanade. If this be his intention, set a red light in the upper room at the southwest corner of the palace, that the falcon may take heed.

"Peasant," said the duke, sternly, "you have heard these words. Who gave you this message to bring?"

"My lord duke," said David, sincerely, "I will tell you. A lady gave it me. She said her mother was ill, and that this writing would fetch her uncle to her bedside. I do not know the meaning of the letter, but I will swear that she is beautiful and good."

"Describe the woman," commanded the duke, "and how you came to be her dupe."

"Describe her!" said David with a tender smile. "You would command words to perform miracles. Well, she is made of sunshine and deep shade. She is slender, like the alders, and moves with their grace. Her eyes change while you gaze into them; now round, and then half shut as the sun peeps between two clouds. When she comes, heaven is all about her; when she leaves, there is chaos and a scent of hawthorn blossoms. She came to me in the Rue Conti, number twenty-nine."

"It is the house," said the duke, turning to the king, "that we have been watching. Thanks to the poet's tongue, we have a picture of the infamous Countess Quebedaux."

"Sire and my lord duke," said David, earnestly, "I hope my poor words have done no injustice. I have looked into that lady's eyes. I will stake my life that she is an angel, letter or no letter."

The duke looked at him steadily. "I will put you to the proof," he said, slowly. "Dressed as the king, you shall, yourself, attend mass in his carriage at midnight. Do you accept the test?"

David smiled. "I have looked into her eyes," he said. "I had my proof there. Take yours how you will."

Half an hour before twelve the Duke d'Aumale, with his own hands, set a red lamp in a southwest window of the palace. At ten minutes to the hour, David, leaning on his arm, dressed as the king, from top to toe, with his head bowed in his cloak, walked slowly from the royal apartments to the waiting carriage. The duke assisted him inside and closed the door. The carriage whirled away along its route to the cathedral.

On the *qui vive* in a house at the corner of the Rue Esplanade was Captain Tetreau with twenty men, ready to pounce upon the conspirators when they should appear.

But it seemed that, for some reason, the plotters had slightly altered their plans. When the royal carriage had reached the Rue Christopher, one square nearer than the Rue Esplanade, forth from it burst Captain Desrolles, with his band of would-be regicides, and assailed the equipage. The guards upon the carriage, though surprised at the premature attack, descended and fought valiantly. The noise of conflict attracted the force of Captain Tetreau, and they came pelting down the street to the rescue. But, in the meantime, the desperate Desrolles had torn open the door of the king's carriage, thrust his weapon against the body of the dark figure inside, and fired.

Now, with loyal reinforcements at hand, the street rang with cries and the rasp of steel, but the frightened horses had dashed away. Upon the cushions lay the dead body of the poor mock king and poet, slain by a ball from the pistol of Monseigneur, the Marquis de Beaupertuys.

THE MAIN ROAD *Three leagues, then, the road ran, and turned into a puzzle. It joined with another and a larger road at right angles. David stood, uncertain, for a while, and then sat himself to rest upon its side.*

Whither those roads led he knew not. Either way there seemed to lie a great world full of chance and peril. And then, sitting there, his eyes fell upon a bright star, one that he and Yvonne had named for theirs. That set him thinking of Yvonne, and he wondered if he had not been too hasty. Why should he leave her and his home because a few hot words had come between them? Was love so brittle a thing that jealousy, the very proof of it, could break it? Mornings always brought a cure for the little heartaches of evening. There was yet time for him to return home without any one in the sweetly sleeping village of Vernoy being the wiser. His heart was Yvonne's; there where he had lived always he could write his poems and find his happiness.

David rose, and shook off his unrest and the wild mood that had tempted him. He set his face steadfastly back along the road he had come. By the time he had retravelled the road to Vernoy, his desire to rove was gone. He passed the sheepfold, and the sheep scurried, with a drumming flutter, at his late footsteps, warming his heart by the homely sound. He crept without noise into his little room and lay there, thankful that his feet had escaped the distress of new roads that night.

How well he knew woman's heart! The next evening Yvonne was at the well in the road where the young congregated in order that the *curé* might have business. The corner of her eye was engaged in a search for David, albeit her set mouth seemed unrelenting. He saw the look; braved the mouth, drew from it a recantation and, later, a kiss as they walked homeward together.

Three months afterward they were married. David's father was shrewd and prosperous. He gave them a wedding that was heard of three leagues away. Both the young people were favorites in the village. There was a procession in the streets, a dance on the green; they had the marionettes and a tumbler out from Dreux to delight the guests.

Then a year, and David's father died. The sheep and the cottage descended to him. He already had the seemliest wife in the village. Yvonne's milk pails and her brass kettles were bright—*ouf!* they blinded you in the sun when you passed that way. But you must keep your eyes upon her yard, for flower beds were so neat and gay they restored to you your sight. And you might hear her sing, aye, as far as the double chestnut tree above Père Gruneau's blacksmith forge.

But a day came when David drew out paper from a long-shut drawer, and began to bite the end of a pencil. Spring had come again and touched his heart. Poet he must have been, for now Yvonne was well-nigh forgotten. This fine new loveliness of earth held him with its witchery and grace. The perfume from her woods and meadows stirred him strangely. Daily had he gone forth with his flock, and brought it safe at night. But now he stretched himself under the hedge and pieced words together on his bits of paper. The sheep strayed, and the wolves, perceiving that difficult poems make easy mutton, ventured from the woods and stole his lambs.

David's stock of poems grew larger and his flock smaller. Yvonne's nose and temper waxed sharp and her talk blunt. Her pans and kettles grew dull, but her eyes had caught their flash. She pointed out to the poet that his neglect was reducing the flock and bringing woe upon the household. David hired a boy to guard the sheep, locked himself in the little room in the top of the cottage, and wrote more poems. The boy, being a poet by nature, but not furnished with an outlet in the way of writing, spent his time in slumber. The wolves lost no time in discovering that poetry and sleep are practically the same; so the flock steadily grew smaller. Yvonne's ill temper increased at an equal rate. Sometimes she would stand in the yard and rail at David through his high window. Then you could hear her as far as the double chestnut tree above Père Gruneau's blacksmith forge.

M. Papineau, the kind, wise, meddling old notary, saw this, as he saw everything at which his nose pointed. He went to David, fortified himself with a great pinch of snuff, and said:

"Friend Mignot, I affixed the seal upon the marriage certificate of your father. It would distress me to be obliged to attest a paper signifying the bankruptcy of his son. But that is what you are coming to. I speak as an old friend. Now, listen to what I have to say. You have your heart set, I perceive, upon poetry. At Dreux, I have a friend, one Monsieur Bril—Georges Bril. He lives in a little cleared space in a houseful of books. He is a learned man; he visits Paris each year; he himself has written books. He will tell you when the catacombs were made, how they found out the names of the stars, and why the plover has a long bill. The meaning and the form of poetry is to him as intelligent as the baa of a sheep is to you. I will give you a letter to him, and you shall take him your poems and let him read them. Then you will know if you shall write more, or give your attention to your wife and business."

"Write the letter," said David. "I am sorry you did not speak of this sooner."

At sunrise the next morning he was on the road to Dreux with the precious roll of poems under his arm. At noon he wiped the dust from his feet at the door of Monsieur Bril. That learned man broke the seal of M. Papineau's letter, and sucked up its contents through his gleaming spectacles as the sun draws water. He took David inside to his study and sat him down upon a little island beat upon by a sea of books.

Monsieur Bril had a conscience. He flinched not even at a mass manuscript the thickness of a finger length and rolled to an incorrigible curve. He broke the back of the roll against his knee and began to read. He slighted nothing; he bored into the lump as a worm into a nut, seeking for a kernel.

Meanwhile, David sat, marooned, trembling in the spray of so much literature. It roared in his ears. He held no chart or compass for voyaging in that sea. Half the world, he thought, must be writing books.

Monsieur Bril bored to the last page of the poems. Then he took off his spectacles and wiped them with his handkerchief.

"My old friend, Papineau, is well?" he asked.

"In the best of health," said David.

"How many sheep have you, Monsieur Mignot?"

"Three hundred and nine, when I counted them yesterday. The flock has had ill fortune. To that number it has decreased from eight hundred and fifty."

"You have a wife and a home, and lived in comfort. The sheep brought you plenty. You went into the fields with them and lived in the keen air and ate the sweet bread of contentment. You had but to be vigilant and recline there upon nature's breast, listening to the whistle of the blackbirds in the grove. Am I right thus far?"

"It was so," said David.

"I have read all your verses," continued Monsieur Bril, his eyes wandering about his sea of books as if he conned the horizon for a sale. "Look yonder, through that window, Monsieur Mignot; tell me what you see in that tree."

"I see a crow," said David, looking.

"There is a bird," said Monsieur Bril, "that shall assist me where I am disposed to shirk a duty. You know that bird, Monsieur Mignot; he is the philosopher of the air. He is happy through submission to his lot. None so merry or full-crawed as he with his whimsical eye and rollicking step. The fields yield him what he desires. He never grieves that his plumage is not gay, like the oriole's. And you have heard, Monsieur Mignot, the notes that nature has given him? Is the nightingale any happier, do you think?"

David rose to his feet. The crow cawed harshly from his tree.

"I thank you, Monsieur Bril," he said, slowly. "There was not, then, one nightingale note among all those croaks?"

"I could not have missed it," said Monsieur Bril, with a sigh. "I read every word. Live your poetry, man; do not try to write it any more."

"I thank you," said David, again. "And now I will be going back to my sheep."

"If you would dine with me," said the man of books, "and overlook the smart of it, I will give you reasons at length."

"No," said the poet, "I must be back in the fields cawing at my sheep."

Back along the road to Vernoy he trudged with his poems under his arm. When he reached his village he turned into the shop of one Zeigler, a Jew out of Armenia, who sold anything that came to his hand.

"Friend," said David, "wolves from the forest harass my sheep on the hills. I must purchase firearms to protect them. What have you?"

"A bad day, this, for me, friend Mignot," said Zeigler, spreading his hands, "for I perceive that I must sell you a weapon that will not fetch a tenth of its value. Only last week I bought from a peddler a wagon full of goods that he procured at a sale by a *commissionaire* of the crown. The sale was of the château and belongings of a great lord—I know not his title—who has been banished for conspiracy against the king. There are some choice firearms in the lot. This pistol—oh, a weapon fit for a prince! —it shall be only forty francs to you, friend Mignot—if I lost ten by the sale. But perhaps an arquebuse——"

"This will do," said David, throwing the money on the counter. "Is it charged?"

"I will charge it," said Zeigler. "And, for ten francs more, add a store of powder and ball."

David laid his pistol under his coat and walked to his cottage. Yvonne was not there. Of late she had taken to gadding much among the neighbors. But a fire was glowing in the kitchen stove. David opened the door of it and thrust his poems in upon the coals. As they blazed up they made a singing, harsh sound in the flue.

"The song of the crow!" said the poet.

He went up to his attic room and closed the door. So quiet was the village that a score of people heard the roar of the great pistol. They flocked thither, and up the stairs where the smoke, issuing, drew their notice.

The man laid the body of the poet upon his bed, awkwardly arranging it to conceal the torn plumage of the poor black crow. The women chattered in a luxury of zealous pity. Some of them ran to tell Yvonne.

M. Papineau, whose nose had brought him there among the first, picked up the weapon and ran his eye over its silver mountings with a mingled air of connoisseurship and grief.

"The arms," he explained, aside, to the *curé*, "and crest of Monseigneur, the Marquis de Beaupertuys."

The Enchanted Profile

THERE ARE few Caliphesses. Women are Scheherazades by birth, predilection, instinct, and arrangement of the vocal cords. The thousand and one stories are being told every day by hundreds of thousands of viziers' daughters to their respective sultans. But the bow-string will get some of 'em yet if they don't watch out.

I heard a story, though, of one Lady Caliph. It isn't precisely an Arabian Nights story, because it brings in Cinderella, who flourished her dishrag in another epoch and country. So, if you don't mind the mixed dates (which seem to give it an Eastern flavor, after all), we'll get along.

In New York there is an old, old hotel. You have seen woodcuts of it in the magazines. It was built—let's see—at a time when there was nothing above Fourteenth Street except the old Indian trail to Boston and Hammerstein's office. Soon the old hostelry will be torn down. And, as the stout walls are riven apart and the bricks go roaring down the chutes, crowds of citizens will gather at the nearest corners and weep over the destruction of a dear old landmark. Civic pride is strong in New Bagdad; and the wettest weeper and the loudest howler against the iconoclasts will be the man (originally from Terre Haute) whose fond memories of the old hotel are limited to his having been kicked out from its free-lunch counter in 1873.

At the hotel always stopped Mrs. Maggie Brown. Mrs. Brown was a bony woman of sixty, dressed in the rustiest black, and carrying a handbag made, apparently, from the hide of the original animal that Adam decided to call an alligator. She always occupied a small parlor and bedroom at the top of the hotel at a rental of two dollars per day. And always, while she was there, each day came hurrying to see her many men, sharp-faced, anxious-looking, with only seconds to spare. For Maggie Brown was said to be the third richest woman in the world; and these solicitous gentlemen were only the city's wealthiest brokers and business men seeking trifling loans of half a dozen millions or so from the dingy old lady with the pre-historic handbag.

The stenographer and typewriter of the Acropolis Hotel (there! I've let the name of it out!) was Miss Ida Bates. She was a hold-over from the Greek classics. There wasn't a flaw in her looks. Some old-timer in paying his regards to a lady said: "To have loved her was a liberal education." Well, even to have looked over the black hair and neat white shirtwaist of Miss Bates was equal to a full course in any correspondence school in the country. She sometimes did a little typewriting for me and, as she refused to take the money in advance, she came to look upon me as something of a friend and protégé. She had unfailing kindliness and good nature; and not even a whitelead drummer or a fur importer had ever dared to cross the dead line of good behavior in her presence. The entire force of the Acropolis, from the owner, who lived in Vienna, down to the head porter, who had been bedridden for sixteen years, would have sprung to her defence in a moment.

One day I walked past Miss Bates's little sanctum Remingtorium, and saw in her place a black-haired unit—unmistakably a person—pounding with each of her forefingers upon the keys. Musing on the mutability of temporal affairs, I passed on. The next day I went on a two weeks' vacation. Returning, I strolled through the lobby of the Acropolis, and saw, with a little warm glow of auld lang syne, Miss Bates, as Grecian and kind and flawless as ever, just putting the cover on her machine. The hour for closing had come; but she asked me in to sit for a few minutes in the dictation chair. Miss Bates explained her absence and return to the Acropolis Hotel in words identical with or similar to these following:

"Well, Man, how are the stories coming?"

"Pretty regularly," said I. "About equal to their going."

"I'm sorry," said she. "Good typewriting is the main thing in a story. You've missed me, haven't you?"

"No one," said I, "whom I have ever known knows as well as you do how to space properly belt buckles, semicolons, hotel guests, and hairpins. But you've been away too. I saw a package of peppermint-pepsin in your place the other day."

"I was going to tell you about it," said Miss Bates, "if you hadn't interrupted me.

"Of course, you know about Maggie Brown, who stops here. Well, she's worth $40,000,000. She lives in Jersey in a ten-dollar flat. She's always got more cash on hand than half a dozen business candidates for vice-president. I don't know whether she carries it in her stocking or not, but I know she's mighty popular down in the part of the town where they worship the golden calf.

"Well, about two weeks ago, Mrs. Brown stops at the door and rubbers at me for ten minutes. I'm sitting with my side to her, striking off some manifold copies of a copper-mine proposition for a nice old man from Tonopah. But I always see everything all around me. When I'm hard at work I can see things through my side-combs; and I can leave one button unbuttoned in the back of my shirtwaist and see who's behind me. I didn't look around, because I make from eighteen to twenty dollars a week, and I didn't have to.

"That evening at knocking-off time she sends for me to come up to her apartment. I expected to have to typewrite about two thousand words of notes-of-hand, liens, and contracts, with a ten-cent tip in sight; but I went. Well, Man, I was certainly surprised. Old Maggie Brown had turned human.

" 'Child,' says she, 'you're the most beautiful creature I ever saw in my life. I want you to quit your work and come and live with me. I've no kith or kin,' says she, 'except a husband and a son or two, and I hold no communication with any of 'em. They're extravagant burdens on a hard-working woman. I want you to be a daughter to me. They say I'm stingy and mean, and the papers print lies about my doing my own cooking and washing. It's a lie,' she goes on. 'I put my washing out, except the handkerchiefs and stockings and petticoats and collars, and light stuff like that. I've got forty million dollars in cash and stocks and bonds that are as negotiable as Standard Oil, preferred, at a church fair. I'm a lonely old woman and I need companionship. You're the most beautiful human being I ever saw,' says she. 'Will you come and live with me? I'll show 'em whether I can spend money or not,' she says.

"Well, Man, what would you have done? Of course, I fell to it. And, to tell you the truth, I began to like old Maggie. It wasn't all on account of the forty millions and what she could do for me. I was kind of lonesome in the world, too. Everybody's got to have somebody they can explain to about the pain in their left shoulder and how fast patent-leather shoes wear out when they begin to crack. And you can't talk about such things to men you meet in hotels—they're looking for just such openings.

"So I gave up my job in the hotel and went with Mrs. Brown. I certainly seemed to have a mash on her. She'd look at me for half an hour at a time when I was sitting, reading, or looking at the magazines.

"One time I says to her: 'Do I remind you of some deceased relative or friend of your childhood, Mrs. Brown? I've noticed you give me a pretty good optical inspection from time to time.'

" 'You have a face,' she says, 'exactly like a dear friend of mine—the best friend I ever had. But I like you for yourself, child, too,' she says.

"And say, Man, what do you suppose she did? Loosened up like a Marcel wave in the surf at Coney. She took me to a swell dressmaker and gave her *à la carte* to fit me out—money no object. They were rush orders, and madame locked the front door and put the whole force to work.

"Then we moved to—where do you think?—no; guess again—that's right—the Hotel Bonton. We had a six-room apartment; and it cost $100 a day. I saw the bill. I began to love that old lady.

"And then, Man, when my dresses began to come in—oh, I won't tell you about 'em! you couldn't understand. And I began to call her Aunt Maggie. You've read about Cinderella, of course. Well, what Cinderella said when the prince fitted that 3½ A on her foot was a hard-luck story compared to the things I told myself.

"Then Aunt Maggie says she is going to give me a coming-out banquet in the Bonton that'll make moving Vans of all the old Dutch families on Fifth Avenue.

" 'I've been out before, Aunt Maggie,' says I. 'But I'll come out again. But you know,' says I, 'that this is one of the swellest hotels in the city. And you know—pardon me—that it's hard to get a bunch of notables together unless you've trained for it.'

" 'Don't fret about that, child,' says Aunt Maggie. 'I don't send out invitations—I issue orders. I'll have fifty guests here that couldn't be brought together again at any reception unless it were given by King Edward or William Travers Jerome. They are men, of course, and all of 'em either owe me money or intend to. Some of their wives won't come, but a good many will.'

"Well, I wish you could have been at that banquet. The dinner service was all gold and cut glass. There were about forty men and eight ladies present besides Aunt Maggie and I. You'd never have known the third richest woman in the world. She had on a new black silk dress with so much passementerie on it that it sounded exactly like a hailstorm I heard once when I was staying all night with a girl that lived on a top-floor studio.

"And my dress!—say, Man, I can't waste the words on you. It was all hand-made lace—where there was any of it at all—and it cost $300. I saw the bill. The men were all baldheaded or white-sidewhiskered, and they kept up a running fire of light repartee about 3-per cent, and Bryan and the cotton crop.

"On the left of me was something that talked like a banker, and on my right was a young fellow who said he was a newspaper artist. He was the only—well, I was going to tell you.

"After the dinner was over Mrs. Brown and I went up to the apartment. We had to squeeze our way through a mob of reporters all the way through the halls. That's one of the things money does for you. Say, do you happen to know a newspaper artist named Lathrop—a tall man with nice eyes and an easy way of talking? No, I don't remember what paper he works on. Well, all right.

"When we got upstairs Mrs. Brown telephones for the bill right away. It came, and it was $600. I saw the bill. Aunt Maggie fainted. I got her on a lounge and opened the bead-work.

"'Child,' says she, when she got back to the world, 'what was it? A raise of rent or an income-tax?'

"'Just a little dinner,' says I. 'Nothing to worry about—hardly a drop in the bucket-shop. Sit up and take notice—a dispossess notice, if there's no other kind.'

"But, say, Man, do you know what Aunt Maggie did? She got cold feet! She hustled me out of that Hotel Bonton at nine the next morning. We went to a rooming-house on the lower West Side. She rented one room that had water on the floor below and light on the floor above. After we got moved all you could see in the room was about $1,500 worth of new swell dresses and a one-burner gas-stove.

"Aunt Maggie had had a sudden attack of the hedges. I guess everybody has got to go on a spree once in their life. A man spends his on highballs, and a woman gets woozy on clothes. But with forty million dollars—say! I'd like to have a picture of—but, speaking of pictures, did you ever run across a newspaper artist named Lathrop—a tall—oh, I asked you that before, didn't I? He was mighty nice to me at the dinner. His voice just suited me. I guess he must have thought I was to inherit some of Aunt Maggie's money.

"Well, Mr. Man, three days of that light-housekeeping was plenty for me. Aunt Maggie was affectionate as ever. She'd hardly let me get out of her sight. But let me tell you. She was a hedger from Hedgersville, Hedger County. Seventy-five cents a day was the limit she set. We cooked our own meals in the room. There I was, with a thousand dollars' worth of the latest things in clothes, doing stunts over a one-burner gas-stove.

"As I say, on the third day I flew the coop. I couldn't stand for throwing together a fifteen-cent kidney stew while wearing, at the same time, a $150 house-dress, with Valenciennes lace insertion. So I goes into the closet and puts on the cheapest dress Mrs. Brown had bought for me—it's the one I've got on now—not so bad for $75, is it? I'd left all my own clothes in my sister's flat in Brooklyn.

"'Mrs. Brown, formerly "Aunt Maggie,"' says I to her, 'I am going to extend my feet alternately, one after the other, in such a manner and direction that this tenement will recede from me in the quickest possible time. I am no worshipper of money,' says I, 'but there are some things I can't stand. I can stand the fabulous monster that I've read about that blows hot birds and cold bottles with the same breath. But I can't stand a quitter,' says I. 'They say you've got forty million dollars—well, you'll never have any less. And I was beginning to like you, too,' says I.

"Well, the late Aunt Maggie kicks till the tears flow. She offers to move into a swell room with a two-burner stove and running water.

"'I've spent an awful lot of money, child,' says she. 'We'll have to economize for a while. You're the most beautiful creature I ever laid eyes on,' she says, 'and I don't want you to leave me.'

"Well, you see me, don't you? I walked straight to the Acropolis and asked for my job back, and I got it. How did you say your writings were getting along? I know you've lost out some by not having me to typewrite 'em. Do you ever have 'em illustrated? And, by the way, did you ever happen to know a newspaper artist —oh, shut up! I know I asked you before. I wonder what paper he works on? It's funny, but I couldn't help thinking that he wasn't thinking about the money he might have been thinking I was thinking I'd get from old Maggie Brown. If I only knew some of the newspaper editors I'd——"

The sound of an easy footstep came from the doorway. Ida Bates saw who it was with her back-hair comb. I saw her turn pink, perfect statue that she was—a miracle that I share with Pygmalion only.

"Am I excusable?" she said to me—adorable petitioner that she became. "It's—it's Mr. Lathrop. I wonder if it really wasn't the money—I wonder, if after all, he——"

Of course, I was invited to the wedding. After the ceremony I dragged Lathrop aside.

"You an artist," said I, "and haven't figured out why Maggie Brown conceived such a strong liking for Miss Bates—that was? Let me show you."

The bride wore a simple white dress as beautifully draped as the costumes of the ancient Greeks. I took some leaves from one of the decorative wreaths in the little parlor, and made a chaplet of them, and placed them on née Bates' shining chestnut hair, and made her turn her profile to her husband.

"By jingo!" said he. "Isn't Ida's head a dead ringer for the lady's head on the silver dollar?"

The Passing of Black Eagle

FOR SOME MONTHS of a certain year a grim bandit infested the Texas border along the Rio Grande. Peculiarly striking to the optic nerve was this notorious marauder. His personality secured him the title of "Black Eagle, the Terror of the Border." Many fearsome tales are on record concerning the doings of him and his followers. Suddenly, in the space of a single minute, Black Eagle vanished from earth. He was never heard of again. His own band never even guessed the mystery of his disappearance. The border ranches and settlements feared he would come again to ride and ravage the mesquite flats. He never will. It is to disclose the fate of Black Eagle that this narrative is written.

The initial movement of the story is furnished by the foot of a bartender in St. Louis. His discerning eye fell upon the form of Chicken Ruggles as he pecked with avidity at the free lunch. Chicken was a "hobo." He had a long nose like the bill of a fowl, an inordinate appetite for poultry, and a habit of gratifying it without expense, which accounts for the name given him by his fellow vagrants.

Physicians agree that the partaking of liquids at meal times is not a healthy practice. The hygiene of the saloon promulgates the opposite. Chicken had neglected to purchase a drink to accompany his meal. The bartender rounded the counter, caught the injudicious diner by the ear with a lemon squeezer, led him to the door and kicked him into the street.

Thus the mind of Chicken was brought to realize the signs of coming winter. The night was cold; the stars shone with unkindly brilliancy; people were hurrying along the streets in two egotistic, jostling streams. Men had donned their overcoats, and Chicken knew to an exact percentage the increased difficulty of coaxing dimes from those buttoned-in vest pockets. The time had come for his annual exodus to the South.

A little boy, five or six years old, stood looking with covetous eyes in a confectioner's window. In one small hand he held an empty two-ounce vial; in the other he grasped tightly something flat and round, with a shining milled edge. The scene presented a field of operations commensurate to Chicken's talents and daring. After sweeping the horizon to make sure that no official tug was cruising near, he insidiously accosted his prey. The boy, having been early taught by his household to regard altruistic advances with extreme suspicion, received the overtures coldly.

Then Chicken knew that he must make one of those desperate, nerve-shattering plunges into speculation that fortune sometimes requires of those who would win her favor. Five cents was his capital, and this he must risk against the chance of winning what lay within the close grasp of the youngster's chubby hand. It was a fearful lottery, Chicken knew. But he must accomplish his end by strategy, since he had a wholesome terror of plundering infants by force. Once, in a park, driven by hunger, he had committed an onslaught upon a bottle of peptonized infant's food in the possession of an occupant of a baby carriage. The outraged infant had so promptly opened its mouth and pressed the button that communicated with the welkin that help arrived, and Chicken did his thirty days in a snug coop. Wherefore he was, as he said, "leary of kids."

Beginning artfully to question the boy concerning his choice of sweets, he gradually drew out the information he wanted. Mamma said he was to ask the drug-store man for ten cents' worth of paregoric in the bottle; he was to keep his hand shut tight over the dollar; he must not stop to talk to any one in the street; he must ask the drug-store man to wrap up the change and put it in the pocket of his trousers. Indeed, they had pockets —two of them! And he liked chocolate creams best.

Chicken went into the store and turned plunger. He invested his entire capital in C. A. N. D. Y. stocks, simply to pave the way to the greater risk following.

He gave the sweets to the youngster, and had the satisfaction of perceiving that confidence was established. After that it was easy to obtain leadership of the expedition, to take the investment by the hand and lead it to a nice drug store he knew of in the same block. There Chicken, with a parental air, passed over the dollar and called for the medicine, while the boy crunched his candy, glad to be relieved of the responsibility of the purchase. And then the successful investor searching his pockets, found an overcoat button—the extent of his winter trousseau—and, wrapping it carefully, placed the ostensible change in the pocket of confiding juvenility. Setting the youngster's face homeward, and patting him benevolently on the back—for Chicken's heart was as soft as those of his feathered namesakes—the speculator quit the market with a profit of 1,700 per cent. on his invested capital.

Two hours later an Iron Mountain freight engine pulled out of the railroad yards, Texas bound, with a string of empties. In one of the cattle cars, half buried in excelsior, Chicken lay at ease. Beside him in his nest was a quart bottle of very poor whisky and a paper bag of bread and cheese. Mr. Ruggles, in his private car, was on his trip south for the winter season.

For a week that car was trundled southward, shifted, laid over, and manipulated after the manner of rolling stock, but Chicken stuck to it, leaving it only at necessary times to satisfy his hunger and thirst. He knew it must go down to the cattle country, and San Antonio, in the heart of it, was his goal. There the air was salubrious and mild; the people indulgent and long-suffering. The bartenders there would not kick him. If he should eat too long or too often at one place they would swear at him as if by rote and without heat. They swore so drawlingly, and they rarely paused short of their full vocabulary, which was copious, so that Chicken had often gulped a good meal during the process of the vituperative prohibition. The season there was always spring-like; the plazas were pleasant at night, with music and gayety: except during the slight and infrequent cold snaps one could sleep comfortably out of doors in case the interiors should develop inhospitality.

At Texarkana his car was switched to the I. and G. N. Then still southward it trailed until, at length, it crawled across the Colorado bridge at Austin, and lined out, straight as an arrow, for the run to San Antonio.

When the freight halted at that town Chicken was fast asleep. In ten minutes the train was off again for Laredo, the end of the road. Those empty cattle cars were for distribution along the line at points from which the ranches shipped their stock.

When Chicken awoke his car was stationary. Looking out between the slats he saw it was a bright, moonlit night. Scrambling out, he saw his car with three others abandoned on a little siding in a wild and lonesome country. A cattle pen and chute stood on one side of the track. The railroad bisected a vast, dim ocean of prairie, in the midst of which Chicken, with his futile rolling stock, was as completely stranded as was Robinson with his land-locked boat.

A white post stood near the rails. Going up to it, Chicken read the letters at the top, S. A. 90. Laredo was nearly as far to the south. He was almost a hundred miles from any town. Coyotes began to yelp in the mysterious sea around him. Chicken felt lonesome. He had lived in Boston without an education, in Chicago without nerve, in Philadelphia without a sleeping place, in New York without a pull, and in Pittsburg sober, and yet he had never felt so lonely as now.

Suddenly through the intense silence, he heard the whicker of a horse. The sound came from the side of the track toward the east, and Chicken began to explore timorously in that direction. He stepped high along the mat of curly mesquite grass, for he was afraid of everything there might be in this wilderness—snakes, rats, brigands, centipedes, mirages, cowboys, fandangoes, tarantulas, tamales—he had read of them in the story papers. Rounding a clump of prickly pear that reared high its fantastic and menacing array of rounded heads, he was struck to shivering terror by a snort and a thunderous plunge, as the horse, himself startled, bounded away some fifty yards, and then resumed his grazing. But here was the one thing in the desert that Chicken did not fear. He had been reared on a farm; he had handled horses, understood them, and could ride.

Approaching slowly and speaking soothingly, he followed the animal, which, after its first flight, seemed gentle enough, and secured the end of the twenty-foot lariat that dragged after him in the grass. It required him but a few moments to contrive the rope into an ingenious nose-bridle, after the style of the Mexican *borsal.* In another he was upon the horse's back and off at a splendid lope, giving the animal free choice of direction. "He will take me some where," said Chicken to himself.

It would have been a thing of joy, that untrammelled gallop over the moonlit prairie, even to Chicken, who loathed exertion, but that his mood was not for it. His head ached; a growing thirst was upon him; the "somewhere" whither his lucky mount might convey him was full of dismal peradventure.

And now he noted that the horse moved to a definite goal. Where the prairie lay smooth he kept his course straight as an arrow's toward the east. Deflected by hill or arroyo or impracticable spinous brakes, he quickly flowed again into the current, charted by his unerring instinct. At last, upon the side of a gentle rise, he suddenly subsided to a complacent walk. A stone's cast away stood a little mott of coma trees; beneath it a *jacal* such as the Mexicans erect—a one-room house of upright poles daubed with clay and roofed with grass or tule reeds. An experienced eye would have estimated the spot as the headquarters of a small sheep ranch. In the moonlight the ground in the nearby corral showed pulverized to a level smoothness by the hoofs of the sheep. Everywhere was carelessly distributed the paraphernalia of the place—ropes, bridles, saddles, sheep pelts, wool sacks, feed troughs, and camp litter. The barrel of drinking water stood in the end of the two-horse wagon near the door. The harness was piled, promiscuous, upon the wagon tongue, soaking up the dew.

Chicken slipped to earth, and tied the horse to a tree. He halloed again and again, but the house remained quiet. The door stood open, and he entered cautiously. The light was sufficient for him to see that no one was at home. He struck a match and lighted a lamp that stood on a table. The room was that of a bachelor ranchman who was content with the necessaries of life. Chicken rummaged intelligently until he found what he had hardly dared hope for—a small brown jug that still contained something near a quart of his desire.

Half an hour later, Chicken—now a gamecock of hostile aspect —emerged from the house with unsteady steps. He had drawn upon the absent ranchman's equipment to replace his own ragged attire. He wore a suit of coarse brown ducking, the coat being a sort of rakish bolero, jaunty to a degree. Boots he had donned, and spurs that whirred with every lurching step. Buckled around him was a belt full of cartridges with a big six-shooter in each of its two holsters.

Prowling about, he found blankets, a saddle and bridle with which he caparisoned his steed. Again mounting, he rode swiftly away, singing a loud and tuneless song.

Bud King's band of desperadoes, outlaws and horse and cattle thieves were in camp at a secluded spot on the bank of the Frio. Their depredations in the Rio Grande country, while no bolder than usual, had been advertised more extensively, and Captain Kinney's company of rangers had been ordered down to look after them. Consequently, Bud King, who was a wise general, instead of cutting out a hot trail for the upholders of the law, as his men wished to do, retired for the time to the prickly fastnesses of the Frio valley.

Though the move was a prudent one, and not incompatible with Bud's well-known courage, it raised dissension among the members of the band. In fact, while they thus lay ingloriously *perdu* in the brush, the question of Bud King's fitness for the leadership was argued, with closed doors, as it were, by his followers. Never before had Bud's skill or efficiency been brought to criticism; but his glory was waning (and such is glory's fate) in the light of a newer star. The sentiment of the band was crystallizing into the opinion that Black Eagle could lead them with more luster, profit, and distinction.

This Black Eagle—sub-titled the "Terror of the Border"—had been a member of the gang about three months.

One night while they were in camp on the San Miguel waterhole a solitary horseman on the regulation fiery steed dashed in among them. The newcomer was of portentous and devastating aspect. A beak-like nose with a predatory curve projected above a mass of bristling, blue-black whiskers. His eye was cavernous and fierce. He was spurred, sombreroed, booted, garnished with revolvers, abundantly drunk, and very much unafraid. Few people in the country drained by the Rio Bravo would have cared thus to invade alone the camp of Bud King. But this fell bird swooped fearlessly upon them and demanded to be fed.

Hospitality in the prairie country is not limited. Even if your enemy pass your way you must feed him before you shoot him. You must empty your larder into him before you empty your lead. So the stranger of undeclared intentions was set down to a mighty feast.

A talkative bird he was, full of most marvellous loud tales and exploits, and speaking a language at times obscure but never colorless. He was a new sensation to Bud King's men, who rarely encountered new types. They hung, delighted, upon his vainglorious boasting, the spicy strangeness of his lingo, his contemptuous familiarity with life, the world, and remote places, and the extravagant frankness with which he conveyed his sentiments.

To their guest the band of outlaws seemed to be nothing more than a congregation of country bumpkins whom he was "stringing for grub" just as he would have told his stories at the back door of a farmhouse to wheedle a meal. And, indeed, his ignorance was not without excuse, for the "bad man" of the Southwest does not run to extremes. Those brigands might justly have been taken for a little party of peaceable rustics assembled for a fish-fry or pecan gathering. Gentle of manner, slouching of gait, soft-voiced, unpicturesquely clothed; not one of them presented to the eye any witness of the desperate records they had earned.

For two days the glittering stranger within the camp was feasted. Then, by common consent, he was invited to become a member of the band. He consented, presenting for enrollment the prodigious name of "Captain Montressor." This was immediately overruled by the band, and "Piggy" substituted as a compliment to the awful and insatiate appetite of its owner.

Thus did the Texas border receive the most spectacular brigand that ever rode its chaparral.

For the next three months Bud King conducted business as usual, escaping encounters with law officers and being content with reasonable profits. The band ran off some very good companies of horses from the ranges, and a few bunches of fine cattle which they got safely across the Rio Grande and disposed of to fair advantage. Often the band would ride into the little villages and Mexican settlements, terrorizing the inhabitants and plundering for the provisions and ammunition they needed. It was during these bloodless raids that Piggy's ferocious aspect and frightful voice gained him a renown more widespread and glorious than those other gentle-voiced and sad-faced desperadoes could have acquired in a lifetime.

The Mexicans, most apt in nomenclature, first called him The Black Eagle, and used to frighten the babes by threatening them with tales of the dreadful robber who carried off little children in his great beak. Soon the name extended, and Black Eagle, the Terror of the Border, became a recognized factor in exaggerated newspaper reports and ranch gossip.

The country from the Nueces to the Rio Grande was a wild but fertile stretch, given over to the sheep and cattle ranches. Range was free; the inhabitants were few; the law was mainly a letter, and the pirates met with little opposition until the flaunting and garish Piggy gave the band undue advertisement. Then Kinney's ranger company headed for those precincts, and Bud King knew that it meant grim and sudden war or else temporary retirement. Regarding the risk to be unnecessary, he drew off his band to an almost inaccessible spot on the bank of the Frio. Wherefore, as has been said, dissatisfaction arose among the members, and impeachment proceedings against Bud were premeditated, with Black Eagle in high favor for the succession. Bud King was not unaware of the sentiment, and he called aside Cactus Taylor, his trusted lieutenant, to discuss it.

"If the boys," said Bud, "ain't satisfied with me, I'm willin' to step out. They're buckin' against my way of handlin' 'em. And 'specially because I concludes to hit the brush while Sam Kinney is ridin' the line. I saves 'em from bein' shot or sent up on a state contract, and they up and says I'm no good."

"It ain't so much that," explained Cactus, "as it is they're plum locoed about Piggy. They want them whiskers and that nose of his to split the wind at the head of the column."

"There's somethin' mighty seldom about Piggy," declared Bud, musingly. "I never yet see anything on the hoof that he exactly grades up with. He can shore holler a plenty, and he straddles a hoss from where you laid the chunk. But he ain't never been smoked yet. You know, Cactus, we ain't had a row since he's been with us. Piggy's all right for skearin' the greaser kids and layin' waste a cross-roads store. I reckon he's the finest canned oyster buccaneer and cheese pirate that ever was, but how's his appetite for fightin'? I've knowed some citizens you'd think was starvin' for trouble get a bad case of dyspepsy the first dose of lead they had to take."

"He talks all spraddled out," said Cactus, "'bout the rookuses he's been in. He claims to have saw the elephant and hearn the owl."

"I know," replied Bud, using the cow-puncher's expressive phrase of skepticism, "but it sounds to me!"

This conversation was held one night in camp while the other members of the band—eight in number—were sprawling around the fire, lingering over their supper. When Bud and Cactus ceased talking they heard Piggy's formidable voice holding forth to the others as usual while he was engaged in checking, though never satisfying, his ravening appetite.

"Wat's de use," he was saying, "of chasin' little red cowses and hosses 'round for t'ousands of miles? Dere ain't nuttin' in it. Gallopin' t'rough dese bushes and briers, and gettin' a t'irst dat a brewery couldn't put out, and missin' meals! Say! You know what I'd do if I was main finger of dis bunch? I'd stick up a train. I'd blow de express car and make hard dollars where you guys get wind. Youse makes me tired. Dis sook-cow kind of cheap sport gives me a pain."

Later on, a deputation waited on Bud. They stood on one leg, chewed mesquite twigs and circumlocuted, for they hated to hurt his feelings. Bud foresaw their business, and made it easy for them. Bigger risks and larger profits was what they wanted.

The suggestion of Piggy's about holding up a train had fired their imagination and increased their admiration for the dash and boldness of the instigator. They were such simple, artless, and custom-bound bush-rangers that they had never before thought of extending their habits beyond the running off of live-stock and the shooting of such of their acquaintances as ventured to interfere.

Bud acted "on the level," agreeing to take a subordinate place in the gang until Black Eagle should have been given a trial as leader.

After a great deal of consultation, studying of time-tables and discussion of the country's topography, the time and place for carrying out their new enterprise was decided upon. At that time there was a feedstuff famine in Mexico and a cattle famine in certain parts of the United States, and there was a brisk international trade. Much money was being shipped along the railroads that connected the two republics. It was agreed that the most promising place for the contemplated robbery was at Espina, a little station on the I. and G. N., about forty miles north of Laredo. The train stopped there one minute; the country around was wild and unsettled; the station consisted of but one house in which the agent lived.

Black Eagle's band set out, riding by night. Arriving in the vicinity of Espina they rested their horses all day in a thicket a few miles distant.

The train was due at Espina at 10:30 P.M. They could rob the train and be well over the Mexican border with their booty by daylight the next morning.

To do Black Eagle justice, he exhibited no signs of flinching from the responsible honors that had been conferred upon him.

He assigned his men to their respective posts with discretion, and coached them carefully as to their duties. On each side of the track four of the band were to lie concealed in the chaparral. Gotch-Ear Rodgers was to stick up the station agent. Bronco Charlie was to remain with the horses, holding them in readiness. At a spot where it was calculated the engine would be when the train stopped, Bud King was to lie hidden on one side, and Black Eagle himself on the other. The two would get the drop on the engineer and fireman, force them to descend and proceed to the rear. Then the express car would be looted, and the escape made. No one was to move until Black Eagle gave the signal by firing his revolver. The plan was perfect.

At ten minutes to train time every man was at his post, effectually concealed by the thick chaparral that grew almost to the rails. The night was dark and lowering, with a fine drizzle falling from the flying gulf clouds. Black Eagle crouched behind a bush within five yards of the track. Two six-shooters were belted around him. Occasionally he drew a large black bottle from his pocket and raised it to his mouth.

A star appeared far down the track which soon waxed into the headlight of the approaching train. It came on with an increasing roar; the engine bore down upon the ambushing desperadoes with a glare and a shriek like some avenging monster come to deliver them to justice. Black Eagle flattened himself upon the ground. The engine, contrary to their calculations, instead of stopping between him and Bud King's place of concealment, passed fully forty yards farther before it came to a stand.

The bandit leader rose to his feet and peered around the bush. His men all lay quiet, awaiting the signal. Immediately opposite Black Eagle was a thing that drew his attention. Instead of being a regular passenger train it was a mixed one. Before him stood a box car, the door of which, by some means, had been left slightly open. Black Eagle went up to it and pushed the door farther open. An odor came forth—a damp, rancid, familiar, musty, intoxicating, beloved odor stirring strongly at old memories of happy days and travels. Black Eagle sniffed at the witching smell as the returned wanderer smells of the rose that twines his boyhood's cottage home. Nostalgia seized him. He put his hand inside. Excelsior—dry, springy, curly, soft, enticing, covered the floor. Outside the drizzle had turned to a chilling rain.

The train bell clanged. The bandit chief unbuckled his belt and cast it, with its revolvers, upon the ground. His spurs followed quickly, and his broad sombrero. Black Eagle was moulting. The train started with a rattling jerk. The ex-Terror of the Border scrambled into the box car and closed the door. Stretched luxuriously upon the excelsior, with the black bottle clasped closely to his breast, his eyes closed, and a foolish, happy smile upon his terrible features Chicken Ruggles started upon his return trip.

Undisturbed, with the band of desperate bandits lying motionless, awaiting the signal to attack, the train pulled out from Espina. As its speed increased, and the black masses of chaparral went whizzing past on either side, the express messenger, lighting his pipe, looked through his window and remarked, feelingly:

"What a jim-dandy place for a hold-up!"

A Retrieved Reformation

A GUARD came to the prison shoe-shop, where Jimmy Valentine was assiduously stitching uppers, and escorted him to the front office. There the warden handed Jimmy his pardon, which had been signed that morning by the governor. Jimmy took it in a tired kind of way. He had served nearly ten months of a four-year sentence. He had expected to stay only about three months, at the longest. When a man with as many friends on the outside as Jimmy Valentine had is received in the "stir" it is hardly worth while to cut his hair.

"Now, Valentine," said the warden, "you'll go out in the morning. Brace up, and make a man of yourself. You're not a bad fellow at heart. Stop cracking safes, and live straight."

"Me?" said Jimmy, in surprise. "Why, I never cracked a safe in my life."

"Oh, no," laughed the warden. "Of course not. Let's see, now. How was it you happened to get sent up on that Springfield job? Was it because you wouldn't prove an alibi for fear of compromising somebody in extremely high-toned society? Or was it simply a case of a mean old jury that had it in for you? It's always one or the other with you innocent victims."

"Me?" said Jimmy, still blankly virtuous. "Why, warden, I never was in Springfield in my life!"

"Take him back, Cronin," smiled the warden, "and fix him up with outgoing clothes. Unlock him at seven in the morning, and let him come to the bull-pen. Better think over my advice, Valentine."

At a quarter past seven on the next morning Jimmy stood in the warden's outer office. He had on a suit of the villainously fitting, ready-made clothes and a pair of the stiff, squeaky shoes that the state furnishes to its discharged compulsory guests.

The clerk handed him a railroad ticket and the five-dollar bill with which the law expected him to rehabilitate himself into good citizenship and prosperity. The warden gave him a cigar, and shook hands. Valentine, 9762, was chronicled on the books "Pardoned by Governor," and Mr. James Valentine walked out into the sunshine.

Disregarding the song of the birds, the waving green trees, and the smell of the flowers, Jimmy headed straight for a restaurant. There he tasted the first sweet joys of liberty in the shape of a broiled chicken and a bottle of white wine—followed by a cigar a grade better than the one the warden had given him. From there he proceeded leisurely to the depot. He tossed a quarter into the hat of a blind man sitting by the door, and boarded his train. Three hours set him down in a little town near the state line. He went to the café of one Mike Dolan and shook hands with Mike, who was alone behind the bar.

"Sorry we couldn't make it sooner, Jimmy, me boy," said Mike. "But we had that protest from Springfield to buck against, and the governor nearly balked. Feeling all right?"

"Fine," said Jimmy. "Got my key?"

He got his key and went upstairs, unlocking the door of a room at the rear. Everything was just as he had left it. There on the floor was still Ben Price's collar-button that had been torn from that eminent detective's shirt-band when they had over-powered Jimmy to arrest him.

Pulling out from the wall a folding-bed, Jimmy slid back a panel in the wall and dragged out a dust-covered suitcase. He opened this and gazed fondly at the finest set of burglar's tools in the East. It was a complete set, made of specially tempered steel, the latest designs in drills, punches, braces and bits, jimmies, clamps, and augers, with two or three novelties invented by Jimmy himself, in which he took pride. Over nine hundred dollars they had cost him to have made at ——, a place where they make such things for the profession.

In half an hour Jimmy went downstairs and through the café. He was now dressed in tasteful and well-fitting clothes, and carried his dusted and cleaned suitcase in his hand.

"Got anything on?" asked Mike Dolan, genially.

"Me?" said Jimmy, in a puzzled tone. "I don't understand. I'm representing the New York Amalgamated Short Snap Biscuit Cracker and Frazzled Wheat Company."

This statement delighted Mike to such an extent that Jimmy had to take a seltzer-and-milk on the spot. He never touched "hard" drinks.

A week after the release of Valentine, 9762, there was a neat job of safe-burglary done in Richmond, Indiana, with no clue to the author. A scant eight hundred dollars was all that was secured. Two weeks after that a patented, improved, burglar-proof safe in Logansport was opened like a cheese to the tune of fifteen hundred dollars, currency; securities and silver untouched. That began to interest the rogue-catchers. Then an old-fashioned bank-safe in Jefferson City became active and threw out of its crater an eruption of bank-notes amounting to five thousand dollars. The losses were now high enough to bring the matter up into Ben Price's class of work. By comparing notes, a remarkable similarity in the methods of the burglaries was noticed. Ben Price investigated the scenes of the robberies, and was heard to remark:

"That's Dandy Jim Valentine's autograph. He's resumed business. Look at that combination knob—jerked out as easy as pulling up a radish in wet weather. He's got the only clamps that can do it. And look how clean those tumblers were punched out! Jimmy never has to drill but one hole. Yes, I guess I want Mr. Valentine. He'll do his bit next time without any short-time or clemency foolishness."

Ben Price knew Jimmy's habits. He had learned them while working up the Springfield case. Long jumps, quick get-aways, no confederates, and a taste for good society—these ways had helped Mr. Valentine to become noted as a successful dodger of retribution. It was given out that Ben Price had taken up the trail of the elusive cracksman, and other people with burglar-proof safes felt more at ease.

One afternoon Jimmy Valentine and his suitcase climbed out of the mail-hack in Elmore, a little town five miles off the railroad down in the black-jack country of Arkansas. Jimmy, looking like an athletic young senior just home from college, went down the board sidewalk toward the hotel.

A young lady crossed the street, passed him at the corner and entered a door over which was the sign "The Elmore Bank." Jimmy Valentine looked into her eyes, forgot what he was, and became another man. She lowered her eyes and colored slightly. Young men of Jimmy's style and looks were scarce in Elmore.

Jimmy collared a boy that was loafing on the steps of the bank as if he were one of the stock-holders, and began to ask him questions about the town, feeding him dimes at intervals. By and by the young lady came out, looking royally unconscious of the young man with the suitcase, and went her way.

"Isn't that young lady Miss Polly Simpson?" asked Jimmy, with specious guile.

"Naw," said the boy. "She's Annabel Adams. Her pa owns this bank. What'd you come to Elmore for? Is that a gold watch-chain? I'm going to get a bulldog. Got any more dimes?"

Jimmy went to the Planters' Hotel, registered as Ralph D. Spencer, and engaged a room. He leaned on the desk and declared his platform to the clerk. He said he had come to Elmore to look for a location to go into business. How was the shoe business, now, in the town? He had thought of the shoe business. Was there an opening?

The clerk was impressed by the clothes and manner of Jimmy. He, himself, was something of a pattern of fashion to the thinly gilded youth of Elmore, but he now perceived his shortcomings. While trying to figure out Jimmy's manner of tying his four-in-hand he cordially gave information.

Yes, there ought to be a good opening in the shoe line. There wasn't an exclusive shoe-store in the place. The dry-goods and general stores handled them. Business in all lines was fairly good. Hoped Mr. Spencer would decide to locate in Elmore. He would find it a pleasant town to live in, and the people very sociable.

Mr. Spencer thought he would stop over in the town a few days and look over the situation. No, the clerk needn't call the boy. He would carry up his suitcase, himself; it was rather heavy.

Mr. Ralph Spencer, the phœnix that arose from Jimmy Valentine's ashes—ashes left by the flame of a sudden and alternative attack of love—remained in Elmore, and prospered. He opened a shoe-store and secured a good run of trade.

Socially he was also a success, and made many friends. And he accomplished the wish of his heart. He met Miss Annabel Adams, and became more and more captivated by her charms.

At the end of a year the situation of Mr. Ralph Spencer was this: he had won the respect of the community, his shoe-store was flourishing, and he and Annabel were engaged to be married in two weeks. Mr. Adams, the typical, plodding, country banker, approved of Spencer. Annabel's pride in him almost equalled her affection. He was as much at home in the family of Mr. Adams and that of Annabel's married sister as if he were already a member.

One day Jimmy sat down in his room and wrote this letter, which he mailed to the safe address of one of his old friends in St. Louis:

Dear Old Pal:

I want you to be at Sullivan's place, in Little Rock, next Wednesday night at nine o'clock. I want you to wind up some little matters for me. And, also, I want to make you a present of my kit of tools. I know you'll be glad to get them —you couldn't duplicate the lot for a thousand dollars. Say,

Billy, I've quit the old business—a year ago. I've got a nice store. I'm making an honest living, and I'm going to marry the finest girl on earth two weeks from now. It's the only life, Billy—the straight one. I wouldn't touch a dollar of another man's money now for a million. After I get married I'm going to sell out and go West, where there won't be so much danger of having old scores brought up against me. I tell you, Billy, she's an angel. She believes in me; and I wouldn't do another crooked thing for the whole world. Be sure to be at Sully's, for I must see you. I'll bring along the tools with me.

Your old friend,
Jimmy

On the Monday night after Jimmy wrote this letter, Ben Price jogged unobtrusively into Elmore in a livery buggy. He lounged about town in his quiet way until he found out what he wanted to know. From the drug-store across the street from Spencer's shoe-store he got a good look at Ralph D. Spencer.

"Going to marry the banker's daughter are you, Jimmy?" said Ben to himself, softly. "Well, I don't know!"

The next morning Jimmy took breakfast at the Adamses. He was going to Little Rock that day to order his wedding-suit and buy something nice for Annabel. That would be the first time he had left town since he came to Elmore. It had been more than a year now since those last professional "jobs," and he thought he could safely venture out.

After breakfast quite a family party went down town together —Mr. Adams, Annabel, Jimmy, and Annabel's married sister with her two little girls, aged five and nine. They came by the hotel where Jimmy still boarded, and he ran up to his room and brought along his suitcase. Then they went on to the bank. There stood Jimmy's horse and buggy and Dolph Gibson, who was going to drive him over to the railroad station.

All went inside the high, carved oak railings into the banking-

room—Jimmy included, for Mr. Adams's future son-in-law was welcome anywhere. The clerks were pleased to be greeted by the
good-looking, agreeable young man who was going to marry Miss
Annabel. Jimmy set his suitcase down. Annabel, whose heart was
bubbling with happiness and lively youth, put on Jimmy's hat
and picked up the suitcase. "Wouldn't I make a nice drummer?"
said Annabel. "My! Ralph, how heavy it is. Feels like it was full of
gold bricks."

"Lot of nickel-plated shoe-horns in there," said Jimmy, coolly,
"that I'm going to return. Thought I'd save express charges by taking them up. I'm getting awfully economical."

The Elmore Bank had just put in a new safe and vault. Mr.
Adams was very proud of it, and insisted on an inspection by
every one. The vault was a small one, but it had a new patented
door. It fastened with three solid steel bolts thrown simultaneously
with a single handle, and had a time-lock. Mr. Adams beamingly
explained its workings to Mr. Spencer, who showed a courteous
but not too intelligent interest. The two children, May and
Agatha, were delighted by the shining metal and funny clock and
knobs.

While they were thus engaged Ben Price sauntered in and
leaned on his elbow, looking casually inside between the railings.
He told the teller that he didn't want anything; he was just waiting for a man he knew.

Suddenly there was a scream or two from the women, and a
commotion. Unperceived by the elders, May, the nine-year-old
girl, in a spirit of play, had shut Agatha in the vault. She had
then shot the bolts and turned the knob of the combination as she
had seen Mr. Adams do.

The old banker sprang to the handle and tugged at it for a moment. "The door can't be opened," he groaned. "The clock hasn't
been wound nor the combination set."

Agatha's mother screamed again, hysterically.

"Hush!" said Mr. Adams, raising his trembling hand. "All be
quiet for a moment, Agatha!" he called as loudly as he could:

"Listen to me." During the following silence they could just hear the faint sound of the child wildly shrieking in the dark vault in a panic of terror.

"My precious darling!" wailed the mother. "She will die of fright! Open the door! Oh, break it open! Can't you men do something?"

"There isn't a man nearer than Little Rock who can open that door," said Mr. Adams, in a shaky voice. "My God! Spencer, what shall we do? That child—she can't stand it long in there. There isn't enough air, and, besides, she'll go into convulsions from fright."

Agatha's mother, frantic now, beat the door of the vault with her hands. Somebody wildly suggested dynamite. Annabel turned to Jimmy, her large eyes full of anguish, but not yet despairing. To a woman nothing seems quite impossible to the powers of the man she worships.

"Can't you do something, Ralph—*try*, won't you?"

He looked at her with a queer, soft smile on his lips and in his keen eyes.

"Annabel," he said, "give me that rose you are wearing, will you?"

Hardly believing that she heard him aright, she unpinned the bud from the bosom of her dress, and placed it in his hand. Jimmy stuffed it into his vest-pocket, threw off his coat and pulled up his shirt-sleeves. With that act Ralph D. Spencer passed away and Jimmy Valentine took his place.

"Get away from the door, all of you," he commanded, shortly.

He set his suitcase on the table, and opened it out flat. From that time on he seemed to be unconscious of the presence of any one else. He laid out the shining, queer implements swiftly and orderly, whistling softly to himself as he always did when at work. In a deep silence and immovable, the others watched him as if under a spell.

In a minute Jimmy's pet drill was biting smoothly into the steel door. In ten minutes—breaking his own burglarious record—he threw back the bolts and opened the door.

Agatha, almost collapsed, but safe, was gathered into her mother's arms.

Jimmy Valentine put on his coat, and walked outside the railings toward the front door. As he went he thought he heard a far-away voice that he once knew call "Ralph!" But he never hesitated.

At the door a big man stood somewhat in his way.

"Hello, Ben!" said Jimmy, still with his strange smile. "Got around at last, have you? Well, let's go. I don't know that it makes much difference, now."

And then Ben Price acted rather strangely.

"Guess you're mistaken, Mr. Spencer," he said. "Don't believe I recognize you. Your buggy's waiting for you, ain't it?"

And Ben Price turned and strolled down the street.

Friends in San Rosario

THE WEST-BOUND stopped at San Rosario on time at 8:20 A.M. A man with a thick black-leather wallet under his arm left the train and walked rapidly up the main street of the town. There were other passengers who also got off at San Rosario, but they either slouched limberly over to the railroad eating-house or the Silver Dollar saloon, or joined the groups of idlers about the station.

Indecision had no part in the movements of the man with the wallet. He was short in stature, but strongly built, with very light, closely trimmed hair, smooth, determined face, and aggressive, gold-rimmed nose glasses. He was well dressed in the prevailing Eastern style. His air denoted a quiet but conscious reserve force, if not actual authority.

After walking a distance of three squares he came to the center of the town's business area. Here another street of importance crossed the main one, forming the hub of San Rosario's life and commerce. Upon one corner stood the postoffice. Upon another Rubensky's Clothing Emporium. The other two diagonally opposing corners were occupied by the town's two banks, the First National and the Stockmen's National. Into the First National Bank of San Rosario the newcomer walked, never slowing his brisk step until he stood at the cashier's window. The bank opened for business at nine, and the working force was already assembled, each member preparing his department for the day's business. The cashier was examining the mail when he noticed the stranger standing at his window.

"Bank doesn't open 'til nine," he remarked, curtly, but without feeling. He had had to make that statement so often to early birds since San Rosario adopted city banking hours.

"I am well aware of that," said the other man, in cool, brittle tones. "Will you kindly receive my card?"

The cashier drew the small, spotless parallelogram inside the bars of his wicket, and read:

| J. F. C. NETTLEWICK |
| NATIONAL BANK EXAMINER |

"Oh—er—will you walk around inside, Mr.—er—Nettlewick. Your first visit—didn't know your business, of course. Walk right around, please."

The examiner was quickly inside the sacred precincts of the bank, where he was ponderously introduced to each employee in turn by Mr. Edlinger, the cashier—a middle-aged gentleman of deliberation, discretion, and method.

"I was kind of expecting Sam Turner round again, pretty soon," said Mr. Edlinger. "Sam's been examining us now for about four years. I guess you'll find us all right, though considering the tightness in business. Not overly much money on hand, but able to stand the storms, sir, stand the storms."

"Mr. Turner and I have been ordered by the Comptroller to exchange districts," said the examiner, in his decisive, formal tones. "He is covering my old territory in southern Illinois and Indiana. I will take the cash first, please."

Perry Dorsey, the teller, was already arranging his cash on the counter for the examiner's inspection. He knew it was right to a cent, and he had nothing to fear, but he was nervous and flustered. So was every man in the bank. There was something so icy and swift, so impersonal and uncompromising about this man that his very presence seemed an accusation. He looked to be a man who would never make nor overlook an error.

Mr. Nettlewick first seized the currency, and with a rapid, almost juggling motion, counted it by packages. Then he spun the sponge cup toward him and verified the count by bills. His thin, white fingers flew like some expert musician's upon the keys of a piano. He dumped the gold upon the counter with a crash, and the coins whined and sang as they skimmed across the marble slab from the tips of his nimble digits. The air was full of fractional currency when he came to the halves and quarters. He counted the last nickel and dime. He had the scales brought, and he weighed every sack of silver in the vault. He questioned Dorsey concerning each of the cash memoranda—certain checks, charge slips, etc., carried over from the previous day's work—with unimpeachable courtesy, yet with something so mysteriously momentous in his frigid manner, that the teller was reduced to pink cheeks and a stammering tongue.

This newly imported examiner was so different from Sam Turner. It had been Sam's way to enter the bank with a shout, pass the cigars, and tell the latest stories he had picked up on his rounds. His customary greeting to Dorsey had been, "Hello, Perry! Haven't skipped out with the boodle yet, I see." Turner's way of counting the cash had been different too. He would finger the packages of bills in a tired kind of way, and then go into the vault and kick over a few sacks of silver, and the thing was done. Halves and quarters and dimes? Not for Sam Turner. "No chicken feed for me," he would say when they were set before him. "I'm not in the agricultural department." But, then, Turner was a Texan, an old friend of the bank's president, and had known Dorsey since he was a baby.

While the examiner was counting the cash, Major Thomas B. Kingman—known to every one as "Major Tom"—the president of the First National, drove up to the side door with his old dun horse and buggy, and came inside. He saw the examiner busy with the money, and, going into the little "pony corral," as he called it, in which his desk was railed off, he began to look over his letters.

Earlier, a little incident had occurred that even the sharp eyes of the examiner had failed to notice. When he had begun his work at the cash counter, Mr. Edlinger had winked significantly at Roy Wilson, the youthful bank messenger, and nodded his head slightly toward the front door. Roy understood, got his hat and walked leisurely out, with his collector's book under his arm. Once outside, he made a beeline for the Stockmen's National. That bank was also getting ready to open. No customers had, as yet, presented themselves.

"Say, you people!" cried Roy, with the familiarity of youth and long acquaintance, "you want to get a move on you. There's a new bank examiner over at the First, and he's a stem-winder. He's counting nickels on Perry, and he's got the whole outfit bluffed. Mr. Edlinger gave me the tip to let you know."

Mr. Buckley, president of the Stockmen's National—a stout, elderly man, looking like a farmer dressed for Sunday—heard Roy from his private office at the rear and called him.

"Has Major Kingman come down to the bank yet?" he asked of the boy.

"Yes, sir, he was just driving up as I left," said Roy.

"I want you to take him a note. Put it into his own hands as soon as you get back."

Mr. Buckley sat down and began to write.

Roy returned and handed to Major Kingman the envelope containing the note. The major read it, folded it, and slipped it into his vest pocket. He leaned back in his chair for a few moments as if he were meditating deeply, and then rose and went into the vault. He came out with the bulky, old-fashioned leather note case stamped on the back in gilt letters, "Bills Discounted." In this were the notes due the bank with their attached securities, and the major, in his rough way, dumped the lot upon his desk and began to sort them over.

By this time Nettlewick had finished his count of the cash. His pencil fluttered like a swallow over the sheet of paper on which he had set his figures. He opened his black wallet, which seemed to be also a kind of secret memorandum book, made a few rapid figures in it, wheeled and transfixed Dorsey with the glare of his spectacles. That look seemed to say: "You're safe this time, but——"

"Cash all correct," snapped the examiner. He made a dash for the individual bookkeeper, and, for a few minutes there was a fluttering of ledger leaves and a sailing of balance sheets through the air.

"How often do you balance your pass-books?" he demanded, suddenly.

"Er—once a month," faltered the individual bookkeeper, wondering how many years they would give him.

"All right," said the examiner, turning and charging upon the general bookkeeper, who had the statements of his foreign banks and their reconcilement memoranda ready. Everything there was found to be all right. Then the stub book of the certificates of deposit. Flutter—flutter—zip—zip—check! All right, list of overdrafts, please. Thanks. H'm-m. Unsigned bills of the bank next. All right.

Then came the cashier's turn, and easy-going Mr. Edlinger rubbed his nose and polished his glasses nervously under the quick fire of questions concerning the circulation, undivided profits, bank real estate, and stock ownership.

Presently Nettlewick was aware of a big man towering above him at his elbow—a man sixty years of age, rugged and hale, with a rough, grizzled beard, a mass of gray hair, and a pair of penetrating blue eyes that confronted the formidable glasses of the examiner without a flicker.

"Er—Major Kingman, our president—er—Mr. Nettlewick," said the cashier.

Two men of very different types shook hands. One was a finished product of the world of straight lines, conventional methods, and formal affairs. The other was something freer, wider, and nearer to nature. Tom Kingman had not been cut to any pattern. He had been mule-driver, cowboy, ranger, soldier, sheriff, prospector and cattleman. Now, when he was bank president, his old comrades from the prairies, of the saddle, tent, and trail, found no change in him. He had made his fortune when Texas cattle were at the high tide of value, and had organized the First National Bank of San Rosario. In spite of his largeness of heart and sometimes unwise generosity toward his old friends, the bank had prospered, for Major Tom Kingman knew men as well as he knew cattle. Of late years the cattle business had known a depression, and the major's bank was one of the few whose losses had not been great.

"And now," said the examiner, briskly, pulling out his watch, "the last thing is the loans. We will take them up now, if you please."

He had gone through the First National at almost record-breaking speed—but thoroughly, as he did everything. The running order of the bank was smooth and clean, and that had facilitated his work. There was but one other bank in the town. He received from the Government a fee of twenty-five dollars for each bank that he examined. He should be able to go over those loans and discounts in half an hour. If so, he could examine the other bank immediately afterward, and catch the 11:45, the only other train that day in the direction he was working. Otherwise, he would have to spend the night and Sunday in this uninteresting Western town. That was why Mr. Nettlewick was rushing matters.

"Come with me, sir," said Major Kingman, in his deep voice, that united the Southern drawl with the rhythmic twang of the West. "We will go over them together. Nobody in the bank knows those notes as I do. Some of 'em are a little wobbly on their legs, and some are mavericks without extra many brands on their backs, but they'll 'most all pay out at the round-up."

The two sat down at the president's desk. First, the examiner went through the notes at lightning speed, and added up their total, finding it to agree with the amount of loans carried on the book of daily balances. Next, he took up the larger loans, inquiring scrupulously into the condition of their endorsers or

securities. The new examiner's mind seemed to course and turn
and make unexpected dashes hither and thither like a blood-
hound seeking a trail. Finally he pushed aside all the notes
except a few, which he arranged in a neat pile before him, and
began a dry, formal little speech.

"I find, sir, the condition of your bank to be very good, considering the poor crops and the depression in the cattle interests
of your state. The clerical work seems to be done accurately and
punctually. Your past-due paper is moderate in amount, and
promises only a small loss. I would recommend the calling in of
your large loans, and the making of only sixty and ninety day or
call loans until general business revives. And now, there is one
thing more, and I will have finished with the bank. Here are
six notes aggregating something like $40,000. They are secured,
according to their faces, by various stocks, bonds, shares, etc., to
the value of $70,000. Those securities are missing from the notes
to which they should be attached. I suppose you have them in
the safe or vault. You will permit me to examine them."

Major Tom's light-blue eyes turned unflinchingly toward the
examiner.

"No, sir," he said, in a low but steady tone; "those securities
are neither in the safe nor the vault. I have taken them. You
may hold me personally responsible for their absence."

Nettlewick felt a slight thrill. He had not expected this. He
had struck a momentous trail when the hunt was drawing to a
close.

"Ah!" said the examiner. He waited a moment, and then continued: "May I ask you to explain more definitely?"

"The securities were taken by me," repeated the major. "It
was not for my own use, but to save an old friend in trouble.
Come in here, sir, and we'll talk it over."

He led the examiner into the bank's private office at the rear,
and closed the door. There was a desk, and a table, and half-a-
dozen leather-covered chairs. On the wall was the mounted head
of a Texas steer with horns five feet from tip to tip. Opposite

hung the major's old cavalry saber that he had carried at Shiloh and Fort Pillow.

Placing a chair for Nettlewick, the major seated himself by the window, from which he could see the post-office and the carved limestone front of the Stockmen's National. He did not speak at once, and Nettlewick felt, perhaps, that the ice should be broken by something so near its own temperature as the voice of official warning.

"Your statement," he began, "since you have failed to modify it, amounts, as you must know, to a very serious thing. You are aware, also, of what my duty must compel me to do. I shall have to go before the United States Commissioner and make——"

"I know, I know," said Major Tom, with a wave of his hand. "You don't suppose I'd run a bank without being posted on national banking laws and the revised statutes! Do your duty. I'm not asking any favors. But I spoke of my friend. I did want you to hear me tell about Bob."

Nettlewick settled himself in his chair. There would be no leaving San Rosario for him that day. He would have to telegraph to the Comptroller of the Currency; he would have to swear out a warrant before the United States Commissioner for the arrest of Major Kingman; perhaps he would be ordered to close the bank on account of the loss of the securities. It was not the first crime the examiner had unearthed. Once or twice the terrible upheaval of human emotions that his investigations had loosed had almost caused a ripple in his official calm. He had seen bank men kneel and plead and cry like women for a chance —an hour's time—the overlooking of a single error. One cashier had shot himself at his desk before him. None of them had taken it with the dignity and coolness of this stern old Westerner. Nettlewick felt that he owed it to him at least to listen if he wished to talk. With his elbow on the arm of his chair, and his square chin resting upon the fingers of his right hand, the bank examiner waited to hear the confession of the president of the First National Bank of San Rosario.

"When a man's your friend," began Major Tom, somewhat di-
dactically, "for forty years, and tried by water, fire, earth, and
cyclones, when you can do him a little favor you feel like doing
it."

("Embezzle for him $70,000 worth of securities," thought the
examiner.)

"We were cowboys together, Bob and I," contined the major,
speaking slowly, and deliberately, and musingly, as if his thoughts
were rather with the past than the critical present, "and we pros-
pected together for gold and silver over Arizona, New Mexico,
and a good part of California. We were both in the war of sixty-
one, but in different commands. We've fought Indians and horse
thieves side by side; we've starved for weeks in a cabin in the
Arizona mountains, buried twenty feet deep in snow; we've ridden herd together when the wind blew so hard the lightning
couldn't strike—well, Bob and I have been through some rough
spells since the first time we met in the branding camp of
the old Anchor-Bar ranch. And during that time we've found it
necessary more than once to help each other out of tight places.
In those days it was expected of a man to stick to his friend, and
he didn't ask any credit for it. Probably next day you'd need him
to get at your back and help stand off a band of Apaches, or put
a tourniquet on your leg above a rattlesnake bite and ride for
whisky. So, after all, it was give and take, and if you didn't stand
square with your pardner, why, you might be shy one when you
needed him. But Bob was a man who was willing to go further
than that. He never played a limit.

"Twenty years ago I was sheriff of this county and I made Bob
my chief deputy. That was before the boom in cattle when we
both made our stake. I was sheriff and collector, and it was a
big thing for me then. I was married, and we had a boy and a
girl—a four and a six year old. There was a comfortable house
next to the courthouse, furnished by the county, rent free, and I
was saving some money. Bob did most of the office work. Both of
us had seen rough times and plenty of rustling and danger, and I

tell you it was great to hear the rain and the sleet dashing against the windows of nights, and be warm and safe and comfortable, and know you could get up in the morning and be shaved and have folks call you 'mister.' And then, I had the finest wife and kids that ever struck the range, and my old friend with me enjoying the first fruits of prosperity and white shirts, and I guess I was happy. Yes, I was happy about that time."

The major sighed and glanced casually out of the window. The bank examiner changed his position, and leaned his chin upon his other hand.

"One winter," continued the major, "the money for the county taxes came pouring in so fast that I didn't have time to take the stuff to the bank for a week. I just shoved the checks into a cigar box and the money into a sack, and locked them in the big safe that belonged in the sheriff's office.

"I had been overworked that week, and was about sick, anyway. My nerves were out of order, and my sleep at night didn't seem to rest me. The doctor had some scientific name for it, and I was taking medicine. And so, added to the rest, I went to bed at night with that money on my mind. Not that there was much need of being worried, for the safe was a good one, and nobody but Bob and I knew the combination. On Friday night there was about $6,500 in cash in the bag. On Saturday morning I went to the office as usual. The safe was locked, and Bob was writing at his desk. I opened the safe, and the money was gone. I called Bob, and roused everybody in the courthouse to announce the robbery. It struck me that Bob took it pretty quiet, considering how much it reflected upon both him and me.

"Two days went by and we never got a clew. It couldn't have been burglars, for the safe had been opened by the combination in the proper way. People must have begun to talk, for one afternoon in comes Alice—that's my wife—and the boy and girl, and Alice stamps her foot, and her eyes flash, and she cries out, 'The lying wretches—Tom, Tom!' and I catch her in a faint, and bring her 'round little by little, and she lays her head down and cries

and cries for the first time since she took Tom Kingman's name
and fortunes. And Jack and Zilla—the youngsters—they were always wild as tigers cubs to rush at Bob and climb all over him
whenever they were allowed to come to the courthouse—they
stood and kicked their little shoes, and herded together like
scared partridges. They were having their first trip down into the
shadows of life. Bob was working at his desk, and he got up and
went out without a word. The grand jury was in session then, and
the next morning Bob went before them and confessed that he
stole the money. He said he lost it in a poker game. In fifteen
minutes they had found a true bill and sent me the warrant to
arrest the man with whom I'd been closer than a thousand
brothers for many a year.

"I did it, and then I said to Bob, pointing: 'There's my house,
and here's my office, and up there's Maine, and out that way is
California, and over there is Florida—and that's your range 'til
court meets. You're in my charge, and I take the responsibility.
You be here when you're wanted.'

" 'Thanks, Tom,' he said, kind of carelessly; 'I was sort of
hoping you wouldn't lock me up. Court meets next Monday, so,
if you don't object, I'll just loaf around the office until then.
I've got one favor to ask, if it isn't too much. If you'd let the kids
come out in the yard once in a while and have a romp I'd like
it.'

" 'Why not?' I answered him. 'They're welcome, and so are
you. And come to my house the same as ever.' You see, Mr. Nettlewick, you can't make a friend of a thief, but neither can you
make a thief of a friend, all at once."

The examiner made no answer. At that moment was heard the
shrill whistle of a locomotive pulling into the depot. That was
the train on the little, narrow-gauge road that struck into San
Rosario from the south. The major cocked his ear and listened for
a moment, and looked at his watch. The narrow-gauge was in
on time—10:35. The major continued.

"So Bob hung around the office, reading the papers and smoking. I put another deputy to work in his place, and, after a while, the first excitement of the case wore off.

"One day when we were alone in the office Bob came over to where I was sitting. He was looking sort of grim and blue—the same look he used to get when he'd been up watching for Indians all night or herd-riding.

"'Tom,' says he, 'it's harder than standing off redskins; it's harder than lying in the lava desert forty miles from water; but I'm going to stick it out to the end. You know that's been my style. But if you'd tip me the smallest kind of a sign—if you'd just say, "Bob I understand," why, it would makes it lots easier.'

"I was surprised. 'I don't know what you mean, Bob,' I said. 'Of course, you know that I'd do anything under the sun to help you that I could. But you've got me guessing.'

"'All right, Tom,' was all he said, and he went back to his newspaper and lit another cigar.

"It was the night before the court met when I found out what he meant. I went to bed that night with the same old, light-headed, nervous feeling come back upon me. I dropped off to sleep about midnight. When I woke I was standing half dressed in one of the courthouse corridors. Bob was holding one of my arms, our family doctor the other and Alice was shaking me and half crying. She had sent for the doctor without my knowing it, and when he came they had found me out of bed and missing, and had begun a search.

"'Sleep-walking,' said the doctor.

"All of us went back to the house, and the doctor told us some remarkable stories about the strange things people had done while in that condition. I was feeling rather chilly after my trip out, and, as my wife was out of the room at the time, I pulled open the door of an old wardrobe that stood in the room and dragged out a big quilt I had seen in there. With it tumbled out the bag of money for stealing which Bob was to be tried—and convicted—in the morning.

"'How the jumping rattlesnakes did that get there?' I yelled, and all hands must have seen how surprised I was. Bob knew in a flash.

" 'You darned old snoozer,' he said, with the old-time look on his face, 'I saw you put it there. I watched you open the safe and take it out, and I followed you. I looked through the window and saw you hide it in that wardrobe.'

" 'Then, you blankety-blank, flop-eared, sheep-headed coyote, what did you say you took it for?'

" 'Because,' said Bob, simply, 'I didn't know you were asleep.'

"I saw him glance toward the door of the room where Jack and Zilla were, and I knew then what it meant to be a man's friend from Bob's point of view."

Major Tom paused, and again directed his glance out of the window. He saw someone in the Stockmen's National Bank reach and draw a yellow shade down the whole length of its plate-glass, big front window, although the position of the sun did not seem to warrant such a defensive movement against its rays.

Nettlewick sat up straight in his chair. He had listened patiently, but without consuming interest, to the major's story. It had impressed him as irrelevant to the situation, and it could certainly have no effect upon the consequences. Those Western people, he thought, had an exaggerated sentimentality. They were not business-like. They needed to be protected from their friends. Evidently the major had concluded. And what he had said amounted to nothing.

"May I ask," said the examiner, "if you have anything further to say that bears directly upon the question of those abstracted securities?"

"Abstracted securities, sir!" Major Tom turned suddenly in his chair, his blue eyes flashing upon the examiner. "What do you mean, sir?"

He drew from his coat pocket a batch of folded papers held together by a rubber band, tossed them into Nettlewick's hands, and rose to his feet.

"You'll find those securities there, sir, every stock, bond, and share of 'em. I took them from the notes while you were counting the cash. Examine and compare them for yourself."

The major led the way back into the banking room. The examiner, astounded, perplexed, nettled, at sea, followed. He felt that he had been made the victim of something that was not exactly a hoax, but that left him in the shoes of one who had been played upon, used, and then discarded, without even an inkling of the game. Perhaps, also, his official position had been irreverently juggled with. But there was nothing he could take hold of. An official report of the matter would be an absurdity. And, somehow, he felt that he would never know anything more about the matter than he did then.

Frigidly, mechanically, Nettlewick examined the securities, found them to tally with the notes, gathered his black wallet, and rose to depart.

"I will say," he protested, turning the indignant glare of his glasses upon Major Kingman, "that your statements—your misleading statements, which you have not condescended to explain —do not appear to be quite the thing, regarded either as business or humor. I do not understand such motives or actions."

Major Tom looked down at him serenely and not unkindly.

"Son," he said, "there are plenty of things in the chaparral, and on the prairies, and up the cañons that you don't understand. But I want to thank you for listening to a garrulous old man's prosy story. We old Texans love to talk about our adventures and our old comrades, and the home folks have long ago learned to run when we begin with 'Once upon a time,' so we have to spin our yarns to the stranger within our gates."

The major smiled, but the examiner only bowed coldly, and abruptly quitted the bank. They saw him travel diagonally across the street in a straight line and enter the Stockmen's National Bank.

Major Tom sat down at his desk and drew from his vest pocket the note Roy had given him. He had read it once, but hurriedly, and now, with something like a twinkle in his eyes, he read it again. These were the words he read:

Dear Tom:
I hear there's one of Uncle Sam's greyhounds going through you, and that means that we'll catch him inside of a couple of hours, maybe. Now, I want you to do something for me. We've got just $2,200 in the bank, and the law requires that we have $20,000. I let Ross and Fisher have $18,000 late yesterday afternoon to buy up that Gibson bunch of cattle. They'll realize $40,000 in less than thirty days on the transaction, but that won't make my cash on hand look any prettier to that bank examiner. Now, I can't show him those notes, for they're just plain notes of hand without any security in sight, but you know very well that Pink Ross and Jim Fisher are two of the finest white men God ever made, and they'll do the square thing. You remember Jim Fisher—he was the one who shot that faro dealer in El Paso. I wired Sam Bradshaw's bank to send me $20,000, and it will get in on the narrow-gauge at 10:35. You can't let a bank examiner in to count $2,200 and close your doors. Tom, you hold that examiner. Hold him. Hold him if you have to rope him and sit on his head. Watch our front window after the narrow-gauge gets in, and when we've got the cash inside we'll pull down the shade for a signal. Don't turn him loose till then. I'm counting on you, Tom.
                              Your Old Pard,
                                   Bob Buckley,
                         Prest. Stockmen's National

The major began to tear the note into small pieces and throw them into his waste basket. He gave a satisfied little chuckle as he did so.

"Confounded old reckless cowpuncher!" he growled, contentedly, "that pays him some on account for what he tried to do for me in the sheriff's office twenty years ago."

The Renaissance at Charleroi

GRANDEMONT Charles was a little Creole gentleman, aged thirty-four, with a bald spot on the top of his head and the manners of a prince. By day he was a clerk in a cotton broker's office in one of those cold, rancid mountains of oozy brick, down near the levee in New Orleans. By night, in his three-story-high *chambre garnie* in the old French Quarter he was again the last male descendant of the Charles family, that noble house that had lorded it in France. and had pushed its way smiling, rapiered, and courtly into Louisiana's early and brilliant days. Of late years the Charleses had subsided into the more republican but scarcely less royally carried magnificence and ease of plantation life along the Mississippi. Perhaps Grandemont was even Marquis de Brassé. There was that title in the family. But a marquis on seventy-five dollars per month! *Vraiment!* Still, it has been done on less.

Grandemont had saved out of his salary the sum of six hundred dollars. Enough, you would say, for any man to marry on. So, after a silence of two years on that subject, he reopened that most hazardous question to Mlle. Adèle Fauquier, riding down to Meade d'Or, her father's plantation. Her answer was the same that it had been any time during the last ten years: "First find my brother, Monsieur Charles."

This time he had stood before her, perhaps discouraged by a love so long and hopeless, being dependent upon a contingency so unreasonable, and demanded to be told in simple words whether she loved him or no.

Adèle looked at him steadily out of her gray eyes that betrayed no secrets and answered, a little more softly:

"Grandemont, you have no right to ask that question unless you can do what I ask of you. Either bring back brother Victor to us or the proof that he died."

Somehow, though five times thus rejected, his heart was not so heavy when he left. She had not denied that she loved. Upon what shallow waters can the bark of passion remain afloat! Or, shall we play the doctrinaire, and hint that at thirty-four the tides of life are calmer and cognizant of many sources instead of but one—as at four-and-twenty?

Victor Fauquier would never be found. In those early days of his disappearance there was money to the Charles name, and Grandemont had spent the dollars as if they were picayunes in trying to find the lost youth. Even then he had small hope of success, for the Mississippi gives up a victim from its oily tangles only at the whim of its malign will.

A thousand times had Grandemont conned in his mind the scene of Victor's disappearance. And, at each time that Adèle had set her stubborn but pitiful alternative against his suit, still clearer it repeated itself in his brain.

The boy had been the family favorite: daring, winning, reckless. His unwise fancy had been captured by a girl on the plantation—the daughter of an overseer. Victor's family was in ignorance of the intrigue, as far as it had gone. To save them the inevitable pain that his course promised, Grandemont strove to prevent it. Omnipotent money smoothed the way. The overseer and his daughter left, between a sunset and dawn, for an undesignated bourne. Grandemont was confident that this stroke would bring the boy to reason. He rode over to Meade d'Or to talk with him. The two strolled out of the house and grounds, crossed the road, and mounting the levee, walked its broad path while they conversed. A thundercloud was hanging, imminent, above,

but, as yet, no rain fell. At Grandemont's disclosure of his interference in the clandestine romance, Victor attacked him, in a
wild and sudden fury. Grandemont, though of slight frame, possessed muscles of iron. He caught the wrists amid a shower of
blows descending upon him, bent the lad backward and stretched
him upon the levee path. In a little while the gust of passion was
spent, and he was allowed to rise. Calm now, but a powder mine
where he had been but a whiff of the tantrums, Victor extended
his hand toward the dwelling house of Meade d'Or.

"You and they," he cried, "have conspired to destroy my happiness. None of you shall ever look upon my face again."

Turning, he ran swiftly down the levee, disappearing in the
darkness, Grandemont followed as well as he could, calling to
him, but in vain. For longer than an hour he pursued the search.
Descending the side of the levee, he penetrated the rank density
of weeds and willows that undergrew the trees until the river's
edge, shouting Victor's name. There was never an answer, though
once he thought he heard a bubbling scream from the dun waters sliding past. Then the storm broke, and he returned to the
house drenched and dejected.

There he explained the boy's absence sufficiently, he thought,
not speaking of the tangle that had led to it, for he hoped that
Victor would return as soon as his anger had cooled. Afterward,
when the threat was made good and they saw his face no more, he
found it difficult to alter his explanations of that night, and there
clung a certain mystery to the boy's reasons for vanishing as well
as to the manner of it.

It was on that night that Grandemont first perceived a new
and singular expression in Adèle's eyes whenever she looked at
him. And through the years following that expression was always
there. He could not read it, for it was born of a thought she would
never otherwise reveal.

Perhaps, if he had known that Adèle had stood at the gate on
that unlucky night, where she had followed, lingering to await
the return of her brother and lover, wondering why they had

chosen so tempestuous an hour and so black a spot to hold converse—if he had known that a sudden flash of lightning had revealed to her sight that short, sharp struggle as Victor was sinking under his hands, he might have explained everything, and she——

I know not what she would have done. But one thing is clear —there was something besides her brother's disappearance between Grandemont's pleadings for her hand and Adèle's "yes." Ten years had passed, and what she had seen during the space of that lightning flash remained an indelible picture. She had loved her brother, but was she holding out for the solution of that mystery or for the "Truth"! Women have been known to reverence it, even as an abstract principle. It is said there have been a few who, in the matter of their affections, have considered a life to be a small thing as compared with a lie. That I do not know. But, I wonder, had Grandemont cast himself at her feet crying that his hand had sent Victor to the bottom of that inscrutable river, and that he could no longer sully his love with a lie, I wonder if—I wonder what she would have done!

But, Grandemont Charles, Arcadian little gentleman, never guessed the meaning of that look in Adèle's eyes; and from this last bootless payment of his devoirs he rode away as rich as ever in honor and love, but poor in hope.

That was in September. It was during the first winter month that Grandemont conceived his idea of the *renaissance*. Since Adèle would never be his, and wealth without her were useless trumpery, why need he add to that hoard of slowly harvested dollars? Why should he even retain that hoard?

Hundreds were the cigarettes he consumed over his claret, sitting at the little polished tables in the Royal street cafés while thinking over his plan. By and by he had it perfect. It would cost, beyond doubt, all the money he had, but—*le jeu vaut la chandelle* —for some hours he would be once more a Charles of Charleroi. Once again should the nineteenth of January, that most significant day in the fortunes of the house of Charles, be fittingly observed. On that date the French king had seated a Charles by his side at table; on that date Armand Charles, Marquis de Brassé, landed, like a brilliant meteor, in New Orleans; it was the date of his mother's wedding; of Grandemont's birth. Since Grandemont could remember until the breaking up of the family that anniversary had been the synonym for feasting, hospitality, and proud commemoration.

Charleroi was the old family plantation, lying some twenty miles down the river. Years ago the estate had been sold to discharge the debts of its too-bountiful owners. Once again it had changed hands, and now the must and mildew of litigation had settled upon it. A question of heirship was in the courts, and the dwelling house of Charleroi, unless the tales told of ghostly powdered and laced Charleses haunting its unechoing chambers were true, stood uninhabited.

Grandemont found the solicitor in chancery who held the keys pending the decision. He proved to be an old friend of the family. Grandemont explained briefly that he desired to rent the house for two or three days. He wanted to give a dinner at his old home to a few friends. That was all.

"Take it for a week—a month, if you will," said the solicitor; "but do not speak to me of rental." With a sigh he concluded: "The dinners I have eaten under that roof, *mon fils!*"

There came to many of the old-established dealers in furniture, china, silverware, decorations, and household fittings at their stores on Canal, Chartres, St. Charles and Royal streets, a quiet young man with a little bald spot on the top of his head, distinguished manners, and the eye of a *connoisseur*, who explained what he wanted. To hire the complete and elegant equipment of a dining-room, hall, reception-room, and cloak-rooms. The goods were to be packed and sent, by boat, to the Charleroi landing, and would be returned within three or four days. All damage or loss to be promptly paid for.

Many of those old merchants knew Grandemont by sight, and the Charleses of old by association. Some of them were of Creole stock and felt a thrill of responsive sympathy with the magnificently indiscreet design of this impoverished clerk who would revive but for a moment the ancient flame of glory with the fuel of his savings.

"Choose what you want," they said to him. "Handle everything carefully. See that the damage bill is kept low, and the charges for the loan will not oppress you."

To the wine merchants next; and here a doleful slice was lopped from the six hundred. It was an exquisite pleasure to Grandemont once more to pick among the precious vintages. The champagne bins lured him like the abodes of sirens, but these he was forced to pass. With his six hundred he stood before them as a child with a penny stands before a French doll. But he bought with taste and discretion of other wines—Chablis, Moselle, Château d'Or, Hochheimer, and port of right age and pedigree.

The matter of the cuisine gave him some studious hours until he suddenly recollected André—André, their old *chef*—the most sublime master of French Creole cookery in the Mississippi Valley. Perhaps he was yet somewhere about the plantation. The solicitor had told him that the place was still being cultivated, in accordance with a compromise agreement between the litigants.

On the next Sunday after the thought Grandemont rode, horseback, down to Charleroi. The big, square house with its two long ells looked blank and cheerless with its closed shutters and doors.

The shrubbery in the yard was ragged and riotous. Fallen leaves from the grove littered the walks and porches. Turning down the lane at the side of the house, Grandemont rode on to the quarters of the plantation hands. He found the workers streaming back from church, careless, happy, and bedecked in gay yellows, reds, and blues.

Yes, André was still there; his wool a little grayer; his mouth as wide; his laughter as ready as ever. Grandemont told him of his plan, and the old *chef* swayed with pride and delight. With a sigh of relief, knowing that he need have no further concern until the serving of that dinner was announced, he placed in André's hands a liberal sum for the cost of it, giving *carte blanche* for its creation.

Among the blacks were also a number of the old house servants. Absalom, the former major domo, and a half-dozen of the younger men, once waiters and attachés of the kitchen, pantry, and other domestic departments, crowded around to meet "*M'shi Grande.*" Absalom guaranteed to marshal, of these, a corps of assistants that would perform with credit the serving of the dinner.

After distributing a liberal largesse among the faithful, Grandemont rode back to town well pleased. There were many other smaller details to think of and provide for, but eventually the scheme was complete, and now there remained only the issuance of the invitations to his guests.

Along the river within the scope of a score of miles dwelt some half-dozen families with whose princely hospitality that of the Charleses had been contemporaneous. They were the proudest and most august of the old régime. Their small circle had been a brilliant one; their social relations close and warm; their houses full of rare welcome and discriminating bounty. Those friends, said Grandemont, should once more, if never again, sit at Charleroi on a nineteenth of January to celebrate the festal day of his house.

Grandemont had his cards of invitation engraved. They were expensive, but beautiful. In one particular their good taste might have been disputed; but the Creole allowed himself that one feather in the cap of his fugacious splendor. Might he not be allowed, for the one day of the *renaissance*, to be "Grandemont du Puy Charles, of Charleroi"? He sent the invitations out early in January so that the guests might not fail to receive due notice.

At eight o'clock in the morning of the nineteenth, the lower coast steamboat *River Belle* gingerly approached the long unused landing at Charleroi. The bridge was lowered, and a swarm of the plantation hands streamed along the rotting pier, bearing ashore a strange assortment of freight. Great shapeless bundles and bales and packets swathed in cloths and bound with ropes; tubs and urns of palms, evergreens, and tropical flowers; tables, mirrors, chairs, couches, carpets, and pictures—all carefully bound and padded against the dangers of transit.

Grandemont was among them, the busiest there. To the safe conveyance of certain large hampers eloquent with printed cautions to delicate handling he gave his superintendence, for they contained the fragile china and glassware. The dropping of of one of those hampers would have cost him more than he could have saved in a year.

The last article unloaded, the *River Belle* backed off and continued her course down stream. In less than an hour everything had been conveyed to the house. And came then Absalom's task, directing the placing of the furniture and wares. There was plenty of help, for that day was always a holiday in Charleroi, and the Negroes did not suffer the old traditions to lapse. Almost the entire population of the quarters volunteered their aid. A score of piccaninnies were sweeping at the leaves in the yard. In the big kitchen at the rear André was lording it with his old-time magnificence over his numerous sub-cooks and scullions. Shutters were flung wide; dust spun in clouds; the house echoed to voices and the tread of busy feet. The prince had come again, and Charleroi woke from its long sleep.

The full moon, as she rose across the river that night and peeped above the levee, saw a sight that had been long missing from her orbit. The old plantation house shed a soft and alluring radiance from every window. Of its two-score rooms only four had been refurnished—the large reception chamber, the dining hall, and two smaller rooms for the convenience of the expected guests. But lighted wax candles were set in the windows of every room.

The dining hall was the *chef-d'œuvre*. The long table, set with twenty-five covers, sparkled like a winter landscape with its snowy napery and china and the icy gleam of crystal. The chaste beauty of the room had required small adornment. The polished floor burned to a glowing ruby with the reflection of candlelight. The rich wainscoting reached halfway to the ceiling. Along and above this had been set the relieving lightness of a few water-color sketches of fruit and flower.

The reception chamber was fitted in a simple but elegant style. Its arrangement suggested nothing of the fact that on the morrow the rooms would again be cleared and abandoned to the dust and the spider. The entrance hall was imposing with palms and ferns and the light of an immense candelabrum.

At seven o'clock Grandemont, in evening dress, with pearls— a family passion—in his spotless linen, emerged from somewhere. The invitations had specified eight as the dining hour. He drew an armchair upon the porch, and sat there, smoking cigarettes and half dreaming.

The moon was an hour high. Fifty yards back from the gate stood the house, under its noble grove. The road ran in front, and then came the grass-grown levee and the insatiate river beyond. Just above the levee top a tiny red light was creeping down and a tiny green one was creeping up. Then the passing steamers saluted, and the hoarse din startled the drowsy silence of the melancholy lowlands. The stillness returned, save for the little voices of the night—the owl's recitative, the capriccio of the crickets, the concerto of the frogs in the grass. The piccaninnies and the dawdlers from the quarters had been dismissed to their confines, and the mêlée of the day was reduced to an orderly and intelligent silence. The six colored waiters, in their white jackets, paced, cat-footed, about the table, pretending to arrange where all was beyond betterment. Absalom, in black and shining pumps, posed, superior, here and there where the lights set off his grandeur. And Grandemont rested in his chair, waiting for his guests.

He must have drifted into a dream—and an extravagant one— for he was master of Charleroi and Adèle was his wife. She was coming out to him now; he could hear her steps; he could feel her hand upon his shoulder——

"Pardon moi, M'shi Grande"—it was Absalom's hand touching him, it was Absalom's voice, speaking the *patois* of the blacks— "but it is eight o'clock."

Eight o'clock. Grandemont sprang up. In the moonlight he could see the row of hitching posts outside the gate. Long ago the horses of the guests should have stood there. They were vacant.

A chanted roar of indignation, a just, waxing bellow of affront and dishonored genius came from André's kitchen, filling the house with rhythmic protest. The beautiful dinner, the pearl of a dinner, the little excellent superb jewel of a dinner! But one moment more of waiting and not even the thousand thunders of black pigs of the quarters would touch it!

"They are a little late," said Grandemont, calmly. "They will come soon. Tell André to hold back dinner. And ask him if, by some chance, a bull from the pastures has broken, roaring, into the house."

He seated himself again to his cigarettes. Though he had said it, he scarcely believed Charleroi would entertain company that night. For the first time in history the invitation of a Charles had been ignored. So simple in courtesy and honor was Grandemont and, perhaps, so serenely confident in the prestige of his name, that the most likely reasons for his vacant board did not occur to him.

Charleroi stood by a road traveled daily by people from those plantations whither his invitations had gone. No doubt even on the day before the sudden reanimation of the old house they had driven past and observed the evidences of long desertion and decay. They had looked at the corpse of Charleroi and then at Grandemont's invitations, and, though the puzzle or tasteless hoax or whatever the thing meant left them perplexed, they would not seek its solution by the folly of a visit to that deserted house.

The moon was now above the grove, and the yard was pied with deep shadows save where they lightened in the tender glow of outpouring candlelight. A crisp breeze from the river hinted at the possibility of frost when the night should have become older. The grass at one side of the steps was specked with the white stubs of Grandemont's cigarettes. The cotton-broker's clerk sat in his chair with the smoke spiralling above him. I doubt that he once thought of the little fortune he had so impotently squandered. Perhaps it was compensation enough for him to sit thus at Charleroi for a few retrieved hours. Idly his mind wandered in and out many fanciful paths of memory. He smiled to himself as a paraphrased line of Scripture strayed into his mind: "A certain *poor* man made a feast."

He heard the sound of Absalom coughing a note of summons. Grandemont stirred. This time he had not been asleep—only drowsing.

"Nine o'clock, M'shi Grande," said Absalom in the uninflected voice of a good servant who states a fact unqualified by personal opinion.

Grandemont rose to his feet. In their time all the Charleses had been proven, and they were gallant losers.

"Serve dinner," he said, calmly. And then he checked Absalom's movement to obey, for something clicked the gate latch and was coming down the walk towards the house. Something that shuffled its feet and muttered to itself as it came. It stopped in the current of light at the foot of the steps and spake, in the universal whine of the gadding mendicant.

"Kind sir, could you spare a poor hungry man, out of luck, a little to eat? And to sleep in the corner of a shed? For"—the thing concluded, irrelevantly—"I can sleep now. There are no mountains to dance reels in the night; and the copper kettles are all scoured bright. The iron band is still around my ankle, and a link, if it is your desire I should be chained."

It set a foot upon the step and drew up the rags that hung upon the limb. Above the distorted shoe, caked with dust of a hundred leagues, they saw the link and the iron band. The clothes of the tramp were wrecked to piebald tatters by sun and rain and wear. A mat of brown, tangled hair and beard covered his head and face, out of which his eyes stared distractedly. Grandemont noticed that he carried in one hand a white, square card.

"What is that?" he asked.

"I picked it up, sir, at the side of the road." The vagabond handed the card to Grandemont. "Just a little to eat, sir. A little parched corn, a *tortilla*, or a handful of beans. Goat's meat I cannot eat. When I cut their throats they cry like children."

Grandemont held up the card. It was one of his own invitations to dinner. No doubt someone had cast it away from a passing carriage after comparing it with the tenantless house at Charleroi.

"From the hedges and highways bid them come," he said to himself, softly smiling. And then to Absalom: "Send Louis to me."

Louis, once his own body-servant, came promptly, in his white jacket.

"This gentleman," said Grandemont, "will dine with me. Furnish him with bath and clothes. In twenty minutes have him ready and dinner served."

Louis approached the disreputable guest with the suavity due to a visitor to Charleroi, and spirited him away to inner regions.

Promptly, in twenty minutes, Absalom announced dinner, and, a moment later, the guest was ushered into the dining hall where Grandemont waited, standing, at the head of the table. The attentions of Louis had transformed the stranger into something resembling the polite animal. Clean linen and an old evening suit that had been sent down from town to clothe a waiter had worked a miracle with his exterior. Brush and comb had partially subdued the wild disorder of his hair. Now he might have passed for no more extravagant a thing than one of those *poseurs* in art and music who affect such oddity of guise. The man's countenance and demeanor, as he approached the table, exhibited nothing of the awkwardness or confusion to be expected from his Arabian Nights change. He allowed Absalom to seat him at Grandemont's right hand with the manner of one thus accustomed to be waited upon.

"It grieves me," said Grandemont, "to be obliged to exchange names with a guest. My own name is Charles."

"In the mountains," said the wayfarer, "they call me Gringo. Along the roads they call me Jack."

"I prefer the latter," said Grandemont. "A glass of wine with you, Mr. Jack."

Course after course was served by the supernumerous waiters. Grandemont, inspired by the results of André's exquisite skill in cookery and his own in the selection of wines, became the model host, talkative, witty, and genial. The guest was fitful in conversation. His mind seemed to be sustaining a succession of waves of dementia followed by intervals of comparative lucidity. There was the glassy brightness of recent fever in his eyes. A long course of it must have been the cause of his emaciation and weakness, his distracted mind, and the dull pallor that showed even through the tan of wind and sun.

"Charles," he said to Grandemont—for thus he seemed to interpret his name—"you never saw the mountains dance, did you?"

"No, Mr. Jack," answered Grandemont, gravely, "the spectacle has been denied me. But, I assure you, I can understand it must be a diverting sight. The big ones, you know, white with snow on the tops, waltzing—*décolleté*, we may say."

"You first scour the kettles," said Mr. Jack, leaning toward him excitedly, "to cook the beans in the morning, and you lie down on a blanket and keep quite still. Then they come out and dance for you. You would go out and dance with them but you are chained every night to the centre pole of the hut. You believe the mountains dance, don't you, Charlie?"

"I contradict no traveler's tales," said Grandemont, with a smile.

Mr. Jack laughed loudly. He dropped his voice to a confidential whisper.

"You are a fool to believe it," he went on. "They don't really dance. It's the fever in your head. It's the hard work and the bad water that does it. You are sick for weeks and there is no medicine.

The fever comes on every evening, and then you are as strong as two men. One night the *compañía* are lying drunk with *mescal*. They have brought back sacks of silver dollars from a ride, and they drink to celebrate. In the night you file the chain in two and go down the mountain. You walk for miles—hundreds of them. By and by the mountains are all gone, and you come to the prairies. They do not dance at night; they are merciful, and you sleep. Then you come to the river, and it says things to you. You follow it down, down, but you can't find what you are looking for."

Mr. Jack leaned back in his chair, and his eyes slowly closed. The food and wine had steeped him in a deep calm. The tense strain had been smoothed from his face. The languor of repletion was claiming him. Drowsily he spoke again.

"It's bad manners—I know—to go to sleep—at table—but—that was—such a good dinner—Grande, old fellow."

Grande! The owner of the name started and set down his glass. How should this wretched tatterdemalion whom he had invited, Caliph-like, to sit at his feast know his name?

Not at first, but soon, little by little, the suspicion, wild and unreasonable as it was, stole into his brain. He drew out his watch with hands that almost balked him by their trembling, and opened the back case. There was a picture there—a photograph fixed to the inner side.

Rising, Grandemont shook Mr. Jack by the shoulder. The weary guest opened his eyes. Grandemont held the watch.

"Look at this picture, Mr. Jack. Have you ever——"

"*My sister Adèle!*"

The vagrant's voice rang loud and sudden through the room. He started to his feet, but Grandemont's arms were about him, and Grandemont was calling him "Victor!—Victor Fauquier! *Merci, merci, mon Dieu!*"

Too far overcome by sleep and fatigue was the lost one to talk that night. Days afterward, when the tropic *calentura* had cooled in his veins, the disordered fragments he had spoken were completed in shape and sequence. He told the story of his angry flight, of toils and calamities on sea and shore, of his ebbing and flowing fortune in southern lands, and of his latest peril when, held a captive, he served menially in a stronghold of bandits in the Sonora Mountains of Mexico. And of the fever that seized him there and his escape and delirium, during which he strayed, perhaps led by some marvelous instinct, back to the river on whose bank he had been born. And of the proud and stubborn thing in his blood that had kept him silent through all those years, clouding the honor of one, though he knew it not, and keeping apart two loving hearts. "What a thing is love!" you may say. And if I grant it, you shall say, with me: "What a thing is pride!"

On a couch in the reception chamber Victor lay, with a dawning understanding in his heavy eyes and peace in his softened countenance. Absalom was preparing a lounge for the transient master of Charleroi, who, to-morrow, would be again the clerk of a cotton broker, but also——

"To-morrow," Grandemont was saying, as he stood by the couch of his guest, speaking the words with his face shining as must have shone the face of Elijah's charioteer when he announced the glories of that heavenly journey—"To-morrow I will take you to Her."

Whistling Dick's Christmas Stocking

IT WAS with much caution that Whistling Dick slid back the door of the box-car, for Article 5716, City Ordinances, authorized (perhaps unconstitutionally) arrest on suspicion, and he was familiar of old with this ordinance. So, before climbing out, he surveyed the field with all the care of a good general.

He saw no change since his last visit to this big, almsgiving, long-suffering city of the South, the cold weather paradise of the tramps. The levee where his freight-car stood was pimpled with dark bulks of merchandise. The breeze reeked with the well-remembered, sickening smell of the old tarpaulins that covered bales and barrels. The dun river slipped along among the shipping with an oily gurgle. Far down toward Chalmette he could see the great bend in the stream, outlined by the row of electric lights. Across the river Algiers lay, a long, irregular blot, made darker by the dawn which lightened the sky beyond. An industrious tug or two, coming for some early sailing ship, gave a few appalling toots, that seemed to be the signal for breaking day. The Italian luggers were creeping nearer their landing, laden with early vegetables and shellfish. A vague roar, subterranean in quality, from dray wheels and street cars, began to make itself heard and felt; and the ferryboats, the Mary Anns of water craft, stirred sullenly to their menial morning tasks.

Whistling Dick's red head popped suddenly back into the car. A sight too imposing and magnificent for his gaze had been added to the scene. A vast, incomparable policeman rounded a pile of rice sacks and stood within twenty yards of the car. The daily miracle of the dawn, now being performed above Algiers, received the flattering attention of this specimen of municipal official splendor. He gazed with unbiased dignity at the faintly glowing colors until, at last, he turned to them his broad back, as if convinced that legal interference was not needed, and the sunrise might proceed unchecked. So he turned his face to the rice bags, and, drawing a flat flask from an inside pocket, he placed it to his lips and regarded the firmament.

Whistling Dick, professional tramp, possessed a half-friendly acquaintance with this officer. They had met several times before on the levee at night, for the officer, himself a lover of music, had been attracted by the exquisite whistling of the shiftless vagabond. Still, he did not care, under the present circumstances, to renew the acquaintance. There is a difference between meeting a policeman upon a lonely wharf and whistling a few operatic airs with him, and being caught by him crawling out of a freight-car. So Dick waited, as even a New Orleans policeman must move on some time—perhaps it is a retributive law of nature—and before long "Big Fritz" majestically disappeared between the trains of cars.

Whistling Dick waited as long as his judgment advised, and then slid swiftly to the ground. Assuming as far as possible the air of an honest laborer who seeks his daily toil, he moved across the network of railway lines, with the intention of making his way by quiet Girod Street to a certain bench in Lafayette Square, where, according to appointment, he hoped to rejoin a pal known as "Slick," this adventurous pilgrim having preceded him by one day in a cattle-car into which a loose slat had enticed him.

As Whistling Dick picked his way where night still lingered among the big, reeking, musty warehouses, he gave way to the habit that had won for him his title. Subdued, yet clear, with each note as true and liquid as a bobolink's, his whistle tinkled about the dim, cold mountains of brick like drops of rain falling into a hidden pool. He followed an air, but it swam mistily into a swirling current of improvisation. You could cull out the trill of mountain brooks, the staccato of green rushes shivering above the chilly lagoons, the pipe of sleepy birds.

Rounding a corner, the whistler collided with a mountain of blue and brass.

"So," observed the mountain calmly, "you are already pack. Und dere vill not pe frost before two veeks yet! Und you haf forgotten how to vistle. Dere was a valse note in dot last bar."

"Watcher know about it?" said Whistling Dick, with tentative familiarity; "you wit yer little Gherman-band nixcumrous chunes. Watcher know about music? Pick yer ears, and listen agin. Here's de way I whistled it—see?"

He puckered his lips, but the big policeman held up his hand.

"Shtop," he said, "und learn der right way. Und learn also dot a rolling shtone can't vistle for a cent."

Big Fritz's heavy moustache rounded into a circle, and from its depths came a sound deep and mellow as that from a flute. He repeated a few bars of the air the tramp had been whistling. The rendition was cold, but correct, and he emphasized the note he had taken exception to.

"Dot p is p natural, and not p vlat. Py der vay, you petter pe glad I meet you. Von hour later, und I vould haf to put you in a gage to vistle mit der chail pirds. Der orders are to bull all der pums after sunrise."

"To which?"

"To bull der pums—eferybody mitout fisible means. Dirty days is der price, or fifteen tollars."

"Is dat straight, or a game you givin' me?"

"It's der pest tip you efer had. I gif it to you because I pelief you are not so bad as der rest. Und pecause you can vistle 'Der Freischütz' bezzer dan I myself gan. Don't run against any more bolicemans aroundt der corners, but go away from town a few tays. Goot-pye."

So Madame Orleans had at last grown weary of the strange and ruffled brood that came yearly to nestle beneath her charitable pinions.

After the big policeman had departed, Whistling Dick stood for an irresolute minute, feeling all the outraged indignation of a delinquent tenant who is ordered to vacate his premises. He had pictured to himself a day of dreamful ease when he should have joined his pal; a day of lounging on the wharf, munching the bananas and cocoanuts scattered in unloading the fruit steamers; and then a feast along the free-lunch counters from which the easy-going owners were too good-natured or too generous to drive him away, and afterward a pipe in one of the little flowery parks and a snooze in some shady corner of the wharf. But here was a stern order to exile, and one that he knew must be obeyed. So, with a wary eye open for the gleam of brass buttons, he began his retreat toward a rural refuge. A few days in the country need not necessarily prove disastrous. Beyond the possibility of a slight nip of frost, there was no formidable evil to be looked for.

However, it was with a depressed spirit that Whistling Dick passed the old French market on his chosen route down the river. For safety's sake he still presented to the world his portrayal of the part of the worthy artisan on his way to labor. A stall-keeper in the market, undeceived, hailed him by the generic name of his ilk, and "Jack" halted, taken by surprise. The vendor, melted by this proof of his own acuteness, bestowed a foot of Frankfurter and half a loaf, and thus the problem of breakfast was solved.

When the streets, from topographical reasons, began to shun the river bank the exile mounted to the top of the levee, and on its well-trodden path pursued his way. The suburban eye regarded him with cold suspicion, individuals reflected the stern spirit of the city's heartless edict. He missed the seclusion of the crowded town and the safety he could always find in the multitude.

At Chalmette, six miles upon his desultory way, there suddenly menaced him a vast and bewildering industry. A new port was being established; the dock was being built, compresses were going up; picks and shovels and barrows struck at him like serpents from every side. An arrogant foreman bore down upon him, estimating his muscles with the eye of a recruiting-sergeant. Brown men and black men all about him were toiling away. He fled in terror.

By noon he had reached the country of the plantations, the great, sad, silent levels bordering the mighty river. He overlooked fields of sugarcane so vast that their farthest limits melted into the sky. The sugar-making season was well advanced, and the cutters were at work; the wagons creaked drearily after them; the Negro teamsters inspired the mules to greater speed with mellow and sonorous imprecations. Dark-green groves, blurred by the blue of distance, showed where the plantation-houses stood. The tall chimneys of the sugar-mills caught the eye miles distant, like light-houses at sea.

At a certain point Whistling Dick's unerring nose caught the scent of frying fish. Like a pointer to a quail, he made his way down the levee side straight to the camp of a credulous and ancient fisherman, whom he charmed with song and story, so that he dined like an admiral, and then like a philosopher annihilated the worst three hours of the day by a nap under the trees.

When he awoke and again continued his hegira, a frosty sparkle in the air succeeded the drowsy warmth of the day, and as this portent of a chilly night translated itself to the brain of Sir Peregrine, he lengthened his stride and bethought him of shelter. He traveled a road that faithfully followed the convolutions of the levee, running along its base, but whither he knew not. Bushes and rank grass crowded it to the wheel ruts, and out of this ambuscade the pests of the lowlands swarmed after him, humming a keen vicious soprano. And as the night grew nearer, although colder, the whine of the mosquitoes became a greedy, petulant snarl that shut out all other sounds. To his right, against the heavens, he saw a green light moving, and, accompanying it, the masts and funnels of a big incoming steamer, moving as upon a screen at a magic-lantern show. And there were mysterious marshes at his left, out of which came queer gurgling cries and a choked croaking. The whistling vagrant struck up a merry warble to offset these melancholy influences, and it is likely that never before, since Pan himself jiggered it on his reeds, had such sounds been heard in those depressing solitudes.

A distant clatter in the rear quickly developed into the swift beat of horses' hoofs, and Whistling Dick stepped aside into the dew-wet grass to clear the track. Turning his head, he saw approaching a fine team of stylish grays drawing a double surrey. A stout man with a white moustache occupied the front seat, giving all his attention to the rigid lines in his hands. Behind him sat a placid, middle-aged lady and a brilliant-looking girl hardly arrived at young ladyhood. The lap-robe had slipped partly from the knees of the gentleman driving, and Whistling Dick saw two stout canvas bags between his feet—bags such as, while loafing in cities, he had seen warily transferred between express wagons and bank doors. The remaining space in the vehicle was filled with parcels of various sizes and shapes.

As the surrey swept even with the sidetracked tramp, the bright-eyed girl, seized by some merry, madcap impulse, leaned out toward him with a sweet, dazzling smile, and cried, "Mer-ry Christ-mas!" in a shrill, plaintive treble.

Such a thing had not often happened to Whistling Dick, and he felt handicapped in devising the correct response. But lacking time for reflection, he let his instinct decide, and snatching off his battered derby, he rapidly extended it at arm's length, and drew it back with a continuous motion, and shouted a loud, but ceremonious, "Ah, there!" after the flying surrey.

The sudden movement of the girl had caused one of the parcels to become unwrapped, and something limp and black fell from it into the road. The tramp picked it up and found it to be a new black silk stocking, long and fine and slender. It crunched crisply, and yet with a luxurious softness, between his fingers.

"Ther bloomin' little skeezicks!" said Whistling Dick, with a broad grin bisecting his freckled face. "Wot d'yer think of dat, now! Mer-ry Chris-mus! Sounded like a cuckoo clock, dat's what she did. Dem guys is swells, too, bet yer life, an' der old 'un stacks dem sacks of dough down under his trotters like dey was common as dried apples. Been shoppin' fer Chrismus, and de kid's lost one of her new socks w'ot she was goin' to hold up Santy wid. De bloomin' little skeezicks! Wit' her 'Mer-ry Chris-mus!' W'ot 'd yer t'ink! Same as to say, 'Hello, Jack, how goes it?' and as swell as Fift' Av'noo, and as easy as a blowout in Cincinnat'."

Whistling Dick folded the stocking carefully and stuffed it into his pocket.

It was nearly two hours later when he came upon signs of habitation. The buildings of an extensive plantation were brought into view by a turn in the road. He easily selected the planter's residence in a large square building with two wings, with numerous good-sized, well-lighted windows, and broad verandas running around its full extent. It was set upon a smooth lawn, which was faintly lit by the far-reaching rays of the lamps within. A noble grove surrounded it, and old-fashioned shrubbery grew thickly about the walls and fences. The quarters of the hands and the mill buildings were situated at a distance in the rear.

The road was now enclosed on each side by a fence, and presently, as Whistling Dick drew nearer the houses, he suddenly stopped and sniffed the air.

"If dere ain't a hobo stew cookin' somewhere in dis immediate precinct," he said to himself, "me nose has quit tellin' de trut'."

Without hesitation he climbed the fence to windward. He found himself in an apparently disused lot, where piles of old bricks were stacked, and rejected, decaying lumber. In a corner he saw the faint glow of a fire that had become little more than a bed of living coals, and he thought he could see some dim human forms sitting or lying about it. He drew nearer, and by the light of a little blaze that suddenly flared up he saw plainly the fat figure of a ragged man in an old brown sweater and cap.

"Dat man," said Whistling Dick to himself softly, "is a dead ringer for Boston Harry. I'll try him wit' de high sign."

He whistled one or two bars of a rag-time melody, and the air was immediately taken up, and then quickly ended with a peculiar run. The first whistler walked confidently up to the fire. The fat man looked up and spake in a loud, asthmatic wheeze:

"Gents, the unexpected but welcome addition to our circle is Mr. Whistling Dick, an old friend of mine for whom I fully vouches. The waiter will lay another cover at once. Mr. W. D. will join us at supper, during which function he will enlighten us in regard to the circumstances that give us the pleasure of his company."

"Chewin' de stuffin' out'n de dictionary, as usual, Boston," said Whistling Dick; "but t'anks all de same for de invitashun. I guess I finds meeself here about de same way as yous guys. A cop gimme de tip dis mornin'. Yous workin' on dis farm?"

"A guest," said Boston sternly, "shouldn't never insult his entertainers until he's filled up wid grub. 'Tain't good business sense. Workin'!—but I will restrain myself. We five—me, Deaf Pete, Blinky, Goggles, and Indiana Tom—got put on to this scheme of Noo Orleans to work visiting gentlemen upon her dirty streets, and we hit the road last evening just as the tender hues of twilight had flopped down upon the daisies and things. Blinky, pass the empty oyster-can at your left to the empty gentleman at your right."

For the next ten minutes the gang of roadsters paid their undivided attention to the supper. In an old five-gallon kerosene can they had cooked a stew of potatoes, meat, and onions which they partook of from smaller cans they had found scattered about the vacant lot.

Whistling Dick had known Boston Harry of old, and knew him to be one of the shrewdest and most successful of his brotherhood. He looked like a prosperous stock-drover or a solid merchant from some country village. He was stout and hale, with a ruddy, always smoothly shaven face. His clothes were strong and neat, and he gave special attention to his decent-appearing shoes. During the past ten years he had acquired a reputation for working a larger number of successfully managed confidence games than any of his acquaintances, and he had not a day's work to be counted against him. It was rumored among his associates that he had saved a considerable amount of money. The four other men were fair specimens of the slinking, ill-clad, noisome genus who carried their labels of "suspicious" in plain view.

After the bottom of the large can had been scraped, and pipes lit at the coals, two of the men called Boston aside and spake with him lowly and mysteriously. He nodded decisively, and then said aloud to Whistling Dick:

"Listen, sonny, to some plain talky-talk. We five are on a lay. I've guaranteed you to be square, and you're to come in on the profits equal with the boys, and you've got to help. Two hundred hands on this plantation are expecting to be paid a week's wages to-morrow morning. To-morrow's Christmas, and they want to lay off. Says the boss: 'Work from five to nine in the morning to get a train load of sugar off, and I'll pay every man cash down for the week and a day extra.' They say: 'Hooray for the boss! It goes.' He drives to Noo Orleans to-day, and fetches back the cold dollars. Two thousand and seventy-four fifty is the amount. I got the figures from a man who talks too much, who got 'em from the bookkeeper. The boss of this plantation thinks he's going to pay this wealth to the hands. He's got it down wrong; he's going to pay it to us. It's going to stay in the leisure class, where it belongs. Now, half of this haul goes to me, and the other half the rest of you may divide. Why the difference? I represent the brains. It's my scheme. Here's the way we're going to get it. There's some company at supper in the house, but they'll leave about nine. They've just happened in for an hour or so. If they don't go pretty soon, we'll work the scheme anyhow. We want all night to get away good with the dollars. They're heavy. About nine o'clock Deaf Pete and Blinky'll go down the road about a quarter beyond the house, and set fire to a big cane-field there that the cutters haven't touched yet. The wind's just right to have it roaring in two minutes. The alarm'll be given, and every man Jack about the place will be down there in ten minutes, fighting fire. That'll leave the money sacks and the women alone in the house for us to handle. You've heard cane burn? Well, there's mighty few women can screech loud enough to be heard above its crackling. The thing's dead safe. The only danger is in being caught before we can get far enough away with the money. Now, if you——"

"Boston," interrupted Whistling Dick, rising to his feet, "t'anks for de grub yous fellers has given me, but I'll be movin' on now."

"What do you mean?" asked Boston, also rising.

"W'y, you can count me outer dis deal. You oughter know that. I'm on de bum all right enough, but dat other t'ing don't go wit' me. Burglary is no good. I'll say good night and many t'anks fer——"

Whistling Dick had moved away a few steps as he spoke, but he stopped very suddenly. Boston had covered him with a short revolver of roomy calibre.

"Take your seat," said the tramp leader. "I'd feel mighty proud of myself if I let you go and spoil the game. You'll stick right in this camp until we finish the job. The end of that brick pile is your limit. You go two inches beyond that, and I'll have to shoot. Better take it easy, now."

"It's my way of doin'," said Whistling Dick. "Easy goes. You can depress de muzzle of dat twelve-incher, and run 'em back on de trucks. I remains, as de newspapers says, 'in yer midst.'"

"All right," said Boston, lowering his piece, as the other returned and took his seat again on a projecting plank in a pile of timber. "Don't try to leave; that's all. I wouldn't miss this chance even if I had to shoot an old acquaintance to make it go. I don't want to hurt anybody specially, but this thousand dollars I'm going to get will fix me for fair. I'm going to drop the road, and start a saloon in a little town I know about. I'm tired of being kicked around."

Boston Harry took from his pocket a cheap silver watch and held it near the fire.

"It's a quarter to nine," he said. "Pete, you and Blinky start. Go down the road past the house and fire the cane in a dozen places. Then strike for the levee, and come back on it, instead of the road, so you won't meet anybody. By the time you get back the men will all be striking out for the fire, and we'll break for the house and collar the dollars. Eveybody cough up what matches he's got."

The two surly tramps made a collection of all the matches in the party, Whistling Dick contributing his quota with propitiatory alacrity, and then they departed in the dim starlight in the direction of the road.

Of the three remaining vagrants, two, Goggles and Indiana Tom, reclined lazily upon convenient lumber and regarded Whistling Dick with undisguised disfavor. Boston, observing that the dissenting recruit was disposed to remain peaceably, relaxed a little of his vigilance. Whistling Dick arose presently and strolled leisurely up and down keeping carefully within the territory assigned him.

"Dis planter chap," he said, pausing before Boston Harry, "w'ot makes yer t'ink he's got de tin in de house wit' 'im?"

"I'm advised of the facts in the case," said Boston. "He drove to Noo Orleans and got it, I say, to-day. Want to change your mind now and come in?"

"Naw, I was just askin'. Wot kind o' team did de boss drive?"

"Pair of grays."

"Double surrey?"

"Yep."

"Women folks along?"

"Wife and kid. Say, what morning paper are you trying to pump news for?"

"I was just conversin' to pass de time away. I guess dat team passed me in de road dis evenin'. Dat's all."

As Whistling Dick put his hands into his pockets and continued his curtailed beat up and down by the fire, he felt the silk stocking he had picked up in the road.

"Ther bloomin' little skeezicks," he muttered, with a grin.

As he walked up and down he could see, through a sort of natural opening or lane among the trees, the planter's residence some seventy-five yards distant. The side of the house toward him exhibited spacious, well-lighted windows through which a soft radiance streamed, illuminating the broad veranda and some extent of the lawn beneath.

"What's that you said?" asked Boston, sharply.

"Oh, nuttin' 't all," said Whistling Dick, lounging carelessly, and kicking meditatively at a little stone on the ground.

"Just as easy," continued the warbling vagrant softly to himself, "an' sociable an' swell, an' sassy, wit' her 'Mer-ry Chris-mus.' Wot d'yer t'ink, now!"

Dinner, two hours late, was being served in the Bellemeade plantation dining-room.

The dining-room and all its appurtenances spoke of an old régime that was here continued rather than suggested to the memory. The plate was rich to the extent that its age and quaintness alone saved it from being showy; there were interesting names signed in the corners of the pictures on the walls; the viands were of the kind that bring a shine into the eyes of gourmets. The service was swift, silent, lavish, as in the days when the waiters were assets like the plate. The names by which the planter's family and their visitors addressed one another were historic in the annals of two nations. Their manners and conversation had that most difficult kind of ease—the kind that still preserves punctilio. The planter himself seemed to be the dynamo that generated the larger portion of the gaiety and wit. The younger ones at the board found it more than difficult to turn back on him his guns of raillery and banter. It is true, the young men attempted to storm his works repeatedly, incited by the hope of gaining the approbation of their fair companions; but even when they sped a well-aimed shaft, the planter forced them to feel defeat by the tremendous discomfiting thunder of the laughter with which he accompanied his retorts. At the head of the table, serene, matronly, benevolent, reigned the mistress of the house, placing here and there the right smile, the right word, the encouraging glance.

The talk of the party was too desultory, too evanescent to follow, but at last they came to the subject of the tramp nuisance, one that had of late vexed the plantations for many miles around. The planter seized the occasion to direct his good-natured fire of raillery at the mistress, accusing her of encouraging the plague. "They swarm up and down the river every winter," he said. "They overrun New Orleans, and we catch the surplus, which is generally the worst part. And, a day or two ago, Madame New Orleans, suddenly discovering that she can't go shopping without brushing her skirts against great rows of the vagabonds sunning themselves on the banquettes, says to the police: 'Catch 'em all,' and the police catch a dozen or two, and the remaining three or four thousand overflow up and down the levees, and madame there"—pointing tragically with the carving-knife at her—"feeds them. They won't work, they defy my overseers, and they make friends with my dogs; and you, madame, feed them before my eyes and intimidate me when I would interfere. Tell us, please, how many to-day did you thus incite to future laziness and depredation?"

"Six, I think," said madame, with a reflective smile; "but you know two of them offered to work, for you heard them yourself."

The planter's disconcerting laugh rang out again.

"Yes, at their own trades. And one was an artificial-flower maker, and the other a glass-blower. Oh, they were looking for work! Not a hand would they consent to lift to labor of any other kind."

"And another one," continued the soft-hearted mistress, "used quite good language. It was really extraordinary for one of his class. And he carried a watch. And had lived in Boston. I don't believe they are all bad. They have always seemed to me to rather lack development. I always look upon them as children with whom wisdom has remained at a standstill while whiskers have continued to grow. We passed one this evening as we were driving home who had a face as good as it was incompetent. He was whistling the intermezzo from 'Cavalleria' and blowing the spirit of Mascagni himself into it."

A bright-eyed young girl who sat at the left of the mistress leaned over and said in a confidential undertone:

"I wonder, Mamma, if that tramp we passed on the road found my stocking, and do you think he will hang it up to-night? Now I can hang up but one. Do you know why I wanted a new pair of silk stockings when I have plenty? Well, old Aunt Judy says, if you hang up two that have never been worn, Santa Claus will fill one with good things, and Monsieur Pambe will place in the other payment for all the words you have spoken—good or bad— on the day before Christmas. That's why I've been unusually nice and polite to everyone to-day. Monsieur Pambe, you know, is a witch gentleman! he——"

The words of the young girl were interrupted by a startling thing.

Like the wraith of some burned-out shooting star, a black streak came crashing though the window-pane and upon the table, where it shivered into fragments a dozen pieces of crystal and china ware, and then glanced between the heads of the guests to the wall, imprinting therein a deep, round indentation, at which, to-day, the visitor to Bellemeade marvels as he gazes upon it and listens to this tale as it is told.

The women screamed in many keys, and the men sprang to their feet, and would have laid their hands upon their swords had not the verities of chronology forbidden.

The planter was the first to act; he sprang to the intruding missile and held it up to view.

"By Jupiter!" he cried. "A meteoric shower of hosiery! Has communication at last been established with Mars?"

"I should say—ahem!—Venus," ventured a young gentleman visitor, looking hopefully for approbation toward the unresponsive young-lady visitors.

The planter held at arm's length the unceremonious visitor—a long dangling black stocking. "It's loaded," he announced.

As he spoke he reversed the stocking, holding it by the toe, and down from it dropped a roundish stone, wrapped about by a piece of yellowish paper. "Now for the first interstellar message of the century!" he cried; and nodding to the company, who had crowded about him, he adjusted his glasses with provoking deliberation, and examined it closely. When he finished he had changed from the jolly host to the practical decisive man of business. He immediately struck a bell, and said to the silent-footed mulatto man who responded: "Go and tell Mr. Wesley to get Reeves and Maurice and about ten stout hands they can rely upon, and come to the hall door at once. Tell him to have the men arm themselves, and bring plenty of ropes and plough lines. Tell him to hurry." And then he read aloud from the paper these words:

To the Gent of de Hous:
   Dere is five tuff hobocs xcept meself in the vaken lot near de road war de old brick piles is. Dey got me stuck up wid a gun see and I taken dis means of comunikaten. 2 of der lads is gone down to set fire to de cain field below de hous and when yous fellers goes to turn de hoes on it de hole gang is goin to rob de house of de money yoo gotto pay off wit say git a move on ye say de kid dropt dis sock in der rode tel her mery crismus de same as she told me. Ketch de bums down de rode first and den sen a relefe core to get me out of soke youres truly,

Whistlen Dick

There was some quiet, but rapid, maneuvering at Bellemeade during the ensuing half hour, which ended in five disgusted and sullen tramps being captured and locked securely in an out-house pending the coming of the morning and retribution. For another result, the visiting young gentlemen had secured the unqualified worship of the visiting young ladies by their distinguished and heroic conduct. For still another, behold Whistling Dick, the hero, seated at the planter's table, feasting upon viands his experience had never before included, and waited upon by admiring femininity in shapes of such beauty and "swellness" that even his ever-full mouth could scarcely prevent him from whistling. He was made to disclose in detail his adventure with the evil gang of Boston Harry, and how he cunningly wrote the note and wrapped it around the stone and placed it in the toe of the stocking, and, watching his chance, sent it silently, with a wonderful centrifugal momentum, like a comet, at one of the big lighted windows of the dining-room.

The planter vowed that the wanderer should wander no more; that his was a goodness and an honesty that should be rewarded, and that a debt of gratitude had been made that must be paid; for had he not saved them from a doubtless imminent loss, and maybe a greater calamity? He assured Whistling Dick that he might consider himself a charge upon the honor of Bellemeade; that a position suited to his powers would be found for him at once, and hinted that the way would be heartily smoothed for him to rise to as high places of emolument and trust as the plantation afforded.

But now, they said, he must be weary, and the immediate thing to consider was rest and sleep. So the mistress spoke to a servant, and Whistling Dick was conducted to a room in the wing of the house occupied by the servants. To this room, in a few minutes, was brought a portable tin bathtub filled with water, which was placed on a piece of oiled cloth upon the floor. There the vagrant was left to pass the night.

By the light of the candle he examined the room. A bed, with the covers neatly turned back, revealed snowy pillows and sheets. A worn, but clean, red carpet covered the floor. There was a dresser with a beveled mirror, a washstand with a flowered bowl and pitcher; the two or three chairs were softly upholstered. A little table held books, papers, and a day-old cluster of roses in a jar. There were towels on a rack and soap in a white dish.

Whistling Dick set his candle on a chair and placed his hat carefully under the table. After satisfying what we must suppose to have been his curiosity by a sober scrutiny, he removed his coat, folded it, and laid it upon the floor, near the wall, as far as possible from the unused bathtub. Taking his coat for a pillow, he stretched himself luxuriously upon the carpet.

When, on Christmas morning, the first streaks of dawn broke above the marshes, Whistling Dick awoke and reached instinctively for his hat. Then he remembered that the skirts of Fortune had swept him into their folds on the night previous, and he went to the window and raised it, to let the fresh breath of the morning cool his brow and fix the yet dream-like memory of his good luck within his brain.

As he stood there, certain dread and ominous sounds pierced the fearful hollow of his ear.

The force of plantation workers, eager to complete the shortened task allotted to them, were all astir. The mighty din of the ogre Labor shook the earth, and the poor tattered and forever disguised Prince in search of his fortune held tight to the window-sill even in the enchanted castle, and trembled.

Already from the bosom of the mill came the thunder of rolling barrels of sugar, and (prison-like sounds) there was a great rattling of chains as the mules were harried with stimulant imprecations to their places by the wagon-tongues. A little vicious "dummy" engine, with a train of flat cars in tow, stewed and fumed on the plantation tap of the narrow-gauge railroad, and a toiling, hurrying, hallooing stream of workers were dimly seen in the half darkness loading the train with the weekly output of sugar. Here was a poem, an epic—nay, a tragedy—with work, the curse of the world, for its theme.

The December air was frosty, but the sweat broke out upon Whistling Dick's face. He thrust his head out of the window and looked down. Fifteen feet below him, against the wall of the house, he could make out that a border of flowers grew, and by that token he overhung a bed of soft earth.

Softly as a burglar goes, he clambered out upon the sill, lowered himself until he hung by his hands alone, and then dropped safely. No one seemed to be about upon this side of the house. He dodged low and skimmed swiftly across the yard to the low fence. It was an easy matter to vault this, for a terror urged him such as lifts the gazelle over the thorn bush when the lion pursues. A crash through the dew-drenched weeds on the roadside, a clutching, slippery rush up the grassy side of the levee to the footpath at the summit, and—he was free!

The east was blushing and brightening. The wind, himself a vagrant rover, saluted his brother upon the cheek. Some wild geese, high above, gave cry. A rabbit skipped along the path before him, free to turn to the right or to the left as his mood should send him. The river slid past, and certainly no one could tell the ultimate abiding place of its waters.

A small, ruffled, brown-breasted bird, sitting upon a dogwood sapling, began a soft, throaty, tender little piping in praise of the dew which entices foolish worms from their holes; but suddenly he stopped, and sat with his head turned sidewise, listening.

From the path along the levee there burst forth a jubilant, stirring, buoyant, thrilling whistle, loud and keen and clear as the cleanest notes of the piccolo. The soaring sound rippled and trilled and arpeggioed as the songs of wild birds do not; but it had a wild free grace that, in a way, reminded the small brown bird of something familiar, but exactly what he could not tell. There was in it the bird call, or reveille, that all birds know; but a great waste of lavish, unmeaning things that art had added and arranged, besides, and that were quite puzzling and strange; and the little brown bird sat with his head on one side until the sound died away in the distance.

The little bird did not know that the part of that strange warbling that he understood was just what kept the warbler without his breakfast; but he knew very well that the part he did not understand did not concern him, so he gave a little flutter of his wings and swooped down like a brown bullet upon a big fat worm that was wriggling along the levee path.

From
CABBAGES AND KINGS

❀

The Lotus and the Bottle

WILLARD GEDDIE, consul for the United States in Coralio, was working leisurely on his yearly report. Goodwin, who had strolled in as he did daily for a smoke on the much coveted porch, had found him so absorbed in his work that he departed after roundly abusing the consul for his lack of hospitality.

"I shall complain to the civil service department," said Goodwin; —"or is it a department?—perhaps it's only a theory. One gets neither civility nor service from you. You won't talk; and you won't set out anything to drink. What kind of a way is that of representing your government?"

Goodwin strolled out and across to the hotel to see if he could bully the quarantine doctor into a game on Coralio's solitary billiard table. His plans were completed for the interception of the fugtives from the capital; and now it was but a waiting game that he had to play.

The consul was interested in his report. He was only twenty-four; and he had not been in Coralio long enough for his enthusiasm to cool in the heat of the tropics—a paradox that may be allowed between Cancer and Capricorn.

So many thousand bunches of bananas, so many thousand

oranges and cocoanuts, so many ounces of gold dust, pounds of rubber, coffee, indigo and sarsaparilla—actually, exports were twenty per cent. greater than for the previous year!

A little thrill of satisfaction ran through the consul. Perhaps, he thought, the State Department, upon reading his introduction, would notice—and then he leaned back in his chair and laughed. He was getting as bad as the others. For the moment he had forgotten that Coralio was an insignificant town in an insignificant republic lying along the by-ways of a second-rate sea. He thought of Gregg, the quarantine doctor, who subscribed for the London *Lancet*, expecting to find it quoting his reports to the home Board of Health concerning the yellow fever germ. The consul knew that not one in fifty of his acquaintances in the States had ever heard of Coralio. He knew that two men, at any rate, would have to read his report—some underling in the State Department and a compositor in the Public Printing Office. Perhaps the typesticker would note the increase of commerce in Coralio, and speak of it, over the cheese and beer, to a friend.

He had just written: "Most unaccountable is the supineness of the large exporters in the United States in permitting the French and German houses to practically control the trade interests of this rich and productive country"—when he heard the hoarse notes of a steamer's siren.

Geddie laid down his pen and gathered his Panama hat and umbrella. By the sound he knew it to be the *Valhalla*, one of the line of fruit vessels plying for the Vesuvius Company. Down to *niños* of five years, everyone in Coralio could name you each incoming steamer by the note of her siren.

The consul sauntered by a roundabout, shaded way to the beach. By reason of long practice he gauged his stroll so accurately that by the time he arrived on the sandy shore the boat of the customs officials was rowing back from the steamer, which had been boarded and inspected according to the laws of Anchuria.

There is no harbor at Coralio. Vessels of the draught of the *Valhalla* must ride an anchor a mile from shore. When they take on fruit it is conveyed on lighters and freighter sloops. At Solitas, where there was a fine harbor, ships of many kinds were to be seen, but in the roadstead off Coralio scarcely any save the fruiters paused. Now and then a tramp coaster, or a mysterious brig from Spain, or a saucy French barque would hang innocently for a few days in the offing. Then the custom-house crew would become doubly vigilant and wary. At night a sloop or two would be making strange trips in and out along the shore; and in the morning the stock of Three-Star Hennessey, wines and drygoods in Coralio would be found vastly increased. It has also been said that the customs officials jingled more silver in the pockets of their red-striped trousers, and that the record books showed no increase in import duties received.

The customs boat and the *Valhalla* gig reached the shore at the same time. When they grounded in the shallow water there was still five yards of rolling surf between them and dry sand. Then half-clothed Caribs dashed into the water, and brought in on their backs the *Valhalla's* purser and the little native officials in their cotton undershirts, blue trousers with red stripes, and flapping straw hats.

At college Geddie had been a treasure as a first-baseman. He now closed his umbrella, stuck it upright in the sand, and stooped, with his hands resting upon his knees. The purser, burlesquing the pitcher's contortions, hurled at the consul the heavy roll of news-papers, tied with a string, that the steamer always brought for him. Geddie leaped high and caught the roll with a sounding "thwack." The loungers on the beach—about a third of the popu-lation of the town—laughed and applauded delightedly. Every week they expected to see that roll of papers delivered and re-ceived in that same manner, and they were never disappointed. Innovations did not flourish in Coralio.

The consul re-hoisted his umbrella and walked back to the consulate.

This home of a great nation's representative was a wooden structure of two rooms, with a native-built gallery of poles, bamboo and nipa palm running on three sides of it. One room was the official apartment, furnished chastely with a flat-top desk, a hammock, and three uncomfortable cane-seated chairs. Engravings of the first and latest president of the country represented hung against the wall. The other room was the consul's living apartment.

It was eleven o'clock when he returned from the beach, and therefore breakfast time. Chanca, the Carib woman who cooked for him, was just serving the meal on the side of the gallery facing the sea—a spot famous as the coolest in Coralio. The breakfast consisted of shark's fin soup, stew of land crabs, breadfruit, a boiled iguana steak, aguacates, a freshly cut pineapple, claret and coffee.

Geddie took his seat, and unrolled with luxurious laziness his bundle of newspapers. Here in Coralio for two days or longer he would read of goings-on in the world very much as we of the world read those whimsical contributions to inexact science that assume to portray the doings of the Martians. After he had finished with the papers they would be sent on the rounds of the other English-speaking residents of the town.

The paper that came first to his hand was one of those bulky mattresses of printed stuff upon which the readers of certain New York journals are supposed to take their Sabbath literary nap. Opening this the consul rested it upon the table, supporting its weight with the aid of the back of a chair. Then he partook of his meal deliberately, turning the leaves from time to time and glancing half idly at the contents.

Presently he was struck by something familiar to him in a picture—a half-page, badly printed reproduction of a photograph of a vessel. Languidly interested, he leaned for a nearer scrutiny and a view of the florid headlines of the column next to the picture.

Yes: he was not mistaken. The engraving was of the eight-hundred-ton yacht *Idalia*, belonging to "that prince of good fellows, Midas of the money market, and society's pink of perfection, J. Ward Tolliver."

Slowly sipping his black coffee, Geddie read the column of print. Following a listed statement of Mr. Tolliver's real estate and bonds, came a description of the yacht's furnishings, and then the grain of news no bigger than a mustard seed. Mr. Tolliver, with a party of favored guests, would sail the next day on a six weeks' cruise along the Central American and South American coasts and among the Bahama Islands. Among the guests were Mrs. Cumberland Payne and Miss Ida Payne, of Norfolk.

The writer, with the fatuous presumption that was demanded of him by his readers, had concocted a romance suited to their palates. He bracketed the names of Miss Payne and Mr. Tolliver until he had well-nigh read the marriage ceremony over them. He played coyly and insinuatingly upon the strings of "*on dit*" and "Madame Rumor" and "a little bird" and "no one would be surprised," and ended with congratulations.

Geddie, having finished his breakfast, took his papers to the edge of the gallery, and sat there in his favorite steamer chair with his feet on the bamboo railing. He lighted a cigar, and looked out upon the sea. He felt a glow of satisfaction at finding he was so little disturbed by what he had read. He told himself that he had conquered the distress that had sent him, a voluntary exile, to this far land of the lotus. He could never forget Ida, of course; but there was no longer any pain in thinking about her. When they had had that misunderstanding and quarrel he had impulsively sought his consulship with the desire to retaliate upon her by detaching himself from her world and presence. He had succeeded thoroughly in that. During the twelve months of his life in Coralio no word had passed between them, though he had sometimes heard of her through the dilatory correspondence with the few friends to whom he still wrote. Still he could not repress a little thrill of satisfaction at knowing that she had not yet married Tolliver or any one else. But evidently Tolliver had not yet abandoned hope.

Well, it made no difference to him now. He had eaten of the lotus. He was happy and content in this land of perpetual afternoon. Those old days of life in the States seemed like an irritating dream. He hoped Ida would be as happy as he was. The climate as balmy as that of distant Avalon; the fetterless, idyllic round of enchanted days; the life among this indolent, romantic people—a life full of music, flowers, and low laughter; the influence of the imminent sea and mountains, and the many shapes of love and magic and beauty that bloomed in the white tropic nights—with all he was more than content. Also, there was Paula Brannigan.

Geddie intended to marry Paula—if, of course, she would consent; but he felt rather sure that she would do that. Somehow, he kept postponing his proposal. Several times he had been quite near to it; but a mysterious something always held him back. Perhaps it was only the unconscious, instinctive conviction that the act would sever the last tie that bound him to his old world.

He could be very happy with Paula. Few of the native girls could be compared with her. She had attended a convent school in New Orleans for two years; and when she chose to display her accomplishments no one could detect any difference between her and the girls of Norfolk and Manhattan. But it was delicious to see her at home dressed, as she sometimes was, in the native costume, with bare shoulders and flowing sleeves.

Bernard Brannigan was the great merchant of Coralio. Besides his store, he maintained a train of pack mules, and carried on a lively trade with the interior towns and villages. He had married a native lady of high Castilian descent, but with a tinge of Indian brown showing through her olive cheek. The union of the Irish and the Spanish had produced, as it so often has, an offshoot of rare beauty and variety. They were very excellent people indeed, and the upper story of their house was ready to be placed at the service of Geddie and Paula as soon as he should make up his mind to speak about it.

By the time two hours were whiled away the consul tired of

reading. The papers lay scattered about him on the gallery. Reclining there, he gazed dreamily out upon an Eden. A clump of banana plants interposed their broad shields between him and the sun. The gentle slope from the consulate to the sea was covered with the dark-green foliage of lemon-trees and orange-trees just bursting into bloom. A lagoon pierced the land like a dark, jagged crystal, and above it a pale ceiba-tree rose almost to the clouds. The waving cocoanut palms on the beach flared their decorative green leaves against the slate of an almost quiescent sea. His senses were cognizant of brilliant scarlet and ochres amid the vert of the coppice, of odors of fruit and bloom and the smoke from Chanca's clay oven under the calabash-tree; of the treble laughter of the native women in their huts, the song of the robin, the salt taste of the breeze, the diminuendo of the faint surf running along the shore—and, gradually, of a white speck, growing to a blur, that introduced itself upon the drab prospect of the sea.

Lazily interested, he watched this blur increase until it became the *Idalia* steaming at full speed, coming down the coast. Without changing his position he kept his eyes upon the beautiful white yacht as she drew swiftly near and came opposite to Coralio. Then, sitting upright, he saw her float steadily past and on. Scarcely a mile of sea had separated her from the shore. He had seen the frequent flash of her polished brass work and the stripes of her deck-awnings—so much, and no more. Like a ship on a magic lantern slide the *Idalia* had crossed the illuminated circle of the consul's little world, and was gone. Save for the tiny cloud of smoke that was left hanging over the brim of the sea, she might have been an immaterial thing, a chimera of his idle brain.

Geddie went into his office and sat down to dawdle over his report. If the reading of the article in the paper had left him unshaken, this silent passing of the *Idalia* had done for him still more. It had brought the calm and peace of a situation from which all uncertainty had been erased. He knew that men sometimes hope without being aware of it. Now, since she had come two thousand miles and had passed without a sign, not even his unconscious self need cling to the past any longer.

After dinner, when the sun was low behind the mountains, Geddie walked on the little strip of beach under the cocoanuts. The wind was blowing mildly landward, and the surface of the sea was rippled by tiny wavelets.

A miniature breaker, spreading with a soft "swish" upon the sand, brought with it something round and shiny that rolled back again as the wave receded. The next influx beached it clear, and Geddie picked it up. The thing was a long-necked wine bottle of colorless glass. The cork had been driven in tightly to the level of the mouth, and the end covered with dark-red sealing-wax. The bottle contained only what seemed to be a sheet of paper, much curled from the manipulation it had undergone while being inserted. In the sealing-wax was the impression of a seal—probably of a signet-ring, bearing the initials of a monogram; but the impression had been hastily made, and the letters were past anything more certain than a shrewd conjecture. Ida Payne had always worn a signet-ring in preference to any other finger decoration. Geddie thought he could make out the familiar "I P"; and a queer sensation of disquietude went over him. More personal and intimate was this reminder of her than had been the sight of the vessel she was doubtless on. He walked back to his house, and set the bottle on his desk.

Throwing off his hat and coat, and lighting a lamp—for the night had crowded precipitately upon the brief twilight—he began to examine his piece of sea salvage.

By holding the bottle near the light and turning it judiciously, he made out that it contained a double sheet of note-paper filled with close writing; further, that the paper was of the same size and shade as that always used by Ida; and that, to the best of his belief, the handwriting was hers. The imperfect glass of the bottle so distorted the rays of light that he could read no word of the writing; but certain capital letters, of which he caught comprehensive glimpses, were Ida's, he felt sure.

There was a little smile both of perplexity and amusement in Geddie's eyes as he set the bottle down, and laid three cigars side by side on his desk. He fetched his steamer chair from the gallery, and stretched himself comfortably. He would smoke those three cigars while considering the problem.

For it amounted to a problem. He almost wished that he had not found the bottle; but the bottle was there. Why should it have drifted in from the sea, whence come so many disquieting things, to disturb his peace?

In this dreamy land, where time seemed so redundant, he had fallen into the habit of bestowing much thought upon even trifling matters.

He began to speculate upon many fanciful theories concerning the story of the bottle, rejecting each in turn.

Ships in danger of wreck or disablement sometimes cast forth such precarious messengers calling for aid. But he had seen the *Idalia* not three hours before, safe and speeding. Suppose the crew had mutinied and imprisoned the passengers below, and the message was one begging for succor! But, premising such an improbable outrage, would the agitated captives have taken the pains to fill four pages of note-paper with carefully penned arguments to their rescue?

Thus by elimination he soon rid the matter of the more unlikely theories, and was reduced—though aversely—to the less assailable one that the bottle contained a message to himself. Ida knew he was in Coralio; she must have launched the bottle while the yacht was passing and the wind blowing fairly toward the shore.

As soon as Geddie reached this conclusion a wrinkle came between his brows and a stubborn look settled around his mouth. He sat looking out through the doorway at the gigantic fire-flies traversing the quiet streets.

If this was a message to him from Ida, what could it mean save an overture toward a reconciliation? And if that, why had she not used the safe methods of the post instead of this uncertain and even flippant means of communication? A note in an empty bottle, cast into the sea! There was something light and frivolous about it, if not actually contemptuous.

The thought stirred his pride and subdued whatever emotions had been resurrected by the finding of the bottle.

Geddie put on his coat and hat and walked out. He followed a street that led him along the border of the little plaza where a band was playing and people were rambling, care-free and indolent. Some timorous *señoritas* scurrying past with fire-flies tangled in the jetty braids of their hair glanced at him with shy, flattering eyes. The air was languorous with the scent of jasmin and orange-blossoms.

The consul stayed his steps at the house of Bernard Brannigan. Paula was swinging in a hammock on the gallery. She rose from it like a bird from its nest. The color came to her cheek at the sound of Geddie's voice.

He was charmed at the sight of her costume—a flounced muslin dress, with a little jacket of white flannel, all made with neatness and style. He suggested a stroll, and they walked out to the old Indian well on the hill road. They sat on the curb, and there Geddie made the expected but long-deferred speech. Certain though he had been that she would not say him nay, he was thrilled with joy at the completeness and sweetness of her surrender. Here was surely a heart made for love and steadfastness. Here was no caprice or questionings or captious standards of convention.

When Geddie kissed Paula at her door that night he was happier than he had ever been before. "Here in this hollow lotus land, ever to live and lie reclined" seemed to him, as it has seemed to many mariners, the best as well as the easiest. His future would be an ideal one. He had attained a Paradise without a serpent. His Eve would be indeed a part of him, unbeguiled, and therefore more beguiling. He had made his decision to-night, and his heart was full of serene, assured content.

Geddie went back to his house whistling that finest and saddest love song, "La Golondrina." At the door his tame monkey leaped down from his shelf, chattering briskly. The consul turned to his desk to get him some nuts he usually kept there. Reaching in the half-darkness, his hand struck against the bottle. He started as if he had touched the cold rotundity of a serpent.

He had forgotten that the bottle was there.

He lighted the lamp and fed the monkey. Then, very deliberately, he lighted a cigar, and took the bottle in his hand, and walked down the path to the beach.

There was a moon, and the sea was glorious. The breeze had shifted, as it did each evening, and was now rushing steadily seaward.

Stepping to the water's edge, Geddie hurled the unopened bottle far out into the sea. It disappeared for a moment, and then shot upward twice its length. Geddie stood still, watching it. The moonlight was so bright that he could see it bobbing up and down with the little waves. Slowly it receded from the shore, flashing and turning as it went. The wind was carrying it out to sea. Soon it became a mere speck, doubtfully discerned at irregular intervals; and then the mystery of it was swallowed up by the greater mystery of the ocean. Geddie stood still upon the beach, smoking and looking out upon the water.

"Simon!—Oh, Simon!—wake up there, Simon!" bawled a sonorous voice at the edge of the water.

Old Simon Cruz was a half-breed fisherman and smuggler who lived in a hut on the beach. Out of his earliest nap Simon was thus awakened.

He slipped on his shoes and went outside. Just landing from one of the *Valhalla's* boats was the third mate of that vessel, who was an acquaintance of Simon's, and three sailors from the fruiter.

"Go up, Simon," called the mate, "and find Dr. Gregg or Mr. Goodwin or anybody that's a friend to Mr. Geddie, and bring 'em here at once."

"Saints of the skies!" said Simon, sleepily, "nothing has happened to Mr. Geddie?"

"He's under that tarpauling," said the mate, pointing to the boat, "and he's rather more than half drowned. We seen him from the steamer nearly a mile out from shore, swimmin' like mad after a bottle that was floatin' in the water, outward bound. We lowered the gig and started for him. He nearly had his hand on the bottle, when he gave out and went under. We pulled him out in time to save him, maybe; but the doctor is the one to decide that."

"A bottle?" said the old man, rubbing his eyes. He was not yet fully awake. "Where is the bottle?"

"Driftin' along out there some'eres," said the mate, jerking his thumb toward the sea. "Get on with you, Simon."

Shoes

JOHN DE GRAFFENREID ATWOOD ate of the lotus, root, stem, and flower. The tropics gobbled him up. He plunged enthusiastically into his work, which was to try to forget Rosine.

Now, they who dine on the lotus rarely consume it plain. There is a sauce *au diable* that goes with it; and the distillers are the chefs who prepare it. And on Johnny's menu card it read "brandy." With a bottle between them, he and Billy Keogh would sit on the porch of the little consulate at night and roar out great, indecorous songs, until the natives, slipping hastily past, would shrug a shoulder and mutter things to themselves about the *"Americanos diablos."*

One day Johnny's *mozo* brought the mail and dumped it on the table. Johnny leaned from his hammock, and fingered the four or five letters dejectedly. Keogh was sitting on the edge of the table chopping lazily with a paper knife at the legs of a centipede that was crawling among the stationery. Johnny was in that phase of lotus-eating when all the world tastes bitter in one's mouth.

"Same old thing!" he complained. "Fool people writing for information about the country. They want to know all about raising fruit, and how to make a fortune without work. Half of 'em don't even send stamps for a reply. They think a consul hasn't anything to do but write letters. Slit those envelopes for me, old man, and see what they want. I'm feeling too rocky to move."

Keogh, acclimated beyond all possibility of ill-humor, drew his

chair to the table with smiling compliance on his rose-pink countenance, and began to slit open the letters. Four of them were
from citizens in various parts of the United States who seemed
to regard the consul at Coralio as a cyclopædia of information. They asked long lists of questions, numerically arranged,
about the climate, products, possibilities, laws, business chances,
and statistics of the country in which the consul had the honor of
representing his own government.

"Write 'em, please, Billy," said that inert official, "just a line, re-
ferring them to the latest consular report. Tell 'em the State Department will be delighted to furnish the literary gems. Sign my
name. Don't let your pen scratch, Billy; it'll keep me awake."

"Don't snore," said Keogh, amiably, "and I'll do your work for
you. You need a corps of assistants, anyhow. Don't see how you
ever get out a report. Wake up a minute!—here's one more letter
—it's from your own town, too—Dalesburg."

"That so?" murmured Johnny, showing a mild obligatory interest. "What's it about?"

"Postmaster writes," explained Keogh. "Says a citizen of the
town wants some facts and advice from you. Says the citizen has
an idea in his head of coming down where you are and opening a shoe store. Wants to know if you think the business
would pay. Says he's heard of the boom along this coast, and wants
to get in on the ground floor."

In spite of the heat and his bad temper, Johnny's hammock
swayed with his laughter. Keogh laughed too; and the pet monkey
on the top shelf of the bookcase chattered in shrill sympathy
with the ironical reception of the letter from Dalesburg.

"Great bunions!" exclaimed the consul. "Shoe store! What'll
they ask about next, I wonder? Overcoat factory, I reckon. Say,
Billy—of our 3,000 citizens, how many do you suppose ever had on
a pair of shoes?"

Keogh reflected judicially.

"Let's see—there's you and me and——"

"Not me," said Johnny, promptly and incorrectly, holding up a foot encased in a disreputable deerskin *zapato*. "I haven't been a victim to shoes in months."

"But you've got 'em, though," went on Keogh. "And there's Goodwin and Blanchard and Geddie and old Lutz and Doc Gregg and that Italian that's agent for the banana company, and there's old Delgado—no; he wears sandals. And, oh, yes; there's Madama Ortiz, 'what kapes the hotel'—she had on a pair of red slippers at the *baile* the other night. And Miss Pasa, her daughter, that went to school in the States—she brought back some civilized notions in the way of footgear. And there's the *commandante's* sister that dresses up her feet on feast-days—and Mrs. Geddie, who wears a two with a Castilian instep—and that's about all the ladies. Let's see—don't some of the soldiers at the *cuartel*—no that's so; they're allowed shoes only when on the march. In barracks they turn their little toeses out to grass."

" 'Bout right," agreed the consul. "Not over twenty out of the three thousand ever felt leather on their walking arrangements. Oh, yes; Coralio is just the town for an enterprising shoe store— that doesn't want to part with its goods. Wonder if old Patterson is trying to jolly me! He always was full of things he called jokes. Write him a letter, Billy. I'll dictate it. We'll jolly him back a few."

Keogh dipped his pen, and wrote at Johnny's dictation. With many pauses, filled in with smoke and sundry travellings of the bottle and glasses, the following reply to the Dalesburg communication was perpetrated:

Mr. Obadiah Patterson,
    Dalesburg, Ala.
    Dear Sir: In reply to your favor of July 2d, I have the honor to inform you that, according to my opinion, there is no place on the habitable globe that presents to the eye stronger evidence of the need of a first-class shoe store than does the town of Coralio. There are 3,000 inhabitants in the place, and not a single shoe store! The situation speaks for itself. This coast is rapidly becoming the goal of enterprising busi-

ness men, but the shoe business is one that has been sadly overlooked or neglected. In fact, there are a considerable number of our citizens actually without shoes at present.

Besides the want above mentioned, there is also a crying need for a brewery, a college of higher mathematics, a coal yard, and a clean and intellectual Punch and Judy show. I have the honor to be, sir,

Your Obt. Servant,
John de Graffenreid Atwood,
U. S. Consul at Coralio.

P. S.—Hello! Uncle Obadiah. How's the old burg racking along? What would the government do without you and me? Look out for a green-headed parrot and a bunch of bananas soon, from your old friend

Johnny

"I throw in that postscript," explained the consul, "so Uncle Obadiah won't take offence at the official tone of the letter! Now, Billy, you get that correspondence fixed up, and send Pancho to the post-office with it. The *Ariadne* takes the mail out to-morrow if they make up that load of fruit to-day."

The night programme in Coralio never varied. The recreations of the people were soporific and flat. They wandered about, barefoot and aimless, speaking lowly and smoking cigar or cigarette. Looking down on the dimly lighted ways one seemed to see a threading maze of brunette ghosts tangled with a procession of insane fire-flies. In some houses the thrumming of lugubrious guitars added to the depression of the *triste* night. Giant tree-frogs rattled in the foliage as loudly as the end man's "bones" in a minstrel troupe. By nine o'clock the streets were almost deserted.

Not at the consulate was there often a change of bill. Keogh would come there nightly, for Coralio's one cool place with the little seaward porch of that official residence.

The brandy would be kept moving; and before midnight sentiment would begin to stir in the heart of the self-exiled consul. Then he would relate to Keogh the story of his ended romance.

Each night Keogh would listen patiently to the tale, and be ready with untiring sympathy.

"But don't you think for a minute"—thus Johnny would always conclude his woeful narrative—"that I'm grieving about that girl, Billy. I've forgotten her. She never enters my mind. If she were to enter that door right now, my pulse wouldn't gain a beat. That's all over long ago."

"Don't I know it?" Keogh would answer. "Of course you've forgotten her. Proper thing to do. Wasn't quite O. K. of her to listen to the knocks that—er—Dink Pawson kept giving you."

"Pink Dawson!"—a world of contempt would be in Johnny's tones—"Poor white trash! That's what he was. Had five hundred acres of farming land, though; and that counted. Maybe I'll have a chance to get back at him some day. The Dawsons weren't anybody. Everybody in Alabama knows the Atwoods. Say, Billy—did you know my mother was a De Graffenreid?"

"Why, no," Keogh would say; "is that so?" He had heard it some three hundred times.

"Fact. The De Graffenreids of Hancock County. But I never think of that girl any more, do I, Billy?"

"Not for a minute, my boy," would be the last sounds heard by the conqueror of Cupid.

At this point Johnny would fall into a gentle slumber, and Keogh would saunter out to his own shack under the calabash tree at the edge of the plaza.

In a day or two the letter from the Dalesburg postmaster and its answer had been forgotten by the Coralio exiles. But on the 26th day of July the fruit of the reply appeared upon the tree of events.

The *Andador*, a fruit steamer that visited Coralio regularly, drew into the offing and anchored. The beach was lined with spectators while the quarantine doctor and the custom-house crew rowed out to attend to their duties.

An hour later Bill Keogh lounged into the consulate, clean and cool in his linen clothes, and grinning like a pleased shark.

"Guess what?" he said to Johnny, lounging in his hammock.

"Too hot to guess," said Johnny, lazily.

"Your shoe-store man's come," said Keogh, rolling the sweet morsel on his tongue, "with a stock of goods big enough to supply the continent as far down as Terra del Fuego. They're carting his cases over to the custom-house now. Six barges full they brought ashore and have paddled back for the rest. Oh, ye saints in glory! won't there be regalements in the air when he gets onto the joke and has an interview with Mr. Consul? It'll be worth nine years in the tropics just to witness that one joyful moment."

Keogh loved to take his mirth easily. He selected a clean place on the matting and lay upon the floor. The walls shook with his enjoyment. Johnny turned half over and blinked.

"Don't tell me," he said, "that anybody was fool enough to take that letter seriously."

"Four-thousand-dollar stock of goods!" gasped Keogh, in ecstasy. "Talk about coals to Newcastle! Why didn't he take a shipload of palm-leaf fans to Spitzbergen while he was about it? Saw the old codger on the beach. You ought to have been there when he put on his specs and squinted at the five hundred or so barefooted citizens standing around."

"Are you telling the truth, Billy?" asked the consul, weakly.

"Am I? You ought to see the buncoed gentleman's daughter he brought along. Looks! She makes the brick-dust señoritas here look like tar-babies."

"Go on," said Johnny, "if you can stop that asinine giggling. I hate to see a grown man make a laughing hyena of himself."

"Name is Hemstetter," went on Keogh. "He's a—— Hello! what's the matter now?"

Johnny's moccasined feet struck the floor with a thud as he wriggled out of his hammock.

"Get up, you idiot," he said, sternly, "or I'll brain you with this inkstand. That's Rosine and her father. Gad! what a drivelling idiot old Patterson is! Get up, here, Billy Keogh, and help me. What the devil are we going to do? Has all the world gone crazy?"

Keogh rose and dusted himself. He managed to regain a decorous demeanor.

"Situation has got to be met, Johnny," he said, with some success at seriousness. "I didn't think about its being your girl until you spoke. First thing to do is to get them comfortable quarters. You go down and face the music, and I'll trot out to Goodwin's and see if Mrs. Goodwin won't take them in. They've got the decentest house in town."

"Bless you, Billy!" said the consul. "I knew you wouldn't desert me. The world's bound to come to an end, but maybe we can stave it off for a day or two."

Keogh hoisted his umbrella and set out for Goodwin's house. Johnny put on his coat and hat. He picked up the brandy bottle, but set it down again without drinking, and marched bravely down to the beach.

In the shade of the custom-house walls he found Mr. Hemstetter and Rosine surrounded by a mass of gaping citizens. The customs officers were ducking and scraping, while the captain of the *Andador* interpreted the business of the new arrivals. Rosine looked healthy and very much alive. She was gazing at the strange scenes around her with amused interest. There was a faint blush upon her round cheek as she greeted her old admirer. Mr. Hemstetter shook hands with Johnny in a very friendly way. He was an oldish, impractical man—one of that numerous class of erratic business men who are forever dissatisfied, and seeking a change.

"I am very glad to see you, John—may I call you John?" he said. "Let me thank you for your prompt answer to our postmaster's letter of inquiry. He volunteered to write to you on my behalf. I was looking about for something different in the way of a business in which the profits would be greater. I had noticed in the papers that this coast was receiving much attention from investors. I am extremely grateful for your advice to come. I sold out everything that I possess, and invested the proceeds in as fine a stock of shoes as could be bought in the North. You have a picturesque town here, John. I hope business will be as good as your letter justifies me in expecting."

Johnny's agony was abbreviated by the arrival of Keogh, who hurried up with the news that Mrs. Goodwin would be much pleased to place rooms at the disposal of Mr. Hemstetter and his daughter. So there Mr. Hemstetter and Rosine were at once conducted and left to recuperate from the fatigue of the voyage, while Johnny went down to see that the cases of shoes were safely stored in the customs warehouse pending their examination by the officials. Keogh, grinning like a shark, skirmished about to find Goodwin, to instruct him not to expose to Mr. Hemstetter the true state of Coralio as a shoe market until Johnny had been given a chance to redeem the situation, if such a thing were possible.

That night the consul and Keogh held a desperate consultation on the breezy porch of the consulate.

"Send 'em back home," began Keogh, reading Johnny's thoughts.

"I would," said Johnny, after a little silence; "but I've been lying to you, Billy."

"All right about that," said Keogh, affably.

"I've told you hundreds of times," said Johnny, slowly, "that I had forgotten that girl, haven't I?"

"About three hundred and seventy-five," admitted the monument of patience.

"I lied," repeated the consul, "every time. I never forget her for one minute. I was an obstinate ass for running away just because she said 'No' once. And I was too proud a fool to go back. I talked with Rosine a few minutes this evening up at Goodwin's. I found out one thing. You remember that farmer fellow who was always after her?"

"Dink Pawson?" asked Keogh.

"Pink Dawson. Well, he wasn't a hill of beans to her. She says she didn't believe a word of the things he told her about me. But I'm sewed up now, Billy. That tomfool letter we sent ruined whatever chance I had left. She'll despise me when she finds out that her old father has been made the victim of a joke that a decent school boy wouldn't have been guilty of. Shoes! Why he couldn't sell twenty pairs of shoes in Coralio if he kept store here for twenty years. You put a pair of shoes on one of these Caribs or Spanish brown boys and what'd he do? Stand on his head and squeal until he'd kicked 'em off. None of 'em ever wore shoes and they never will. If I send 'em back home I'll have to tell the whole story, and what'll she think of me? I want that girl worse than ever, Billy, and now when she's in reach I've lost her forever because I tried to be funny when the thermometer was at 102."

"Keep cheerful," said the optimistic Keogh. "And let 'em open the store. I've been busy myself this afternoon. We can stir up a temporary boom in foot-gear anyhow. I'll buy six pairs when the doors open. I've been around and seen all the fellows and explained the catastrophe. They'll all buy shoes like they was centipedes. Frank Goodwin will take cases of 'em. The Geddies want about eleven pairs between 'em. Clancy is going to invest the savings of weeks, and even old Doc Gregg wants three pairs of alligator-hide slippers if they've got any tens. Blanchard got a look at Miss Hemstetter; and as he's a Frenchman, no less than a dozen pairs will do for him."

"A dozen customers," said Johnny, "for a $4,000 stock of shoes! It won't work. There's a big problem here to figure out. You go home, Billy, and leave me alone. I've got to work at it all by myself. Take that bottle of Three-star along with you—no, sir; not another ounce of booze for the United States consul. I'll sit here tonight and pull out the think stop. If there's a soft place on this proposition anywhere I'll land on it. If there isn't there'll be another wreck to the credit of the gorgeous tropics."

Keogh left, feeling that he could be of no use. Johnny laid a handful of cigars on a table and stretched himself in a steamer chair. When the sudden daylight broke, silvering the harbor ripples, he was still sitting there. Then he got up, whistling a little tune, and took his bath.

At nine o'clock he walked down to the dingy little cable office and hung for half an hour over a blank. The result of his application was the following message, which he signed and had transmitted at a cost of $33:

To Pinkney Dawson,
    Dalesburg, Ala.
    Draft for $100 comes to you next mail. Ship me immediately 500 pounds stiff, dry cockleburrs. New use here in arts. Market price twenty cents pound. Further orders likely. Rush.

Ships

Within a week a suitable building had been secured in the Calle Grande, and Mr. Hemstetter's stock of shoes arranged upon their shelves. The rent of the store was moderate; and the stock made a fine showing of neat white boxes, attractively displayed.

Johnny's friends stood by him loyally. On the first day Keogh strolled into the store in a casual kind of way about once every hour, and bought shoes. After he had purchased a pair each of extension soles, congress gaiters, button kids, low-quartered calfs, dancing pumps, rubber boots, tans of various hues, tennis shoes and flowered slippers, he sought out Johnny to be prompted as to names of other kinds that he might inquire for. The other English-speaking residents also played their parts nobly by buying often and liberally. Keogh was grand marshal, and made them distribute their patronage, thus keeping up a fair run of custom for several days.

Mr. Hemstetter was gratified by the amount of business done thus far; but expressed surprise that the natives were so backward with their custom.

"Oh, they're awfully shy," explained Johnny, as he wiped his forehead nervously. "They'll get the habit pretty soon. They'll come with a rush when they do come."

One afternoon Keogh dropped into the consul's office, chewing an unlighted cigar thoughtfully.

"Got anything up your sleeve?" he inquired of Johnny. "If you have it's about time to show it. If you can borrow some gent's hat in the audience, and make a lot of customers for an idle stock of shoes come out of it, you'd better spiel. The boys have all laid in enough foot-wear to last 'em ten years; and there's nothing doing in the shoe store but dolcy far nienty. I just came by there. Your venerable victim was standing in the door, gazing through his specs at the bare toes passing by his emporium. The natives here have got the true artistic temperament. Me and Clancy took eighteen tintypes this morning in two hours. There's been but one pair of shoes sold all day. Blanchard went in and bought a pair of fur-lined house-slippers because he thought he saw Miss Hemstetter go into the store. I saw him throw the slippers into the lagoon afterwards."

"There's a Mobile fruit steamer coming in to-morrow or next day," said Johnny. "We can't do anything until then."

"What are you going to do—try to create a demand?"

"Political economy isn't your strong point," said the consul, impudently. "You can't create a demand. But you can create a necessity for a demand. That's what I am going to do."

Two weeks after the consul sent his cable, a fruit steamer brought him a huge, mysterious brown bale of some unknown commodity. Johnny's influence with the custom-house people was sufficiently strong for him to get the goods turned over to him without the usual inspection. He had the bale taken to the consulate and snugly stowed in the back room.

That night he ripped open a corner of it and took out a handful of the cockleburrs. He examined them with the care with which a warrior examines his arms before he goes forth to battle for his lady-love and life. The burrs were the ripe August product, as hard as filberts, and bristling with spines as tough and sharp as needles. Johnny whistled softly a little tune, and went out to find Billy Keogh.

Later in the night, when Coralio was steeped in slumber, he and Billy went forth into the deserted streets with their coats bulging like balloons. All up and down the Calle Grande they went, sowing the sharp burrs carefully in the sand, along the narrow sidewalks, in every foot of grass between the silent houses. And then they took the side streets and byways, missing none. No place where the foot of man, woman or child might fall was slighted. Many trips they made to and from the prickly hoard. And then, nearly at the dawn, they laid themselves down to rest calmly, as great generals do after planning a victory according to the revised tactics, and slept, knowing that they had sowed with the accuracy of Satan sowing tares and the perseverance of Paul planting.

With the rising sun came the purveyors of fruits and meats, and arranged their wares in and around the little market-house. At one end of the town near the seashore the market-house stood; and the sowing of the burrs had not been carried that far. The dealers waited long past the hour when their sales usually began. None came to buy. "*Qué hay?*" they began to exclaim, one to another.

At their accustomed time, from every 'dobe and palm hut and grass-thatched shack and dim *patio* glided women—black women, brown women, lemon-colored women, women dun and yellow and tawny. They were the marketers starting to purchase the family supply of cassava, plantains, meat, fowls, and tortillas. Décolleté they were and bare-armed and bare-footed, with a single skirt reaching below the knee. Stolid and ox-eyed, they stepped from their doorways into the narrow paths or upon the soft grass of the streets.

The first to emerge uttered ambiguous squeals, and raised one foot quickly. Another step and they sat down, with shrill cries of alarm, to pick at the new and painful insects that had stung them upon the feet. "*Qué picadores diablos!*" they screeched to one another across the narrow ways. Some tried the grass instead of the paths, but there they were also stung and bitten by the strange little prickly balls. They plumped down in the grass, and added their lamentations to those of their sisters in the sandy paths. All through the town was heard the plaint of the feminine jabber. The venders in the market still wondered why no customers came.

Then men, lords of the earth, came forth. They, too, began to hop, to dance, to limp, and to curse. They stood stranded and foolish, or stooped to pluck at the scourge that attacked their feet and ankles. Some loudly proclaimed the pest to be poisonous spiders of an unknown species.

And then the children ran out for their morning romp. And now to the uproar was added the howls of limping infants and cockleburred childhood. Every minute the advancing day brought forth fresh victims.

Doña Maria Castillas y Buenventura de las Casas stepped from her honored doorway, as was her daily custom, to procure fresh bread from the *panadería* across the street. She was clad in a skirt of flowered yellow satin, a chemise of ruffled linen, and wore a purple mantilla from the looms of Spain. Her lemon-tinted feet, alas! were bare. Her progress was majestic, for were not her ancestors hidalgos of Aragon? Three steps she made across the velvety grass, and set her aristocratic sole upon a bunch of Johnny's burrs. Doña Maria Castillas y Buenventura de las Casas emitted a yowl even as a wildcat. Turning about, she fell upon hands and knees, and crawled—ay, like a beast of the field she crawled back to her honorable door-sill.

Don Señor Ildefonso Federico Valdazar, *Juez de la Paz*, weighing twenty stone, attempted to convey his bulk to the *pulpería* at the corner of the plaza in order to assuage his matutinal thirst. The first plunge of his unshod foot into the cool grass struck a concealed mine. Don Ildefonso fell like a crumpled cathedral, crying out that he had been fatally bitten by a deadly scorpion. Everywhere were the shoeless citizens hopping, stumbling, limping, and picking from their feet the venomous insects that had come in a single night to harass them.

The first to perceive the remedy was Estebán Delgado, the barber, a man of travel and education. Sitting upon a stone, he plucked burrs from his toes, and made oration:

"Behold, my friend, these bugs of the devil! I know them well. They soar through the skies in swarms like pigeons. These are the dead ones that fell during the night. In Yucatan I have seen them as large as oranges. Yes! There they hiss like serpents, and have wings like bats. It is the shoes—the shoes that one needs! *Zapatos —zapatos para mí!*"

Estebán hobbled to Mr. Hemstetter's store, and bought shoes. Coming out, he swaggered down the street with impunity, reviling loudly the bugs of the devil. The suffering ones sat up or stood upon one foot and beheld the immune barber. Men, women, and childen took up the cry: "*Zapatos! zapatos!*"

The necessity for the demand had been created. The demand followed. That day Mr. Hemstetter sold three hundred pairs of shoes.

"It is really surprising," he said to Johnny, who came up in the evening to help him straighten out the stock, "how trade is picking up. Yesterday I made but three sales."

"I told you they'd whoop things up when they got started," said the consul.

"I think I shall order a dozen more cases of goods, to keep the stock up," said Mr. Hemstetter, beaming through his spectacles.

"I wouldn't send in any orders yet," advised Johnny. "Wait till you see how the trade holds up."

Each night Johnny and Keogh sowed the crop that grew dollars by day. At the end of ten days two-thirds of the stock of shoes had been sold; and the stock of cockleburrs was exhausted. Johnny cabled to Pink Dawson for another 500 pounds, paying twenty cents per pound as before. Mr. Hemstetter carefully made up an order for $1,500 worth of shoes from Northern firms. Johnny hung about the store until this order was ready for the mail, and succeeded in destroying it before it reached the postoffice.

That night he took Rosine under the mango tree by Goodwin's porch, and confessed everything. She looked him in the eye, and said: "You are a very wicked man. Father and I will go back home. You say it was a joke? I think it is a very serious matter."

But at the end of half an hour's argument the conversation had been turned upon a different subject. The two were considering the respective merits of pale blue and pink wall paper with which the old colonial mansion of the Atwoods in Dalesburg was to be decorated after the wedding.

On the next morning Johnny confessed to Mr. Hemstetter. The shoe merchant put on his spectacles, and said through them: "You strike me as being a most extraordinary young scamp. If I had not managed this enterprise with good business judgment my entire stock of goods might have been a complete loss. Now, how do you propose to dispose of the rest of it?"

When the second invoice of cockleburrs arrived Johnny loaded them and the remainder of the shoes into a schooner, and sailed down the coast to Alazan.

There, in the same dark and diabolical manner, he repeated his success; and came back with a bag of money and not so much as a shoestring.

And then he besought his great Uncle of the waving goatee and starred vest to accept his resignation, for the lotus no longer lured him. He hankered for the spinach and cress of Dalesburg.

The services of Mr. William Terence Keogh as acting consul, *pro tem.*, were suggested and accepted, and Johnny sailed with the Hemstetters back to his native shores.

Keogh slipped into the sinecure of the American consulship with the ease that never left him even in such high places. The tintype establishment was soon to become a thing of the past, although its deadly work along the peaceful and helpless Spanish Main was never effaced. The restless partners were about to be off again, scouting ahead of the slow ranks of Fortune. But now they would take different ways. There were rumors of a promising uprising in Peru; and thither the martial Clancy would turn his adventurous steps. As for Keogh, he was figuring in his mind and on quires of Government letter-heads a scheme that dwarfed the art of misrepresenting the human countenance upon tin.

"What suits me," Keogh used to say, "in the way of a business proposition is something diversified that looks like a longer shot than it is—something in the way of a genteel graft that isn't worked enough for the correspondence schools to be teaching it by mail. I take the long end; but I like to have at least as good a chance to win as a man learning to play poker on an ocean steamer, or running for governor of Texas on the Republican ticket. And when I cash in my winnings, I don't want to find any widows' and orphans' chips in my stack."

The grass-grown globe was the green table on which Keogh gambled. The games he played were of his own invention. He was no grubber after the diffident dollar. Nor did he care to follow it with horn and hounds. Rather he loved to coax it with egregious and brilliant flies from its habitat in the waters of strange streams. Yet Keogh was a business man; and his schemes, in spite of their singularity, were as solidly set as the plans of a building contractor. In Arthur's time Sir William Keogh would have been a Knight of the Round Table. In these modern days he rides abroad, seeking the Graft instead of the Grail.

Three days after Johnny's departure, two small schooners appeared off Coralio. After some delay a boat put off from one of them, and brought a sunburned young man ashore. This young man had a shrewd and calculating eye; and he gazed with amazement at the strange things that he saw. He found on the beach some one who directed him to the consul's office; and thither he made his way at a nervous gait.

Keogh was sprawled in the official chair, drawing caricatures of his uncle's head on an official pad of paper. He looked up at his visitor.

"Where's Johnny Atwood?" inquired the sunburned young man, in a business tone.

"Gone," said Keogh, working carefully at Uncle Sam's necktie.

"That's just like him," remarked the nut-brown one, leaning

against the table. "He always was a fellow to gallivant around instead of 'tending to business. Will he be in soon?"

"Don't think so," said Keogh, after a fair amount of deliberation.

"I s'pose he's out at some of his tomfoolery," conjectured the visitor, in a tone of virtuous conviction. "Johnny never would stick to anything long enough to succeed. I wonder how he manages to run his business here, and never be 'round to look after it."

"I'm looking after the business just now," admitted the *pro tem.* consul.

"Are you—then, say!—where's the factory?"

"What factory?" asked Keogh, with a mildly polite interest.

"Why, the factory where they use them cockleburrs. Lord knows what they use 'em for, anyway! I've got the basements of both them ships out there loaded with 'em. I'll give you a bargain in this lot. I've had every man, woman, and child around Dalesburg that wasn't busy pickin' 'em for a month. I hired these ships to bring 'em over. Everybody thought I was crazy. Now, you can have this lot for fifteen cents a pound, delivered on land. And if you want more I guess old Alabam' can come up to the demand. Johnny told me when he left home that if he struck anything down here that there was any money in he'd let me in on it. Shall I drive the ships in and hitch?"

A look of supreme, almost incredulous, delight dawned in Keogh's ruddy countenance. He dropped his pencil. His eyes turned upon the sunburned young man with joy in them mingled with fear lest his ecstasy should prove a dream.

"For God's sake, tell me," said Keogh, earnestly, "are you Dink Pawson?"

"My name is Pinkney Dawson," said the cornerer of the cockleburr market.

Billy Keogh slid rapturously and gently from his chair to his favorite strip of matting on the floor.

There were not many sounds in Coralio on that sultry afternoon. Among those that were may be mentioned a noise of enraptured and unrighteous laughter from a prostrate Irish-

American, while a sunburned young man, with a shrewd eye, looked on him with wonder and amazement. Also the "tramp, tramp, tramp" of many well-shod feet in the streets outside. Also the lonesome wash of the waves that beat along the historic shores of the Spanish Main.

Masters of Arts

A TWO-INCH STUB of a blue pencil was the wand with which Keogh performed the preliminary acts of his magic. So, with this he covered paper with diagrams and figures while he waited for the United States of America to send down to Coralio a successor to Atwood, resigned.

The new scheme that his mind had conceived, his stout heart indorsed, and his blue pencil corroborated, was laid around the characteristics and human frailties of the new president of Anchuria. These characteristics, and the situation out of which Keogh hoped to wrest a golden tribute, deserve chronicling contributive to the clear order of events.

President Losada—many called him Dictator—was a man whose genius would have made him conspicuous even among Anglo-Saxons, had not that genius been intermixed with other traits that were petty and subversive. He had some of the lofty patriotism of Washington (the man he most admired), the force of Napoleon, and much of the wisdom of the sages. These characteristics might have justified him in the assumption of the title of "The Illustrious Liberator," had they not been accompanied by a stupendous and amazing vanity that kept him in the less worthy ranks of the dictators.

Yet he did his country great service. With a mighty grasp he shook it nearly free from the shackles of ignorance and sloth and the vermin that fed upon it, and all but made it a power in the council of nations. He established schools and hospitals, built roads, bridges, railroads and palaces, and bestowed generous subsidies upon the arts and sciences. He was the absolute despot and the idol of his people. The wealth of the country poured into his hands. Other presidents had been rapacious without reason. Losada amassed enormous wealth, but his people had their share of the benefits.

The joint in his armor was his insatiate passion for monuments and tokens commemorating his glory. In every town he caused to be erected statues of himself bearing legends in praise of his greatness. In the walls of every public edifice, tablets were fixed reciting his splendor and the gratitude of his subjects. His statuettes and portraits were scattered throughout the land in every house and hut. One of the sycophants in his court painted him as St. John, with a halo and a train of attendants in full uniform. Losada saw nothing incongruous in this picture, and had it hung in a church in the capital. He ordered from a French sculptor a marble group including himself with Napoleon, Alexander the Great, and one or two others whom he deemed worthy of the honor.

He ransacked Europe for decorations, employing policy, money and intrigue to cajole the orders he coveted from kings and rulers. On state occasions his breast was covered from shoulder to shoulder with crosses, stars, golden roses, medals and ribbons. It was said that the man who could contrive for him a new decoration, or invent some new method of extolling his greatness, might plunge a hand deep into the treasury.

This was the man upon whom Billy Keogh had his eye. The gentle buccaneer had observed the rain of favors that fell upon those who ministered to the president's vanities, and he did not deem it his duty to hoist his umbrella against the scattering drops of liquid fortune.

In a few weeks the new consul arrived, releasing Keogh from his temporary duties. He was a young man fresh from college, who lived for botany alone. The consulate at Coralio gave him the opportunity to study tropical flora. He wore smoked glasses, and carried a green umbrella. He filled the cool, back porch of the consulate with plants and specimens so that space for a bottle and chair was not to be found. Keogh gazed on him sadly, but without rancour, and began to pack his gripsack. For his new plot against stagnation along the Spanish Main required of him a voyage overseas.

Soon came the *Karlsefin* again—she of the trampish habits—gleaning a cargo of cocoanuts for a speculative descent upon the New York market. Keogh was booked for a passage on the return trip.

"Yes, I'm going to New York," he explained to the group of his countrymen that had gathered on the beach to see him off. "But I'll be back before you miss me. I've undertaken the art education of this piebald country, and I'm not the man to desert it while it's in the early throes of tintypes."

With this mysterious declaration of his intentions Keogh boarded the *Karlsefin*.

Ten days later, shivering, with the collar of his thin coat turned high, he burst into the studio of Carolus White at the top of a tall building in Tenth Street, New York City.

Carolus White was smoking a cigarette and frying sausages over an oil stove. He was only twenty-three, and had noble theories about art.

"Billy Keogh!" exclaimed White, extending the hand that was not busy with the frying pan. "From what part of the uncivilized world, I wonder!"

"Hello, Carry," said Keogh, dragging forward a stool, and holding his fingers close to the stove. "I'm glad I found you so soon. I've been looking for you all day in the directories and art galleries. The free-lunch man on the corner told me where you were, quick. I was sure you'd be painting pictures yet."

Keogh glanced about the studio with the shrewd eye of a connoisseur in business.

"Yes, you can do it," he declared, with many gentle nods of his head. "That big one in the corner with the angels and green clouds and band-wagon is just the sort of thing we want. What would you call that, Carry—scene from Coney Island, ain't it?"

"That," said White, "I had intended to call 'The Translation of Elijah,' but you may be nearer right than I am."

"Name doesn't matter," said Keogh, largely; "it's the frame and the varieties of paint that does the trick. Now, I can tell you in a minute what I want. I've come on a little voyage of two thousand miles to take you in with me on a scheme. I thought of you as soon as the scheme showed itself to me. How would you like to go back with me and paint a picture? Ninety days for the trip, and five thousand dollars for the job."

"Cereal food or hair-tonic posters?" asked White.

"It isn't an ad."

"What kind of a picture is it to be?"

"It's a long story," said Keogh.

"Go ahead with it. If you don't mind, while you talk I'll just keep my eye on these sausages. Let 'em get one shade deeper than a Vandyke brown and you spoil 'em."

Keogh explained his project. They were to return to Coralio, where White was to pose as a distinguished American portrait painter who was touring in the tropics as a relaxation from his arduous and remunerative professional labors. It was not an unreasonable hope, even to those who had trod in the beaten paths of business, that an artist with so much prestige might secure a commission to perpetuate upon canvas the lineaments of the president, and secure a share of the *pesos* that were raining upon the caterers to his weaknesses.

Keogh had set his price at ten thousand dollars. Artists had been paid more for portraits. He and White were to share the expenses of the trip, and divide the possible profits. Thus he laid the scheme before White, whom he had known in the West before one declared for Art and the other became a Bedouin.

Before long the two machinators abandoned the rigor of the bare studio for a snug corner of a café. There they sat far into the night, with old envelopes and Keogh's stub of blue pencil between them.

At twelve o'clock White doubled up in his chair, with his chin on his fist, and shut his eyes at the unbeautiful wall-paper.

"I'll go you, Billy," he said, in the quiet tones of decision. "I've got two or three hundred saved up for sausages and rent; and I'll take the chance with you. Five thousand! It will give me two years in Paris and one in Italy. I'll begin to pack to-morrow."

"You'll begin in ten minutes," said Keogh. "It's to-morrow now. The *Karlsefin* starts back at four P.M. Come on to your painting shop, and I'll help you."

For five months in the year Coralio is the Newport of Anchuria. Then only does the town possess life. From November to March it is practically the seat of the government. The president with his official family sojourns there; and society follows him. The pleasure-loving people make the season one long holiday of amusement and rejoicing. *Fiestas*, balls, games, sea bathing, processions and small theatres contribute to their enjoyment. The famous Swiss band from the capital plays in the little plaza every evening, while the fourteen carriages and vehicles in the town circle in funereal but complacent procession. Indians from the interior mountains, looking like prehistoric stone idols, come down to peddle their handiwork in the streets. The people throng the narrow ways, a chattering, happy, careless stream of buoyant humanity. Preposterous children rigged out with the shortest of ballet skirts and gilt wings, howl, underfoot, among the effervescent crowds. Especially is the arrival of the presidential party, at the opening of the season, attended with pomp, show and patriotic demonstrations of enthusiasm and delight.

When Keogh and White reached their destination, on the return trip of the *Karlsefin*, the gay winter season was well begun. As they stepped upon the beach they could hear the band playing in the plaza. The village maidens, with fire-flies already fixed in their dark locks, were gliding, barefoot and coy-eyed, along the paths. Dandies in white linen, swinging their canes, were beginning their seductive strolls. The air was full of human essence, of artificial enticement, of coquetry, indolence, pleasure—the man-made sense of existence.

The first two or three days after their arrival were spent in pre-liminaries. Keogh escorted the artist about town, introducing him to the little circle of English-speaking residents and pulling what-ever wires he could to effect the spreading of White's fame as a painter. And then Keogh planned a more spectacular demonstra-tion of the idea he wished to keep before the public.

He and White engaged rooms in the Hotel de los Estranjeros. The two were clad in new suits of immaculate duck, with Ameri-can straw hats, and carried canes of remarkable uniqueness and inutility. Few caballeros in Coralio—even the gorgeously uni-formed officers of the Anchurian army—were as conspicuous for ease and elegance of demeanor as Keogh and his friend, the great American painter, Señor White.

White set up his easel on the beach and made striking sketches of the mountain and sea views. The native population formed at his rear in a vast, chattering semicircle to watch his work. Keogh, with his care for details, had arranged for himself a pose which he carried out with fidelity. His rôle was that of friend to the great artist, a man of affairs and leisure. The visible emblem of his position was a pocket camera.

"For branding the man who owns it," said he, "a genteel dilet-tante with a bank account and an easy conscience, a steam-yacht ain't in it with a camera. You see a man doing nothing but loafing around making snapshots, and you know right away he reads up well in 'Bradstreet.' You notice these old millionaire boys—soon as they get through taking everything else in sight they go to taking photographs. People are more impressed by a kodak than they are by a title or a four-carat scarf-pin." So Keogh strolled blandly about Coralio, snapping the scenery and the shrinking señoritas, while White posed conspicuously in the higher re-gions of art.

Two weeks after their arrival, the scheme began to bear fruit.

An aide-de-camp of the president drove to the hotel in a dashing victoria. The president desired that Señor White come to the Casa Morena for an informal interview.

Keogh gripped his pipe tightly between his teeth. "Not a cent less than ten thousand," he said to the artist—"remember the price. And in gold or its equivalent—don't let him stick you with this bargain-counter stuff they call money here."

"Perhaps it isn't that he wants," said White.

"Get out!" said Keogh, with splendid confidence. "I know what he wants. He wants his picture painted by the celebrated young American painter and filibuster now sojourning in this down-trodden country. Off you go."

The victoria sped away with the artist. Keogh walked up and down, puffing great clouds of smoke from his pipe, and waited. In an hour the victoria swept again to the door of the hotel, deposited White, and vanished. The artist dashed up the stairs, three at a step. Keogh stopped smoking, and became a silent interrogation point.

"Landed," exclaimed White, with his boyish face flushed with elation. "Billy, you are a wonder. He wants a picture. I'll tell you all about it. By Heavens! that dictator chap is a corker! He's a dictator clear down to his finger-ends. He's a kind of combination of Julius Cæsar, Lucifer and Chauncey Depew done in sepia. Polite and grim—that's his way. The room I saw him in was about ten acres big, and looked like a Mississippi steamboat with its gilding and mirrors and white paint. He talks English better than I can ever hope to. The matter of the price came up. I mentioned ten thousand. I expected him to call the guard and have me taken out and shot. He didn't move an eyelash. He just waved one of his chestnut hands in a careless way, and said, 'Whatever you say.' I am to go back to-morrow and discuss with him the details of the picture."

Keogh hung his head. Self-abasement was easy to read in his downcast countenance.

"I'm failing, Carry," he said, sorrowfully. "I'm not fit to handle these man's-size schemes any longer. Peddling oranges in a push-cart is about the suitable graft for me. When I said ten thousand, I swear I thought I had sized up that brown man's limit to within two cents. He'd have melted down for fifteen thousand just as easy. Say—Carry—you'll see the old man Keogh safe in some nice, quiet idiot asylum, won't you, if he makes a break like that again?"

The Casa Morena, although only one story in height, was a building of brown stone, luxurious as a palace in its interior. It stood on a low hill in a walled garden of splendid tropical flora at the upper edge of Coralio. The next day the president's carriage came again for the artist. Keogh went out for a walk along the beach, where he and his "picture box" were now familiar sights. When he returned to the hotel White was sitting in a steamer-chair on the balcony.

"Well," said Keogh, "did you and His Nibs decide on the kind of chromo he wants?"

White got up and walked back and forth on the balcony a few times. Then he stopped and laughed strangely. His face was flushed, and his eyes were bright with a kind of angry amusement.

"Look here, Billy," he said, somewhat roughly, "when you first came to me in my studio and mentioned a picture, I thought you wanted a Smashed Oats or a Hair Tonic poster painted on a range of mountains or the side of a continent. Well, either of those jobs would have been Art in its highest form compared to the one you've steered me against. I can't paint that picture, Billy. You've got to let me out. Let me try to tell you what that barbarian wants. He had it all planned out and even a sketch made of his idea. The old boy doesn't draw badly at all. But, ye goddesses of Art! listen to the monstrosity he expects me to paint. He wants himself in the centre of the canvas, of course. He is to be painted as Jupiter sitting on Olympus, with the clouds at his feet. At one side of him stands George Washington, in full regimentals, with his hand on the president's shoulder. An angel with outstretched wings hovers overhead, and is placing a laurel wreath on the president's head, crowning him—Queen of the May, I suppose. In the background is to be cannon, more angels and soldiers. The man who would paint that picture would have to have the soul of a dog, and would deserve to go down into oblivion without even a tin can tied to his tail to sound his memory."

Little beads of moisture crept out all over Billy Keogh's brow. The stub of his blue pencil had not figured out a contingency like this. The machinery of his plan had run with flattering smoothness until now. He dragged another chair upon the balcony, and got White back to his heat. He lit his pipe with apparent calm.

"Now, sonny," he said, with gentle grimness, "you and me will have an Art to Art talk. You've got your art and I've got mine. Yours is the real Pierian stuff that turns up its nose at bock-beer signs and oleographs of the Old Mill. Mine's the art of Business. This was my scheme, and it worked out like two-and-two. Paint that president man as Old King Cole, or Venus, or a landscape, or a fresco, or a bunch of lilies, or anything he thinks he looks like. But get the paint on the canvas and collect the spoils. You wouldn't throw me down, Carry, at this stage of the game. Think of that ten thousand."

"I can't help thinking of it," said White, "and that's what hurts. I'm tempted to throw every ideal I ever had down in the mire, and steep my soul in infamy by painting that picture. That five thousand meant three years of foreign study to me, and I'd almost sell my soul for that."

"Now it ain't as bad as that," said Keogh, soothingly. "It's a business proposition. It's so much paint and time against money. I don't fall in with your idea that that picture would so everlastingly jolt the art side of the question. George Washington was all right, you know, and nobody could say a word against the angel. I don't think so bad of that group. If you was to give Jupiter a pair of epaulets and a sword, and kind of work the clouds around to look like a blackberry patch, it wouldn't make such a bad battle scene. Why, if we hadn't already settled on the price, he ought to pay an extra thousand for Washington, and the angel ought to raise it five hundred."

"You don't understand, Billy," said White, with an uneasy laugh. "Some of us fellows who try to paint have big notions about Art. I wanted to paint a picture some day that people would stand before and forget that it was made of paint. I wanted it to creep into them like a bar of music and mushroom there like a soft bullet. And I wanted 'em to go away and ask, 'What else has he done?' And I didn't want 'em to find a thing; not a portrait nor a magazine cover nor an illustration nor a drawing of a girl—nothing but *the* picture. That's why I've lived on fried sausages, and tried to keep true to myself. I persuaded myself to do this portrait for the chance it might give to me to study abroad. But this howling, screaming caricature! Good Lord! can't you see how it is?"

"Sure," said Keogh, as tenderly as he would have spoken to a child, and he laid a long fore-finger on White's knee. "I see. It's bad to have your art all slugged up like that. I know. You wanted to paint a big thing like the panorama of the battle of Gettysburg. But let me kalsomine you a little mental sketch to consider. Up to date we're out $385.50 on this scheme. Our capital took every cent both of us could raise. We've got about enough left to get back to New York on. I need my share of that ten thousand. I want to work a copper deal in Idaho, and make a hundred thousand. That's the business end of the thing. Come down off your art perch, Carry, and let's land that hatful of dollars."

"Billy," said White, with an effort, "I'll try. I won't say I'll do it, but I'll try. I'll go at it, and put it through if I can."

"That's business," said Keogh heartily. "Good boy! Now, here's another thing—rush that picture—crowd it through as quick as you can. Get a couple of boys to help you mix the paint if necessary. I've picked up some pointers around town. The people here are beginning to get sick of Mr. President. They say he's been too free with concessions; and they accuse him of trying to make a dicker with England to sell out the country. We want that picture done and paid for before there's any row."

In the great *patio* of Casa Morena, the president caused to be stretched a huge canvas. Under this White set up his temporary studio. For two hours each day the great man sat to him.

White worked faithfully. But, as the work progressed, he had seasons of bitter scorn, of infinite self-contempt, of sullen gloom and sardonic gaiety. Keogh, with the patience of a great general, soothed, coaxed, argued—kept him at the picture.

At the end of a month White announced that the picture was completed—Jupiter, Washington, angels, clouds, cannon and all. His face was pale and his mouth drawn straight when he told Keogh. He said the president was much pleased with it. It was to be hung in the National Gallery of Statesmen and Heroes. The artist had been requested to return to Casa Morena on the following day to receive payment. At the appointed time he left the hotel, silent under his friend's joyful talk of their success.

An hour later he walked into the room where Keogh was waiting, threw his hat on the floor, and sat upon the table.

"Billy," he said, in strained and laboring tones, "I've a little money out West in a small business that my brother is running. It's what I've been living on while I've been studying art. I'll draw out my share and pay you back what you've lost on this scheme."

"Lost!" exclaimed Keogh, jumping up. "Didn't you get paid for the picture?"

"Yes, I got paid," said White. "But just now there isn't any picture, and there isn't any pay. If you care to hear about it, here are the edifying details. The president and I were looking at the painting. His secretary brought a bank draft on New York for ten thousand dollars and handed it to me. The moment I touched it I went wild. I tore it into little pieces and threw them on the floor. A workman was repainting the pillars inside the *patio*. A bucket of his paint happened to be convenient. I picked up his brush and slapped a quart of blue paint all over that ten-thousand-dollar nightmare. I bowed, and walked out. The president didn't move or speak. That was one time he was taken by surprise. It's tough on you, Billy, but I couldn't help it."

There seemed to be excitement in Coralio. Outside there was a confused, rising murmur pierced by high-pitched cries. "*Abajo el traidor—Muerte al traidor!*" were the words they seemed to form.

"Listen to that!" exclaimed White, bitterly: "I know that much Spanish. They're shouting, 'Down with the traitor!' I heard them before. I felt that they meant me. I was a traitor to Art. The picture had to go."

" 'Down with the blank fool' would have suited your case better," said Keogh with fiery emphasis. "You tear up ten thousand dollars like an old rag because the way you've spread on five dollars' worth of paint hurts your conscience. Next time I pick a side-partner in a scheme the man has got to go before a notary and swear he never even heard the word 'ideal' mentioned."

Keogh strode from the room, white-hot. White paid little attention to his resentment. The scorn of Billy Keogh seemed a trifling thing beside the greater self-scorn he had escaped.

In Coralio the excitement waxed. An outburst was imminent. The cause of this demonstration of displeasure was the presence in the town of a big, pink-cheeked Englishman, who, it was said, was an agent of his government come to clinch the bargain by which the president placed his people in the hands of a foreign power. It was charged that not only had he given away priceless concessions, but that the public debt was to be transferred into the hands of the English, and the custom-houses turned over to them as a guarantee. The long-enduring people had determined to make their protest felt.

On that night, in Coralio and in other towns, their ire found vent. Yelling mobs, mercurial but dangerous, roamed the streets. They overthrew the great bronze statue of the president that stood in the centre of the plaza, and hacked it to shapeless pieces. They tore from public buildings the tablets set there proclaiming the glory of the "Illustrious Liberator." His pictures in the government office were demolished. The mobs even attacked the Casa

Morena, but were driven away by the military, which remained faithful to the executive. All the night terror reigned.

The greatness of Losada was shown by the fact that by noon the next day order was restored, and he was still absolute. He issued proclamations denying positively that any negotiations of any kind had been entered into with England. Sir Stafford Vaughn, the pink-cheeked Englishman, also declared in placards and in public print that his presence there had no international significance. He was a traveller without guile. In fact (so he stated), he had not even spoken with the president or been in his presence since his arrival.

During this disturbance, White was preparing for his homeward voyage in the steamship that was to sail within two or three days. About noon, Keogh, the restless, took his camera out with the hope of speeding the lagging hours. The town was now as quiet as if peace had never departed from her perch on the red-tiled roofs.

About the middle of the afternoon, Keogh hurried back to the hotel with something decidedly special in his air. He retired to the little room where he developed his pictures.

Later on he came out to White on the balcony, with a luminous, grim, predatory smile on his face.

"Do you know what that is?" he asked, holding up a 4 × 5 photograph mounted on cardboard.

"Snap-shot of a señorita sitting in the sand—alliteration unintentional," guessed White, lazily.

"Wrong," said Keogh with shining eyes. "It's a slung-shot. It's a can of dynamite. It's a gold mine. It's a sight-draft on your president man for twenty thousand dollars—yes, sir—twenty thousand this time, and no spoiling the picture. No ethics of art in the way. Art! You with your smelly little tubes! I've got you skinned to death with a kodak. Take a look at that."

White took the picture in his hand, and gave a long whistle.

"Jove," he exclaimed, "but wouldn't that stir up a row in town if you let it be seen. How in the world did you get it, Billy?"

"You know that high wall around the president man's back garden? I was up there trying to get a bird's-eye of the town. I happened to notice a chink in the wall where a stone and a lot of plaster had slid out. Thinks I, I'll take a peep through to see how Mr. President's cabbages are growing. The first thing I saw was him and this Sir Englishman sitting at a little table about twenty feet away. They had the table all spread over with documents, and they were hobnobbing over them as thick as two pirates. 'Twas a nice corner of the garden, all private and shady with palms and orange trees, and they had a pail of champagne set by handy in the grass. I knew then was the time for me to make my big hit in Art. So I raised the machine up to the crack, and pressed the button. Just as I did so them old boys shook hands on the deal—you see they took that way in the picture."

Keogh put on his coat and hat.

"What are you going to do with it?" asked White.

"Me," said Keogh in a hurt tone, "why, I'm going to tie a pink ribbon to it and hang it on the what-not, of course. I'm surprised at you. But while I'm out you just try to figure out what ginger-cake potentate would be most likely to want to buy this work of art for his private collection—just to keep it out of circulation."

The sunset was reddening the tops of the cocoanut palms when Billy Keogh came back from Casa Morena. He nodded to the artist's questioning gaze; and lay down on a cot with his hands under the back of his head.

"I saw him. He paid the money like a little man. They didn't want to let me in at first. I told 'em it was important. Yes, that president man is on the plenty-able list. He's got a beautiful business system about the way he uses his brains. All I had to do was to hold up the photograph so he could see it, and name the price. He just smiled, and walked over to a safe and got the cash. Twenty one-thousand-dollar brand-new United States Treasury notes he laid on the table, like I'd pay out a dollar and a quarter. Fine notes, too—they crackled with a sound like burning the brush off a ten-acre lot."

"Let's try the feel of one," said White, curiously. "I never saw a thousand-dollar bill." Keogh did not immediately respond.

"Carry," he said, in an absent-minded way, "you think a heap of your art, don't you?"

"More," said White, frankly, "than has been for the financial good of myself and my friends."

"I thought you were a fool the other day," went on Keogh, quietly, "and I'm not sure now that you wasn't. But if you was, so am I. I've been in some funny deals, Carry, but I've always managed to scramble fair, and match my brains and capital against the other fellow's. But when it comes to—well, when you've got the other fellow cinched, and the screws on him, and he's got to put up—why, it don't strike me as being a man's game. They've got a name for it, you know; it's—confound you, don't you understand? A fellow feels—it's something like that blamed art of yours —he—well, I tore that photograph up and laid the pieces on that stack of money and shoved the whole business back across the table. 'Excuse me, Mr. Losada,' I said, 'but I guess I've made a mistake in the price. You get the photo for nothing.' Now, Carry, you get out the pencil, and we'll do some more figuring. I'd like to save enough out of our capital for you to have some fried sausages in your joint when you get back to New York."

"The Rose of Dixie"

WHEN *The Rose of Dixie* magazine was started by a stock company in Toombs City, Georgia, there was never but one candidate for its chief editorial position in the minds of its owners. Col. Aquila Telfair was the man for the place. By all the rights of learning, family, reputation, and Southern traditions, he was its foreordained, fit, and logical editor. So, a committee of the patriotic Georgia citizens who had subscribed the founding fund of $100,000 called upon Colonel Telfair at his residence, Cedar Heights, fearful lest the enterprise and the South should suffer by his possible refusal.

The colonel received them in his great library, where he spent most of his days. The library had descended to him from his father. It contained ten thousand volumes, some of which had been published as late as the year 1861. When the deputation arrived, Colonel Telfair was seated at his massive white-pine centre-table, reading Burton's "Anatomy of Melancholy." He arose and shook hands punctiliously with each member of the committee. If you were familiar with *The Rose of Dixie* you will remember the colonel's portrait, which appeared in it from time to time. You could not forget the long, carefully brushed white hair, the hooked, high-bridged nose, slightly twisted to the left; the keen eyes under the still black eyebrows; the classic mouth beneath the drooping white mustache, slightly frazzled at the ends.

The committee solicitously offered him the position of managing editor, humbly presenting an outline of the field that the publication was designed to cover and mentioning a comfortable salary. The colonel's lands were growing poorer each year and were much cut up by red gullies. Besides, the honor was not one to be refused.

In a forty-minute speech of acceptance, Colonel Telfair gave an outline of English literature from Chaucer to Macaulay, refought the battle of Chancellorsville, and said that, God helping him, he would so conduct *The Rose of Dixie* that its fragrance and beauty would permeate the entire world, hurling back into the teeth of the Northern minions their belief that no genius or good could exist in the brains and hearts of the people whose property they had destroyed and whose rights they had curtailed.

Offices for the magazine were partitioned off and furnished in the second floor of the First National Bank building; and it was for the colonel to cause *The Rose of Dixie* to blossom and flourish or to wilt in the balmy air of the land of flowers.

The staff of assistants and contributors that Editor-Colonel Telfair drew about him was a peach. It was a whole crate of Georgia peaches. The first assistant editor, Tolliver Lee Fairfax, had had a father killed during Pickett's charge. The second assistant, Keats Unthank, was the nephew of one of Morgan's Raiders. The book reviewer, Jackson Rockingham, had been the youngest soldier in the Confederate army, having appeared on the field of battle with a sword in one hand and a milk-bottle in the other. The art editor, Roncesvalles Sykes, was a third cousin to a nephew of Jefferson Davis. Miss Lavinia Terhune, the colonel's stenographer and typewriter, had an aunt who had once been kissed by Stonewall Jackson. Tommy Webster, the head office boy, got his job by having recited Father Ryan's poems, complete, at the commencement exercises of the Toombs City High School. The girls who wrapped and addressed the magazines were members of old Southern families in Reduced Circumstances. The cashier was a scrub named Hawkins, from Ann Arbor, Michigan, who had recommendations and a bond from a guarantee company filed with the owners. Even Georgia stock companies sometimes realize that it takes live ones to bury the dead.

Well, sir, if you believe me, *The Rose of Dixie* blossomed five times before anybody heard of it except the people who buy their hooks and eyes in Toombs City. Then Hawkins climbed off his stool and told on 'em to the stock company. Even in Ann Arbor he had been used to having his business propositions heard of at least as far away as Detroit. So an advertising manager was engaged—Beauregard Fitzhugh Banks—a young man in a lavender necktie, whose grandfather had been the Exalted High Pillowslip of the Kuklux Klan.

In spite of which *The Rose of Dixie* kept coming out every month. Although in every issue it ran photos of either the Taj Mahal or the Luxembourg Gardens, or Carmencita or La Follette, a certain number of people bought it and subscribed for it. As a boom for it, Editor-Colonel Telfair ran three different views of Andrew Jackson's old home, "The Hermitage," a full-page engraving of the second battle of Manasses, entitled "Lee to the Rear!" and a five-thousand-word biography of Belle Boyd in the same number. The subscription list that month advanced 118. Also there were poems in the same issue by Leonina Vashti Haricot (pen-name), related to the Haricots of Charleston, South Carolina, and Bill Thompson, nephew of one of the stockholders. And an article from a special society correspondent describing a tea-party given by the swell Boston and English set, where a lot of tea was spilled overboard by some of the guests masquerading as Indians.

One day a person whose breath would easily cloud a mirror, he was so much alive, entered the office of *The Rose of Dixie*. He was a man about the size of a real-estate agent, with a self-tied tie and a manner that he must have borrowed conjointly from W. J.

Bryan, Hackenschmidt, and Hetty Green. He was shown into the editor-colonel's *pons asinorum*. Colonel Telfair rose and began a Prince Albert bow.

"I'm Thacker," said the intruder, taking the editor's chair— "T. T. Thacker, of New York."

He dribbled hastily upon the colonel's desk some cards, a bulk manila envelope, and a letter from the owners of *The Rose of Dixie*. This letter introduced Mr. Thacker, and politely requested Colonel Telfair to give him a conference and whatever information about the magazine he might desire.

"I've been corresponding with the secretary of the magazine owners for some time," said Thacker, briskly. "I'm a practical magazine man myself, and a circulation booster as good as any, if I do say it. I'll guarantee an increase of anywhere from ten thousand to a hundred thousand a year for any publication that isn't printed in a dead language. I've had my eye on *The Rose of Dixie* ever since it started. I know every end of the business from editing to setting up the classified ads. Now, I've come down here to put a good bunch of money in the magazine, if I can see my way clear. It ought to be made to pay. The secretary tells me it's losing money. I don't see why a magazine in the South, if it's properly handled, shouldn't get a good circulation in the North, too."

Colonel Telfair leaned back in his chair and polished his gold-rimmed glasses.

"Mr. Thacker," said he, courteously but firmly, "*The Rose of Dixie* is a publication devoted to the fostering and the voicing of Southern genius. Its watchword, which you may have seen on the cover, is 'Of, For, and By the South.'"

"But you wouldn't object to a Northern circulation, would you?" asked Thacker.

"I suppose," said the editor-colonel, "that it is customary to open the circulation lists to all. I do not know. I have nothing to do with the business affairs of the magazine. I was called upon to assume editorial control of it, and I have devoted to its conduct such poor literary talents as I may possess and whatever store of erudition I may have acquired."

"Sure," said Thacker. "But a dollar is a dollar anywhere, North, South, or West—whether you're buying codfish, goober peas, or Rocky Ford cantaloupes. Now, I've been looking over your November number. I see one here on your desk. You don't mind running over it with me?

"Well, your leading article is all right. A good write-up of the cotton-belt with plenty of photographs is a winner any time. New York is always interested in the cotton crop. And this sensational account of the Hatfield-McCoy feud, by a schoolmate of a niece of the Governor of Kentucky, isn't such a bad idea. It happened so long ago that most people have forgotten it. Now, here's a poem three pages long called 'The Tyrant's Foot,' by Lorella Lascelles. I've pawed around a good deal over manuscripts, but I never saw her name on a rejection slip."

"Miss Lascelles," said the editor, "is one of our most widely recognized Southern poetesses. She is closely related to the Alabama Lascelles family, and made with her own hands the silken Confederate banner that was presented to the governor of that state at his inauguration."

"But why," persisted Thacker, "is the poem illustrated with a view of the M. & O. Railroad depot at Tuscaloosa?"

"The illustration," said the colonel, with dignity, "shows a corner of the fence surrounding the old homestead where Miss Lascelles was born."

"All right," said Thacker. "I read the poem, but I couldn't tell whether it was about the depot or the battle of Bull Run. Now, here's a short story called 'Rosie's Temptation,' by Fosdyke Piggott. It's rotten. What is a Piggott, anyway?"

"Mr. Piggott," said the editor, "is a brother of the principal stockholder of the magazine."

"All's right with the world—Piggott passes," said Thacker. "Well, this article on Arctic exploration and the one on tarpon fishing might go. But how about this write-up of the Atlanta,

New Orleans, Nashville, and Savannah breweries? It seems to consist mainly of statistics about their output and the quality of their beer. What's the chip over the bug?"

"If I understand your figurative language," answered Colonel Telfair, "it is this: the article you refer to was handed to me by the owners of the magazine with instructions to publish it. The literary quality of it did not appeal to me. But, in a measure, I feel impelled to conform, in certain matters, to the wishes of the gentlemen who are interested in the financial side of *The Rose*."

"I see," said Thacker. "Next we have two pages of selections from 'Lalla Rookh,' by Thomas Moore. Now, what Federal prison did Moore escape from, or what's the name of the F. F. V. family that he carries as a handicap?"

"Moore was an Irish poet who died in 1852," said Colonel Telfair, pityingly. "He is a classic. I have been thinking of reprinting his translation of Anacreon serially in the magazine."

"Look out for the copyright laws," said Thacker, flippantly. "Who's Bessie Belleclair, who contributes the essay on the newly completed waterworks plant in Milledgeville?"

"The name, sir," said Colonel Telfair, "is the *nom de guerre* of Miss Elvira Simpkins. I have not the honor of knowing the lady; but her contribution was sent us by Congressman Brower, of her native state. Congressman Brower's mother was related to the Polks of Tennessee."

"Now, see here, Colonel," said Thacker, throwing down the magazine, "this won't do. You can't successfully run a magazine for one particular section of the country. You've got to make a universal appeal. Look how the Northern publications have catered to the South and encouraged the Southern writers. And you've got to go far and wide for your contributors. You've got to buy stuff according to its quality, without any regard to the pedigree of the author. Now, I'll bet a quart of ink that this Southern parlor organ you've been running has never played a note that originated above Mason & Hamlin's line. Am I right?"

"I have carefully and conscientiously rejected all contributions from that section of the country—if I understand your figurative language aright," replied the colonel.

"All right. Now, I'll show you something."

Thacker reached for his thick manila envelope and dumped a mass of typewritten manuscript on the editor's desk.

"Here's some truck," said he, "that I paid cash for, and brought along with me."

One by one he folded back the manuscripts and showed their first pages to the colonel.

"Here are four short stories by four of the highest priced authors in the United States—three of 'em living in New York, and one commuting. There's a special article on Vienna-bred society by Tom Vampson. Here's an Italian serial by Captain Jack—no—it's the other Crawford. Here are three separate exposés of city governments by Sniffings, and here's a dandy entitled 'What Women Carry in Dress-Suit Cases'—a Chicago newspaper woman hired herself out for five years as a lady's maid to get that information. And here's a Synopsis of Preceding Chapters of Hall Caine's new serial to appear next June. And here's a couple of pounds of *vers de société* that I got at a rate from the clever magazines. That's the stuff that people everywhere want. And now here's a write-up with photographs at the ages of four, twelve, twenty-two, and thirty of George B. McClellan. It's a prognostication. He's bound to be elected Mayor of New York. It'll make a big hit all over the country. He——"

"I beg your pardon," said Colonel Telfair, stiffening in his chair. "What was the name?"

"Oh, I see," said Thacker, with half a grin. "Yes, he's a son of the General. We'll pass that manuscript up. But, if you'll excuse me, Colonel, it's a magazine we're trying to make go off—not the first gun at Fort Sumter. Now, here's a thing that's bound to get next to you. It's an original poem by James Whitcomb Riley. J. W. himself. You know what that means to a magazine. I won't tell you what I had to pay for that poem; but I'll tell you this— Riley can make more money writing with a fountain-pen than you or I can with one that lets the ink run. I'll read you the last two stanzas:

> "Pa lays around 'n' loafs all day,
>   'N' reads and makes us leave him be.
> He lets me do just like I please,
>   'N' when I'm bad he laughs at me,
>   'N' when I holler loud 'n' say
>   Bad words 'n' then begin to tease
> The cat, 'n' pa just smiles, ma's mad
>   'N' gives me Jesse crost her knees.
>   I always wondered why that wuz—
>   I guess it's cause
>   Pa never does.

> " 'N' after all the lights are out
>   I'm sorry 'bout it; so I creep
> Out of my trundle bed to ma's
>   'N' say I love her a whole heap,
> 'N' kiss her, 'n' I hug her tight.
>   'N' it's too dark to see her eyes,
> But every time I do I know
>   She cries 'n' cries 'n' cries 'n' cries.
>   I always wondered why that wuz—
>   I guess it's cause
>   Pa never does.

"That's the stuff," continued Thacker. "What do you think of that?"

"I am not unfamiliar with the works of Mr. Riley," said the colonel deliberately. "I believe he lives in Indiana. For the last ten years I have been somewhat of a literary recluse, and am familiar with nearly all the books in the Cedar Heights library. I am also of the opinion that a magazine should contain a certain amount of poetry. Many of the sweetest singers of the South have already contributed to the pages of *The Rose of Dixie*. I, myself, have thought of translating from the original for publication in its pages the works of the great Italian poet Tasso. Have you ever drunk from the fountain of this immortal poet's lines, Mr. Thacker?"

"Not even a demi-Tasso," said Thacker. "Now, let's come to the point, Colonel Telfair. I've already invested some money in this as a flyer. That bunch of manuscripts cost me $4,000. My object was to try a number of them in the next issue—I believe you make up less than a month ahead—and see what effect it has on the circulation. I believe that by printing the best stuff we can get in the North, South, East, or West we can make the magazine go. You have there the letter from the owning company asking you to coöperate with me in the plan. Let's chuck out some of this slush that you've been publishing just because the writers are related to the Skoopdoodles of Skoopdoodle County. Are you with me?"

"As long as I continue to be the editor of *The Rose*," said Colonel Telfair, with dignity, "I shall be its editor. But I desire also to conform to the wishes of its owners if I can do so conscientiously."

"That's the talk," said Thacker, briskly. "Now, how much of this stuff I've brought can we get into the January number? We want to begin right away."

"There is yet space in the January number," said the editor, "for about eight thousand words, roughly estimated."

"Great!" said Thacker. "It isn't much, but it'll give the readers some change from goobers, governors, and Gettysburg. I'll leave the selection of the stuff I brought to fill the space to you, as it's all good. I've got to run back to New York, and I'll be down again in a couple of weeks."

Colonel Telfair slowly swung his eye-glasses by their broad, black ribbon.

"The space in the January number that I referred to," said he, measuredly, "has been held open purposely, pending a decision that I have not yet made. A short time ago a contribution was submitted to *The Rose of Dixie* that is one of the most remarkable literary efforts that has ever come under my observation. None but a master mind and talent could have produced it. It would about fill the space that I have reserved for its possible use."

Thacker looked anxious.

"What kind of stuff is it?" he asked. "Eight thousand words sounds suspicious. The oldest families must have been collaborating. Is there going to be another secession?"

"The author of the article," continued the colonel, ignoring Thacker's allusions, "is a writer of some reputation. He has also distinguished himself in other ways. I do not feel at liberty to reveal to you his name—at least not until I have decided whether or not to accept his contribution."

"Well," said Thacker, nervously, "is it a continued story, or an account of the unveiling of the new town pump in Whitmire, South Carolina, or a revised list of General Lee's body-servants, or what?"

"You are disposed to be facetious," said Colonel Telfair, calmly. "The article is from the pen of a thinker, a philosopher, a lover of mankind, a student, and a rhetorician of high degree."

"It must have been written by a syndicate," said Thacker. "But, honestly, Colonel, you want to go slow. I don't know of any eight-thousand-word single doses of written matter that are read by anybody these days, except Supreme Court briefs and reports of murder trials. You haven't by any accident gotten hold of a copy of one of Daniel Webster's speeches, have you?"

Colonel Telfair swung a little in his chair and looked steadily from under his bushy eyebrows at the magazine promoter.

"Mr. Thacker," he said, gravely, "I am willing to segregate the somewhat crude expression of your sense of humor from the solicitude that your business investments undoubtedly have conferred upon you. But I must ask you to cease your jibes and derogatory comments upon the South and the Southern people. They, sir, will not be tolerated in the office of *The Rose of Dixie* for one moment. And before you proceed with more of your covert insinuations that I, the editor of this magazine, am not a competent judge of the merits of the matter submitted to its consideration, I beg that you will first present some evidence or proof that you are my superior in any way, shape, or form relative to the question in hand."

"Oh, come, Colonel," said Thacker, good-naturedly. "I didn't do anything like that to you. It sounds like an indictment by the fourth assistant attorney-general. Let's get back to business. What's this 8,000 to 1 shot about?"

"The article," said Colonel Telfair, acknowledging the apology by a slight bow, "covers a wide area of knowledge. It takes up theories and questions that have puzzled the world for centuries, and disposes of them logically and concisely. One by one it holds up to view the evils of the world, points out the way of eradicating them, and then conscientiously and in detail commends the good. There is hardly a phase of human life that it does not discuss wisely, calmly, and equitably. The great policies of governments, the duties of private citizens, the obligations of home life, ethics, morality—all these important subjects are handled with a calm wisdom and confidence that I must confess has captured my admiration."

"It must be a crackerjack," said Thacker, impressed.

"It is a great contribution to the world's wisdom," said the colonel. "The only doubt remaining in my mind as to the tremendous advantage it would be to us to give it publication in *The Rose of Dixie* is that I have not yet sufficient information about the author to give his work publicity in our magazine."

"I thought you said he is a distinguished man," said Thacker.

"He is," replied the colonel, "both in literary and in other more diversified and extraneous fields. But I am extremely careful about the matter that I accept for publication. My contributors are people of unquestionable repute and connections, which fact can be verified at any time. As I said, I am holding this article until I can acquire more information about its author. I do not know whether I will publish it or not. If I decide against it, I shall be much pleased, Mr. Thacker, to substitute the matter that you are leaving with me in its place."

Thacker was somewhat at sea.

"I don't seem to gather," said he, "much about the gist of this inspired piece of literature. It sounds more like a dark horse than Pegasus to me."

"It is a human document," said the colonel-editor, confidently, "from a man of great accomplishments who, in my opinion, has obtained a stronger grasp on the world and its outcomes than that of any man living to-day."

Thacker rose to his feet excitedly.

"Say!" he said. "It isn't possible that you've cornered John D. Rockefeller's memoirs, is it? Don't tell me that all at once."

"No, sir," said Colonel Telfair. "I am speaking of mentality and literature, not of the less worthy intricacies of trade."

"Well, what's the trouble about running the article," asked Thacker, a little impatiently, "if the man's well known and has got the stuff?"

Colonel Telfair sighed.

"Mr. Thacker," said he, "for once I have been tempted. Nothing has yet appeared in *The Rose of Dixie* that has not been from the pen of one of its sons or daughters. I know little about the author of this article except that he has acquired prominence in a section of the country that has always been inimical to my heart and mind. But I recognize his genius; and, as I have told you, I have instituted an investigation of his personality. Perhaps it will be futile. But I shall pursue the inquiry. Until that is finished, I must leave open the question of filling the vacant space in our January number."

Thacker arose to leave.

"All right, Colonel," he said, as cordially as he could. "You use your own judgment. If you've really got a scoop or something that will make 'em sit up, run it instead of my stuff. I'll drop in again in about two weeks. Good luck!"

Colonel Telfair and the magazine promoter shook hands.

Returning a fortnight later, Thacker dropped off a very rocky Pullman at Toombs City. He found the January number of the magazine made up and the forms closed.

The vacant space that had been yawning for type was filled by an article that was headed thus:

SECOND MESSAGE TO CONGRESS
Written for
THE ROSE OF DIXIE
BY
A Member of the Well-Known
BULLOCH FAMILY, OF GEORGIA
T. ROOSEVELT

A *Poor Rule*

I HAVE always maintained, and asserted from time to time, that woman is no mystery; that man can foretell, construe, subdue, comprehend, and interpret her. That she is a mystery has been foisted by herself upon credulous mankind. Whether I am right or wrong we shall see. As "Harper's Drawer" used to say in by-gone years: "The following good story is told of Miss——, Mr.——, Mr.——, and Mr.——."

We shall have to omit "Bishop X" and "the Rev.——," for they do not belong.

In those days Paloma was a new town on the line of the Southern Pacific. A reporter would have called it a "mushroom" town; but it was not. Paloma was first, and last, of the toadstool variety.

The train stopped there at noon for the engine to drink and for the passengers both to drink and to dine. There was a new yellow-pine hotel, also a wool warehouse, and perhaps three dozen box residences. The rest was composed of tents, cow ponies, "black-waxy" mud, and mesquite-trees, all bound round by a horizon. Paloma was an about-to-be city. The houses represented faith; the tents hope; the twice-a-day train, by which you might leave, creditably sustained the rôle of charity.

The Parisian Restaurant occupied the muddiest spot in the town while it rained, and the warmest when it shone. It was operated, owned, and perpetrated by a citizen known as Old

Man Hinkle, who had come out of Indiana to make his fortune
in this land of condensed milk and sorghum.

There was a four-room, unpainted, weather-boarded box house
in which the family lived. From the kitchen extended a "shelter"
made of poles covered with chaparral brush. Under this was a
table and two benches, each twenty feet long, the product of Paloma home carpentry. Here was set forth the roast mutton, the
stewed apples, boiled beans, soda-biscuits, puddinorpie, and hot
coffee of the Parisian menu.

Ma Hinkle and a subordinate known to the ears as "Betty,"
but denied to the eyesight, presided at the range. Pa Hinkle
himself, with salamandrous thumbs, served the scalding viands.
During rush hours a Mexican youth, who rolled and smoked
cigarettes between courses, aided him in waiting on the guests.
As is customary at Parisian banquets I placed the sweets at the
end of my wordy menu.

Ileen Hinkle!

The spelling is correct, for I have seen her write it. No doubt
she had been named by ear; but she so splendidly bore the orthog-
raphy that Tom Moore himself (had he seen her) would have
endorsed the phonography.

Ileen was the daughter of the house, and the first Lady Cashier to invade the territory south of an east-and-west line drawn
through Galveston and Del Rio. She sat on a high stool in a
rough pine grandstand—or was it a temple?—under the shelter
at the door of the kitchen. There was a barbed-wire protection in
front of her, with a little arch under which you passed your
money. Heaven knows why the barbed wire; for every man who
dined Parisianly there would have died in her service. Her duties
were light; each meal was a dollar; you put it under the arch,
and she took it.

I set out with the intent to describe Ileen Hinkle to you. Instead, I must refer you to the volume of Edmund Burke entitled:
*A Philosophical Inquiry into the Origin of Our Ideas of the Sub-
lime and Beautiful.* It is an exhaustive treatise, dealing first

with the primitive conceptions of beauty—roundness and smoothness, I think they are, according to Burke. It is well said. Rotundity is a patent charm; as for smoothness—the more new wrinkles a woman acquires, the smoother she becomes.

Ileen was a strictly vegetable compound, guaranteed under the Pure Ambrosia and Balm-of-Gilead Act of the year of the fall of Adam. She was a fruit-stand blonde—strawberries, peaches, cherries, etc. Her eyes were wide apart, and she possessed the calm that precedes a storm that never comes. But it seems to me that words (at any rate per) are wasted in an effort to describe the beautiful. Like fancy, "It is engendered in the eyes." There are three kinds of beauties—I was foreordained to be homiletic; I can never stick to a story.

The first is the freckle-faced, snub-nosed girl whom you like. The second is Maude Adams. The third is, or are, the ladies in Bouguereau's paintings. Ileen Hinkle was the fourth. She was the mayoress of Spotless Town. There were a thousand golden apples coming to her as Helen of the Troy laundries.

The Parisian Restaurant was within a radius. Even from beyond its circumference men rode in to Paloma to win her smiles. They got them. One meal—one smile—one dollar. But, with all her impartiality, Ileen seemed to favor three of her admirers above the rest. According to the rules of politeness, I will mention myself last.

The first was an artificial product known as Bryan Jacks—a name that had obviously met with reverses. Jacks was the outcome of paved cities. He was a small man made of some material resembling flexible sandstone. His hair was the color of a brick Quaker meeting-house; his eyes were twin cranberries; his mouth was like the aperture under a drop-letters-here sign.

He knew every city from Bangor to San Francisco, thence north to Portland, thence S. 45 E. to a given point in Florida. He had mastered every art, trade, game, business, profession, and sport in the world, had been present at, or hurrying on his way to, every headline event that had occurred between oceans since he was five years old. You might open the atlas, place your finger at random upon the name of a town, and Jacks would tell you the front names of three prominent citizens before you could close it again. He spoke patronizingly and even disrespectfully of Broadway, Beacon Hill, Michigan, Euclid, and Fifth avenues, and the St. Louis Four Courts. Compared with him as a cosmopolite, the Wandering Jew would have seemed a mere hermit. He had learned everything the world could teach him, and he would tell you about it.

I hate to be reminded of Pollok's "Course of Time," and so do you; but every time I saw Jacks I would think of the poet's description of another poet by the name of G. G. Byron who "Drank early; deeply drank—drank draughts that common millions might have quenched; then died of thirst because there was no more to drink."

That fitted Jacks, except that, instead of dying, he came to Paloma, which was about the same thing. He was a telegrapher and station-and-express agent at seventy-five dollars a month. Why a young man who knew everything and could do everything was content to serve in such an obscure capacity I never could understand, although he let out a hint once that it was as a personal favor to the president and stockholders of the S. P. Ry. Co.

One more line of description, and I turn Jacks over to you. He wore bright blue clothes, yellow shoes, and a bow tie made of the same cloth as his shirt.

My rival No. 2 was Bud Cunningham, whose services had been engaged by a ranch near Paloma to assist in compelling refractory cattle to keep within the bounds of decorum and order. Bud was the only cowboy off the stage that I ever saw who looked like one on it. He wore the sombrero, the chaps, and the handkerchief tied at the back of his neck.

Twice a week Bud rode in from the Val Verde Ranch to sup at the Parisian Restaurant. He rode a many-high-handed Kentucky horse at a tremendously fast lope, which animal he would rein up so suddenly under the big mesquite at the corner of the brush shelter that his hoofs would plough canals yards long in the loam.

Jacks and I were regular boarders at the restaurant, of course.

The front room of the Hinkle House was as neat a little parlor as there was in the black-waxy country. It was all willow rocking-chairs, and home-knit tidies, and albums, and conch shells in a row. And a little upright piano in one corner.

Here Jacks and Bud and I—or sometimes one or two of us, according to our good-luck—used to sit of evenings when the tide of trade was over, and "visit" Miss Hinkle.

Ileen was a girl of ideas. She was destined for higher things (if there can be anything higher) than taking in dollars all day through a barbed-wire wicket. She had read and listened and thought. Her looks would have formed a career for a less ambitious girl; but, rising superior to mere beauty, she must establish something in the nature of a *salon*—the only one in Paloma.

"Don't you think that Shakespeare was a great writer?" she would ask, with such a pretty little knit of her arched brows that the late Ignatius Donnelly, himself, had he seen it, could scarcely have saved his Bacon.

Ileen was of the opinion, also, that Boston is more cultured than Chicago; that Rosa Bonheur was one of the greatest of women painters; that Westerners are more spontaneous and open-hearted than Easterners; that London must be a very foggy city, and that California must be quite lovely in the springtime. And of many other opinions indicating a keeping up with the world's best thought.

These, however, were but gleaned from hearsay and evidence: Ileen had theories of her own. One, in particular, she disseminated to us untiringly. Flattery she detested. Frankness and honesty of speech and action, she declared, were the chief mental ornaments of man and woman. If ever she could like any one, it would be for those qualities.

"I'm awfully weary," she said, one evening, when we three musketeers of the mesquite were in the little parlor, "of having compliments on my looks paid to me. I know I'm not beautiful."

(Bud Cunningham told me afterward that it was all he could do to keep from calling her a liar when she said that.)

"I'm only a little Middle-Western girl," went on Ileen, "who just wants to be simple and neat, and tries to help her father make a humble living."

(Old Man Hinkle was shipping a thousand silver dollars a month, clear profit, to a bank in San Antonio.)

Bud twisted around in his chair and bent the rim of his hat, from which he could never be persuaded to separate. He did not know whether she wanted what she said she wanted or what she knew she deserved. Many a wiser man has hesitated at deciding. Bud decided.

"Why—ah, Miss Ileen, beauty, as you might say, ain't everything. Not sayin' that you haven't your share of good looks, I always admired more than anything else about you the nice, kind way you treat your ma and pa. Any one what's good to their parents and is a kind of homebody don't specially need to be too pretty."

Ileen gave him one of her sweetest smiles. "Thank you, Mr. Cunningham," she said. "I consider that one of the finest compliments I've had in a long time. I'd so much rather hear you say that than to hear you talk about my eyes and hair. I'm glad you believe me when I say I don't like flattery."

Our cue was there for us. Bud had made a good guess. You couldn't lose Jacks. He chimed in next.

"Sure thing, Miss Ileen," he said; "the good-lookers don't always win out. Now, you ain't bad looking, of course—but that's nix-cum-rous. I knew a girl once in Dubuque with a face like a cocoanut, who could skin the cat twice on a horizontal bar without changing hands. Now, a girl might have the California peach crop mashed to a marmalade and not be able to do that. I've seen—er—worse lookers than *you*, Miss Ileen; but what I like about you is the business way you've got of doing things. Cool and wise—that's the winning way for a girl. Mr. Hinkle told me the other day you'd never taken in a lead silver dollar or a plugged one since you've been on the job. Now, that's the stuff for a girl—that's what catches me."

Jacks got his smile, too.

"Thank you, Mr. Jacks," said Ileen. "If you only knew how I appreciate any one's being candid and not a flatterer! I get so tired of people telling me I'm pretty. I think it is the loveliest thing to have friends who tell you the truth."

Then I thought I saw an expectant look on Ileen's face as she glanced toward me. I had a wild, sudden impulse to dare fate, and tell her of all the beautiful handiwork of the Great Artificer she was the most exquisite—that she was a flawless pearl gleaming pure and serene in a setting of black mud and emerald prairies—that she was—a—a corker; and that as for mine, I cared not if she were as cruel as a serpent's tooth to her fond parents, or if she couldn't tell a plugged dollar from a bridle buckle, if I might sing, chant, praise, glorify, and worship her peerless and wonderful beauty.

But I refrained. I feared the fate of a flatterer. I had witnessed her delight at the crafty and discreet words of Bud and Jacks. No! Miss Hinkle was not one to be beguiled by the plated-silver tongue of a flatterer. So I joined the ranks of the candid and honest. At once I became mendacious and didactic.

"In all ages, Miss Hinkle," said I, "in spite of the poetry and romance of each, intellect in woman has been admired more than beauty. Even in Cleopatra, herself, men found more a charm in her queenly mind than in her looks."

"Well, I should think so!" said Ileen. "I've seen pictures of her that weren't so much. She had an awfully long nose."

"If I may say so," I went on, "you remind me of Cleopatra, Miss Ileen."

"Why, my nose isn't so long!" said she, opening her eyes wide and touching that comely feature with a dimpled forefinger.

"Why—er—I mean," said I—"I mean as to mental endowments."

"Oh!" said she; and then I got my smile just as Bud and Jacks got theirs.

"Thank every one of you," she said, very, very sweetly, "for being so frank and honest with me. That's the way I want you to be always. Just tell me plainly and truthfully what you think, and we'll all be the best friends in the world. And now, because you've been so good to me, and understand so well how I dislike people who do nothing but pay me exaggerated compliments, I'll sing and play a little for you."

Of course, we expressed our thanks and joy; would have been better pleased if Ileen had remained in her low rocking-chair face to face with us and let us gaze upon her. For she was no Adelina Patti—not even on the farewellest of the diva's farewell tours. She had a cooing little voice like that of a turtle-dove that could almost fill the parlor when the windows and doors were closed, and Betty was not rattling the lids of the stove in the kitchen. She had a gamut that I estimate at about eight inches on the piano; and her runs and trills sounded like the clothes bubbling in your grandmother's iron wash-pot. Believe that she must have been beautiful when I tell you that it sounded like music to us.

Ileen's musical taste was catholic. She would sing through a pile of sheet music on the left-hand top of the piano, laying each slaughtered composition on the right-hand top. The next evening she would sing from right to left. Her favorites were Mendelssohn, and Moody and Sankey. By request she always wound up with "Sweet Violets" and "When the Leaves Begin to Turn."

When we left at ten o'clock the three of us would go down to Jacks' little wooden station and sit on the platform, swinging our feet and trying to pump one another for clues as to which way Miss Ileen's inclinations seemed to lean. That is the way of rivals —they do not avoid and glower at one another; they convene and converse and construe—striving by the art politic to estimate the strength of the enemy.

One day there came a dark horse to Paloma, a young lawyer who at once flaunted his shingle and himself spectacularly upon the town. His name was C. Vincent Vesey. You could see at a glance that he was a recent graduate of a Southwestern law school. His Prince Albert coat, light striped trousers, broad-brimmed soft black hat, and narrow white muslin bow tie proclaimed that more loudly than any diploma could. Vesey was a compound of Daniel Webster, Lord Chesterfield, Beau Brummel, and Little Jack Horner. His coming boomed Paloma. The next day after he arrived an addition to the town was surveyed and laid off in lots.

Of course, Vesey, to further his professional fortunes, must mingle with the citizenry and outliers of Paloma. And, as well as with the soldier men, he was found to seek popularity with the gay dogs of the place. So Jacks and Bud Cunningham and I came to be honored by his acquaintance.

The doctrine of predestination would have been discredited had not Vesey seen Ileen Hinkle and become fourth in the tourney. Magnificently, he boarded at the yellow-pine hotel instead of the Parisian Restaurant; but he came to be a formidable visitor in the Hinkle parlor. His competition reduced Bud to an inspired increase of profanity, drove Jacks to an outburst of slang so weird that it sounded more horrible than the most trenchant of Bud's imprecations, and made me dumb with gloom.

For Vesey had the rhetoric. Words flowed from him like oil from a gusher. Hyperbole, compliment, praise, appreciation, honeyed gallantry, golden opinions, eulogy, and unveiled panegyric vied with one another for preëminence in his speech. We had small hopes that Ileen could resist his oratory and Prince Albert.

But a day came that gave us courage.

About dusk one evening I was sitting on the little gallery in front of the Hinkle parlor, waiting for Ileen to come, when I heard voices inside. She had come into the room with her father, and Old Man Hinkle began to talk to her. I had observed before that he was a shrewd man, and not unphilosophic.

"Ily," said he, "I notice there's three or four young fellers that have been callin' to see you regular for quite a while. Is there any one of 'em you like better than another?"

"Why, pa," she answered, "I like all of 'em very well. I think Mr. Cunningham and Mr. Jacks and Mr. Harris are very nice young men. They are so frank and honest in everything they say to me. I haven't known Mr. Vesey very long, but I think he's a very nice young man, he's so frank and honest in everything he says to me."

"Now, that's what I'm gittin' at," says old Hinkle. "You've always been sayin' you like people what tell the truth and don't go humbuggin' you with compliments and bogus talk. Now, suppose you make a test of these fellers, and see which one of 'em will talk the straightest to you."

"But how'll I do it, pa?"

"I'll tell you how. You know you sing a little bit, Ily; you took music lessons nearly two years in Logansport. It wasn't long, but it was all we could afford then. And your teacher said you didn't have any voice, and it was a waste of money to keep on. Now, suppose you ask the fellers what they think of your singin', and see what each one of 'em tells you. The man that'll tell you the truth about it 'll have a mighty lot of nerve, and 'll do to tie to. What do you think of the plan?"

"All right, pa," said Ileen. "I think it's a good idea. I'll try it."

Ileen and Mr. Hinkle went out of the room through the inside door. Unobserved, I hurried down to the station. Jacks was at his telegraph table waiting for eight o'clock to come. It was Bud's night in town, and when he rode in I repeated the conversation to them both. I was loyal to my rivals, as all true admirers of all Ileens should be.

Simultaneously the three of us were smitten by an uplifting thought. Surely this test would eliminate Vesey from the contest. He, with his unctuous flattery, would be driven from the lists. Well we remembered Ileen's love of frankness and honesty —how she treasured truth and candor above vain compliment and blandishment.

Linking arms, we did a grotesque dance of joy up and down the platform, singing "Muldoon Was a Solid Man" at the top of our voices.

That evening four of the willow rocking-chairs were filled besides the lucky one that sustained the trim figure of Miss Hinkle. Three of us waited with suppressed excitement the application of the test. It was tried on Bud first.

"Mr. Cunningham," said Ileen, with her dazzling smile, after she had sung: "When the Leaves Begin to Turn," "what do you really think of my voice? Frankly and honestly, now, as you know I want you to always be toward me."

Bud squirmed in his chair at his chance to show the sincerity that he knew was required of him.

"Tell you the truth, Miss Ileen," he said, earnestly, "you ain't got much more voice than a weasel—just a little squeak, you know. Of course, we all like to hear you sing, for it's kind of sweet and soothin' after all, and you look most mighty well sittin' on the piano-stool as you do faced around. But as for real singin'—I reckon you couldn't call it that."

I looked closely at Ileen to see if Bud had overdone his frankness, but her pleased smile and sweetly spoken thanks assured me that we were on the right track.

"And what do you think, Mr. Jacks?" she asked next.

"Take it from me," said Jacks, "you ain't in the prima donna class. I've heard 'em warble in every city in the United States; and I tell you your vocal output don't go. Otherwise, you've got the grand opera bunch sent to the soap factory—in looks, I mean; for the high screeches generally look like Mary Ann on her Thursday out. But nix for the gargle work. Your epiglottis ain't a real side-stepper—its footwork ain't good."

With a merry laugh at Jacks' criticism, Ileen looked inquiringly at me.

I admit that I faltered a little. Was there not such a thing as being too frank? Perhaps I even hedged a little in my verdict; but I stayed with the critics.

"I am not skilled in scientific music, Miss Ileen," I said, "but frankly I cannot praise very highly the singing voice that Nature has given you. It has long been a favorite comparison that a great singer sings like a bird. Well, there are birds and birds. I would say that your voice reminds me of the thrush's—throaty and not strong, nor of much compass or variety—but still—er—sweet—in—er—its—way, and—er——"

"Thank you, Mr. Harris," interrupted Miss Hinkle. "I knew I could depend upon your frankness and honesty."

And then C. Vincent Vesey drew back one sleeve from his snowy cuff, and the water came down at Lodore.

My memory cannot do justice to his masterly tribute to that priceless, God-given treasure—Miss Hinkle's voice. He raved over it in terms that, if they had been addressed to the morning stars when they sang together, would have made that stellar choir explode in a meteoric shower of flaming self-satisfaction.

He marshalled on his white finger-tips the grand opera stars of all the continents, from Jenny Lind to Emma Abbott, only to depreciate their endowments. He spoke of larynxes, of chest notes, of phrasing, arpeggios, and other strange paraphernalia of the throaty art. He admitted, as though driven to a corner, that Jenny Lind had a note or two in the high register that Miss Hinkle had not yet acquired—but—"!!!"—that was a mere matter of practice and training.

And, as a peroration, he predicted—solemnly predicted—a career in vocal art for the "coming star of the Southwest—and one of which grand old Texas may well be proud," hitherto unsurpassed in the annals of musical history.

When we left at ten, Ileen gave each of us her usual warm, cordial handshake, entrancing smile, and invitation to call again. I could not see that one was favored above or below another—but three of us knew—we knew.

We knew that frankness and honesty had won, and that the rivals now numbered three instead of four.

Down at the station Jacks brought out a pint bottle of the

proper stuff, and we celebrated the downfall of a blatant interloper.

Four days went by without anything happening worthy of recount.

On the fifth, Jacks and I, entering the brush arbor for our supper, saw the Mexican youth, instead of a divinity in a spotless waist and a navy-blue skirt, taking in the dollars through the barbed-wire wicket.

We rushed into the kitchen, meeting Pa Hinkle coming out with two cups of hot coffee in his hands.

"Where's Ileen?" we asked, in recitative.

Pa Hinkle was a kindly man. "Well, gents," said he, "it was a sudden notion she took; but I've got the money, and I let her have her way. She's gone to a corn—conservatory in Boston for four years for to have her voice cultivated. Now, excuse me to pass, gents, for this coffee's hot, and my thumbs is tender."

That night there were four instead of three of us sitting on the station platform and swinging our feet. C. Vincent Vesey was one of us. We discussed things while dogs barked at the moon that rose, as big as a five-cent piece or a flour-barrel, over the chaparral.

And what we discussed was whether it is better to lie to a woman or to tell her the truth.

And as all of us were young then, we did not come to a decision.

The Last of the Troubadours

INEXORABLY Sam Galloway saddled his pony. He was going away from the Rancho Altito at the end of a three months' visit. It is not to be expected that a guest should put up with wheat coffee and biscuits yellow-streaked with saleratus for longer than that. Nick Napoleon, the big Negro man cook, had never been able to make good biscuits. Once before, when Nick was cooking at the Willow Ranch, Sam had been forced to fly from his *cusine*, after only a six weeks' sojourn.

On Sam's face was an expression of sorrow, deepened with regret and slightly tempered by the patient forgiveness of a connoisseur who cannot be understood. But very firmly and inexorably he buckled his saddle-cinches, looped his take-rope and hung it to his saddle-horn, tied his slicker and coat on the cantle, and looped his quirt on his right wrist. The Merrydews (householders of the Rancho Altito), men, women, children, and servants, vassals, visitors, employés, dogs, and casual callers, were grouped in the "gallery" of the ranch house, all with face set to the tune of melancholy and grief. For, as the coming of Sam Galloway to any ranch, camp, or cabin between the rivers Frio or Bravo del Norte aroused joy, so his departure caused mourning and distress.

And then, during absolute silence, except for the bumping of a hind elbow of a hound dog as he pursued a wicked flea, Sam tenderly and carefully tied his guitar across his saddle on top of his slicker and coat. The guitar was in a green duck bag; and if you catch the significance of it, it explains Sam.

Sam Galloway was the Last of the Troubadours. Of course you know about the troubadours. The encyclopædia says they flourished between the eleventh and the thirteenth centuries. What they flourished doesn't seem clear—you may be pretty sure it wasn't a sword: maybe it was a fiddle-bow, or a forkful of spaghetti, or a lady's scarf. Anyhow, Sam Galloway was one of 'em.

Sam put on a martyred expression as he mounted his pony. But the expression on his face was hilarious compared with the one on his pony's. You see, a pony gets to know his rider mighty well, and it is not unlikely that cow ponies in pastures and at hitching racks had often guyed Sam's pony for being ridden by a guitar player instead of by a rollicking, cussing, all-wool cowboy. No man is a hero to his saddle-horse. And even an escalator in a department store might be excused for tripping up a troubadour.

Oh, I know I'm one; and so are you. You remember the stories you memorize and the card tricks you study and that little piece on the piano—how does it go—ti-tum-te-tum-ti-tum—those little Arabian Ten-Minute Entertainments that you furnish when you go up to call on your rich Aunt Jane. You should know that *omnæ personæ in tres partes divisæ sunt.* Namely: Barons, Troubadours, and Workers. Barons have no inclination to read such folderol as this; and Workers have no time: so I know you must be a Troubadour, and that you will understand Sam Galloway. Whether we sing, act, dance, write, lecture, or paint, we are only troubadours; so let us make the worst of it.

The pony with the Dante Alighieri face, guided by the pressure of Sam's knees, bore that wandering minstrel sixteen miles southeastward. Nature was in her most benignant mood. League after league of delicate, sweet flowerets made fragrant the gently undulating prairie. The east wind tempered the spring warmth; wool-white clouds flying in from the Mexican Gulf hindered the direct rays of the April sun. Sam sang songs as he rode. Under his pony's bridle he had tucked some sprigs of chaparral to keep away the deer flies. Thus crowned, the long-faced quadruped looked more Dantesque than before, and, judging by his countenance, seemed to think of Beatrice.

Straight as topography permitted, Sam rode to the sheep ranch of old man Ellison. A visit to a sheep ranch seemed to him desirable just then. There had been too many people, too much noise, argument, competition, confusion, at Rancho Altito. He had never conferred upon old man Ellison the favour of sojourning at his ranch; but he knew he would be welcome. The troubadour is own passport everywhere. The Workers in the castle let down the drawbridge to him, and the Baron sets him at the his left hand at table in the banquet hall. There ladies smile upon him and applaud his songs and stories, while the Workers bring boars' heads and flagons. If the Baron nods once or twice in his carved oaken chair, he does not do it maliciously.

Old man Ellison welcomed the troubadour flatteringly. He had often heard praises of Sam Galloway from other ranchmen who had been complimented by his visits, but had never aspired to such a honor for his own humble barony. I say barony because old man Ellison was the Last of the Barons. Of course, Mr. Bulwer-Lytton lived too early to know him or he wouldn't have conferred that sobriquet upon Warwick. In life it is the duty and the function of the Baron to provide work for the Workers and lodging and shelter for the Troubadours.

Old man Ellison was a shrunken old man, with a short, yellow-white beard and a face lined and seamed by past-and-gone smiles. His ranch was a little two-room box house in a grove of hackberry trees in the lonesomest part of the sheep country. His household consisted of a Kiowa Indian man cook, four hounds, a pet sheep, and a half-tamed coyote chained to a fence-post. He owned 3,000 sheep, which he ran on two sections of leased land and many thousands of acres neither leased nor owned. Three or four times a year some one who spoke his language would ride up to his gate and exchange a few bald ideas with him. Those were red-letter days to old man Ellison. Then in what illuminated, embossed, and gorgeously decorated capitals must have been written the day on which a troubadour—a troubadour who, according to the encyclopædia, should have flourished between the eleventh and the thirteenth centuries—drew rein at the gates of his baronial castle!

Old man Ellison's smiles came back and filled his wrinkles when he saw Sam. He hurried out of the house in his shuffling, limping way to greet him.

"Hello, Mr. Ellison," called Sam, cheerfully. "Thought I'd drop over and see you a while. Notice you've had fine rains on your range. They ought to make good grazing for your spring lambs."

"Well, well, well," said old man Ellison. "I'm mighty glad to see you, Sam. I never thought you'd take the trouble to ride over to as out-of-the-way an old ranch as this. But you're mighty welcome. 'Light. I've got a sack of new oats in the kitchen—shall I bring out a feed for your hoss?"

"Oats for him?" said Sam, derisively. "No, sir-ee. He's as fat as a pig now on grass. He don't get rode enough to keep him in condition. I'll just turn him in the horse pasture with a drag rope on if you don't mind."

I am positive that never during the eleventh and thirteenth centuries did Baron, Troubadour, and Worker amalgamate as harmoniously as their parallels did that evening at old man Ellison's sheep ranch. The Kiowa's biscuits were light and tasty and his coffee strong. Ineradicable hospitality and appreciation glowed on old man Ellison's weather-tanned face. As for the troubadour, he said to himself that he had stumbled upon pleasant places indeed. A well-cooked, abundant meal, a host whom his lightest attempt to entertain seemed to delight far beyond the merits of the exertion, and the reposeful atmosphere that his sensitive soul at that time craved united to confer upon him a satisfaction and luxurious ease that he had seldom found on his tours of the ranches.

After the delectable supper, Sam untied the green duck bag and took out his guitar. Not by way of payment, mind you— neither Sam Galloway nor any other of the true troubadours are lineal descendants of the late Tommy Tucker. You have read of Tommy Tucker in the works of the esteemed but often obscure Mother Goose. Tommy Tucker sang for his supper. No true troubadour would do that. He would have his supper, and then sing for Art's sake.

Sam Galloway's repertoire comprised about fifty funny stories and between thirty and forty songs. He by no means stopped there. He could talk through twenty cigarettes on any topic that you brought up. And he never sat up when he could lie down; and never stood when he could sit. I am strongly disposed to linger with him, for I am drawing a portrait as well as a blunt pencil and a tattered thesaurus will allow.

I wish you could have seen him: he was small and tough and inactive beyond the power of imagination to conceive. He wore an ultramarine-blue woollen shirt laced down the front with a pearl-gray, exaggerated sort of shoestring, indestructible brown duck clothes, inevitable high-heeled boots with Mexican spurs, and a Mexican straw sombrero.

That evening Sam and old man Ellison dragged their chairs out under the hackberry trees. They lighted cigarettes; and the troubadour gaily touched his guitar. Many of the songs he sang were the weird, melancholy, minor-keyed *canciones* that he had learned from the Mexican sheep herders and *vaqueros*. One, in particular, charmed and soothed the soul of the lonely baron. It was a favourite song of the sheep herders, beginning: "*Huile, huile, palomita*," which being translated means, "Fly, fly, little dove." Sam sang it for old man Ellison many times that evening.

The troubadour stayed on at the old man's ranch. There was peace and quiet and appreciation there, such as he had not found in the noisy camps of the cattle kings. No audience in the world

could have crowned the work of poet, musician, or artist with
more worshipful and unflagging approval than that bestowed
upon his efforts by old man Ellison. No visit by a royal personage
to a humble woodchopper or peasant could have been received
with more flattering thankfulness and joy.

On a cool, canvas-covered cot in the shade of the hackberry
trees Sam Galloway passed the greater part of his time. There he
rolled his brown paper cigarettes, read such tedious literature as
the ranch afforded, and added to his repertoire of improvisations
that he played so expertly on his guitar. To him, as a slave minis-
tering to a great lord, the Kiowa brought cool water from the red
jar hanging under the brush shelter, and food when he called for
it. The prairie zephyrs fanned him mildly; mocking-birds at morn
and eve competed with but scarce equalled the sweet melodies of
his lyre; a perfumed stillness seemed to fill all his world. While
old man Ellison was pottering among his flocks of sheep on his
mile-an-hour pony, and while the Kiowa took his siesta in the
burning sunshine at the end of the kitchen, Sam would lie on his
cot thinking what a happy world he lived in, and how kind it is to
the ones whose mission in life it is to give entertainment and
pleasure. Here he had food and lodging as good as he had ever
longed for; absolute immunity from care or exertion or strife; an
endless welcome, and a host whose delight at the sixteenth repeti-
tion of a song or a story was as keen as at its initial giving. Was
there ever a troubadour of old who struck upon as royal a castle
in his wanderings? While he lay thus, meditating upon his blessings, little brown cottontails would shyly frolic through the yard;
a covey of white-topknotted blue quail would run past, in single
file, twenty yards away; a *paisano* bird, out hunting for tarantulas,
would hop upon the fence and salute him with sweeping flour-
ishes of its long tail. In the eighty-acre horse pasture the pony
with the Dantesque face grew fat and almost smiling. The troubadour was at the end of his wanderings.

Old man Ellison was his own *vaciero*. That means that he supplied his sheep camps with wood, water, and rations by his own

labors instead of hiring a *vacïero*. On small ranches it is often done.

One morning he started for the camp of Encarnación Felipe de la Cruz y Monto Piedras (one of his sheep herders) with the week's usual rations of brown beans, coffee, meal, and sugar. Two miles away on the trail from old Fort Ewing he met, face to face, a terrible being called King James, mounted on a fiery, prancing, Kentucky-bred horse.

King James's real name was James King; but people reversed it because it seemed to fit him better, and also because it seemed to please his majesty. King James was the biggest cattleman between the Alamo plaza in San Antone and Bill Hopper's saloon in Brownsville. Also he was the loudest and most offensive bully and braggart and bad man in southwest Texas. And he always made good whenever he bragged; and the more noise he made the more dangerous he was. In the story papers it is always the quiet, mild-mannered man with light blue eyes and a low voice who turns out to be really dangerous; but in real life and in this story such is not the case. Give me my choice between assaulting a large, loud-mouthed rough-houser and an inoffensive stranger with blue eyes sitting quietly in a corner, and you will see something doing in the corner every time.

King James, as I intended to say earlier, was a fierce, two-hundred-pound, sunburned, blond man, as pink as an October strawberry, and with two horizontal slits under shaggy red eyebrows for eyes. On that day he wore a flannel shirt that was tan-colored, with the exception of certain large areas which were darkened by transudations due to the summer sun. There seemed to be other clothing and garnishings about him, such as brown duck trousers stuffed into immense boots, and red handkerchiefs and revolvers; and a shotgun laid across his saddle and a leather belt with millions of cartridges shining in it—but your mind skidded off such accessories; what held your gaze was just the two little horizontal slits that he used for eyes.

This was the man that old man Ellison met on the trail; and

when you count up in the baron's favor that he was sixty-five and weighed ninety-eight pounds and had heard of King James's record and that he (the baron) had a hankering for the *vita simplex* and had no gun with him and wouldn't have used it if he had, you can't censure him if I tell you that the smiles with which the troubadour had filled his wrinkles went out of them and left them plain wrinkles again. But he was not the kind of baron that flies from danger. He reined in the mile-an-hour pony (no difficult feat), and saluted the formidable monarch.

King James expressed himself with royal directness.

"You're that old snoozer that's running sheep on this range, ain't you? What right have you got to do it? Do you own the land, or lease any?"

"I have two sections leased from the state," said old man Ellison, mildly.

"Not by no means, you haven't," said King James. "Your lease expired yesterday; and I had a man at the land office on the minute to take it up. You don't control a foot of grass in Texas. You sheep men have got to git. Your time's up. It's a cattle country, and there ain't any room in it for snoozers. This range you've got your sheep on is mine. I'm putting up a wire fence, forty by sixty miles; and if there's a sheep inside of it when it's done it'll be a dead one. I'll give you a week to move yours away. If they ain't gone by then, I'll send six men over here with Winchesters to make mutton out of the whole lot. And if I find you here at the same time this is what you'll get."

King James patted the breech of his shotgun warningly.

Old man Ellison rode on to the camp of Encarnación. He sighed many times, and the wrinkles in his face grew deeper. Rumors that the old order was about to change had reached him before. The end of Free Grass was in sight. Other troubles, too, had been accumulating upon his shoulders. His flocks were decreasing instead of growing; the price of wool was declining at every clip; even Bradshaw, the storekeeper at Frio City, at whose store he bought his ranch supplies, was dunning him for his last six months' bill and threatening to cut him off. And so this last greatest calamity suddenly dealt out to him by the terrible King James was a crusher.

When the old man got back to the ranch at sunset he found Sam Galloway lying on his cot, propped against a roll of blankets and wool sacks, fingering his guitar.

"Hello, Uncle Ben," the troubadour called, cheerfully. "You rolled in early this evening. I been trying a new twist on the Spanish Fandango to-day. I just about got it. Here's how she goes —listen."

"That's fine, that's mighty fine," said old man Ellison, sitting on the kitchen step and rubbing his white, Scotch-terrier whiskers. "I reckon you've got all the musicians beat east and west, Sam, as far as the roads are cut out."

"Oh, I don't know," said Sam reflectively. "But I certainly do get there on variations. I guess I can handle anything in five flats about as well as any of 'em. But you look kind of fagged out, Uncle Ben—ain't you feeling right well this evening?"

"Little tired; that's all, Sam. If you ain't played yourself out, let's have that Mexican piece that starts off with: '*Huile, huile, palomita.*' It seems that that song always kind of soothes and comforts me after I've been riding far or anything bothers me."

"Why, *seguramente, señor,*" said Sam. "I'll hit her up for you as often as you like. And before I forget about it, Uncle Ben, you want to jerk Bradshaw up about them last hams he sent us. They're just a little bit strong."

A man sixty-five years old, living on a sheep ranch and beset by a complication of disasters, cannot successfully and continuously dissemble. Moreover, a troubadour has eyes quick to see unhappiness in others around him—because it disturbs his own ease. So, on the next day, Sam again questioned the old man about his air of sadness and abstraction. Then old man Ellison told him the story of King James's threats and orders and that pale melancholy and red ruin appeared to have marked him for their own. The troubadour took the news thoughtfully. He had heard much about King James.

On the third day of the seven days of grace allowed him by the autocrat of the range, old man Ellison drove his buckboard to Frio City to fetch some necessary supplies for the ranch. Bradshaw was hard but not implacable. He divided the old man's order by two, and let him have a little more time. One article secured was a new, fine ham for the pleasure of the troubadour.

Five miles out of Frio City on his way home the old man met King James riding into town. His majesty could never look anything but fierce and menacing, but to-day his slits of eyes appeared to be a little wider than they usually were.

"Good day," said the king, gruffly. "I've been wanting to see you. I hear it said by a cowman from Sandy yesterday that you was from Jackson County, Mississippi, originally. I want to know if that's a fact."

"Born there," said old man Ellison, "and raised there till I was twenty-one."

"This man says," went on King James, "that he thinks you was related to the Jackson County Reeveses. Was he right?"

"Aunt Caroline Reeves," said the old man, "was my half-sister."

"She was my aunt," said King James. "I run away from home when I was sixteen. Now, let's re-talk over some things that we discussed a few days ago. They call me a bad man; and they're only half right. There's plenty of room in my pasture for your bunch of sheep and their increase for a long time to come. Aunt Caroline used to cut out sheep in cake dough and bake 'em for me. You keep your sheep where they are, and use all the range you want. How's your finances?"

The old man related his woes in detail, dignifiedly, with restraint and candor.

"She used to smuggle extra grub into my school basket—I'm speaking of Aunt Caroline," said King James. "I'm going over to Frio City to-day, and I'll ride back by your ranch to-morrow. I'll draw $2,000 out of the bank there and bring it over to you; and I'll tell Bradshaw to let you have anything you want on credit. You are bound to have heard the old saying at home, that the Jackson County Reeveses and Kings would stick closer by each other than chestnut burs. Well, I'm a King yet whenever I run across a Reeves. So you look out for me along about sundown to-morrow, and don't you worry about nothing. Shouldn't wonder if the dry spell don't kill out the young grass."

Old man Ellison drove happily ranchward. Once more the smiles filled out his wrinkles. Very suddenly, by the magic of kinship and the good that lies somewhere in all hearts, his troubles had been removed.

On reaching the ranch he found that Sam Galloway was not there. His guitar hung by its buckskin string to a hackberry limb, moaning as the gulf breeze blew across its masterless strings.

The Kiowa endeavored to explain.

"Sam, he catch pony," said he, "and say he ride to Frio City. What for no can damn sabe. Say he come back to-night. Maybe so. That all."

As the first stars came out the troubadour rode back to his haven. He pastured his pony and went into the house, his spurs jingling martially.

Old man Ellison sat at the kitchen table, having a tin cup of before-supper coffee. He looked contented and pleased.

"Hello, Sam," said he, "I'm darned glad to see ye back. I don't know how I managed to get along on this ranch, anyhow, before ye dropped in to cheer things up. I'll bet ye've been skylarking around with some of them Frio City gals, now, that's kept ye so late."

And then old man Ellison took another look at Sam's face and saw that the minstrel had changed to the man of action.

And while Sam is unbuckling from his waist old man Ellison's six-shooter, that the latter had left behind when he drove to town, we may well pause to remark that anywhere and whenever a troubadour lays down the guitar and takes up the sword trouble is sure to follow. It is not the expert thrust of Athos nor the cold skill of Aramis nor the iron wrist of Porthos that we have to fear —it is the Gascon's fury—the wild and unacademic attack of the troubadour—the sword of D'Artagnan.

"I done it," said Sam. "I went over to Frio City to do it. I couldn't let him put the skibunk on you, Uncle Ben. I met him in Summer's saloon. I knowed what to do. I said a few things to him that nobody else heard. He reached for his gun first—half a dozen fellows saw him do it—but I got mine unlimbered first. Three doses I gave him—right around the lungs, and a saucer could have covered up all of 'em. He won't bother you no more."

"This—is—King—James—you speak—of?" asked old man Ellison, while he sipped his coffee.

"You bet it was. And they took me before the county judge; and the witnesses what saw him draw his gun first was all there. Well, of course, they put me under $300 bond to appear before the court, but there was four or five boys on the spot ready to sign the bail. He won't bother you no more, Uncle Ben. You ought to have seen how close them bullet holes was together. I reckon playing a guitar as much as I do must kind of limber a fellow's trigger finger a little, don't you think, Uncle Ben?"

Then there was a little silence in the castle except for the spluttering of a venison steak that the Kiowa was cooking.

"Sam," said old man Ellison, stroking his white whiskers with a tremulous hand, "would you mind getting the guitar and playing that '*Huile, huile, palomita*' piece once or twice? It always seems to be kind of soothing and comforting when a man's tired and fagged out."

There is no more to be said, except that the title of the story is wrong. It should have been called "The Last of the Barons." There never will be an end to the troubadours; and now and then it does seem that the jingle of their guitars will drown the sound of the muffled blows of the pickaxes and trip hammers of all the Workers in the world.

Makes the Whole World Kin

THE BURGLAR stepped inside the window quickly, and then he took his time. A burglar who respects his art always takes his time before taking anything else.

The house was a private residence. By its boarded front door and untrimmed Boston ivy the burglar knew that the mistress of it was sitting on some oceanside piazza telling a sympathetic man in a yachting cap that no one had ever understood her sensitive, lonely heart. He knew by the light in the third-story front windows, and by the lateness of the season, that the master of the house had come home, and would soon extinguish his light and retire. For it was September of the year and of the soul, in which season the house's good man comes to consider roof gardens and stenographers as vanities, and to desire the return of his mate and the more durable blessings of decorum and the moral excellencies.

The burglar lighted a cigarette. The guarded glow of the match illuminated his salient points for a moment. He belonged to the third type of burglars.

This third type has not yet been recognized and accepted. The police have made us familiar with the first and second. Their classification is simple. The collar is the distinguishing mark.

When a burglar is caught who does not wear a collar he is described as a degenerate of the lowest type, singularly vicious and depraved, and is suspected of being the desperate criminal who stole the handcuffs out of Patrolman Hennessy's pocket in 1878 and walked away to escape arrest.

The other well-known type is the burglar who wears a collar. He is always referred to as a Raffles in real life. He is invariably a gentleman by daylight, breakfasting in a dress suit, and posing as a paperhanger, while after dark he plies his nefarious occupation of burglary. His mother is an extremely wealthy and respected resident of Ocean Grove, and when he is conducted to his cell he asks at once for a nail file and the *Police Gazette.* He always has a wife in every State in the Union and fiancées in all the Territories, and the newspapers print his matrimonial gallery out of their stock of cuts of the ladies who were cured by only one bottle after having been given up by five doctors, experiencing great relief after the first dose.

The burglar wore a blue sweater. He was neither a Raffles nor one of the chefs from Hell's Kitchen. The police would have been baffled had they attempted to classify him. They have not yet heard of the respectable, unassuming burglar who is neither above nor below his station.

This burglar of the third class began to prowl. He wore no masks, dark lanterns, or gum shoes. He carried a 38-calibre revolver in his pockets, and he chewed peppermint gum thoughtfully.

The furniture of the house was swathed in its summer dust protectors. The silver was far away in safe-deposit vaults. The burglar expected no remarkable "haul." His objective point was that dimly lighted room where the master of the house should be sleeping heavily after whatever solace he had sought to lighten the burden of his loneliness. A "touch" might be made there to the extent of legitimate, fair professional profits—loose money, a watch, a jeweled stick-pin—nothing exorbitant or beyond reason. He had seen the window left open and had taken the chance.

The burglar softly opened the door of the lighted room. The gas was turned low. A man lay in the bed asleep. On the dresser lay many things in confusion—a crumpled roll of bills, a watch, keys, three poker chips, crushed cigars, a pink silk hair bow, and an unopened bottle of bromo-seltzer for a bulwark in the morning.

The burglar took three steps toward the dresser. The man in

the bed suddenly uttered a squeaky groan and opened his eyes. His right hand slid under his pillow, but remained there.

"Lay still," said the burglar in conversational tone. Burglars of the third type do not hiss. The citizen in the bed looked at the round end of the burglar's pistol and lay still.

"Now hold up both your hands," commanded the burglar.

The citizen had a little, pointed, brown-and-gray beard, like that of a painless dentist. He looked solid, esteemed, irritable, and disgusted. He sat up in bed and raised his right hand above his head.

"Up with the other one," ordered the burglar. "You might be amphibious and shoot with your left. You can count two, can't you? Hurry up, now."

"Can't raise the other one," said the citizen with a contortion of his lineaments.

"What's the matter with it?"

"Rheumatism in the shoulder."

"Inflammatory?"

"Was. The inflammation has gone down."

The burglar stood for a moment or two, holding his gun on the afflicted one. He glanced at the plunder on the dresser and then, with a half-embarrassed air back at the man in the bed. Then he, too, made a sudden grimace.

"Don't stand there making faces," snapped the citizen, bad-humoredly. "If you've come to burgle why don't you do it? There's some stuff lying around."

"'Scuse me," said the burglar, with a grin; "but it just socked me one, too. Its good for you that rheumatism and me happens to be old pals. I got it in my left arm, too. Most anybody but me would have popped you when you wouldn't hoist that left claw of yours."

"How long have you had it?" inquired the citizen.

"Four years. I guess that ain't all. Once you've got it, it's you for a rheumatic life—that's my judgment."

"Ever try rattlesnake oil?" asked the citizen interestedly.

"Gallons," said the burglar. "If all the snakes I've used the oil of was strung out in a row they'd reach eight times as far as Saturn, and the rattles could be heard at Valparaiso, Indiana, and back."

"Some use Chiselum's Pills," remarked the citizen.

"Fudge!" said the burglar. "Took 'em five months. No good. I had some relief the year I tried Finkelham's Extract, Balm of Gilead poultices, and Pott's Pain Pulverizer; but I think it was the buckeye I carried in my pocket what done the trick."

"Is yours worse in the morning or at night?" asked the citizen.

"Night," said the burglar; "just when I'm busiest. Say, take down that arm of your—I guess you won't—— Say! did you ever try Blickerstaff's Blood Builder?"

"I never did. Does yours come in paroxysms or is it a steady pain?"

The burglar sat down on the foot of the bed and rested his gun on his crossed knee.

"It jumps," said he. "It strikes me when I ain't looking for it. I had to give up second-story work because I got stuck sometimes half-way up. Tell you what—I don't believe the bloomin' doctors know what is good for it."

"Same here. I've spent a thousand dollars without getting any relief. Yours swell any?"

"Of mornings. And when it's goin' to rain—great Christopher!"

"Me, too," said the citizen. "I can tell when a streak of humidity the size of a tablecloth starts from Florida on its way to New York. And if I pass a theatre where there's an 'East Lynne' matinée going on, the moisture starts my left arm jumping like a tooth-ache."

"It's undiluted—hades!" said the burglar.

"You're dead right," said the citizen.

The burglar looked down at his pistol and thrust it into his pocket with an awkward attempt at ease.

"Say, old man," he said, constrainedly, "ever try opodeldoc?"

"Slop!" said the citizen angrily. "Might as well rub on restaurant butter."

"Sure," concurred the burglar. "It's a salve suitable for little Minnie when the kitty scratches her finger. I'll tell you what! We're up against it. I only find one thing that eases her up. Hey? Little old sanitary, ameliorating, lest-we-forget Booze. Say—this job's off—'scuse me—get on your clothes and let's go out and have some. 'Scuse the liberty, but—ouch! There she goes again!"

"For a week," said the citizen, "I haven't been able to dress myself without help. I'm afraid Thomas is in bed, and——"

"Climb out," said the burglar, "I'll help you get into your duds."

The conventional returned as a tidal wave and flooded the citizen. He stroked his brown-and-gray beard.

"It's very unusual——" he began.

"Here's your shirt," said the burglar, "fall out. I know a man who said Omberry's Ointment fixed him in two weeks so he could use both hands in tying his four-in-hand."

As they were going out the door the citizen turned and started back.

"'Liked to forgot my money," he explained; "laid it on the dresser last night."

The burglar caught him by the right sleeve.

"Come on," he said, bluffly. "I ask you. Leave it alone. I've got the price. Ever try witch hazel and oil of wintergreen?"

Jimmy Hayes and Muriel

Supper was over, and there had fallen upon the camp the silence that accompanies the rolling of corn-husk cigarettes. The water hole shone from the dark earth like a patch of fallen sky. Coyotes yelped. Dull thumps indicated the rocking-horse movements of the hobbled ponies as they moved to fresh grass. A half-troop of the Frontier Battalion of Texas Rangers were distributed about the fire.

A well-known sound—the fluttering and scraping of chaparral against wooden stirrups—came from the thick brush above the camp. The rangers listened cautiously. They heard a loud and cheerful voice call out reassuringly:

"Brace up, Muriel, old girl, we're 'most there now! Been a long ride for ye, ain't it, ye old antediluvian handful of animated carpet-tacks? Hey, now, quit a tryin' to kiss me! Don't hold on to my neck so tight—this here paint hoss ain't any too shore-footed, let me tell ye. He's liable to dump us both off if we don't watch out."

Two minutes of waiting brought a tired "paint" pony single-footing into camp. A gangling youth of twenty lolled in the saddle. Of the "Muriel" whom he had been addressing, nothing was to be seen.

"Hi, fellows!" shouted the rider, cheerfully. "This here's a letter fer Lieutenant Manning."

He dismounted, unsaddled, dropped the coils of his stake-rope, and got his hobbles from the saddle-horn. While Lieutenant Manning, in command, was reading the letter, the newcomer rubbed solicitously at some dried mud in the loops of the hobbles, showing a consideration for the forelegs of his mount.

"Boys," said the lieutenant, waving his hand to the rangers, "this is Mr. James Hayes. He's a new member of the company. Captain McLean sends him down from El Paso. The boys will see that you have some supper, Hayes, as soon as you get your pony hobbled."

The recruit was received cordially by the rangers. Still, they observed him shrewdly and with suspended judgment. Picking a comrade on the border is done with ten times the care and discretion with which a girl chooses a sweetheart. On your "side-kicker's" nerve, loyalty, aim, and coolness your own life may depend many times.

After a hearty supper Hayes joined the smokers about the fire. His appearance did not settle all the questions in the minds of his brother rangers. They saw simply a loose, lank youth with tow-colored sunburned hair and a berry-brown, ingenuous face that wore a quizzical, good-natured smile.

"Fellows," said the new ranger, "I'm goin' to interduce to you a lady friend of mine. Ain't ever heard anybody call her a beauty, but you'll all admit she's got some fine points about her. Come along, Muriel!"

He held open the front of his blue flannel shirt. Out of it crawled a horned frog. A bright red ribbon was tied jauntily around its spiky neck. It crawled to its owner's knee and sat there motionless.

"This here Muriel," said Hayes, with an oratorical wave of his hand, "has got qualities. She never talks back, she always stays at home, and she's satisfied with one red dress for every day and Sunday, too."

"Look at that blame insect!" said one of the rangers with a grin. "I've seen plenty of them horny frogs, but I never knew anybody to have one for a side-partner. Does the blame thing know you from anybody else?"

"Take it over there and see," said Hayes.

The stumpy little lizard known as the horned frog is harmless. He has the hideousness of the prehistoric monsters whose reduced descendant he is, but he is gentler than the dove.

The ranger took Muriel from Hayes's knee and went back to his seat on a roll of blankets. The captive twisted and clawed and struggled vigorously in his hand. After holding it for a moment or two, the ranger set it upon the ground. Awkwardly, but swiftly, the frog worked its four oddly moving legs until it stopped close by Hayes's foot.

"Well, dang my hide!" said the other ranger. "The little cuss knows you. Never thought them insects had that much sense!"

II Jimmy Hayes became a favorite in the ranger camp. He had an endless store of good nature, and a mild, perennial quality of humor that is well adapted to camp life. He was never without his horned frog. In the bosom of his shirt during rides, on his knee or shoulder in camp, under his blankets at night, the ugly little beast never left him.

Jimmy was a humorist of a type that prevails in the rural South and West. Unskilled in originating methods of amusing or in witty conceptions, he had hit upon a comical idea and clung to it reverently. It had seemed to Jimmy a very funny thing to have about his person, with which to amuse his friends, a tame horned frog with a red ribbon around its neck. As it was a happy idea, why not perpetuate it?

The sentiments existing between Jimmy and the frog cannot be exactly determined. The capability of the horned frog for lasting affection is a subject upon which we have no symposiums. It is easier to guess Jimmy's feelings. Muriel was his *chef d'œuvre* of wit, and as such he cherished her. He caught flies for her, and shielded her from sudden northers. Yet his care was half selfish, and when the time came she repaid him a thousand fold. Other

Muriels have thus overbalanced the light attentions of other Jimmies.

Not at once did Jimmy attain full brotherhood with his comrades. They loved him for his simplicity and drollness, but there hung above him a great sword of suspended judgment. To make merry in camp is not all of a ranger's life. There are horse-thieves to trail, desperate criminals to run down, bravos to battle with, bandits to rout out of the chaparral, peace and order to be compelled at the muzzle of a six-shooter. Jimmy had been "'most generally a cow-puncher," he said; he was inexperienced in ranger methods of warfare. Therefore the rangers speculated apart and solemnly as to how he would stand fire. For, let it be known, the honor and pride of each ranger company is the individual bravery of its members.

For two months the border was quiet. The rangers lolled, listless, in camp. And then—bringing joy to the rusting guardians of the frontier—Sebastiano Saldar, an eminent Mexican desperado and cattle-thief, crossed the Rio Grande with his gang and began to lay waste the Texas side. There were indications that Jimmy Hayes would soon have the opportunity to show his mettle. The rangers patrolled with alacrity, but Saldar's men were mounted like Lochinvar, and were hard to catch.

One evening, about sundown, the rangers halted for supper after a long ride. Their horses stood panting, with their saddles on. The men were frying bacon and boiling coffee. Suddenly, out of the brush, Sebastiano Saldar and his gang dashed upon them with blazing six-shooters and high-voiced yells. It was a neat surprise. The rangers swore in annoyed tones, and got their Winchesters busy; but the attack was only a spectacular dash of the purest Mexican type. After the florid demonstration the raiders galloped away, yelling, down the river. The rangers mounted and pursued; but in less than two miles the fagged ponies labored so that Lieutenant Manning gave the word to abandon the chase and return to the camp.

Then it was discovered that Jimmy Hayes was missing. Some

one remembered having seen him run for his pony when the attack began, but no one had set eyes on him since. Morning came, but no Jimmy. They searched the country around, on the theory that he had been killed or wounded, but without success. Then they followed after Saldar's gang, but it seemed to have disappeared. Manning concluded that the wily Mexican had recrossed the river after his theatric farewell. And, indeed, no further depredations from him were reported.

This gave the rangers time to nurse a soreness they had. As has been said, the pride and honor of the company is the individual bravery of its members. And now they believed that Jimmy Hayes had turned coward at the whiz of Mexican bullets. There was no other deduction. Buck Davis pointed out that not a shot was fired by Saldar's gang after Jimmy was seen running for his horse. There was no way for him to have been shot. No, he had fled from his first fight, and afterward he would not return, aware that the scorn of his comrades would be a worse thing to face than the muzzles of many rifles.

So Manning's detachment of McLean's company, Frontier Battalion, was gloomy. It was the first blot on its escutcheon. Never before in the history of the service had a ranger shown the white feather. All of them had liked Jimmy Hayes, and that made it worse.

Days, weeks, and months went by, and still that little cloud of unforgotten cowardice hung above the camp.

III Nearly a year afterward—after many camping grounds and many hundreds of miles guarded and defended—Lieutenant Manning, with almost the same detachment of men, was sent to a point only a few miles below their old camp on the river to look after some smuggling there. One afternoon, while they were riding through a dense mesquite flat, they came upon a patch of open hog-wallow prairie. There they rode upon the scene of an unwritten tragedy.

In a big hog-wallow lay the skeletons of three Mexicans. Their clothing alone served to identify them. The largest of the figures had once been Sebastiano Saldar. His great, costly sombrero, heavy with gold ornamentation—a hat famous all along the Rio Grande—lay there pierced by three bullets. Along the ridge of the hog-wallow rested the rusting Winchesters of the Mexicans—all pointing in the same direction.

The rangers rode in that direction for fifty yards. There, in a little depression of the ground, with his rifle still bearing upon the three, lay another skeleton. It had been a battle of extermination. There was nothing to identify the solitary defender. His clothing —such as the elements had left distinguishable—seemed to be of the kind that any ranchman or cowboy might have worn.

"Some cow-puncher," said Manning, "that they caught out alone. Good boy! He put up a dandy scrap before they got him. So that's why we didn't hear from Don Sebastiano any more!"

And then, from beneath the weather-beaten rags of the dead man, there wriggled out a horned frog with a faded red ribbon around its neck, and sat upon the shoulder of its long quiet master. Mutely it told the story of the untried youth and the swift "paint" pony—how they had outstripped all their comrades that day in the pursuit of the Mexican raiders, and how the boy had gone down upholding the honor of the company.

The ranger troop herded close, and a simultaneous wild yell arose from their lips. The outburst was at once a dirge, an apology, an epitaph, and a pæan of triumph. A strange requiem, you may say, over the body of a fallen comrade; but if Jimmy Hayes could have heard it he would have understood.

The Adventures of Shamrock Jolnes

I AM so fortunate as to count Shamrock Jolnes, the great New York detective, among my muster of friends. Jolnes is what is called the "inside man" of the city detective force. He is an expert in the use of the typewriter, and it is his duty, whenever there is a "murder mystery" to be solved, to sit at a desk telephone at headquarters and take down the message of "cranks" who 'phone in their confessions to having committed the crime.

But on certain "off" days when confessions are coming in slowly and three or four newspapers have run to earth as many different guilty persons, Jolnes will knock about the town with me, exhibiting, to my great delight and instruction, his marvellous powers of observation and deduction.

The other day I dropped in at Headquarters and found the great detective gazing thoughtfully at a string that was tied tightly around his little finger.

"Good morning, Whatsup," he said, without turning his head. "I'm glad to notice that you've had your house fitted up with electric lights at last."

"Will you please tell me," I said, in surprise, "how you knew that? I am sure that I never mentioned the fact to any one, and the wiring was a rush order not completed until this morning."

"Nothing easier," said Jolnes, genially. "As you came in I caught the odor of the cigar you are smoking. I know an expensive cigar; and I know that not more than three men in New York can afford to smoke cigars and pay gas bills too at the present time. That was an easy one. But I am working just now on a little problem of my own."

"Why have you that string on your finger?" I asked.

"That's the problem," said Jolnes. "My wife tied that on this morning to remind me of something I was to send up to the house. Sit down, Whatsup, and excuse me for a few moments."

The distinguished detective went to a wall telephone, and stood with the receiver to his ear for probably ten minutes.

"Were you listening to a confession?" I asked, when he had returned to his chair.

"Perhaps," said Jolnes, with a smile, "it might be called something of the sort. To be frank with you, Whatsup, I've cut out the dope. I've been increasing the quantity for so long that morphine doesn't have much effect on me any more. I've got to have something more powerful. That telephone I just went to is connected with a room in the Waldorf where there's an author's reading in progress. Now, to get at the solution of this string."

After five minutes of silent pondering, Jolnes looked at me, with a smile, and nodded his head.

"Wonderful man!" I exclaimed; "already?"

"It is quite simple," he said, holding up his finger. "You see that knot? That is to prevent my forgetting. It is, therefore, a forget-me-knot. A forget-me-not is a flower. It was a sack of flour that I was to send home!"

"Beautiful!" I could not help crying out in admiration.

"Suppose we go out for a ramble," suggested Jolnes.

"There is only one case of importance on hand now. Old man McCarty, one hundred and four years old, died from eating too many bananas. The evidence points so strongly to the Mafia that the police have surrounded the Second Avenue Katzenjammer Gambrinus Club No. 2, and the capture of the assassin is only the matter of a few hours. The detective force has not yet been called on for assistance."

Jolnes and I went out and up the street toward the corner, where we were to catch a surface car.

Halfway up the block we met Rheingelder, an acquaintance of ours, who held a City Hall position.

"Good morning, Rheingelder," said Jolnes, halting. "Nice breakfast that was you had this morning."

Always on the lookout for the detective's remarkable feats of deduction, I saw Jolnes's eyes flash for an instant upon a long yellow splash on the shirt bosom and a smaller one upon the chin of Rheingelder—both undoubtedly made by the yolk of an egg.

"Oh, dot is some of your detectiveness," said Rheingelder, shaking all over with a smile. "Vell, I bet you trinks and cigars all around dot you cannot tell vot I haf eaten for breakfast."

"Done," said Jolnes. "Sausage, pumpernickel, and coffee."

Rheingelder admitted the correctness of the surmise and paid the bet. When we had proceeded on our way I said to Jolnes:

"I thought you looked at the egg spilled on his chin and shirt front."

"I did," said Jolnes. "That is where I began my deduction. Rheingelder is a very economical, saving man. Yesterday eggs dropped in the market to twenty-eight cents per dozen. To-day they are quoted at forty-two. Rheingelder ate eggs yesterday, and to-day he went back to his usual fare. A little thing like this isn't anything, Whatsup; it belongs to the primary arithmetic class."

When we boarded the street car we found the seats all occupied —principally by ladies. Jolnes and I stood on the rear platform.

About the middle of the car there sat an elderly man with a short, gray beard, who looked to be the typical, well-dressed New Yorker. At successive corners other ladies climbed aboard, and soon three or four of them were standing over the man, clinging to straps and glaring meaningly at the man who occupied the coveted seat. But he resolutely retained his place.

"We New Yorkers," I remarked to Jolnes, "have about lost our manners, as far as the exercise of them in public goes."

"Perhaps so," said Jolnes, lightly; "but the man you evidently refer to happens to be a very chivalrous and courteous gentleman from Old Virginia. He is spending a few days in New York with his wife and two daughters, and he leaves for the South to-night."

"You know him, then?" I said, in amazement.

"I never saw him before we stepped on the car," declared the detective, smilingly.

"By the gold tooth of the Witch of Endor!" I cried, "if you can construe all that from his appearance you are dealing in nothing else than black art."

"The habit of observation—nothing more," said Jolnes. "If the old gentleman gets off the car before we do, I think I can demonstrate to you the accuracy of my deduction."

Three blocks farther along the gentleman rose to leave the car. Jolnes addressed him at the door:

"Pardon me, sir, but are you not Colonel Hunter, of Norfolk, Virginia?"

"No, suh," was the extremely courteous answer. "My name, suh, is Ellison—Major Winfield R. Ellison, from Fairfax County, in the same state. I know a good many people, suh, in Norfolk—the Goodriches, the Tollivers, and the Crabtrees, suh, but I never had the pleasure of meeting yo' friend, Colonel Hunter. I am happy to say, suh, that I am going back to Virginia to-night, after having spent a week in yo' city with my wife and three daughters. I shall be in Norfolk in about ten days, and if you will give me yo' name, suh, I will take pleasure in looking up Colonel Hunter and telling him that you inquired after him, suh."

"Thank you," said Jolnes; "tell him that Reynolds sent his regards, if you will be so kind."

I glanced at the great New York detective and saw that a look of intense chagrin had come upon his clear-cut features. Failure in the slightest point always galled Shamrock Jolnes.

"Did you say your *three* daughters?" he asked of the Virginia gentleman.

"Yes, suh, my three daughters, all as fine girls as there are in Fairfax County," was the answer.

With that Major Ellison stopped the car and began to descend the step.

Shamrock Jolnes clutched his arm.

"One moment, sir," he begged, in an urbane voice in which I alone detected the anxiety—"am I not right in believing that one of the young ladies is an *adopted* daughter?"

"You are, suh," admitted the major, from the ground, "but how the devil you knew it, suh, is mo' than I can tell."

"And mo' than I can tell, too," I said, as the car went on.

Jolnes was restored to his calm, observant serenity by having wrested victory from his apparent failure; so after we got off the car he invited me into a café promising to reveal the process of his latest wonderful feat.

"In the first place," he began after we were comfortably seated, "I knew the gentleman was no New Yorker because he was flushed and uneasy and restless on account of the ladies that were standing, although he did not rise and give them his seat. I decided from his appearance that he was a Southerner rather than a Westerner.

"Next I began to figure out his reason for not relinquishing his seat to a lady when he evidently felt strongly, but not over-poweringly, impelled to do so. I very quickly decided upon that. I noticed that one of his eyes had received a severe jab in one corner, which was red and inflamed, and that all over his face were tiny round marks about the size of the end of an uncut lead pencil. Also upon both of his patent-leather shoes were a number of deep imprints shaped like ovals cut off square at one end.

"Now, there is only one district in New York City where a man is bound to receive scars and wounds and indentations of that sort—and that is along the sidewalks of Twenty-third Street and a portion of Sixth Avenue south of there. I knew from the imprints of trampling French heels on his feet and the marks of countless jabs in the face from umbrellas and parasols carried

by women in the shopping district that he had been in conflict
with the amazonian troops. And as he was a man of intelligent
appearance, I knew he would not have braved such dangers unless he had been dragged thither by his own women folk. Therefore, when he got on the car his anger at the treatment he had
received was sufficient to make him keep his seat in spite of his
traditions of Southern chivalry."

"That is all very well," I said, "but why did you insist upon
daughters—and especially two daughters? Why couldn't a wife
alone have taken him shopping?"

"There had to be daughters," said Jolnes, calmly. "If he had
only a wife, and she near his own age, he could have bluffed her
into going alone. If he had a young wife she would prefer to go
alone. So there you are."

"I'll admit that," I said; "but, now, why two daughters? And
how, in the name of all the prophets, did you guess that one was
adopted when he told you he had three?"

"Don't say guess," said Jolnes, with a touch of pride in his air;
"there is no such word in the lexicon of ratiocination. In
Major Ellison's buttonhole there was a carnation and a rosebud
backed by a geranium leaf. No woman ever combined a carnation
and a rosebud into a boutonnière. Close your eyes, Whatsup,
and give the logic of your imagination a chance. Cannot you
see the lovely Adele fastening the carnation to the lapel so that
papa may be gay upon the street? And then the romping Edith
May dancing up with sisterly jealousy to add her rosebud to the
adornment?"

"And then," I cried, beginning to feel enthusiasm, "when he
declared that he had three daughters——"

"I could see," said Jolnes, "one in the background who added
no flower; and I knew that she must be——"

"Adopted!" I broke in. "I give you every credit; but how did
you know he was leaving for the South to-night?"

"In his breast pocket," said the great detective, "something
large and oval made a protuberance. Good liquor is scarce on

trains, and it is a long journey from New York to Fairfax County."

"Again, I must bow to you," I said. "And tell me this, so that my last shred of doubt will be cleared away; why did you decide that he was from Virginia?"

"It was very faint, I admit," answered Shamrock Jolnes, "but no trained observer could have failed to detect the odor of mint in the car."

From
ROLLING STONES

❁

The Friendly Call

WHEN I used to sell hardware in the West, I often "made" a little town called Saltillo, in Colorado. I was always certain of securing a small or a larger order from Simon Bell, who kept a general store there. Bell was one of those six-foot, low-voiced products, formed from a union of the West and the South. I liked him. To look at him you would think he should be robbing stage coaches or juggling gold mines with both hands; but he would sell you a paper of tacks or a spool of thread, with ten times more patience and courtesy than any saleslady in a city department store.

I had a twofold object in my last visit to Saltillo. One was to sell a bill of goods; the other to advise Bell of a chance that I knew of by which I was certain he could make a small fortune.

In Mountain City, a town on the Union Pacific, five times larger than Saltillo, a mercantile firm was about to go to the wall. It had a lively and growing custom, but was on the edge of dissolution and ruin. Mismanagement and the gambling habits of one of the partners explained it. The condition of the firm was not yet public property. I had my knowledge of it from a private source. I knew that, if the ready cash were offered, the stock and good will could be bought for about one fourth their value.

On arriving in Saltillo I went to Bell's store. He nodded to me, smiled his broad, lingering smile, went on leisurely selling some candy to a little girl, then came around the counter and shook hands.

"Well," he said (his invariably preliminary jocosity at every call I made), "I suppose you are out here making kodak pictures of the mountains. It's the wrong time of the year to buy any hardware, of course."

I told Bell about the bargain in Mountain City. If he wanted to take advantage of it, I would rather have missed a sale than have him over-stocked in Saltillo.

"It sounds good," he said, with enthusiasm. "I'd like to branch out and do a bigger business, and I'm obliged to you for mentioning it. But—well, you come and stay at my house to-night and I'll think about it."

It was then after sundown and time for the larger stores in Saltillo to close. The clerks in Bell's put away their books, whirled the combination of the safe, put on their coats and hats and left for their homes. Bell padlocked the big, double wooden front doors, and we stood, for a moment, breathing the keen fresh mountain air coming across the foothills.

A big man walked down the street and stopped in front of the high porch of the store. His long, black moustache, black eyebrows, and curly black hair contrasted queerly with his light, pink complexion, which belonged, by rights, to a blonde. He was about forty, and wore a white vest, a white hat, a watch chain made of five-dollar gold pieces linked together, and a rather well-fitting two-piece gray suit of the cut that college boys of eighteen are wont to affect. He glanced at me distrustfully, and then at Bell with coldness and, I thought, something of enmity in his expression.

"Well," asked Bell, as if he were addressing a stranger, "did you fix up that matter?"

"Did I!" the man answered, in a resentful tone. "What do you suppose I've been here two weeks for? The business is to be settled tonight. Does that suit you, or have you got something to kick about?"

"It's all right," said Bell. "I knew you'd do it."

"Of course you did," said the magnificent stranger. "Haven't I done it before?"

"You have," admitted Bell. "And so have I. How do you find it at the hotel?"

"Rocky grub. But I ain't kicking. Say—can you give me any pointers about managing that—affair? It's my first deal in that line of business, you know."

"No, I can't," answered Bell, after some thought. "I've tried all kinds of ways. You'll have to try some of your own."

"Tried soft soap?"

"Barrels of it."

"Tried a saddle girth with a buckle on the end of it?"

"Never none. Started to once; and here's what I got."

Bell held out his right hand. Even in the deepening twilight I could see on the back of it a long, white scar, that might have been made by a claw or a knife or some sharp-edged tool.

"Oh, well," said the florid man, carelessly, "I'll know what to do later on."

He walked away without another word. When he had gone ten steps he turned and called to Bell:

"You keep well out of the way when the goods are delivered, so there won't be any hitch in the business."

"All right," answered Bell, "I'll attend to my end of the line."

This talk was scarcely clear in its meaning to me; but as it did not concern me, I did not let it weigh upon my mind. But the singularity of the other man's appearance lingered with me for a while; and as we walked toward Bell's house I remarked to him:

"Your customer seems to be a surly kind of fellow—not one that you'd like to be snowed in with in a camp on a hunting trip."

"He is that," assented Bell, heartily. "He reminds me of a rat-tlesnake that's been poisoned by the bite of a tarantula."

"He doesn't look like a citizen of Saltillo," I went on.

"No," said Bell, "he lives in Sacramento. He's down here on a little business trip. His name is George Ringo, and he's been my best friend—in fact, the only friend I ever had—for twenty years."

I was too surprised to make any further comment.

Bell lived in a comfortable, plain, square, two-story white house on the edge of the little town. I waited in the parlor—a room depressingly genteel—furnished with red plush, straw matting, looped-up lace curtains, and a glass case large enough to contain a mummy, full of mineral specimens.

While I waited I heard, upstairs, that unmistakable sound in-stantly recognized the world over—a bickering woman's voice, rising as her anger and fury grew. I could hear, between the gusts, the temperate rumble of Bell's tones, striving to oil the troubled waters.

The storm subsided soon; but not before I had heard the woman say, in a lower, concentrated tone, rather more carrying than her high-pitched railings: "This is the last time. I tell you— the last time. Oh, you *will* understand."

The household seemed to consist of only Bell and his wife and a servant or two. I was introduced to Mrs. Bell at supper.

At first sight she seemed to be a handsome woman, but I soon perceived that her charm had been spoiled. An uncon-trolled petulance, I thought, and emotional egotism, an absence of poise and a habitual dissatisfaction had marred her woman-hood. During the meal, she showed that false gayety, spurious kindliness and reactionary softness that mark the woman addicted to tantrums. Withal, she was a woman who might be at-tractive to many men.

After supper, Bell and I took our chairs outside, set them on the grass in the moonlight and smoked. The full moon is a witch. In her light, truthful men dig up for you nuggets of purer gold; while liars squeeze out brighter colors from the tubes of their invention. I saw Bell's broad, slow smile come out upon his face and linger there.

"I reckon you think George and me are a funny kind of friends," he said. "The fact is we never did take much interest in each other's company. But his idea and mine, of what a friend should be, was always synonymous and we lived up to it, strict, all these years. Now, I'll give you an idea of what our idea is.

"A man don't need but one friend. The fellow who drinks your liquor and hangs around you, slapping you on the back and taking up your time, telling you how much he likes you, ain't a friend, even if you did play marbles at school and fish in the same creek with him. As long as you don't need a friend one of that kind may answer. But a friend, to my mind, is one you can deal with on a strict reciprocity basis like me and George have always done.

"A good many years ago, him and me was connected in a number of ways. We put our capital together and run a line of freight wagons in New Mexico, and we mined some and gambled a few. And then, we got into trouble of one or two kinds; and I reckon that got us on a better understandable basis than anything else did, unless it was the fact that we never had much personal use for each other's ways. George is the vainest man I ever see, and the biggest brag. He could blow the biggest geyser in the Yosemite valley back into its hole with one whisper. I am a quiet man, and fond of studiousness and thought. The more we used to see each other, personally, the less we seemed to like to be together. If he ever had slapped me on the back and snivelled over me like I've seen men do to what they called their friends, I know I'd have had a rough-and-tumble with him on the spot. Same way with George. He hated my ways as bad as I did his. When we were mining, we lived in separate tents, so as not to intrude our obnoxiousness on each other.

"But after a long time, we begun to know each of us could depend on the other when we were in a pinch, up to his last dollar, word of honor or perjury, bullet, or drop of blood we had in the world. We never even spoke of it to each other, because that would have spoiled it. But we tried it out, time after time, until we came to know. I've grabbed my hat and jumped a freight and rode 200 miles to identify him when he was about to be hung by mistake, in Idaho, for a train robber. Once, I laid sick of typhoid in a tent in Texas, without a dollar or a change of clothes, and sent for George in Boise City. He came on the next train. The first thing he did before speaking to me, was to hang up a little looking glass on the side of the tent and curl his moustache and rub some hair dye on his head. His hair is naturally a light reddish. Then he gave me the most scientific cussing I ever had, and took off his coat.

" 'If you wasn't a Moses-meek little Mary's lamb, you wouldn't have been took down this way,' says he. 'Haven't you got gumption enough not to drink swamp water or fall down and scream whenever you have a little colic or feel a mosquito bite you?' He made me a little mad.

" 'You've got the bedside manners of a Piute medicine man,' says I. 'And I wish you'd go away and let me die a natural death. I'm sorry I sent for you.'

" 'I've a mind to,' says George, 'for nobody cares whether you live or die. But now I've been tricked into coming, I might as well stay until this little attack of indigestion or nettle rash or whatever it is, passes away.'

"Two weeks afterward, when I was beginning to get around again, the doctor laughed and said he was sure that my friend's keeping me mad all the time did more than his drugs to cure me.

"So that's the way George and me was friends. There wasn't any sentiment about it—it was just give and take, and each of us knew that the other was ready for the call at any time.

"I remember, once, I played a sort of joke on George, just to try him. I felt a little mean about it afterward, because I never ought to have doubted he'd do it.

"We was both living in a little town in the San Luis valley, running some flocks of sheep and a few cattle. We were partners, but, as usual, we didn't live together. I had an old aunt, out from the East, visiting for the summer, so I rented a little cottage. She soon had a couple of cows and some pigs and chickens to make the place look like home. George lived alone in a little cabin half a mile out of town.

"One day a calf that we had, died. That night I broke its bones, dumped it into a coarse sack and tied it up with wire. I put on an old shirt, tore a sleeve 'most out of it, and the collar half off, tangled up my hair, put some red ink on my hands and splashed some of it over my shirt and face. I must have looked like I'd been having the fight of my life. I put the sack in a wagon and drove out to George's cabin. When I halloed, he come out in a yellow dressing-gown, a Turkish cap, and patent leather shoes. George always was a great dresser.

"I dumped the bundle to the ground.

"'Sh-sh!' says I, kind of wild in my way. 'Take that and bury it, George, out somewhere behind your house—bury it just like it is. And don——'

"'Don't get excited,' says George. 'And for the Lord's sake go and wash your hands and face and put on a clean shirt.'

"And he lights his pipe, while I drove away at a gallop. The next morning he drops around to our cottage, where my aunt was fiddling with her flowers and truck in the front yard. He bends himself and bows and makes compliments as he could do, when so disposed, and begs a rose bush from her, saying he had turned up a little land back of his cabin, and wanted to plant something on it by way of usefulness and ornament. So my aunt, flattered, pulls up one of her biggest by the roots and gives it to him. Afterward I see it growing where he planted it, in a place where the grass had been cleared off and the dirt levelled. But neither George nor me ever spoke of it to each other again."

The moon rose higher, possibly drawing water from the sea, pixies from their dells, and certainly more confidences from Simms Bell, the friend of a friend.

"There come a time, not long afterward," he went on, "when I was able to do a good turn for George Ringo. George had made a little pile of money in beeves and he was up in Denver, and he showed up when I saw him, wearing deer-skin vests, yellow shoes, clothes like the awnings in front of drug stores, and his hair dyed so blue that it looked black in the dark. He wrote me to come up there, quick—that he needed me, and to bring the best outfit of clothes I had. I had 'em on when I got the letter, so I left on the next train. George was——"

Bell stopped for half a minute, listening intently.

"I thought I heard a team coming down the road," he explained. "George was at a summer resort on a lake near Denver and was putting on as many airs as he knew how. He had rented a little two-room cottage, and had a Chihuahua dog and a hammock and eight different kinds of walking sticks.

" 'Simms,' he says to me, 'there's a widow woman here that's petering the soul out of me with her intentions. I can't get out of her way. It ain't that she ain't handsome and agreeable, in a sort of style, but her attentions is serious, and I ain't ready for to marry nobody and settle down. I can't go to no festivity nor sit on the hotel piazza or mix in any of the society round-ups, but what she cuts me out of the herd and puts her daily brand on me. I like this here place,' goes on George, 'and I'm making a hit here in the most censorious circles, so I don't want to have to run away from it. So I sent for you.'

" 'What do you want me to do?' I asks George.

" 'Why,' says he, 'I want you to head her off. I want you to cut me out. I want you to come to the rescue. Suppose you seen a wildcat about for to eat me, what would you do?'

" 'Go for it,' says I.

" 'Correct,' says George. 'Then go for this Mrs. De Clinton the same.'

" 'How am I to do it?' I asks. 'By force and awfulness or in some gentler and less lurid manner?'

" 'Court her,' George says, 'get her off my trail. Feed her. Take her out in boats. Hang around her and stick to her. Get her mashed on you if you can. Some women are pretty big fools. Who knows but what she might take a fancy to you.'

"'Had you ever thought,' I asks, 'of repressing your fatal fascinations in her presence; of squeezing a harsh note in the melody of your siren voice, of veiling your beauty—in other words, of giving her the bounce yourself?'

"George sees no essence of sarcasm in my remark. He twists his moustache and looks at the points of his shoes.

"'Well, Simms,' he said, 'you know how I am about the ladies. I can't hurt none of their feelings. I'm by nature polite and esteemful of their intents and purposes. This Mrs. De Clinton don't appear to be the suitable sort for me. Besides, I ain't a marrying man by all means.'

"'All right,' said I, 'I'll do the best I can in the case.'

"So I bought a new outfit of clothes and a book on etiquette and made a dead set for Mrs. De Clinton. She was a fine-looking woman, cheerful and gay. At first, I almost had to hobble her to keep her from loping around at George's heels; but finally I got her so she seemed glad to go riding with me and sailing on the lake; and she seemed real hurt on the mornings when I forgot to send her a bunch of flowers. Still, I didn't like the way she looked at George, sometimes, out of the corner of her eye. George was having a fine time now, going with the whole bunch just as he pleased. Yes'm," continued Bell, "she certainly was a fine-looking woman at that time. She's changed some since, as you might have noticed at the supper table."

"What!" I exclaimed.

"I married Mrs. De Clinton," went on Bell. "One evening while we were up at the lake. When I told George about it, he opened his mouth and I thought he was going to break our traditions and say something grateful, but he swallowed it back.

"'All right,' says he, playing with his dog. 'I hope you won't have too much trouble. Myself, I'm not never going to marry.'

"That was three years ago," said Bell. "We came here to live. For a year we got along medium fine. And then everything changed. For two years I've been having something that rhymes first-class with my name. You heard the row upstairs this evening? That was a merry welcome compared to the usual average. She's tired of me and of this little town life and she rages all day, like a panther in a cage. I stood it until two weeks ago and then I had to send out The Call. I located George in Sacramento. He started the day he got my wire."

Mrs. Bell came out of the house swiftly toward us. Some strong excitement or anxiety seemed to possess her, but she smiled a faint hostess smile, and tried to keep her voice calm.

"The dew is falling," she said, "and it's growing rather late. Wouldn't you gentlemen rather come into the house?"

Bell took some cigars from his pocket and answered: "It's most too fine a night to turn in yet. I think Mr. Ames and I will walk out along the road a mile or so and have another smoke. I want to talk with him about some goods that I want to buy."

"Up the road or down the road?" asked Mrs. Bell.

"Down," said Bell.

I thought she breathed a sigh of relief.

When we had gone a hundred yards and the house became concealed by trees, Bell guided me into the thick grove that lined the road and back through them toward the house again. We stopped within twenty yards of the house, concealed by the dark shadows. I wondered at this maneuver. And then I heard in the distance coming down the road beyond the house, the regular hoofbeats of a team of horses. Bell held his watch in a ray of moonlight.

"On time, within a minute," he said. "That's George's way."

The team slowed up as it drew near the house and stopped in a patch of black shadows. We saw the figure of a woman carrying a heavy valise move swiftly from the other side of the house, and hurry to the waiting vehicle. Then it rolled away briskly in the direction from which it had come.

I looked at Bell inquiringly, I suppose. I certainly asked him no question.

"She's running away with George," said Bell, simply. "He's kept me posted about the progress of the scheme all along. She'll get a divorce in six months and then George will marry her. He never helps anybody halfway. It's all arranged between them."

I began to wonder what friendship was, after all.

When we went into the house, Bell began to talk easily on other subjects; and I took his cue. By and by the big chance to buy out the business in Mountain City came back to my mind and I began to urge it upon him. Now that he was free, it would be easier for him to make the move; and he was sure of a splendid bargain.

Bell was silent for some minutes, but when I looked at him I fancied that he was thinking of something else—that he was not considering the project.

"Why, no, Mr. Ames," he said, after a while, "I can't make that deal. I'm awful thankful to you, though, for telling me about it. But I've got to stay here. I can't go to Mountain City."

"Why?" I asked.

"Missis Bell," he replied, "won't live in Mountain City. She hates the place and wouldn't go there. I've got to keep right on here in Saltillo."

"Mrs. Bell!" I exclaimed, too puzzled to conjecture what he meant.

"I ought to explain," said Bell. "I know George and I know Mrs. Bell. He's impatient in his ways. He can't stand things that fret him, long, like I can. Six months, I give them—six months of married life, and there'll be another disunion. Mrs. Bell will come back to me. There's no other place for her to go. I've got to stay here and wait. At the end of six months, I'll have to grab a satchel and catch the first train. For George will be sending out The Call."

Sound and Fury

PERSONS OF THE DRAMA Mr. Penne   *An Author*
                            Miss Lore   *An Amanuensis*

SCENE *Workroom of* Mr. Penne's *popular novel factory.*

MR. PENNE Good morning, Miss Lore. Glad to see you so prompt. We should finish that June installment for the *Epoch* to-day. Leverett is crowding me for it. Are you quite ready? We will resume where we left off yesterday. (*Dictates.*) "Kate, with a sigh, rose from his knees, and——"

MISS LORE Excuse me; you mean "rose from *her* knees," in stead of "his," don't you?

MR. PENNE Er—no—"his," if you please. It is the love scene in the garden. (*Dictates.*) "Rose from his knees where, blushing with youth's bewitching coyness, she had rested for a moment after Cortland had declared his love. The hour was one of supreme and tender joy. When Kate—scene that Cortland never——"

MISS LORE Excuse me; but wouldn't it be more grammatical to say "when Kate *saw*," instead of "seen"?

MR. PENNE The context will explain. (*Dictates.*) "When Kate —scene that Cortland never forgot—came tripping across the lawn it seemed to him the fairest sight that earth had ever offered to his gaze."

MISS LORE Oh!

MR. PENNE (*dictates*) "Kate had abandoned herself to the joy of her newfound love so completely that no shadow of her former grief was cast upon it. Cortland, with his arm firmly entwined about her waist, knew nothing of her sighs——"

MISS LORE   Goodness! If he couldn't tell her size with his arm around——

MR. PENNE (*frowning*)   "Of her sighs and tears of the previous night."

MISS LORE   Oh!

MR. PENNE (*dictates*)   "To Cortland the chief charm of this girl was her look of innocence and unworldliness. Never had nun——"

MISS LORE   How about changing that to "never had any"?

MR. PENNE (*emphatically*)   "Never had nun in cloistered cell a face more sweet and pure."

MISS LORE   Oh!

MR. PENNE (*dictates*)   "But now Kate must hasten back to the house lest her absence be discovered. After a fond farewell she turned and sped lightly away. Cortland's gaze followed her. He watched her rise——"

MISS LORE   Excuse me, Mr. Penne; but how could he watch her eyes while her back was turned toward him?

MR. PENNE (*with extreme politeness*)   Possibly you would gather my meaning more intelligently if you would wait for the conclusion of the sentence. (*Dictates.*) "Watched her rise as gracefully as a fawn as she mounted the eastern terrace."

MISS LORE   Oh!

MR. PENNE (*dictates*)   "And yet Cortland's position was so far above that of this rustic maiden that he dreaded to consider the social upheaval that would ensue should he marry her. In no uncertain tones the traditional voices of his caste and world cried out loudly to him to let her go. What should follow——"

MISS LORE (*looking up with a start*)   I'm sure I can't say, Mr. Penne. Unless (*with a giggle*) you would want to add "Gallegher."

MR. PENNE (*coldly*)   Pardon me. I was not seeking to impose upon you the task of a collaborator. Kindly consider the question as a part of the text.

MISS LORE   Oh!

MR. PENNE (*dictates*)   "On one side was love and Kate; on the other side his heritage of social position and family pride. Would love win? Love, that the poets tell us will last forever!" (*Perceives that* Miss Lore *looks fatigued, and looks at his watch.*) That's a good long stretch. Perhaps we'd better knock off a bit.

(Miss Lore *does not reply.*)

MR. PENNE   I said, Miss Lore, we've been at it quite a long time—wouldn't you like to knock off for a while?

MISS LORE   Oh! Were you addressing me before? I put what you said down. I thought it belonged in the story. It seemed to fit in all right. Oh, no; I'm not tired.

MR. PENNE   Very well, then, we will continue. (*Dictates.*) "In spite of these qualms and doubts, Cortland was a happy man. That night at the club he silently toasted Kate's bright eyes in a bumper of the rarest vintage. Afterward he set out for a stroll with, as Kate on——"

MISS LORE   Excuse me, Mr. Penne, for venturing a suggestion; but don't you think you might state that in a less coarse manner?

MR. PENNE (*astounded*)   Wh-wh—I'm afraid I fail to understand you.

MISS LORE   His condition. Why not say he was "full" or "intoxicated"? It would sound much more elegant than the way you express it.

MR. PENNE (*still darkly wandering*)   Will you kindly point out, Miss Lore, where I have intimated that Cortland was "full," if you prefer that word?

MISS LORE (*calmly consulting her stenographic notes*)   It is right here, word for word. (*Reads.*) "Afterwards he set out for a stroll with a skate on."

MR. PENNE (*with peculiar emphasis*)   Ah! And now will you kindly take down the expurgated phrase? (*Dictates.*) "Afterward he set out for a stroll with, as Kate on one occasion had fancifully told him, her spirit leaning upon his arm."

MISS LORE Oh!

MR. PENNE (*dictates*) Chapter thirty-four. Heading—"What Kate Found in the Garden." "That fragrant summer morning brought gracious tasks to all. The bees were at the honeysuckle blossoms on the porch. Kate, singing a little song, was training the riotous branches of her favorite woodbine. The sun, himself, had rows——"

MISS LORE Shall I say "had risen"?

MR. PENNE (*very slowly and with desperate deliberation*) "The —sun—himself—had—rows—of—blushing—pinks—and—hollyhocks—and—hyacinths—waiting—that—he—might—dry—their —dew-drenched—cups."

MISS LORE Oh!

MR. PENNE (*dictates*) "The earliest trolley, scattering the birds from its pathway like some marauding cat, brought Cortland over from Oldport. He had forgotten his fair——"

MISS LORE Hm! Wonder how he got the conductor to——

MR. PENNE (*very loudly*) "Forgotten his fair and roseate visions of the night in the practical light of the sober morn."

MISS LORE Oh!

MR. PENNE (*dictates*) "He greeted her with his usual smile and manner. 'See the waves,' he cried, pointing to the heaving waters of the sea, 'ever wooing and returning to the rock-bound shore.' 'Ready to break,' Kate said, with——"

MISS LORE My! One evening he has his arm around her, and the next morning he's ready to break her head! Just like a man!

MR. PENNE (*with suspicious calmness*) There are times, Miss Lore, when a man becomes so far exasperated that even a woman—— But suppose we finish the sentence. (*Dictates.*) " 'Ready to break,' Kate said, with the thrilling look of a soul-awakened woman, 'into foam and spray, destroying themselves upon the shore they love so well.' "

MISS LORE Oh!

MR. PENNE (*dictates*) "Cortland in Kate's presence heard faintly the voice of caution. Thirty years had not cooled his ardor. It was in his power to bestow great gifts upon this girl. He still retained the beliefs that he had at twenty." (*To* Miss Lore, *wearily*) I think that will be enough for the present.

MISS LORE (*wisely*) Well, if he had the twenty that he believed he had, it might buy her a rather nice one.

MR. PENNE (*faintly*) The last sentence was my own. We will discontinue for the day, Miss Lore.

MISS LORE Shall I come again to-morrow?

MR. PENNE (*helpless under the spell*) If you will be so good. (*Exit* Miss Lore.)

ASBESTOS CURTAIN

From
WHIRLIGIGS

❀

The Theory and the Hound

NOT MANY days ago my old friend from the tropics, J. P. Bridger, United States consul on the island of Ratona, was in the city. We had wassail and jubilee and saw the Flatiron building, and missed seeing the Bronxless menagerie by about a couple of nights. And then, at the ebb tide, we were walking up a street that parallels and parodies Broadway.

A woman with a comely and mundane countenance passed us, holding in leash a wheezing, vicious, waddling brute of a yellow pug. The dog entangled himself with Bridger's legs and mumbled his ankles in a snarling, peevish, sulky bite. Bridger, with a happy smile, kicked the breath out of the brute; the woman showered us with a quick rain of well-conceived adjectives that left us in no doubt as to our place in her opinion, and we passed on. Ten yards farther an old woman with disordered white hair and her bankbook tucked well hidden beneath her tattered shawl begged. Bridger stopped and disinterred for her a quarter from his holiday waistcoat.

On the next corner a quarter of a ton of well-clothed man with a rice-powdered, fat, white jowl, stood holding the chain of a devil-born bull-dog whose forelegs were strangers by the length of a dachshund. A little woman in a last-season's hat confronted him and wept, which was plainly all she could do, while he cursed her in low, sweet, practised tones.

Bridger smiled again—strictly to himself—and this time he took out a little memorandum book and made a note of it. This he had no right to do without due explanation, and I said so.

"It's a new theory," said Bridger, "that I picked up down in Ratona. I've been gathering support for it as I knock about. The world isn't ripe for it yet, but—well, I'll tell you; and then you run your mind back along the people you've known and see what you make of it."

And so I cornered Bridger in a place where they have artificial palms and wine; and he told me the story which is here in my words and on his responsibility.

One afternoon at three o'clock, on the island of Ratona, a boy raced along the beach screaming, "*Pájaro*, ahoy!"

Thus he made known the keenness of his hearing and the justice of his discrimination in pitch.

He who first heard and made oral proclamation concerning the toot of an approaching steamer's whistle, and correctly named the steamer, was a small hero in Ratona—until the next steamer came. Wherefore, there was rivalry among the barefoot youth of Ratona, and many fell victims to the softly blown conch shells of sloops which, as they enter harbor, sound surprisingly like a distant steamer's signal. And some could name you the vessel when its call, in your duller ears, sounded no louder than the sigh of the wind through the branches of the cocoanut palms.

But to-day he who proclaimed the *Pájaro* gained his honors. Ratona bent its ear to listen; and soon the deep-tongued blast grew louder and nearer, and at length Ratona saw above the line of palms on the low "point" the two black funnels of the fruiter slowly creeping toward the mouth of the harbor.

You must know that Ratona is an island twenty miles off the south of a South American republic. It is a port of that republic; and it sleeps sweetly in a smiling sea, toiling not nor spinning;

fed by the abundant tropics where all things "ripen, cease and fall toward the grave."

Eight hundred people dream life away in a green-embowered village that follows the horseshoe curve of its bijou harbor. They are mostly Spanish and Indian mestizos, with a shading of San Domingo Negroes, a lightening of pure-blood Spanish officials, and a slight leavening of the froth of three or four pioneering white races. No steamers touch at Ratona save the fruit steamers which take on their banana inspectors there on their way to the coast. They leave Sunday newspapers, ice, quinine, bacon, watermelons, and vaccine matter at the island and that is about all the touch Ratona gets with the world.

The *Pájaro* paused at the mouth of the harbor, rolling heavily in the swell that sent the whitecaps racing beyond the smooth water inside. Already two dories from the village—one conveying fruit inspectors, the other going for what it could get—were half-way out to the steamer.

The inspector's dory was taken on board with them, and the *Pájaro* steamed away for the mainland for its load of fruit.

The other boat returned to Ratona bearing a contribution from the *Pájaro's* store of ice, the usual roll of newspapers, and one passenger—Taylor Plunkett, sheriff of Chatham County, Kentucky.

Bridger, the United States consul at Ratona, was cleaning his rifle in the official shanty under a bread-fruit tree twenty yards from the water of the harbor. The consul occupied a place somewhat near the tail of his political party's procession. The music of the band wagon sounded very faintly to him in the distance. The plums of office went to others. Bridger's share of the spoils—the consulship at Ratona—was little more than a prune—a dried prune from the boarding-house department of the public crib. But $900 yearly was opulence in Ratona. Besides, Bridger had contracted a passion for shooting alligators in the lagoons near his consulate, and he was not unhappy.

He looked up from a careful inspection of his rifle lock and saw a broad man filling his doorway. A broad, noiseless, slow-moving man sunburned almost to the brown of Vandyke. A man of forty-five, neatly clothed in homespun, with scanty light hair, a close-clipped brown-and-gray beard and pale-blue eyes expressing mildness and simplicity.

"You are Mr. Bridger, the consul," said the broad man. "They directed me here. Can you tell me what those big bunches of things like gourds are in those trees that look like feather dusters along the edge of the water?"

"Take that chair," said the consul, reoiling his cleaning rag. "No, the other one—that bamboo thing won't hold you. Why, they're cocoanuts—green cocoanuts. The shell of 'em is always a light green before they're ripe."

"Much obliged," said the other man, sitting down carefully. "I didn't quite like to tell the folks at home they were olives unless I was sure about it. My name is Plunkett. I'm sheriff of Chatham County, Kentucky. I've got extradition papers in my pocket authorizing the arrest of a man on this island. They've been signed by the President of this country, and they're in correct shape. The man's name is Wade Williams. He's in the cocoanut raising business. What he's wanted for is the murder of his wife two years ago. Where can I find him?"

The consul squinted an eye and looked through his rifle barrel.

"There's nobody on the island who calls himself 'Williams,'" he remarked.

"Didn't suppose there was," said Plunkett mildly. "He'll do by any other name."

"Besides myself," said Bridger, "there are only two Americans on Ratona—Bob Reeves and Henry Morgan."

"The man I want sells cocoanuts," suggested Plunkett.

"You see that cocoanut walk extending up to the point?" said the consul, waving his hand toward the open door. "That belongs to Bob Reeves. Henry Morgan owns half the trees to loo'ard on the island."

"One month ago," said the sheriff, "Wade Williams wrote a confidential letter to a man in Chatham County, telling him where he was and how he was getting along. The letter was lost; and the person that found it gave it away. They sent me after him, and I've got the papers. I reckon he's one of your cocoanut men for certain."

"You've got his picture, of course," said Bridger. "It might be Reeves or Morgan, but I'd hate to think it. They're both as fine fellows as you'd meet in an all-day auto ride."

"No," doubtfully answered Plunkett; "there wasn't any picture of Williams to be had. And I never saw him myself. I've been sheriff only a year. But I've got a pretty accurate description of him. About 5 feet 11; dark hair and eyes; nose inclined to be Roman; heavy about the shoulders; strong, white teeth, with none missing; laughs a good deal, talkative; drinks considerably but never to intoxication; looks you square in the eye when talking; age thirty-five. Which one of your men does that description fit?"

The consul grinned broadly.

"I'll tell you what you do," he said, laying down his rifle and slipping on his dingy black alpaca coat. "You come along, Mr. Plunkett, and I'll take you up to see the boys. If you can tell which one of 'em your description fits better than it does the other you have the advantage of me."

Bridger conducted the sheriff out and along the hard beach close to which the tiny houses of the village were distributed. Immediately back of the town rose sudden, small, thickly wooded hills. Up one of these, by means of steps cut in the hard clay, the consul led Plunkett. On the very verge of an eminence was perched a two-room wooden cottage with a thatched roof. A Carib woman was washing clothes outside. The consul ushered the sheriff to the door of the room that overlooked the harbor.

Two men were in the room, about to sit down, in their shirt sleeves, to a table spread for dinner. They bore little resemblance one to the other in detail; but the general description given by Plunkett could have been justly applied to either. In height, color of hair, shape of nose, build, and manners each of them tallied with it. They were fair types of jovial, ready-witted, broad-

gauged Americans who had gravitated together for companionship in an alien land.

"Hello, Bridger!" they called in unison at sight of the consul.
"Come and have dinner with us!" And then they noticed Plunkett
at his heels, and came forward with hospitable curiosity.

"Gentlemen," said the consul, his voice taking an unaccus-
tomed formality, "this is Mr. Plunkett. Mr. Plunkett—Mr. Reeves
and Mr. Morgan."

The cocoanut barons greeted the newcomer joyously. Reeves
seemed about an inch taller than Morgan, but his laugh was not
quite as loud. Morgan's eyes were deep brown; Reeves's were
black. Reeves was the host and busied himself with fetching other
chairs and calling to the Carib woman for supplemental table
ware. It was explained that Morgan lived in a bamboo shack to
"loo'ard," but that every day the two friends dined together.
Plunkett stood still during the preparations, looking about mildly
with his pale-blue eyes. Bridger looked apologetic and uneasy.

At length two other covers were laid and the company was
assigned to places. Reeves and Morgan stood side by side across
the table from the visitors. Reeves nodded genially as a signal for
all to seat themselves. And then suddenly Plunkett raised his hand
with a gesture of authority. He was looking straight between
Reeves and Morgan.

"Wade Williams," he said quietly, "you are under arrest for
murder."

Reeves and Morgan instantly exchanged a quick, bright glance,
the quality of which was interrogation, with a seasoning of surprise.
Then, simultaneously they turned to the speaker with a puzzled
and frank deprecation in their gaze.

"Can't say that we understand you, Mr. Plunkett," said Morgan,
cheerfully. "Did you say 'Williams'?"

"What's the joke, Bridgy?" asked Reeves, turning to the consul
with a smile.

Before Bridger could answer, Plunkett spoke again.

"I'll explain," he said, quietly. "One of you don't need any explanation, but this is for the other one. One of you is Wade Williams of Chatham County, Kentucky. You murdered your wife on May 5, two years ago, after ill-treating and abusing her continually for five years. I have the proper papers in my pocket for taking you back with me, and you are going. We will return on the fruit steamer that comes back by this island to-morrow to leave its inspectors. I acknowledge, gentlemen, that I'm not quite sure which one of you is Williams. But Wade Williams goes back to Chatham County to-morrow. I want you to understand that."

A great sound of merry laughter from Morgan and Reeves went out over the still harbor. Two or three fishermen in the fleet of sloops anchored there looked up at the house of the *diablos Americanos* on the hill and wondered.

"My dear Mr. Plunkett," cried Morgan, conquering his mirth, "the dinner is getting cold. Let us sit down and eat. I am anxious to get my spoon into that shark-fin soup. Business afterward."

"Sit down, gentlemen, if you please," added Reeves, pleasantly. "I am sure Mr. Plunkett will not object. Perhaps a little time may be of advantage to him in identifying—the gentleman he wishes to arrest."

"No objections, I'm sure," said Plunkett, dropping into his chair heavily. "I'm hungry myself. I didn't want to accept the hospitality of you folks without giving you notice; that's all."

Reeves set bottles and glasses on the table.

"There's cognac," he said, "and anisada, and Scotch 'smoke,' and rye. Take your choice."

Bridger chose rye, Reeves poured three fingers of Scotch for himself, Morgan took the same. The sheriff, against much protestation, filled his glass from the water bottle.

"Here's to the appetite," said Reeves, raising his glass, "of Mr. Williams!" Morgan's laugh and his drink encountering sent him into a choking-splutter. All began to pay attention to the dinner, which was well cooked and palatable.

"Williams!" called Plunkett, suddenly and sharply.

All looked up wonderingly. Reeves found the sheriff's mild eye resting upon him. He flushed a little.

"See here," he said, with some asperity, "my name's Reeves, and I don't want you to——" But the comedy of the thing came to his rescue and he ended with a laugh.

"I suppose, Mr. Plunkett," said Morgan, carefully seasoning an alliagator pear, "that you are aware of the fact that you will import a good deal of trouble for yourself into Kentucky if you take back the wrong man—that is, of course, if you take anybody back?"

"Thank you for the salt," said the sheriff. "Oh, I'll take somebody back. It'll be one of you two gentlemen. Yes, I know I'll get stuck for damages if I make a mistake. But I'm going to try to get the right man."

"I'll tell you what you do," said Morgan, leaning forward with a jolly twinkle in his eyes. "You take me. I'll go without any trouble. The cocoanut business hasn't panned out well this year, and I'd like to make some extra money out of your bondsmen."

"That's not fair," chimed in Reeves. "I got only $16 a thousand for my last shipment. Take me, Mr. Plunkett."

"I'll take Wade Williams," said the sheriff, patiently, "or I'll come pretty close to it."

"It's like dining with a ghost," remarked Morgan, with a pretended shiver. "The ghost of a murderer, too! Will somebody pass the toothpicks to the shade of the naughty Mr. Williams?"

Plunkett seemed as unconcerned as if he were dining at his own table in Chatham County. He was a gallant trencherman, and the strange tropic viands tickled his palate. Heavy, commonplace, almost slothful in his movements, he appeared to be devoid of all the cunning and watchfulness of the sleuth. He even ceased to observe, with any sharpness or attempted discrimination, the two men, one of whom he had undertaken with surprising self-confidence to drag away upon the serious charge of wife-murder. Here, indeed, was a problem set before him that if wrongly solved would have amounted to his serious discomfiture, yet there he sat puzzling his soul (to all appearances) over the novel flavor of a broiled iguana cutlet.

The consul felt a decided discomfort. Reeves and Morgan were his friends and pals; yet the sheriff from Kentucky had a certain right to his official aid and moral support. So Bridger sat the silentest around the board and tried to estimate the peculiar situation. His conclusion was that both Reeves and Morgan, quick-witted, as he knew them to be, had conceived at the moment of Plunkett's disclosure of his mission—and in the brief space of a lightning flash—the idea that the other might be the guilty Williams; and that each of them had decided in that moment loyally to protect his comrade against the doom that threatened him. This was the consul's theory, and if he had been a bookmaker at a race of wits for life and liberty he would have offered heavy odds against the plodding sheriff from Chatham County, Kentucky.

When the meal was concluded the Carib woman came and removed the dishes and cloth. Reeves strewed the table with excellent cigars, and Plunkett, with the others, lighted one of these with evident gratification.

"I may be dull," said Morgan, with a grin and a wink at Bridger; "but I want to know if I am. Now, I say this is all a joke of Mr. Plunkett's concocted to frighten two babes-in-the-woods. Is this Williamson to be taken seriously or not?"

"'Williams,'" corrected Plunkett, gravely. "I never got off any jokes in my life. I know I wouldn't travel 2,000 miles to get off a poor one as this would be if I didn't take Wade Williams back with me. Gentlemen!" continued the sheriff, now letting his mild eyes travel impartially from one of the company to another, "see if you can find any joke in this case. Wade Williams is listening to the words I utter now; but out of politeness I will speak of him as a third person. For five years he made his wife lead the life of a dog—No; I'll take that back. No dog in Kentucky was ever treated as she was. He spent the money that she brought him —spent it at races, at the card table, and on horses and hunting. He was a good fellow to his friends, but a cold, sullen demon at home. He wound up the five years of neglect by striking her with his closed hand—a hand as hard as a stone—when she was ill and weak from suffering. She died the next day; and he skipped. That's all there is to it. It's enough. I never saw Williams; but I knew his wife. I'm not a man to tell half. She and I were keeping company when she met him. She went to Louisville on a visit and saw him there. I'll admit that he spoilt my chances in no time. I lived then on the edge of the Cumberland Mountains. I was elected sheriff of Chatham County a year after Wade Williams killed his wife. My official duty sends me out here after him; but I'll admit that there's personal feeling, too. And he's going back with me. Mr.—er—Reeves, will you pass me a match?"

"Awfully imprudent of Williams," said Morgan, putting his feet up against the wall, "to strike a Kentucky lady. Seems to me I've heard they were scrappers."

"Bad, bad Williams," said Reeves, pouring out more "Scotch."

The two men spoke lightly, but the consul saw and felt the tension and the carefulness in their actions and words. "Good old fellows," he said to himself; "they're both all right. Each of 'em is standing by the other like a little brick church."

And then a dog walked into the room where they sat—a black-and-tan hound, long-eared, lazy, confident of welcome.

Plunkett turned his head and looked at the animal, which halted, confidently, within a few feet of his chair.

Suddenly the sheriff, with a deep-mouthed oath, left his seat and bestowed upon the dog a vicious and heavy kick, with his ponderous shoe.

The hound, heart-broken, astonished, with flapping ears and in-curved tail, uttered a piercing yelp of pain and surprise.

Reeves and the consul remained in their chairs, saying nothing, but astonished at the unexpected show of intolerance from the easy-going man from Chatham County.

But Morgan, with a suddenly purpling face, leaped to his feet and raised a threatening arm above the guest.

"You—brute!" he shouted, passionately; "why did you do that?"

Quickly the amenities returned, Plunkett muttered some indistinct apology and regained his seat. Morgan with a decided effort controlled his indignation and also returned to his chair.

And then Plunkett, with the spring of a tiger, leaped around the corner of the table and snapped handcuffs on the paralyzed Morgan's wrists.

"Hound-lover and woman-killer!" he cried; "get ready to meet your God."

When Bridger had finished I asked him:

"Did he get the right man?"

"He did," said the consul.

"And how did he know?" I inquired, being in a kind of bewilderment.

"When he put Morgan in the dory," answered Bridger, "the next day to take him aboard the *Pájaro*, this man Plunkett stopped to shake hands with me and I asked him the same question.

"'Mr. Bridger,' said he. 'I'm a Kentuckian, and I've seen a great deal of both men and animals. And I never yet saw a man that was overfond of horses and dogs but what was cruel to women.'"

The Ransom of Red Chief

IT LOOKED like a good thing: but wait till I tell you. We were down South, in Alabama—Bill Driscoll and myself—when this kidnapping idea struck us. It was, as Bill afterward expressed it, "during a moment of temporary mental apparition"; but we didn't find that out till later.

There was a town down there, as flat as a flannel-cake, and called Summit, of course. It contained inhabitants of as undeleterious and self-satisfied a class of peasantry as ever clustered around a Maypole.

Bill and me had a joint capital of about six hundred dollars, and we needed just two thousand dollars more to pull off a fraudulent town-lot scheme in Western Illinois with. We talked it over on the front steps of the hotel. Philoprogenitoveness, says we, is strong in semi-rural communities; therefore, and for other reasons, a kidnapping project ought to do better there than in the radius of newspapers that send reporters out in plain clothes to stir up talk about such things. We knew that Summit couldn't get after us with anything stronger than constables and, maybe, some lackadaisical bloodhounds and a diatribe or two in the *Weekly Farmers' Budget*. So, it looked good.

We selected for our victim the only child of a prominent citizen named Ebenezer Dorset. The father was respectable and tight, a mortgage fancier and a stern, upright collection-plate passer and forecloser. The kid was a boy of ten, with bas-relief freckles, and hair the color of the cover of the magazine you buy at the news-stand when you want to catch a train. Bill and me figured that Ebenezer would melt down for a ransom of two thousand dollars to a cent. But wait till I tell you.

About two miles from Summit was a little mountain, covered with a dense cedar brake. On the rear elevation of this mountain was a cave. There we stored provisions.

One evening after sundown, we drove in a buggy past old Dorset's house. The kid was in the street, throwing rocks at a kitten on the opposite fence.

"Hey, little boy!" says Bill, "would you like to have a bag of candy and a nice ride?"

The boy catches Bill neatly in the eye with a piece of brick.

"That will cost the old man an extra five hundred dollars," says Bill, climbing over the wheel.

That boy put up a fight like a welter-weight cinnamon bear; but, at last, we got him down in the bottom of the buggy and drove away. We took him up to the cave, and I hitched the horse in the cedar brake. After dark I drove the buggy to the little village, three miles away, where we had hired it, and walked back to the mountain.

Bill was pasting court-plaster over the scratches and bruises on his features. There was a fire burning behind the big rock at the entrance of the cave, and the boy was watching a pot of boiling coffee, with two buzzard tail-feathers stuck in his red hair. He points a stick at me when I come up, and says:

"Ha! cursed paleface, do you dare to enter the camp of Red Chief, the terror of the plains?"

"He's all right now," says Bill, rolling up his trousers and examining some bruises on his shins. "We're playing Indian. We're making Buffalo Bill's show look like magic-lantern views of Palestine in the town hall. I'm Old Hank, the Trapper, Red Chief's captive, and I'm to be scalped at daybreak. By Geronimo! that kid can kick hard."

Yes, sir, that boy seemed to be having the time of his life. The fun of camping out in a cave had made him forget that he was a captive himself. He immediately christened me Snake-eye, the Spy, and announced that, when his braves returned from the war-path, I was to be broiled at the stake at the rising of the sun.

Then we had supper; and he filled his mouth full of bacon and bread and gravy, and began to talk. He made a during-dinner speech something like this:

"I like this fine. I never camped out before; but I had a pet 'possum once, and I was nine last birthday. I hate to go to school. Rats ate up sixteen of Jimmy Talbot's aunt's speckled hen's eggs. Are there any real Indians in these woods? I want some more gravy. Does the trees moving make the wind blow? We had five puppies. What makes your nose so red, Hank? My father has lots of money. Are the stars hot? I whipped Ed Walker twice, Saturday. I don't like girls. You dassent catch toads unless with a string. Do oxen make any noise? Why are oranges round? Have you got beds to sleep on in this cave? Amos Murray has got six toes. A parrot can talk, but a monkey or a fish can't. How many does it take to make twelve?"

Every few minutes he would remember that he was a pesky redskin, and pick up his stick rifle and tiptoe to the mouth of the cave to rubber for the scouts of the hated paleface. Now and then he would let out a war-whoop that made Old Hank the Trapper shiver. That boy had Bill terrorized from the start.

"Red Chief," says I to the kid, "would you like to go home?"

"Aw, what for?" says he. "I don't have any fun at home. I hate to go to school. I like to camp out. You won't take me back home again, Snake-eye, will you?"

"Not right away," says I. "We'll stay here in the cave awhile."

"All right!" says he. "That'll be fine. I never had such fun in all my life."

We went to bed about eleven o'clock. We spread down some wide blankets and quilts and put Red Chief between us. We weren't afraid he'd run away. He kept us awake for three hours, jumping up and reaching for his rifle and screeching: "Hist! pard," in mine and Bill's ears, as the fancied crackle of a twig or the rustle of a leaf revealed to his young imagination the stealthy approach of the outlaw band. At last, I fell into a troubled sleep, and dreamed that I had been kidnapped and chained to a tree by a ferocious pirate with red hair.

Just at daybreak, I was awakened by a series of awful screams from Bill. They weren't yells, or howls, or shouts, or whoops, or yawps, such as you'd expect from a manly set of vocal organs— they were simply indecent, terrifying, humiliating screams, such as women emit when they see ghosts or caterpillars. It's an awful thing to hear a strong, desperate, fat man scream incontinently in a cave at daybreak.

I jumped up to see what the matter was. Red Chief was sitting on Bill's chest, with one hand twined in Bill's hair. In the other he had the sharp case-knife we used for slicing bacon; and he was industriously and realistically trying to take Bill's scalp, according to the sentence that had been pronounced upon him the evening before.

I got the knife away from the kid and made him lie down again. But, from that moment, Bill's spirit was broken. He laid down on his side of the bed, but he never closed an eye again in sleep as long as that boy was with us. I dozed off for a while, but along toward sun-up I remembered that Red Chief had said I was to be burned at the stake at the rising of the sun. I wasn't nervous or afraid; but I sat up and lit my pipe and leaned against a rock.

"What you getting up so soon for, Sam?" asked Bill.

"Me?" says I. "Oh, I got a kind of pain in my shoulder. I thought sitting up would rest it."

"You're a liar!" says Bill. "You're afraid. You was to be burned at sunrise, and you was afraid he'd do it. And he would, too, if he could find a match. Ain't it awful, Sam? Do you think anybody will pay out money to get a little imp like that back home?"

"Sure," said I. "A rowdy kid like that is just the kind that parents dote on. Now, you and the Chief get up and cook breakfast, while I go up on the top of this mountain and reconnoitre."

I went up on the peak of the little mountain and ran my eye over the contiguous vicinity. Over towards Summit I expected to see the sturdy yeomanry of the village armed with scythes and pitchforks beating the countryside for the dastardly kidnappers. But what I saw was a peaceful landscape dotted with one man ploughing with a dun mule. Nobody was dragging the creek; no couriers dashed hither and yon, bringing tidings of no news to the distracted parents. There was a sylvan attitude of somnolent sleepiness pervading that section of the external outward surface of Alabama that lay exposed to my view. "Perhaps," says I to myself, "it has not yet been discovered that the wolves have borne away the tender lambkin from the fold. Heaven help the wolves!" says I, and I went down the mountain to breakfast.

When I got to the cave I found Bill backed up against the side of it, breathing hard, and the boy threatening to smash him with a rock half as big as a cocoanut.

"He put a red-hot boiled potato down my back," explained Bill, "and then mashed it with his foot; and I boxed his ears. Have you got a gun about you, Sam?"

I took the rock away from the boy and kind of patched up the argument. "I'll fix you," says the kid to Bill. "No man ever yet struck the Red Chief but he got paid for it. You better beware!"

After breakfast the kid takes a piece of leather with strings wrapped around it out of his pocket and goes outside the cave unwinding it.

"What's he up now?" says Bill, anxiously. "You don't think he'll run away, do you, Sam?"

"No fear of it," says I. "He don't seem to be much of a home body. But we've got to fix up some plan about the ransom. There don't seem to be much excitement around Summit on account of his disappearance; but maybe they haven't realized yet that he's gone. His folks may think he's spending the night with Aunt Jane or one of the neighbors. Anyhow, he'll be missed to-day. To-night we must get a message to his father demanding the two thousand dollars for his return."

Just then we heard a kind of war-whoop, such as David might have emitted when he knocked out the champion Goliath. It was a sling that Red Chief had pulled out of his pocket, and he was whirling it around his head.

I dodged, and heard a heavy thud and a kind of a sigh from Bill, like a horse gives out when you take his saddle off. A nigger-head rock the size of an egg had caught Bill just behind his left ear. He loosened himself all over and fell in the fire across the frying pan of hot water for washing the dishes. I dragged him out and poured cold water on his head for half an hour.

By and by, Bill sits up and feels behind his ear and says: "Sam, do you know who my favorite Biblical character is?"

"Take it easy," says I. "You'll come to your senses presently."

"King Herod," says he. "You won't go away and leave me here alone, will you, Sam?"

I went out and caught that boy and shook him until his freckles rattled.

"If you don't behave," says I, "I'll take you straight home. Now, are you going to be good, or not?"

"I was only funning," says he, sullenly. "I didn't mean to hurt Old Hank. But what did he hit me for? I'll behave, Snake-eye, if you won't send me home, and if you'll let me play the Black Scout to-day."

"I don't know the game," says I. "That's for you and Mr. Bill to decide. He's your playmate for the day. I'm going away for a while, on business. Now, you come in and make friends with him and say you are sorry for hurting him, or home you go, at once."

I made him and Bill shake hands, and then I took Bill aside and told him I was going to Poplar Grove, a little village three miles from the cave, and find out what I could about how the kidnapping had been regarded in Summit. Also, I thought it best to send a peremptory letter to old man Dorset that day, demanding the ransom and dictating how it should be paid.

"You know, Sam," says Bill, "I've stood by you without batting an eye in earthquakes, fire and flood—in poker games, dynamite outrages, police raids, train robberies, and cyclones. I never lost my nerve yet till we kidnapped that two-legged skyrocket of a kid. He's got me going. You won't leave me long with him, will you, Sam?"

"I'll be back some time this afternoon," says I. "You must keep the boy amused and quiet till I return. And now we'll write the letter to old Dorset."

Bill and I got paper and pencil and worked on the letter while Red Chief, with a blanket wrapped around him, strutted up and down, guarding the mouth of the cave. Bill begged me tearfully to make the ransom fifteen hundred dollars instead of two thousand. "I ain't attempting," says he, "to decry the celebrated moral aspect of parental affection, but we're dealing with humans, and it ain't human for anybody to give up two thousand dollars for that forty-pound chunk of freckled wildcat. I'm willing to take a chance at fifteen hundred dollars. You can charge the difference up to me."

So, to relieve Bill, I acceded, and we collaborated a letter that ran this way:

Ebenezer Dorset, Esq.:
   We have your boy concealed in a place far from Summit. It is useless for you or the most skilful detectives to attempt to find him. Absolutely, the only terms on which you can have him restored to you are these: We demand fifteen hundred dollars in large bills for his return; the money to be left at midnight to-night at the same spot and in the same box as your reply—as hereinafter described. If you agree to these terms, send your answer in writing by a solitary messenger to-night at half-past eight o'clock. After crossing Owl Creek on the road to Poplar Grove, there are three large trees about a hundred yards apart, close to the fence of the wheat field on the right-hand side. At the bottom of the fence-post, opposite the third tree, will be found a small pasteboard box.
   The messenger will place the answer in this box and return immediately to Summit.

If you attempt any treachery or fail to comply with our demand as stated, you will never see your boy again.

If you pay the money as demanded, he will be returned to you safe and well within three hours. These terms are final, and if you do not accede to them no further communication will be attempted.

                                        Two Desperate Men

I addressed this letter to Dorset, and put it in my pocket. As I was about to start, the kid comes up to me and says:

"Aw, Snake-eye, you said I could play the Black Scout while you was gone."

"Play it, of course," says I. "Mr. Bill will play with you. What kind of a game is it?"

"I'm the Black Scout," says Red Chief, "and I have to ride to the stockade to warn the settlers that the Indians are coming. I'm tired of playing Indian myself. I want to be the Black Scout."

"All right," says I. "It sounds harmless to me. I guess Mr. Bill will help you foil the pesky savages."

"What am I to do?" asks Bill, looking at the kid suspiciously.

"You are the hoss," says Black Scout. "Get down on your hands and knees. How can I ride to the stockade without a hoss?"

"You'd better keep him interested," said I, "till we get the scheme going. Loosen up."

Bill gets down on his all fours, and a look comes in his eye like a rabbit's when you catch it in a trap.

"How far is it to the stockade, kid?" he asks, in a husky manner of voice.

"Ninety miles," says the Black Scout. "And you have to hump yourself to get there on time. Whoa, now!"

The Black Scout jumps on Bill's back and digs his heels in his side.

"For Heaven's sake," says Bill, "hurry back, Sam, as soon as you can. I wish we hadn't made the ransom more than a thousand. Say, you quit kicking me or I'll get up and warm you good."

I walked over to Poplar Grove and sat around the post-office and store, talking with the chaw-bacons that came in to trade. One whiskerando says that he hears Summit is all upset on account of Elder Ebenezer Dorset's boy having been lost or stolen. That was all I wanted to know. I bought some smoking tobacco, referred casually to the price of black-eyed peas, posted my letter surreptitiously, and came away. The post-master said the mail-carrier would come by in an hour to take the mail to Summit.

When I got back to the cave Bill and the boy were not to be found. I explored the vicinity of the cave, and risked a yodel or two, but there was no response.

So I lighted my pipe and sat down on a mossy bank to await developments.

In about half an hour I heard the bushes rustle, and Bill wabbled out into the little glade in front of the cave. Behind him was the kid, stepping softly like a scout, with a broad grin on his face. Bill stopped, took off his hat, and wiped his face with a red handkerchief. The kid stopped about eight feet behind him.

"Sam," says Bill, "I suppose you'll think I'm a renegade, but I couldn't help it. I'm a grown person with masculine proclivities and habits of self-defense, but there is a time when all systems of egotism and predominance fail. The boy is gone. I sent him home. All is off. There was martyrs in old times," goes on Bill, "that suffered death rather than give up the particular graft they enjoyed. None of 'em ever was subjugated to such supernatural tortures as I have been. I tried to be faithful to our articles of depredation; but there came a limit."

"What's the trouble, Bill?" I asks him.

"I was rode," says Bill, "the ninety miles to the stockade, not barring an inch. Then, when the settlers was rescued, I was given oats. Sand ain't a palatable substitute. And then, for an hour I had to try to explain to him why there was nothin' in holes, how a road can run both ways, and what makes the grass green. I tell you, Sam, a human can only stand so much. I takes him by the neck of his clothes and drags him down the mountain. On the way he kicks my legs black and blue from the knees down; and I've got to have two or three bites on my thumb and hand cauterized.

"But he's gone"—continues Bill—"gone home. I showed him the road to Summit and kicked him about eight feet nearer there at one kick. I'm sorry we lose the ransom; but it was either that or Bill Driscoll to the madhouse."

Bill is puffing and blowing, but there is a look of ineffable peace and growing content on his rose-pink features.

"Bill," says I, "there isn't any heart disease in your family, is there?"

"No," says Bill, "nothing chronic except malaria and accidents. Why?"

"Then you might turn around," says I, "and have a look behind you."

Bill turns and sees the boy, and loses his complexion and sits down plump on the ground and begins to pluck aimlessly at grass and little sticks. For an hour I was afraid of his mind. And then I told him that my scheme was to put the whole job through immediately and that we would get the ransom and be off with it by midnight if old Dorset fell in with our proposition. So Bill braced up enough to give the kid a weak sort of a smile and a promise to play the Russian in a Japanese war with him as soon as he felt a little better.

I had a scheme for collecting that ransom without danger of being caught by counterplots that ought to commend itself to professional kidnappers. The tree under which the answer was to be left—and the money later on—was close to the road fence with big, bare fields on all sides. If a gang of constables should be watching for any one to come for the note, they could see him a long way off crossing the fields or in the road. But no, sirree! At half-past eight I was up in that tree as well hidden as a tree toad, waiting for the messenger to arrive.

Exactly on time, a half-grown boy rides up the road on a bicycle, locates the pasteboard box at the foot of the fence-post, slips a folded piece of paper into it, and pedals away again back toward Summit.

I waited an hour and then concluded the thing was square. I slid down the tree, got the note, slipped along the fence till I struck the woods, and was back at the cave in another half an hour. I opened the note, got near the lantern, and read it to Bill. It was written with a pen in a crabbed hand, and the sum and substance of it was this:

Two Desperate Men.

Gentlemen: I received your letter to-day by post, in regard to the ransom you ask for the return of my son. I think you are a little high in your demands, and I hereby make you a counter-proposition, which I am inclined to believe you will accept. You bring Johnny home and pay me two hundred and fifty dollars in cash, and I agree to take him off your hands. You had better come at night, for the neighbors believe he is lost, and I couldn't be responsible for what they would do to anybody they saw bringing him back. Very respectfully,
                                        Ebenezer Dorset

"Great pirates of Penzance," says I; "of all the impudent——"

But I glanced at Bill, and hesitated. He had the most appealing look in his eyes I ever saw on the face of a dumb or a talking brute.

"Sam," says he, "what's two hundred and fifty dollars, after all? We've got the money. One more night of this kid will send me to a bed in Bedlam. Besides being a thorough gentleman, I think Mr. Dorset is a spendthrift for making us such a liberal offer. You ain't going to let the chance go, are you?"

"Tell you the truth, Bill," says I, "this little he ewe lamb has somewhat got on my nerves too. We'll take him home, pay the ransom, and make our getaway."

We took him home that night. We got him to go to telling him that his father had bought a silver-mounted rifle and a pair of moccasins for him, and we were to hunt bears the next day.

It was just twelve o'clock when we knocked at Ebenezer's

front door. Just at the moment when I should have been abstracting the fifteen hundred dollars from the box under the tree, according to the original proposition, Bill was counting out two hundred and fifty dollars into Dorset's hand.

When the kid found out we were going to leave him at home he started up a howl like a calliope and fastened himself as tight as a leech to Bill's leg. His father peeled him away gradually, like a porous plaster.

"How long can you hold him?" asks Bill.

"I'm not as strong as I used to be," says old Dorset, "but I think I can promise you ten minutes."

"Enough," says Bill. "In ten minutes I shall cross the Central, Southern, and Middle Western States, and be legging it trippingly for the Canadian border."

And, as dark as it was, and as fat as Bill was, and as good a runner as I am, he was a good mile and a half out of Summit before I could catch up with him.

The Whirligig of Life

JUSTICE-OF-THE-PEACE Benaja Widdup sat in the door of his office smoking his elder-stem pipe. Halfway to the Zenith the Cumberland range rose blue-gray in the afternoon haze. A speckled hen swaggered down the main street of the "settlement," cackling foolishly.

Up the road came a sound of creaking axles, and then a slow cloud of dust, and then a bull-cart bearing Ransie Bilbro and his wife. The cart stopped at the Justice's door, and the two climbed down. Ransie was a narrow six feet of sallow brown skin and yellow hair. The imperturbability of the mountains hung upon him like a suit of armor. The woman was calicoed, angled, snuff-brushed, and weary with unknown desires. Through it all gleamed a faint protest of cheated youth unconscious of its loss.

The Justice of the Peace slipped his feet into his shoes, for the sake of dignity, and moved to let them enter.

"We-all," said the woman, in a voice like the wind blowing through pine boughs, "wants a divo'ce." She looked at Ransie to see if he noted any flaw or ambiguity or evasion or partiality or self-partisanship in her statement of their business.

"A divo'ce," repeated Ransie, with a solemn nod. "We-all can't git along together nohow. It's lonesome enough fur to live in the mount'ins when a man and woman keers fur one another. But when she's a-spittin' like a wildcat or a-sullenin' like a hoot-owl in the cabin, a man ain't got no call to live with her."

"When he's a no-'count varmint," said the woman, without any especial warmth, "a-traipsin' along of scalawags and moonshiners and a-layin' on his back pizen 'ith co'n whiskey, and a-pesterin' folks with a pack o' hungry, triflin' houn's to feed!"

"When she keeps a-throwin' skillet lids," came Ransie's antiphony, "and slings b'ilin' water on the best coon-dog in the Cumberlands, and sets herself again' cookin' a man's victuals, and keeps him awake o' nights accusin' him of a sight of doin's!"

"When he's al'ays a-fightin' the revenues, and gits a hard name in the mount'ins fur a mean man, who's gwine to be able fur to sleep o' nights?"

The Justice of the Peace stirred deliberately to his duties. He placed his one chair and a wooden stool for his petitioners. He opened his book of statutes on the table and scanned the index. Presently he wiped his spectacles and shifted his inkstand.

"The law and the statutes," said he, "air silent on the subjeck of divo'ce as fur as the jurisdiction of this co't air concerned. But, accordin' to equity and the Constitution and the golden rule, it's a bad barg'in that can't run both ways. If a justice of the peace can marry a couple, it's plain that he is bound to be able to divo'ce 'em. This here office will issue a decree of divo'ce and abide by the decision of the Supreme Co't to hold it good."

Ransie Bilbro drew a small tobacco-bag from his trousers pocket. Out of this he shook upon the table a five-dollar note. "Sold a b'arskin and two foxes fur that," he remarked. "It's all the money we got."

"The regular price of a divo'ce in this co't," said the Justice, "air five dollars." He stuffed the bill into the pocket of his homespun vest with a deceptive air of indifference. With much bodily toil and mental travail he wrote the decree upon half a sheet of foolscap, and then copied it upon the other. Ransie Bilbro and his wife listened to his reading of the document that was to give them freedom:

Know all men by these presents that Ransie Bilbro and his wife, Ariela Bilbro, this day personally appeared before me and promises that hereinafter they will neither love, honor, nor obey each other, neither for better nor worse, being of sound mind and body, and accept summons for divorce according to the peace and dignity of the State. Herein fail not, so help you God. Benaja Widdup, justice of the peace in and for the county of Piedmont, State of Tennessee.

The Justice was about to hand one of the documents to Ransie. The voice of Ariela delayed the transfer. Both men looked at her. Their dull masculinity was confronted by something sudden and unexpected in the woman.

"Judge, don't you give him that air paper yit. 'Tain't all settled, nohow. I got to have my rights first. I got to have my ali-money. 'Tain't no kind of a way to do fur a man to divo'ce his wife 'thout her havin' a cent fur to do with. I'm a-layin' off to be a-goin' up to brother Ed's up on Hogback Mount'in. I'm bound fur to hev a pa'r of shoes and some snuff and things besides. Ef Rance kin affo'd a divo'ce, let him pay me ali-money."

Ransie Bilbro was stricken to dumb perplexity. There had been no previous hint of alimony. Women were always bringing up startling and unlooked-for issues.

Justice Benaja Widdup felt that the point demanded judicial decision. The authorities were also silent on the subject of alimony. But the woman's feet were bare. The trail to Hogback Mountain was steep and flinty.

"Ariela Bilbro," he asked, in official tones, "how much did you 'low would be good and sufficient ali-money in the case befo' the co't?"

"I 'lowed," she answered, "fur the shoes and all, to say five dollars. That ain't much fur ali-money, but I reckon that'll git me up to brother Ed's."

"The amount," said the Justice, "air not onreasonable. Ransie Bilbro, you air ordered by the co't to pay the plaintiff the sum of five dollars befo' the decree of divo'ce air issued."

"I hain't no mo' money," breathed Ransie, heavily. "I done paid you all I had."

"Otherwise," said the Justice, looking severely over his spectacles, "you air in contempt of co't."

"I reckon if you gimme till to-morrow," pleaded the husband, "I mout be able to rake or scrape it up somewhars. I never looked for to be a-payin' no ali-money."

"The case air adjourned," said Benaja Widdup, "till to-morrow, when you'all will present yo'selves and obey the order of the co't. Followin' of which the decrees of divo'ce will be delivered." He sat down in the door and began to loosen a shoe-string.

"We mout as well go down to Uncle Ziah's," decided Ransie, "and spend the night." He climbed into the cart on one side, and Ariela climbed in one the other. Obeying the flat of his rope, the little red bull slowly came around on a tack, and the cart crawled away in the nimbus arising from its wheels.

Justice-of-the-peace Benaja Widdup smoked his elder-stem pipe. Late in the afternoon he got his weekly paper, and read it until the twilight dimmed its lines. Then he lit the tallow candle on his table, and read until the moon rose, marking the time for supper. He lived in the double log cabin on the slope near the girdled poplar. Going home to supper he crossed a little branch darkened by a laurel thicket. The dark figure of a man stepped from the laurels and pointed a rifle at his breast. His hat was pulled down low, and something covered most of his face.

"I want yo' money," said the figure, "'thout any talk. I'm gettin' nervous, and my finger's a-wabblin' on this here trigger."

"I've only got f-f-five dollars," said the Justice, producing it from his vest pocket.

"Roll it up," came the order, "and stick it in the end of this here gun-bar'l."

The bill was crisp and new. Even fingers that were clumsy and trembling found little difficulty in making a spill of it and inserting it (this with less ease) into the muzzle of the rifle.

"Now I reckon you kin be goin' along," said the robber.

The Justice lingered not on his way.

The next day came the little red bull, drawing the cart to the office door. Justice Benaja Widdup had his shoes on, for he was expecting the visit. In his presence Ransie Bilbro handed to his wife a five-dollar bill. The official's eyes sharply viewed it. It seemed to curl up as though it had been rolled and inserted into the end of a gun-barrel. But the Justice refrained from comment. It is true that other bills might be inclined to curl. He handed each one a decree of divorce. Each stood awkwardly silent, slowly folding the guarantee of freedom. The woman cast a shy glance full of constraint at Ransie.

"I reckon you'll be goin' back up to the cabin," she said, "along 'ith the bull-cart. There's bread in the tin box settin' on the shelf. I put the bacon in the bilin'-pot to keep the hounds from gettin' it. Don't forget to wind the clock to-night."

"You air a-goin' to your brother Ed's?" asked Ransie, with fine unconcern.

"I was 'lowin' to get along up thar afore night. I ain't sayin' as they'll pester theyselves any to make me welcome, but I hain't nowhar else fur to go. It's a right smart ways, and I reckon I better be goin'. I'll be a-sayin' good-bye, Ranse—that is, if you keer fur to say so."

"I don't know as anybody's a hound dog," said Ransie, in a martyr's voice, "fur to not want to say good-bye—'less you air so anxious to git away that you don't want me to say it."

Ariela was silent. She folded the five-dollar bill and her decree carefully, and placed them in the bosom of her dress. Benaja Widdup watched the money disappear with mournful eyes behind his spectacles.

And then with his next words he achieved rank (as his thoughts ran) with either the great crowd of the world's sympathizers or the little crowd of its great financiers.

"Be kind o' lonesome in the old cabin to-night, Ransie," she said.

Ransie Bilbro stared out at the Cumberlands, clear blue now in the sunlight. He did not look at Ariela.

"I 'low it might be lonesome," he said; "but when folks gits mad and wants a divo'ce, you can't make folks stay."

"There's others wanted a divo'ce," said Ariela, speaking to the wooden stool. "Besides, nobody don't want nobody to stay."

"Nobody never said they didn't."

"Nobody never said they did. I reckon I better start on now to brother Ed's."

"Nobody can't wind that old clock."

"Want me to go along 'ith you in the cart and wind it fur you, Ranse?"

The mountaineer's countenance was proof against emotion. But he reached out a big hand and enclosed Ariela's thin brown one. Her soul peeped out once through her impassive face, hallowing it.

"Them hounds sha'n't pester you no more," said Ransie. "I reckon I been mean and low down. You wind that clock, Ariela."

"My heart hit's in that cabin, Ranse," she whispered, "along 'ith you. I ain't a-goin' to git mad no more. Le's be startin', Ranse, so's we kin git home by sundown."

Justice-of-the-peace Benaja Widdup interposed as they started for the door, forgetting his presence.

"In the name of the State of Tennessee," he said, "I forbid you-all to be a-defyin' of its laws and statutes. This co't is mo' than willin' and full of joy to see the clouds of discord and misunderstandin' rollin' away from two lovin' hearts, but it air the duty of the co't to p'eserve the morals and integrity of the State. The co't reminds you that you air no longer man and wife, but air divo'ced by regular decree, and as such air not entitled to the benefits and 'purtenances of the mattermonal estate."

Ariela caught Ransie's arm. Did those words mean that she must lose him now when they had just learned the lesson of life?

"But the co't air prepared," went on the Justice, "fur to remove the disabilities set up by the decree of divo'ce. The co't air on hand to perform the solemn ceremony of marri'ge, thus fixin' things up and enablin' the parties in the case to resume the honor'ble and elevatin' state of mattermony which they desires. The fee fur performin' said ceremony will be, in this case, to wit, five dollars."

Ariela caught the gleam of promise in his words. Swiftly her hand went to her bosom. Freely as an alighting dove the bill fluttered to the Justice's table. Her sallow cheek colored as she stood hand in hand with Ransie and listened to the reuniting words.

Ransie helped her into the cart, and climbed in beside her. The little red bull turned once more, and they set out, handclasped, for the mountains.

Justice-of-the-peace Benaja Widdup sat in his door and took off his shoes. Once again he fingered the bill tucked down in his vest pocket. Once again he smoked his elder-stem pipe. Once again the speckled hen swaggered down the main street of the "settlement," cackling foolishly.

A Blackjack Bargainer

THE MOST disreputable thing in Yancey Goree's law office was Goree himself, sprawled in his creaky old armchair. The rickety little office, built of red brick, was set flush with the street—the main street of the town of Bethel.

Bethel rested upon the foot-hills of the Blue Ridge. Above it the mountains were piled to the sky. Far below it the turbid Catawba gleamed yellow along its disconsolate valley.

The June day was at its sultriest hour. Bethel dozed in the tepid shade. Trade was not. It was so still that Goree, reclining in his chair, distinctly heard the clicking of the chips in the grand-jury room, where the "court-house gang" was playing poker. From the open back door of the office a well-worn path meandered across the grassy lot to the court-house. The treading out of that path had cost Goree all he ever had—first inheritance of a few thousand dollars, next the old family home, and, latterly, the last shreds of his self-respect and manhood. The "gang" had cleaned him out. The broken gambler had turned drunkard and parasite; he had lived to see this day come when the men who had stripped him denied him a seat at the game. His word was no longer to be taken. The daily bout at cards had arranged itself accordingly, and to him was assigned the ignoble part of the onlooker. The sheriff, the county clerk, a sportive deputy, a gay attorney, and a chalk-faced man hailing "from the valley," sat at table, and the sheared one was thus tacitly advised to go and grow more wool.

Soon wearying of his ostracism, Goree had departed for his office, muttering to himself as he unsteadily traversed the unlucky pathway. After a drink of corn whiskey from a demijohn under the table, he had flung himself into the chair, staring, in a sort of maudlin apathy, out at the mountains immersed in the summer haze. The little white patch he saw away up on the side of Blackjack was Laurel, the village near which he had been born and bred. There, also, was the birthplace of the feud between the Gorees and the Coltranes. Now no direct heir of the Gorees survived except this plucked and singed bird of misfortune. To the Coltranes, also, but one male supporter was left—Colonel Abner Coltrane, a man of substance and standing, a member of the State Legislature, and a contemporary with Goree's father. The feud had been a typical one of the region; it had left a red record of hate, wrong, and slaughter.

But Yancey Goree was not thinking of feuds. His befuddled brain was hopelessly attacking the problem of the future maintenance of himself and his favorite follies. Of late, old friends of the family had seen to it that he had whereof to eat and a place to sleep, but whiskey they would not buy for him, and he must have whiskey. His law business was extinct; no case had been intrusted to him in two years. He had been a borrower and a sponge, and it seemed that if he fell no lower it would be from lack of opportunity. One more chance—he was saying to himself—if he had one more stake at the game, he thought he could win; but he had nothing left to sell, and his credit was more than exhausted.

He could not help smiling, even in his misery, as he thought of the man to whom, six months before, he had sold the old Goree homestead. There had come from "back yan'" in the mountains two of the strangest creatures, a man named Pike Garvey and his wife. "Back yan'," with a wave of the hand toward the hills, was understood among the mountaineers to designate the remotest fastnesses, the unplumbed gorges, the haunts of lawbreakers, the wolf's den, and the boudoir of the bear. In the cabin far up on

Blackjack's shoulder, in the wildest part of these retreats, this odd couple had lived for twenty years. They had neither dog nor children to mitigate the heavy silence of the hills. Pike Garvey was little known in the settlements, but all who had dealt with him pronounced him "crazy as a loon." He acknowledged no occupation save that of a squirrel hunter, but he "moonshined" occasionally by way of diversion. Once the "revenues" had dragged him from his lair, fighting silently and desperately like a terrier, and he had been sent to state's prison for two years. Released, he popped back into his hole like an angry weasel.

Fortune, passing over many anxious wooers, made a freakish flight into Blackjack's bosky pockets to smile upon Pike and his faithful partner.

One day a party of spectacled, knickerbockered, and altogether absurd prospectors invaded the vicinity of the Garveys' cabin. Pike lifted his squirrel rifle off the hook and took a shot at them at long range on the chance of their being revenues. Happily he missed, and the unconscious agents of good luck drew nearer, disclosing their innocence of anything resembling law or justice. Later on, they offered the Garveys an enormous quantity of ready, green, crisp money for their thirty-acre patch of cleared land, mentioning, as an excuse for such a mad action, some irrelevant and inadequate nonsense about a bed of mica underlying the said property.

When the Garveys became possessed of so many dollars that they faltered in computing them, the deficiencies of life on Blackjack began to grow prominent. Pike began to talk of new shoes, a hogshead of tobacco to set in the corner, a new lock to his rifle; and, leading Martella to a certain spot on the mountainside, he pointed out to her how a small cannon—doubtless a thing not beyond the scope of their fortune in price—might be planted so as to command and defend the sole accessible trail to the cabin, to the confusion of revenues and meddling strangers forever.

But Adam reckoned without his Eve. These things represented to him the applied power of wealth, but there slumbered in his dingy cabin an ambition that soared far above his primitive wants. Somewhere in Mrs. Garvey's bosom still survived a spot of femininity unstarved by twenty years of Blackjack. For so long a time the sounds in her ears had been the scaly-barks dropping in the woods at noon, and the wolves singing among the rocks at night, and it was enough to have purged her vanities. She had grown fat and sad and yellow and dull. But when the means came, she felt a rekindled desire to assume the perquisites of her sex—to sit at tea tables; to buy inutile things; to whitewash the hideous veracity of life with a little form and ceremony. So she coldly vetoed Pike's proposed system of fortifications, and announced that they would descend upon the world, and gyrate socially.

And thus, at length, it was decided, and the thing done. The village of Laurel was their compromise between Mrs. Garvey's preference for one of the large valley towns and Pike's hankering for primeval solitudes. Laurel yielded a halting round of feeble social distractions comportable with Martella's ambitions, and was not entirely without recommendation to Pike, its contiguity to the mountains presenting advantages for sudden retreat in case fashionable society should make it advisable.

Their descent upon Laurel had been coincident with Yancey Goree's feverish desire to convert property into cash, and they bought the old Goree homestead, paying four thousand dollars ready money into the spendthrift's shaking hand.

Thus it happened that while the disreputable last of the Gorees sprawled in his disreputable office, at the end of his row, spurned by the cronies whom he had gorged, strangers dwelt in the halls of his fathers.

A cloud of dust was rolling slowly up the parched street, with something traveling in the midst of it. A little breeze wafted the cloud to one side, and a new, brightly painted carryall, drawn by a slothful gray horse, became visible. The vehicle deflected from the middle of the street as it neared Goree's office, and stopped in the gutter directly in front of his door.

On the front seat sat a gaunt, tall man, dressed in black broadcloth, his rigid hands incarcerated in yellow kid gloves. On the back seat was a lady who triumphed over the June heat. Her stout form was armored in a skin-tight silk dress of the description known as "changeable," being a gorgeous combination of shifting hues. She sat erect, waving a much-ornamented fan, with her eyes fixed stonily far down the street. However Martella Garvey's heart might be rejoicing at the pleasures of her new life, Blackjack had done his work with her exterior. He had carved her countenance to the image of emptiness and inanity; had imbued her with the stolidity of his crags and the reserve of his hushed interiors. She always seemed to hear, whatever her surroundings were, the scaly-barks falling and pattering down the mountainside. She could always hear the awful silence of Blackjack sounding through the stillest of nights.

Goree watched this solemn equipage, as it drove to his door, with only faint interest but when the lank driver wrapped the reins about his whip, and awkwardly descended, and stepped into the office, he rose unsteadily to receive him, recognizing Pike Garvey, the new, the transformed, the recently civilized.

The mountaineer took the chair Goree offered him. They who cast doubts upon Garvey's soundness of mind had a strong witness in the man's countenance. His face was too long, a dull saffron in hue, and immobile as a statue's. Pale-blue, unwinking round eyes without lashes added to the singularity of his gruesome visage. Goree was at a loss to account for the visit.

"Everything all right at Laurel, Mr. Garvey?" he inquired.

"Everything all right, sir, and mighty pleased is Missis Garvey and me with the property. Missis Garvey likes yo' old place, and she likes the neighborhood. Society is what she 'lows she wants, and she is gettin' of it. The Rogerses, the Hapgoods, the Pratts, and the Troys hev been to see Missis Garvey, and she hev et meals to most of thar houses. The best folks hev axed her to differ'nt of doin's. I cyan't say, Mr. Goree, that sech things suits me—fur me, give me them thar." Garvey's huge yellow-gloved hand flourished in the direction of the mountains. "That's whar I b'long, 'mongst the wild honey bees and the b'ars. But that ain't what I come fur to say, Mr. Goree. Thar's somethin' you got what me and Missis Garvey wants to buy."

"Buy!" echoed Goree. "From me?" Then he laughed harshly. "I reckon you are mistaken about that. I sold out to you, as you yourself expressed it, 'lock, stock, and barrel.' There isn't even a ramrod left to sell."

"You've got it; and we 'uns want it. 'Take the money,' says Missis Garvey, 'and buy it fa'r and squar'.'"

Goree shook his head. "The cupboard's bare," he said.

"We've riz," pursued the mountaineer, undeflected from his object, "a heap. We was pore as possums, and now we could hev folks to dinner every day. We been reco'nized, Missis Garvey says, by the best society. But there's somethin' we need we ain't got. She says it ought to been put in the 'ventory ov the sale, but it 'tain't thar. 'Take the money, then,' she says, 'and buy it fa'r and squar'.'"

"Out with it," said Goree, his racked nerves growing impatient.

Garvey threw his slouch hat upon the table, and leaned forward, fixing his unblinking eyes upon Goree's.

"There's a old feud," he said, distinctly and slowly, "'tween you 'uns and the Coltranes."

Goree frowned ominously. To speak of his feud to a feudist is a serious breach of the mountain etiquette. The man from "back yan'" knew it as well as the lawyer did.

"Na offense," he went on, "but purely in the way of business. Missis Garvey hev studied all about feuds. Most of the quality folks in the mountains hev 'em. The Settles and the Goforths, the Rankins and the Boyds, the Silers and the Galloways, hev all been cyarin' on feuds f'om twenty to a hundred year. The last man to drap was when yo' uncle, Jedge Paisley Goree, 'journed co't and shot Len Coltrane f'om the bench. Missis Garvey and me, we come f'om the po' white trash. Nobody wouldn't pick a feud with we'uns, no mo'n with a fam'ly of treetoads. Quality people everywhar, says Missis Garvey, has feuds. We 'uns ain't quality, but we're buyin' into it as fur as we can. 'Take the money, then,' says Missis Garvey, 'and buy Mr. Goree's feud, fa'r and squar'.'"

The squirrel hunter straightened a leg half across the room, drew a roll of bills from his pocket, and threw them on the table.

"Thar's two hundred dollars, Mr. Goree, what you would call a fa'r price for a feud that's been 'lowed to run down like yourn hev. Thar's only you left to cyar' on yo' side of it, and you'd make mighty po' killin'. I'll take it off yo' hands, and it'll set me and Missis Garvey up among the quality. Thar's the money."

The little roll of currency on the table slowly untwisted itself, writhing and jumping as its folds relaxed. In the silence that followed Garvey's last speech the rattling of the poker chips in the court-house could be plainly heard. Goree knew that the sheriff had just won a pot, for the subdued whoop with which he always greeted a victory floated across the square upon the crinkly heat waves. Beads of moisture stood on Goree's brow. Stooping, he drew the wicker-covered demijohn from under the table, and filled a tumbler from it.

"A little corn liquor, Mr. Garvey? Of course you are joking about—what you spoke of? Opens quite a new market, doesn't it? Feuds, prime, two-fifty to three. Feuds, slightly damaged—two hundred, I believe you said, Mr. Garvey?"

Goree laughed self-consciously.

The mountaineer took the glass Goree handed him, and drank the whiskey without a tremor of the lids of his staring eyes. The lawyer applauded the feat by a look of envious admiration. He poured his own drink, and took it like a drunkard, by gulps, and with shudders at the smell and taste.

"Two hundred," repeated Garvey. "Thar's the money."

A sudden passion flared up in Goree's brain. He struck the table with his fist. One of the bills flipped over and touched his hand. He flinched as if something had stung him.

"Do you come to me," he shouted, "seriously with such a ridiculous, insulting, darn-fool proposition?"

"It's fa'r and squar'," said the squirrel hunter, but he reached out his hand as if to take back the money; and then Goree knew that his own flurry of rage had not been from pride or resentment, but from anger at himself, knowing that he would set foot in the deeper depths that were being opened to him. He turned in an instant from an outraged gentleman to an anxious chafferer recommending his goods.

"Don't be in a hurry, Garvey," he said, his face crimson and his speech thick. "I accept your p-p-proposition, though it's dirt cheap at two hundred. A t-trade's all right when both p-purchaser and b-buyer are s-satisfied. Shall I w-wrap it up for you, Mr. Garvey?"

Garvey rose, and shook out his broadcloth. "Missis Garvey will be pleased. You air out of it, and it stands Coltrane and Garvey. Just a scrap ov writin', Mr. Goree, you bein' a lawyer, to show we traded."

Goree seized a sheet of paper and a pen. The money was clutched in his moist hand. Everything else suddenly seemed to grow trivial and light.

"Bill of sale, by all means. 'Right, title, and interest in and to' . . . 'forever warrant and——' No, Garvey, we'll have to leave out that 'defend,'" said Goree with a loud laugh. "You'll have to defend this title yourself."

The mountaineer received the amazing screed that the lawyer handed him, folded it with immense labor, and placed it carefully in his pocket.

Goree was standing near the window. "Step here," he said, raising his finger, "and I'll show you your recently purchased enemy. There he goes, down the other side of the street."

The mountaineer crooked his long frame to look through the window in the direction indicated by the other. Colonel Abner Coltrane, an erect, portly gentleman of about fifty wearing the inevitable long, double-breasted frock coat of the Southern lawmaker, and an old high silk hat, was passing on the opposite sidewalk. As Garvey looked, Goree glanced at his face. If there be such a thing as a yellow wolf, here was its counterpart. Garvey snarled as his unhuman eyes followed the moving figure, disclosing long amber-colored fangs.

"Is that him? Why, that's the man who sent me to the pen'tentiary once!"

"He used to be district attorney," said Goree, carelessly. "And, by the way, he's a first-class shot."

"I kin hit a squirrel's eye at a hundred yard," said Garvey. "So that thar's Coltrane! I made a better trade than I was thinkin'. I'll take keer of this feud, Mr. Goree, better'n you ever did!"

He moved toward the door, but lingered there, betraying a slight perplexity.

"Anything else to-day?" inquired Goree with frothy sarcasm. "Any family traditions, ancestral ghosts, or skeletons in the closet? Prices as low as the lowest."

"Thar was another thing," replied the unmoved squirrel hunter, "that Missis Garvey was thinkin' of. 'Tain't so much in my line as t'other, but she wanted partic'lar that I should inquire, and ef you was willin', 'pay fur it,' she says, 'fa'r and squar'.' Thar's a buryin' groun', as you know, Mr. Goree, in the yard of yo' old place, under the cedars. Them that lies thar is yo' folks what was killed by the Coltranes. The monyments has the names on 'em. Missis Garvey says a fam'ly buryin' groun' is a sho' sign of quality. She says ef we git the feud, thar's somethin' else ought to go with it. The names on them monyments is 'Goree,' but they can be changed to ourn by——"

"Go! Go!" screamed Goree, his face turning purple. He stretched out both hands toward the mountaineer, his fingers hooked and shaking. "Go, you ghoul! Even a Ch-Chinaman protects the g-graves of his ancestors—go!"

The squirrel hunter slouched out of the door to his carryall. While he was climbing over the wheel, Goree was collecting, with feverish celerity, the money that had fallen from his hand to the floor. As the vehicle slowly turned about, the sheep with a coat of newly grown wool was hurrying, in indecent haste, along the path to the courthouse.

At three o'clock in the morning they brought him back to his office, shorn and unconscious. The sheriff, the sportive deputy, the county clerk, and the gay attorney carried him, the chalk-faced man "from the valley" acting as escort.

"On the table," said one of them, and they deposited him there among the litter of his unprofitable books and papers.

"Yance thinks a lot of a pair of deuces when he's liquored up," sighed the sheriff, reflectively.

"Too much," said the gay attorney. "A man has no business to play poker who drinks as much as he does. I wonder how much he dropped to-night."

"Close to two hundred. What I wonder is whar he got it. Yance ain't had a cent fur over a month, I know."

"Struck a client, maybe. Well, let's get home before daylight. He'll be all right when he wakes up, except for a sort of beehive about the cranium."

The gang slipped away through the early morning twilight. The next eye to gaze upon the miserable Goree was the orb of day. He peered through the uncurtained window, first deluging the sleeper in a flood of faint gold, but soon pouring upon the mottled red of his flesh a searching, white, summer heat. Goree stirred, half unconsciously, among the table's débris, and turned his face from the window. His movement dislodged a heavy law book, which crashed upon the floor. Opening his eyes, he saw, bending over him, a man in a black frock coat. Looking higher, he discovered a well-worn silk hat, and beneath it the kindly, smooth face of Colonel Abner Coltrane.

A little uncertain of the outcome, the colonel waited for the other to make some sign of recognition. Not in twenty years had male members of these two families faced each other in peace. Goree's eyelids puckered as he strained his blurred sight toward this visitor, and then he smiled serenely.

"Have you brought Stella and Lucy over to play?" he said, calmly.

"Do you know me, Yancey?" asked Coltrane.

"Of course I do. You brought me a whip with a whistle in the end."

So he had—twenty-four years ago; when Yancey's father was his best friend.

Goree's eyes wandered about the room. The colonel understood. "Lie still, and I'll bring you some," said he. There was a pump in the yard at the rear, and Goree closed his eyes, listening with rapture to the click of its handle and the bubbling of the falling stream. Coltrane brought a pitcher of the cool water, and held it for him to drink. Presently Goree sat up—a most forlorn object, his summer suit of flax soiled and crumpled, his discreditable head tousled and unsteady. He tried to wave one of his hands toward the colonel.

"Ex-excuse—everything, will you?" he said. "I must have drunk too much whiskey last night, and gone to bed on the table." His brows knitted into a puzzled frown.

"Out with the boys a while?" asked Coltrane, kindly.

"No, I went nowhere. I haven't had a dollar to spend in the last two months. Struck the demijohn too often, I reckon, as usual."

Colonel Coltrane touched him on the shoulder.

"A little while ago, Yancey," he began, "you asked me if I had brought Stella and Lucy over to play. You weren't quite awake then, and must have been dreaming you were a boy again. You are awake now, and I want you to listen to me. I have come from Stella and Lucy to their old playmate, and to my old friend's son. They know that I am going to bring you home with me, and you will find them as ready with a welcome as they were in the old days. I want you to come to my house and stay until you are yourself again, and as much longer as you will. We heard of your being down in the world, and in the midst of temptation, and we agreed that you should come over and play at our house once more. Will you come, my boy? Will you drop our old family trouble and come with me?"

"Trouble!" said Goree, opening his eyes wide. "There was never any trouble between us that I know of. I'm sure we've always been the best of friends. But, good Lord, Colonel, how could I go to your home as I am—a drunken wretch, a miserable, degraded spendthrift and gambler——"

He lurched from the table to his armchair, and began to weep maudlin tears, mingled with genuine drops of remorse and shame. Coltrane talked to him persistently and reasonably, reminding him of the simple mountain pleasures of which he had once been so fond, and insisting upon the genuineness of the invitation.

Finally he landed Goree by telling him he was counting upon his help in the engineering and transportation of a large amount of felled timber from a high mountainside to a waterway. He knew that Goree had once invented a device for this purpose—a series of slides and chutes—upon which he had justly prided himself. In an instant the poor fellow, delighted at the idea of his being of use to any one, had paper spread upon the table, and was drawing rapid but pitifully shaky lines in demonstration of what he could and would do.

The man was sickened of the husks; his prodigal heart was turning again toward the mountains. His mind was yet strangely clogged, and his thoughts and memories were returning to his brain one by one, like carrier pigeons over a stormy sea. But Coltrane was satisfied with the progress he had made.

Bethel received the surprise of its existence that afternoon when a Coltrane and a Goree rode amicably together through the town. Side by side they rode, out from the dusty streets and gaping townspeople, down across the creek bridge, and up toward the mountain. The prodigal had brushed and washed and combed himself to a more decent figure, but he was unsteady in the saddle, and he seemed to be deep in the contemplation of some vexing problem. Coltrane left him in his mood, relying upon the influence of changed surroundings to restore his equilibrium.

Once Goree was seized with a shaking fit, and almost came to a collapse. He had to dismount and rest at the side of the road. The colonel, foreseeing such a condition, had provided a small flask of whiskey for the journey but when it was offered to him Goree refused it almost with violence, declaring he would never touch it again. By and by he was recovered, and went quietly enough for a mile or two. Then he pulled up his horse suddenly, and said:

"I lost two hundred dollars last night, playing poker. Now, where did I get that money?"

"Take it easy, Yancey. The mountain air will soon clear it up. We'll go fishing, first thing, at the Pinnacle Falls. The trout are jumping there like bullfrogs. We'll take Stella and Lucy along, and have a picnic on Eagle Rock. Have you forgotten how a hickory-cured-ham sandwich tastes, Yancey, to a hungry fisherman?"

Evidently the colonel did not believe the story of his lost wealth; so Goree retired again into brooding silence.

By late afternoon they had traveled ten of the twelve miles between Bethel and Laurel. Half a mile this side of Laurel lay the old Goree place; a mile or two beyond the village lived the Coltranes. The road was now steep and laborious, but the compensations were many. The tilted aisles of the forest were opulent with leaf and bird and bloom. The tonic air put to shame the pharmacopœia. The glades were dark with mossy shade, and bright with shy rivulets winking from the ferns and laurels. On the lower side they viewed, framed in the near foliage, exquisite sketches of the far valley swooning in its opal haze.

Coltrane was pleased to see that his companion was yielding to the spell of the hills and woods. For now they had but to skirt the base of Painter's Cliff; to cross Elder Branch and mount the hill beyond, and Goree would have to face the squandered home of his fathers. Every rock he passed, every tree, every foot of the roadway, was familiar to him. Though he had forgotten the woods, they thrilled him like the music of *"Home, Sweet Home."*

They rounded the cliff, descended into Elder Branch, and paused there to let the horses drink and splash in the swift water. On the right was a rail fence that cornered there, and followed the road and stream. Inclosed by it was the old apple orchard of the home place; the house was yet concealed by the brow of the steep hill. Inside and along the fence, pokeberries, elders, sassafras, and sumac grew high and dense. At a rustle of their branches, both Goree and Coltrane glanced up, and saw a long, yellow, wolfish face above the fence, staring at them with pale, unwinking eyes. The head quickly disappeared; there was a violent swaying of the bushes, and an ungainly figure ran up through the apple orchard in the direction of the house zigzagging among the trees.

"That's Garvey," said Coltrane; "the man you sold out to. There's no doubt but he's considerably cracked. I had to send him up for moonshining once, several years ago, in spite of the fact that I believed him irresponsible. Why, what's the matter, Yancey?"

Goree was wiping his forehead, and his face had lost its color. "Do I look queer, too?" he asked, trying to smile. "I'm just remembering a few more things." Some of the alcohol had evaporated from his brain. "I recollect now where I got that two hundred dollars."

"Don't think of it," said Coltrane, cheerfully. "Later on we'll figure it all out together."

They rode out of the branch, and when they reached the foot of the hill Goree stopped again.

"Did you ever suspect I was a very vain kind of fellow, Colonel?" he asked. "Sort of foolish proud about appearances?"

The colonel's eyes refused to wander to the soiled, sagging suit of flax and the faded slouch hat.

"It seems to me," he replied, mystified, but humoring him, "I remember a young buck about twenty, with the tightest coat, the sleekest hair, and the prancingest saddle horse in the Blue Ridge."

"Right you are," said Goree, eagerly. "And it's in me yet, though it don't show. Oh, I'm as vain as a turkey gobbler, and as proud as Lucifer. I'm going to ask you to indulge this weakness of mine in a little matter."

"Speak out, Yancey. We'll create you Duke of Laurel and Baron of Blue Ridge, if you choose; and you shall have a feather out of Stella's peacock's tail to wear in your hat."

"I'm in earnest. In a few minutes we'll pass the house up there on the hill where I was born, and where my people have lived for nearly a century. Strangers live there now—and look at me! I am about to show myself to them ragged and poverty-stricken, a wastrel and a beggar. Colonel Coltrane, I'm ashamed to do it. I want you to let me wear your coat and hat until we are out of sight beyond. I know you think it a foolish pride, but I want to make as good a showing as I can when I pass the old place."

"Now, what does this mean?" said Coltrane to himself, as he compared his companion's sane looks and quiet demeanor with his strange request. But he was already unbuttoning the coat, assenting readily, as if the fancy were in no wise to be considered strange.

The coat and hat fitted Goree well. He buttoned the former about him with a look of satisfaction and dignity. He and Coltrane were nearly the same size—rather tall, portly, and erect. Twenty-five years were between them, but in appearance they might have been brothers. Goree looked older than his age; his face was puffy and lined; the colonel had the smooth, fresh complexion of a temperate liver. He put on Goree's disreputable old flax coat and faded slouch hat.

"Now," said Goree, taking up the reins, "I'm all right. I want you to ride about ten feet in the rear as we go by, Colonel, so that they can get a good look at me. They'll see I'm no back number yet, by any means. I guess I'll show up pretty well to them once more, anyhow. Let's ride on."

He set out up the hill at a smart trot, the colonel following, as he had been requested.

Goree sat straight in the saddle, with head erect, but his eyes were turned to the right, sharply scanning every shrub and fence and hiding-place in the old homestead yard. Once he muttered to himself, "Will the crazy fool try it, or did I dream half of it?"

It was when he came opposite the little family burying ground that he saw what he had been looking for—a puff of white smoke, coming from the thick cedars in one corner. He toppled so slowly to the left that Coltrane had time to urge his horse to that side, and catch him with one arm.

The squirrel hunter had not overpraised his aim. He had sent the bullet where he intended, and where Goree had expected that it would pass—through the breast of Colonel Abner Coltrane's black frock coat.

Goree leaned heavily against Coltrane, but he did not fall. The horses kept pace, side by side, and the colonel's arm kept him steady. The little white houses of laurel shone through the trees, half a mile away. Goree reached out one hand and groped until it rested upon Coltrane's fingers, which held his bridle.

"Good friend," he said, and that was all.

Thus did Yancey Goree, as he rode past his old home, make, considering all things, the best showing that was in his power.

One Dollar's Worth

THE JUDGE of the United States court of the district lying along the Rio Grande border found the following letter one morning in his mail:

Judge:

When you sent me up for four years you made a talk. Among other hard things, you called me a rattlesnake. Maybe I am one—anyhow, you hear me rattling now. One year after I got to the pen, my daughter died of—well, they said it was poverty and the disgrace together. You've got a daughter, Judge, and I'm going to make you know how it feels to lose one. And I'm going to bite that district attorney that spoke against me. I'm free now, and I guess I've turned to rattlesnake all right. I feel like one. I don't say much, but this is my rattle. Look out what I strike.

Yours respectfully,
Rattlesnake

Judge Derwent threw the letter carelessly aside. It was nothing new to receive such epistles from desperate men whom he had been called up to judge. He felt no alarm. Later on he showed the letter to Littlefield, the young district attorney, for Littlefield's name was included in the threat, and the judge was punctilious in matters between himself and his fellow men.

Littlefield honored the rattle of the writer, as far as it concerned himself, with a smile of contempt; but he frowned a little over the reference to the Judge's daughter, for he and Nancy Derwent were to be married in the fall.

Littlefield went to the clerk of the court and looked over the records with him. They decided that the letter might have been sent by Mexico Sam, a half-breed border desperado who had been imprisoned for manslaughter four years before. Then official duties crowded the matter from his mind, and the rattle of the revengeful serpent was forgotten.

Court was in session at Brownsville. Most of the cases to be tried were charges of smuggling, counterfeiting, post-office robberies, and violations of Federal laws along the border. One case was that of a young Mexican, Rafael Ortiz, who had been rounded up by a clever deputy marshal in the act of passing a counterfeit silver dollar. He had been suspected of many such deviations from rectitude, but this was the first time that anything provable had been fixed upon him. Ortiz languished cozily in jail, smoking brown cigarettes and waiting for trial. Kilpatrick, the deputy, brought the counterfeit dollar and handed it to the district attorney in his office in the court-house. The deputy and a reputable druggist were prepared to swear that Ortiz paid for a bottle of medicine with it. The coin was a poor counterfeit, soft, dull-looking, and made principally of lead. It was the day before the morning on which the docket would reach the case of Ortiz, and the district attorney was preparing himself for the trial.

"Not much need of having in high-priced experts to prove the coin's queer, is there, Kil?" smiled Littlefield, as he thumped the dollar down upon the table, where it fell with no more ring than would have come from a lump of putty.

"I guess the Greaser's as good as behind the bars," said the deputy, easing up his holsters. "You've got him dead. If it had been just one time, these Mexicans can't tell good money from bad; but this little yaller rascal belongs to a gang of counterfeiters, I know. This is the first time I've been able to catch him doing the trick. He's got a girl down there in them Mexican jacals on the river bank. I seen her one day when I was watching him. She's as pretty as a red heifer in a flower bed."

Littlefield shoved the counterfeit dollar into his pocket, and slipped his memoranda of the case into an envelope. Just then a bright, winsome face, as frank and jolly as a boy's, appeared in the doorway, and in walked Nancy Derwent.

"Oh, Bob, didn't court adjourn at twelve to-day until to-morrow?" she asked of Littlefield.

"It did," said the district attorney, "and I'm very glad of it. I've got a lot of rulings to look up, and——"

"Now, that's just like you. I wonder you and Father don't turn to law books or rulings or something! I want you to take me out plover-shooting this afternoon. Long Prairie is just alive with them. Don't say no, please! I want to try my new twelve-bore hammerless. I've sent to the livery stable to engage Fly and Bess for the buckboard; they stand fire so nicely. I was sure you would go."

They were to be married in the fall. The glamour was at its height. The plovers won the day—or, rather, the afternoon—over the calf-bound authorities. Littlefield began to put his papers away.

There was a knock at the door. Kilpatrick answered it. A beautiful, dark-eyed girl with a skin tinged with the faintest lemon color walked into the room. A black shawl was thrown over her head and wound once around her neck.

She began to talk in Spanish, a voluble, mournful stream of melancholy music. Littlefield did not understand Spanish. The deputy did, and he translated her talk by portions, at intervals holding up his hands to check the flow of her words.

"She came to see you, Mr. Littlefield. Her name's Joya Treviñas. She wants to see you about—well, she's mixed up with that Rafael Ortiz. She's his—she's his girl. She says he's innocent. She says she made the money and got him to pass it. Don't you believe her, Mr. Littlefield. That's the way with these Mexican girls;

they'll lie, steal, or kill for a fellow when they get stuck on him. Never trust a woman that's in love!"

"Mr. Kilpatrick!"

Nancy Derwent's indignant exclamation caused the deputy to flounder for a moment in attempting to explain that he had mis-quoted his own sentiments, and then he went on with the translation:

"She says she's willing to take his place in the jail if you'll let him out. She says she was down sick with the fever, and the doctor said she'd die if she didn't have medicine. That's why he passed the lead dollar on the drug store. She says it saved her life. This Rafael seems to be her honey, all right; there's a lot of stuff in her talk about love and such things that you don't want to hear."

It was an old story to the district attorney.

"Tell her," said he, "that I can do nothing. The case comes up in the morning, and he will have to make his fight before the court."

Nancy Derwent was not so hardened. She was looking with sympathetic interest at Joya Treviñas and at Littlefield alternately. The deputy repeated the district attorney's words to the girl. She spoke a sentence or two in a low voice, pulled her shawl closely about her face, and left the room.

"What did she say then?" asked the district attorney.

"Nothing special," said the deputy. "She said: 'If the life of the one'—let's see how it went—'Si la vida de ella a quien tu amas—if the life of the girl you love is ever in danger, remember Rafael Ortiz.'"

Kilpatrick strolled out through the corridor in the direction of the marshal's office.

"Can't you do anything for them, Bob?" asked Nancy. "It's such a little thing—just one counterfeit dollar—to ruin the happiness of two lives! She was in danger of death, and he did it to save her. Doesn't the law know the feeling of pity?"

"It hasn't a place in jurisprudence, Nan," said Littlefield, "especially *in re* the district attorney's duty. I'll promise you that the prosecution will not be vindictive; but the man is as good as convicted when the case is called. Witnesses will swear to his passing the bad dollar which I have in my pocket at this moment as 'Exhibit A.' There are no Mexicans on the jury, and it will vote Mr. Greaser guilty without leaving the box."

The plover-shooting was fine that afternoon, and in the excitement of the sport the case of Rafael and the grief of Joya Treviñas was forgotten. The district attorney and Nancy Derwent drove out from the town three miles along a smooth, grassy road, and then struck across a rolling prairie toward a heavy line of timber on Piedra Creek. Beyond this creek lay Long Prairie, the favorite haunt of the plover. As they were nearing the creek they heard the galloping of a horse to their right, and saw a man with black hair and a swarthy face riding toward the woods at a tangent, as if he had come up behind them.

"I've seen that fellow somewhere," said Littlefield, who had a memory for faces, "but I can't exactly place him. Some ranchman, I suppose, taking a short cut home."

They spent an hour on Long Prairie, shooting from the buckboard. Nancy Derwent, an active, outdoor Western girl, was pleased with her twelve-bore. She had bagged within two brace of her companion's score.

They started homeward at a gentle trot. When within a hundred yards of Piedra Creek a man rode out of the timber directly toward them.

"It looks like the man we saw coming over," remarked Miss Derwent.

As the distance between them lessened, the district attorney suddenly pulled up his team sharply, with his eyes fixed upon the advancing horseman. That individual had drawn a Winchester from its scabbard on his saddle and thrown it over his arm.

"Now I know you, Mexico Sam!" muttered Littlefield to himself. "It *was* you who shook your rattles in that gentle epistle."

Mexico Sam did not leave things long in doubt. He had a nice eye in all matters relating to firearms, so when he was within good rifle range, but outside of danger from No. 8 shot, he threw up his Winchester and opened fire upon the occupants of the buckboard.

The first shot cracked the back of the seat within the two-inch space between the shoulders of Littlefield and Miss Derwent. The next went through the dashboard and Littlefield's trouser leg.

The district attorney hustled Nancy out of the buckboard to the ground. She was a little pale, but asked no question. She had the frontier instinct that accepts conditions in an emergency without superfluous argument. They kept their guns in hand, and Littlefield hastily gathered some handfuls of cartridges from the pasteboard box on the seat and crowded them into his pockets.

"Keep behind the horses, Nan," he commanded. "That fellow is a ruffian I sent to prison once. He's trying to get even. He knows our shot won't hurt him at that distance."

"All right, Bob," said Nancy, steadily. "I'm not afraid. But you come close, too. Whoa, Bess; stand still, now!"

She stroked Bess's mane. Littlefield stood with his gun ready, praying that the desperado would come within range.

But Mexico Sam was playing his vendetta along safe lines. He was a bird of different feather from the plover. His accurate eye drew an imaginary line of circumference around the area of danger from bird-shot, and upon this line he rode. His horse wheeled to the right, and as his victims rounded to the safe side of their equine breastwork he sent a ball through the district attorney's hat. Once he miscalculated in making a detour, and overstepped his margin. Littlefield's gun flashed, and Mexico Sam ducked his head to the harmless patter of the shot. A few of them stung his horse, which pranced promptly back to the safety line.

The desperado fired again. A little cry came from Nancy Derwent. Littlefield whirled, with blazing eyes, and saw the blood trickling down her cheek.

"I'm not hurt, Bob—only a splinter struck me. I think he hit one of the wheel-spokes."

"Lord!" groaned Littlefield. "If I only had a charge of buckshot!"

The ruffian got his horse still, and took careful aim. Fly gave a snort and fell in the harness, struck in the neck. Bess, now disabused of the idea that plover were being fired at, broke her traces and galloped wildly away. Mexican Sam sent a ball neatly through the fullness of Nancy Derwent's shooting jacket.

"Lie down—lie down!" snapped Littlefield. "Close to the horse —flat on the ground—so." He almost threw her upon the grass against the back of the recumbent Fly. Oddly enough, at that moment the words of the Mexican girl returned to his mind:

"If the life of the girl you love is ever in danger, remember Rafael Ortiz."

Littlefield uttered an exclamation.

"Open fire on him, Nan, across the horse's back! Fire as fast as you can! You can't hurt him, but keep him dodging shot for one minute while I try to work a little scheme."

Nancy gave a quick glance at Littlefield, and saw him take out his pocket-knife and open it. Then she turned her face to obey orders, keeping up a rapid fire at the enemy.

Mexico Sam waited patiently until this innocuous fusillade ceased. He had plenty of time, and he did not care to risk the chance of a bird-shot in his eye if it could be avoided by a little caution. He pulled his heavy Stetson low down over his face until the shots ceased. Then he drew a little nearer, and fired with careful aim at what he could see of his victims above the fallen horse.

Neither of them moved. He urged his horse a few steps nearer. He saw the district attorney rise to one knee, and deliberately level his shotgun. He pulled his hat down and awaited the harmless rattle of the tiny pellets.

The shotgun blazed with a heavy report. Mexico Sam sighed, turned limp all over, and slowly fell from his horse—a dead rattlesnake.

At ten o'clock the next morning court opened, and the case of the United States *versus* Rafael Ortiz was called. The district attorney, with his arm in a sling, rose and addressed the court.

"May it please your honor," he said, "I desire to enter a *nolle pros.* in this case. Even though the defendant should be guilty, there is not sufficient evidence in the hands of the government to secure a conviction. The piece of counterfeit coin upon the identity of which the case was built is not now available as evidence. I ask, therefore, that the case be stricken off."

At the noon recess, Kilpatrick strolled into the district attorney's office.

"I've just been down to take a squint at old Mexico Sam," said the deputy. "They've got him laid out. Old Mexico was a tough outfit, I reckon. The boys was wonderin' down there what you shot him with. Some said it must have been nails. I never see a gun carry anything to make holes like he had."

"I shot him," said the district attorney, "with Exhibit A of your counterfeiting case. Lucky thing for me—and somebody else— that it was as bad money as it was! It sliced up into slugs very nicely. Say, Kil, can't you go down to the jacals and find where that Mexican girl lives? Miss Derwent wants to know."

THE VOICE OF THE CITY

❁

A *Lickpenny Lover*

THERE WERE 3,000 girls in the Biggest Store. Masie was one of them. She was eighteen and a saleslady in the gents' gloves. Here she became versed in two varieties of human beings—the kind of gents who buy their gloves in department stores and the kind of women who buy gloves for unfortunate gents. Besides this wide knowledge of the human species, Masie had acquired other information. She had listened to the promulgated wisdom of the 2,999 other girls and had stored it in a brain that was as secretive and wary as that of a Maltese cat. Perhaps nature, foreseeing that she would lack wise counsellors, had mingled the saving ingredient of shrewdness along with her beauty, as she has endowed the silver fox of the priceless fur above the other animals with cunning.

For Masie was beautiful. She was a deep-tinted blonde, with the calm poise of a lady who cooks butter cakes in a window. She stood behind her counter in the Biggest Store; and as you closed your hand over the tapeline for your glove measure you thought of Hebe; and as you looked again you wondered how she had come by Minerva's eyes.

When the floorwalker was not looking Masie chewed tutti frutti;

when he was looking she gazed up as if at the clouds and smiled wistfully.

That is the shopgirl smile, and I enjoin you to shun it unless you are well fortified with callosity of the heart, caramels, and a congeniality for the capers of Cupid. This smile belonged to Masie's recreation hours and not to the store; but the floorwalker must have his own. He is the Shylock of the stores. When he comes nosing around the bridge of his nose is a toll-bridge. It is goo-goo eyes or "git" when he looks toward a pretty girl. Of course not all floorwalkers are thus. Only a few days ago the papers printed news of one over eighty years of age.

One day Irving Carter, painter, millionaire, traveller, poet, automobilist, happened to enter the Biggest Store. It is due to him to add that his visit was not voluntary. Filial duty took him by the collar and dragged him inside, while his mother philandered among the bronze and terra-cotta statuettes.

Carter strolled across to the glove counter in order to shoot a few minutes on the wing. His need for gloves was genuine; he had forgotten to bring a pair with him. But his action hardly calls for apology, because he had never heard of glove-counter flirtations.

As he neared the vicinity of his fate he hesitated, suddenly conscious of this unknown phase of Cupid's less worthy profession.

Three or four cheap fellows, sonorously garbed, were leaning over the counters, wrestling with the mediatorial hand-coverings, while giggling girls played vivacious seconds to their lead upon the strident string of coquetry. Carter would have retreated, but he had gone too far. Masie confronted him behind her counter with a questioning look in eyes as coldly, beautifully, warmly blue as the glint of summer sunshine on an iceberg drifting in Southern seas.

And then Irving Carter, painter, millionaire, etc., felt a warm flush rise to his aristocratically pale face. But not from diffidence. The blush was intellectual in origin. He knew in a moment that he stood in the ranks of the ready-made youths who wooed the giggling girls at other counters. Himself leaned against the oaken trysting place of a cockney Cupid with a desire in his heart for the favor of a glove salesgirl. He was no more than Bill and Jack and Mickey. And then he felt a sudden tolerance for them, and an elating, courageous contempt for the conventions upon which he had fed, and an unhesitating determination to have this perfect creature for his own.

When the gloves were paid for and wrapped Carter lingered for a moment. The dimples at the corners of Masie's damask mouth deepened. All gentlemen who bought gloves lingered in just that way. She curved an arm, showing like Psyche's through her shirt-waist sleeve, and rested an elbow upon the show-case edge.

Carter had never before encountered a situation of which he had not been perfect master. But now he stood far more awkward than Bill or Jack or Mickey. He had no chance of meeting this beautiful girl socially. His mind struggled to recall the nature and habits of shop-girls as he had read or heard of them. Somehow he had received the idea that they sometimes did not insist too strictly upon the regular channels of introduction. His heart beat loudly at the thought of proposing an unconventional meeting with this lovely and virginal being. But the tumult in his heart gave him courage.

After a few friendly and well-received remarks on general subjects, he laid his card by her hand on the counter.

"Will you please pardon me," he said, "if I seem too bold; but I earnestly hope you will allow me the pleasure of seeing you again. There is my name; I assure you that it is with the greatest respect that I ask the favor of becoming one of your fr—— acquaintances. May I not hope for the privilege?"

Masie knew men—especially men who buy gloves. Without hesitation she looked him frankly and smilingly in the eyes, and said:

"Sure. I guess you're right. I don't usually go out with strange gentlemen, though. It ain't quite ladylike. When should you want to see me again?"

"As soon as I may," said Carter. "If you would allow me to call at your home, I——"

Masie laughed musically. "Oh, gee, no!" she said emphatically. "If you could see our flat once! There's five of us in three rooms. I'd just like to see ma's face if I was to bring a gentleman friend there!"

"Anywhere, then," said the enamored Carter, "that will be convenient to you."

"Say," suggested Masie, with a bright-idea look in her peach-blow face; "I guess Thursday night will about suit me. Suppose you come to the corner of Eighth Avenue and Forty-eighth Street at 7:30. I live right near the corner. But I've got to be back home by eleven. Ma never lets me stay out after eleven."

Carter promised gratefully to keep the tryst, and then hastened to his mother, who was looking about for him to ratify her purchase of a bronze Diana.

A salesgirl, with small eyes and an obtuse nose, strolled near Masie, with a friendly leer.

"Did you make a hit with his nobs, Masie?" she asked, familiarly.

"The gentleman asked permission to call," answered Masie, with the grand air, as she slipped Carter's card into the bosom of her waist.

"Permission to call!" echoed small eyes, with a snigger. "Did he say anything about dinner in the Waldorf and a spin in his auto afterward?"

"Oh, cheese it!" said Masie, wearily. "You've been used to swell things, I don't think. You've had a swelled head ever since that hosecart driver took you out to a chop suey joint. No, he never mentioned the Waldorf; but there's a Fifth Avenue address on his card, and if he buys the supper you can bet your life there won't be no pigtail on the waiter what takes the order."

As Carter glided away from the Biggest Store with his mother in his electric runabout, he bit his lip with a dull pain at his heart. He knew that love had come to him for the first time in all the twenty-nine years of his life. And that the object of it should make so readily an appointment with him at a street corner,

434 _Tales of O. Henry_

though it was a step toward his desires, tortured him with misgivings.

Carter did not know the shopgirl. He did not know that her home is often either a scarcely habitable tiny room or a domicile filled to overflowing with kith and kin. The street corner is her parlor, the park is her drawing room; the avenue is her garden walk; yet for the most part she is as inviolate mistress of herself in them as is my lady inside her tapestried chamber.

One evening at dusk, two weeks after their first meeting, Carter and Masie strolled arm-in-arm into a little, dimly-lit park. They found a bench, tree-shadowed and secluded, and sat there.

For the first time his arm stole gently around her. Her golden-bronze head slid restfully against his shoulder.

"Gee!" sighed Masie, thankfully. "Why didn't you ever think of that before?"

"Masie," said Carter, earnestly, "you surely know that I love you. I ask you sincerely to marry me. You know me well enough by this time to have no doubts of me. I want you, and I must have you. I care nothing for the difference in our stations."

"What is the difference?" asked Masie, curiously.

"Well, there isn't any," said Carter, quickly, "except in the minds of foolish people. It is in my power to give you a life of luxury. My social position is beyond dispute, and my means are ample."

"They all say that," remarked Masie. "It's the kid they all give you. I suppose you really work in a delicatessen or follow the races. I ain't as green as I look."

"I can furnish you all the proofs you want," said Carter, gently, "And I want you, Masie. I loved you the first day I saw you."

"They all do," said Masie, with an amused laugh, "to hear 'em talk. If I could meet a man that got stuck on me the third time he'd seen me I think I'd get mashed on him."

"Please don't say such things," pleaded Carter. "Listen to me, dear. Ever since I first looked into your eyes you have been the only woman in the world for me."

"Oh, ain't you the kidder!" smiled Masie. "How many other girls did you ever tell that?"

But Carter persisted. And at length he reached the flimsy, fluttering little soul of the shopgirl that existed somewhere deep down in her lovely bosom. His words penetrated the heart whose very lightness was its safest armor. She looked up at him with eyes that saw. And a warm glow visited her cool cheeks. Tremblingly, awfully, her moth wings closed, and she seemed about to settle upon the flower of love. Some faint glimmer of life and its possibilities on the other side of her glove counter dawned upon her. Carter felt the change and crowded the opportunity.

"Marry me, Masie," he whispered, softly, "and we will go away from this ugly city to beautiful ones. We will forget work and business, and life will be one long holiday. I know where I should take you—I have been there often. Just think of a shore where summer is eternal, where the waves are always rippling on the lovely beach and the people are happy and free as children. We will sail to those shores and remain there as long as you please. In one of those far-away cities there are grand and lovely palaces and towers full of beautiful pictures and statues. The streets of the city are water, and one travels about in——"

"I know," said Masie, sitting up suddenly. "Gondolas."

"Yes," smiled Carter.

"I thought so," said Masie.

"And then," continued Carter, "we will travel on and see whatever we wish in the world. After the European cities we will visit India and the ancient cities there, and ride on elephants and see the wonderful temples of the Hindoos and the Brahmins and the Japanese gardens and the camel trains and chariot races in Persia, and all the queer sights of foreign countries. Don't you think you would like it, Masie?"

Masie rose to her feet.

"I think we had better be going home," she said, coolly. "It's getting late."

Carter humored her. He had come to know her varying, thistledown moods, and that it was useless to combat them. But he felt a certain happy triumph. He had held for a moment, though but by a silken thread, the soul of his wild Psyche, and hope was stronger within him. Once she had folded her wings and her cool hand had closed about his own.

At the Biggest Store the next day Masie's chum, Lulu, waylaid her in an angle of the counter.

"How are you and your swell friend making it?" she asked.

"Oh, him?" said Masie, patting her side curls. "He ain't in it any more. Say, Lu, what do you think that fellow wanted me to do?"

"Go on the stage?" guessed Lulu, breathlessly.

"Nit; he's too cheap a guy for that. He wanted me to marry him and go down to Coney Island for a wedding tour!"

Dougherty's Eye-Opener

BIG JIM DOUGHERTY was a sport. He belonged to that race of men. In Manhattan it is a distinct race. They are the Caribs of the North—strong, artful, self-sufficient, clannish, honorable within the laws of their race, holding in lenient contempt neighboring tribes who bow to the measure of Society's tape-line. I refer, of course, to the titled nobility of sportdom. There is a class which bears as a qualifying adjective the substantive belonging to a wind instrument made of a cheap and base metal. But the tin mines of Cornwall never produced the material for manufacturing descriptive nomenclature for "Big Jim" Dougherty.

The habitat of the sport is the lobby or the outside corner of certain hotels and combination restaurants and cafés. They are mostly men of different sizes, running from small to large; but they are unanimous in the possession of a recently shaven, blue-black cheek and chin and dark overcoats (in season) with black velvet collars.

Of the domestic life of the sport little is known. It has been said that Cupid and Hymen sometimes take a hand in the game and copper the queen of hearts to lose. Daring theorists have averred —not content with simply saying—that a sport often contracts a spouse, and even incurs descendants. Sometimes he sits in the game of politics; and then at chowder picnics there is a revelation of a Mrs. Sport and little Sports in glazed hats with tin pails.

But mostly the sport is Oriental. He believes his women-folk should not be too patent. Somewhere behind grilles or flower-ornamented fire escapes they await him. There, no doubt, they tread on rugs from Teheran and are diverted by the bulbul and play upon the dulcimer and feed upon sweetmeats. But away from his home the sport is an integer. He does not, as men of other races in Manhattan do, become the convoy in his unoccupied hours of fluttering laces and high heels that tick off delectably the happy seconds of the evening parade. He herds with his own race at corners, and delivers a commentary in his Carib lingo upon the passing show.

"Big Jim" Dougherty had a wife, but he did not wear a button portrait of her upon his lapel. He had a home in one of those brown-stone, iron-railed streets on the west side that look like a recently excavated bowling alley of Pompeii.

To this home of his Mr. Dougherty repaired each night when the hour was so late as to promise no further diversion in the arch domains of sport. By that time the occupant of the monoga-mistic harem would be in dreamland, the bulbul silenced and the hour propitious for slumber.

"Big Jim" always arose at twelve, meridian, for breakfast, and soon afterward he would return to the rendezvous of his "crowd."

He was always vaguely conscious that there was a Mrs. Dough-erty. He would have received without denial the charge that the quiet, neat, comfortable little woman across the table at home was his wife. In fact, he remembered pretty well that they had been married for nearly four years. She would often tell him about the cute tricks of Spot, the canary, and the light-haired lady that lived in the window of the flat across the street.

"Big Jim" Dougherty even listened to this conversation of hers sometimes. He knew that she would have a nice dinner ready for him every evening at seven when he came for it. She some-times went to matinées, and she had a talking machine with six dozen records. Once when her Uncle Amos blew in on a wind from up-state she went with him to the Eden Musée. Surely these things were diversions enough for any woman.

One afternoon Mr. Dougherty finished his breakfast, put on his hat and got away fairly for the door. When his hand was on the knob he heard his wife's voice.

"Jim," she said, firmly, "I wish you would take me out to dinner this evening. It has been three years since you have been outside the door with me."

"Big Jim" was astounded. She had never asked anything like this before. It had the flavor of a totally new proposition. But he was a game sport.

"All right," he said. "You be ready when I come at seven. None of this 'wait two minutes till I primp an hour or two' kind of business, now, Dele."

"I'll be ready," said his wife, calmly.

At seven she descended the stone steps in the Pompeian bowling alley at the side of "Big Jim" Dougherty. She wore a dinner gown made of a stuff that the spiders must have woven, and of a color that a twilight sky must have contributed. A light coat with many admirably unnecessary capes and adorably inutile ribbons floated downward from her shoulders. Fine feathers do make fine birds; and the only reproach in the saying is for the man who refuses to give up his earnings for the ostrich-tip industry.

"Big Jim" Dougherty was troubled. There was a being at his side whom he did not know. He thought of the sober-hued plumage that this bird of paradise was accustomed to wear in her cage, and this winged revelation puzzled him. In some way she reminded him of the Delia Cullen that he had married four years before. Shyly and rather awkwardly he stalked at her right hand.

"After dinner I'll take you back home, Dele," said Mr. Dougherty, "and then I'll drop back up to Seltzer's with the boys. You can have swell chuck to-night if you want it. I made a winning on Anaconda yesterday so you can go as far as you like."

Mr. Dougherty had intended to make the outing with his unwonted wife an inconspicuous one. Uxoriousness was a weakness that the precepts of the Caribs did not countenance. If any of his friends of the track, the billiard cloth or the square circle had wives they had never complained of the fact in public. There were a number of table d'hôte places on the cross streets near the broad and shining way; and to one of these he had proposed to escort her, so that the bushel might not be removed from the light of his domesticity.

But while on the way Mr. Dougherty altered those intentions. He had been casting stealthy glances at his attractive companion and he was seized with the conviction that she was no selling plater. He resolved to parade with his wife past Seltzer's café, where at this time a number of his tribe would be gathered to view the daily evening processions. Yes; and he would take her to dine at Hoogley's, the swellest slow-lunch warehouse on the line, he said to himself.

The congregation of smooth-faced tribal gentlemen were on watch at Seltzer's. As Mr. Dougherty and his reorganized Delia passed they stared, momentarily petrified, and then removed their hats—a performance as unusual to them as was the astonishing innovation presented to their gaze by "Big Jim." On the latter gentleman's impassive face there appeared a slight flicker of triumph—a faint flicker, no more to be observed than the expression called there by the draft of little casino to a four-card spade flush.

Hoogley's was animated. Electric lights shone—as, indeed, they were expected to do. And the napery, the glassware, and the flowers also meritoriously performed the spectacular duties required of them. The guests were numerous, well-dressed, and gay.

A waiter—not necessarily obsequious—conducted "Big Jim" Dougherty and his wife to a table.

"Play that menu straight across for what you like, Dele," said "Big Jim." "It's you for a trough of the gilded oats to-night. It strikes me that maybe we've been sticking too fast to home fodder."

"Big Jim's" wife gave her order. He looked at her with respect.

She had mentioned truffles; and he had not known that she knew what truffles were. From the wine list she designated an appropriate and desirable brand. He looked at her with some admiration.

She was beaming with the innocent excitement that woman derives from the exercise of her gregariousness. She was talking to him about a hundred things with animation and delight. And as the meal progressed her cheeks, colorless from a life indoors, took on a delicate flush. "Big Jim" looked around the room and saw that none of the women there had her charm. And then he thought of the three years she had suffered immurement, uncomplaining, and a flush of shame warmed him, for he carried fair play as an item in his creed.

But when the Honorable Patrick Corrigan, leader in Dougherty's district and a friend of his, saw them and came over to the table, matters got to the three-quarter stretch. The Honorable Patrick was a gallant man, both in deeds and words. As for the Blarney stone, his previous actions toward it must have been pronounced. Heavy damages for breach of promise could surely have been obtained had the Blarney stone seen fit to sue the Honorable Patrick.

"Jimmy, old man!" he called; he clapped Dougherty on the back; he shone like a midday sun upon Delia.

"Honorable Mr. Corrigan—Mrs. Dougherty," said "Big Jim."

The Honorable Patrick became a fountain of entertainment and admiration. The waiter had to fetch a third chair for him; he made another at the table, and the wineglasses were refilled.

"You selfish old rascal!" he exclaimed, shaking an arch finger at "Big Jim," "to have kept Mrs. Dougherty a secret from us."

And then "Big Jim" Dougherty, who was no talker, sat dumb, and saw the wife who had dined every evening for three years at home, blossom like a fairy flower. Quick, witty, charming, full of light and ready talk, she received the experienced attack of the Honorable Patrick on the field of repartee and surprised, vanquished, delighted him. She unfolded her long-closed petals and around her the room became a garden. They tried to include "Big Jim" in the conversation, but he was without a vocabulary.

And then a stray bunch of politicians and good fellows who lived for sport came into the room. They saw "Big Jim" and the leader, and over they came and were made acquainted with Mrs. Dougherty. And in a few minutes she was holding a salon. Half a dozen men surrounded her, courtiers all, and six found her capable of charming. "Big Jim" sat, grim, and kept saying to himself: "Three years, three years!"

The dinner came to an end. The Honorable Patrick reached for Mrs. Dougherty's cloak; but that was a matter of action instead of words, and Dougherty's big hand got it first by two seconds.

While the farewells were being said at the door the Honorable Patrick smote Dougherty mightily between the shoulders.

"Jimmy, me boy," he declared, in a giant whisper, "the madam is a jewel of the first water. Ye're a lucky dog."

"Big Jim" walked homeward with his wife. She seemed quite as pleased with the lights and show windows in the streets as with the admiration of the men in Hoogley's. As they passed Seltzer's they heard the sound of many voices in the café. The boys would be starting the drinks around now and discussing past performances.

At the door of their home Delia paused. The pleasure of the outing radiated softly from her countenance. She could not hope for Jim of evenings, but the glory of this one would lighten her lonely hours for a long time.

"Thank you for taking me out, Jim," she said, gratefully. "You'll be going back to Seltzer's now, of course."

"To —— with Seltzer's," said "Big Jim," emphatically. "And d—— Pat Corrigan! Does he think I haven't got any eyes?"

And the door closed behind both of them.

The Defeat of the City

ROBERT WALMSLEY'S descent upon the city resulted in a Kilkenny struggle. He came out of the fight victor by a fortune and a reputation. On the other hand, he was swallowed up by the city. The city gave him what he demanded and then branded him with its brand. It remodelled, cut, trimmed, and stamped him to the pattern it approves. It opened its social gates to him and shut him in on a close-cropped, formal lawn with the select herd of ruminants. In dress, habits, manners, provincialism, routine, and narrowness he acquired that charming insolence, that irritating completeness, that sophisticated crassness, that over-balanced poise that makes the Manhattan gentleman so delightedly small in his greatness.

One of the up-state rural counties pointed with pride to the successful young metropolitan lawyer as a product of its soil. Six years earlier this county had removed the wheat straw from between its huckleberry-stained teeth and emitted a derisive and bucolic laugh as old man Walmsley's freckle-faced "Bob" abandoned the certain three-per-diem meals of the one-horse farm for the discontinuous quick lunch counters of the three-ringed metropolis. At the end of the six years no murder trial, coaching party, automobile accident or cotillion was complete in which the name of Robert Walmsley did not figure. Tailors waylaid him in the street to get a new wrinkle from the cut of his unwrinkled trousers. Hyphenated fellows in the clubs and members of the oldest subpœnaed families were glad to clap him on the back and allow him three letters of his name.

But the Matterhorn of Robert Walmsley's success was not scaled until he married Alicia Van Der Pool. I cite the Matterhorn, for just so high and cool and white and inaccessible was this daughter of the old burghers. The social Alps that ranged about her—over whose bleak passes a thousand climbers struggled—reached only to her knees. She towered in her own atmosphere, serene, chaste, prideful, wading in no fountains, dining no monkeys, breeding no dogs for bench shows. She was a Van Der Pool. Fountains were made to play for her; monkeys were made for other people's ancestors; dogs, she understood, were created to be companions of blind persons and objectionable characters who smoked pipes.

This was the Matterhorn that Robert Walmsley accomplished. If he found, with the good poet with the game foot and artificially curled hair, that he who ascends to mountain tops will find the loftiest peaks most wrapped in clouds and snow, he concealed his chilblains beneath a brave and smiling exterior. He was a lucky man and knew it, even though he were imitating the Spartan boy with an ice-cream freezer beneath his doublet frappéeing the region of his heart.

After a brief wedding tour abroad, the couple returned to create a decided ripple in the calm cistern (so placid and cool and sunless it is) of the best society. They entertained at their red brick mausoleum of ancient greatness in an old square that is a cemetery of crumbled glory. And Robert Walmsley was proud of his wife; although while one of his hands shook his guests' the other held tightly to his alpenstock and thermometer.

One day Alicia found a letter written to Robert by his mother. It was an unerudite letter, full of crops and motherly love and farm notes. It chronicled the health of the pig and the recent red calf, and asked concerning Robert's in return. It was a letter direct from the soil, straight from home, full of biographies of bees, tales of turnips, pæans of new-laid eggs, neglected parents and the slump in dried apples.

"Why have I not been shown your mother's letters?" asked Alicia. There was always something in her voice that made you think of lorgnettes, of accounts at Tiffany's, of sledges smoothly gliding on the trail from Dawson to Forty Mile, of the tinkling of pendent prisms on your grandmothers' chandeliers, of snow lying on a convent roof; of a police sergeant refusing bail. "Your mother," continued Alicia, "invites us to make a visit to the farm. I have never seen a farm. We will go there for a week or two, Robert."

"We will," said Robert, with the grand air of an associate Supreme Justice concurring in an opinion. "I did not lay the invitation before you because I thought you would not care to go. I am much pleased at your decision."

"I will write to her myself," answered Alicia, with a faint foreshadowing of enthusiasm. "Félice shall pack my trunks at once. Seven, I think, will be enough. I do not suppose that your mother entertains a great deal. Does she give many house parties?"

Robert arose, and as attorney for rural places filed a demurrer against six of the seven trunks. He endeavored to define, picture, elucidate, set forth and describe a farm. His own words sounded strange in his ears. He had not realized how thoroughly urbsidized he had become.

A week passed and found them landed at the little country station five hours out from the city. A grinning, stentorian, sarcastic youth driving a mule to a spring wagon hailed Robert savagely.

"Hallo, Mr. Walmsley. Found your way back at last, have you? Sorry I couldn't bring in the automobile for you, but dad's bull-tonguing the ten-acre clover patch with it to-day. Guess you'll excuse my not wearing a dress suit over to meet you—it ain't six o'clock yet, you know."

"I'm glad to see you, Tom," said Robert, grasping his brother's hand. "Yes, I've found my way at last. You've a right to say 'at last.' It's been over two years since the last time. But it will be oftener after this, my boy."

Alicia, cool in the summer heat as an Arctic wraith, white as a Norse snow maiden in her flimsy muslin and fluttering lace parasol, came round the corner of the station; and Tom was stripped of his assurance. He became chiefly eyesight clothed in blue jeans, and on the homeward drive to the mule alone did he confide in language the inwardness of his thoughts.

They drove homeward. The low sun dropped a spendthrift flood of gold upon the fortunate fields of wheat. The cities were far away. The road lay curling around wood and dale and hill like a ribbon lost from the robe of careless summer. The wind followed like a whinnying colt in the track of Phœbus's steeds.

By and by the farmhouse peeped gray out of its faithful grove; they saw the long lane with its convoy of walnut trees running from the road to the house; they smelled the wild rose and the breath of cool, damp willows in the creek's bed. And then in unison all the voices of the soil began a chant addressed to the soul of Robert Walmsley. Out of the tilted aisles of the dim wood they came hollowly; they chirped and buzzed from the parched grass; they trilled from the ripples of the creek ford; they floated up in clear Pan's pipe notes from the dimming meadows; the whippoorwills joined in as they pursued midges in the upper air; slow-going cow-bells struck out a homely accompaniment—and this was what each one said: "You've found your way back at last, have you?"

The old voices of the soil spoke to him. Leaf and bud and blossom conversed with him in the old vocabulary of his careless youth—the inanimate things, the familiar stones and rails, the gates and furrows and roofs and turns of road had an eloquence, too, and a power in the transformation. The country had smiled and he had felt the breath of it, and his heart was drawn as if in a moment back to his old love. The city was far away.

This rural atavism, then, seized Robert Walmsley and possessed him. A queer thing he noticed in connection with it was that

Alicia, sitting at his side, suddenly seemed to him a stranger. She did not belong to this recurrent phase. Never before had she seemed so remote, so colorless and high—so intangible and unreal. And yet he had never admired her more than when she sat there by him in the rickety spring wagon, chiming no more with his mood and with her environment than the Matterhorn chimes with a peasant's cabbage garden.

That night when the greetings and the supper were over, the entire family, including Buff, the yellow dog, bestrewed itself upon the front porch. Alicia, not haughty but silent, sat in the shadow dressed in an exquisite pale-gray tea gown. Robert's mother discoursed to her happily concerning marmalade and lumbago. Tom sat on the top step; Sisters Millie and Pam on the lowest step to catch the lightning bugs. Mother had the willow rocker. Father sat in the big armchair with one of its arms gone. Buff sprawled in the middle of the porch in everybody's way. The twilight pixies and pucks stole forth unseen and plunged other poignant shafts of memory into the heart of Robert. A rural madness entered his soul. The city was far away.

Father sat without his pipe, writhing in his heavy boots, a sacrifice to rigid courtesy. Robert shouted: "No, you don't!" He fetched the pipe and lit it; he seized the old gentleman's boots and tore them off. The last one slipped suddenly, and Mr. Robert Walmsley, of Washington Square, tumbled off the porch backward with Buff on top of him, howling fearfully. Tom laughed sarcastically.

Robert tore off his coat and vest and hurled them into a lilac bush.

"Come out here, you landlubber," he cried to Tom, "and I'll put grass seed on your back. I think you called me a 'dude' a while ago. Come along and cut your capers."

Tom understood the invitation and accepted it with delight. Three times they wrestled on the grass, "side holds," even as the giants of the mat. And twice was Tom forced to bite grass at the hands of the distinguished lawyer. Dishevelled, panting, each still boasting of his own prowess, they stumbled back to the porch. Millie cast a pert reflection upon the qualities of a city brother. In an instant Robert had secured a horrid katydid in his fingers and bore down upon her. Screaming wildly, she fled up the lane pursued by the avenging glass of form. A quarter of a mile and they returned, she full of apology to the victorious "dude." The rustic mania possessed him unabatedly.

"I can do up a cowpenful of you slow hayseeds," he proclaimed, vaingloriously. "Bring on your bulldogs, your hired men, and your log-rollers."

He turned handsprings on the grass that prodded Tom to envious sarcasm. And then, with a whoop, he clattered to the rear and brought back Uncle Ike, a battered colored retainer of the family, with his banjo, and strewed sand on the porch and danced "Chicken in the Bread Tray" and did buck-and-wing wonders for half an hour longer. Incredibly wild and boisterous things he did. He sang, he told stories that set all but one shrieking, he played the yokel, the humorous clodhopper; he was mad, mad with the revival of the old life in his blood.

He became so extravagant that once his mother sought gently to reprove him. Then Alicia moved as though she were about to speak, but she did not. Through it all she sat immovable, a slim, white spirit in the dusk that no man might question or read.

By and by she asked permission to ascend to her room, saying that she was tired. On her way she passed Robert. He was standing in the door, the figure of vulgar comedy, with ruffled hair, reddened face and unpardonable confusion of attire—no trace there of the immaculate Robert Walmsley, the courted clubman and ornament of select circles. He was doing a conjuring trick with some household utensils, and the family, now won over to him without exception, was beholding him with worshipful admiration.

As Alicia passed in Robert started suddenly. He had forgotten for the moment that she was present. Without a glance at him she went on upstairs.

After that the fun grew quiet. An hour passed in talk, and then Robert went up himself.

She was standing by the window when he entered their room. She was still clothed as when they were on the porch. Outside and crowding against the window was a giant apple tree, full blossomed.

Robert sighed and went near the window. He was ready to meet his fate. A confessed vulgarian, he foresaw the verdict of justice in the shape of that still, whiteclad form. He knew the rigid lines that a Van Der Pool would draw. He was a peasant gamboling indecorously in the valley, and the pure, cold, white, unthawed summit of the Matterhorn could not but frown on him. He had been unmasked by his own actions. All the polish, the poise, the form that the city had given him had fallen from him like an ill-fitting mantle at the first breath of a country breeze. Dully he awaited the approaching condemnation.

"Robert," said the calm, cool voice of his judge, "I thought I married a gentleman."

Yes, it was coming. And yet, in the face of it, Robert Walmsley was eagerly regarding a certain branch of the apple tree upon which he used to climb out of that very window. He believed he could do it now. He wondered how many blossoms there were on the tree—ten millions? But here was someone speaking again:

"I thought I married a gentleman," the voice went on, "but——"

Why had she come and was standing so close by his side?

"But I find that I have married"—was this Alicia talking?— "something better—a man—Bob, dear, kiss me, won't you?"

The city was far away.

The Shocks of Doom

THERE IS an aristocracy of the public parks and even of the vagabonds who use them for their private apartments. Vallance
felt rather than knew this, but when he stepped down out of his
world into chaos his feet brought him directly to Madison Square.

Raw and astringent as a schoolgirl—of the old order—young
May breathed austerely among the budding trees. Vallance buttoned his coat, lighted his last cigarette and took his seat upon
a bench. For three minutes he mildly regretted the last hundred of his last thousand that it had cost him when the bicycle
cop put an end to his last automobile ride. Then he felt in every
pocket and found not a single penny. He had given up his apartment that morning. His furniture had gone toward certain debts.
His clothes, save what were upon him, had descended to his
man-servant for back wages. As he sat, there was not in the
whole city for him a bed or a broiled lobster or a streetcar fare or
a carnation for his buttonhole unless he should obtain them by
sponging on his friends or by false pretenses. Therefore he had
chosen the park.

And all this was because an uncle had disinherited him, and cut
down his allowance from liberality to nothing. And all that was
because his nephew had disobeyed him concerning a certain
girl, who comes not into the story—therefore, all readers who
brush their hair towards its roots may be warned to read no further. There was another nephew, of a different branch, who

had once been the prospective heir and favorite. Being without grace or hope, he had long ago disappeared in the mire. Now drag-nets were out for him; he was to be rehabilitated and restored. And so Vallance fell grandly as Lucifer to the lowest pit, joining the tattered ghosts in the little park.

Sitting there he leaned far back on the hard bench and laughed a jet of cigarette smoke up to the lowest tree branches. The sudden severing of all his life's ties had brought him a free, thrilling, almost joyous elation. He felt precisely the sensation of the aëronaut when he cuts loose his parachute and lets his balloon drift away.

The hour was nearly ten. Not many loungers were on the benches. The park-dweller, though a stubborn fighter against autumnal coolness, is slow to attack the advance line of spring's chilly cohorts.

Then arose one from a seat near the leaping fountain, and came and sat himself at Vallance's side. He was either young or old; cheap lodging-houses had flavored him mustily; razors and combs had passed him by; in him drink had been bottled and sealed in the devil's bond. He begged a match, which is the form of introduction among park benchers, and then he began to talk.

"You're not one of the regulars," he said to Vallance. "I know tailored clothes when I see 'em. You just stopped for a moment on your way through the park. Don't mind my talking to you for a while? I've got to be with somebody. I'm afraid—I'm afraid. I've told two or three of those bummers over there about it. They think I'm crazy. Say—let me tell you—all I've had to eat to-day was a couple of bretzels and an apple. To-morrow I'll stand in line to inherit three millions; and that restaurant you see over there with the autos around it will be too cheap for me to eat in. Don't believe it, do you?"

"Without the slightest trouble," said Vallance, with a laugh. "I lunched there yesterday. To-night I couldn't buy a five-cent cup of coffee."

"You don't look like one of us. Well, I guess those things

happen. I used to be a high-flyer myself—some years ago. What knocked you out of the game?"

"I—oh, I lost my job," said Vallance.

"It's undiluted Hades, this city," went on the other. "One day you're eating from China; the next you are eating in China—a chop-suey joint. I've had more than my share of hard luck. For five years I've been little better than a panhandler. I was raised up to live expensively and do nothing. Say—I don't mind telling you —I've got to talk to somebody, you see, because I'm afraid—I'm afraid. My name's Ide. You wouldn't think that old Paulding, one of the millionaires on Riverside Drive, was my uncle, would you? Well, he is. I lived in his house once, and had all the money I wanted. Say, haven't you got the price of a couple of drinks about you—er—what's your name——"

"Dawson," said Vallance. "No; I'm sorry to say that I'm all in financially."

"I've been living for a week in a coal cellar on Division Street," went on Ide, "with a crook they call 'Blinky' Morris. I didn't have anywhere else to go. While I was out to-day a chap with some papers in his pocket was there, asking for me. I didn't know but what he was a fly cop, so I didn't go around again till after dark. There was a letter there he had left for me. Say—Dawson, it was from a big downtown lawyer, Mead. I've seen his sign on Ann Street. Paulding wants me to play the prodigal nephew—wants me to come back and be his heir again and blow in his money. I'm to call at the lawyer's office at ten to-morrow and step into my old shoes again—heir to three million, Dawson, and $10,000 a year pocket money. And—I'm afraid—I'm afraid."

The vagrant leaped to his feet and raised both trembling arms above his head. He caught his breath and moaned hysterically.

Vallance seized his arm and forced him back to the bench.

"Be quiet!" he commanded with something like disgust in his tones. "One would think you had lost a fortune, instead of being about to acquire one. Of what are you afraid?"

Ide cowered and shivered on the bench. He clung to Vallance's sleeve, and even in the dim glow of the Broadway lights the latest disinherited one could see drops on the other's brow wrung out by some strange terror.

"Why, I'm afraid something will happen to me before morning. I don't know what—something to keep me from coming into that money. I'm afraid a tree will fall on me—I'm afraid a cab will run over me, or a stone drop on me from a housetop, or something. I never was afraid before. I've sat in this park a hundred nights as calm as a graven image without knowing where my breakfast was to come from. But now it's different. I love money, Dawson—I'm happy as a god when it's trickling through my fingers, and people are bowing to me, with the music and the flowers and fine clothes all around. As long as I knew I was out of the game I didn't mind. I was even happy sitting here ragged and hungry, listening to the fountain jump and watching the carriages go up the avenue. But it's in reach of my hand again now—almost—and I can't stand it to wait twelve hours, Dawson—I can't stand it. There are fifty things that could happen to me—I could go blind—I might be attacked with heart disease—the world might come to an end before I could——"

Ide sprang to his feet again, with a shriek. People stirred on the benches and began to look. Vallance took his arm.

"Come and walk," he said, soothingly. "And try to calm yourself. There is no need to become excited or alarmed. Nothing is going to happen to you. One night is like another."

"That's right," said Ide. "Stay with me, Dawson—that's a good fellow. Walk around with me awhile. I never went to pieces like this before, and I've had a good many hard knocks. Do you think you could hustle something in the way of a little lunch, old man? I'm afraid my nerve's too far gone to try any panhandling."

Vallance led his companion up almost deserted Fifth Avenue, and then westward along the Thirties toward Broadway. "Wait here a few minutes," he said, leaving Ide in a quiet and shadowed spot. He entered a familiar hotel, and strolled toward the bar quite in his old assured way.

"There's a poor devil outside, Jimmy," he said to the bartender, "who says he's hungry and looks it. You know what they do when you give them money. Fix up a sandwich or two for him; and I'll see that he doesn't throw it away."

"Certainly, Mr. Vallance," said the bartender. "They ain't all fakes. Don't like to see anybody go hungry."

He folded a liberal supply of the free lunch into a napkin. Vallance went with it and joined his companion. Ide pounced upon the food ravenously. "I haven't had any free lunch as good as this in a year," he said. "Aren't you going to eat any, Dawson?"

"I'm not hungry—thanks," said Vallance.

"We'll go back to the Square," said Ide. "The cops won't bother us there. I'll roll up the rest of this ham and stuff for our breakfast. I won't eat any more; I'm afraid I'll get sick. Suppose I'd die of cramps or something to-night, and never get to touch that money again! It's eleven hours yet till time to see that lawyer. You won't leave me, will you, Dawson? I'm afraid something might happen. You haven't any place to go, have you?"

"No," said Vallance, "nowhere to-night. I'll have a bench with you."

"You take it cool," said Ide, "if you've told it to me straight. I should think a man put on the bum from a good job just in one day would be tearing his hair."

"I believe I've already remarked," said Vallance, laughing, "that I would have thought that a man who was expecting to come into a fortune on the next day would be feeling pretty easy and quiet."

"It's funny business," philosophized Ide, "about the way people take things, anyhow. Here's your bench, Dawson, right next to mine. The light don't shine in your eyes here. Say, Dawson, I'll get the old man to give you a letter to somebody about a job when I get back home. You've helped me a lot to-night. I don't believe I could have gone through the night if I hadn't struck you."

"Thank you," said Vallance. "Do you lie down or sit up on these when you sleep?"

For hours Vallance gazed almost without winking at the stars through the branches of the trees and listened to the sharp slapping of horses' hoofs on the sea of asphalt to the south. His mind was active but his feelings were dormant. Every emotion seemed to have been eradicated. He felt no regrets, no fears, no pain or discomfort. Even when he thought of the girl, it was as of an inhabitant of one of those remote stars at which he gazed. He remembered the absurd antics of his companion and laughed softly, yet without a feeling of mirth. Soon the daily army of milk wagons made of the city a roaring drum to which they marched. Vallance fell asleep on his comfortless bench.

At ten o'clock on the next day the two stood at the door of Lawyer Mead's office in Ann Street.

Ide's nerves fluttered worse than ever when the hour approached; and Vallance could not decide to leave him a possible prey to the dangers he dreaded.

When they entered the office, Lawyer Mead looked at them wonderingly. He and Vallance were old friends. After his greeting, he turned to Ide, who stood with white face and trembling limbs before the expected crisis.

"I sent a second letter to your address last night, Mr. Ide," he said. "I learned this morning that you were not there to receive it. It will inform you that Mr. Paulding has reconsidered his offer to take you back into favor. He has decided not to do so, and desires you to understand that no change will be made in the relations existing between you and him."

Ide's trembling suddenly ceased. The color came back to his face, and he straightened his back. His jaw went forward half an inch, and a gleam came into his eye. He pushed back his battered hat with one hand, and extended the other, with levelled fingers, toward the lawyer. He took a long breath and then laughed sardonically.

"Tell old Paulding he may go to the devil," he said, loudly and clearly, and turned and walked out of the office with a firm and lively step.

Lawyer Mead turned on his heel to Vallance and smiled.

"I am glad you came in," he said, genially. "Your uncle wants you to return home at once. He is reconciled to the situation that led to his hasty action, and desires to say that all will be as——"

"Hey, Adams!" cried Lawyer Mead, breaking his sentence, and calling to his clerk. "Bring a glass of water—Mr. Vallance has fainted."

Squaring the Circle

AT THE HAZARD of wearying youth this tale of vehement emotions must be prefaced by a discourse on geometry.

Nature moves in circles; Art in straight lines. The natural is rounded; the artificial is made up of angles. A man lost in the snow wanders, in spite of himself, in perfect circles; the city man's feet, denaturalized by rectangular streets and floors, carry him ever away from himself.

The round eyes of childhood typify innocence; the narrow line of the flirt's optic proves the invasion of art. The horizontal mouth is the mark of determined cunning; who has not read Nature's most spontaneous lyric in lips rounded for the candid kiss?

Beauty is Nature in perfection; circularity is its chief attribute. Behold the full moon, the enchanting gold ball, the domes of splendid temples, the huckleberry pie, the wedding ring, the circus ring, the ring for the waiter, and the "round" of drinks.

On the other hand, straight lines show that Nature has been deflected. Imagine Venus's girdle transformed into a "straight front!"

When we begin to move in straight lines and turn sharp corners our natures begin to change. The consequence is that Nature, being more adaptive than Art, tries to conform to its sterner regulations. The result is often a rather curious product—for instance: A prize chrysanthemum, wood alcohol whiskey, a Republican Missouri, cauliflower *au gratin*, and a New Yorker.

Nature is lost quickest in a big city. The cause is geometrical, not moral. The straight lines of its streets and architecture, the rectangularity of its laws and social customs, the undeviating pavements, the hard, severe, depressing, uncompromising rules of all its ways—even of its recreation and sports—coldly exhibit a sneering defiance of the curved line of Nature.

Wherefore, it may be said that the big city has demonstrated the problem of squaring the circle. And it may be added that this mathematical introduction precedes an account of the fate of a Kentucky feud that was imported to the city that has a habit of making its importations conform to its angles.

The feud began in the Cumberland Mountains between the Folwell and the Harkness families. The first victim of the home-spun vendetta was a 'possum dog belonging to Bill Harkness. The Harkness family evened up this dire loss by laying out the chief of the Folwell clan. The Folwells were prompt at repartee. They oiled up their squirrel rifles and made it feasible for Bill Harkness to follow his dog to a land where the 'possums come down when treed without the stroke of an ax.

The feud flourished for forty years. Harknesses were shot at the plough, through their lamp-lit cabin windows, coming from camp-meetings, asleep, in duello, sober and otherwise, singly and in family groups, prepared and unprepared. Folwells had the branches of their family tree lopped off in similar ways, as the traditions of their country prescribed and authorized.

By and by the pruning left but a single member of each family. And then Cal Harkness, probably reasoning that further pursuance of the controversy would give a too decided personal flavor to the feud, suddenly disappeared from the relieved Cumberlands, baulking the avenging hand of Sam, the ultimate opposing Folwell.

A year afterward Sam Folwell learned that his hereditary, un-suppressed enemy was living in New York City. Sam turned over the big iron washpot in the yard, scraped off some of the soot, which he mixed with lard and shined his boots with the compound. He put on his store clothes of butternut dyed black, a white shirt and collar, and packed a carpet-sack with Spartan *lingerie*. He took his squirrel rifle from its hooks, but put it back again with a sigh. However ethical and plausible the habit might be in the Cumberlands, perhaps New York would not swallow his pose of hunting squirrels among the skyscrapers along Broadway. An ancient but reliable Colt's revolver that he resurrected from a bureau drawer seemed to proclaim itself the pink of weapons for metropolitan adventure and vengeance. This and a hunting-knife in a leather sheath, Sam packed in the carpet-sack. As he started, muleback, for the lowland railroad station the last Folwell turned in his saddle and looked grimly at the little cluster of white-pine slabs in the clump of cedars that marked the Folwell burying-ground.

Sam Folwell arrived in New York in the night. Still moving and living in the free circles of nature, he did not perceive the formidable, pitiless, restless, fierce angles of the great city waiting in the dark to close about the rotundity of his heart and brain and mould him to the form of its millions of reshaped victims. A cabby picked him out of the whirl, as Sam himself had often picked a nut from a bed of wind-tossed autumn leaves, and whisked him away to a hotel commensurate to his boots and carpet-sack.

On the next morning the last of the Folwells made his sortie into the city that sheltered the last Harkness. The Colt was thrust beneath his coat and secured by a narrow leather belt; the hunting-knife hung between his shoulder-blades, with the haft an inch below his coat collar. He knew this much—that Cal Harkness drove an express wagon somewhere in that town, and that he, Sam Folwell, had come to kill him. And as he stepped upon the sidewalk the red came into his eye and the feud-hate into his heart.

The clamor of the central avenues drew him thitherward. He had half expected to see Cal coming down the street in his shirt-sleeves with a jug and a whip in his hand, just as he would have seen him in Frankfort or Laurel City. But an hour went by and Cal did not appear. Perhaps he was waiting in ambush, to shoot him from a door or a window. Sam kept a sharp eye on doors and windows for a while.

About noon the city tired of playing with its mouse and suddenly squeezed him with its straight lines.

Sam Folwell stood where two great, rectangular arteries of the city cross. He looked four ways, and saw the world hurled from its orbit and reduced by spirit level and tape to an edged and cornered plane. All life moved on tracks, in grooves, according to system, within boundaries, by rote. The root of life was the cube root; the measure of existence was square measure. People streamed by in straight rows; the horrible din and crash stupefied him.

Sam leaned against the sharp corner of a stone building. Those faces passed him by thousands, and none of them were turned toward him. A sudden foolish fear that he had died and was a spirit, and that they could not see him, seized him. And then the city smote him with loneliness.

A fat man dropped out of the stream and stood a few feet distant, waiting for his car. Sam crept to his side and shouted above the tumult into his ear:

"The Rankinses' hogs weighed more'n ourn a whole passel, but the mast in thar neighborhood was a fine chance better than what it was down——"

The fat man moved away unostentatiously, and bought roasted chestnuts to cover his alarm.

Sam felt the need of a drop of mountain dew. Across the street men passed in and out through swinging doors. Brief glimpses could be had of a glistening bar and its bedeckings. The feudist crossed and essayed to enter. Again had Art eliminated the familiar circle. Sam's hand found no door-knob—it slid, in vain, over a rectangular brass plate and polished oak with nothing even so large as a pin's head upon which his fingers might close.

Abashed, reddened, heartbroken, he walked away from the bootless door and sat upon a step. A locust club tickled him in the ribs.

"Take a walk for yourself," said the policeman. "You've been loafing around here long enough."

At the next corner a shrill whistle sounded in Sam's ear. He wheeled around and saw a black-browed villain scowling at him over peanuts heaped on a steaming machine. He started across the street. An immense engine, running without mules, with the voice of a bull and the smell of a smoky lamp, whizzed past, grazing his knee. A cab-driver bumped him with a hub and explained to him that kind words were invented to be used on other occasions. A motorman clanged his bell wildly and, for once in his life, corroborated a cab-driver. A large lady in a changeable silk waist dug an elbow into his back, and a newsy pensively pelted him with banana rinds, murmuring, "I hates to do it —but if anybody seen me let it pass!"

Cal Harkness, his day's work over and his express wagon stabled, turned the sharp edge of the building that, by the cheek of architects, is modelled upon a safety razor. Out of the mass of hurrying people his eye picked up, three yards away, the surviving bloody and implacable foe of his kith and kin.

He stopped short and wavered for a moment, being unarmed and sharply surprised. But the keen mountaineer's eye of Sam Folwell had picked him out.

There was a sudden spring, a ripple in the stream of passers-by and the sound of Sam's voice crying:

"Howdy, Cal! I'm durned glad to see ye."

And in the angles of Broadway, Fifth Avenue, and Twenty-third Street the Cumberland feudists shook hands.

The Memento

MISS LYNNETTE D'ARMANDE turned her back on Broadway. This was but tit for tat, because Broadway had often done the same thing to Miss D'Armande. Still, the "tats" seemed to have it, for the ex-leading lady of the "Reaping the Whirlwind" company had everything to ask of Broadway, while there was no vice-versa.

So Miss Lynnette D'Armande turned the back of her chair to her window that overlooked Broadway, and sat down to stitch in time the lisle-thread heel of a black silk stocking. The tumult and glitter of the roaring Broadway beneath her window had no charm for her; what she greatly desired was the stifling air of a dressing-room on that fairyland street and the roar of an audience gathered in that capricious quarter. In the meantime, those stockings must not be neglected. Silk does wear out so, but—after all, isn't it just the only goods there is?

The Hotel Thalia looks on Broadway as Marathon looks on the sea. It stands like a gloomy cliff above the whirlpool where the tides of two great thoroughfares clash. Here the player-bands gather at the end of their wanderings to loosen the buskin and dust the sock. Thick in the streets around it are booking-offices, theatres, agents, schools, and the lobster-palaces to which those thorny paths lead.

Wandering through the eccentric halls of the dim and fusty Thalia, you seem to have found yourself in some great ark or caravan about to sail, or fly, or roll away on wheels. About the house lingers a sense of unrest, of expectation, of transientness, even of anxiety and apprehension. The halls are a labyrinth. Without a guide, you wander like a lost soul in a Sam Lloyd puzzle.

Turning any corner, a dressing-sack or a *cul-de-sac* may bring you up short. You meet alarming tragedians stalking in bath-robes in search of rumored bathrooms. From hundreds of rooms come the buzz of talk, scraps of new and old songs, and the ready laughter of the convened players.

Summer has come; their companies have disbanded, and they take their rest in their favorite caravansary, while they besiege the managers for engagements for the coming season.

At this hour of the afternoon the day's work of tramping the rounds of the agents' offices is over. Past you, as you ramble distractedly through the mossy halls, flit audible visions of houris, with veiled, starry eyes, flying tag-ends of things and a swish of silk, bequeathing to the dull hallways an odor of gaiety and a memory of *frangipanni*. Serious young comedians, with versatile Adam's apples, gather in doorways and talk of Booth. Far-reaching from somewhere comes the smell of ham and red cabbage, and the crash of dishes on the American plan.

The indeterminate hum of life in the Thalia is enlivened by the discreet popping—at reasonable and salubrious intervals—of beer-bottle corks. Thus punctuated, life in the genial hostel scans easily—the comma being the favorite mark, semicolons frowned upon, and periods barred.

Miss D'Armande's room was a small one. There was room for her rocker between the dresser and the wash-stand if it were placed longitudinally. On the dresser were its usual accoutrements, plus the ex-leading lady's collected souvenirs of road engagements and photographs of her dearest and best professional friends.

At one of these photographs she looked twice or thrice as she darned, and smiled friendlily.

"I'd like to know where Lee is just this minute," she said, half-aloud.

If you had been privileged to view the photograph thus flattered, you would have thought at the first glance that you saw the picture of a many-petalled white flower, blown through the air by a storm. But the floral kingdom was not responsible for that swirl of petalous whiteness.

You saw the filmy, brief skirt of Miss Rosalie Ray as she made a complete heels-over-head turn in her wistaria-entwined swing, far out from the stage, high above the heads of the audience. You saw the camera's inadequate representation of the graceful, strong kick, with which she, at this exciting moment, sent flying, high and far, the yellow silk garter that each evening spun from her agile limb and descended upon the delighted audience below.

You saw, too, amid the black-clothed, mainly masculine patrons of select vaudeville a hundred hands raised with the hope of staying the flight of the brilliant aërial token.

Forty weeks of the best circuits this act had brought Miss Rosalie Ray, for each of two years. She did other things during her twelve minutes—a song and dance, imitations of two or three actors who are but imitations of themselves, and a balancing feat with a step-ladder and feather-duster; but when the blossom-decked swing was let down from the flies, and Miss Rosalie sprang smiling into the seat, with the golden circlet conspicuous in the place whence it was soon to slide and become a soaring and coveted guerdon—then it was that the audience rose in its seat as a single man—or presumably so—and indorsed the specialty that made Miss Ray's name a favorite in the booking-offices.

At the end of two years Miss Ray suddenly announced to her dear friend, Miss D'Armande, that she was going to spend the summer at an antediluvian village on the north shore of Long Island, and that the stage would see her no more.

Seventeen minutes after Miss Lynnette D'Armande had expressed her wish to know the whereabouts of her old chum, there were sharp raps at her door.

Doubt not that it was Rosalie Ray. At the shrill command to enter she did so, with something of a tired flutter, and dropped a heavy hand-bag on the floor. Upon my word, it was Rosalie, in a loose, travel-stained automobileless coat, closely tied brown veil with yard-long flying ends, gray walking suit, and tan oxfords with lavender over-gaiters.

When she threw off her veil and hat, you saw a pretty enough face, now flushed and disturbed by some unusual emotion, and restless, large eyes with discontent marring their brightness. A heavy pile of dull auburn hair, hastily put up, was escaping in crinkly, waving strands and curling, small locks from the confining combs and pins.

The meeting of the two was not marked by the effusion vocal, gymnastical, osculatory, and catechetical that distinguishes the greetings of their unprofessional sisters in society. There was a brief clinch, two simultaneous labial dabs, and they stood on the same footing of the old days. Very much like the short salutations of soldiers or of travellers in foreign wilds are the welcomes between the strollers at the corners of their criss-cross roads.

"I've got the hall-room two flights up above yours," said Rosalie, "but I came straight to see you before going up. I didn't know you were here till they told me."

"I've been in since the last of April," said Lynnette. "And I'm going on the road with a 'Fatal Inheritance' Company. We open next week in Elizabeth. I thought you'd quit the stage, Lee. Tell me about yourself."

Rosalie settled herself with a skilful wriggle on the top of Miss D'Armande's wardrobe trunk, and leaned her head against the papered wall. From long habit, thus can peripatetic leading ladies and their sisters make themselves as comfortable as though the deepest armchairs embraced them.

"I'm going to tell you, Lynn," she said, with a strangely sardonic and yet carelessly resigned look on her youthful face. "And then to-morrow I'll strike the old Broadway trail again, and wear some more paint off the chairs in the agents' offices. If anybody had told me any time in the last three months up to four o'clock this afternoon that I'd ever listen to that 'Leave-your-name-and-address' rot of the booking bunch again, I'd have given 'em the real Mrs. Fiske laugh. Loan me a handkerchief, Lynn. Gee! but those Long Island trains are fierce. I've got enough soft-coal cinders on my face to go on and play *Topsy* without using the cork. And, speaking of corks—got anything to drink, Lynn?"

Miss D'Armande opened a door of the washstand and took out a bottle.

"There's nearly a pint of Manhattan. There's a cluster of carnations in the drinking glass, but——"

"Oh, pass the bottle. Save the glass for company. Thanks! That hits the spot. The same to you. My first drink in three months!

"Yes, Lynn, I quit the stage at the end of last season. I quit it because I was sick of the life. And especially because my heart and soul were sick of men—of the kind of men we stage people have to be up against. You know what the game is to us—it's a fight against 'em all the way down the line from the manager who wants us to try his new motor-car to the bill-posters who want to call us by our front names.

"And the men we have to meet after the show are the worst of all. The stage-door kind, and the manager's friends who take us to supper and show their diamonds and talk about seeing 'Dan' and 'Dave' and 'Charlie' for us. They're beasts, and I hate 'em.

"I tell you, Lynn, it's the girls like us on the stage that ought to be pitied. It's girls from good homes that are honestly ambitious and work hard to rise in the profession, but never do get there. You hear a lot of sympathy sloshed around on chorus girls and their fifteen dollars a week. Piffle! There ain't a sorrow in the chorus that a lobster cannot heal.

"If there's any tears to shed, let 'em fall for the actress that gets a salary of from thirty to forty-five dollars a week for taking a leading part in a bum show. She knows she'll never do any better; but she hangs on for years, hoping for the 'chance' that never comes.

"And the fool plays we have to work in! Having another girl roll you around the stage by the hind legs in a 'Wheelbarrow Chorus' in a musical comedy is dignified drama compared with the idiotic things I've had to do in the thirty-centers.

"But what I hated most was the men—the men leering and blathering at you across tables, trying to buy you with Würzburger or Extra Dry, according to their estimate of your price. And the men in the audiences, clapping, yelling, snarling, crowding, writhing, gloating—like a lot of wild beasts, with their eyes fixed on you, ready to eat you up if you come in reach of their claws. Oh, how I hate 'em!

"Well, I'm not telling you much about myself, am I, Lynn?

"I had two hundred dollars saved up, and I cut the stage the first of the summer. I went over on Long Island and found the sweetest little village that ever was, called Soundport, right on the water. I was going to spend the summer there, and study up on elocution, and try to get a class in the fall. There was an old widow lady with a cottage near the beach who sometimes rented a room or two just for company, and she took me in. She had another boarder, too—the Reverend Arthur Lyle.

"Yes, he was the head-liner. You're on, Lynn. I'll tell you all of it in a minute. It's only a one-act play.

"The first time he walked on, Lynn, I felt myself going; the first lines he spoke, he had me. He was different from the men in audiences. He was tall and slim, and you never heard him come in the room, but you *felt* him. He had a face like a picture of a knight—like one of that Round Table bunch—and a voice like a 'cello solo. And his manners!

"Lynn, if you'd take John Drew in his best drawing-room scene and compare the two, you'd have John arrested for disturbing the peace.

"I'll spare you the particulars; but in less than a month Arthur and I were engaged. He preached at a little one-night stand of a Methodist church. There was to be a parsonage the size of a lunchwagon, and hens and honeysuckles when we were married. Arthur used to preach to me a good deal about Heaven, but he never could get my mind quite off those honeysuckles and hens.

"No; I didn't tell him I'd been on the stage. I hated the business and all that went with it; I'd cut it out forever, and I didn't see any use of stirring things up. I was a good girl, and I didn't have anything to confess, except being an elocutionist, and that was about all the strain my conscience would stand.

"Oh, I tell you, Lynn, I was happy. I sang in the choir and attended the sewing society, and recited that 'Annie Laurie' thing with the whistling stunt in it, 'in a manner bordering upon the professional,' as the weekly village paper reported it. And Arthur and I went rowing, and walking in the woods, and clamming, and that poky little village seemed to me the best place in the world. I'd have been happy to live there always, too, if——

"But one morning old Mrs. Gurley, the widow lady, got gossipy while I was helping her string beans on the back porch, and began to gush information, as folks who rent out their rooms usually do. Mr. Lyle was her idea of a saint on her earth—as he was mine, too. She went over all his virtues and graces, and wound up by telling me that Arthur had had an extremely romantic love-affair, not long before, that had ended unhappily. She didn't seem to be on to the details, but she knew that he had been hit pretty hard. He was paler and thinner, she said, and he had some kind of a remembrance or keepsake of the lady in a little rosewood box that he kept locked in his desk drawer in his study.

" 'Several times,' says she, 'I've seen him gloomerin' over that box of evenings, and he always locks it up right away if anybody comes into the room.'

"Well, you can imagine how long it was before I got Arthur by the wrist and led him down stage and hissed in his ear.

"That same afternoon we were lazying around in a boat among the waterlilies at the edge of the bay.

" 'Arthur,' says I, 'you never told me you'd had another love-affair. But Mrs. Gurley did,' I went on, to let him know I knew. I hate to hear a man lie.

" 'Before you came,' says he, looking me frankly in the eye, 'there was a previous affection—a strong one. Since you know of it, I will be perfectly candid with you.'

" 'I am waiting,' says I.

" 'My dear Ida,' says Arthur—of course I went by my real name, while I was in Soundport—'this former affection was a spiritual one, in fact. Although the lady aroused my deepest sentiments, and was, as I thought, my ideal woman, I never met her, and never spoke to her. It was an ideal love. My love for you, while no less ideal, is different. You wouldn't let that come between us.'

" 'Was she pretty?' I asked.

" 'She was very beautiful,' said Arthur.

" 'Did you see her often?' I asked.

" 'Something like a dozen times,' says he.

" 'Always from a distance?' says I.

" 'Always from quite a distance,' says he.

" 'And you loved her?' I asked.

" 'She seemed my ideal beauty and grace—and soul,' says Arthur.

" 'And this keepsake that you keep under lock and key, and moon over at times, is that a remembrance from her?'

" 'A memento,' says Arthur, 'that I have treasured.'

" 'Did she send it to you?'

" 'It came from her,' says he.

" 'In a roundabout way?' I asked.

" 'Somewhat roundabout,' says he, 'and yet rather direct.'

" 'Why didn't you ever meet her?' I asked. 'Were your positions in life so different?'

" 'She was far above me,' says Arthur. 'Now, Ida,' he goes on, 'this is all of the past. You're not going to be jealous, are you?'

" 'Jealous!' says I. 'Why, man, what are you talking about? It makes me think ten times as much of you as I did before I knew about it.'

"And it did, Lynn—if you can understand it. That ideal love was a new one on me, but it struck me as being the most beautiful and glorious thing I'd ever heard of. Think of a man loving a woman he'd never even spoken to, and being faithful just to what his mind and heart pictured her! Oh, it sounded great to me. The men I'd always known come at you with either diamonds, knockout drops, or a raise of salary—and their ideals!—well, we'll say no more.

"Yes, it made me think more of Arthur than I did before. I couldn't be jealous of that far-away divinity that he used to worship, for I was going to have him myself. And I began to look upon him as a saint on earth, just as old lady Gurley did.

"About four o'clock this afternoon a man came to the house for Arthur to go and see somebody that was sick among his church bunch. Old lady Gurley was taking her afternoon snore on the couch, so that left me pretty much alone.

"In passing by Arthur's study I looked in, and saw his bunch of keys hanging in the drawer of his desk, where he'd forgotten 'em. Well, I guess we're all to the Mrs. Bluebeard now and then, ain't we, Lynn? I made up my mind I'd have a look at that memento he kept so secret. Not that I cared what it was—it was just curiosity.

"While I was opening the drawer I imagined one or two things it might be. I thought it might be a dried rosebud she'd dropped down to him from a balcony, or maybe a picture of her he'd cut out of a magazine, she being so high up in the world.

"I opened the drawer, and there was the rosewood casket about the size of a gent's collar box. I found the little key in the bunch that fitted it, and raised the lid.

"I took one look at that memento, and then I went to my room and packed my trunk. I threw a few things into my grip, gave my hair a flirt or two with a side-comb, put on my hat, and went in and gave the old lady's foot a kick. I'd tried awfully hard to use proper and correct language while I was there for Arthur's sake, and I had the habit down pat, but it left me then.

" 'Stop sawing gourds,' says I, 'and sit up and take notice. The ghost's about to walk. I'm going away from here, and I owe you eight dollars. The expressman will call for my trunk.'

"I handed her the money.

"'Dear me, Miss Crosby!' said she. 'Is anything wrong? I thought you were pleased here. Dear me, young women are so hard to understand, and so different from what you expect 'em to be.'

"'You're damn right,' says I. 'Some of 'em are. But you can't say that about men. *When you know one man you know 'em all!* That settles the human race question.'

"And then I caught the four-thirty-eight, soft-coal unlimited; and here I am."

"You didn't tell me what was in that box, Lee," said Miss D'Armande, anxiously.

"One of those yellow silk garters that I used to kick off my leg into the audience during that old vaudeville swing act of mine. Is there any of the cocktail left, Lynn?"

The Trimmed Lamp

OF COURSE there are two sides to the question. Let us look at the other. We often hear "shop-girls" spoken of. No such persons exist. There are girls who work in shops. They make their living that way. But why turn their occupation into an adjective? Let us be fair. We do not refer to the girls who live on Fifth Avenue as "marriage-girls."

Lou and Nancy were chums. They came to the big city to find work because there was not enough to eat at their homes to go around. Nancy was nineteen; Lou was twenty. Both were pretty, active country girls who had no ambition to go on the stage.

The little cherub that sits up aloft guided them to a cheap and respectable boarding-house. Both found positions and became wage-earners. They remained chums. It is at the end of six months that I would beg you to step forward and be introduced to them. Maddlesome Reader: My Lady Friends, Miss Nancy and Miss Lou. While you are shaking hands please take notice—cautiously—of their attire. Yes, cautiously; for they are as quick to resent a stare as a lady in a box at the horse show is.

Lou is a piece-work ironer in a hand laundry. She is clothed in a badly fitting purple dress, and her hat plume is four inches too long; but her ermine muff and scarf cost $25, and its fellow beasts will be ticketed in the windows at $7.98 before the season is over. Her cheeks are pink, and her light blue eyes bright. Contentment radiates from her.

Nancy you would call a shop-girl—because you have the habit. There is no type; but a perverse generation is always seeking a type; so this is what the type should be. She has the high-ratted pompadour and the exaggerated straight-front. Her skirt is shoddy, but has the correct flare. No furs protect her against the bitter spring air, but she wears her short broadcloth jacket as jauntily as though it were Persian lamb! On her face and in her eyes, remorseless type-seeker, is the typical shop-girl expression. It is a look of silent but contemptuous revolt against cheated womanhood; of sad prophecy of the vengeance to come. When she laughs her loudest the look is still there. The same look can be seen in the eyes of Russian peasants; and those of us left will see it some day on Gabriel's face when he comes to blow us up. It is a look that should wither and abash man; but he has been known to smirk at it and offer flowers—with a string tied to them.

Now lift your hat and come away, while you receive Lou's cheery "See you again," and the sardonic, sweet smile of Nancy that seems, somehow, to miss you and go fluttering like a white moth up over the housetops to the stars.

The two waited on the corner for Dan. Dan was Lou's steady company. Faithful? Well, he was on hand when Mary would have had to hire a dozen subpoena servers to find her lamb.

"Ain't you cold, Nancy?" said Lou. "Say, what a chump you are for working in that old store for $8 a week! I made $18.50 last week. Of course ironing ain't as swell work as selling lace behind a counter, but it pays. None of us ironers make less than $10. And I don't know that it's any less respectful work, either."

"You can have it," said Nancy, with uplifted nose. "I'll take my eight a week and hall bedroom. I like to be among nice things and swell people. And look what a chance I've got! Why, one of our glove girls married a Pittsburg—a steel maker, or blacksmith or something—the other day worth a million dollars. I'll catch a swell myself some time. I ain't bragging on my looks or anything; but I'll take my chances where there's big prizes offered. What show would a girl have in a laundry?"

"Why, that's where I met Dan," said Lou, triumphantly. "He came in for his Sunday shirt and collars and saw me at the first board, ironing. We all try to get to work at the first board. Ella Maginnis was sick that day, and I had her place. He said he noticed my arms first, how round and white they was. I had my sleeves rolled up. Some nice fellows come into laundries. You can tell 'em by their bringing their clothes in suitcases, and turning in the door sharp and sudden."

"How can you wear a waist like that, Lou?" said Nancy, gazing down at the offending article with sweet scorn in her heavy-lidded eyes. "It shows fierce taste."

"This waist?" said Lou, with wide-eyed indignation. "Why, I paid $16 for this waist. It's worth twenty-five. A woman left it to be laundered, and never called for it. The boss sold it to me. It's got yards and yards of hand embroidery on it. Better talk about that ugly, plain thing you've got on."

"This ugly, plain thing," said Nancy, calmly, "was copied from one that Mrs. Van Alstyne Fisher was wearing. The girls say her bill in the store last year was $12,000. I made mine, myself. It cost me $1.50. Ten feet away you couldn't tell it from hers."

"Oh, well," said Lou, good-naturedly, "if you want to starve and put on airs, go ahead. But I'll take my job and good wages; and after hours give me something as fancy and attractive to wear as I am able to buy."

But just then Dan came—a serious young man with a ready-made necktie, who had escaped the city's brand of frivolity—an electrician earning $30 per week who looked upon Lou with the sad eyes of Romeo, and thought her embroidered waist a web in which any fly should delight to be caught.

"My friend, Mr. Owens—shake hands with Miss Danforth," said Lou.

"I'm mighty glad to know you, Miss Danforth," said Dan, with outstretched hand. "I've heard Lou speak of you so often."

"Thanks," said Nancy, touching his fingers with the tips of her cool ones, "I've heard her mention you—a few times."

Lou giggled.

"Did you get that handshake from Mrs. Van Alstyne Fisher, Nance?" she asked.

"If I did, you can feel safe in copying it," said Nancy.

"Oh, I couldn't use it at all. It's too stylish for me. It's intended to set off diamond rings, that high shake is. Wait till I get a few and then I'll try it."

"Learn it first," said Nancy, wisely, "and you'll be more likely to get the rings."

"Now, to settle this argument," said Dan, with his ready, cheerful smile, "let me make a proposition. As I can't take both of you up to Tiffany's and do the right thing, what do you say to a little vaudeville? I've got the tickets. How about looking at stage diamonds since we can't shake hands with the real sparklers?"

The faithful squire took his place close to the curb; Lou next, a little peacocky in her bright and pretty clothes; Nancy on the inside, slender, and soberly clothed as the sparrow, but with the true Van Alstyne Fisher walk—thus they set out for their evening's moderate diversion.

I do not suppose that many look upon a great department store as an education institution. But the one in which Nancy worked was something like that to her. She was surrounded by beautiful things that breathed of taste and refinement. If you live in an atmosphere of luxury, luxury is yours whether your money pays for it, or another's.

The people she served were mostly women whose dress, manners, and position in the social world were quoted as criterions. From them Nancy began to take toll—the best from each according to her view.

From one she would copy and practise a gesture, from another an eloquent lifting of an eyebrow, from others, a manner of walking, of carrying a purse, of smiling, of greeting a friend, of addressing "inferiors in station." From her best beloved model, Mrs. Van Alstyne Fisher, she made requisition for that excellent thing, a soft, low voice as clear as silver and as perfect in articulation as the notes of a thrush. Suffused in the aura of this high social refinement and good breeding, it was impossible for her to escape a deeper effect of it. As good habits are said to be better than good principles, so, perhaps, good manners are better than good habits. The teachings of your parents may not keep alive your New England conscience; but if you sit on a straight-back chair and repeat the words "prisms and pilgrims" forty times the devil will flee from you. And when Nancy spoke in the Van Alstyne Fisher tones she felt the thrill of *noblesse oblige* to her very bones.

There was another source of learning in the great departmental school. Whenever you see three or four shop-girls gather in a bunch and jingle their wire bracelets as an accompaniment to apparently frivolous conversation, do not think that they are there for the purpose of criticizing the way Ethel does her back hair. The meeting may lack the dignity of the deliberative bodies of man; but it has all the importance of the occasion on which Eve and her first daughter first put their heads together to make Adam understand his proper place in the household. It is Woman's Conference for Common Defense and Exchange of Strategical Theories of Attack and Repulse upon and against the World, which is a Stage, and Man, its Audience who Persists in Throwing Bouquets Thereupon. Woman, the most helpless of the young of any animal—with the fawn's grace but without its fleetness; with the bird's beauty but without its power of flight; with the honeybee's burden of sweetness but without its—— Oh, let's drop that simile—some of us may have been stung.

During this council of war they pass weapons one to another, and exchange stratagems that each has devised and formulated out of the tactics of life.

"I says to 'im," says Sadie, "ain't you the fresh thing! Who do you suppose I am, to be addressing such a remark to me? And what do you think he says back to me?"

The heads, brown, black, flaxen, red, and yellow bob together; the answer is given; and the parry to the thrust is decided upon, to be used by each thereafter in passages-at-arms with the common enemy, man.

Thus Nancy learned the art of defense; and to women successful defense means victory.

The curriculum of a department store is a wide one. Perhaps no other college could have fitted her as well for her life's ambition—the drawing of a matrimonial prize.

Her station in the store was a favored one. The music room was near enough for her to hear and become familiar with the works of the best composers—at least to acquire the familiarity that passed for appreciation in the social world in which she was vaguely trying to set a tentative and aspiring foot. She absorbed the educating influence of art wares, of costly and dainty fabrics, of adornments that are almost culture to women.

The other girls soon became aware of Nancy's ambition. "Here comes your millionaire, Nancy," they would call to her whenever any man who looked the rôle approached her counter. It got to be a habit of men, who were hanging about while their women folk were shopping, to stroll over to the handkerchief counter and dawdle over the cambric squares. Nancy's imitation high-bred air and genuine dainty beauty was what attracted. Many men thus came to display their graces before her. Some of them may have been millionaires; others were certainly no more than their sedulous apes. Nancy learned to discriminate. There was a window at the end of the handkerchief counter; and she could see the rows of vehicles waiting for the shoppers in the street below. She looked and perceived that automobiles differ as well as do their owners.

Once a fascinating gentleman bought four dozen handkerchiefs, and wooed her across the counter with a King Cophetua air. When he had gone one of the girls said:

"What's wrong, Nance, that you didn't warm up to that fellow? He looks the swell article, all right, to me."

"Him?" said Nancy, with her coolest, sweetest, most impersonal, Van Alstyne Fisher smile; "not for mine. I saw him drive up outside. A 12 H. P. machine and an Irish chauffeur! And you saw what kind of handkerchiefs he bought—silk! And he's got dactylis on him. Give me the real thing or nothing, if you please."

Two of the most "refined" women in the store—a forelady and a cashier—had a few "swell gentlemen friends" with whom they now and then dined. Once they included Nancy in an invitation. The dinner took place in a spectacular café whose tables are engaged for New Year's Eve a year in advance. There were two "gentlemen friends"—one without any hair on his head—high living ungrew it; and we can prove it—the other a young man whose worth and sophistication he impressed upon you in two convincing ways—he swore that all the wine was corked; and he wore diamond cuff buttons. This young man perceived irresistible excellencies in Nancy. His taste ran to shop-girls; and here was one that added the voice and manners of her own high social world to the franker charms of her own caste. So, on the following day, he appeared in the store and made her a serious proposal of marriage over a box of hemstitched, grass-bleached Irish linens. Nancy declined. A brown pompadour ten feet away had been using her eyes and ears. When the rejected suitor had gone she heaped carboys of upbraidings and horror upon Nancy's head.

"What a terrible little fool you are! That fellow's a millionaire —he's a nephew of old Van Skittles himself. And he was talking on the level, too. Have you gone crazy, Nance?"

"Have I?" said Nancy. "I didn't take him, did I? He isn't a millionaire so hard that you could notice it, anyhow. His family only allows him $20,000 a year to spend. The bald-headed fellow was guying him about it the other night at supper."

The brown pompadour came nearer and narrowed her eyes.

"Say, what do you want?" she inquired, in a voice hoarse for lack of chewing-gum. "Ain't that enough for you? Do you want to be a Mormon, and marry Rockefeller and Gladstone Dowie and the King of Spain and the whole bunch? Ain't $20,000 a year good enough for you?"

Nancy flushed a little under the level gaze of the black, shallow eyes.

"It wasn't altogether the money, Carrie," she explained. "His friend caught him in a rank lie the other night at dinner. It was about some girl he said he hadn't been to the theater with. Well, I can't stand a liar. Put everything together—I don't like him; and that settles it. When I sell out it's not going to be on any bargain day. I've got to have something that sits up in a chair like a man, anyhow. Yes. I'm looking out for a catch; but it's got to be able to do something more than make a noise like a toy bank."

"The physiopathic ward for yours!" said the brown pompadour, walking away.

These high ideas, if not ideals—Nancy continued to cultivate on $8 per week. She bivouacked on the trail of the great unknown "catch" eating her dry bread and tightening her belt day by day. On her face was the faint, soldierly, sweet, grim smile of the pre-ordained man-hunter. The store was her forest; and many times she raised her rifle at game that seemed broad-antlered and big; but always some deep unerring instinct—perhaps of the huntress, perhaps of the woman—made her hold her fire and take up the trail again.

Lou flourished in the laundry. Out of her $18.50 per week she paid $6 for her room and board. The rest went mainly for clothes. Her opportunities for bettering her taste and manners were few compared with Nancy's. In the steaming laundry there was nothing but work, work and her thoughts of the evening pleasures to come. Many costly and showy fabrics passed under her iron; and it may be that her growing fondness for dress was thus transmitted to her through the conducting metal.

When the day's work was over Dan awaited her outside, her faithful shadow in whatever light she stood.

Sometimes he cast an honest and troubled glance at Lou's clothes that increased in conspicuity rather than in style; but this was no disloyalty; he deprecated the attention they called to her in the streets.

And Lou was no less faithful to her chum. There was a law that Nancy should go with them on whatsoever outings they might take. Dan bore the extra burden heartily and in good cheer. It might be said that Lou furnished the color, Nancy the tone, and Dan the weight of the distraction-seeking trio. The escort, in his neat but obviously ready-made suit, his ready-made tie and unfailing, genial, ready-made wit never startled or clashed. He was of that good kind that you are likely to forget while they are present, but remember distinctly after they are gone.

To Nancy's superior taste the flavor of these ready-made pleasures was sometimes a little bitter: but she was young; and youth is a gourmand, when it cannot be a gourmet.

"Dan is always wanting me to marry him right away," Lou told her once. "But why should I? I'm independent. I can do as I please with the money I earn; and he never would agree for me to keep on working afterward. And say, Nance, what do you want to stick to that old store for, and half starve and half dress yourself? I could get you a place in the laundry right now if you'd come. It seems to me that you could afford to be a little less stuck-up if you could make a good deal more money."

"I don't think I'm stuck-up, Lou," said Nancy, "But I'd rather live on half rations and stay where I am. I suppose I've got the habit. It's the chance that I want. I don't expect to be always behind a counter. I'm learning something new every day. I'm right up against refined and rich people all the time—even if I do only wait on them; and I'm not missing any pointers that I see passing around."

"Caught your millionaire yet?" asked Lou with her teasing laugh.

"I haven't selected one yet," answered Nancy. "I've been looking them over."

"Goodness! the idea of picking over 'em! Don't you ever let

one get by you, Nance—even if he's a few dollars shy. But of course you're joking—millionaires don't think about working girls like us."

"It might be better for them if they did," said Nancy, with cool wisdom. "Some of us could teach them how to take care of their money."

"If one was to speak to me," laughed Lou, "I know I'd have a duck-fit."

"That's because you don't know any. The only difference between swells and other people is you have to watch 'em closer. Don't you think that red silk lining is just a little bit too bright for that coat, Lou?"

Lou looked at the plain, dull olive jacket of her friend.

"Well, no, I don't—but it may seem so beside that faded-looking thing you've got on."

"This jacket," said Nancy, complacently, "has exactly the cut and fit of one that Mrs. Van Alstyne Fisher was wearing the other day. The material cost me $3.98. I suppose hers cost about $100 more."

"Oh, well," said Lou, lightly, "it don't strike me as millionaire bait. Shouldn't wonder if I catch one before you do, anyway."

Truly it would have taken a philosopher to decide upon the values of the theories held by the two friends. Lou, lacking that certain pride and fastidiousness that keeps stores and desks filled with girls working for the barest living, thumped away gaily with her iron in the noisy and stifling laundry. Her wages supported her even beyond the point of comfort; so that her dress profited until sometimes she cast a sidelong glance of impatience at the neat but inelegant apparel of Dan—Dan the constant, the immutable, the undeviating.

As for Nancy, her case was one of tens of thousands. Silk and jewels and laces and ornaments and the perfume and music of the fine world of good-breeding and taste—these were made for woman; they are her equitable portion. Let her keep near them if they are a part of life to her, and if she will. She is no traitor to herself, as Esau was; for she keeps her birthright and the pottage she earns is often very scant.

In this atmosphere Nancy belonged; and she throve in it and ate her frugal meals and schemed over her cheap dresses with a determined and contented mind. She already knew woman; and she was studying man, the animal, both as to his habits and eligibility. Some day she would bring down the game that she wanted; but she promised herself it would be what seemed to her the biggest and the best, and nothing smaller.

Thus she kept her lamp trimmed and burning to receive the bridegroom when he should come.

But another lesson she learned, perhaps unconsciously. Her standard of values began to shift and change. Sometimes the dollar-mark grew blurred in her mind's eye, and shaped itself into letters that spelled such words as "truth" and "honor" and now and then just "kindness." Let us make a likeness of one who hunts the moose or elk in some mighty wood. He sees a little dell, mossy and embowered, where a rill trickles, babbling to him of rest and comfort. At these times the spear of Nimrod himself grows blunt.

So, Nancy wondered sometimes if Persian lamb was always quoted at its market value by the hearts that it covered.

One Thursday evening Nancy left the store and turned across Sixth Avenue westward to the laundry. She was expected to go with Lou and Dan to a musical comedy.

Dan was just coming out of the laundry when she arrived. There was a queer, strained look on his face.

"I thought I would drop around to see if they had heard from her," he said.

"Heard from who?" asked Nancy. "Isn't Lou there?"

"I thought you knew," said Dan. "She hasn't been here or at the house where she lived since Monday. She moved all her things from there. She told one of the girls in the laundry she might be going to Europe."

"Hasn't anybody seen her anywhere?" asked Nancy.

Dan looked at her with his jaws set grimly, and a steely gleam in his steady gray eyes.

"They told me in the laundry," he said, harshly, "that they saw her pass yesterday—in an automobile. With one of the millionaires, I suppose, that you and Lou were forever busying your brains about."

For the first time Nancy quailed before a man. She laid her hand that trembled slightly on Dan's sleeve.

"You've no right to say such a thing to me, Dan—as if I had anything to do with it!"

"I didn't mean it that way," said Dan, softening. He fumbled in his vest pocket.

"I've got the tickets for the show to-night," he said, with a gallant show of lightness. "If you——"

Nancy admired pluck whenever she saw it.

"I'll go with you, Dan," she said.

Three months went by before Nancy saw Lou again.

At twilight one evening the shop-girl was hurrying home along the border of a little quiet park. She heard her name called, and wheeled about in time to catch Lou rushing into her arms.

After the first embrace they drew their heads back as serpents do, ready to attack or to charm, with a thousand questions trembling on their swift tongues. And then Nancy noticed that prosperity had descended upon Lou, manifesting itself in costly furs, flashing gems, and creations of the tailor's art.

"You little fool!" cried Lou, loudly and affectionately. "I see you are still working in that store, and as shabby as ever. And how about that big catch you were going to make—nothing doing yet, I suppose?"

And then Lou looked, and saw that something better than prosperity had descended upon Nancy—something that shone brighter than gems in her eyes and redder than a rose in her cheeks, and that danced like electricity anxious to be loosed from the tip of her tongue.

"Yes, I'm still in the store," said Nancy, "but I'm going to leave it next week. I've made my catch—the biggest catch in the world. You won't mind now Lou, will you?—I'm going to be married to Dan—to Dan!—he's my Dan now—why, Lou!"

Around the corner of the park strolled one of those new-crop, smooth-faced young policemen that are making the force more endurable—at least to the eye. He saw a woman with an expensive fur coat and diamond-ringed hands crouching down against the iron fence of the park sobbing turbulently, while a slender, plainly dressed working girl leaned close, trying to console her. But the Gibsonian cop, being of the new order, passed on, pretending not to notice, for he was wise enough to know that these matters are beyond help so far as the power he represents is concerned, though he rap the pavement with his nightstick till the sound goes up to the furthermost stars.

Two Thanksgiving Day Gentlemen

THERE IS one day that is ours. There is one day when all we Americans who are not self-made go back to the old home to eat saleratus biscuits and marvel how much nearer to the porch the old pump looks than it used to. Bless the day. President Roosevelt gives it to us. We hear some talk of the Puritans, but don't just remember who they were. Bet we can lick 'em, anyhow, if they try to land again. Plymouth Rocks? Well, that sounds more familiar. Lots of us have had to come down to hens since the Turkey Trust got its work in. But somebody in Washington is leaking out advance information to 'em about these Thanksgiving proclamations.

The big city east of the cranberry bogs has made Thanksgiving Day an institution. The last Thursday in November is the only day in the year on which it recognizes the part of America lying across the ferries. It is the one day that is purely American. Yes, a day of celebration, exclusively American.

And now for the story which is to prove to you that we have traditions on this side of the ocean that are becoming older at a much rapider rate than those of England are—thanks to our git-up and enterprise.

Stuffy Pete took his seat on the third bench to the right as you enter Union Square from the east, at the walk opposite the fountain. Every Thanksgiving Day for nine years he had taken his seat there promptly at 1 o'clock. For every time he had done so things had happened to him—Charles Dickensy things that swelled his waistcoat above his heart, and equally on the other side.

But to-day Stuffy Pete's appearance at the annual trysting place seemed to have been rather the result of habit than of the yearly hunger which, as the philanthropists seem to think, afflicts the poor at such extended intervals.

Certainly Pete was not hungry. He had just come from a feast that had left him of his powers barely those of respiration and locomotion. His eyes were like two pale gooseberries firmly imbedded in a swollen and gravy-smeared mask of putty. His breath came in short wheezes; a senatorial roll of adipose tissue denied a fashionable set to his upturned coat collar. Buttons that had been sewed upon his clothes by kind Salvation fingers a week before flew like pop-corn, strewing the earth around him. Ragged he was, with a split shirt front open to the wishbone; but the November breeze, carrying fine snowflakes, brought him only a grateful coolness. For Stuffy Pete was overcharged with the caloric produced by a super-bountiful dinner, beginning with oysters and ending with plum pudding, and including (it seemed to him) all the roast turkey and baked potatoes and chicken salad and squash pie and ice cream in the world. Wherefore he sat, gorged, and gazed upon the world with after-dinner contempt.

The meal had been an unexpected one. He was passing a red brick mansion near the beginning of Fifth Avenue, in which lived two old ladies of ancient family and a reverence for traditions. They even denied the existence of New York, and believed that Thanksgiving Day was declared solely for Washington Square. One of their traditional habits was to station a servant at the postern gate with orders to admit the first hungry wayfarer that came along after the hour of noon had struck, and banquet him to a finish. Stuffy Pete happened to pass by on his way to the park, and the seneschals gathered him in and upheld the custom of the castle.

After Stuffy Pete had gazed straight before him for ten minutes he was conscious of a desire for a more varied field of vision. With a tremendous effort he moved his head slowly to the left. And then his eyes bulged out fearfully, and his breath ceased, and the rough-shod ends of his short legs wriggled and rustled on the gravel.

For the Old Gentleman was coming across Fourth Avenue toward his bench.

Every Thanksgiving Day for nine years the Old Gentleman had come there and found Stuffy Pete on his bench. That was a thing that the Old Gentleman was trying to make a tradition of. Every Thanksgiving Day for nine years he had found Stuffy there, and had led him to a restaurant and watched him eat a big dinner. They do those things in England unconsciously. But this is a young country, and nine years is not so bad. The Old Gentleman was a stanch American patriot, and considered himself a pioneer in American tradition. In order to become picturesque we must keep on doing one thing for a long time without ever letting it get away from us. Something like collecting the weekly dimes in industrial insurance. Or cleaning the streets.

The Old Gentleman moved, straight and stately, toward the Institution that he was rearing. Truly, the annual feeding of Stuffy Pete was nothing national in its character, such as the Magna Charta or jam for breakfast was in England. But it was a step. It was almost feudal. It showed, at least, that a Custom was not impossible to New Y—ahem!—America.

The Old Gentleman was thin and tall and sixty. He was dressed all in black, and wore the old-fashioned kind of glasses that won't stay on your nose. His hair was whiter and thinner than it had been last year, and he seemed to make more use of his big, knobby cane with the crooked handle.

As his established benefactor came up Stuffy wheezed and shuddered like some woman's over-fat pug when a street dog bristles up at him. He would have flown, but all the skill of Santos-Dumont could not have separated him from his bench. Well had the myrmidons of the two old ladies done their work.

"Good morning," said the Old Gentleman. "I am glad to perceive that the vicissitudes of another year have spared you to move in health about the beautiful world. For that blessing alone this day of thanksgiving is well proclaimed to each of us. If you will come with me, my man, I will provide you with a dinner that should make your physical being accord with the mental."

That is what the Old Gentleman said every time. Every Thanksgiving Day for nine years. The words themselves almost formed an Institution. Nothing could be compared with them except the Declaration of Independence. Always before they had been music in Stuffy's ears. But now he looked up at the Old Gentleman's face with tearful agony in his own. The fine snow almost sizzled when it fell upon his perspiring brow. But the Old Gentleman shivered a little and turned his back to the wind.

Stuffy had always wondered why the Old Gentleman spoke his speech rather sadly. He did not know that it was because he was wishing every time that he had a son to succeed him. A son who would come there after he was gone—a son who would stand proud and strong before some subsequent Stuffy, and say: "In memory of my father." Then it would be an Institution.

But the Old Gentleman had no relatives. He lived in rented rooms in one of the decayed old family brownstone mansions in one of the quiet streets east of the park. In the winter he raised fuchsias in a little conservatory the size of a steamer trunk. In the spring he walked in the Easter parade. In the summer he lived at a farmhouse in the New Jersey hills, and sat in a wicker armchair, speaking of a butterfly, the ornithoptera amphrisius, that he hoped to find some day. In the autumn he fed Stuffy a dinner. These were the Old Gentleman's occupations.

Stuffy Pete looked up at him for a half minute, stewing and helpless in his own self-pity. The Old Gentleman's eyes were bright with the giving-pleasure. His face was getting more lined each year, but his little black necktie was in as jaunty a bow as ever, and his linen was beautiful and white, and his gray mustache was curled gracefully at the ends. And then Stuffy made a noise that sounded like peas bubbling in a pot. Speech was intended;

and as the Old Gentleman had heard the sounds nine times before, he rightly construed them into Stuffy's old formula of acceptance.

"Thankee, sir. I'll go with ye, and much obliged. I'm very hungry, sir."

The coma of repletion had not prevented from entering Stuffy's mind the conviction that he was the basis of an Institution. His Thanksgiving appetite was not his own; it belonged by all the sacred rights of established custom, if not by the actual Statute of Limitations, to this kind old gentleman who had preëmpted it. True, America is free; but in order to establish tradition some one must be a repetend—a repeating decimal. The heroes are not all heroes of steel and gold. See one here that wielded only weapons of iron, badly silvered, and tin.

The Old Gentleman led his annual protégé southward to the restaurant, and to the table where the feast had always occurred. They were recognized.

"Here comes de old guy," said a waiter, "dat blows dat same bum to a meal every Thanksgiving."

The Old Gentleman sat across the table glowing like a smoked pearl at his corner-stone of future ancient Tradition. The waiters heaped the table with holiday food—and Stuffy, with a sigh that was mistaken for hunger's expression, raised knife and fork and carved for himself a crown of imperishable bay.

No more valiant hero ever fought his way through the ranks of an enemy. Turkey, chops, soups, vegetables, pies, disappeared before him as fast as they could be served. Gorged nearly to the uttermost when he entered the restaurant, the smell of food had almost caused him to lose his honor as a gentleman, but he rallied like a true knight. He saw the look of beneficent happiness on the Old Gentleman's face—a happier look than even the fuchsias and the ornithoptera amphrisius had ever brought to it—and he had not the heart to see it wane.

In an hour Stuffy leaned back with a battle won.

"Thankee kindly, sir," he puffed like a leaky steam pipe; "thankee kindly for a hearty meal."

Then he arose heavily with glazed eyes and started toward the kitchen. A waiter turned him about like a top, and pointed him toward the door. The Old Gentleman carefully counted out $1.30 in silver change, leaving three nickels for the waiter.

They parted as they did each year at the door, the Old Gentleman going south, Stuffy north.

Around the first corner Stuffy turned, and stood for one minute. Then he seemed to puff out his rags as an owl puffs out his feathers, and fell to the sidewalk like a sunstricken horse.

When the ambulance came the young surgeon and the driver cursed softly at his weight. There was no smell of whiskey to justify a transfer to the patrol wagon, so Stuffy and his two dinners went to the hospital. There they stretched him on a bed and began to test him for strange diseases, with the hope of getting a chance at some problem with the bare steel.

And lo! an hour later another ambulance brought the Old Gentleman. And they laid him on another bed and spoke of appendicitis, for he looked good for the bill.

But pretty soon one of the young doctors met one of the young nurses whose eyes he liked, and stopped to chat with her about the cases.

"That nice old gentleman over there, now," he said, "you wouldn't think that was a case of almost starvation. Proud old family, I guess. He told me he hadn't eaten a thing for three days."

The Making of a New Yorker

BESIDES MANY THINGS, Raggles was a poet. He was called a tramp; but that was only an elliptical way of saying that he was a philosopher, an artist, a traveller, a naturalist, and a discoverer. But most of all he was a poet. In all his life he never wrote a line of verse; he lived his poetry. His Odyssey would have been a Limerick, had it been written. But, to linger with the primary proposition, Raggles was a poet.

Raggles's specialty, had he been driven to ink and paper, would have been sonnets to the cities. He studied cities as women study their reflections in mirrors; as children study the glue and sawdust of a dislocated doll; as the men who write about wild animals study the cages in the zoo. A city to Raggles was not merely a pile of bricks and mortar, peopled by a certain number of inhabitants; it was a thing with soul characteristic and distinct; an individual conglomeration of life, with its own peculiar essence, flavor, and feeling. Two thousand miles to the north and south, east and west, Raggles wandered in poetic fervor, taking the cities to his breast. He footed it on dusty roads, or sped magnificently in freight cars, counting time as of no account. And when he had found the heart of a city and listened to its secret confession, he strayed on, restless, to another. Fickle Raggles!—but perhaps he had not met the civic corporation that could engage and hold his critical fancy.

Through the ancient poets we have learned that the cities are feminine. So they were to poet Raggles; and his mind carried a concrete and clear conception of the figure that symbolized and typified each one that he had wooed.

Chicago seemed to swoop down upon him with a breezy suggestion of Mrs. Partington, plumes and patchouli, and to disturb his rest with a soaring and beautiful song of future promise. But Raggles would awake to a sense of shivering cold and a haunting impression of ideals lost in a depressing aura of potato salad and fish.

Thus Chicago affected him. Perhaps there is a vagueness and inaccuracy in the description; but that is Raggles's fault. He should have recorded his sensations in magazine poems.

Pittsburg impressed him as the play of "Othello" performed in the Russian language in a railroad station by Dockstader's minstrels. A royal and generous lady this Pittsburg, though—homely, hearty, with flushed face, washing the dishes in a silk dress and white kid slippers, and bidding Raggles sit before the roaring fireplace and drink champagne with his pigs' feet and fried potatoes.

New Orleans had simply gazed down upon him from a balcony. He could see her pensive, starry eyes and catch the flutter of her fan, and that was all. Only once he came face to face with her. It was at dawn, when she was flushing the red bricks of the banquette with a pail of water. She laughed and hummed a chansonette and filled Raggles's shoes with ice-cold water. Allons!

Boston construed herself to the poetic Raggles in an erratic and singular way. It seemed to him that he had drunk cold tea and that the city was a white, cold cloth that had been bound tightly around his brow to spur him to some unknown but tremendous mental effort. And, after all, he came to shovel snow for a livelihood; and the cloth, becoming wet, tightened its knots and could not be removed.

Indefinite and unintelligible ideas, you will say; but your disapprobation should be tempered with gratitude, for these are poets' fancies—and suppose you had come upon them in verse!

One day Raggles came and laid siege to the heart of the great city of Manhattan. She was the greatest of all; and he wanted to learn her note in the scale; to taste and appraise and classify and solve and label her and arrange her with the other cities that had given him up the secret of their individuality. And here we cease to be Raggles's translator and become his chronicler.

Raggles landed from a ferry-boat one morning and walked into the core of the town with the blasé air of a cosmopolite. He was dressed with care to play the rôle of an "unidentified man." No country, race, class, clique, union, party clan, or bowling association could have claimed him. His clothing, which had been donated to him piece-meal by citizens of different height, but same number of inches around the heart, was not yet as uncomfortable to his figure as those specimens of raiment, self-measured, that are railroaded to you by transcontinental tailors with a suit case, suspenders, silk handkerchief and pearl studs as a bonus. Without money—as a poet should be—but with the ardor of an astronomer discovering a new star in the chorus of the milky way, or a man who has seen ink suddenly flow from his fountain pen, Raggles wandered into the great city.

Late in the afternoon he drew out of the roar and commotion with a look of dumb terror on his countenance. He was defeated, puzzled, discomfited, frightened. Other cities had been to him as long primer to read; as country maidens quickly to fathom; as send-price-of-subscription-with-answer rebuses to solve; as oyster cocktails to swallow; but here was one as cold, glittering, serene, impossible as a four-carat diamond in a window to a lover outside fingering damply in his pocket his ribbon-counter salary.

The greetings of the other cities he had known—their homespun kindliness, their human gamut of rough charity, friendly curses, garrulous curiosity, and easily estimated credulity or indifference. This city of Manhattan gave him no clue; it was walled against him. Like a river of adamant it flowed past him in the streets. Never an eye was turned upon him; no voice spoke to him. His heart yearned for the clap of Pittsburg's sooty hand on his shoulder; for Chicago's menacing but social yawp in his ear; for the pale and eleemosynary stare through the Bostonian eyeglass—even for the precipitate but unmalicious boot-toe of Louisville or St. Louis.

On Broadway Raggles, successful suitor of many cities, stood, bashful, like any country swain. For the first time he experienced the poignant humiliation of being ignored. And when he tried to reduce this brilliant, swiftly changing, ice-cold city to a formula he failed utterly. Poet though he was, it offered him no color similes, no points of comparison, no flaw in its polished facets, no handle by which he could hold it up and view its shape and structure, as he familiarly and often contemptuously had done with other towns. The houses were interminable ramparts loopholed for defence; the people were bright but bloodless spectres passing in sinister and selfish array.

The thing that weighed heaviest on Raggles's soul and clogged his poet's fancy was the spirit of absolute egotism that seemed to saturate the people as toys are saturated with paint. Each one that he considered appeared a monster of abominable and insolent conceit. Humanity was gone from them; they were toddling idols of stone and varnish, worshipping themselves and greedy for though oblivious of worship from their fellow graven images. Frozen, cruel, implacable, impervious, cut to an identical pattern, they hurried on their ways like statues brought by some miracle to motion, while soul and feeling lay unaroused in the reluctant marble.

Gradually Raggles became conscious of certain types. One was an elderly gentleman with a snow-white, short beard, pink, unwrinkled face, and stony, sharp blue eyes, attired in the fashion of a gilded youth, who seemed to personify the city's wealth, ripeness and frigid unconcern. Another type was a woman, tall, beautiful, clear as a steel engraving, goddess-like, calm, clothed like the princesses of old, with eyes as coldly blue as the reflection of sunlight on a glacier. And another was a by-product of this town of marionettes—a broad, swaggering, grim, threateningly sedate fellow, with a jowl as large as a harvested wheat field, the complexion of a baptized infant, and the knuckles of a prize-fighter. This type leaned against cigar signs and viewed the world with frappéd contumely.

A poet is a sensitive creature, and Raggles soon shriveled in the bleak embrace of the undecipherable. The chill, sphinx-like, ironical, illegible, unnatural, ruthless expression of the city left him downcast and bewildered. Had it no heart? Better the woodpile, the scolding of vinegar-faced housewives at back doors, the kindly spleen of bartenders behind provincial free-lunch counters, the amiable truculence of rural constables, the kicks, arrests, and happy-go-lucky chances of the other vulgar, loud, crude cities than this freezing heartlessness.

Raggles summoned his courage and sought alms from the populace. Unheeding, regardless, they passed on without the wink of an eyelash to testify that they were conscious of his existence. And then he said to himself that this fair but pitiless city of Manhattan was without a soul; that its inhabitants were mannikins moved by wires and springs, and that he was alone in a great wilderness.

Raggles started to cross the street. There was a blast, a roar, a hissing and a crash as something struck him and hurled him over and over six yards from where he had been. As he was coming down like the stick of a rocket the earth and all the cities thereof turned to a fractured dream.

Raggles opened his eyes. First an odor made itself known to him—an odor of the earliest spring flowers of Paradise. And then a hand soft as a falling petal touched his brow. Bending over him was the woman clothed like the princess of old, with blue eyes, now soft and humid with human sympathy. Under his head on the pavement were silks and furs. With Raggles's hat in his hand and with his face pinker than ever from a vehement outburst of oratory against reckless driving, stood the elderly gentleman who personified the city's wealth and ripeness. From a near-by café hurried the by-product with the vast jowl and baby complexion, bearing a glass full of crimson fluid that suggested delightful possibilities.

"Drink dis, sport," said the by-product, holding the glass to Raggles's lips.

Hundreds of people huddled around in a moment, their faces wearing the deepest concern. Two flattering and gorgeous policemen got into the circle and pressed back the overplus of Samaritans. An old lady in a black shawl spoke loudly of camphor; a newsboy slipped one of his papers beneath Raggles's elbow, where it lay on the muddy pavement. A brisk young man with a notebook was asking for names.

A bell clanged importantly, and the ambulance cleaned a lane through the crowd. A cool surgeon slipped into the midst of affairs.

"How do you feel, old man?" asked the surgeon, stooping easily to his task. The princess of silks and satins wiped a red drop or two from Raggles's brow with a fragrant cobweb.

"Me?" said Raggles, with a seraphic smile, "I feel fine."

He had found the heart of his new city.

In three days they let him leave his cot for the convalescent ward in the hospital. He had been in there an hour when the attendants heard sounds of conflict. Upon investigation they found that Raggles had assaulted and damaged a brother convalescent—a glowering transient whom a freight train collision had sent in to be patched up.

"What's all this about?" inquired the head nurse.

"He was runnin' down me town," said Raggles.

"What town?" asked the nurse.

"Noo York," said Raggles.

A *Harlem* Tragedy

HARLEM.

Mrs. Fink had dropped into Mrs. Cassidy's flat one flight below.

"Ain't it a beaut?" said Mrs. Cassidy.

She turned her face proudly for her friend Mrs. Fink to see. One eye was nearly closed, with a great, greenish-purple bruise around it. Her lip was cut and bleeding a little and there were red finger-marks on each side of her neck.

"My husband wouldn't ever think of doing that to me," said Mrs. Fink, concealing her envy.

"I wouldn't have a man," declared Mrs. Cassidy, "that didn't beat me up at least once a week. Shows he thinks something of you. Say! but that last dose Jack gave me wasn't no homeopathic one. I can see stars yet. But he'll be the sweetest man in town for the rest of the week to make up for it. This eye is good for theater tickets and a silk shirt waist at the very least."

"I should hope," said Mrs. Fink, assuming complacency, "that Mr. Fink is too much of a gentleman ever to raise his hand against me."

"Oh, go on, Maggie!" said Mrs. Cassidy, laughing and applying witch hazel, "you're only jealous. Your old man is too frappéed and slow to ever give you a punch. He just sits down and practises physical culture with a newspaper when he comes home—now ain't that the truth?"

"Mr. Fink certainly peruses of the papers when he comes home," acknowledged Mrs. Fink, with a toss of her head; "but he certainly don't ever make no Steve O'Donnell out of me just to amuse himself—that's a sure thing."

Mrs. Cassidy laughed the contented laugh of the guarded and happy matron. With the air of Cornelia exhibiting her jewels, she drew down the collar of her kimono and revealed another treasured bruise, maroon-colored, edged with olive and orange—a bruise now nearly well, but still to memory dear.

Mrs. Fink capitulated. The formal light in her eye softened to envious admiration. She and Mrs. Cassidy had been chums in the downtown paper-box factory before they had married, one year before. Now she and her man occupied the flat above Mame and her man. Therefore she could not put on airs with Mame.

"Don't it hurt when he soaks you?" asked Mrs. Fink, curiously.

"Hurt!"—Mrs. Cassidy gave a soprano scream of delight. "Well, say—did you ever have a brick house fall on you?—well, that's just the way it feels—just like when they're digging you out of the ruins. Jack's got a left that spells two matinées and a new pair of Oxfords—and his right!—well, it takes a trip to Coney and six pairs of openwork silk lisle threads to make that good."

"But what does he beat you for?" inquired Mrs. Fink, with wide-open eyes.

"Silly!" said Mrs. Cassidy, indulgently. "Why, because he's full. It's generally on Saturday nights."

"But what cause do you give him?" persisted the seeker after knowledge.

"Why, didn't I marry him? Jack comes in tanked up; and I'm here, ain't I? Who else has he got a right to beat? I'd just like to catch him once beating anybody else! Sometimes it's because supper ain't ready; and sometimes it's because it is. Jack ain't particular about causes. He just lushes till he remembers he's married, and then he makes for home and does me up. Saturday nights I just move the furniture with sharp corners out of the way, so I won't cut my head when he gets his work in. He's got a left swing that jars you! Sometimes I take the count in the first round; but when I feel like having a good time during the week or want some new rags I come up again for more punishment. That's what I done last night. Jack knows I've been wanting a black silk waist for a month, and I didn't think just one black eye would bring it. Tell you what, Mag, I'll bet you the ice cream he brings it to-night."

Mrs. Fink was thinking deeply.

"My Mart," she said, "never hit me a lick in his life. It's just like you said, Mame; he comes in grouchy and ain't got a word to say. He never takes me out anywhere. He's a chair-warmer at home for fair. He buys me things, but he looks so glum about it that I never appreciate 'em."

Mrs. Cassidy slipped an arm around her chum.

"You poor thing!" she said. "But everybody can't have a husband like Jack. Marriage wouldn't be no failure if they was all like him. These discontented wives you hear about—what they need is a man to come home and kick their slats in once a week, and then make it up in kisses, and chocolate creams. That'd give 'em some interest in life. What I want is a masterful man that slugs you when he's jagged and hugs you when he ain't jagged. Preserve me from the man that ain't got the sand to do neither!"

Mrs. Fink sighed.

The hallways were suddenly filled with sound. The door flew open at the kick of Mr. Cassidy. His arms were occupied with bundles. Mame flew and hung about his neck. Her sound eye sparkled with the love light that shines in the eye of the Maori maid when she recovers consciousness in the hut of the wooer who has stunned and dragged her there.

"Hello, old girl!" shouted Mr. Cassidy. He shed his bundles and lifted her off her feet in a mighty hug. "I got tickets for Barnum & Bailey's, and if you'll bust the string of one of them bundles I guess you'll find that silk waist—why, good evening, Mrs. Fink—I didn't see you at first. How's old Mart coming along?"

"He's very well, Mr. Cassidy—thanks," said Mrs. Fink. "I must

500 Tales of O. Henry

be going along up now. Mart'll be home for supper soon. I'll
bring you down the pattern you want to-morrow, Mame."

Mrs. Fink went up to her flat and had a little cry. It was a mean-
ingless cry, the kind of cry that only a woman knows about,
a cry from no particular cause, altogether an absurd cry; the
most transient and the most hopeless cry in the repertory of
grief. Why had Martin never thrashed her? He was as big and
strong as Jack Cassidy. Did he not care for her at all? He never
quarrelled; he came home and lounged about silent, glum, idle.
He was a fairly good provider, but he ignored the spices of life.

Mrs. Fink's ship of dreams was becalmed. Her captain ranged between plum duff and his hammock. If only he would shiver his
timbers or stamp his foot on the quarter-deck now and then!
And she had thought to sail so merrily, touching at ports in
the Delectable Isles! But now, to vary the figure, she was ready to
throw up the sponge, tired out, without a scratch to show for all
those tame rounds with her sparring partner. For one moment
she almost hated Mame—Mame, with her cuts and bruises, her
salve of presents and kisses; her stormy voyage with her fighting,
brutal, loving mate.

Mr. Fink came home at 7. He was permeated with the curse of
domesticity. Beyond the portals of his cozy home he cared not to
roam, to roam. He was the man who had caught the street car,
the anaconda that had swallowed its prey, the tree that lay as it
had fallen.

"Like the supper, Mart?" asked Mrs. Fink, who had striven over
it.

"M-m-m-yep," grunted Mr. Fink.

After supper he gathered his newspapers to read. He sat in his
stocking feet.

Arise, some new Dante, and sing me the befitting corner of
perdition for the man who sitteth in the house in his stockinged
feet. Sisters in Patience who by reason of ties or duty have endured
it in silk, yarn, cotton, lisle thread or woollen—does not the new
canto belong?

The next day was Labor Day. The occupations of Mr. Cassidy and Mr. Fink ceased for one passage of the sun. Labor, triumphant, would parade and otherwise disport itself.

Mrs. Fink took Mrs. Cassidy's pattern down early. Mame had on her new silk waist. Even her damaged eye managed to emit a holiday gleam. Jack was fruitfully penitent, and there was a hilarious scheme for the day afoot, with parks and picnics and Pilsener in it.

A rising, indignant jealousy seized Mrs. Fink as she returned to her flat above. Oh, happy Mame, with her bruises and her quick-following balm! But was Mame to have a monopoly of happiness? Surely Martin Fink was as good a man as Jack Cassidy. Was his wife to go always unbelabored and uncaressed? A sudden, brilliant breathless idea came to Mrs. Fink. She would show Mame that there were husbands as able to use their fists and perhaps to be as tender afterward as any Jack.

The holiday promised to be a nominal one with the Finks. Mrs. Fink had the stationary washtubs in the kitchen filled with a two-weeks' wash that had been soaking overnight. Mr. Fink sat in his stockinged feet reading a newspaper. Thus Labor Day presaged to speed.

Jealousy surged high in Mrs. Fink's heart and higher still surged an audacious resolve. If her man would not strike her—if he would not so far prove his manhood, his prerogative and his interest in conjugal affairs, he must be prompted to do his duty.

Mr. Fink lit his pipe and peacefully rubbed an ankle with a stockinged toe. He reposed in the state of matrimony like a lump of unblended suet in a pudding. This was his level Elysium— to sit at ease vicariously girdling the world in print amid the wifely splashing of suds and the agreeable smells of breakfast dishes departed and dinner ones to come. Many ideas were far from his mind; but the furthest one was the thought of beating his wife.

Mrs. Fink turned on the hot water and set the washboards in the suds. Up from the flat below came the gay laugh of Mrs. Cassidy.

It sounded like a taunt, a flaunting of her own happiness in the face of the unslugged bride above. Now was Mrs. Fink's time.

Suddenly she turned like a fury upon the man reading.

"You lazy loafer!" she cried, "must I work my arms off washing and toiling for the ugly likes of you? Are you a man or are you a kitchen hound?"

Mr. Fink dropped his paper, motionless from surprise. She feared that he would not strike—that the provocation had been insufficient. She leaped at him and struck him fiercely in the face with her clenched hand. In that instant she felt a thrill of love for him such as she had not felt for many a day. Rise up, Martin Fink, and come into your kingdom! Oh, she must feel the weight of his hand now—just to show that he cared—just to show that he cared!

Mr. Fink sprang to his feet—Maggie caught him again on the jaw with a wide swing of her other hand. She closed her eyes in that fearful, blissful moment before his blow should come —she whispered his name to herself—she leaned to the expected shock, hungry for it.

In the flat below Mr. Cassidy, with a shamed and contrite face, was powdering Mame's eye in preparation for their junket. From the flat above came the sound of a woman's voice, high-raised, a bumping, a stumbling and a shuffling, a chair overturned—unmistakable sounds of domestic conflict.

"Mart and Mag scrapping?" postulated Mr. Cassidy. "Didn't know they ever indulged. Shall I trot up and see if they need a sponge holder?"

One of Mrs. Cassidy's eyes sparkled like a diamond. The other twinkled at least like paste.

"Oh, oh," she said, softly and without apparent meaning in the feminine ejaculatory manner. "I wonder if—wonder if! Wait, Jack, till I go up and see."

Up the stairs she sped. As her foot struck the hallway above out from the kitchen door of her flat wildly flounced Mrs. Fink.

"Oh, Maggie," cried Mrs. Cassidy, in a delighted whisper; "did he? Oh, did he?"

Mrs. Fink ran and laid her face upon her chum's shoulder and sobbed hopelessly.

Mrs. Cassidy took Maggie's face between her hands and lifted it gently. Tear-stained it was, flushing and paling, but its velvety, pink-and-white, becomingly freckled surface was unscratched, unbruised, unmarred by the recreant fist of Mr. Fink.

"Tell me, Maggie," pleaded Mame, "or I'll go in there and find out. What was it? Did he hurt you—what did he do?"

Mrs. Fink's face went down again despairingly on the bosom of her friend.

"For God's sake don't open that door, Mame," she sobbed. "And don't ever tell nobody—keep it under your hat. He—he never touched me, and—he's—oh, Gawd—he's washin' the clothes—he's washin' the clothes!"

The Last Leaf

In a little district west of Washington Square the streets have run crazy and broken themselves into small strips called "places." These "places" make strange angles and curves. One street crosses itself a time or two. An artist once discovered a valuable possibility in this street. Suppose a collector with a bill for paints, paper and canvas should, in traversing this route, suddenly meet himself coming back, without a cent having been paid on account!

So, to quaint old Greenwich Village the art people soon came prowling, hunting for north windows and eighteenth-century gables and Dutch attics and low rents. Then they imported some pewter mugs and a chafing dish or two from Sixth Avenue, and became a "colony."

At the top of a squatty, three-story brick Sue and Johnsy had their studio. "Johnsy" was familiar for Joanna. One was from Maine; the other from California. They had met at the *table d'hôte* of an Eighth Street "Delmonico's," and found their tastes in art, chicory salad and bishop sleeves so congenial that the joint studio resulted.

That was in May. In November a cold, unseen stranger, whom the doctors called Pneumonia, stalked about the colony, touching one here and there with his icy fingers. Over on the east side this ravager strode boldly, smiting his victims by scores, but his feet trod slowly through the maze of the narrow and moss-grown "places."

Mr. Pneumonia was not what you would call a chivalric old gentleman. A mite of a little woman with blood thinned by California zephyrs was hardly fair game for the red-fisted, short-breathed old duffer. But Johnsy he smote; and she lay, scarcely moving, on her painted iron bedstead, looking through the small Dutch window-panes at the blank side of the next brick house.

One morning the busy doctor invited Sue into the hallway with a shaggy, gray eyebrow.

"She has one chance in—let us say, ten," he said, as he shook down the mercury in his clinical thermometer. "And that chance is for her to want to live. This way people have of lining-up on the side of the undertaker makes the entire pharmacopœia look silly. Your little lady has made up her mind that she's not going to get well. Has she anything on her mind?"

"She—she wanted to paint the Bay of Naples some day," said Sue.

"Paint?—bosh! Has she anything on her mind worth thinking about twice—a man, for instance?"

"A man?" said Sue, with a jew's-harp twang in her voice. "Is a man worth—but, no, doctor; there is nothing of the kind."

"Well, it is the weakness, then," said the doctor. "I will do all that science, so far as it may filter through my efforts, can accomplish. But whenever my patient begins to count the carriages in her funeral procession I subtract 50 per cent. from the curative power of medicines. If you will get her to ask one question about the new winter styles in cloak sleeves I will promise you a one-in-five chance for her, instead of one in ten."

After the doctor had gone Sue went into the workroom and cried a Japanese napkin to a pulp. Then she swaggered into Johnsy's room with her drawing board, whistling ragtime.

Johnsy, lay, scarcely making a ripple under the bedclothes, with her face toward the window. Sue stopped whistling, thinking she was asleep.

She arranged her board and began a pen-and-ink drawing to illustrate a magazine story. Young artists must pave their way to

Tales of O. Henry

Art by drawing pictures for magazine stories that young authors write to pave their way to Literature.

As Sue was sketching a pair of elegant horseshow riding trousers and a monocle on the figure of the hero, an Idaho cowboy, she heard a low sound, several times repeated. She went quickly to the bedside.

Johnsy's eyes were open wide. She was looking out the window and counting—counting backward.

"Twelve," she said, and a little later "eleven"; and then "ten," and "nine"; and then "eight" and "seven," almost together.

Sue looked solicitously out of the window. What was there to count? There was only a bare, dreary yard to be seen, and the blank side of the brick house twenty feet away. An old, old ivy vine, gnarled and decayed at the roots, climbed half way up the brick wall. The cold breath of autumn had stricken its leaves from the vine until its skeleton branches clung, almost bare, to the crumbling bricks.

"What is it, dear?" asked Sue.

"Six," said Johnsy, in almost a whisper. "They're falling faster now. Three days ago there were almost a hundred. It made my head ache to count them. But now it's easy. There goes another one. There are only five left now."

"Five what, dear? Tell your Sudie."

"Leaves. On the ivy vine. When the last one falls I must go, too. I've known that for three days. Didn't the doctor tell you?"

"Oh, I never heard of such nonsense," complained Sue, with magnificent scorn. "What have old ivy leaves to do with your getting well? And you used to love that vine, so, you naughty girl. Don't be a goosey. Why, the doctor told me this morning that your chances for getting well real soon were—let's see exactly what he said—he said the chances were ten to one! Why, that's almost as good a chance as we have in New York when we ride on the street cars or walk past a new building. Try to take some broth now, and let Sudie go back to her drawing, so she can sell the editor man with it, and buy port wine for her sick child, and pork chops for her greedy self."

"You needn't get any more wine," said Johnsy, keeping her eyes fixed out the window. "There goes another. No, I don't want any broth. That leaves just four. I want to see the last one fall before it gets dark. Then I'll go, too."

"Johnsy, dear," said Sue, bending over her, "will you promise me to keep your eyes closed, and not look out the window until I am done working? I must hand those drawings in by to-morrow. I need the light, or I would draw the shade down."

"Couldn't you draw in the other room?" asked Johnsy, coldly.

"I'd rather be here by you," said Sue. "Besides, I don't want you to keep looking at those silly ivy leaves."

"Tell me as soon as you have finished," said Johnsy, closing her eyes, and lying white and still as a fallen statue, "because I want to see the last one fall. I'm tired of waiting. I'm tired of thinking. I want to turn loose my hold on everything, and go sailing down, down, just like one of those poor, tired leaves."

"Try to sleep," said Sue. "I must call Behrman up to be my model for the old hermit miner. I'll not be gone a minute. Don't try to move 'til I come back."

Old Behrman was a painter who lived on the ground floor beneath them. He was past sixty and had a Michael Angelo's Moses beard curling down from the head of a satyr along the body of an imp. Behrman was a failure in art. Forty years he had wielded the brush without getting near enough to touch the hem of his Mistress's robe. He had been always about to paint a masterpiece, but had never yet begun it. For several years he had painted nothing except now and then a daub in the line of commerce or advertising. He earned a little by serving as a model to those young artists in the colony who could not pay the price of a professional. He drank gin to excess, and still talked of his coming masterpiece. For the rest he was a fierce little old man, who scoffed terribly at softness in any one, and who regarded himself as especial mastiff-in-waiting to protect the two young artists in the studio above.

Sue found Behrman smelling strongly of juniper berries in his dimly lighted den below. In one corner was a blank canvas on an easel that had been waiting there for twenty-five years to receive the first line of the masterpiece. She told him of Johnsy's fancy, and how she feared she would, indeed, light and fragile as a leaf herself, float away, when her slight hold upon the world grew weaker.

Old Behrman, with his red eyes plainly streaming, shouted his contempt and derision for such idiotic imaginings.

"Vass!" he cried. "Is dere people in de world mit der foolishness to die because leafs dey drop off from a confounded vine? I haf not heard of such a thing. No, I will not bose as a model for your fool hermit-dunder-head. Vy do you allow dot silly pusiness to come in der brain of her? Ach, dot poor leetle Miss Yohnsy."

"She is very ill and weak," said Sue, "and the fever has left her mind morbid and full of strange fancies. Very well, Mr. Behrman, if you do not care to pose for me, you needn't. But I think you are a horrid old—old flibbertigibbet."

"You are just like a woman!" yelled Behrman. "Who said I will not bose? Go on. I come mit you. For half an hour I haf peen trying to say dot I am ready to bose. Gott! dis is not any blace in which one so goot as Miss Yohnsy shall lie sick. Some day I vill baint a masterpiece, and ve shall all go away. Gott! yes."

Johnsy was sleeping when they went upstairs. Sue pulled the shade down to the window-sill, and motioned Behrman into the other room. In there they peered out the window fearfully at the ivy vine. Then they looked at each other for a moment without speaking. A persistent, cold rain was falling, mingled with snow. Behrman, in his old blue shirt, took his seat as the hermit miner on an upturned kettle for a rock.

When Sue awoke from an hour's sleep the next morning she

found Johnsy with dull, wide-open eyes staring at the drawn green shade.

"Pull it up; I want to see," she ordered, in a whisper.

Wearily Sue obeyed.

But, lo! after the beating rain and fierce gusts of wind that had endured through the livelong night, there yet stood out against the brick wall one ivy leaf. It was the last on the vine. Still dark green near its stem, but with its serrated edges tinted with the yellow of dissolution and decay, it hung bravely from a branch some twenty feet above the ground.

"It is the last one," said Johnsy. "I thought it would surely fall during the night. I heard the wind. It will fall to-day, and I shall die at the same time."

"Dear, dear!" said Sue, leaning her worn face down to the pillow, "think of me, if you won't think of yourself. What would I do?"

But Johnsy did not answer. The lonesomest thing in all the world is a soul when it is making ready to go on its mysterious, far journey. The fancy seemed to possess her more strongly as one by one the ties that bound her to friendship and to earth were loosed.

The day wore away, and even through the twilight they could see the lone ivy leaf clinging to its stem against the wall. And then, with the coming of the night the north wind was again loosed, while the rain still beat against the windows and pattered down from the low Dutch eaves.

When it was light enough Johnsy, the merciless, commanded that the shade be raised.

The ivy leaf was still there.

Johnsy lay for a long time looking at it. And then she called to Sue, who was stirring her chicken broth over the gas stove.

"I've been a bad girl, Sudie," said Johnsy. "Something has made that last leaf stay there to show me how wicked I was. It is a sin to want to die. You may bring me a little broth now, and some milk with a little port in it, and—no; bring me a hand-mirror first, and then pack some pillows about me, and I will sit up and watch you cook."

An hour later she said:

"Sudie, some day I hope to paint the Bay of Naples."

The doctor came in the afternoon, and Sue had an excuse to go into the hallway as he left.

"Even chances," said the doctor, taking Sue's thin, shaking hand in his. "With good nursing you'll win. And now I must see another case I have downstairs. Behrman, his name is—some kind of an artist, I believe. Pneumonia, too. He is an old, weak man, and the attack is acute. There is no hope for him; but he goes to the hospital to-day to be made more comfortable."

The next day the doctor said to Sue: "She's out of danger. You've won. Nutrition and care now—that's all."

And that afternoon Sue came to the bed where Johnsy lay, contentedly knitting a very blue and very useless woollen shoulder scarf, and put one arm around her, pillows and all.

"I have something to tell you, white mouse," she said. "Mr. Behrman died of pneumonia to-day in the hospital. He was ill only two days. The janitor found him on the morning of the first day in his room downstairs helpless with pain. His shoes and clothing were wet through and icy cold. They couldn't imagine where he had been on such a dreadful night. And then they found a lantern, still lighted, and a ladder that had been dragged from its place, and some scattered brushes, and a palette with green and yellow colors mixed on it, and—look out the window, dear, at the last ivy leaf on the wall. Didn't you wonder why it never fluttered or moved when the wind blew? Ah, darling, it's Behrman's masterpiece—he painted it there the night that the last leaf fell."

The Count and the Wedding Guest

ONE EVENING when Andy Donovan went to dinner at his Second Avenue boarding-house, Mrs. Scott introduced him to a new boarder, a young lady, Miss Conway. Miss Conway was small and unobtrusive. She wore a plain, snuffy-brown dress, and bestowed her interest, which seemed languid, upon her plate. She lifted her diffident eyelids and shot one perspicuous, judicial glance at Mr. Donovan, politely murmured his name, and returned to her mutton. Mr. Donovan bowed with the grace and beaming smile that were rapidly winning for him social, business and political advancement, and erased the snuffy-brown one from the tablets of his consideration.

Two weeks later Andy was sitting on the front steps enjoying his cigar. There was a soft rustle behind and above him and Andy turned his head—and had his head turned.

Just coming out of the door was Miss Conway. She wore a night-black dress of crêpe de—crêpe de—oh, this thin black goods. Her hat was black, and from it drooped and fluttered an ebon veil, filmy as a spider's web. She stood on the top step and drew on black silk gloves. Not a speck of white or a spot of color about her dress anywhere. Her rich golden hair was drawn, with scarcely a ripple, into a shining, smooth knot low on her neck. Her face was plain rather than pretty, but it was now illuminated and made almost beautiful by her large gray eyes that gazed above the houses across the street into the sky with an expression of the most appealing sadness and melancholy.

Gather the idea, girls—all black, you know, with the preference for *crêpe de*—oh, *crêpe de Chine*—that's it. All black, and that sad, faraway look, and the hair shining under the black veil (you have to be a blonde, of course), and try to look as if, although your young life had been blighted just as it was about to give a hop-skip-and-a-jump over the threshold of life, a walk in the park might do you good, and be sure to happen out the door at the right moment, and—oh, it'll fetch 'em every time. But it's fierce, now, how cynical I am, ain't it?—to talk about mourning costumes this way.

Mr. Donovan suddenly reinscribed Miss Conway upon the tablets of his consideration. He threw away the remaining inch and a quarter of his cigar, that would have been good for eight minutes yet, and quickly shifted his center of gravity to his low-cut patent leathers.

"It's a fine, clear evening, Miss Conway," he said; and if the Weather Bureau could have heard the confident emphasis of his tones it would have hoisted the square white signal, and nailed it to the mast.

"To them that has the heart to enjoy it, it is, Mr. Donovan," said Miss Conway, with a sigh.

Mr. Donovan, in his heart, cursed fair weather. Heartless weather! It should hail and blow and snow to be consonant with the mood of Miss Conway.

"I hope none of your relatives—I hope you haven't sustained a loss?" ventured Mr. Donovan.

"Death has claimed," said Miss Conway, hesitating—"not a relative, but one who—but I will not intrude my grief upon you, Mr. Donovan."

"Intrude?" protested Mr. Donovan. "Why, say, Miss Conway, I'd be delighted, that is, I'd be sorry—I mean I'm sure nobody could sympathize with you truer than I would."

Miss Conway smiled a little smile. And oh, it was sadder than her expression in repose.

" 'Laugh, and the world laughs with you; weep, and they give you the laugh,'" she quoted. "I have learned that, Mr. Donovan. I have no friends or acquaintances in this city. But you have been kind to me. I appreciate it highly."

He had passed her the pepper twice at the table.

"It's tough to be alone in New York—that's a cinch," said Mr. Donovan. "But, say—whenever this little old town does loosen up and get friendly it goes the limit. Say you took a little stroll in the park, Miss Conway—don't you think it might chase away some of your mullygrubs? And if you'd allow me——"

"Thanks, Mr. Donovan. I'd be pleased to accept of your escort if you think the company of one whose heart is filled with gloom could be anyways agreeable to you."

Through the open gates of the iron-railed, old, downtown park, where the elect once took the air, they strolled, and found a quiet bench.

There is this difference between the grief of youth and that of old age; youth's burden is lightened by as much of it as another shares; old age may give and give, but the sorrow remains the same.

"He was my fiancé," confided Miss Conway, at the end of an hour. "We were going to be married next spring. I don't want you to think that I am stringing you, Mr. Donovan, but he was a real Count. He had an estate and a castle in Italy. Count Fernando Mazzini was his name. I never saw the beat of him for elegance. Papa objected, of course, and once we eloped, but Papa overtook us, and took us back. I thought sure Papa and Fernando would fight a duel. Papa has a livery business—in P'kipsee, you know.

"Finally, Papa came 'round, all right, and said we might be married next spring. Fernando showed him proofs of his title and wealth, and then went over to Italy to get the castle fixed up for us. Papa's very proud and, when Fernando wanted to give me several thousand dollars for my trousseau he called him down something awful. He wouldn't even let me take a ring or any presents from him. And when Fernando sailed I came to the city and got a position as cashier in a candy store.

"Three days ago I got a letter from Italy, forwarded from P'kipsee, saying that Fernando had been killed in a gondola accident.

"That is why I am in mourning. My heart, Mr. Donovan, will remain forever in his grave. I guess I am poor company, Mr. Donovan, but I cannot take any interest in no one. I should not care to keep you from gayety and your friends who can smile and entertain you. Perhaps you would prefer to walk back to the house?"

Now, girls, if you want to observe a young man hustle out after a pick and shovel, just tell him that your heart is in some other fellow's grave. Young men are grave-robbers by nature. Ask any widow. Something must be done to restore that missing organ to weeping angels in *crêpe de Chine*. Dead men certainly get the worst of it from all sides.

"I'm awful sorry," said Mr. Donovan, gently. "No, we won't walk back to the house just yet. And don't say you haven't no friends in this city, Miss Conway. I'm awful sorry, and I want you to believe I'm your friend, and that I'm awful sorry."

"I've got his picture here in my locket," said Miss Conway, after wiping her eyes with her handkerchief. "I never showed it to anybody; but I will to you, Mr. Donovan, because I believe you to be a true friend."

Mr. Donovan gazed long and with much interest at the photograph in the locket that Miss Conway opened for him. The face of Count Mazzini was one to command interest. It was a smooth, intelligent, bright, almost a handsome face—the face of a strong, cheerful man who might well be a leader among his fellows.

"I have a larger one, framed, in my room," said Miss Conway. "When we return I will show you that. They are all I have to remind me of Fernando. But he ever will be present in my heart, that's a sure thing."

A subtle task confronted Mr. Donovan—that of supplanting

the unfortunate Count in the heart of Miss Conway. This his admiration for her determined him to do. But the magnitude of the undertaking did not seem to weigh upon his spirits. The sympathetic but cheerful friend was the rôle he essayed; and he played it so successfully that the next half-hour found them conversing pensively across two plates of ice-cream, though yet there was no diminution of the sadness in Miss Conway's large gray eyes.

Before they parted in the hall that evening she ran upstairs and brought down the framed photograph wrapped lovingly in a white silk scarf. Mr. Donovan surveyed it with inscrutable eyes.

"He gave me this the night he left for Italy," said Miss Conway. "I had the one for the locket made from this."

"A fine-looking man," said Mr. Donovan, heartily. "How would it suit you, Miss Conway, to give me the pleasure of your company to Coney next Sunday afternoon?"

A month later they announced their engagement to Mrs. Scott and the other boarders. Miss Conway continued to wear black.

A week after the announcement the two sat on the same bench in the downtown park, while the fluttering leaves of the trees made a dim kinetoscopic picture of them in the moonlight. But Donovan had worn a look of abstracted gloom all day. He was so silent to-night that love's lips could not keep back any longer the question that love's heart propounded.

"What's the matter, Andy, you are so solemn and grouchy to-night?"

"Nothing, Maggie."

"I know better. Can't I tell? You never acted this way before. What is it?"

"It's nothing much, Maggie."

"Yes it is; and I want to know. I'll bet it's some other girl you are thinking about. All right. Why don't you go get her if you want her? Take your arm away, if you please."

"I'll tell you then," said Andy, wisely, "but I guess you won't understand it exactly. You've heard of Mike Sullivan, haven't you? 'Big Mike' Sullivan, everybody calls him."

"No, I haven't," said Maggie. "And I don't want to, if he makes you act like this. Who is he?"

"He's the biggest man in New York," said Andy, almost reverently. "He can about do anything he wants to with Tammany or any other old thing in the political line. He's a mile high and as broad as East River. You say anything against Big Mike, and you'll have a million men on your collarbone in about two seconds. Why, he made a visit over to the old country awhile back, and the kings took to their holes like rabbits.

"Well, Big Mike's a friend of mine. I ain't more than deuce-high in the district as far as influence goes, but Mike's as good a friend to a little man, or a poor man as he is to a big one. I met him to-day on the Bowery, and what do you think he does? Comes up and shakes hands. 'Andy,' says he, 'I've been keeping cases on you. You've been putting in some good licks over on your side of the street, and I'm proud of you. What'll you take to drink?' He takes a cigar and I take a highball. I told him I was going to get married in two weeks. 'Andy,' says he, 'send me an invitation, so I'll keep in mind of it, and I'll come to the wedding.' That's what Big Mike says to me; and he always does what he says.

"You don't understand it, Maggie, but I'd have one of my hands cut off to have Big Mike Sullivan at our wedding. It would be the proudest day of my life. When he goes to a man's wedding, there's a guy being married that's made for life. Now, that's why I'm maybe looking sore to-night."

"Why don't you invite him, then, if he's so much to the mustard?" said Maggie, lightly.

"There's a reason why I can't," said Andy, sadly. "There's a reason why he mustn't be there. Don't ask me what it is, for I can't tell you."

"Oh, I don't care," said Maggie. "It's something about politics, of course. But it's no reason why you can't smile at me."

"Maggie," said Andy, presently, "do you think as much of me as you did of your—as you did of the Count Mazzini?"

He waited a long time, but Maggie did not reply. And then, suddenly she leaned against his shoulder and began to cry—to cry and shake with sobs, holding his arm tightly, and wetting the *crêpe de Chine* with tears.

"There, there, there!" soothed Andy, putting aside his own trouble. "And what is it, now?"

"Andy," sobbed Maggie, "I've lied to you, and you'll never marry me, or love me any more. But I feel that I've got to tell. Andy, there never was so much as the little finger of a count. I never had a beau in my life. But all the other girls had; and they talked about 'em; and that seemed to make the fellows like 'em more. And, Andy, I look swell in black—you know I do. So I went out to a photograph store and bought that picture, and had a little one made for my locket, and made up all that story about the Count and about his being killed, so I could wear black. And nobody can love a liar, and you'll shake me, Andy, and I'll die for shame. Oh, there never was anybody I liked but you—and that's all."

But instead of being pushed away, she found Andy's arm folding her closer. She looked up and saw his face cleared and smiling.

"Could you—could you forgive me, Andy?"

"Sure," said Andy. "It's all right about that. Back to the cemetery for the Count. You've straightened everything out, Maggie. I was in hopes you would before the wedding-day. Bully girl!"

"Andy," said Maggie, with a somewhat shy smile, after she had been thoroughly assured of forgiveness, "did you believe all that story about the Count?"

"Well, not to any large extent," said Andy, reaching for his cigar case; "because it's Big Mike Sullivan's picture you've got in that locket of yours."

The Robe of Peace

Mysteries follow one another so closely in a great city that the reading public and the friends of Johnny Bellchambers have ceased to marvel at his sudden and unexplained disappearance nearly a year ago. This particular mystery has now been cleared up, but the solution is so strange and incredible to the mind of the average man that only a select few who were in close touch with Bellchambers will give it full credence.

Johnny Bellchambers, as is well known, belonged to the intrinsically inner circle of the *élite.* Without any of the ostentation of the fashionable ones who endeavor to attract notice by eccentric display of wealth and show he still was *au fait* in everything that gave deserved lustre to his high position in the ranks of society.

Especially did he shine in the matter of dress. In this he was the despair of imitators. Always correct, exquisitely groomed, and possessed of an unlimited wardrobe, he was conceded to be the best-dressed man in New York, and, therefore, in America. There was not a tailor in Gotham who would not have deemed it a precious boon to have been granted the privilege of making Bellchambers' clothes without a cent of pay. As he wore them, they would have been a priceless advertisement. Trousers were his especial passion. Here nothing but perfection would be noticed. He would have worn a patch as quickly as he would have overlooked a wrinkle. He kept a man in his apartments always busy pressing his ample supply. His friends said that three hours was the limit of time that he would wear these garments without exchanging.

Bellchambers disappeared very suddenly. For three days his absence brought no alarm to his friends, and then they began to operate the usual methods of inquiry. All of them failed. He had left absolutely no trace behind. Then the search for a motive was instituted, but none was found. He had no enemies, he had no debts, there was no woman. There were several thousand dollars in his bank to his credit. He had never showed any tendency toward mental eccentricity; in fact, he was of a particularly calm and well-balanced temperament. Every means of tracing the vanished man was made use of, but without avail. It was one of those cases—more numerous in late years—where men seem to have gone out like the flame of a candle, leaving not even a trail of smoke as a witness.

In May, Tom Eyres and Lancelot Gilliam, two of Bellchambers' old friends, went for a little run on the other side. While pottering around in Italy and Switzerland, they happened, one day, to hear of a monastery in the Swiss Alps that promised something outside of the ordinary tourist-beguiling attractions. The monastery was almost inaccessible to the average sight-seer, being on an extremely rugged and precipitous spur of the mountains. The attractions it possessed but did not advertise were, first, an exclusive and divine cordial made by the monks that was said to far surpass benedictine and chartreuse. Next a huge brass bell so purely and accurately cast that it had not ceased sounding since it was first rung three hundred years ago. Finally, it was asserted that no Englishman had ever set foot within its walls. Eyres and Gilliam decided that these three reports called for investigation.

It took them two days with the aid of two guides to reach the monastery of St. Gondrau. It stood upon a frozen, wind-swept crag with the snow piled about it in treacherous, drifting masses. They were hospitably received by the brothers whose duty it was to entertain the infrequent guest. They drank of the precious cordial, finding it rarely potent and reviving. They listened to the great, ever-echoing bell and learned that they were pioneer travelers, in those gray stone walls, over the Englishman whose restless feet have trodden nearly every corner of the earth.

At three o'clock on the afternoon they arrived, the two young Gothamites stood with good Brother Cristofer in the great, cold hallway of the monastery to watch the monks march past on their way to the refectory. They came slowly, pacing by twos, with their heads bowed, treading noiselessly with sandaled feet upon the rough stone flags. As the procession slowly filed past, Eyres suddenly gripped Gilliam by the arm. "Look," he whispered, eagerly, "at the one just opposite you now—the one on this side, with his hand at his waist—if that isn't Johnny Bellchambers then I never saw him!"

Gilliam saw and recognized the lost glass of fashion.

"What the deuce," said he, wonderingly, "is old Bell doing here? Tommy, it surely can't be he! Never heard of Bell having a turn for the religious. Fact is, I've heard him say things when a four-in-hand didn't seem to tie up just right that would bring him up for court-martial before any church."

"It's Bell, without a doubt," said Eyres, firmly, "or I'm pretty badly in need of an oculist. But think of Johnny Bellchambers, the Royal High Chancellor of swell togs and the Mahatma of pink teas, up here in cold storage doing penance in a snuff-colored bathrobe! I can't get it straight in my mind. Let's ask the jolly old boy that's doing the honors."

Brother Cristofer was appealed to for information. By that time the monks had passed into the refectory. He could not tell to which one they referred. Bellchambers? Ah, the brothers of St. Gondrau abandoned their worldly names when they took the vows. Did the gentlemen wish to speak with one of the brothers?

If they would come to the refectory and indicate the one they wished to see, the reverend abbot in authority would, doubtless, permit it.

Eyres and Gilliam went into the dining hall and pointed out to Brother Cristofer the man they had seen. Yes, it was Johnny Bellchambers. They saw his face plainly now, as he sat among the dingy brothers, never looking up, eating broth from a coarse, brown bowl.

Permission to speak to one of the brothers was granted to the two travelers by the abbot, and they waited in a reception room for him to come. When he did come, treading softly in his sandals, both Eyres and Gilliam looked at him in perplexity and astonishment. It was Johnny Bellchambers, but he had a different look. Upon his smooth-shaven face was an expression of ineffable peace, of rapturous attainment, of perfect and complete happiness. His form was proudly erect, his eyes shone with a serene and gracious light. He was as neat and well-groomed as in the old New York days, but how differently was he clad! Now he seemed clothed in but a single garment—a long robe of rough brown cloth, gathered by a cord at the waist, and falling in straight, loose folds nearly to his feet. He shook hands with his visitors with his old ease and grace of manner. If there was any embarrassment in that meeting it was not manifested by Johnny Bellchambers. The room had no seats; they stood to converse.

"Glad to see you, old man," said Eyres, somewhat awkwardly. "Wasn't expecting to find you up here. Not a bad idea, though, after all. Society's an awful sham. Must be a relief to shake the giddy whirl and retire to—er—contemplation and—er—prayer and hymns, and those things."

"Oh, cut that, Tommy," said Bellchambers, cheerfully. "Don't be afraid that I'll pass around the plate. I go through these thing-um-bobs with the rest of these old boys because they are the rules. I'm Brother Ambrose here, you know. I'm given just ten minutes to talk to you fellows. That's rather a new design in waistcoats you have on, isn't it, Gilliam? Are they wearing those things on Broadway now?"

"It's the same old Johnny," said Gilliam, joyfully. "What the devil—I mean why—— Oh, confound it! what did you do it for, old man?"

"Peel the bathrobe," pleaded Eyres, almost tearfully, "and go back with us. The old crowd'll go wild to see you. This isn't in your line, Bell. I know half a dozen girls that wore the willow on the quiet when you shook us in that unaccountable way. Hand in your resignation, or get a dispensation, or whatever you have to do to get a release from this ice factory. You'll get catarrh here, Johnny—and—— My God! you haven't any socks on!"

Bellchambers looked down at his sandaled feet and smiled.

"You fellows don't understand," he said, soothingly. "It's nice of you to want me to go back, but the old life will never know me again. I have reached here the goal of all my ambitions. I am entirely happy and contented. Here I shall remain for the remainder of my days. You see this robe that I wear?" Bellchambers caressingly touched the straight-hanging garment: "At last I have found something that will not bag at the knees. I have attained——"

At that moment the deep boom of the great brass bell reverberated through the monastery. It must have been a summons to immediate devotions, for Brother Ambrose bowed his head, turned and left the chamber without another word. A slight wave of his hand as he passed through the stone doorway seemed to say a farewell to his old friends. They left the monastery without seeing him again.

And this is the story that Tommy Eyres and Lancelot Gilliam brought back with them from their latest European tour.

A Ramble in Aphasia

My wife and I parted on that morning in precisely our usual
manner. She left her second cup of tea to follow me to the front
door. There she plucked from my lapel the invisible strand of
lint (the universal act of woman to proclaim ownership) and bade
me take care of my cold. I had no cold. Next came her kiss of
parting—the level kiss of domesticity flavored with Young Hy-
son. There was no fear of the extemporaneous, of variety spicing
her infinite custom. With the deft touch of long malpractice, she
dabbed awry my well-set scarf pin; and then, as I closed the door,
I heard her morning slippers pattering back to her cooling tea.

When I set out I had no thought or premonition of what was to
occur. The attack came suddenly.

For many weeks I had been toiling, almost night and day, at a
famous railroad law case that I won triumphantly but a few days
previously. In fact, I had been digging away at the law almost
without cessation for many years. Once or twice good Doctor
Volney, my friend and physician, had warned me.

"If you don't slacken up, Bellford," he said, "you'll go suddenly
to pieces. Either your nerves or your brain will give way. Tell me,
does a week pass in which you do not read in the papers of a case
of aphasia—of some man lost, wandering nameless, with his past
and his identity blotted out—and all from that little brain clot
made by overwork or worry?"

"I always thought," said I, "that the clot in those instances was
really to be found on the brains of the newspaper reporters."

Doctor Volney shook his head.

"The disease exists," he said. "You need a change or a rest. Court-room, office, and home—there is the only route you travel. For recreation you—read law books. Better take warning in time."

"On Thursday nights," I said, defensively, "my wife and I play cribbage. On Sundays she reads to me the weekly letter from her mother. That law books are not a recreation remains yet to be established."

That morning as I walked I was thinking of Doctor Volney's words. I was feeling as well as I usually did—possibly in better spirits than usual.

I woke with stiff and cramped muscles from having slept long on the incommodious seat of a day coach. I leaned my head against the seat and tried to think. After a long time I said to myself: "I must have a name of some sort." I searched my pockets. Not a card; not a letter; not a paper or monogram could I find. But I found in my coat pocket nearly $3,000 in bills of large denomination. "I must be some one, of course," I repeated to myself, and began to consider.

The car was well crowded with men, among whom, I told myself, there must have been some common interest, for they intermingled freely, and seemed in the best good humor and spirits. One of them—a stout, bespectacled gentleman enveloped in a decided odor of cinnamon and aloes—took the vacant half of my seat with a friendly nod, and unfolded a newspaper. In the intervals between his periods of reading, we conversed, as travelers will, on current affairs. I found myself able to sustain the conversation on such subjects with credit, at least to my memory. By and by my companion said:

"You are one of us, of course. Fine lot of men the West sends in this time. I'm glad they held the convention in New York; I've never been East before. My name's R. P. Bolder—Bolder & Son, of Hickory Grove, Missouri."

Though unprepared, I rose to the emergency, as men will when put to it.

Now must I hold a christening, and be at once babe, parson, and parent. My senses came to the rescue of my slower brain. The insistent odor of drugs from my companion supplied one idea; a glance at his newspaper, where my eye met a conspicuous advertisement, assisted me further.

"My name," said I, glibly, "is Edward Pinkhammer. I am a druggist, and my home is in Cornopolis, Kansas."

"I knew you were a druggist," said my fellow traveler, affably. "I saw the callous spot on your right forefinger where the handle of the pestle rubs. Of course, you are a delegate to our National Convention."

"Are all these men druggists?" I asked, wonderingly.

"They are. This car came through from the West. And they're your old-time druggists, too—none of your patent tablet-and-granule pharmashootists that use slot machines instead of a prescription desk. We percolate our own paregoric and roll our own pills, and we ain't above handling a few garden seeds in the spring, and carrying a side line of confectionery and shoes. I tell you, Hampinker, I've got an idea to spring on this convention—new ideas is what they want. Now, you know the shelf bottles of tartar emetic and Rochelle salt Ant. et. Pot. Tart. and Sod. et. Pot. Tart.—one's poison, you know, and the other's harmless. It's easy to mistake one label for the other. Where do druggists mostly keep 'em? Why, as far apart as possible, on different shelves. That's wrong. I say keep 'em side by side, so when you want one you can always compare it with the other and avoid mistakes. Do you catch the idea?"

"It seems to me a very good one," I said.

"All right! When I spring it on the convention you back it up. We'll make some of these Eastern orange-phosphate-and-massage-cream professors that think they're the only lozenges in the market look like hypodermic tablets."

"If I can be of any aid," I said, warming, "the two bottles of—
er——"

"Tartrate of antimony and potash, and tartrate of soda and
potash."

"Shall henceforth sit side by side," I concluded, firmly.

"Now, there's another thing," said Mr. Bolder. "For an excip-
ient in manipulating a pill mass which do you prefer—the magnesia carbonate or the pulverized glycerrhiza radix?"

"The—er—magnesia," I said. It was easier to say than the other
word.

Mr. Bolder glanced at me distrustfully through his spectacles.

"Give me the glycerrhiza," said he. "Magnesia cakes."

"Here's another one of these fake aphasia cases," he said,
presently, handing me his newspaper, and laying his finger upon
an article. "I don't believe in 'em. I put nine out of ten of 'em
down as frauds. A man gets sick of his business and his folks and
wants to have a good time. He skips out somewhere, and when
they find him he pretends to have lost his memory—don't know
his own name, and won't even recognize the strawberry mark on
his wife's left shoulder. Aphasia! Tut! Why can't they stay at home
and forget?"

I took the paper and read, after the pungent headlines, the
following:

Denver, June 12.—Elwyn C. Bellford, a prominent lawyer,
is mysteriously missing from his home since three days ago,
and all efforts to locate him have been in vain. Mr. Bellford is
a well-known citizen of the highest standing, and has enjoyed
a large and lucrative law practice. He is married and owns a
fine home and the most extensive private library in the State.
On the day of his disappearance, he drew quite a large sum of
money from his bank. No one can be found who saw him after
he left the bank. Mr. Bellford was a man of singularly quiet
and domestic tastes, and seemed to find his happiness in his
home and profession. If any clue at all exists to his strange
disappearance, it may be found in the fact that for some

months he has been deeply absorbed in an important law case in connection with the Q. Y. and Z. Railroad Company. It is feared that overwork may have affected his mind. Every effort is being made to discover the whereabouts of the missing man.

"It seems to me you are not altogether uncynical, Mr. Bolder," I said, after I had read the despatch. "This has the sound, to me, of a genuine case. Why should this man, prosperous, happily married, and respected, choose suddenly to abandon everything? I know that these lapses of memory do occur, and that men do find themselves adrift without a name, a history, or a home."

"Oh, gammon and jalap!" said Mr. Bolder. "It's larks they're after. There's too much education nowadays. Men know about aphasia, and they use it for an excuse. The women are wise, too. When it's all over they look you in the eye, as scientific as you please, and say: 'He hypnotized me.'"

Thus Mr. Bolder diverted, but did not aid me with his comments and philosophy.

We arrived in New York about ten at night. I rode in a cab to a hotel, and I wrote my name "Edward Pinkhammer" in the register. As I did so I felt pervade me a splendid, wild, intoxicating buoyancy—a sense of unlimited freedom, of newly attained possibilities. I was just born into the world. The old fetters—whatever they had been—were stricken from my hands and feet. The future lay before me a clear road such as an infant enters, and I could set out upon it equipped with a man's learning and experience.

I thought the hotel clerk looked at me five seconds too long. I had no baggage.

"The Druggists' Convention," I said. "My trunk has somehow failed to arrive." I drew out a roll of money.

"Ah!" said he, showing an auriferous tooth, "we have quite a number of the Western delegates stopping here." He struck a bell for the boy.

I endeavored to give color to my rôle.

"There is an important movement on foot among us Westerners," I said, "in regard to a recommendation to the convention that the bottles containing the tartrate of antimony and potash, and the tartrate of sodium and potash be kept in a contiguous position on the shelf."

"Gentleman to three-fourteen," said the clerk, hastily. I was whisked away to my room.

The next day I bought a trunk and clothing, and began to live the life of Edward Pinkhammer. I did not tax my brain with endeavors to solve problems of the past.

It was a piquant and sparkling cup that the great island city held up to my lips. I drank it gratefully. The keys of Manhattan belong to him who is able to bear them. You must be either the city's guest or its victim.

The following few days were as gold and silver. Edward Pinkhammer, yet counting back to his birth by hours only, knew the rare joy of having come upon so diverting a world full-fledged and unrestrained. I sat entranced on the magic carpets provided in theatres and roof-gardens, that transported one into strange and delightful lands full of frolicsome music, pretty girls, and grotesque, drolly extravagant parodies upon human kind. I went here and there at my own dear will, bound by no limits of space, time, or comportment. I dined in weird cabarets, at weirder *tables d'hôte* to the sound of Hungarian music and the wild shouts of mercurial artists and sculptors. Or, again, where the night life quivers in the electric glare like a kinetoscopic picture, and the millinery of the world, and its jewels, and the ones whom they adorn, and the men who make all three possible are met for good cheer and the spectacular effect. And among all these scenes that I have mentioned I learned one thing that I never knew before. And that is that the key to liberty is not in the hands of License, but Convention holds it. Comity has a toll-gate at which you must pay, or you may not enter the land of Freedom. In all the glitter, the seeming disorder, the parade, the abandon, I saw this law, unobtrusive, yet like iron, prevail. Therefore, in Manhattan you must obey these unwritten laws, and then you will be freest of the free. If you decline to be bound by them, you put on shackles.

Sometimes, as my mood urged me, I would seek the stately, softly murmuring palm rooms, redolent with high-born life and delicate restraint, in which to dine. Again I would go down to the waterways in steamers packed with vociferous, bedecked, unchecked love-making clerks and shop-girls to their crude pleasures on the island shores. And there was always Broadway—glistening, opulent, wily, varying, desirable Broadway—growing upon one like an opium habit.

One afternoon as I entered my hotel a stout man with a big nose and a black mustache blocked my way in the corridor. When I would have passed around him, he greeted me with offensive familiarity.

"Hallo, Bellford!" he cried, loudly. "What the deuce are you doing in New York? Didn't know anything could drag you away from that old book den of yours. Is Mrs. B. along or is this a little business run alone, eh?"

"You have made a mistake, sir," I said, coldly, releasing my hand from his grasp. "My name is Pinkhammer. You will excuse me."

The man dropped to one side, apparently astonished. As I walked to the clerk's desk I heard him call to a bell boy and say something about telegraph blanks.

"You will give me my bill," I said to the clerk, "and have my baggage brought down in half an hour. I do not care to remain where I am annoyed by confidence men."

I moved that afternoon to another hotel, a sedate, old-fashioned one on lower Fifth Avenue.

There was a restaurant a little way off Broadway where one could be served almost *al fresco* in a tropic array of screening flora. Quiet and luxury and a perfect service made it an ideal place in which to take luncheon or refreshment. One afternoon I was there picking my way to a table among the ferns when I felt my sleeve caught.

"Mr. Bellford!" exclaimed an amazingly sweet voice.

I turned quickly to see a lady seated alone—a lady of about thirty, with exceedingly handsome eyes, who looked at me as though I had been her very dear friend.

"You were about to pass me," she said, accusingly. "Don't tell me you did not know me. Why should we not shake hands—at least once in fifteen years?"

I shook hands with her at once. I took a chair opposite her at the table. I summoned with my eyebrows a hovering waiter. The lady was philandering with an orange ice. I ordered a *crème de menthe*. Her hair was reddish bronze. You could not look at it, because you could not look away from her eyes. But you were conscious of it as you are conscious of sunset while you look into the profundities of a wood at twilight.

"Are you sure you know me?" I asked.

"No," she said, smiling, "I was never sure of that."

"What would you think," I said, a little anxiously, "if I were to tell you that my name is Edward Pinkhammer from Cornopolis, Kansas?"

"What would I think?" she repeated with a merry glance. "Why, that you had not brought Mrs. Bellford to New York with you, of course. I do wish you had. I would have liked to see Marian." Her voice lowered slightly—"You haven't changed much, Elwyn."

I felt her wonderful eyes searching mine and my face more closely.

"Yes, you have," she amended, and there was a soft, exultant note in her latest tones; "I see it now. You haven't forgotten. You haven't forgotten for a year or a day or an hour. I told you you never could."

I poked my straw anxiously in the *crème de menthe*.

"I'm sure I beg your pardon," I said, a little uneasy at her gaze. "But that is just the trouble. I have forgotten. I've forgotten everything."

She flouted my denial. She laughed deliciously at something she seemed to see in my face.

"I've heard of you at times," she went on. "You're quite a big lawyer out West—Denver, isn't it, or Los Angeles? Marian must be very proud of you. You knew, I suppose, that I married six months after you did. You may have seen it in the papers. The flowers alone cost two thousand dollars."

She had mentioned fifteen years. Fifteen years is a long time.

"Would it be too late," I asked, somewhat timorously, "to offer you congratulations?"

"Not if you dare do it," she answered, with such fine intrepidity that I was silent, and began to crease patterns on the cloth with my thumb nail.

"Tell me one thing," she said, leaning toward me rather eagerly —"a thing I have wanted to know for many years—just from a woman's curiosity, of course—have you ever dared since that night to touch, smell, or look at white roses—at white roses wet with rain and dew?"

I took a sip of *crème de menthe*.

"It would be useless, I suppose," I said, with a sigh, "for me to repeat that I have no recollection at all about these things. My memory is completely at fault. I need not say how much I regret it."

The lady rested her arms upon the table, and again her eyes disdained my words and went traveling by their own route direct to my soul. She laughed softly, with a strange quality in the sound—it was a laugh of happiness—yes, and of content—and of misery. I tried to look away from her.

"You lie, Elwyn Bellford," she breathed, blissfully. "Oh, I know you lie!"

I gazed dully into the ferns.

"My name is Edward Pinkhammer," I said. "I came with the delegates to the Druggists' National Convention. There is a movement on foot for arranging a new position for the bottles of tartrate and antimony and tartrate of potash, in which, very likely, you would take little interest."

A shining landau stopped before the entrance. The lady rose. I took her hand, and bowed.

"I am deeply sorry," I said to her, "that I cannot remember. I could explain, but fear you would not understand. You will not concede Pinkhammer; and I really cannot at all conceive of the— the roses and other things."

"Good-bye, Mr. Bellford," she said, with her happy, sorrowful smile, as she stepped into her carriage.

I attended the theatre that night. When I returned to my hotel, a quiet man in dark clothes, who seemed interested in rubbing his finger nails with a silk handkerchief, appeared, magically, at my side.

"Mr. Pinkhammer," he said, casually, giving the bulk of his attention to his forefinger, "may I request you to step aside with me for a little conversation? There is a room here."

"Certainly," I answered.

He conducted me into a small, private parlor. A lady and a gentleman were there. The lady, I surmised, would have been unusually good-looking had her features not been clouded by an expression of keen worry and fatigue. She was of a style of figure and possessed coloring and features that were agreeable to my fancy. She was in a traveling dress; she fixed upon me an earnest look of extreme anxiety, and pressed an unsteady hand to her bosom. I think she would have started forward, but the gentleman arrested her movement with an authoritative motion of his hand. He then came, himself, to meet me. He was a man of forty, a little gray about the temples, and with a strong, thoughtful face.

"Bellford, old man," he said, cordially, "I'm glad to see you again. Of course we know everything is all right. I warned you, you know, that you were overdoing it. Now, you'll go back with us, and be yourself again in no time."

I smiled ironically.

"I have been 'Bellforded' so often," I said, "that it has lost its edge. Still, in the end, it may grow wearisome. Would you be willing at all to entertain the hypothesis that my name is Edward Pinkhammer, and that I never saw you before in my life?"

Before the man could reply a wailing cry came from the woman. She sprang past his detaining arm. "Elwyn!" she sobbed, and cast herself upon me, and clung tight. "Elwyn," she cried again, "don't break my heart. I am your wife—call my name once—just once. I could see you dead rather than this way."

I unwound her arms respectfully, but firmly.

"Madame," I said, severely, "pardon me if I suggest that you accept a resemblance too precipitately. It is a pity," I went on, with an amused laugh, as the thought occurred to me, "that this Bellford and I could not be kept side by side upon the same shelf like tartrates of sodium and antimony for purposes of identification. In order to understand this allusion," I concluded airily, "it may be necessary for you to keep an eye on the proceedings of the Druggists' National Convention."

The lady turned to her companion, and grasped his arm.

"What is it, Doctor Volney? Oh, what is it?" she moaned.

He led her to the door.

"Go to your room for a while," I heard him say. "I will remain and talk with him. His mind? No, I think not—only a portion of the brain. Yes, I am sure he will recover. Go to your room and leave me with him."

The lady disappeared. The man in dark clothes also went outside, still manicuring himself in a thoughtful way. I think he waited in the hall.

"I would like to talk with you a while, Mr. Pinkhammer, if I may," said the gentleman who remained.

"Very well, if you care to," I replied, "and will excuse me if I take it comfortably; I am rather tired." I stretched myself upon a couch by a window and lit a cigar. He drew a chair near by.

"Let us speak to the point," he said, soothingly. "Your name is not Pinkhammer."

"I know that as well as you do," I said coolly. "But a man must

Tales of O. Henry

have a name of some sort. I can assure you that I do not extravagantly admire the name of Pinkhammer. But when one christens one's self suddenly, the fine names do not seem to suggest themselves. But, suppose it had been Scheringhausen or Scroggins! I think I did very well with Pinkhammer."

"Your name," said the other man, seriously, "is Elwyn C. Bellford. You are one of the first lawyers in Denver. You are suffering from an attack of aphasia, which has caused you to forget your identity. The cause of it was over-application to your profession, and perhaps a life too bare of natural recreation and pleasures. The lady who has just left the room is your wife."

"She is what I would call a fine-looking woman," I said, after a judicial pause. "I particularly admire the shade of brown in her hair."

"She is a wife to be proud of. Since your disappearance, nearly two weeks ago, she has scarcely closed her eyes. We learned that you were in New York through a telegram sent by Isidore Newman, a traveling man from Denver. He said that he had met you in a hotel here, and that you did not recognize him."

"I think I remember the occasion," I said. "The fellow called me 'Bellford,' if I am not mistaken. But don't you think it about time, now, for you to introduce yourself?"

"I am Robert Volney—Doctor Volney. I have been your close friend for twenty years and your physician for fifteen. I came with Mrs. Bellford to trace you as soon as we got the telegram. Try, Elwyn, old man—try to remember!"

"What's the use to try?" I asked, with a little frown. "You say you are a physician. Is aphasia curable? When a man loses his memory does it return slowly, or suddenly?"

"Sometimes gradually and imperfectly; sometimes as suddenly as it went."

"Will you undertake the treatment of my case, Doctor Volney?" I asked.

"Old friend," said he, "I'll do everything in my power, and will have done everything that science can do to cure you."

"Very well," said I. "Then you will consider that I am your patient. Everything is in confidence now—professional confidence."

"Of course," said Doctor Volney.

I got up from the couch. Someone had set a vase of white roses on the centre table—a cluster of white roses, freshly sprinkled and fragrant. I threw them far out of the window, and then I laid myself upon the couch again.

"It will be best, Bobby," I said, "to have this cure happen suddenly. I'm rather tired of it all, anyway. You may go now and bring Marian in. But, oh, Doc," I said, with a sigh, as I kicked him on the shin—"good old Doc—it was glorious!"

A Night in New Arabia

THE GREAT CITY of Bagdad-on-the-Subway is caliph-ridden. Its palaces, bazaars, khans, and byways are thronged with Al Rashids in diverse disguises, seeking diversion and victims for their unbridled generosity. You can scarcely find a poor beggar whom they are willing to let enjoy the spoils unsuccored, nor erect unfortunate upon whom they will not reshower the means of fresh misfortune. You will hardly find anywhere a hungry one who has not had the opportunity to tighten his belt in gift libraries, nor a poor pundit who has not blushed at the holiday basket of celery-crowned turkey forced resoundingly through his door by the eleemosynary press.

So then, fearfully through the Harun-haunted streets creep the one-eyed calenders, the Little Hunchback and the Barber's Sixth Brother, hoping to escape the ministrations of the roving horde of caliphoid sultans.

Entertainment for many Arabian nights might be had from the histories of those who have escaped the largesse of the army of Commanders of the Faithful. Until dawn you might sit on the enchanted rug and listen to such stories as are told of the powerful genie Roc-Ef-El-Er who sent the Forty Thieves to soak up the oil plant of Ali Baba; of the good Caliph Kar-Neg-Ghe, who gave away palaces; of the Seven Voyages of Sailbad, the Sinner, who frequented wooden excursion steamers among the islands; of the Fisherman and the Bottle; of the Barmecides' Boarding house; of Aladdin's rise to wealth by means of his Wonderful Gas-meter.

But now, there being ten sultans to one Scheherazade, she is held too valuable to be in fear of the bowstring. In consequence the art of narrative languishes. And, as the lesser caliphs are hunting the happy poor and the resigned unfortunate from cover to cover in order to heap upon them strange mercies and mysterious benefits, too often comes the report from Arabian headquarters that the captive refused "to talk."

This reticence, then, in the actors who perform the sad comedies of their philanthropy-scourged world, must, in a degree, account for the shortcomings of this painfully gleaned tale, which shall be called

The Story of the Caliph Who Alleviated His Conscience

Old Jacob Spraggins mixed for himself some Scotch and lithia water at his $1,200 oak sideboard. Inspiration must have resulted from its imbibition, for immediately afterward he struck the quartered oak soundly with his fist and shouted to the empty dining room:

"By the coke ovens of hell, it must be that ten thousand dollars! If I can get that squared, it'll do the trick."

Thus, by the commonest artifice of the trade, having gained your interest, the action of the story will now be suspended, leaving you grumpily to consider a sort of doll biography beginning fifteen years before.

When old Jacob was young Jacob he was a breaker boy in a Pennsylvania coal mine. I don't know what a breaker boy is; but his occupation seems to be standing by a coal dump with a wan look and a dinner-pail to have his picture taken for magazine articles. Anyhow, Jacob was one. But, instead of dying of overwork at nine, and leaving his helpless parents and brothers at the mercy of the union strikers' reserve fund, he hitched up his galluses, put a dollar or two in a side proposition now and then, and at forty-five was worth $20,000,000.

There now! it's over. Hardly had time to yawn, did you? I've seen biographies that—— But let us dissemble.

I want you to consider Jacob Spraggins, Esq., after he had arrived at the seventh stage of his career. The stages meant art, first, humble origin; second, deserved promotion; third, stockholder; fourth, capitalist; fifth, trust magnate; sixth, rich malefactor; seventh, caliph; eight, *x*. The eighth stage shall be left to the higher mathematics.

At fifty-five Jacob retired from active business. The income of a czar was still rolling in on him from coal, iron, real estate, oil, railroads, manufactories, and corporations, but none of it touched Jacob's hands in a raw state. It was a sterilized increment, carefully cleaned and dusted and fumigated until it arrived at its ultimate stage of untainted, spotless checks in the white fingers of his private secretary. Jacob built a three-million-dollar palace on a corner lot fronting on Nabob Avenue, city of New Bagdad, and began to feel the mantle of the late H. A. Rashid descending upon him. Eventually Jacob slipped the mantle under his collar, tied it in a neat four-in-hand, and became a licensed harrier of our Mesopotamian proletariat.

When a man's income becomes so large that the butcher actually sends him the kind of steak he orders he begins to think about his soul's salvation. Now, the various stages or classes of rich men must not be forgotten. The capitalist can tell you to a dollar the amount of his wealth. The trust magnate "estimates" it. The rich malefactor hands you a cigar and denies that he has bought the P. D. & Q. The caliph merely smiles and talks about Hammerstein and the musical lasses. There is a record of tremendous altercation at breakfast in a "Where-to-Dine-Well" tavern between a magnate and his wife, the rift within the loot being that the wife calculated their fortune at a figure $3,000,000 higher than did her future *divorcé*. Oh, well, I, myself, heard a similar quarrel between a man and his wife because he found fifty cents less in his pockets than he thought he had. After all, we are all human —Count Tolstoi, R. Fitzsimmons, Peter Pan, and the rest of us.

Don't lose heart because the story seems to be degenerating into a sort of moral essay for intellectual readers.

There will be dialogue and stage business pretty soon.

When Jacob first began to compare the eyes of the needle with the camels in the zoo he decided upon organized charity. He had his secretary send a check for one million to the Universal Benevolent Association of the globe. You may have looked down through a grating in front of a decayed warehouse for a nickel that you had dropped through. But that is neither here nor there. The Association acknowledged receipt of his favor of the 24th ult. with enclosure as stated. Separated by a double line, but still mighty close to the matter under the caption of "Oddities of the Day's News" in an evening paper, Jacob Spraggins read that one "Jasper Spargyous" had "donated $100,000 to the U. B. A. of G." A camel may have a stomach for each day in the week; but I dare not venture to accord him whiskers, for fear of the Great Displeasure at Washington; but if he have whiskers, surely not one of them will seem to have been inserted in the eye of a needle by that effort of that rich man to enter the K. of H. The right is reserved to reject any and all bids; signed, S. Peter, secretary and gate-keeper.

Next, Jacob selected the best endowed college he could scare up and presented it with a $200,000 laboratory. The college did not maintain a scientific course, but it accepted the money and built an elaborate lavatory instead, which was no diversion of funds so far as Jacob ever discovered.

The faculty met and invited Jacob to come over and take his A B C degree. Before sending the invitations they smiled, cut out the C, added the proper punctuation marks, and all was well.

While walking on the campus before being capped and gowned, Jacob saw two professors strolling near by. Their voices, long adapted to indoor acoustics, undesignedly reached his ear.

"There goes the latest *chevalier d'industrie*," said one of them, "to buy a sleeping powder from us. He gets his degree to-morrow."

"*In foro conscientiæ*," said the other. "Let's 'eave 'arf a brick at 'im."

Jacob ignored the Latin, but the brick pleasantry was not too hard for him. There was no mandragora in the honorary draught of learning that he had bought. That was before the passage of the Pure Food and Drugs Act.

Jacob wearied of philanthropy on a large scale.

"If I could see folks made happier," he said to himself—"If I could see 'em myself and hear 'em express their gratitude for what I done for 'em it would make me feel better. This donatin' funds to institutions and societies is about as satisfactory as dropping money into a broken slot machine."

So Jacob followed his nose, which led him through unswept streets to the homes of the poorest.

"The very thing!" said Jacob. "I will charter two river steamboats, pack them full of these unfortunate children and—say ten thousand dolls and drums and a thousand freezers of ice cream, and give them a delightful outing up the Sound. The sea breezes on that trip ought to blow the taint off some of this money that keeps coming in faster than I can work it off my mind."

Jacob must have leaked some of his benevolent intentions, for an immense person with a bald face and a mouth that looked as if it ought to have a "Drop Letters Here" sign over it hooked a finger around him and set him in a space between a barber's pole and a stack of ash cans. Words came out of the postoffice slit—smooth, husky words with gloves on 'em, but sounding as if they might turn to bare knuckles any moment.

"Say, Sport, do you know where you are at? Well, dis is Mike O'Grady's district you're buttin' into—see? Mike's got de stomach-ache privilege for every kid in dis neighborhood—see? And if dere's any picnics or red balloons to be dealt out here, Mike's money pays for 'em—see? Don't you butt in, or something'll be handed to you. Youse d—— settlers and reformers with your social ologies and your millionaire detectives have got dis district in a hell of a fix, anyhow. With your college students and professors rough-housing de sodawater stands and dem rubber-nick coaches fillin' de streets, de folks down here are 'fraid to go out of de houses. Now, you leave 'em to Mike. Dey belongs to him, and he knows how to handle 'em. Keep on your own side of de town. Are you some wiser now, uncle, or do you want to scrap wit' Mike O'Grady for de Santa Claus belt in dis district?"

Clearly, that spot in the moral vineyard was preëmpted. So Caliph Spraggins menaced no more the people in the bazaars of the East Side. To keep down his growing surplus he doubled his donations to organized charity, presented the Y. M. C. A. of his native town with a $10,000 collection of butterflies, and sent a check to the famine sufferers in China big enough to buy new emerald eyes and diamond-filled teeth for all their gods. But none of these charitable acts seemed to bring peace to the caliph's heart. He tried to get a personal note into his benefactions by tipping bellboys and waiters $10 and $20 bills. He got well snickered at and derided for that by the minions who accept with respect gratuities commensurate to the service performed. He sought out an ambitious and talented but poor young woman, and bought for her the star part in a new comedy. He might have gotten rid of $50,000 more of his cumbersome money in this philanthropy if he had not neglected to write letters to her. But she lost the suit for lack of evidence, while his capital still kept piling up, and his *optikos needleorum camelibus*—or rich man's disease—was unrelieved.

In Caliph Spraggins's $3,000,000 home lived his sister Henrietta, who used to cook for the coal miners in a twenty-five-cent eating house in Coketown, Pa., and now would have offered John Mitchell only two fingers of her hand to shake. And his daughter Celia, nineteen, back from boarding-school and from being polished off by private instructors in the restaurant languages and those études and things.

Celia is the heroine. Lest the artist's delineation of her charms on this very page humbug your fancy, take from me her authorized description. She was a nice-looking, awkward, loud, rather bashful, brown-haired girl, with a sallow complexion, bright eyes, and a perpetual smile. She had a wholesome,

Spraggins-inherited love for plain food, loose clothing, and the society of the lower classes. She had too much health and youth to feel the burden of wealth. She had a wide mouth that kept the peppermint-pepsin tablets rattling like hail from the slot-machine wherever she went, and she could whistle hornpipes. Keep this picture in mind; and let the artist do his worst.

Celia looked out of her window one day and gave her heart to the grocer's young man. The receiver thereof was at that moment engaged in conceding immortality to his horse and calling down upon him the ultimate fate of the wicked; so he did not notice the transfer. A horse should stand still when you are lifting a crate of strictly new-laid eggs out of the wagon.

Young lady reader, you would have liked that grocer's young man yourself. But you wouldn't have given him your heart, because you are saving it for a riding-master, or a shoe-manufacturer with a torpid liver, or something quiet but rich in gray tweeds at Palm Beach. Oh, I know about it. So I am glad the grocer's young man was for Celia, and not for you.

The grocer's young man was slim and straight and as confident and easy in his movements as the man in the back of the magazines who wears the new frictionless roller suspenders. He wore a gray bicycle cap on the back of his head, and his hair was straw-colored and curly, and his sunburned face looked like one that smiled a good deal when he was not preaching the doctrine of everlasting punishment to delivery-wagon horses. He slung imported A1 fancy groceries about as though they were only the stuff he delivered at boarding-houses; and when he picked up his whip, your mind instantly recalled Mr. Tackett and his air with the buttonless foils.

Tradesmen delivered their goods at a side gate at the rear of the house. The grocer's wagon came about ten in the morning. For three days Celia watched the driver when he came, finding something new each time to admire in the lofty and almost contemptuous way he had of tossing around the choicest gifts of

Pomona, Ceres, and the canning factories. Then she consulted Annette.

To be explicit, Annette McCorkle, the second housemaid who deserves a paragraph herself. Annette Fletcherized large numbers of romantic novels which she obtained at a free public library branch (donated by one of the biggest caliphs in the business). She was Celia's sidekicker and chum, though Aunt Henrietta didn't know it, you may hazard a bean or two.

"Oh, canary-bird seed!" exclaimed Annette. "Ain't it a corkin' situation? You a heiress, and fallin' in love with him on sight! He's a sweet boy, too, and above his business. But he ain't suspectible like the common run of grocers' assistants. He never pays no attention to me."

"He will to me," said Celia.

"Riches——" began Annette, unsheathing the not unjustifiable feminine sting.

"Oh, you're not so beautiful," said Celia, with her wide, disarming smile. "Neither am I; but he shan't know that there's any money mixed up with my looks, such as they are. That's fair. Now, I want you to lend me one of your caps and an apron, Annette."

"Oh, marshmallows!" cried Annette. "I see. Ain't it lovely? It's just like 'Lurline, the Left-Handed; or, A Buttonhole Maker's Wrongs.' I'll bet he'll turn out to be a count."

There was a long hallway (or "passageway," as they call it in the land of the Colonels) with one side latticed, running along the rear of the house. The grocer's young man went through this to deliver his goods. One morning he passed a girl in there with shining eyes, sallow complexion, and wide, smiling mouth, wearing a maid's cap and apron. But as he was cumbered with a basket of Early Drumhead lettuce and Trophy tomatoes and three bunches of asparagus and six bottles of the most expensive Queen olives, he saw no more than that she was one of the maids.

But on his way out he came up behind her, and she was whistling "Fisher's Hornpipe" so loudly and clearly that all the piccolos in the world should have disjointed themselves and crept into their cases for shame.

The grocer's young man stopped and pushed back his cap until it hung on his collar button behind.

"That's out o' sight, Kid," said he.

"My name is Celia, if you please," said the whistler, dazzling him with a three-inch smile.

"That's all right. I'm Thomas McCleod. What part of the house do you work in?"

"I'm the—the second parlor maid."

"Do you know the 'Falling Waters'?"

"No," said Celia, "we don't know anybody. We got rich too quick—that is, Mr. Spraggins did."

"I'll make you acquainted," said Thomas McCleod. "It's a strathspey—a first cousin to a hornpipe."

If Celia's whistling put the piccolos out of commission, Thomas McCleod's surely made the biggest flutes hunt their holes. He could actually whistle *bass*.

When he stopped Celia was ready to jump into his delivery wagon and ride with him clear to the end of the pier and on to the ferryboat of the Charon line.

"I'll be around to-morrow at 10:15," said Thomas, "with some spinach and a case of carbonic."

"I'll practice that what-you-may-call-it," said Celia. "I can whistle a fine second."

The processes of courtship are personal, and do not belong to general literature. They should be chronicled in detail only in advertisements of iron tonics and in the secret by-laws of the Woman's Auxiliary of the Ancient Order of the Rat Trap. But genteel writing may contain a description of certain stages of its progress without intruding upon the province of the X-ray or of park policemen.

A day came when Thomas McCleod and Celia lingered at the end of the latticed "passage."

"Sixteen a week isn't much," said Thomas, letting his cap rest on his shoulder blades.

Celia looked through the lattice-work and whistled a dead march. Shopping with Aunt Henrietta the day before, she had paid that much for a dozen handkerchiefs.

"Maybe I'll get a raise next month," said Thomas. "I'll be around to-morrow at the same time with a bag of flour and the laundry soap."

"All right," said Celia. "Annette's married cousin pays only $20 a month for a flat in the Bronx."

Never for a moment did she count on the Spraggins money. She knew Aunt Henrietta's invincible pride of caste and pa's mightiness as a Colossus of cash, and she understood that if she chose Thomas she and her grocer's young man might go whistle for their living.

Another day came, Thomas violating the dignity of Nabob Avenue with "The Devil's Dream," whistled keenly between his teeth.

"Raised to eighteen a week yesterday," he said. "Been pricing flats around Morningside. You want to start untying those apron strings and unpinning that cap, old girl."

"Oh, Tommy!" said Celia, with her broadest smile. "Won't that be enough? I got Betty to show me how to make a cottage pudding. I guess we could call it a flat pudding if we wanted to."

"And tell no lie," said Thomas.

"And I can sweep and polish and dust—of course, a parlor maid learns that. And we could whistle duets of evenings."

"The old man said he'd raise me to twenty at Christmas if Bryan couldn't think of any harder name to call a Republican than a 'postponer,'" said the grocer's young man.

"I can sew," said Celia; "and I know that you must make the gas company's man show his badge when he comes to look at the meter; and I know how to put up quince jam and window curtains."

"Bully! you're all right, Cele. Yes, I believe we can pull it off on eighteen."

As he was jumping into the wagon the second parlor maid braved discovery by running swiftly to the gate.

"And, oh, Tommy, I forgot," she called, softly, "I believe I could make your neckties."

"Forget it," said Thomas, decisively.

"And another thing," she continued. "Sliced cucumbers at night will drive away cockroaches."

"And sleep, too, you bet," said Mr. McCleod. "Yes, I believe if I have a delivery to make on the West Side this afternoon I'll look in at a furniture store I know over there."

It was just as the wagon dashed away that old Jacob Spraggins struck the sideboard with his fist and made the mysterious remark about ten thousand dollars that you perhaps remember. Which justifies the reflection that some stories, as well as life, and puppies thrown into wells, move around in circles. Painfully but briefly we must shed light on Jacob's words.

The foundation of his fortune was made when he was twenty. A poor coal-digger (ever hear of a rich one?) had saved a dollar or two and bought a small tract of land on a hillside on which he tried to raise corn. Not a nubbin. Jacob, whose nose was a divining-rod, told him there was a vein of coal beneath. He bought the land from the miner for $125 and sold it a month afterward for $10,000. Luckily the miner had enough left of his sale money to drink himself into a black coat opening in the back, as soon as he heard the news.

And so, forty years afterward, we find Jacob illuminated with the sudden thought that if he could make restitution of this sum of money to the heirs or assigns of the unlucky miner, respite and Nepenthe might be his.

And now must come swift action, for we have here some four thousand words and not a tear shed and never a pistol, joke, safe, nor bottle cracked.

Old Jacob hired a dozen private detectives to find the heirs, if any existed, of the old miner, Hugh McLeod.

Get the point? Of course I know as well as you do that Thomas is going to be the heir. I might have concealed the name; but why always hold back your mystery till the end? I say, let it come near the middle so people can stop reading there if they want to.

After the detectives had trailed false clues about three thousand dollars—I mean miles—they corner Thomas at the grocery and got his confession that Hugh McLeod had been his grandfather, and that there were no other heirs. They arranged a meeting for him and old Jacob one morning in one of their offices.

Jacob liked the young man very much. He liked the way he looked straight at him when he talked, and the way he threw his bicycle cap over the top of a rose-colored vase on the centre-table.

"There was a slight flaw in Jacob's system of restitution. He did not consider that the act, to be perfect, should include confession. So he represented himself to be the agent of the purchaser of the land who had sent him to refund the sale price for the ease of his conscience.

"Well, sir," said Thomas, "this sounds to me like an illustrated postcard from South Boston with 'We're having a good time here' written on it. I don't know the game. Is this ten thousand dollars money, or do I have to save so many coupons to get it?"

Old Jacob counted out to him twenty five-hundred-dollar bills.

That was better, he thought, than a check. Thomas put them thoughtfully into his pocket.

"Grandfather's best thanks," he said, "to the party who sends it."

Jacob talked on, asking him about his work, how he spent his leisure time, and what his ambitions were. The more he saw and heard of Thomas, the better he liked him. He had not met many young men in Bagdad so frank and wholesome.

"I would like to have you visit my house," he said. "I might help you in investing or laying out your money. I am a very wealthy man. I have a daughter about grown, and I would like for you to know her. There are not many young men I would care to have call on her."

"I'm obliged," said Thomas. "I'm not much at making calls. It's generally the side entrance for mine. And, besides, I'm engaged to a girl that has the Delaware peach crop killed in the blossom. She's a parlor maid in a house where I deliver goods. She won't be working there much longer, though. Say, don't forget to give your friend my grandfather's best regards. You'll excuse me now; my wagon's outside with a lot of green stuff that's got to be delivered. See you again, sir."

At eleven Thomas delivered some bunches of parsley and lettuce at the Spraggins mansion. Thomas was only twenty-two; so, as he came back, he took out the handful of five-hundred-dollar bills and waved them carelessly. Annette took a pair of eyes as big as creamed onions to the cook.

"I told you he was a count," she said, after relating. "He never would carry on with me."

"But you say he showed money," said the cook.

"Hundreds of thousands," said Annette. "Carried around loose in his pockets. And he never would look at me."

"It was paid to me to-day," Thomas was explaining to Celia outside. "It came from my grandfather's estate. Say, Cele, what's the use of waiting now? I'm going to quit the job to-night. Why can't we get married next week?"

"Tommy," said Celia, "I'm no parlor maid. I've been fooling you. I'm Miss Spraggins—Celia Spraggins. The newspapers say I'll be worth forty million dollars some day."

Thomas pulled his cap down straight on his head for the first time since we have known him.

"I suppose then," said he, "I suppose then you'll not be marrying me next week. But you *can* whistle."

"No," said Celia, "I'll not be marrying you next week. My father would never let me marry a grocer's clerk. But I'll marry you to-night, Tommy, if you say so."

Old Jacob Spraggins came home at 9:30 P.M., in his motor car. The make of it you will have to surmise sorrowfully; I am giving you unsubsidized fiction; had it been a street car I could have told you its voltage and the number of flat wheels it had. Jacob called for his daughter; he had bought a ruby necklace for her, and wanted to hear her say what a kind, thoughtful, dear old dad he was.

There was a brief search in the house for her, and then came Annette, glowing with the pure flame of truth and loyalty well mixed with envy and histrionics.

"Oh, sir," said she, wondering if she should kneel, "Miss Celia's just this minute running away out of the side gate with a young man to be married. I couldn't stop her, sir. They went in a cab."

"What young man?" roared old Jacob.

"A millionaire, if you please, sir—a rich nobleman in disguise. He carries his money with him, and the red peppers and the onions was only to blind us, sir. He never did seem to take to me."

Jacob rushed out in time to catch his car. The chauffeur had been delayed by trying to light a cigarette in the wind.

"Here, Gaston, or Mike, or whatever you call yourself, scoot around the corner quicker than blazes and see if you can see a cab. If you do, run it down."

There was a cab in sight a block away. Gaston, or Mike, with his eyes half shut and his mind on his cigarette, picked up the trail, neatly crowded the cab to the curb, and pocketed it.

"What t'ell you doin'?" yelled the cabman.

"Pa!" shrieked Celia.

"Grandfather's remorseful friend's agent!" said Thomas. "Wonder what's on his conscience now."

"A thousand thunders!" said Gaston, or Mike. "I have no other match."

"Young man," said old Jacob, severely, "how about that parlor maid you were engaged to?"

A couple of years afterward old Jacob went into the office of his private secretary.

"The amalgamated Missionary Society solicits a contribution of $30,000 toward the conversion of the Koreans," said the secretary.

"Pass 'em up," said Jacob.

"The University of Plumville writes that its yearly endowment fund of $50,000 that you bestowed upon it is past due."

"Tell 'em it's been cut out."

"The Scientific Society of Clam Cove, Long Island, asks for $10,000 to buy alcohol to preserve specimens."

"Waste basket."

"The Society for Providing Healthful Recreation for Working Girls wants $20,000 from you to lay out a golf course."

"Tell 'em to see an undertaker.

"Cut 'em all out," went on Jacob. "I've quit being a good thing. I need every dollar I can scrape or save. I want you to write to the directors of every company that I'm interested in and recommend a 10 per cent. cut in salaries. And say—I noticed half a cake of soap lying in a corner of the hall as I came in. I want you to speak to the scrub-woman about waste. I've got no money to throw away. And say—we've got vinegar pretty well in hand, haven't we?"

"The Globe Spice & Seasons Company," said the secretary, "controls the market at present."

"Raise vinegar two cents a gallon. Notify all our branches."

Suddenly Jacob Spraggins's plump red face relaxed into a pulpy grin. He walked over to the secretary's desk and showed a small red mark on his thick forefinger.

"Bit it," he said, "darned if he didn't, and he ain't had the tooth three weeks—Jaky McLeod, my Celia's kid. He'll be worth a hundred millions by the time he is twenty-one if I can pile it up for him."

As he was leaving, old Jacob turned at the door, and said:

"Better make that vinegar raise three cents instead of two. I'll be back in an hour and sign the letters."

The true history of the Caliph Harun Al Rashid relates that toward the end of his reign he wearied of philanthropy, and caused to be beheaded all his former favorites and companions of his "Arabian Nights" rambles. Happy are we in these days of enlightenment when the only death warrant the caliphs can serve on us is in the form of a trademan's bill.

Proof of the Pudding

SPRING WINKED a vitreous optic at Editor Westbrook of the *Minerva Magazine,* and deflected him from his course. He had lunched in his favorite corner of a Broadway hotel, and was returning to his office when his feet became entangled in the lure of the vernal coquette. Which is by way of saying that he turned eastward in Twenty-sixth Street, safely forded the spring freshet of vehicles in Fifth Avenue, and meandered along the walks of budding Madison Square.

The lenient air and the settings of the little park almost formed a pastorale, the color motif was green—the presiding shade at the creation of man and vegetation.

The callow grass between the walks was the color of verdigris, a poisonous green, reminiscent of the horde of derelict humans that had breathed upon the soil during the summer and autumn. The bursting tree buds looked strangely familiar to those who had botanized among the garnishings of the fish course of a forty-cent dinner. The sky above was of that pale aquamarine tint that hall-room poets rhyme with "true" and "Sue" and "coo." The one natural and frank color visible was the ostensible green of the newly painted benches—a shade between the color of a pickled cucumber and that of a last year's fast-black cravenette raincoat. But, to the city-bred eye of Editor Westbrook, the landscape appeared a masterpiece.

And now, whether you are of those who rush in, or of the gentle concourse that fears to tread, you must follow in a brief invasion of the editor's mind.

Editor Westbrook's spirit was contented and serene. The April number of the *Minerva* had sold its entire edition before the tenth day of the month—a newsdealer in Keokuk had written that he could have sold fifty copies more if he had had 'em. The owners of the magazine had raised his (the editor's) salary; he had just installed in his home a jewel of a recently imported cook who was afraid of policemen; and the morning papers had published in full a speech he had made at a publishers' banquet. Also there were echoing in his mind the jubilant notes of a splendid song that his charming young wife had sung to him before he left his up-town apartment that morning. She was taking enthusiastic interest in her music of late, practising early and diligently. When he had complimented her on the improvement in her voice she had fairly hugged him for joy at his praise. He felt, too, the benign, tonic medicament of the trained nurse, Spring, tripping softly down the wards of the convalescent city.

While Editor Westbrook was sauntering between the rows of park benches (already filling with vagrants and the guardians of lawless childhood) he felt his sleeve grasped and held. Suspecting that he was about to be panhandled, he turned a cold and unprofitable face, and saw that his captor was—Dawe—Shackleford Dawe, dingy, almost ragged, the genteel scarcely visible in him through the deeper lines of the shabby.

While the editor is pulling himself out of his surprise a flashlight biography of Dawe is offered.

He was a fiction writer and one of Westbrook's old acquaintances. At one time they might have called each other old friends. Dawe had some money in those days, and lived in a decent apartment house near Westbrook's. The two families often went to theatres and dinners together. Mrs. Dawe and Mrs. Westbrook became "dearest" friends. Then one day a little tentacle of the octopus, just to amuse itself, ingurgitated Dawe's capital, and he moved to the Gramercy Park neighborhood where one, for a few groats per week, may sit upon one's trunk under eight-branched chandeliers and opposite Carrara marble mantels and watch the mice play upon the floor. Dawe thought to live by writing fiction. Now and then he sold a story. He submitted many to Westbrook. The *Minerva* printed one or two of them; the rest were returned. Westbrook sent a careful and conscientious personal letter with each rejected manuscript, pointing out in detail his reasons for considering it unavailable. Editor Westbrook had his own clear conception of what constituted good fiction. So had Dawe. Mrs. Dawe was mainly concerned about the constituents of the scanty dishes of food that she managed to scrape together. One day Dawe had been spouting to her about the excellencies of certain French writers. At dinner they sat down to a dish that a hungry school-boy could have encompassed at a gulp. Dawe commented.

"It's Maupassant hash," said Mrs. Dawe. "It may not be art, but I do wish you would do a five-course Marion Crawford serial with an Ella Wheeler Wilcox sonnet for dessert. I'm hungry."

As far as this from success was Shackleford Dawe when he plucked Editor Westbrook's sleeve in Madison Square. That was the first time the editor had seen Dawe in several months.

"Why, Shack, is this you?" said Westbrook, somewhat awkwardly, for the form of his phrase seemed to touch upon the other's changed appearance.

"Sit down for a minute," said Dawe, tugging at his sleeve. "This is my office. I can't come to yours, looking as I do. Oh, sit down—you won't be disgraced. Those half-plucked birds on the other benches will take you for a swell porch-climber. They won't know you are only an editor."

"Smoke, Shack?" said Editor Westbrook, sinking cautiously upon the virulent green bench. He always yielded gracefully when he did yield.

Dawe snapped at the cigar as a kingfisher darts at a sunperch, or a girl pecks at a chocolate cream.

"I have just——" began the editor.

"Oh, I know; don't finish," said Dawe. "Give me a match. You have just ten minutes to spare. How did you manage to get past my office-boy and invade my sanctum? There he goes now, throwing his club at a dog that couldn't read the 'Keep off the Grass' signs."

"How goes the writing?" asked the editor.

"Look at me," said Dawe, "for your answer. Now don't put on that embarrassed, friendly-but-honest look and ask me why I don't get a job as a wine agent or a cab driver. I'm in the fight to a finish. I know I can write good fiction and I'll force you fellows to admit it yet. I'll make you change the spelling of 're-grets' to 'c-h-e-q-u-e' before I'm done with you."

Editor Westbrook gazed through his noseglasses with a sweetly sorrowful, omniscient, sympathetic, skeptical expression—the copyrighted expression of the editor beleaguered by the unavailable contributor.

"Have you read the last story I sent you—'The Alarum of the Soul'?" asked Dawe.

"Carefully. I hesitated over that story, Shack, really I did. It had some good points. I was writing you a letter to send with it when it goes back to you. I regret——"

"Never mind the regrets," said Dawe, grimly. "There's neither salve nor sting in 'em any more. What I want to know is *why*. Come, now; out with the good points first."

"The story," said Westbrook, deliberately, after a suppressed sigh, "is written around an almost original plot. Characteriza-tion—the best you have done. Construction—almost as good, except for a few weak joints which might be strengthened by a few changes and touches. It was a good story, except——"

"I can write English, can't I?" interrupted Dawe.

"I have always told you," said the editor, "that you had a style."

"Then the trouble is the——"

"Same old thing," said Editor Westbrook. "You work up to your climax like an artist. And then you turn yourself into a

photographer. I don't know what form of obstinate madness
possesses you, Shack, but that is what you do with everything
that you write. No. I will retract the comparison with the photographer. Now and then photography, in spite of its impossible
perspective, manages to record a fleeting glimpse of truth. But
you spoil every dénouement by those flat, drab, obliterating
strokes of your brush that I have so often complained of. If you
would rise to the literary pinnacle of your dramatic scenes, and
paint them in the high colors that art requires, the postman
would leave fewer bulky, self-addressed envelopes at your door."

"Oh, fiddles and footlights!" cried Dawe, derisively. "You've
got that old sawmill drama king in your brain yet. When the man
with the black mustache kidnaps golden-haired Bessie you are
bound to have the mother kneel and raise her hands in the spot-
light and say: 'May high heaven witness that I will rest neither
night nor day till the heartless villain that has stolen me child
feels the weight of a mother's vengeance!' "

Editor Westbrook conceded a smile of impervious complacency.

"I think," said he, "that in real life the woman would express
herself in those words or in very similar ones."

"Not in a six hundred nights' run anywhere but on the stage,"
said Dawe, hotly. "I'll tell you what she'd say in real life. She'd
say: 'What! Bessie led away by a strange man? Good Lord! It's
one trouble after another! Get my other hat, I must hurry around
to the the police-station. Why wasn't somebody looking after her,
I'd like to know? For God's sake, get out of my way or I'll never
get ready. Not that hat—the brown one with the velvet bows.
Bessie must have been crazy; she's usually shy of strangers. Is that
too much powder? Lordy! How I'm upset!'

"That's the way she'd talk," continued Dawe. "People in real
life don't fly into heroics and blank verse at emotional crises.
They simply can't do it. If they talk at all on such occasions they
draw from the same vocabulary that they use every day, and
muddle up their words and ideas a little more, that's all."

"Shack," said Editor Westbrook, impressively, "did you ever

pick up the mangled and lifeless form of a child from under the
fender of a street car, and carry it in your arms and lay it down
before the distracted mother? Did you ever do that and listen
to the words of grief and despair as they flowed spontaneously
from her lips?"

"I never did," said Dawe. "Did you?"

"Well, no," said Editor Westbrook, with a slight frown. "But
I can well imagine what she would say."

"So can I," said Dawe.

And now the fitting time had come for Editor Westbrook to
play the oracle and silence his opinionated contributor. It was
not for an unarrived fictionist to dictate words to be uttered
by the heroes and heroines of the *Minerva Magazine*, contrary
to the theories of the editor thereof.

"My dear Shack," said he, "if I know anything of life I know
that every sudden, deep, and tragic emotion in the human heart
calls forth an opposite, concordant, conformable, and propor-
tionate expression of feeling. How much of this inevitable accord
between expression and feeling should be attributed to nature,
and how much to the influence of art, it would be difficult to say.
The sublimely terrible roar of the lioness that has been deprived
of her cubs is dramatically as far above her customary whine and
purr as the kingly and transcendent utterances of Lear are above
the level of his senile vaporings. But it is also true that all men
and women have what may be called a sub-conscious dramatic
sense that is awakened by a sufficiently deep and powerful emotion—a sense unconsciously acquired from literature and the
stage that prompts them to express those emotions in language
befitting their importance and histrionic value."

"And in the name of the seven sacred saddle-blankets of Sagit-
tarius, where did the stage and literature get the stunt?" asked
Dawe.

"From life," answered the editor, triumphantly.

The story writer rose from the bench and gesticulated eloquently but dumbly. He was beggared for words with which to formulate adequately his dissent.

On a bench near by a frowzy loafer opened his red eyes and perceived that his moral support was due a downtrodden brother.

"Punch him one, Jack," he called hoarsely to Dawe. "W'at's he come makin' a noise like a penny arcade for amongst gen'lemen that comes in the Square to set and think?"

Editor Westbrook looked at his watch with an affected show of leisure.

"Tell me," asked Dawe, with truculent anxiety, "what especial faults in 'The Alarm of the Soul' caused you to throw it down?"

"When Gabriel Murray," said Westbrook, "goes to his telephone and is told that his fiancée has been shot by a burglar, he says —I do not recall the exact words, but——"

"I do," said Dawe. "He says: 'Damn Central; she always cuts me off.' (And then to his friend) 'Say, Tommy, does a thirty-two bullet make a big hole? It's kind of hard luck, ain't it? Could you get me a drink from the sideboard, Tommy? No; straight; nothing on the side.'"

"And again," continued the editor, without pausing for argument, "when Berenice opens the letter from her husband informing her that he has fled with the manicure girl, her words are—let me see——"

"She says," interposed the author: "'Well, what do you think of that!'"

"Absurdly inappropriate words," said Westbrook, "presenting an anti-climax—plunging the story into hopeless bathos. Worse yet; they mirror life falsely. No human being ever uttered banal colloquialisms when confronted by sudden tragedy."

"Wrong," said Dawe, closing his unshaven jaws doggedly. "I say no man or woman ever spouts 'high-falutin' talk when they go up against a real climax. They talk naturally and a little worse."

The editor rose from the bench with his air of indulgence and inside information.

"Say, Westbrook," said Dawe, pinning him by the lapel, "would you have accepted 'The Alarum of the Soul' if you had believed that the actions and words of the characters were true to life in the parts of the story that we discussed?"

"It is very likely that I would, if I believed that way," said the editor. "But I have explained to you that I do not."

"If I could prove to you that I am right?"

"I'm sorry, Shack, but I'm afraid I haven't time to argue any further just now."

"I don't want to argue," said Dawe. "I want to demonstrate to you from life itself that my view is the correct one."

"How could you do that?" asked Westbrook, in a surprised tone.

"Listen," said the writer, seriously. "I have thought of a way. It is important to me that my theory of true-to-life fiction be recognized as correct by the magazines. I've fought for it for three years, and I'm down to my last dollar, with two months' rent due."

"I have applied the opposite of your theory," said the editor, "in selecting the fiction for the *Minerva Magazine*. The circulation has gone up from ninety thousand to——"

"Four hundred thousand," said Dawe. "Whereas it should have been boosted to a million."

"You said something to me just now about demonstrating your pet theory."

"I will. If you'll give me about half an hour of your time I'll prove to you that I am right. I'll prove it by Louise."

"Your wife!" exclaimed Westbrook. "How?"

"Well, not exactly by her, but *with* her," said Dawe. "Now, you know how devoted and loving Louise has always been. She thinks I'm the only genuine preparation on the market that bears the old doctor's signature. She's been fonder and more faithful than ever, since I've been cast for the neglected genius part."

"Indeed, she is a charming and admirable life companion," agreed the editor. "I remember what inseparable friends she and Mrs. Westbrook once were. We are both lucky chaps, Shack, to have such wives. You must bring Mrs. Dawe up some evening soon, and we'll have one of those informal chafing-dish suppers that we used to enjoy so much."

"Later," said Dawe. "When I get another shirt. And now I'll tell you my scheme. When I was about to leave home after breakfast— if you can call tea and oatmeal breakfast—Louise told me she was gong to visit her aunt in Eighty-ninth Street. She said she would return home at three o'clock. She is always on time to a minute. It is now——"

Dawe glanced toward the editor's watch pocket.

"Twenty-seven minutes to three," said Westbrook, scanning his timepiece.

"We have just enough time," said Dawe. "We will go to my flat at once. I will write a note, address it to her and leave it on the table where she will see it as she enters the door. You and I will be in the dining room concealed by the portières. In that note I'll say that I have fled from her forever with an affinity who understands the needs of my artistic soul as she never did. When she reads it we will observe her actions and hear her words. Then we will know which theory is the correct one—yours or mine."

"Oh, never!" exclaimed the editor, shaking his head. "That would be inexcusably cruel. I could not consent to have Mrs. Dawe's feelings played upon in such a manner."

"Brace up," said the writer, "I guess I think as much of her as you do. It's for her benefit as well as mine. I've got to get a market for my stories in some way. It won't hurt Louise. She's healthy and sound. Her heart goes as strong as a ninety-eight-cent watch. It'll last for only a minute, and then I'll step out and explain to her. You really owe it to me to give me the chance, Westbrook."

Editor Westbrook at length yielded, though but half willingly. And in the half of him that consented lurked the vivisectionist that is in all of us. Let him who has not used the scalpel rise and stand in his place. Pity 'tis that there are not enough rabbits and guinea-pigs to go around.

The two experimenters in Art left the Square and hurried eastward and then to the south until they arrived in the Gramercy neighborhood. Within its high iron railings the little park had put on its smart coat of vernal green, and was admiring itself in its fountain mirror. Outside the railings the hollow square of crumbling houses, shells of a bygone gentry, leaned as if in ghostly gossip over the forgotten doings of the vanished quality. *Sic transit gloria urbis.*

A block or two north of the Park, Dawe steered the editor again eastward, then, after covering a short distance, into a lofty but narrow flathouse burdened with a floridly over-decorated façade. To the fifth story they toiled, and Dawe, panting, pushed his latch-key into the door of one of the front flats.

When the door opened Editor Westbrook saw, with feelings of pity, how meanly and meagrely the rooms were furnished.

"Get a chair, if you can find one," said Dawe, "while I hunt up pen and ink. Hello, what's this? Here's a note from Louise. She must have left it there when she went out this morning."

He picked up an envelope that lay on the centre-table and tore it open. He began to read the letter that he drew out of it; and once having begun it aloud he so read it through to the end. These are the words that Editor Westbrook heard:

"Dear Shackleford:
"By the time you get this I will be about a hundred miles away and still a-going. I've got a place in the chorus of the Occidental Opera Co., and we start on the road to-day at twelve o'clock. I didn't want to starve to death, and so I decided to make my own living. I'm not coming back. Mrs. Westbrook is going with me. She said she was tired of living with a combination phonograph, iceberg, and dictionary, and she's not coming back, either. We've been practicing the songs and dances for two months on the quiet. I hope you will be successful, and get along all right! Good-bye.
"Louise"

Dawe dropped the letter, covered his face with his trembling hands, and cried out in a deep, vibrating voice:

"*My God, why hast thou given me this cup to drink? Since she is false, then let Thy Heaven's fairest gifts, faith and love, become the jesting by-words of traitors and fiends!*"

Editor Westbrook's glasses fell to the floor. The fingers of one hand fumbled with a button on his coat as he blurted between his pale lips:

"*Say, Shack, ain't that a hell of a note? Wouldn't that knock you off your perch, Shack? Ain't it hell, now, Shack—ain't it?*"

From
WAIFS AND STRAYS

⚜

Hearts and Hands

AT DENVER there was an influx of passengers into the coaches on the eastbound B. & M. express. In one coach there sat a very pretty young woman dressed in elegant taste and surrounded by all the luxurious comforts of an experienced traveler. Among the newcomers were two young men, one of handsome presence with a bold, frank countenance and manner; the other a ruffled, glum-faced person, heavily built and roughly dressed. The two were handcuffed together.

As they passed down the aisle of the coach the only vacant seat offered was a reversed one facing the attractive young woman. Here the linked couple seated themselves. The young woman's glance fell upon them with a distant, swift disinterest; then with a lovely smile brightening her countenance and a tender pink tingeing her rounded cheeks, she held out a little gray-gloved hand. When she spoke her voice, full, sweet, and deliberate, proclaimed that its owner was accustomed to speak and be heard.

"Well, Mr. Easton, if you *will* make me speak first, I suppose I must. Don't you ever recognize old friends when you meet them in the West?"

The younger man roused himself sharply at the sound of her

voice, seemed to struggle with a slight embarrassment which he threw off instantly, and then clasped her fingers with his left hand.

"It's Miss Fairchild," he said, with a smile. "I'll ask you to excuse the other hand; it's otherwise engaged just at present."

He slightly raised his right hand, bound at the wrist by the shining "bracelet" to the left one of his companion. The glad look in the girl's eyes slowly changed to a bewildered horror. The glow faded from her cheeks. Her lips parted in a vague, relaxing distress. Easton, with a little laugh, as if amused, was about to speak again when the other forestalled him. The glum-faced man had been watching the girl's countenance with veiled glances from his keen, shrewd eyes.

"You'll excuse me for speaking, miss, but, I see you're acquainted with the marshal here. If you'll ask him to speak a word for me when we get to the pen he'll do it, and it'll make things easier for me there. He's taking me to Leavenworth prison. It's seven years for counterfeiting."

"Oh!" said the girl, with a deep breath and returning color. "So that is what you are doing out here? A marshal!"

"My dear Miss Fairchild," said Easton, calmly, "I had to do something. Money has a way of taking wings unto itself, and you know it takes money to keep step with our crowd in Washington. I saw this opening in the West, and—well, a marshalship isn't quite as high a position as that of ambassador, but——"

"The ambassador," said the girl, warmly, "doesn't call any more. He needn't ever have done so. You ought to know that. And so now you are one of these dashing Western heroes, and you ride and shoot and go into all kinds of dangers. That's different from the Washington life. You have been missed from the old crowd."

The girl's eyes, fascinated, went back, widening a little, to rest upon the glittering handcuffs.

"Don't you worry about them, miss," said the other man. "All marshals handcuff themselves to their prisoners to keep them from getting away. Mr. Easton knows his business."

"Will we see you again soon in Washington?" asked the girl.

"Not soon, I think," said Easton. "My butterfly days are over, I fear."

"I love the West," said the girl, irrelevantly. Her eyes were shining softly. She looked away out the car window. She began to speak truly and simply, without the gloss of style and manner: "Mamma and I spent the summer in Denver. She went home a week ago because father was slightly ill. I could live and be happy in the West. I think the air here agrees with me. Money isn't everything. But people always misunderstand things and remain stupid——"

"Say, Mr. Marshal," growled the glum-faced man. "This isn't quite fair. I'm needin' a drink, and haven't had a smoke all day. Haven't you talked long enough? Take me in the smoker now, won't you? I'm half dead for a pipe."

The bound travelers rose to their feet, Easton with the same slow smile on his face.

"I can't deny a petition for tobacco," he said, lightly. "It's the one friend of the unfortunate. Good-bye, Miss Fairchild. Duty calls, you know." He held out his hand for a farewell.

"It's too bad you are not going East," she said, reclothing herself with manner and style. "But you must go on to Leavenworth, I suppose?"

"Yes," said Easton, "I must go on to Leavenworth."

The two men sidled down the aisle into the smoker.

The two passengers in a seat near by had heard most of the conversation. Said one of them: "That marshal's a good sort of chap. Some of these Western fellows are all right."

"Pretty young to hold an office like that, isn't he?" asked the other.

"Young!" exclaimed the first speaker, "Why—— Oh! didn't you catch on? Say—did you ever know an officer to handcuff a prisoner to his *right* hand?"